ALABAMA

*Southern Charm Reigns
in Four Inspiring Romances*

KAY
CORNELIUS

BARBOUR
PUBLISHING

D1167171

Politically Correct © 1999 by Kay Cornelius
Toni's Vow © 2003 by Kay Cornelius
Anita's Fortune © 2004 by Kay Cornelius
Mary's Choice © 2004 by Kay Cornelius

ISBN 1-59310-562-2

Cover art by Corbis

Scripture quotations are taken from the HOLY BIBLE, NEW INTERNATIONAL VERSION®. NIV®. Copyright© 1973, 1978, 1984 by International Bible Society. Used by permission of Zondervan. All rights reserved.

Scripture quotations are also taken from the King James Version of the Bible.

Published by Barbour Publishing, Inc., P.O. Box 719, Uhrichsville, Ohio 44683, www.barbourbooks.com

Our mission is to publish and distribute inspirational products offering exceptional value and biblical encouragement to the masses.

 Member of the
Evangelical Christian
Publishers Association

Printed in the United States of America.
5 4 3 2 1

Dear Readers,

Welcome to Rockdale, a lovely small town nestled in the mountains of northeastern Alabama.

Although Rockdale is fictional, the other places described in Alabama are real, and all are located a short distance from Huntsville, where my husband and I have made our home since 1958. We came here from Nashville, where we met while attending Peabody College of Vanderbilt University. I taught secondary English, and Don worked in contracts for NASA and Lockheed-Martin Missiles and Space before his retirement. We now have two grown children and four grandchildren. Don and I are both volunteer instructors for the AARP Mature Driving Course, and in addition to my writing, I find leading the senior ladies' Bible study at our church to be a great blessing. In my spare time, I'm making a sampler afghan with twenty different squares, which may be done some time in 2010, at the rate I'm going now.

I hope you will enjoy meeting some of Rockdale's residents and reading about their lives.

Grace and peace,
Kay Cornelius

Politically Correct

"Who can find a virtuous woman?
for her price is far above rubies. . .
Strength and honour are her clothing;
and she shall rejoice in time to come. . .
Her children arise up and call her blessed;
her husband also, and he praiseth her."
PROVERBS 31:10, 25, 28

Prologue

I n the lobby of a vintage building in the heart of Washington, D.C., Jeremy Warren Winter took a deep, steadying breath before he pushed the UP button on the lone elevator. In a few moments, he would enter the offices of the Edwards Associates Company, where the entire course of his future could be decided in a single interview.

Jeremy ran his finger around his collar, which suddenly seemed too tight. His carefully chosen conservative, button-down white shirt had returned from the laundry stiff with too much starch, and he could almost feel his neck getting redder by the moment. He glanced down at his tasteful blue-and-gray striped tie and felt somewhat reassured. Jeremy thought the tie blended well with his single-breasted navy blue jacket and dove gray trousers. His obviously new, wing-tip oxfords had started to pinch his broad feet, but since he expected to sit down during his interview, he doubted that Mr. Guy Pettibone would notice his discomfort.

Guy Pettibone. Jeremy swallowed hard and wished in vain that his interview with the man who had made and broken so many politicians and would-be politicians was safely concluded and that he was on his way back to Alabama with Mr. Pettibone's stamp of approval. But in a way, it would be a shame to waste the experience of meeting such a man for the first time. In the old days, political careers had been decided in smoke-filled rooms. Now, however, image seemed to be the thing, and no one could beat Guy Pettibone when it came to making a candidate look worthy of being elected.

The elevator arrived, groaning and creaking, and Jeremy glanced at his watch. Assuming that the elevator would take no more than two minutes to bear him to the fifth floor, he should walk into the Edwards Associates office punctually at ten o'clock.

"Be on time. Don't get there too early and certainly don't be late," his uncle Henry had advised him. Jeremy was aware that if ex–United States Senator Henry Marshall had not known Guy Pettibone for many years, the great political consultant would probably never have consented to see an unknown nobody like his nephew.

Well, Uncle Henry's influence might get me past the door, Jeremy thought, *but from there on, it's up to me to make a good impression on Mr. Guy Pettibone.*

"I'll do it," he said aloud just as the wood-paneled elevator shuddered to a stop at the fifth floor and the doors opened with a jerk. Jeremy stepped out of the elevator directly into a reception area. He knew that the Edwards Associates public relations firm had many clients, but he had not expected it to occupy the entire floor.

"May I help you?" Mrs. Barnes, the silver-haired receptionist spoke to Jeremy with polite disdain, as if she could not imagine what business such a crass young man could possibly have with a firm like Edwards Associates.

However, since Jeremy had already determined not to allow anything anyone said or did to affect him, he merely nodded and showed her Mr. Pettibone's letter and then announced, "Mr. Pettibone asked me to come at ten."

The woman glanced at the letter and then back at Jeremy. Did she really look at him with more respect, or was it just his imagination? "I'll tell Mr. Pettibone you're here. You may wait over there."

Jeremy walked to the grouping of chairs she indicated and sat down, careful of the knife-sharp crease in his trousers. Uncle Henry had told him that Guy Pettibone was notorious for accepting or rejecting people on the basis of his first impressions, and Jeremy did not want to be dismissed out of hand because of a flaw in his appearance.

"Don't worry, Jeremy. Guy Pettibone wouldn't even agree to see you if he didn't think you had great potential," Henry Marshall had told him, but Jeremy knew that what he had put down in his resumé was probably far less important than the judgment Guy Pettibone would make when they met face-to-face.

Jeremy shifted in his chair and glanced covertly at his watch. *Of course he'll make me wait,* he thought without anger. Jeremy knew all about such strategies. In fact, Guy Pettibone might even be secretly observing him to see if he seemed uneasy.

I'm nervous enough, all right, Jeremy admitted. However, one of his minor talents had always been an ability to disguise his true feelings. Most of the time Jeremy's expression looked thoughtful, even when he was not trying to appear that way. He seldom smiled (and therefore to great effect when he did), and only rarely did he lose his temper. Such traits might not be highly regarded in some quarters, but they could be quite valuable in a politician.

"Mr. Winter? I'm Mrs. Laura Tate, Mr. Pettibone's secretary. Come this way, please."

Startled, Jeremy looked up at an attractive young matron who had apparently emerged in silence from a hallway behind him.

I suppose that's part of the plan, too, Jeremy thought. He walked beside her down a long corridor that ended at a plain oak door.

Mrs. Tate knocked once, then opened the door and stuck her head inside. "Mr. Pettibone? Mr. Winter is here."

A muffled rumble came from the figure seated in a chair behind the desk. Guy Pettibone sat with his back turned to them, looking out a large window in which, framed in the distance, Jeremy recognized the dome of the United States Capitol Building. In spite of himself, he felt a thrill at the thought that one day he could be a part of what went on in that very place.

"Go ahead." Not until the woman prompted him did Jeremy realize he still stood in the doorway. He started forward, and the figure in the chair turned, then rose and walked toward him.

He's even bigger than Uncle Henry said he was, Jeremy thought in awe. He knew that Guy Pettibone had been an all-American linebacker on a championship Texas college football team and then had played professional ball until injuries ended his career. However, Jeremy had not expected the man to dwarf his own height or to be almost twice as wide. Since Guy Pettibone never gave interviews or allowed his picture to be taken, Jeremy had only his uncle's description to go by. Obviously, much had been left unsaid.

Guy Pettibone's clothing was not what Jeremy had anticipated, either. He wore a suit of some kind of almost iridescent material that changed from shades of brown to red and back again as the big man moved. On his oddly small feet, he wore high-heeled, pointed-toed Western boots fashioned of some strange kind of leather, into which his trousers were tucked, paratrooper style.

"Like these boots? They're ostrich skin. The little holes are where the feathers were," Guy Pettibone said when he saw Jeremy glance at them.

When Mr. Pettibone extended his hand to be shaken, Jeremy noted the gleam of a huge diamond ring on his pinkie finger. Careful to exert just the right amount of firm pressure, Jeremy returned the handshake and waited for Mr. Pettibone to speak again.

Guy Pettibone continued to look closely at Jeremy, and Jeremy looked back, determined to maintain eye contact with this imposing man. "You appear somewhat younger than I expected for thirty. Turn around, boy."

Boy? The man's thick, Texas accent made it a two-syllable word, but Jeremy sensed that it had not been intended as an insult. Dutifully, Jeremy made a low turn, as if publicly modeling his carefully chosen clothes.

"Sit down, sit down." Guy Pettibone waved expansively toward a pair of leather wing chairs in front of his desk. Jeremy sat on the edge of the nearer one, careful to keep his back straight.

"I presume you can talk, boy?" Mr. Pettibone said from the depths of his swiveling desk chair.

"Yes, sir, I can," Jeremy said clearly, "but I'm here today mostly to listen and learn."

Guy Pettibone's expression did not change. He grunted, picked up a riding crop that lay on top of his cluttered desk and leaned back, slapping it absently against the arm of his chair. "That's odd. I thought you'd come to ask me to help you prepare to run for a seat in the next congressional elections. Or perhaps you have an agenda I don't know about?"

Jeremy sensed that he had made a mistake, but he would not compound it by forcing a lame apology. "No, sir. But I know you wouldn't be seeing me if you hadn't already pretty well decided that I was worth your time."

Guy Pettibone slapped the riding crop against his desk and guffawed. "Your uncle said you had a bit of sand in your craw. I like that. Now, tell me just what it is that you want from me, Mr. Winter."

Jeremy had prepared himself for this question, and he spoke without hesitation. "Mr. Pettibone, I was in high school when Uncle Henry went to the Senate. He got me a job as a page, and right then I knew I wanted a career in politics. I've done all I could to prepare myself for public service, but I know it takes more than the desire and a good education to get elected to office these days."

Guy Pettibone raised his eyebrows slightly. "Really? Just what else would you say it takes?"

Ignoring the slightly sarcastic note in Guy Pettibone's voice, Jeremy risked a slight smile. "Money, of course. . .lots of money. But to get that, the help and advice of a political consultant who knows the ins and outs of the system, someone who can guide a candidate through it. And of course, you're absolutely the best there is."

Guy Pettibone leaned back in his chair and crossed his arms over his ample chest. "Flattery doesn't impress me. I know who I am, but I'm still not sure about you." Then with narrowed eyes, he leaned forward and pointed the riding crop directly at Jeremy. "You a drinking man? You ever do drugs?"

Jeremy had to resist the impulse to smile at the questions. "Neither. You could say I'm a world-class designated driver. I picked up a bad case of some kind of strange hepatitis overseas when I was a kid. As a result, I can't ever drink, period. And I've always thought people who did drugs were stupid; my record there is absolutely clean."

"What about your general health?"

Jeremy shrugged. "No problems. I can't even remember the last time I was sick."

Guy Pettibone made another note on his pad. "How long has it been since you had a complete physical exam?"

"Two years, maybe. The doctor said he wished he had my heart rate and blood pressure."

"No doubt," Mr. Pettibone said dryly. "Now tell me about yourself, Mr. Winter."

Jeremy blinked, taken aback by the unexpected request. *I thought that's what I was doing,* he wanted to say. "It's all in my resumé."

Mr. Pettibone sighed and shook his head. "You majored in political science and went to law school and have since been working as one of fifty other non-partners in a Birmingham firm. Big deal. So have dozens of others, maybe all brighter than you. What's different about Jeremy Warren Winter?"

Jeremy prided himself on his ability to think on his feet; he had even said so in his letter to Guy Pettibone. He took a deep breath, his mind already choosing his words. "My family's Alabama roots go way back. I'm not ashamed to say that my grandmother was a full-blooded Cherokee; I got my straight black hair and square face from her. My father's a retired army sergeant major who survived three different tours in Vietnam. Growing up on army bases all over this country and overseas, I learned how to get along with all kinds of people. I went to college on a scholarship, but I worked off and on during law school, which is why it took me so long to finish. Since then, my work in a large law firm convinced me that I don't want to do that the rest of my life. I'd like to get involved in politics as soon as possible."

Guy Pettibone glanced at Jeremy's resumé, then back at him. "I see that you plan to resign from the Birmingham firm and go to this town called Rockdale. Any particular reason?"

Jeremy nodded. "Several. For one thing, it's my home of record, and my grandmother left me property there. I'll be working with Randall Bell for the time being. The Rockdale congressional district seat will be up for grabs if the incumbent retires at the end of the current term. . .and he's hinted he will. I'd like to run for it."

Guy Pettibone nodded and made a note on a blue legal pad. "Yes, I know Congressman Harrison. He's not a well man. What about your party affiliation? Will that be a problem?"

"I'm not sure what you mean."

"The way things are today, a party label can be a straitjacket. We like to see our candidates run in the party where we feel they have the best chance to win. Unless, of course, you aren't willing to change sides."

"I'm not really on either side. In fact, I've even been thinking I might run as an Independent."

Guy Pettibone grunted and made another note. "We'll have to do some research on that one." He leaned back in his chair and again pointed his riding crop at Jeremy. "Just how far are you willing to go to get elected, Mr. Winter?"

Jeremy had expected that he might be asked such a question, and he spoke almost automatically. "I won't do anything illegal or immoral, if that's what you mean."

"I never ask my clients to break the law, and if I ever find out you have, that'll be the end of our relationship. But I can advise you on what you need to do to be elected. If you can't promise to act on my advice, then I don't want you as my client."

"I'd want to know what it involves first," Jeremy said.

Guy Pettibone laughed. "No days like that, Mr. Winter. Either you trust me or you don't. I don't give free samples. If I'm willing to sign an unknown quantity like you as an Edwards Associates client, then you must be willing to let me guide you. Period. End of the discussion. Got it?"

He's good, Jeremy thought admiringly. Being accepted as Guy Pettibone's client would be a giant step toward realizing his ambitions; it was probably the single most important thing that could happen to his political career.

Jeremy nodded. "I understand. I'd have to be pretty crazy to ask for your help and not follow through on your advice."

"Or stupid." Mr. Pettibone opened a desk drawer and withdrew a sheaf of papers. He thumbed through them until he found what he searched for, then handed it across the desk to Jeremy. "Our standard contract," he explained as Jeremy scanned the brief document. "As you can see, we require a retainer on signing, then certain other payments from time to time. Either of us can cancel the agreement with due notice, but there will be no refund of moneys already paid."

Jeremy looked across the desk at Guy Pettibone. "Will I owe you more money when I win?"

Guy Pettibone guffawed again. "You ought to, and that's a pure fact. However, I work for a flat fee, win, lose, or draw, and only on one race at a time. After you've been in the House of Representatives for a couple of terms, you might get a hankering to make a run for the Senate. If so, we'll negotiate again."

Mr. Pettibone's matter-of-fact assumption that he would be elected to the House made Jeremy's heart beat a little faster. He wet his lips and handed the contract back. "This looks fair to me. Where do I sign?"

"Hold it. . . . We need a witness."

Mr. Pettibone spoke into his telephone, and the woman who had brought Jeremy to the office soon entered.

"Mr. Winter will be joining us as a client, Mrs. Tate," he told her.

"How nice," she said politely. Jeremy wondered how many other times she had said the same words to other hopeful young men and women.

"I'm looking forward to it," Jeremy said, although he was not sure at this point exactly all that "it" might entail.

Mrs. Tate handed Jeremy two copies of the contract and showed him where to sign it. After Mr. Pettibone added his illegible scrawl, she signed as a witness and handed one copy to Jeremy. "Here you are, Mr. Winter. Stop by the receptionist's desk on the way out. Mrs. Barnes will take your check and give you a packet of general information."

"What kind of information?" Jeremy asked as Mrs. Tate left the room. "Is this when I get the secret handshake?"

Guy Pettibone ignored Jeremy's feeble attempt at humor. "More like our fax number and that sort of thing." He rose from his chair and stood before Jeremy, who felt dwarfed by comparison. "We have a lot of work to do and not very much time to do it in. It's a good thing you didn't wait any longer to come to me. Use this to take notes. I won't repeat what I'm about to say."

Surprised, Jeremy took the fresh blue legal pad that Guy Pettibone held out, then patted his pocket and realized he did not have a pen.

Seeing Jeremy's problem, Mr. Pettibone handed him a pen from the several in his own shirt pocket. "I'm about to tell you some things that will help you get elected, and the first is to carry a small notebook and a pen with you always, everywhere you go. When you meet people, write down their names or make some note about them on their business cards. File them promptly and consult them often."

Jeremy nodded. "I usually have several pens, but—"

"Let me do the talking," Mr. Pettibone interrupted. "As of five minutes ago, you're paying me to talk to you, not the other way around. Now, about your clothes."

Jeremy glanced down at his carefully selected outfit, then back up to see Mr. Pettibone shaking his head.

"That getup might be fine in the big city, but it's all wrong for that district you aim to represent. In a few days, I'll send you a memo about the look you need. Meanwhile, get yourself some shoes that fit."

Jeremy nodded, chagrined. "What else?"

Mr. Pettibone went back to the desk and picked up Jeremy's resumé. "You don't mention any church affiliation. You're not one of those New Age weirdos, are you?"

Jeremy almost smiled, then quickly thought better of it. "No, sir."

"Then you must find a church and join it as soon as possible."

Jeremy was not sure where Guy Pettibone was going with this suggestion. "Er. . .what sort of church?"

Mr. Pettibone shrugged and waved his hands vaguely in the air. "Oh, any church, as long as it has respected people of the community among its members. Mainstream is your best bet. You don't want to get identified with anything fringe or too trendy. Image, boy, image. It all has to do with the way the community sees you. Religion is in, politically speaking."

"Umm. . .all right." Jeremy made a note, then looked back at Mr. Pettibone, who had apparently noticed something else he did not like in his resumé.

"You're almost thirty years old and you're still single," Guy Pettibone said almost accusingly. "HYBs may get a certain number of women's votes, but in the end they lose a lot more."

"What's a hib?" asked Jeremy, thoroughly confused.

"H–Y–B," Mr. Pettibone explained patiently. "Handsome Young Bachelor. . . HYB. But perhaps you're already engaged or seeing someone?"

Jeremy shook his head. "No, sir. To tell the truth, I've always thought that women were a distraction I didn't have the time or money to afford."

Mr. Pettibone waved his hands and vigorously shook his head. "On the contrary. These days a successful candidate can't afford not to have an attractive wife. I suggest that you start looking around. I'm sure there must be any number of intelligent, good-looking women both willing and able to help you get elected."

Jeremy looked closely at Guy Pettibone, but the man seemed to be absolutely sincere. *He's telling me I should get married,* Jeremy thought with wonder. He made another note on the blue legal pad and looked warily toward his new mentor, almost afraid to hear what he might suggest next.

"Well, what about it? Will you take my advice?"

"I'll see what I can do." If Jeremy's voice lacked conviction, Mr. Pettibone did not seem to notice.

"Very good, Mr. Winter. By the way, I love your name. The minute I saw it, I hoped we could work together. Are you known by Jeremy?"

"Yes. My mother wanted to call me Jere, but Dad said that sounded like a girl's name, so I've always been Jeremy."

"Good. It has a strong sound to it. And the Warren. . .a family name?"

"My mother was a Warren, and there are still lots of them living around Rockdale."

"Excellent! You ought to work up a family tree, maybe even sponsor a family reunion. Besides being a good source of votes, family ties are big and getting bigger."

Jeremy's head had begun to feel light, as if he and reality were no longer in strict contact, but dutifully he made yet another note. "My family," he echoed.

"Your last name is absolutely made to order, you know," Guy Pettibone said. Jeremy raised his eyebrows and waited to hear why. It did not take long.

Mr. Pettibone lifted both arms in the air and made punching gestures with his fists. "Win with Winter! Win, win, Winter! Winner Winter!"

He dropped his hands to his sides and grinned. "Couldn't ask for catchier political slogans than those, eh, Mr. Winter?"

"I suppose not." Jeremy's ears still rang from Mr. Pettibone's enthusiastic cheers, and warily he wondered what other surprises the political consultant might have in store for him.

Mr. Pettibone looked at his watch, then at Jeremy. "I'm sorry, but I have another appointment. If I think of other things to tell you, I'll call. Also, I need you to send regular progress reports. The details are in the material you'll get on your way out."

Jeremy rose and offered Mr. Pettibone his hand. "Thank you, sir. I really appreciate what you're doing for me."

"For us, Mr. Winter, for us. Tell that uncle of yours to come to see me sometime, you hear. Washington misses him."

"Yes, sir, I will."

A few minutes later, Jeremy took the heavy packet from the receptionist and shakily signed the check that officially made him Guy Pettibone's client. In the elevator, he checked his watch, surprised to see that his entire stay at Edwards Associates had lasted less than half an hour.

So little time for so much to happen, Jeremy thought.

14

He walked from the dim lobby and blinked in the bright sunshine. Outwardly he might look the same, but inwardly Jeremy Warren Winter felt almost catastrophically altered.

Jeremy glanced at the words he had scribbled on the blue legal pad, the first commands for his new life as an aspiring politician.

Take notes (names, etc.)
Get new clothes (as per Pettibone)
Go to church (regular one)
Get married (!)
Make family tree (reunions?)

Several large orders for anyone to consider, Jeremy reflected. But Guy Pettibone knew his business. And to get what he wanted, Jeremy would willingly make every effort to do as he had been told.

Chapter 1

Jeremy Warren Winter drove toward Rockdale on a blustery March day that gave little assurance that warmer weather would ever arrive. As he left the highway and turned onto the narrow, two-lane road that would lead him to his new life, Jeremy thought of the changes that had taken place in the weeks since he had become Guy Pettibone's client.

From the way he dressed (loafers instead of wing-tips, more casual jackets and trousers) and wore his hair (longer in front, with part sweeping his forehead) to the car he now drove (a three-year-old, American-made sedan), Jeremy had followed his mentor's every suggestion.

"I rather like your new look," Jeremy's sister, Janice, had said when he stopped by her suburban Birmingham home on his way to Rockdale. She touched the unruly shock of hair above his right eyebrow and smiled. "There's just one thing: You'd better get yourself a stick."

"A stick?" Jeremy repeated.

Janice's dark brown eyes, so like her brother's, sparkled with amusement. "You'll need something to beat off the Rockdale women," she had explained. "I know how small towns operate. Once the word gets out that you're an eligible bachelor, you'll be fair game."

Jeremy's face warmed briefly at the thought. He had not told Janice about Guy Pettibone's admonition that he should get married before campaigning for political office, but he knew she would probably endorse the idea. When Jeremy had turned thirty, Janice had frowned in exasperation when he arrived at his birthday celebration without a date. Jeremy had gone out with only a few young women during his time in Birmingham but none that he had cared for his sister to meet.

"You're not getting younger," she had reminded him. "Don't wait too long to start looking for a wife. All the good prospects will be taken."

"Maybe so, but I haven't yet seen anyone I want to spend the rest of my life with," Jeremy had truthfully replied.

"And at the rate you're going, you never will," Janice had said.

"Don't worry about it. The woman of my dreams could be waiting for me in Rockdale this very moment."

Jeremy had spoken lightly, and Janice had laughed with him. But now, as he came ever closer to Rockdale, Jeremy allowed himself to wonder if his frivolous statement might turn out to be true, after all. The whole idea of marrying for political convenience had been the most distasteful of the many suggestions that Guy Pettibone had made and the only one about which Jeremy had serious reservations.

Mr. Pettibone can't make me marry against my will, Jeremy reminded himself.

If he happened to find someone he really wanted to marry by the time he announced for Wayne Harrison's seat, fine and good. If not, he doubted that Mr. Pettibone would withdraw his aid. After all, their contract had no "marriage clause" as a requirement for Edwards Associates to continue to represent him.

Jeremy nodded as if something had been settled, then realized that he had almost driven past the turnoff to Rockdale. The narrow, blacktop road wound some distance up a steep grade, then snaked down into the protected valley where the town lay.

"Rockdale may be in the middle of nowhere, but it's still the prettiest place this side of heaven," Jeremy's mother had often said of her home town.

She was right about that, Jeremy thought. Even now, without the lush green vegetation that was yet to come, the stark landscape held its own beauty and symmetry.

Skeletal trees interspersed with pines and cedars and a tangle of dormant vines lined both sides of the narrow road, effectively screening the few houses from view. Only an occasional mailbox and the logging roads that intersected the highway gave any hint of civilization. Jeremy passed the spot where a well-remembered, everlasting spring erupted from a cleft in the rocky hillside, only to disappear mysteriously into a hole in the ground a few feet away. He had been only five or six years old when his grandmother had first awed him with the sight. "It's like magic," Jeremy had told her.

His grandmother had nodded and spoken seriously. "In a way, it is, Jeremy. This spring comes from so deep in the earth that it never stops running, even in the driest weather. The Cherokee say it is a gift from God."

It's no wonder my Cherokee ancestors didn't want to leave this place, Jeremy thought. According to his grandmother, in 1838, when the Cherokee were ordered to leave the land they had considered to be theirs from time immemorial, her people had instead gone into hiding in the remote reaches of the forested mountains of northeastern Alabama. Fearing they would also be forced to relocate to that far-off land now known as Oklahoma, several successive generations of the family had stayed on in the deep woods.

When logging finally forced them out, the family had settled in Rockdale, where Jeremy's grandmother, Rebecca, grew up to marry a prosperous white man named Warren, who had made a fortune from timber. However, Jeremy's grandmother never forgot the old Cherokee stories, and, through the years, whenever Jeremy and Janice visited her, Rebecca Warren always repeated the tales to them.

Jeremy sighed, remembering the last time he had seen his grandmother, when he had come to Rockdale one cold November to see his mother laid to rest in the family cemetery on Warren Mountain. He had been fifteen then, living in California, where his father was stationed. Jeremy's grandmother had held him tightly when he said good-bye, and he had promised he would return to Rockdale as usual in the summer.

But instead, Jeremy's uncle had arranged for him to be a page, and he had gone to Washington. After that, Jeremy worked every summer to help pay his own way. His father soon remarried, and Adele, his new wife, wanted no part of the place where Jeremy's mother had lived.

Jeremy's eyes blurred as he recalled his next trip to Rockdale, a few years later, when he returned to bury his grandmother.

"What do you plan to do with Mrs. Warren's property?" Randall Bell had asked Jeremy then. As Rebecca Warren's lawyer, Mr. Bell knew that she had willed most of her money to Janice and all of her property to Jeremy. "You could get a good price for it, I suspect," he had added when Jeremy made no immediate reply.

"I'm not interested in selling," Jeremy had heard himself say, although until that moment, he had not really known just how much he wanted to keep her house.

"Jack Johnson's been renting the pastureland and paying shares on the crops he grows on the other acreage. I'm sure he'll be glad to continue that arrangement," Randall Bell had said.

Jeremy had nodded. "All right. What about the house? It shouldn't sit empty."

"You're right about that. I heard that your sister's about to get married. If she wants to take Mrs. Warren's best furniture and leave the rest, it'll be easier to rent." Seeing that Jeremy looked a bit overwhelmed at the thought, Mr. Bell had added, "I'll be happy to manage things for you until you finish law school," and Jeremy had quickly agreed to let him take care of the property for a percentage of its income.

Because of that relationship, Randall Bell had stayed in touch with Jeremy and followed his career with interest. A few months ago, when he had found out that Jeremy was considering a return to Rockdale, Mr. Bell had offered him a place in his law firm.

"Jim Barrett's been my partner for years, but since his stroke, he seldom comes to the office, and frankly, I could use some help. Of course, what we handle here can't compare with the kind of bigshot stuff you saw in Birmingham," he had added.

"Good, I hope it doesn't," Jeremy had said earnestly, and their deal was sealed with a handshake.

Jeremy touched his brakes, recalling that the SPEED STRICTLY ENFORCED sign at the outskirts of Rockdale meant just that. He had no intention of marring the first impression he would make with his future constituents by getting a speeding ticket. He coasted across the bridge that spanned Rockdale Creek and came to a stop at the first traffic light. From there, he could barely make out the cupola atop the Rock County Courthouse. Opposite the courthouse on the north side of the square, stood the law office of Bell and Barrett, where Jeremy would start to work on Monday morning.

No one will be there now, he thought and kept driving straight on Rockdale Boulevard. He stopped for a red light near the post office and was amused to see that two older women, standing on the steps, seemed to be looking him over pretty thoroughly. Jeremy did not recognize them, but he knew they would probably see to it that his arrival was duly and widely noted.

"Everyone knows your business in a small town, but in a way, that's good," his mother had once said. "I suspect that fact kept me and a lot of others out of trouble when we were growing up."

Jeremy drove past a jumble of small businesses, a strip shopping center, and a huge new chain store. He took the next right onto Warren Road, where a billboard proclaimed: MOUNTAIN LOTS FOR SALE, followed by a telephone number.

Jeremy briefly wondered who would buy land on a place as wild as Warren Mountain, then he rounded a sharp curve in the road and slowed to turn into a rutted driveway. Barely legible, the lettering on the battered rural mailbox still read: WARREN.

"The house needs a great deal of work," Randall Bell had warned Jeremy when he learned he planned to move into it. "I'll be glad to get someone out there if you like."

"No, thanks. I intend to do a lot of it myself. I worked several summers for a building contractor," Jeremy had said.

"All right, but you might change your mind when you see it," Randall Bell had said. "I'm afraid the last tenants weren't very good housekeepers."

Jeremy recalled Randall Bell's words when he saw the house where he had known so many happy times. Its once white clapboards badly needed a coat of paint, the porch swing hung drunkenly on one chain, and a tangle of dead weeds marked the flower garden that had once edged the winter brown bermuda grass lawn.

Nevertheless, something in this old house still said "home" to him as no other place ever could, and Jeremy's breath caught in his throat as he realized that it did, indeed, belong to him. For an instant, he fancied that the house seemed to be waiting for him with an air of expectancy, then he shook his head at his foolishness. A house was nothing more than an inanimate object, and this one might cost a great deal more to repair than he had budgeted.

Jeremy got out of the car and slowly walked toward the house. Probably visioning a pillared southern mansion, Guy Pettibone had been enthusiastic when Jeremy told him he would be living in his ancestral home.

"I'll want pictures of you, standing in front of it, holding a paint can and wearing work clothes," he had told Jeremy when he had said that the house needed repairs.

Jeremy knew that it might be some time before the house looked good enough to be in a picture. But, for better or worse, this old place would be his home, at least when he was not in Washington. He would always need to keep a place in his home district, of course.

Jeremy, realizing his presumption, stopped this thought short and ruefully shook his head. *Hubris,* the Greeks called it, an arrogance from excessive pride that had brought down more than one ambitious man.

All right, Jeremy reminded himself, *I won't let myself even think about going to Washington yet.*

He would not, he could not, forget his political goals. But for now, Jeremy knew that making his house livable and settling into a new way of life in Rockdale would be quite enough to occupy him.

∞

Jeremy's arrival in Rockdale, although unheralded, did not go unnoticed. A strange car always attracted attention, especially if its driver happened to be a lone male. Sally Proffitt and Jenny Suiter, elderly widows and lifelong friends, were standing on the post office steps exchanging gossip when they noticed an unfamiliar car, driven by a dark-haired man, stop at a red light. The man was too far away for them to make out his features, but when the car pulled away and they saw its Birmingham license prefix, Sally and Jenny exchanged knowing glances and nodded.

"That must be the Warren boy," Sally said. "Randall Bell said he'd be coming along any day now."

"I wonder why he left Birmingham? Most young people want to live in cities these days."

Sally shrugged. "Maybe he got in some kind of trouble and had to leave."

"Oh, I doubt that," said Jenny, whose mother and Rebecca Warren had been first cousins, once removed. "Maybe like the Bell girl, he just wanted to come back here to live."

Sally threw her head back and hooted in laughter. "I reckon Joan Bell would like this town even better if she could manage to catch a husband."

Jenny nodded. "She sure hasn't had much luck so far. Maybe her daddy's new law partner will fill the bill."

"I'm sure Randall had that in mind from the start. At any rate, it ought to be interesting to watch what happens."

April Kincaid came out of the post office and stopped for a moment to button her jacket against the chill of the March wind, which was strong enough to ruffle her curly, dark blond hair. Without intending to, April overheard part of the women's conversation and knew they were talking about Mr. Bell, the lawyer, and his daughter, Joan, who had come back to Rockdale to live about the same time that April had arrived. April knew Randall Bell as a lawyer, but although she had seen his daughter around town, they had never met, nor were they likely to.

April dismissed what she had just heard as idle chatter and nodded politely at the women. "Afternoon, Miss Sally, Miss Jenny."

Sally Proffitt returned April's nod. "Hello, April. Does Tom Statum have anything fit to eat tonight?"

It was a question the women asked whenever they saw April, and she always answered them patiently. "Fried chicken's on special, with mashed potatoes and gravy and green beans."

Jenny Suiter made a face. "Ugh! You tell Tom he'd better not try to serve any more of those awful fake mashed potatoes. I could cook up a batch of cardboard that'd taste better."

"And canned green beans would be better than those tasteless frozen things he had last Tuesday night," Sally added.

"I'll be sure to tell Mr. Statum what you said," April promised.

"You do that, now," said Jenny.

"Yes, ma'am. Good-bye, now."

The women silently watched April thrust her hands into her pockets and walk down the steps.

"Strange girl, that one," Sally said.

"Sure keeps to herself, but she's a good waitress."

"Yes, she is. We'll have to sit at one of her tables tonight."

∞

From the moment her father told her that Jeremy Warren was coming back to Rockdale, Joan Bell had been looking forward to seeing him again with great anticipation. She vaguely remembered Jeremy as a skinny, dark-haired boy who had spent several summers with his grandmother. When they came into town, Jeremy stayed close to Mrs. Warren, usually too shy or too afraid to play with the Rockdale children. Even when he did, since Jeremy was three years older than Joan and a boy, to boot, their paths rarely crossed.

Joan had been twelve and sick in bed with a cold at the time Jeremy's mother was buried in Rockdale. But even if Joan had been able to go, it was unlikely that her father would have let her. She was away in college when his grandmother had died, and a few months ago, when Jeremy had come to Rockdale to accept her father's invitation to join his practice, Joan was in Huntsville visiting her aunt.

Since she had not seen Jeremy Warren since they had both grown up, Joan had asked her father about him. "How did he turn out? Is he still thin as a rail?"

"Jeremy's slender, but not thin. And now, more than ever, he looks more like the Warrens," he had said.

"Is he handsome?"

Her father had looked amused. "By whose standards? As picky as you are about men, I'm not about to answer that question."

"I'm not 'picky'. . . . I just happen to have high standards," Joan had replied.

However, Joan had to admit her father's words held a germ of truth. Even given the fact that most of her friends from college had been in no hurry to get married as soon as they graduated, at the age of twenty-seven, Joan was quite ready to walk down the aisle. That she had not already done so was partly her fault, Joan knew. Several times she thought she had found the right man. She had been engaged twice, once long enough to have to return some early wedding gifts. But each time, something had happened to destroy the relationship on which she had pinned her hopes.

"Men today just can't seem to handle commitment," Joan had complained when her last marriage prospect dropped her when she had pressed about his intentions for their future.

"Or maybe they just can't seem to handle you," Randall Bell had replied. "Maybe I shouldn't have tried to be both mother and father to you all these years."

"You know I'd have hated having a stepmother," Joan had said, and her father did not disagree.

Joan had been ten years old when her mother had died, and her father had thrown himself into his work with a zeal that had left little time for anything else. A housekeeper had looked after Joan, and her aunt, who had no children, had been unable or unwilling to let Joan get very close to her. Randall Bell was relieved when Joan went away to college, but last year, when she told him she wanted to return to Rockdale, he had tried to talk her out of it.

"You won't like it. There's nothing in Rockdale for a young woman of your education and talents," he had warned her.

There aren't many eligible men in all of Rock County, Joan knew her father meant. *I know you're disappointed not to be married yet, but coming back here to live isn't likely to make you happy, either.*

Not wanting to think how right her father had been, Joan sighed and picked up a stack of test papers she had put off grading all weekend. She had needed a job, and Mr. Benson, the Rockdale High School principal ever since Joan could remember, had been delighted to welcome one of their own to his faculty.

"Lucky for us that Mrs. Hobbs decided to retire, after all," he had said. "No telling when I'd ever have another opening in social studies."

Lucky isn't the word for it, Joan thought grimly. Her two classes of seniors had suffered through a semester of economics and now struggled with the mysteries of government, while the overwhelming majority of the sophomores taking world history seemed totally uninterested in the subject.

For the time being, however, the job suited Joan's purpose well enough, at least until the end of the school term. After that, if Rockdale had nothing better to offer, then she would be forced to rethink her situation.

Joan sighed, uncapped her red pen, and had just started to mark the first paper when the telephone rang.

"Don't bother to get up. I'll answer it," Randall Bell told his daughter.

He knows it won't be for me, Joan thought sourly. *Even on a Saturday evening, no one in Rockdale is likely to call to invite me out.*

Her father put his newspaper aside and walked into the kitchen to pick up the phone. Through the open door, Joan could hear the surprise in his voice. "Jeremy! I was wondering when I'd hear from you. Are you still in Birmingham?"

Joan raised her head and listened intently to her father's side of the conversation. From it, she concluded that Jeremy Warren had, indeed, arrived in town and was already making himself at home in his grandmother's house.

"I'm surprised the phone company would activate your service on a Saturday," Joan heard her father say, then, "Oh, of course. I forgot you have a cellular phone. What are your supper plans?"

Joan put her papers aside and went into the kitchen. She touched her father's arm to get his attention. "You can invite him over here," she said.

Her father glanced at Joan, then frowned into the receiver. "What did you say? Oh, yes, that's a good idea. Try the new grocery on the boulevard. You went past it to get to Warren Road. Yes, that's right. Well, if you can't come tonight, how about meeting at the club for brunch tomorrow? One o'clock will be fine. I'll see you then."

Randall Bell hung up the telephone and turned to Joan. "That was Jeremy Winter," he said unnecessarily. "He'll be coming to the club tomorrow for brunch."

Joan made no effort to hide her satisfaction. "I'll look forward to seeing your new partner at long last," she said.

Randall Bell looked at Joan without smiling. "I'm sure you will."

∞

Jeremy followed his sister's advice and put sheets on the sagging mattress in the biggest bedroom as his first order of business, then he took the list of staples she had made and headed for the new supermarket he had passed on the way to the house. He had no trouble finding enough of the kind of food that bachelors favor to stave off starvation, at least for a few days. However, when Jeremy had put the food away, he discovered that the oven in his grandmother's old stove no longer worked, and he realized he would not be able to cook the frozen dinner he had planned to have.

Jeremy sighed. He had not counted on having to buy new appliances, and he felt momentarily depressed. *Did I really do the right thing by coming back here?*

Jeremy looked around the dingy kitchen and marveled that his grandmother had been able to produce a seemingly endless supply of tasty food using its ancient equipment.

"Our people never give up," his grandmother liked to remind him. "Once a Warren mind is set to do a thing, that thing will be done, even if it takes our last breath."

"I'm not going to give up," Jeremy said aloud. He was just tired and hungry, that was all.

Jeremy considered his options. He had turned down supper at Randall Bell's house, but there were restaurants in Rockdale. He had not seen any fast-food outlets, but Jeremy recalled a place downtown that served good, although plain, food.

Jeremy reached for his jacket and tried to recall the restaurant's name. He was heading back toward town on the Rockdale Boulevard when it came to him, and he said it out loud. "Statum's. . .that's what it was. Statum's Family Restaurant."

With the fervent hope that it was still operating, Jeremy turned left at the post office and headed for Center Street.

∞

Night after night, the customers of Statum's Family Restaurant followed the same pattern. What April privately called the senior set always arrived by five o'clock and sometimes even before, followed soon after by several working couples who could afford to eat out every night. Families with small children tended to come earlier than those with older children, who always wanted their parents to take them to the new pizza place on the boulevard, with its enticing computer games. A few regulars, mostly singles who disliked eating with noisy children, came last of all, even though they took a risk that the day's specials might be out by then.

April Kincaid had worked at Statum's long enough to know all of the regulars by name. She had quickly learned that Rockdale folks expected such friendliness from her, and even though she had to overcome her natural reserve to do it, April tried to chat with every customer who seemed to want to talk, and that was most of them.

At seven forty-five on this Saturday evening, the senior set, families with young children, and all but one of the families with older children had come and gone, leaving only a scattered handful of diners. Thinking it unlikely that anyone else would come in, April gathered the condiment holders from the vacant tables and went behind the counter to refill them. She rather liked that part of the job because it meant that she would soon be free to remove her white apron and relax while Mr. Statum and the busboy stacked the chairs on the table and swept and mopped the floor.

April had daily thanked God for leading her to this place and blessing her with this job. Tiring and somewhat dull it might be, but when April had needed work, Tom Statum had trusted her enough to let her have it. He was a big, rough man of little education who had been an army cook. When he retired, he came back to his home town and opened this restaurant. April knew she was not the only one that Tom Statum had helped out over the years, but in return for what he had done for her, she tried to be a conscientious waitress.

April had almost finished her task when Mr. Statum called to her, "You have a customer." She looked up to see a tall, dark-haired man standing just inside the

24

doorway, looking around as if uncertain of what he should do next. He wore jeans and a casual flannel shirt, but his leather jacket and loafers told April that this was no logger.

"Are you still open?" he asked. The way he spoke suggested that he was not from around there. *Perhaps that's why I don't recognize him,* April thought.

April picked up a menu as she came from behind the counter and assumed her automatic welcome-customer smile. "Yes, we are. Booth or table?"

"Booth," he said, and April set the menu on the booth he chose, well away from the other diners.

"I'll be right back to take your order," she said.

Behind the counter once more, April took a long, close look at the man and decided she had definitely never seen him before. His nearly black eyebrows formed a straight line that almost grew together over his dark, expressive eyes. With his square jaw and long, straight nose, this man was not handsome in a traditional sense, but his features had character. *I'd definitely remember meeting someone like him,* she thought.

As she filled a glass with ice and added water and Statum's customary lemon slice garnish, Tom Statum walked over to the newcomer and stuck out his hand in greeting.

"Jeremy Winter! I heard you was comin' back here to live. You gonna be livin' in the old home place?"

"Hello, Mr. Statum. It's good to see you again." Even as he spoke, Jeremy was guessing that this man owned the restaurant. "Yes, although I'm still sort of camping out."

The big man grinned. "Say, if you're gonna live in Rockdale, you have to call me Tom, like everybody else does."

April came to the table with Jeremy's water, and Tom introduced them. "April Kincaid, meet Jeremy Winter. He's gonna be livin' here now."

Although April could have felt a bit uncomfortable shaking the hand he offered, Jeremy Winter's fleeting smile assured her he did not take offense at being introduced to her. "Pleased to meet you," she said.

"Take his order. I can see he can use some fattenin' up."

"We're out of fried chicken, but the meat loaf's good."

Jeremy folded the menu and handed it to April. "Then I'll have meat loaf. . . and whatever goes with it."

April usually asked new customers if they preferred rolls or corn bread, but this time, she decided to bring both and see which he ate first. Then next time, she would know without asking.

"That guy's grandmother was a saint on this earth," Tom told April when she passed Jeremy's order on to the cook. "He was a funny lookin' little kid, but he never gave Miz Warren no trouble."

April was glad when a customer came up to the counter to pay his bill. She did not really want to hear any more praise of Jeremy Winter. Whatever he had been like as a boy or what he might be like now should mean absolutely nothing to her.

The Warrens and all their money and all the years they had been one of the most powerful influences in Rockdale all made it more unlikely that any of them, especially anyone like Jeremy Winter, would ever look twice at a nobody like April Kincaid.

Whatever else people might say about me, I know my place, April thought. She felt almost relieved when Mr. Statum told her to go on home, even before the cook had finished assembling Jeremy Winter's order.

"Thanks. It's been a long day," April told him.

She went into the kitchen and untied her apron and tossed it into the laundry bin.

"What kind of bread you want me to put on this meat loaf plate?" asked Sam, the assistant cook.

April hesitated for a moment. Jeremy's speech might not sound distinctly southern, but his roots apparently were.

"Corn bread," she replied and walked out the back door.

Chapter 2

Although the Rockdale Country Club had been built on land donated by his great-grandfather and the Warren family had always been members, Jeremy had seldom gone there. His grandmother, who had little patience with what she called "putting on airs," attended the annual Founders' Dinner but seldom participated in the women's luncheons and parties, which she called "time-wasters."

"Women ought to do something useful, not fritter their days away in idleness," Rebecca Warren had said when her daughter suggested that her mother should take more advantage of her membership.

Later, when Jeremy started spending summers in Rockdale, his mother had wanted him to take swimming lessons at the country club. "I can teach him myself a whole lot easier," his grandmother had replied, and so she did, in a deep pool made by beavers in a part of Rock Creek that meandered through the Warren land.

My grandmother was quite a woman, Jeremy thought as he guided his car through the twin, native-stone pillars that marked the entrance to the Rockdale Country Club. *They don't make many like her anymore.*

The graveled lot was so full that Jeremy had to park a good distance from the entrance. He did not mind the walk, but he was aware that his dark brown tassel loafers would be covered with fine white dust by the time he reached the sprawling, single-story stone building. He wanted to make the best possible first impression on the people who would see him today, people who would be in a position to help or hinder his political ambitions. Accordingly, Jeremy had chosen his clothing with care. Sunday brunch was less formal than an evening dinner, but he suspected that most of the people there would probably have come from church services, so the men would be wearing neckties. Jeremy selected a patterned, brown silk tie, ivory dress shirt, brown wool trousers, and tweed jacket, each approved by Mr. Pettibone's fashion consultant.

His head down against the wind, Jeremy approached the building with the long, loping stride that had helped put him on his high school and college track teams. The thought crossed his mind that he should start working out again. Mr. Pettibone had warned him that campaigning was physically demanding, and although Jeremy knew he was in pretty good shape now, he wanted to stay that way.

I must ask if Rockdale has a gym, he thought, then looked up to see Randall Bell standing in the doorway. He came forward to shake Jeremy's hand and motion him into the stone and cedar foyer.

"Right on time, I see," he noted approvingly. "Come along. Our table is over here."

Many people glanced at them as they entered the dining room, but Mr. Bell did not stop to make any introductions until he reached a table by a glass wall that overlooked the golf course. An attractive young woman with hair almost as dark as Jeremy's own turned and regarded him appraisingly.

"Joan, this is Jeremy Winter. I'm sure you two must have met as children, but you probably don't remember it."

I could never forget meeting anyone so beautiful as you. Jeremy probably would never have spoken the words aloud, even if he and Joan Bell had been alone; it was not his style. He would certainly never say anything like that in the presence of her father, who also happened to be Jeremy's employer.

Be direct but friendly, Jeremy advised himself as he nodded and extended his hand in greeting.

"Hello, Joan. I'm afraid your father's right. I couldn't have picked you out of a police lineup."

Her low, musical laugh was as easy on his ears as her elegant beauty was on his eyes, and Jeremy liked the way she looked him straight in the eye when, without rising from her seat, she took his hand and shook it briefly.

"What a flattering thing to say!" she said ruefully.

"I can assure you that my daughter has never been in a police lineup in her life." Randall Bell's tone confirmed what Jeremy already suspected: His new employer had many fine qualities, but a sense of humor was not necessarily among them.

Joan looked exasperated. "Oh, Daddy, he knows that," she said. She looked back at Jeremy. "The fact is, I only vaguely remember you as a skinny kid with long black hair."

"Well, at least I got rid of the long hair," Jeremy said.

"Now that you two have been properly introduced, let's proceed to the buffet line. I doubt you'd find a better brunch anywhere than we have right here at the Rockdale Country Club."

When her father pulled back her chair and Joan stood, her height surprised Jeremy. In high heels, she matched his five feet, ten inches; he guessed that in flats, Joan would still be only slightly shorter. As they made their way to the buffet, Jeremy admired the unhurried, natural grace of her walk.

Jeremy usually tried not to form too-quick opinions about people he had just met, especially women, but now he found himself making an exception for Joan Bell. *Not bad,* he thought before another idea presented itself. *She's probably engaged. Or even worse, maybe she's divorced.*

Jeremy did not need Guy Pettibone to tell him that marrying a divorced woman would be a great detriment to any candidate for political office.

"You ought to try the shrimp. As the chef likes to say, they're so fresh, they were swimming in the Gulf this time yesterday."

Aware that Joan had spoken to him but not sure what she had said, Jeremy nodded without smiling. Mr. Pettibone had warned him not to smile unless he had a genuine reason. "People don't trust grinners. Some will think you're not serious enough, and others will think you're a phony. When in doubt, always go for wisdom rather than wit."

No one had ever accused Jeremy of being witty, but ever since Mr. Pettibone had cautioned him to be serious, he had felt self-conscious about smiling at all.

"Joan's right," Randall Bell added. "You really ought to try the shrimp."

Belatedly, Jeremy realized what Joan must have said and knew that not responding to it must have made him appear rude. "I'm sure it's delicious, but I can't eat any kind of shellfish."

"How awful to be allergic to such wonderful food!" Joan exclaimed and looked at Jeremy as if she meant it.

When they had filled their plates and returned to the table, Jeremy told them the real reason he passed up the shrimp. "Actually, I never had any trouble with shellfish until I picked up a bad case of hepatitis when I was living in the Far East," Jeremy said. "Since then, I can't eat shellfish or drink alcohol. I was told that doing either would make me deathly ill."

Joan's eyes widened in disbelief. "That's terrible! How deprived can one person be?"

Jeremy looked down at his plate, not quite knowing how seriously to take her reaction. He felt relieved when her father spoke, as if for him.

"Jeremy shouldn't feel at all deprived. In fact, this world would be a better place if more people had the same problem."

"I don't know about that, but there'd certainly be a lot more shrimp swimming in the Gulf," Jeremy said. He did not want Joan to think he felt self-righteous about not drinking.

Joan looked at Jeremy in such open admiration that he felt his face warm. "I'm glad there's a sense of humor hiding behind that grim expression, after all," she said.

"I don't mean to look grim," Jeremy began, but Randall Bell interrupted, speaking to his daughter as if Jeremy were not present.

"He can't help it, his mother being a Warren. They all look that way. But when people get to know Jeremy, I'm sure they won't think of him as 'grim.'"

Joan leaned forward to speak to Jeremy, her expression earnest. "Speaking of getting to know people, Daddy and I were talking about that last night. We'd like to have a party here at the country club so you can meet some people."

"That would be great," Jeremy said, quite sincerely. He needed an opportunity to rub elbows with the important people in Rockdale, and he knew the Bells' guest list would likely include most, if not all, of them.

Joan smiled. "Then since you have no objections, I'll call the club manager tomorrow and see what we can work out."

By the time they finished eating, the sky had clouded, and a cold wind blew into the foyer when Jeremy opened the front door.

"Wait here. I'll bring the car around," Randall Bell instructed Joan when he felt the icy blast.

As her father hurried across the parking lot, Joan turned to Jeremy. "Daddy might not have told you so, but he's really very pleased to have you back in Rockdale."

Jeremy nodded, and Joan smiled slightly and added, "And so am I, Jeremy."

Jeremy intended to murmur something in agreement, but at that moment Randall Bell pulled up to the entrance in his almost-new Cadillac, and Jeremy followed Joan outside to open the car door for her.

"Thanks for the brunch, sir," Jeremy said over the rising wind.

"My pleasure. I'll see you at the office tomorrow morning."

"What time?" Jeremy asked, realizing belatedly that the matter of office hours had never been discussed.

"Eight thirty," Joan said for her father, who nodded.

The car pulled away, and Jeremy stood staring after it for a moment before he thrust his hands deep into his pockets and, bent against the wind, jogged back to his own car.

∞

I think I've made a good start so far, Jeremy told himself that night when he had unpacked the last of the boxes of personal items he had brought from his apartment. He was more certain than ever that he would be able to work with Randall Bell. As for his daughter. . .

Jeremy shook his head in wonder. Joan Bell was an unexpected bonus. Her father had mentioned her to Jeremy in passing, saying his daughter was a teacher and had a master's degree from some out-of-state school, but somehow Jeremy had gotten the impression she did not live in Rockdale. Or perhaps he had told him, and Jeremy's mind had just tuned out the information.

At any rate, now that he had met Joan Bell, Jeremy knew there was no way he could likely tune her out again. In fact, if she proved to meet Guy Pettibone's strict requirements, then Jeremy would no doubt be seeing her a great deal.

"Don't count your chickens before they hatch, son. Dreaming's fine, but doing is better." Here in her house, his grandmother's words seemed to echo from every wall, and Jeremy shook his head at his folly. "Slow and easy wins the race," he said aloud. He intended to achieve his ambitions, all right, but he knew it would not all happen right away.

After all, the incumbent legislator had not yet announced his retirement. But Jeremy wanted to make sure that when the time came, he would be elected to succeed him.

The Rock County courthouse had been built in the 1930s from sand-colored stone cut from the nearby tag end of the Appalachian Mountain chain. Although time and the elements had conspired to dim the building's original elegance, perhaps even to render it unsafe, Rock County officials had never managed to find sufficient funds to replace it. In traditional fashion, the square, three-story building had wide entrance doors on each of its four sides. From the basement, where the county's records were stored, to the pigeon-crowded cupola that crowned the building, many things needed to be done, from painting the walls and replacing the ceilings to cleaning and repairing the floors.

When April Kincaid entered the courthouse on the second Friday morning in March, her nose wrinkled at its distinct odor. To April, it smelled somewhat like an old, wooden-floored school building, coupled with the dust given off by the old records, along with something more that she could not quite pin down. All similar institutions, no matter where they were located, seemed to have the same kinds of unique smells, she decided.

I'd know this was a courthouse, even blindfolded and led here at midnight, April thought. She had first learned about the courthouse smell in another place and at another time, a place and time she did not like to think about now.

April ignored the creaky elevator and started up the wide steps, which sagged in the middle. Several boards groaned loudly as they were stepped on, and April idly wondered how many thousands of people had climbed these stairs in the past sixty years. She often counted each step, a holdover from the old days when April did anything she could to keep from thinking about the place where she was and the reason that she was there.

All that had changed, but old habits die hard and, as she arrived slightly breathless at the third floor, April could have told anyone who cared that she had just climbed sixty-eight steps, including those leading from the street to the south entrance.

She stopped for a moment, both to recover her breath and to see who already waited outside Judge Wayne Oliver's courtroom.

Mrs. Schmidt isn't here yet, April realized. She felt a tiny spark of hope that she might not come, after all. Neither, however, were Toni and Evelyn Trent, the social worker who was responsible for getting her to court on time. Also missing were lawyers representing both sides. April recognized Mr. Benson, the high school principal, and the woman with him, Doris Dodd. As school attendance secretary, her report that Toni was chronically truant was a big part of the girl's present legal troubles.

Knowing that joining them would be awkward, April took a seat on a pewlike bench on the opposite side of the wide hall. A moment later, she heard male voices, then two men entered the hall from stairs opposite those April had used. Even before the older man could introduce the younger to the group that waited outside the courtroom, April recognized them both and drew in a sharp breath.

She had expected Randall Bell, who had been appointed by the court to represent Toni's interests. When she had talked briefly to him about the case, April had resigned herself to the fact that Mr. Bell would probably merely go through the motions of defending the girl. But April had not expected Mr. Bell's tall, slender new partner to be with him, and she tried to recall his first name from their brief meeting at the restaurant.

He's kin to the Warrens; I remember that. But that wasn't the name Tom called him.

Mr. Bell spoke his name at almost the same moment that April remembered it. "Mrs. Dodd, Mr. Benson, this is Jeremy Winter. He's working with me now, and I've asked Judge Oliver to assign him to the Schmidt case in my place."

April's heart sank. As uninterested as Mr. Bell might have been in representing Toni, at least he knew something about her case. Jeremy Winter might be a great lawyer, but he had been in town only a few days. He certainly had not talked to Toni; the girl would have let April know anything that important.

Jeremy was still shaking Mr. Benson's hand when the courtroom door opened, and Judge Oliver's bailiff motioned them to enter.

They can't do anything without Toni, and she's not here yet, April thought as she followed the others into the smallest courtroom on the third floor.

But Toni was already there, sitting alone at the defendant's table, while Evelyn Trent, the gray-haired investigating social worker, sat at the table on the other side of the room. April noted that the girl had followed her advice and had worn a plain white blouse instead of an old tee shirt with her jeans. With her light brown hair pulled back from her thin face, which was devoid of makeup, Toni appeared even younger than her fifteen years.

The girl did not look up when April joined her, but Toni's tightly clasped hands revealed her tension. *No wonder she's uptight,* April thought, *knowing that in only a matter of minutes, the entire course of her future could be decided by strangers.*

The bailiff knocked on the judge's chamber door, then called, "All rise," as Judge Wayne Oliver emerged.

The judge's black robe hung loosely on his gaunt frame, and he almost stumbled as he took his place at the bench. *He's too old to be doing this,* April thought as Judge Oliver's penetrating blue eyes swept the courtroom, resting briefly on each of those gathered there. He cleared his throat, then spoke in a strong voice that belied his fragile appearance.

"In the matter of Toni Schmidt, minor, I have here the petition of Mr. Randall Bell, Miss Schmidt's attorney of record, to excuse himself from this case in favor of Mr. Jeremy Winter." The judge looked directly at Jeremy. "Your credentials appear to be in order, Mr. Winter. Mr. Bell's petition is hereby granted."

The judge banged his gavel, and Jeremy immediately rose. "May I address the court, Your Honor?"

"You may, Mr. Winter."

"Sir, as you are aware, I've been in Rockdale for only a short time, and I need more time to study this case. I request a continuance of thirty days."

Thirty days! April glanced at Toni, whose expression did not change. Toni had learned to mask her emotions, but April knew the girl must be deeply disappointed at this further delay.

"So granted," the judge said so quickly that April knew he had probably not only anticipated the request but had already decided to agree to it. "This hearing is set for one month from now, subject to the court calendar."

With a final bang of his gavel, Judge Oliver left the bench. April stood with the others as he retired to his chambers, then turned to Toni, whose careful mask of indifference was beginning to crumble.

"I don't see why they can't go ahead and get this over with," Toni said.

"I know you're disappointed, but having someone new to represent you could be a good thing."

Toni looked past April as the lawyer who had asked for more time to study the case joined them.

"Miss Schmidt, I know you heard me introduce myself to the judge, but in case you didn't catch my name, I'm Jeremy Winter, and I'm pleased to meet you."

He stuck out his hand, and Toni took it without saying anything. From the way Toni looked at him, April knew the girl did not trust this new lawyer. She nodded briefly to acknowledge the introduction, then looked at April as if she expected April to speak for her.

Jeremy's faintly puzzled look told April that he knew they had met, but he did not recall her name. She was about to tell him who she was and where they had met when he suddenly seemed to remember.

"Your name is April, isn't it? I think we met at DHR—the Department of Human Resources."

"I'm April Kincaid, but I'm not a social worker."

Jeremy Winter took a small notebook from his coat pocket and repeated her name as he wrote it down. "We have met, though?"

April briefly inclined her head. "Yes, the night you came to Rockdale, as a matter of fact. I wait tables at Statum's."

"Of course!" He made another note, then looked from April to Toni as if trying to figure out their connection. "Are you two sisters?" he asked, his question coaxing a smile from Toni.

"Not hardly," Toni said. "I got no real sisters or brothers, either."

"Toni is my friend." April hoped she did not sound defensive. "We both hoped the hearing would take place today."

"Yes, I understand that. I can see that this case has been pending for a while. But I need time if I'm to do my best for you, Miss Schmidt, and I'm sure your friend would agree that the delay is justified."

Toni shrugged her shoulders and looked faintly bored. "Whatever," she said.

Evelyn Trent, the social worker, who had been engaged in conversation with Doris Dodd, came up beside Toni. "It's time to go now," she said.

"April can take me back," Toni said, but Evelyn Trent shook her head.

"You both know the rules," she said, not unkindly. Then she addressed Jeremy directly. "Here's my card if you need to talk to me about anything. I'm out of the office quite a lot, but if you leave a message, I'll get back to you as soon as I can."

"Thank you, Miss Trent. I need to go over a few things with you. I'll want to talk to you, too, Miss Schmidt," he added.

The girl met his level gaze. "My name is Toni," she said.

"Good-bye, Miss Kincaid, Mr. Winter. Come along, Toni," Miss Trent said. Without looking again at either Jeremy or April, Toni turned and followed the social worker from the courtroom.

April turned to Jeremy and spoke earnestly. "Toni has a great deal of potential, Mr. Winter. If the state declares her incorrigible and ships her off to reform school, it could ruin her life."

"Please feel free to call me Jeremy," he said. "I'd like to hear your thoughts about the matter. Can we discuss it over a cup of coffee?"

April hesitated, then she glanced at her no-nonsense wristwatch and shook her head. "I don't have time now. I'll be through work after three this afternoon, though."

Jeremy consulted his notebook and shook his head. "Sorry, but I have an appointment that I expect will tie me up all afternoon. Why don't you call the office and make an appointment to see me at your convenience? Here's my card," he added when she looked uncertain.

She nodded slightly. "All right."

"Good. I'll see you soon, then."

April watched him stride away, looking every bit like a young man in a hurry to make it to the top. She glanced at the card, on which raised black letters proclaimed his name:

JEREMY WARREN WINTER, ATTORNEY-AT-LAW
OFFICE HOURS BY APPOINTMENT

Those words were followed by the office's street address and its telephone and fax machine numbers.

"Pretty fancy for Rockdale," April murmured under her breath. She had heard that Jeremy Winter had been a big-shot lawyer in Birmingham, and apparently he had brought his city ways with him. While he handed out engraved business cards, all anyone ever had to do to see Randall Bell was go to his office. Nine times out of ten, he would be there.

April tucked Jeremy's card inside her billfold, which she carried, manlike, in the back pocket of her jeans, and she wondered what had made him come to a nowhere place like Rockdale.

∞

Randall Bell had just ushered a client out of his office when Jeremy returned from the courthouse, and he motioned to him.

"Come in and tell me how the hearing went," he invited.

"It didn't," Jeremy said. "Judge Oliver granted my request for a thirty-day continuance."

"Good. I thought he would. Of course, in this case, I don't know that it'll help, but at least you'll have some time to study the facts."

"What are they, exactly?" Jeremy asked. "You told me the state wants to declare the girl incorrigible and send her to the Training School. Why?"

Randall Bell pointed to Jeremy's briefcase. "You can read the file. It seems that the girl's stepmother wants her gone, period, and the state agrees."

"I see. What about April Kincaid?"

The older lawyer looked surprised. "She was there? I didn't see her."

"Yes. I thought they were sisters, but she said she's just Toni's friend. I wondered about the connection."

"As far as I know, they're no kin. In fact, nobody knows much about April Kincaid. She just showed up in town one day, and Tom Statum gave her a job. I don't know how she got hooked up with Toni. We talked about the case when I first got it, but she never said why she was so interested in this girl."

"Maybe I'll just ask her," Jeremy said.

"She coming in today?"

"No, but she said she'd make an appointment."

"You'd better tell Edith. She might give her a hard time unless she knows you really want to see her."

"What does your secretary have against April Kincaid? She seems like a nice enough young woman."

"Our secretary," Randall Bell corrected. "Edith doesn't like pro bono cases. If she thinks a potential client can't pay, she isn't always very accommodating."

Jeremy nodded and made a note to have a talk with their secretary, Edith Westleigh, who had informed him they were distant cousins. "You're some kin to every Westleigh in Rock County," she had said with some severity. "I wouldn't go bragging about it, though, if I were you. Hardly one in ten of them are worth the gunpowder it'd take to blow them away."

If Edith had not laughed at the sight of his stricken face, Jeremy might have thought that she was serious. But he had soon learned that this crotchety-appearing, long-lost cousin knew every family in the county and that her judgments about their character seemed to be fairly accurate.

Almost as if she had heard her name mentioned, Edith came to the office door and told Mr. Bell that he had a telephone call. "It's Joan," she added.

Jeremy turned to leave, but Randall Bell motioned for him to stay. "This may concern you," he said, lifting the receiver.

I doubt it, Jeremy thought. Since meeting her the previous Sunday, Jeremy had not seen or talked to Joan Bell, but her father had told him she had made all the arrangements for a "little party" where Jeremy could be introduced to their friends. "Keep your calendar clear for next Saturday night," Randall Bell had warned.

"I'll do that," Jeremy said, although he did not yet have to worry about dealing with more invitations than he could handle.

Jeremy waited while Randall listened to his daughter for a moment, then said, "Yes, he's standing here right now. Maybe you'd better ask him yourself."

"Ask me what?" Jeremy asked, but Randall Bell handed over the receiver without replying to his question.

"Talk to her. I need to look up a file," Randall said.

"Hello, Joan," Jeremy said.

"I'm glad I caught you," she said, her voice barely audible over the background noise. "I thought you might be ready for some home-cooking by now. Daddy and I would like you to join us for supper tonight."

Jeremy glanced at the picture of Joan Bell on her father's desk and was reminded that she was, indeed, quite attractive. "Are you sure you want to cook tonight? I hear that teachers usually feel pretty done-in by the end of the week."

Her low, melodious laugh sent unexpected chill bumps marching down his back. "That's true, so you won't get anything fancy."

"That suits me," Jeremy said.

A loud buzzing sound startled him, and he had trouble hearing Joan. "Oh, there's the bell. I've got to go to my next class. Come about six thirty, okay?"

"Fine," Jeremy started to say just as the telephone line went dead. Apparently, Joan Bell had felt so confident that Jeremy would accept her invitation that she had not even waited to hear him say so.

"My daughter's a strong-willed young woman," Randall Bell had told Jeremy.

I'm strong-willed, too, Jeremy could have said but did not.

At least in some ways he was strong-willed. He knew what he wanted and had some idea of what he must do to get it. Maybe Joan Bell would play a part in helping Jeremy achieve his ambition. . .or maybe she would not.

Only time will tell, he thought.

But, in the meantime, Jeremy certainly did not intend to turn down an invitation to supper.

Chapter 3

Jeremy appeared at the Bells' front door promptly at six thirty, confident he was appropriately dressed in his chino slacks and long-sleeved sport shirt, topped by a casual sweater. He had thought of bringing flowers, but settled instead for a fresh loaf of french bread from the supermarket bakery.

Joan Bell answered the door herself, trim in black slacks and a plaid sweater under her white chef's apron. She smiled in amusement as she took his offering. "When I said supper would be simple, I didn't mean it wouldn't include bread."

Jeremy matched her light tone. "Well, that's a relief. I presumed you'd furnish the water, but I wasn't so sure about the bread."

"Come in. Daddy's in the den."

"Is that you, Jeremy? Come in," Randall Bell called.

Jeremy sniffed appreciatively. "Something smells good," he said.

"That's my special marinara sauce," Joan said. "All I have to do is drain the pasta and toss the salad, then we'll be ready to eat."

"Can I help you?" Jeremy asked perfunctorily, relieved when she shook her head.

"My daughter doesn't like to have anyone watch her cook," Randall Bell said when Jeremy joined him in the den.

"It's just as well. I'm all thumbs in the kitchen."

"So am I. It was lucky for me that Joan came home just after I lost my housekeeper. Otherwise, I'd have to be one of Tom Statum's regulars."

"I remember your housekeeper. Wasn't her name Ellie?"

Randall Bell nodded. "That's right. Her sister, Pearl, worked for your grandmother for many years."

"Everyone in Rockdale seems to be related in some way," Jeremy said.

"Yes, but the town's getting more new blood all the time, and that's good."

For some reason, Jeremy thought of April Kincaid. She had not yet made an appointment to see him, but with several weeks to go before Toni Schmidt's hearing, she still had plenty of time to do so.

"At the barbershop this afternoon, I heard that some company was looking at sites around Rockdale," Jeremy said.

Randall nodded. "That's right," he said and began to tell Jeremy what he knew about it.

They were discussing possible ways the county could attract new industry when, a few minutes later, Joan called them into the dining room.

"I thought I was invited to supper," Jeremy observed when he saw that the table was set with what was obviously fine porcelain and sterling silver, with crystal goblets beside each place. "This looks pretty formal."

"Maybe so, but there's nothing formal about the food," Joan said.

"Joan enjoys playing hostess with her mother's things," Randall Bell added. Her father could not see the face Joan made behind his back, but Jeremy did, and he interpreted it to mean "I'm a grown woman and I'm not playing at anything." He gave her a sympathetic smile and took the chair Joan indicated, to the right of her father's place at the head of the table. She sat to her father's left and bowed her head while her father said a perfunctory blessing.

Jeremy had not heard grace said before a meal in years, probably not since his days with his grandmother. *That's a nice touch,* he thought and was reminded what Mr. Pettibone had said about the necessity for Jeremy to join a church.

"I remember hearing Reverend Jones preach at Grandmother's church," Jeremy said a few minutes later when Joan asked him about people he recalled from his Rockdale summers. "Something about his voice always put me to sleep, but almost as soon as I'd nod off, Grandmother poked me awake with her elbow."

"His sermons must have been pretty dull, all right," Randall Bell said. "Even after he left, the church's membership kept going down. A couple of years ago, the remaining members disbanded the congregation and sold the building."

"I'm sorry to hear that," Jeremy said. His grandmother had told him that Warrens had helped to start that church, which she no doubt expected to last for at least another hundred years.

"As the expression goes, if you're looking for a 'church home,' you should come to First," Joan said.

Jeremy did not have to ask her which "First" she meant. There was only one church in Rockdale known by that name, an impressive, old-fashioned red-brick building with a Gothic spire and a large membership.

"You should feel right at home," Randall Bell agreed. "Most of the lawyers go to First."

"So do doctors and bankers and people like that," Joan added.

"Reverend Whitson, the senior minister, keeps his sermons brief and to the point," her father noted.

"That sounds appealing," Jeremy said.

Joan nodded as if something had been settled. "Then come to the eleven o'clock service this Sunday. We sit about halfway down on the right. We'll save a place for you."

"Thanks," Jeremy said. "I was thinking about doing some work around the house, but I'll try to make it."

Randall Bell nodded his approval. "I hope you can. Our clients like to see us in church."

Jeremy looked at Mr. Bell to see if he had intended to make a joke. But Randall

Bell was not given to joking, and the man appeared to be perfectly serious. *What a hypocritical thing to say about church attendance,* Jeremy thought but immediately felt a twinge of guilt as he realized that his own motives were no better.

"Many people have the idea that all lawyers are crooked," Joan said, as if to explain her father's words, and Jeremy knew she must have noticed his reaction.

"Unfortunately, some are," Randall Bell said. He frowned at Joan. "But legal ethics are hardly a suitable topic of conversation for the supper table. I'm sure we can do better."

"As a matter of fact, we can. I'd like to discuss the party with you," Joan said, addressing Jeremy. "Since the invitations need to go to the printer tomorrow, I want to make sure you approve of the arrangements."

"Whatever you plan will be fine. I really appreciate all you're doing for me," Jeremy said.

Joan looked at him without smiling. "It's our pleasure," she said.

Something in her tone told Jeremy that, although she had said "our," Joan would not necessarily be going to all this trouble for her father's new colleague without some other purpose in mind.

Joan Bell has her own agenda, he told himself. Soon, he supposed, he would find out what it was. In the meantime, unless it was at cross-purposes with his plans, Jeremy was willing to follow her lead.

∞

On Sunday morning, Jeremy slept later than he intended to. He scanned the newspaper headlines while having a sketchy breakfast of coffee and a stale cinnamon roll, then he got out the new navy blue suit that Guy Pettibone's fashion consultant had directed him to purchase.

"This will be an excellent choice for almost any occasion, from weddings and funerals to cocktail parties and dinner dances. . .anything short of a black tie gala," the consultant had said.

"I presume that would include First Church in Rockdale, Alabama," Jeremy told the full-length mirror on the back of his bedroom door. He had been advised to get a mirror because the fashion consultant had said that seeing himself all at once would alert him to any "grooming problems" he might otherwise miss. "There's no point in buying an expensive suit if you don't know what you look like from head to toe."

Jeremy straightened his tie and regarded the rather serious-looking image reflected by his mirror. *If it were a photograph,* he thought, *the caption could read: JEREMY WINTER, SINCERE AND SUCCESSFUL.*

Satisfied that his appearance was about as good as it would get, Jeremy picked up his car keys and went out into the pleasant spring morning for the ten-minute drive to First Church.

Almost as soon as Jeremy entered the huge double doorway, he felt a light touch on his arm and turned to see Joan Bell.

No doubt she has a full-length mirror, too, was Jeremy's first thought. From the top of her head to her well-shod feet, Joan was more than just well groomed. She was a knockout. Her raspberry red suit had a long jacket and a skirt that ended just below the knee, all of which fit as if it had been tailored for her.

"I was afraid you might not see us," she said.

"I don't think anyone could miss that suit," Jeremy said. He meant his words as a compliment, but she smiled ruefully.

"It is loud, isn't it? But this shade of red is my favorite color, and when I saw it in New York last spring, I couldn't resist it."

"I can see why," Jeremy said with admiration. "So you get your clothes in New York?" he added.

Joan's warm, musical laugh attracted several curious stares, and as if suddenly remembering where they were, she took Jeremy's arm and started toward the sanctuary. "No. Daddy and I went up on one of those whirlwind tours. You know the kind, where you see a couple of plays and visit a few museums."

"And shop," Jeremy added.

"Of course," Joan said, smiling.

They reached Randall Bell's pew with the first notes of an organ prelude. After the men exchanged a quiet greeting, Jeremy settled back between Joan and her father and looked around the church. Rows of cushioned, dark wood pews stretched across the width of the sanctuary. On each side wall were many stained-glass windows, each bearing the name of the family that had paid for them. Even though he was too far away to read any of the captions, Jeremy guessed that both the Bells and Randalls had windows bearing their names. Another stained-glass window, this one round and much more elaborate than the others, was set into the wall behind the altar. Although he had never been in it before, the church's interior seemed comfortably familiar, and Jeremy had no doubt that First Church would fit Mr. Pettibone's idea of "mainstream."

With the last notes of the prelude still reverberating against the lofted ceiling, several vestment-clad men came from a rear doorway and took their places on the dais in front of the altar.

Joan leaned toward Jeremy and started whispering their names to him. "The one in the middle is the senior minister, Vance Whitson," she finished, just as that somewhat rotund man came to the lectern to give a brief invocation. As he returned to his chair, a robed choir filled the loft to one side of the altar and sang another invocation. Then the congregation rose for the first hymn, one that Jeremy had never heard, much less tried to sing.

To his daughter's right, Randall Bell sang with much more enthusiasm than skill, but on Jeremy's left, while her lips seemed to be moving, he could not hear Joan at all. *She probably can't sing very well and doesn't want anyone to know it,* he guessed. In the course of the service, in which it seemed to Jeremy that he must have risen and sat at least two dozen times, Joan joined in on all the spoken responses, but he never heard her sing a note.

The robed choir sang an anthem that featured two soloists, a man and a woman. Both had pleasant voices, but Jeremy had trouble understanding the words both they and the choir were singing. After the special music, the other two ministers on the church staff shared the saying of the prayers and led the responsive readings. However, when the senior minister rose to deliver his sermon, they left the dais to sit in the otherwise empty front row. Jeremy settled back, prepared to listen attentively, but when the minister put on his glasses and began to read the sermon, Jeremy's interest waned. There was nothing particularly wrong with the message (which was, as Randall Bell had indicated, mercifully brief), but even as Jeremy heard the words, he had no idea what they had to do with him, and he felt oddly disappointed.

What did you expect? Jeremy asked himself, a question he could not answer. Maybe he did not really know what else, aside from the value of being seen there, he had hoped to gain from attending First Church, but whatever it was, he had not found it.

When the service ended, Joan and Randall Bell began to introduce Jeremy to some of the other members, a process that continued all the way up the aisle, into the foyer, and even to the parking lot. He met assorted doctors and lawyers, merchants and bankers, most with their families.

"Did I miss anyone?" Jeremy asked when they were finally alone again.

Joan laughed. "A few, but they'll probably be at the country club. You are planning to join us for brunch, I hope?"

He hadn't been, but considering the meager fare at his house, Jeremy found the idea appealing. "Yes, but only if you'll let me pay my way this time."

"If you insist," Randall Bell said. "Leave your car here and ride with us."

Once more Jeremy found himself sitting between Randall and Joan Bell. In the much closer confines of the car, Jeremy realized that the aroma he had noticed inside the church had come, not from the altar flowers as he had supposed, but from Joan's perfume.

Pleasant, he thought and almost asked the name of the scent before he realized that that would undoubtedly be a breach of etiquette.

"Well, what did you think of Reverend Whitson?" Randall Bell asked Jeremy when he had safely maneuvered his Cadillac out of the church's parking lot.

"If brevity is the soul of wit, then I suppose he must be really intelligent," Jeremy said.

Randall Bell's matter-of-fact tone reminded Jeremy once again that the older lawyer seemed almost impervious to any attempt at humor. "Yes, he is, but you heard one of his shorter messages. What did you think about it?"

Jeremy hesitated a moment, then decided he might as well be honest. "I really wasn't sure what he said. Does he always read his sermons?"

"Always," Joan said before her father had a chance to reply. "He says that's the only way he can finish on time. If he preached from notes, we'd still be there."

"I see," said Jeremy. Deciding it would be diplomatic to change the subject, Jeremy quickly added a comment about one of the people he had spoken to after the service. "It was good to see Mrs. Dinwiddie again. She and my grandmother were always good friends. I thought she'd probably passed on to her reward by now."

"Mrs. Dinwiddie was my first piano teacher," Joan said.

Without smiling, Randall Bell glanced at her. "And last."

Joan sighed. "Oh, Daddy, you didn't have to remind me of that." She turned to Jeremy and added, "I'm afraid I'm hopelessly tone deaf."

"Even so, you could have practiced," her father reminded her. "I'll always believe that you could have mastered the piano if you'd wanted to."

"Well, I didn't."

Randall Bell took his eyes off the road long enough to frown at his daughter. "My mother played the organ at First Church for forty years. We all hoped that Joan would follow in her footsteps."

"You hoped, Daddy. Grandmother Randall knew better when she tried to teach me 'Twinkle, Twinkle, Little Star,' and it came out sounding like 'Yankee Doodle.'"

Both what they said and the tone with which they spoke told Jeremy that he had managed to spark an old controversy between them, and he suspected that Joan's musical training was not the only thing they did not see the same way. Jeremy had known some male colleagues who had gone back home to live after college, and none had found it easy. Jeremy thought the situation might be different for a daughter, but apparently it was not.

I'd better change the subject again before this gets ugly, Jeremy thought. He had his opportunity almost immediately as the car passed what seemed to be a large estate, barely visible through its massive wrought-iron gates.

"Whose spread is that?" Jeremy asked Randall Bell. *I didn't know anyone in Rockdale had that kind of money,* he added privately.

As if he had understood Jeremy's thoughts, Randall Bell laughed ruefully. "Nobody you'd know. It belongs to a songwriter named Jackie Tyler. He made it big in the music business, and for some reason, he decided to live here part of the year."

"It's supposed to be quite a showplace, but we've never been inside it," Joan added.

To Jeremy's relief, both father and daughter seemed to be in a better mood when they entered the country club. Their progress toward the Bells' usual table slowed as Joan stopped several times to introduce Jeremy to even more people.

"This is my boss, Paul Benson," Joan said when she came to his table.

"We've already met," the high school principal said. He introduced Jeremy to his wife, Sarah, and their teenaged daughters, Ashley and Audra, who regarded Jeremy with great interest.

"I suppose I'll be seeing you in court," Jeremy said to the principal in parting.

"Don't tell me Mr. Benson's having legal troubles!" Joan said when they reached the table where her father was already seated.

"Of course not. He's a witness in a case I inherited from your father," Jeremy replied. He did not know how much Randall Bell told his daughter about his clients' cases, but he guessed it was very little.

"That's all there is to it," Randall agreed. "And speaking of clients, I just saw Fred Liggett over there. I need to talk to him, and it's impossible to catch him in his office. You two go on to the buffet. Don't wait for me."

However, when Randall Bell left, neither Jeremy nor Joan made a move to rise. Jeremy took advantage of her father's absence to tell Joan something that he would not want Randall Bell to hear.

"I admire Mr. Bell tremendously, and I appreciate all that he's doing for me, but if he were my father, I don't think I could stand to live with him."

Joan's face colored briefly, and she smiled ruefully. "Sometimes, neither can I. Being Daddy's little girl again has its disadvantages."

"For what it's worth, I think you're doing a great job of it," Jeremy said.

"It's worth a lot, coming from you, Jeremy," Joan said. She extended a hand toward him, and for a moment, he thought she expected him to shake it, but instead she laid it lightly on his. He turned his palm upward and grasped her hand. He barely had time to press her hand lightly before she quickly withdrew it.

The reason was immediately apparent when Jeremy heard Randall Bell's voice behind him. "I see that you've ignored me, as usual," he said to Joan. "Let's join the line before it gets any longer."

Randall Bell walked away before he could see the almost conspiratorial look that Jeremy and Joan exchanged. However, their glance did not go completely unnoticed.

Ashley Benson's long brown hair screened her face as she leaned over to whisper something in her sister's ear that caused the other girl to look over to the buffet line and giggle.

"It's about time Miss Ding-dong had a boyfriend," Audra whispered back.

Their mother frowned. "Don't whisper in public, girls. It's quite rude."

"What about whispering in private?" Ashley asked. "Is that allowed?"

Mrs. Benson sighed and adopted the expression of a parent who has suffered much and long. "Don't be impudent, Miss Ashley. You and Audra know very well how you ought to behave."

Don't we ever! said the look that Ashley and her year-younger sister exchanged before each murmured a perfunctory, "Yes, ma'am," and resumed eating.

But there was no doubt that tomorrow everyone at Rockdale High School would hear the news that uppity Miss Bell, who could not catch a man with a rope, was sweet on her daddy's new partner and that the poor sap seemed to feel the same way about her.

Chapter 4

April Kincaid, her right hand on the telephone, stood behind the counter at Statum's Family Restaurant some two weeks after Jeremy Winter had told her to make an appointment to see him. April had not meant to ignore his request, but she felt a strange reluctance to talk to the intense young lawyer who had inherited Toni's case. At first, since Toni's hearing was still a month away, it was easy to tell herself that there was still plenty of time. In the back of her mind, April thought that Jeremy Winter might return to the restaurant, but he had not.

I'll call his office tomorrow, April promised herself almost daily, but she never did anything about it. . .until now.

Just as April lifted the receiver to make the call, Mr. Statum came in from the kitchen with a strange look on his face that she could not quite figure out.

"You had a phone call a few minutes ago," he said.

There was nothing unusual about that; April did not have a telephone, and Mr. Statum had never complained about the rare calls she received at his restaurant. He had even urged her to use the restaurant telephone whenever she needed it. But something told April that this call must have been different.

"Who was it from?" she asked.

Tom Statum folded his beefy arms across his chest. "Are you in some kind of trouble, April? I want to know about it if you are."

April's eyes widened in surprised alarm. "What makes you think that?"

"I hear tell that you and that Schmidt girl are still pretty thick. I know you think you can help her and all of that, but don't let her pull you down again."

Although April felt deeply disappointed at Tom's apparent lack of trust, she put aside her own feelings in her concern for Toni. "Did Toni call? Is that it?"

Tom Statum looked slightly embarrassed. "No. It was Jeremy Winter, the new lawyer fellow. Said he wants to talk to you about the Schmidt girl."

Only when April let out her breath in a long sigh did she realize she must have been holding it. Her relief tempered her annoyance, and she made herself speak deliberately. "I told you that Toni's hearing had been postponed. I also thought you knew Mr. Winter is going to represent her. He just wants to talk to me about it."

Tom Statum had started wiping the counter while April talked, more because he was ashamed to look her in the eye than because the spotless surface needed cleaning, she guessed. April had become quite used to having people avoid looking at her in the past, but she felt hurt that Tom Statum, who by now should know her about as well as she knew herself, could still harbor doubts about April.

She sighed deeply and turned away to begin to clip the Daily Special sheet to the stack of waiting menus. Tom watched April for a moment in silence, then he put down his rag and looked directly at her. "Hey, I'm sorry if I said somethin' I shouldn't. Tell you what. Why don't you go on over to that law office and talk to Jeremy right now? I'll finish the menus."

April was touched by Tom's offer, but she still hesitated. "That's okay. I can go after the lunch rush," she said.

"Go now and you'll be back before it even starts," Tom said. "You might as well get it over with."

He knows me pretty well, all right, April thought. She tried to tell herself she had no reason to be concerned about talking to Jeremy Winter. He seemed like a nice man, for a lawyer, and she hoped he would try to do more for Toni than Mr. Bell had.

"All right, I will. . .and thanks."

Tom Statum smiled widely. "No problem, April. Now take off that apron and get out of here."

In the kitchen, April hung her apron on its peg, then closed her eyes in silent prayer. *Lord, just help me do and say the right things to help Toni.*

Feeling better, April hurried out to find Jeremy Winter.

∞

Jeremy had made a note to call April Kincaid in two weeks if she had not already come in to see him by then. When Edith Westleigh confirmed that April had not made an appointment, Jeremy decided to call her himself. The file he had inherited from Randall Bell contained only her work number, and when Jeremy called the restaurant, Tom Statum answered and said that April had not come in yet.

After a brief conversation in which Jeremy had asked Tom to tell April that he needed to see her, Jeremy hung up the telephone. At almost the same instant, Randall Bell entered his office and held out a manila file folder.

"If you find yourself with some free time this morning, this needs to be attended to."

Jeremy eyed the folder warily. "Is that the Morgan title thing?" he asked and was unsurprised when Mr. Bell nodded.

Of all the undesirable chores that Randall Bell had given Jeremy, title searches had been the worst. The oldest records were stored in dusty file boxes on shelves in the courthouse basement. It was impossible to open them without releasing a fine layer of ancient dirt and grit that settled on the searcher's hands, face, and clothing. When Jeremy had completed his first search, he returned to the office as bedraggled and grimy as if he had been mining coal.

"I should have warned you to wear old clothes to do title searches," Mr. Bell had told Jeremy then. "Keep some coveralls or something in the office. Otherwise, you could have a huge dry cleaning bill."

Now Jeremy glanced down at his second-best work outfit, as the consultant had called the dark trousers and lighter sports coat he had chosen to wear that day, and imagined what it would look like after a few hours in the basement archives.

"I can go over as soon as I change. My sweats are in the trunk of my car."

Randall Bell nodded. "Good. It would be a shame to ruin such a nice jacket." He laid the folder on Jeremy's desk and turned to leave, then stopped at the door. "Oh, by the way. . .I'm having lunch at the club today, so I won't be here when you get back."

"I'll put the folder on your desk in case I'm tied up this afternoon," Jeremy said.

Randall Bell lifted one eyebrow as if he doubted Jeremy would have much, if anything, to do that afternoon, but he merely nodded and left without further comment.

Jeremy went to the small parking area behind the office and retrieved a gray fleece top and sweat pants from his trunk, then put them on in his office. When he passed her desk on the way out, Edith Westleigh rolled her eyes at Jeremy. "I reckon I know where you're headed," she said.

"To a hearing before the State Supreme Court, of course," Jeremy replied and was rewarded by a fleeting smile.

A few minutes later, as Jeremy sneezed from the dust raised by the first record book he opened, he tried to tell himself that what he was doing would pay off for him one day. He would not play the part of a small-town lawyer any longer than he had to.

"Slow and easy wins the race," his grandmother had often said to Jeremy when, as a young boy, he became impatient for things he wanted to come to pass at a faster pace. It would take him time to achieve his political ambitions, but Jeremy was convinced that, with Mr. Pettibone's wise counsel, they would be fulfilled.

When I'm elected to Congress, Randall Bell will have to find someone else to do his title searches. Jeremy's satisfaction faded when he saw that the ledger he had wrestled from the shelf was not the one he needed, after all.

Someday, I'll probably look back on all of this and laugh, he told himself as he pushed the book back into its proper place.

Someday. But in the meantime, Jeremy did not find much to laugh about in the present.

∞

Edith Westleigh pulled her glasses down over her nose and peered at April. "Yes?" she asked, her tone suggesting that April might have come there through some great error.

No one can make me feel inferior without my permission, April reminded herself. She drew herself to her full height and lifted her chin. "I'm here to see Mr. Winter," she said with all the authority she could muster.

Edith Westleigh did not look impressed. "Do you have an appointment?"

You know very well I don't. The old April would have said that and more, but the new person she had become understood that putting anyone else down only lowered her own worth. "No, but he left word that he wanted to see me as soon as possible."

I very much doubt that, the secretary's expression said, but her voice remained carefully polite. "I'm sorry, but Mr. Winter isn't in."

April bit her bottom lip, annoyed that she had not thought of that possibility. *I should have had enough sense to call before rushing over here,* she scolded herself, but she made herself speak calmly, nevertheless. "Oh. When will he be back?"

Edith Westleigh picked up a pencil and tapped it against a spiral-bound book lying on the desk. "I'm not sure. Would you like to make an appointment?"

"No." April started to leave, then turned back. "Can you tell me where he went?" April forced herself to smile, and while the secretary did not smile back, she seemed to be thinking about it. "He really needs to see me. He said it was important."

Edith shrugged and nodded toward the courthouse. "Mr. Winter went to search titles in the basement archives. I reckon you can talk to him there, if you don't mind a little dust."

This time April's smile was quite genuine. "Thanks. If I happen to miss Mr. Winter, tell him I came by."

"I'll do that," Edith Westleigh murmured to the young woman's retreating back.

Edith rose from her desk and watched April walk across the street, striding almost like a man.

"She's an odd one, all right," Edith said aloud before she returned to her desk.

∞

April had to ask directions in two different offices before she finally found the room that housed the Rock County deeds archives. She stood in the doorway for a moment and waited for her eyes to adjust to the dim light. At first all she could see were rows and rows of shelves, crowded with a variety of boxes, files, and ledgers. Then someone sneezed, and she looked to the right, where a solitary male figure wearing somewhat rumpled sweat clothes stood before one of the shelves, apparently trying to balance a heavy ledger in one hand while he made notes with the other.

Jeremy Winter, no doubt, April thought, although he certainly did not look much like he did the last time she had seen him. He sneezed again, his legal pad fell to the floor, and he sighed heavily as he stooped to retrieve it.

Not wanting to startle him, April approached Jeremy cautiously and stopped a few feet away. She cleared her throat and waited for him to notice her. When he took the ledger to a table wedged against the far wall, April followed him.

"Mr. Winter?"

Even in the dim light, April saw his momentary surprise when he turned to her. "You're Toni Schmidt's friend," he said, making almost a question.

"Yes. You said you wanted to talk to me?"

A faint smile twitched the corners of his mouth and quickly faded. He made a gesture that took in the room where they stood. "Yes, but in case you haven't noticed, this isn't my office."

Without smiling, April regarded him. "Mr. Statum told me I should see you right away, and your secretary told me where to find you. If you can't talk now—"

"Oh, but I can," Jeremy interrupted. "But I don't have the Schmidt file with me, and I'm not sure I can remember everything I wanted to ask you."

April hesitated for a moment, then squared her shoulders. "I have some time to talk now. I'll tell you what I know about Toni, and if there's anything else you need, I reckon I can always come to your office later."

"Fair enough, if you can stand all this dust." Jeremy pulled out a dilapidated office chair from the other side of the desk and motioned for April to sit in it. Then he turned his ancient swivel chair toward her, found a blank page on his legal pad, and uncapped a fountain pen. "For starters, how long have you known Toni Schmidt?"

April looked down at her hands and wiggled her fingers as if counting. "Four or five months, I reckon."

"I understand that you met when she stole some things from your apartment. What was that all about?"

April looked at Jeremy almost beseechingly. "Toni's not a bad girl, Mr. Winter. I knew that the first time I saw her. When she took the things from my apartment, she was desperate."

"That was after she'd run away from home?" Jeremy asked.

April nodded. "It was really cold that night, and she didn't have any way to keep warm. She took an old quilt and a couple of ratty-looking blankets and left a note saying she was sorry and she'd return my stuff as soon as she could."

Jeremy scribbled on the pad. "I remember seeing a copy of that note in the file. Didn't the police take her in that same night?"

"Yes. They didn't know she had run away until they found her sleeping in the park down by the creek."

"How long had she been gone from home by then?" Jeremy asked.

"A couple of days. Her stepmother says she didn't report her missing because Toni told her she was going to stay with a friend. But Toni says that her stepmother knew she'd run away and was glad of it."

"That's not what the official report says."

"Maybe not, but that's what happened. Mrs. Schmidt told the police they should ask Toni where she got the quilt and blankets, since she knew they weren't hers. I had just come home and found my things missing and called the police, so it didn't take them very long to figure out that Toni took them."

"That must be a record for the Rockdale Police Force," Jeremy said dryly. For years Rockdale's citizens had been aware of the department's poor performance. The police kept drunks off the streets and enforced the traffic laws almost too well, but had less success solving Rockdale's infrequent crimes.

Jeremy replaced the cap on his pen and leaned forward slightly, as if he did not want to miss a word of April's response to his next question. He had learned the ploy at the Birmingham law firm and found that it often made his interviewees say much more than they had perhaps intended.

"The bottom line is that Toni Schmidt had a long history of truancy and petty theft even before she broke into your place. Her stepmother claims she can't handle Toni, and she said under oath that she thought Toni would harm herself or others if she stayed in Rockdale. On paper, it seems the state has ample grounds to declare her incorrigible. What can you tell me about Toni that might help us keep that from happening?"

April took a deep breath and leaned forward slightly. In the short time they had been talking about Toni, Jeremy Winter had already shown more interest in her defense than Randall Bell ever did. Somehow, she knew that this young lawyer had the skill to help Toni, if only she could persuade him to use it on her behalf.

"All her life, nobody ever really wanted Toni, and she's always known it. She was six when she watched her mom die of a drug overdose up in Tennessee. No one knew where her daddy was, and her mom's relatives wouldn't take her, so Toni was passed around from one foster care place to another."

"Then Mr. Schmidt showed up with a woman he said was his wife," Jeremy said when April paused.

April nodded. "He and Marquita got Toni back, but the woman never liked her. Before long, Marquita was getting drunk or high pretty regularly. Sometimes, even when she was sober, she'd beat Toni for no reason."

Jeremy frowned, trying to remember the details of the case. "Where was Mr. Schmidt then?"

April shrugged. "Good question. He disappeared for about a year and then showed up one day, and he and Marquita had a big fight. She left, and he took Toni to his sister's in Chattanooga, where she stayed until her father married this woman named Betty, and they all, including three of Betty's children from another marriage, came here to Rockdale."

"How long ago was that?" Jeremy asked.

"Three years, I think. Anyway, Toni and Betty's kids didn't get along with each other from the first. From what she says, the kids would beat up on each other, then tell their mother that Toni hit them. . .stuff like that."

"Hearsay," Jeremy murmured. "Did her father ever try to help Toni during that time?"

"I doubt it, although Toni won't say much about him. He probably didn't know about a lot of things that happened, because he started driving big rigs about a year after they moved here. He'd be gone for weeks at a time. Things finally got so bad that Betty tried to make Toni's aunt take her. Right after that, Toni's father had a wreck in an ice storm up north and died a few weeks later."

Jeremy nodded. "That was about the time Toni started getting into serious trouble. Understandable, considering everything that had happened to her."

April lifted her hands in a gesture of appeal. "Of course. But DHR and the school system just look at what Toni did and hear her stepmother say she's a bad girl and ought to be put away." April's voice shook with her outrage, but her eyes remained dry.

"And, of course, you don't agree," Jeremy finished for her. "But even if Toni isn't sent to reform school, what sort of life can she have around here with her stepmother?"

April looked surprised. "I thought you'd read the file, Mr. Winter. Whatever it takes, I want to be Toni's guardian."

It was Jeremy's turn to look incredulous, and April found her face warming uncomfortably at his expression. "I guess I missed that part," he said.

"Or maybe Mr. Bell didn't put it in the file to begin with."

"He probably didn't think you were serious. I mean, you're so young yourself."

April raised her chin and looked straight at Jeremy. "I'm ten years older than Toni, and she respects me. Besides, I—" April broke off and looked at her watch, then rose from her chair. "I'm sorry, but I must get back to work."

Jeremy stood and followed her to the door. "Thank you for coming over. I'll call you again after I've reviewed the file," he said.

With anxious eyes, April searched his face. "Do you think you can keep Toni from going to reform school?"

Jeremy's serious expression did not change. "I can try," he said. "I'll need your help."

April's expression matched his. "You've got it," she said, meaning every word.

∞

All the way back to the restaurant, April felt as if she stood poised on the edge of a high cliff. She was just beginning to realize that she would have to answer tough questions about her own past if she applied to be Toni's guardian.

I don't even want to talk to Toni's lawyer about it, April admitted. How could she ever stand up to the facts that would come out in open court?

April closed her eyes briefly. *Lord, I'm out of my depth with this. You're going to have to wade in with me and show me what to do.*

Chapter 5

The party that Joan Bell and her father held in Jeremy's honor the next Friday evening was, by all accounts, a huge success. Nearly all the invited guests came, the food tasted even better than it looked, and almost everyone seemed convinced that Amos Warren's grandson would be a great asset, not only to Rockdale, but also to Rock County and all of Alabama.

Jeremy knew that Joan Bell was responsible for at least part of his success. He was impressed by the simple elegance of her tailored, emerald green suit and matching, flat-heeled slippers. She had swept her long, dark hair back from her face and held it in place with a flat bow of the same satiny fabric as her suit. Joan stayed close by Jeremy's side all evening, whispering names so that he could impress people by seeming to know them even before they could introduce themselves to him. He had already met quite a few of the guests around town or in the law office or the courthouse. Some he had seen at First Church, and he recalled a few others from his past visits, but at least half were total strangers with names as unfamiliar as their faces.

"I must have shaken two hundred hands tonight," Jeremy told Joan when the last guest had left the country club.

"At least that many people were here," she said.

"How do you remember them all? You'd been away from Rockdale a long time yourself. A lot of new people must have arrived while you were gone."

Joan looked pleased at Jeremy's obvious admiration. "That's true, but then, I've always been a people person. I might have no idea of my checkbook balance, but once I put a name with a face, I'll most likely remember that person forever."

Randall Bell joined them in time to hear Joan's last words and nodded to Jeremy. "When the time comes, you couldn't find a better campaign manager than my daughter. Just have someone else take care of your bank account."

Campaign manager? Jeremy cast Joan a startled look, but she had turned away to frown at her father. *Randall Bell must have told her about my plans,* he thought. They had discussed the possibility that Jeremy might eventually run for some political office, and Randall had agreed that that would be a good idea. Although neither had mentioned any particular race by name, Jeremy suspected that his uncle had already spoken to Randall Bell about Harrison's congressional seat.

"Oh, Daddy, why must you always put me down?"

Heeding the edge of anger in Joan's voice, Randall Bell put a placating hand on her arm. "You're just like your mother. All the Birches are entirely too sensitive.

It's no wonder that—" He broke off, apparently thinking better of what he was about to say, and turned his attention to Jeremy. "Sorry. I didn't mean to start a family row. I hope you enjoyed the party."

Jeremy nodded enthusiastically. "Oh, yes, sir. It couldn't have been better. I must have met just about everyone in Rockdale by now."

"You now know most of the people who matter, and that was the idea," Randall Bell said.

"I can't thank you and Joan enough," Jeremy said.

Randall glanced at his daughter and nodded. "Yes, Joan must take all the credit for planning the party. My part is paying for it."

As if Mr. Bell's words were his cue, the club manager emerged from his office holding a sheaf of papers. "May I have a word with you, Mr. Bell?" he called.

"I'll be right there." Randall Bell turned to Jeremy. "This could take some time. I don't want to impose on you, Jeremy, but I'd appreciate it if you'd take Joan home. She's had a long day, and I'm sure she's tired."

Jeremy thought of saying that Joan looked almost as fresh as she had when the evening first began, but since Randall Bell's words and tone of voice were very much like those he used when giving him orders at the office, he didn't. "Of course. I'll be happy to see Joan home."

Joan hesitated for a moment as if she wanted to protest, then she thanked Jeremy and shook a warning finger at her father. "Don't stay out too late, now. Remember we have to get up early tomorrow morning."

"As if you'd let me forget," Randall Bell said with some brusqueness. "I'll see you at the office on Monday, Jeremy."

"Yes, sir."

When Randall Bell walked away from them, Joan took Jeremy's arm and smiled. "Daddy may think I'm on my last legs, but I don't feel a bit tired."

"You don't look it, either. All the same, I'll bring the car to the door," Jeremy said.

Joan's smile was grateful. "All right. I suppose I can handle a little pampering."

On the drive back to the Bells' house, conversation turned to the Bells' weekend plans.

"Daddy has to take a deposition in Memphis, and since my college roommate lives there, I decided to go along."

"It's been awhile since I've visited Memphis," Jeremy said. "Does it still have cool blues and hot barbecue?"

Joan laughed. "Jeremy Winter, I do believe you missed your calling. You sound more like a poet than a lawyer when you talk like that."

Jeremy chuckled. "My old English teachers might disagree."

At the Bells' house, Jeremy got out first and came around to open the door for Joan. It was a small courtesy he had always been willing to offer his female passengers, but few of his dates ever gave him time to do it. Instead, it appeared that they could scarcely wait until the car stopped before getting out, often even before Jeremy had unbuckled his seat belt.

"I wish you were going to Memphis with us," Joan said when they reached her front door and she handed Jeremy the key. He unlocked and opened the door for her but made no move to step inside until she turned back and tugged on his sleeve.

He followed her into the dimly lit foyer and tried to picture himself in Memphis with Joan Bell and her father. *I already see quite enough of Randall Bell in the office,* Jeremy decided.

"I have so much to do around the house, I can't even think about going anywhere yet," he said.

"In that case, you'll just have to settle for a taste of that good barbecue. I'll bring you a sack of ribs."

"That sounds good," Jeremy said. "Have a safe trip. . .and thanks again for the party."

Jeremy's hand already grasped the doorknob, and he had every intention of turning it, opening the door, and leaving. But before he could do so, Joan put her hands on his shoulders and moved toward him. She was kissing his lips almost before Jeremy realized that she intended to do so. The subtle scent of her perfume seemed to reach out to envelop him. Reflexively, without thinking, Jeremy put his left arm around Joan's waist and pulled her even closer, cradling the back of her neck as he returned the kiss.

Joan, who had initiated it, ended the kiss a breathless moment later. She stepped out of Jeremy's embrace and opened the front door. "Good night, Jeremy," she said matter-of-factly. "I'll see you next week."

"I suppose so," he murmured. As the door closed behind him, Jeremy thought he heard Joan's warm laugh, and he wondered what she really thought about him.

Something's not exactly as it ought to be, he told himself, but Jeremy suddenly felt too tired to worry about it.

Her father had said Joan would make a good campaign manager, but Jeremy thought Randall Bell might have had another, more important role in mind for her all along.

"This is my daughter, Joan. Congressman Winter's wife, you know."

Jeremy shook his head at the image his mind had conjured, climbed back into his car, and pulled away from the Bells' house without a backward look.

Even if Jeremy had looked back, he could not have seen Joan at a window in the dark living room, watching to see what he would do.

"When a man looks back, it's a good sign he'll soon return," Joan had always heard.

Joan turned away from the window and touched her fingertips to her lips, which still tingled from the warmth of Jeremy's kiss.

Jeremy Winter isn't going anywhere. I'll see him again. And the next time he leaves this house, I'll make sure he looks back.

∞

On Saturday morning, Jeremy's clock radio came on at the usual time, but instead of music, Jeremy awakened to what seemed to be a local call-in talk show. Before he could stretch far enough to turn it off, he realized that the topic of conversation seemed to be Congressman Harrison, the man who currently represented the Rockdale part of Alabama in Congress.

"I jest wanted ter say that I used ter think that Mr. Harrison was doin' a good job fer us, but of late it seems like he'd ruther stay up there in Washington City than come home an' see what we need down here. I mean, what's he there fer, anyhow?" a man drawled.

Jeremy heard a faint click as the radio announcer disconnected that caller and spoke to the radio audience. "Well, folks, you just heard that feller say that Representative Harrison ought to be replaced. What about it? Anybody out there want to say anything else about our representative?"

After a slight silence, an obviously toothless elderly woman came on the line. "Is this the Call and Tell line?"

"Yes, ma'am, you're on the air. Go ahead with your comment."

"I think Mr. Harrison is a fine man, and I hear the reason he don't come back much no more is 'cause he's been real sick. Look at him next time he does one of them talks of his'n on the TV an' you'll see. The man looks bad."

Jeremy recalled that his grandmother had sometimes said that someone "looked bad."

"Mark my words, they might as well go on and call the undertaker," she would say, and usually she was right.

"Thank you, ma'am. I'm afraid we're out of time for this week's Call and Tell show. Thanks to all of you who called in, and to those of you who didn't get on the air this time, remember we'll be back again next Saturday morning, live from WRCK, located right here in Rockdale, Alabama, the heart of Rock County. Thanks to our fine sponsors. . . ."

Now wide awake, Jeremy sat up and turned off the radio. As he dressed in work jeans and an old tee shirt, he considered the implications of what he had just heard. The rumor that Representative Harrison might be ill had surfaced in Washington several months ago, but apparently the people in his own district were the last to know.

If he's really that sick, he might have to resign before the next election, Jeremy thought. That did not necessarily bode well for him, since Mr. Pettibone had pointed out that Jeremy would need time to build a base of support for his candidacy.

I'll call him Monday and see what he thinks I should do, Jeremy decided.

After making a sketchy breakfast, Jeremy retrieved some gardening tools from the shed behind the house and took them to what had once been a flower bed.

Poor Grandmother, Jeremy thought when he saw how weeds had all but choked out the old roses she had loved so well.

"Thorny they are, Jeremy, but beautiful enough to make up for it," she would say when he complained about the scratches he got helping her prune them.

"It seems to me they'd be even prettier if they didn't have so many stickers," he would say.

"Nothing beautiful comes without some price," she had told him.

As he did with most of his grandmother's sayings, Jeremy had dismissed her words as having nothing to do with his life. "When I grow up, I won't plant anything like these dumb old roses. If I can't have roses without thorns, then I won't have them at all."

Recalling the obstinate boy he had once been, Jeremy shook his head. He pulled on thick work gloves and bent to examine the plants. When he pulled away a tangle of dead grass and last fall's leaves, he saw that, despite their many dead canes, the plants had already begun to put out tender green shoots.

"I think we can save them, Grandmother," he said aloud. It was something that Jeremy had found himself doing ever since he had come back to Rockdale. He knew she was not actually there, of course, and wherever she was, she probably could not hear him, anyway. But a sense of her love for Jeremy was almost palpable everywhere he looked, and he did not feel the slightest bit odd or self-conscious when, at times, he felt compelled to share a thought or two with his grandmother.

Even though his muscles painfully protested that they were unused to such hard labor, Jeremy worked steadily all morning. At noon, he went inside for a sandwich, which he ate standing at the sink. He looked out the window and noticed how Warren Mountain, which rose to a height of some nine hundred feet, had already begun to show signs that the cold, hard winter was about to yield to warmer weather. A hazy golden green tipped the hardwood trees and shrubs near the base of the mountain. Although he had seldom come here in the spring, Jeremy knew that the "bloom line" would, day by day, make its slow advance upward, until the entire hill took on the same golden green hue, followed by a similar progression of darker shades of green as the trees became fully leafed out by early May.

This really is a beautiful place, Jeremy thought. He had lived and traveled literally all over the world, but he had never seen anything that could match the natural beauty of the mountains, lakes, and valleys right here in Rock County, Alabama. "This area has to be the best-kept secret in the whole United States," his mother would say every time she came back to visit. "Why would anyone want to live anywhere else?"

Why, indeed? Jeremy thought. Suddenly reminded of his mother, Jeremy finished his sandwich and decided he had done enough yard work for one day. He showered, put on fresh jeans, combed down his hair, which looked even blacker when it was wet, and walked down the main road to a narrow graveled road that led to the Warren family cemetery.

The small graveyard nestled on a flat plateau between two hills on the east side of Warren Mountain about a half mile from the house. Someone—Jeremy thought it was probably his great-great-great-grandfather—had left enough money to erect a stone fence around it and had established a fund for the cemetery's continued maintenance.

With relief, Jeremy noted that the graves had obviously been recently tended and looked neat. Randall Bell had been seeing to the cemetery since Rebecca Warren's death, and apparently he had done a good job.

That's something I ought to be doing myself now, he thought and made a mental note to speak to Mr. Bell about it. Buried here were Warrens and Ridings and Westleighs and Winters; there was not a single Bell or Randall among them. The Warrens were Jeremy's family, and it was his responsibility to tend their final resting place.

Although his family had never felt a need to visit the cemetery as a means of staying in touch with their loved ones, they always went on Decoration Day, the last Sunday in May. In a kind of minifamily reunion, as many as could get there arrived at the cemetery with fresh or dried flowers—they would have nothing to do with anything artificial—for each grave. The oldest surviving family member present would tell the younger children about their ancestors buried there. Then they all went to church, and after the service, the women would set out on plank-and-sawhorse tables the covered dishes that each family had brought. Everyone spent hours eating and "visiting," then back at the house, Rebecca Warren would offer everyone sandwiches, pound cake, and iced tea, and although they all said they were too full to eat another bite, the food had somehow disappeared.

Jeremy smiled at the memory, which seemed to have happened a very long time ago. He had attended several such Decoration Days when his father was stationed only a few hours' drive away in Georgia. His grandmother had always been a sort of grand marshal for the event, and the family's participation in the tradition had ended with her death.

We should do it again this year, Jeremy thought, even before he recalled that Mr. Pettibone had advised him to have a family reunion. Then Jeremy shook his head as he realized the impossibility of arranging anything like that on such short notice and with the house still needing so much work to make it presentable.

But by next year I ought to be able to swing it, Jeremy thought.

He began a slow circuit of the cemetery, pausing before each grave as he tried to remember how he was related to the people whose names he could barely read on the weathered headstones. The oldest stones were almost illegible, and Jeremy made another note to ask Randall Bell if anyone had information about the people who were buried there.

At his grandmother's grave, Jeremy stopped and read the inscription on her headstone aloud: "A woman of wise counsel who feared the Lord."

Quite a tribute, he thought, *and absolutely true.* Rebecca Warren never took on anything without asking for God's approval.

When Jeremy sighed and stepped away from the tall marker, he heard a muffled cry. He looked up, surprised to see that a young, blond woman stood a few feet away, equally astonished.

"Mr. Winter!" she exclaimed at the same time that Jeremy tentatively spoke her name.

"April Kincaid?"

Her face reddened, and she spread her hands wide as if to apologize for the intrusion. "I'm so sorry. I didn't know anyone was here. I reckon I'm trespassing."

She looked so anxious that Jeremy hastened to reassure her that she had done nothing wrong. "The sign says, 'POSTED—NO HUNTING,' so you're all right." When she still looked as if she doubted it, he added, "Of course, if it did say 'NO TRESPASSING,' I'd have to shoot you."

She smiled then, a small upturning of her mouth that faded all too soon, and Jeremy realized that he had never really noticed what a nice smile she had.

"I'm sure it would be justifiable homicide. Isn't that what you lawyers call it?" April asked.

Jeremy nodded and tried not to stare at her. *There's something different about her today,* he thought but could not decide exactly what. Instead of being pulled back, April's hair hung in tight curls around her face, half-screening it when she ducked her head in embarrassment. And instead of the uniform she wore to wait tables at Statum's, April had on a well-fitting pair of blue jeans, topped by a turtleneck jersey in a light shade of brown that made Jeremy realize that April's eyes were the same warm color as hazelnuts.

"How did you get here?" Jeremy asked, breaking off his gaze to look past her at the graveled lane. "I didn't hear a car."

April almost laughed but managed to stifle the sound at the last minute, as if she did not want to appear to be rude. "That's because I don't have one," she said. "I rode my mountain bike," she added when Jeremy seemed puzzled that she would walk so far.

"I take it you've come here before," he said, making it a question.

She nodded. "I came upon it by accident the first time I rode my bike all the way to the top of Warren Mountain. It's such a beautiful place, and there's some-thing so. . .calming about it that I've been back several times since. I didn't know it belonged to you. I hope you don't mind."

"It doesn't belong to me, exactly," Jeremy said quickly at the anxious tone that had crept back into her voice.

"But these are all your people, aren't they?" April's broad gesture took in the nearby graves.

"Yes. My grandmother and grandfather are buried side by side over there, and the newest headstone marks my grandmother's grave."

"Oh," April said and once more looked distressed. "I'm sorry. . .I had no idea. . .I'll go now," she said and turned to match action to her words.

"You don't have to leave," Jeremy said. "You can stay here as long as you like and come back whenever you want to. It's fine. . .really."

April bobbed her head to acknowledge his invitation. "Thanks. I don't have much time, that's for sure. I usually spend Saturday with Toni, but she had to baby-sit today."

Jeremy looked surprised. "Baby-sit? Does she do that to earn money?"

The guarded look returned to April's face, and she shook her head. "Not hardly. DHR put her in foster care with the Potters. They have two of their own and two other fosters besides Toni. Since she's the oldest, she has to take care of the others when the Potters go somewhere."

Jeremy frowned. "Is that legal?" he asked.

April's sudden laugh startled him. "Mr. Winter, you're the lawyer, remember? I reckon you ought to know that if anybody would."

"I don't know much about family law," Jeremy admitted.

"What kind of law did you study?" she asked.

"I worked with business contracts in Birmingham, but since I got here, I've done a little bit of everything."

"Like title searches," April said.

"Yes. And that reminds me, we should talk some more about Toni's hearing." Jeremy motioned toward a section of the graveyard fence that was flat enough to sit on. "We can sit over there and discuss it now if you have the time."

April hesitated, then she glanced at her watch and shook her head. "I'm sorry, Mr. Winter, but I have to work tonight. I'd better start on back to town."

"I'm sorry you can't stay." Jeremy was somewhat surprised to find that he meant it. "I need to interview Toni next week. I'd like for you to be there, if possible."

April nodded. "I'd like that, too."

"I'll look at my schedule and see when we can set it up. I'll let you know when it'll be."

"Thanks, Mr. Winter. I reckon I'll be seeing you then."

When April turned and started to walk away, Jeremy caught up with her and stopped her. "Wait. There's one more thing."

She looked at him, her hazel eyes betraying her apprehension. "What's that?"

"My name. . . It's Jeremy. I'm not old enough to be 'Mr. Winter.'"

April's small smile returned, then vanished. "All right." She got on her bike and put on her helmet, then looked back at the cemetery. "You don't know how lucky you are to have a family like this," she said in a low voice, then rode away.

"What did you say?" Jeremy called after her, but if April heard him, she gave no sign.

Jeremy stood and looked down the graveled lane a long time after April's black mountain bike had disappeared from view.

I won't mind seeing her again, Jeremy realized.

Chapter 6

With little enthusiasm, Jeremy climbed out of bed the next morning, a cloudy Sunday, and dressed to go to First Church. But when he came to the intersection that would take him to town if he turned left, he turned right instead and drove toward the church where his grandmother and her family before her had worshipped every Sunday.

He knew the building would not look the same, even if it still stood; Randall Bell had said the congregation had disbanded. *It's probably deserted and boarded up,* Jeremy told himself. However, members of his family had started the church, and even though it no longer existed, he felt a compulsion to see it for himself.

"This doesn't look like the same place," Jeremy said aloud a few minutes later when he came to a much larger parking lot than he remembered and saw groups of people, both families and individuals, heading for a rambling structure whose original white frame building had obviously been enlarged with additions on both sides to the rear. The weather-beaten wooden signboard was gone, replaced by one of sturdy metal and fiberglass, with space for changeable messages. Jeremy slowed his car and read it:

ROCKDALE COMMUNITY CHURCH
PROCLAIMING CHRIST IN HOLY BOLDNESS
ALL ARE WELCOME
ED HURLEY, PASTOR

His curiosity aroused, Jeremy turned into the graveled parking lot, over which a layer of fine white dust hung like morning fog, and parked at the end of the row closest to the building. He had no more than gotten out of the car when someone he did not recognize spoke to him, and nearly everyone else he encountered on his way to the church also greeted him. The men shook Jeremy's hand and smiled as if they were really glad to see him, although it was obvious that none of them knew him or realized his connection to their church. The greetings continued into the building itself, where Jeremy saw Tom Statum, the first person whose name he could call.

"Hello, Jeremy," Tom said as they shook hands. "I thought you might come and see what we've made of this place."

"I didn't really know anything about it," Jeremy confessed. "I heard that Grandmother's old church had disbanded, but all of this is a surprise."

"Nobody invited you? Now, that's a real shame," Tom said. He looked as if he had more to say on the subject, but just then a piano began a quiet prelude, and everyone, including the many small children already seated inside the auditorium, immediately quieted.

Tom remained at the door, Jeremy supposed to greet late arrivals, and Jeremy took a moment to survey the old church's interior. Just as he remembered it, the plain clapboards were painted white, and the side windows still had their original panes of brightly colored Italian flash glass, which let in more light than traditional stained-glass windows. The elaborate old carved pulpit and upholstered chairs behind it were gone, replaced by a modern-looking lectern, but the same graceful cherry wood rail still curved around the altar.

As if it had only been a few weeks instead of many years, Jeremy clearly recalled the smoothness of the wood against his hands and forehead as he had knelt there beside his mother and grandmother. Jeremy had really prayed then, something that he had done less and less in the years since.

Almost automatically, Jeremy sought out the pew where his grandmother always sat, the fourth from the front on the right of the center aisle. Jeremy edged past a family with several young children to take his old place near the end. As if to welcome him back, the morning sun suddenly broke through the clouds and sent its beams streaming into the church. Just as he had done as a boy, Jeremy held his hand out to let the rays fall across it, so that his skin appeared in turn to be blue, then yellow, then red.

Jeremy heard a giggle and looked to his left, where a little girl who appeared to be about six or seven gleefully imitated his action.

"I can make colors, too," she told Jeremy before her mother shushed her.

Jeremy smiled at her, then returned his attention to the front of the church, where two men now sat on rather plain chairs behind the pulpit. The older, who had startling white hair and dark eyes, Jeremy assumed to be the pastor, Ed Hurley, according to the sign out front. The younger man, his thin frame topped by wiry red hair, came to the pulpit first and signaled for the congregation to stand. He nodded to the female pianist, who launched into a lively chorus that everyone seemed to know, something about this being the day that the Lord had made.

These people sing as if they really mean the words, Jeremy thought. Then, with almost no break, the tune changed, and everyone began a second, quite different, chorus.

"There, mister." The little girl beside Jeremy tugged on his sleeve and pointed to a folder marked "Choruses" in the pew rack in front of him, but by the time he finally found the one they were singing, the music changed yet again. Although Jeremy had never heard it before, he found the slow, haunting, sweet melody deeply affecting.

"We are standing on holy ground. . .and I know that there are angels all around. . . . Let us praise Jesus now. . . . We are standing on holy ground. . . ."

As they repeated the chorus, Jeremy noticed that many of the worshipers had closed their eyes and held up one or both of their hands. Jeremy tried to imagine the people in First Church becoming so involved in their worship and could not.

After the choruses, the pastor came to the pulpit and motioned for everyone to be seated. "Let us pray," he said.

Just before he bowed his head, Jeremy was surprised to see that the pastor and many of the congregation actually knelt. The prayer itself was also different from what Jeremy expected. Rather than the usual self-conscious exhortations, this pastor almost seemed to be in earnest conversation with a God he obviously revered too much to shout at.

The redheaded song director rose to lead another hymn, which Jeremy knew well enough to sing without looking at the hymnal. On the final chorus, Tom Statum and the other ushers came down the aisle bearing the offering plates. After one of the men offered a brief prayer that the money would be used in God's will and to His glory, they began to collect the offering.

Occupied with taking out his wallet and removing some bills, Jeremy did not look back at the pulpit for some time. But when the first soaring notes of a taped accompaniment got his attention, Jeremy looked up at the singer.

With an almost physical jolt, Jeremy realized two things at once: that the singer had a beautiful voice—and that she was April Kincaid.

Jeremy could not stop staring at her. April wore a simple beige dress with long, full sleeves that fell back from her arms as she raised her hands, palms out, in a gesture similar to the one that Jeremy had seen so many others use that morning. She sang with her head thrown slightly back and her eyes half-closed. Even without being amplified by a microphone, April's surprisingly rich and clear soprano filled the auditorium with glorious sound.

Unlike the soloists at First, April made each word clear, singing with such obvious conviction that Jeremy knew the sentiments must come from her heart.

When she sang about God's grace, every person in the room felt its power and presence among them. As April sang of being redeemed from her sins, some wept openly. She held them all, including Jeremy, spellbound, and when her solo concluded on a steadily sustained high note of triumph, there was a moment of stunned silence. Then, as if they had all been holding their breath for her, everyone exhaled, and from all around the room came cries of, "Praise the Lord!" and, "Amen!" and, "Hallelujah!"

April left the dais with her head down, as if reluctant to acknowledge their praise. Pastor Hurley waited until she had taken a seat in the front row before he stood and came to the pulpit.

"Thank you, April. That was a greater sermon than anything I'll say today. However," he added dryly, "I did prepare a few concluding remarks."

A ripple of laughter ran through the congregation, which then settled back in anticipation.

From where he sat, Jeremy could see only part of the back of April's head, and he had no idea if she had seen him. *Maybe she doesn't know I'm here yet, but she will,* he thought. Each time he had seen April Kincaid, she had seemed different, but hearing her sing today had been Jeremy's biggest surprise so far.

There's something that April isn't telling me about herself, he thought, trying not to keep staring at the pew where she sat.

When Pastor Hurley began to speak, Jeremy gave his full attention to what turned out to be a refreshingly different sermon. Although he regularly cited verses from the open Bible he held in one hand, Pastor Hurley did not consult any notes but spoke with a spontaneous enthusiasm and sincerity that made everything he said seem even more appealing.

On this Palm Sunday, the pastor read from several Gospels the story of Christ's triumphal entry into Jerusalem, then he invited his listeners to picture themselves as part of the crowd that greeted Christ in Jerusalem.

"Maybe you're there out of curiosity to see this man who had done so many startling things. Or maybe it's because you sense that someone who just raised Lazarus from the dead and who had made the blind see and the dumb speak and the deaf hear could also make your life better. If you heard that someone with power like that was coming into Rockdale today, wouldn't you want to get in on it? Hey, I'd be first in line!"

He went on to say that the same power that Christ had shown in His days on earth was still available to all who believed that Jesus was, indeed, the Son of God and that He still lived in the hearts and souls of those who accepted His salvation.

The message put a new and practical slant on a story that had long been familiar to Jeremy, ending in a prayer that included a plea for anyone who had never known what it was to trust in the Lord to accept His invitation to do so.

A young married couple and a teenaged girl came forward and, after greeting them, the pastor announced there would be two special Easter services the following Sunday. He prayed again, and after a last resounding "Amen" from the congregation, the service concluded.

Jeremy wanted to find and speak to April, but he lost sight of her when so many people stopped to introduce themselves and talk to him. When he was finally free to look for her, April had disappeared. He went outside, searching the dwindling cars in the parking lot, but to no effect—April was nowhere to be seen.

"You got car trouble?" Tom Statum asked when he came outside and saw Jeremy standing alone in the parking lot.

Jeremy briefly debated if he should admit that he was looking for April, then decided against it. "No, I'm on my way to the car now."

They were joined by a short, somewhat plump woman with merry, bright eyes whom Tom introduced as his wife, Jeanette.

Mrs. Statum nodded and smiled. "I've heard a lot about you, young man."

"Good, I hope," Jeremy said.

"So far. But in a town like Rockdale, everybody knows your business. Even think about doing something, and it's all over town before you can say 'Jack Robinson.'"

"I'll remember that," Jeremy said. "Nice to meet you, Mrs. Statum. Good-bye, Tom."

Tom stuck out his hand to be shaken. "Good-bye, Jeremy. I hope you'll come back next week. Being Easter, we'll have a real special service."

It will be special if April Kincaid sings again. The thought came to Jeremy's mind immediately, but his better judgment told him that if he said so, the whole town would hear that Jeremy Winter was smitten with Tom Statum's strange little waitress.

Instead, Jeremy responded to Tom's invitation with a noncommittal nod, then turned and started back to his car. Even as he put the key into the ignition, Jeremy scanned the parking lot once more, still hoping to see April. Then he remembered that she had said she did not have a car, and it was highly unlikely that she would ride her bicycle in her Sunday clothes. Therefore, April had no doubt already been given a ride home.

Jeremy was waiting for the traffic to clear so he could leave the parking lot when he idly glanced in the rearview mirror and saw the redheaded song leader come out of the church with April beside him.

The sight evoked a strange sensation that Jeremy scarcely understood. Was the man taking April home as a professional courtesy? Or did he have a more personal interest in her? Jeremy tried to recall if the song leader had worn a wedding band and could not.

It's none of my concern, Jeremy told himself, but his actions betrayed him when he brought his foot down hard on the accelerator, and his tires scratched gravel as the car roared out into the road.

"Who was that?" Ted Brown frowned through the windshield of his ten-year-old Chevrolet at the car speeding away from the church parking lot.

April had caught only a glimpse of the figure behind the wheel, but enough to recognize him. *I'd know Jeremy Winter anywhere,* she admitted to herself but would never say so to anyone else. The thought that he had probably been in church and had heard her sing made April feel oddly uneasy.

"Someone in a big hurry," April said. That much was true, and nothing would be gained by telling Ted Brown that the man was Jeremy Winter.

"That's one of the things wrong with the world today," Ted said. "Everyone's always in such a big hurry to get somewhere else that they don't enjoy being where they are right now."

Where does Jeremy Winter want to go? April wondered, then sighed. Wherever it was, he certainly would not be taking her along.

∞

Early Monday morning, Jeremy arrived at the office hoping to talk to Guy

Pettibone before Randall Bell came in.

"He's out of the office until ten o'clock," Mr. Pettibone's secretary told Jeremy. "Shall I have him call you back?"

"Yes, do that," Jeremy said. Ten o'clock in Washington would be nine o'clock in Rockdale; perhaps he and Mr. Pettibone could still transact their business before Mr. Bell stuck his head into Jeremy's office to discuss that day's work.

While he waited for the call, Jeremy opened Toni Schmidt's file and started making a few preliminary notes about her case. When the time came for him to stand before the judge and argue that Toni should not be sent to reform school, he wanted to be prepared. Seeing April's name in the file, Jeremy was again reminded of her growing appeal to him.

Am I more interested in this case for Toni's sake or for April's?

Jeremy sighed and shook his head in an attempt to stop himself from thinking about April. In order to attain the goals that would ultimately take him far from Rockdale, Jeremy first had to gain the trust of the local people. As Jeanette Statum had said the day before, his every move would be the subject of endless speculation and even more so after his political ambitions came to light. Jeremy did not have to be told that being linked with a woman like April Kincaid could very well undo the work that he had already done, with the help of Joan and Randall Bell, to put himself in a favorable light with the people who mattered.

But all of that is still in the future, he told himself. *I can't be concerned with more than one thing at a time.*

Jeremy returned his attention to Toni Schmidt's file, and he had taken almost two pages of notes before Guy Pettibone returned his call.

"I heard something that I thought you should know," Jeremy said without preamble.

"I know," Mr. Pettibone said. "It looks like Harrison might resign. If so, someone will be appointed to fill out the rest of his term. That could mean trouble."

"I realize that, but what can we do about it?"

After a short silence, Guy Pettibone spoke again. "I'll make a few calls and get back to you. How are things going down there? Any action on the list?"

Jeremy did not have to ask his political consultant what "list" he meant. "I've gotten in touch with some relatives, and I've found a likely church."

"What about the other? Any progress with the wife thing?"

The wife thing? Jeremy stifled his impulse to laugh; the whole idea really was quite preposterous. "I'm sort of seeing someone," Jeremy said.

Mr. Pettibone made a growling sound. "Sort of? There shouldn't be any 'sort of' about it. You need a suitable wife and soon. Get on with it."

"Yes, sir," Jeremy said. "Is there anything else I should do now?"

"Just sit tight. I'll make a few inquiries and get back to you."

Jeremy hung up the telephone, which rang again almost immediately.

Maybe he forgot to tell me something, Jeremy thought as he picked up the receiver.

"Hello, Jeremy. I wanted you to know I kept my promise," Joan Bell said.

For a moment, Jeremy's mind went blank, and he did not know what Joan meant. "How was Memphis?" he asked.

Joan's laugh was warm and rich. "The music was cool and the ribs. . .well, come over for supper tonight and judge for yourself if they're as good as ever."

In the background, Jeremy heard a shrill buzzer and knew she must have called him between classes. "You remembered. Thank you," he said, hoping his false heartiness would disguise his memory lapse.

"I'll take that as a 'yes.' Come about six thirty. See you then."

Jeremy replaced the receiver and sat staring at the telephone for a long moment. He half-wished Joan had not invited him to her house again, but there was no way he could have refused to come without hurting her feelings. He could not afford to do that, especially now that it seemed he might need the Bells' help even sooner than he had anticipated.

"Are you all right?" Mr. Bell's voice roused Jeremy from his reverie, and he turned and nodded.

"Yes, sir. I was just thinking about the Schmidt girl's case."

"You can do that later. The hearing is still more than a week off, and there's a matter I'd like you to see to this morning if you're free."

"Certainly. Will I need my old clothes?"

"No, this doesn't involve a title search. Come into my office, and I'll tell you about it."

Jeremy closed the Schmidt folder and pushed it to one side. For now, it would have to wait, but soon, very soon, he would talk to Toni, and April would be with her during the interview.

I won't forget about you.

That Jeremy's silent pledge was more to April Kincaid than to Toni Schmidt might be unprofessional, but at the moment, it was the way he felt.

Chapter 7

"Did you see who was at the service yesterday?" Tom Statum asked April when she came to work on Monday.

"A bunch of people," April replied. "Anybody in particular?" She had a good idea who Tom was talking about, but since she had not actually seen Jeremy in the congregation, she chose not to mention his name.

Tom looked disappointed. "Jeremy Winter was there. I thought maybe you noticed him, since you have legal business with him and all."

April had turned her back to put on her apron, and she was glad that Tom could not see the way her face warmed at the very mention of Jeremy's name. "No, I didn't see him. I don't see anyone when I'm singing," she added.

"That music was nice yesterday," Tom said. "I can't hardly wait to see what you and Ted will do for Easter services."

"Ted has big plans for the regular worship service, but whatever we do at the sunrise service will have to be simple."

"That's better, anyway, if you ask me. I reckon the Lord don't have to have fancy music, as long as it honors Him."

April tried not to think about Jeremy Winter as she went about her regular duties. Yet, knowing for sure that he had been there at the Community Church and had heard her sing made April vaguely uncomfortable. She sang as an act of worship and as a testimony to her Redeemer, not to impress anyone with her talent. Would Jeremy Winter understand? Many people insisted that April ought to "do something" with her vocal talent. When she replied that she felt she was doing what God wanted her to with His gift, many responded with doubt and disbelief.

"If I had a voice like yours, I sure wouldn't stay in Rockdale," Hoyt Greene had told her. April had gone out with him a few times, but after he had heard her sing, he pestered her about it so much that she had been glad when his company transferred him to Mobile.

As for Jeremy Winter, he had said he wanted her to be there when he interviewed Toni, so she would see him again soon even if, as April suspected, Jeremy Winter never came back to the Community Church.

He's probably more comfortable at First Church, she thought.

∞

Jeremy spent Monday evening at the Bells' house, enjoying the barbecued ribs and all the fixings that went with them that Joan had brought back from Memphis.

After they ate, Randall Bell retreated to the den with his newspaper while

Jeremy helped Joan clear away the dishes.

"Sit here at the kitchen table. I want to show you something," Joan said. She returned a moment later, pulled her chair close to Jeremy's, and opened her high school senior annual. She pointed out various Warrens, Bells, Westleighs, and Randalls. "About half the class is either your cousins or mine."

Jeremy looked at the unfamiliar faces and shook his head. "I never even heard of most of these people."

"You'll have a chance this summer when we have our tenth reunion. I'm in charge of the arrangements, and you can come and meet them. Lots of them will vote for you when you run for office."

Joan spoke so matter-of-factly that at first Jeremy wondered if he had heard her correctly. "What did you say?" he asked.

Her rich laugh told Jeremy that his astonishment had shown. "You don't have to pretend with me, Jeremy. Daddy told me you're planning to go into politics. When you do, you'll need all the support you can get."

She sounds like Guy Pettibone, Jeremy thought. *They'd make a great pair.* But neither Joan nor her father knew that he had hired a political consultant, nor had he specifically mentioned running for Harrison's seat in Congress. Although Joan had given him a perfect opening to tell her his plans, Jeremy felt strangely reluctant to do so.

"I appreciate what you and your father have done to help me already, when I'm practically a stranger—"

Before Jeremy could finish, Joan leaned forward and lightly brushed her lips against his. "Hush," she whispered.

Has she been wearing that perfume all night? Jeremy breathed in the warm scent and closed his eyes. He felt Joan's arms go around his neck and the pressure of her lips increase. Almost involuntarily, Jeremy found himself returning the kiss. Then, recalling the look of glory on April's face when she sang, Jeremy pulled away.

Misunderstanding his reason for breaking off their kiss, Joan put her hand on Jeremy's cheek and spoke in a throaty whisper. "Daddy's watching TV. He's not paying us a bit of attention."

"It's not that—" Jeremy stopped when he realized he did not know what he could say that would explain why he did not want to kiss her.

Joan's eyes narrowed, and she cocked her head to one side, assessing Jeremy as if she had never seen him before. "Daddy said you didn't have any. . .ties. If he's wrong and there's someone else—"

"No, it's not that," Jeremy said hastily. "But I don't want to appear to be using you and your father just to further my own selfish ambitions."

Even as he spoke, Jeremy thought his explanation sounded stiff and unnatural, but Joan seemed to accept it at face value.

"You're entirely too noble for your own good," she murmured and leaned toward him.

Sensing that Joan intended to kiss him again, Jeremy stood so abruptly that he almost overturned his chair. He tried to speak lightly. "You're wrong about that. But as much as I've enjoyed the evening, it's getting late, and we both have to work tomorrow."

Joan looked disappointed, but she did not try to persuade him to stay longer. "I'll see you to the door," she said after Jeremy went into the den and told her father good-bye.

"I think I can find it by myself," he said.

"Maybe so, but as a proper hostess, I can't let you take any risks."

Joan came outside with Jeremy, and he feared that she intended to follow him even farther. "I can find my car, too," he said, still keeping a light tone.

Joan glanced around as if to see if any of their neighbors might be watching, then took Jeremy's hand as if to shake it. "We must continue this discussion later."

Jeremy shook her hand, then immediately dropped it. "Thanks for bringing back the ribs. They were great."

"Any time. After all, a man deserves to have his ribs."

"Tell that to Adam," Jeremy said, surprised that the witticism had come so easily.

Joan's warm laughter followed him to the car, and even after he turned back for a final farewell wave, Jeremy felt that in some strange way, Joan still clung to him.

I'll have to do something about her, Jeremy thought, although he had no idea what.

Joan waved back, aware that it was too dark for him to see her quiet smile of triumph. *Jeremy Winter might pretend to be half-afraid of me,* she thought, *but this time he did look back.* It was just a matter of time until she would have him eating out of her hand.

∞

It took Jeremy two days and many telephone calls to coordinate arrangements for Toni Schmidt to come to his office. Toni arrived there on Thursday afternoon, delivered by Evelyn Trent after Toni's foster mother said she did not have time to pick her up at Rockdale High School.

"She can walk. It won't hurt her," Mrs. Potter argued. However, the social worker had agreed with Jeremy that three miles was a bit too far for Toni to walk, especially since cloudy skies promised possible spring storms.

"Thanks for bringing her, Miss Trent. I'll see that Toni gets home."

The social worker's frosty expression told Jeremy she did not like his suggestion. "Not by yourself you won't," she said.

"Where's April?" Toni asked. "She can go with us."

Jeremy glanced at his watch. "I told her we'd meet at three fifteen. I'm sure she'll be here any minute."

"I'll wait, then," Evelyn Trent said. However, she had just seated herself beside Toni when Edith Westleigh rapped on Jeremy's door, then opened it to admit April.

"Here she is now," Jeremy said unnecessarily. "Can you go with me to take Toni home when we're through here?"

April looked from Jeremy to Evelyn Trent and back again, obviously puzzled by the request. "Yes, as long as I get to work by five o'clock."

"I'm sure we'll be done by then if we start now."

Miss Trent stood and shrugged. "I can take a hint. I know when I'm not wanted."

Jeremy opened his office door for the social worker. "I suppose we'll see you in court. Thanks again for bringing Toni."

"I wondered why the social worker was here," April said when Jeremy returned to his desk and indicated for April to be seated.

"She had to bring me 'cause ol' Miz Prissy Potter's too busy," Toni said with heavy sarcasm.

"I hope you don't call her that to her face," April said.

"Of course not," Toni said impatiently, but it was obvious that she would like to.

"April's right," Jeremy told Toni. "Mrs. Potter will be called to testify concerning your current behavior. It wouldn't be smart to do anything to make her mad at you."

Toni lowered her head and sullenly picked at a hangnail. "I don't, but she hates me anyhow."

April took Toni's hand and spoke with quiet firmness. "I thought we had an agreement about that kind of talk."

"You don't have to live with the Potters," Toni protested.

In an attempt to stop what seemed to be a potential and fruitless argument, Jeremy cleared his throat. "Perhaps we should get started now," he said.

Toni's sullen expression, one that Jeremy had begun to think was habitual, did not change, but April looked relieved. "That's a good idea," she said.

∞

An hour and fifteen minutes later, Jeremy had determined that Toni Schmidt would almost rather go to reform school than to have to stay on with the Potters, but under no circumstances would she ever want to live under the same roof as her stepmother. Toni's response about what she wanted to do—to stay on in Rockdale with April as her guardian until she graduated from high school—was equally emphatic.

"What will you do then?" Jeremy asked.

"Join the Marines," Toni said without hesitation.

Knowing that Toni seemed unable to joke about anything, Jeremy stifled his impulse to laugh. "You certainly don't want reform school on your record, then," he said.

April nodded. "That's what I keep telling Toni."

Jeremy glanced at his watch, then closed the file folder and replaced the cap on his pen. "I think we've done about all we can for now," he said. "It's time to take Toni home."

"It's no home to me," Toni muttered darkly, but neither April nor Jeremy responded to her statement, and the girl remained silent during the drive to the Potters.

"Turn right at the next intersection," April directed a few minutes later.

"I didn't realize the Potters lived so far out," Jeremy said when he finally reached a two-story frame house where several chickens scratched listlessly in an almost bare yard.

"Yeah, there's nothing like the country life," Toni said with her usual sarcasm.

"Toni, Toni, Toni!"

Several children came running out of the house and threw their arms around Toni's knees as soon as she got out of the car.

For a moment, Toni's face softened, but she spoke to them roughly. "Hey, you guys, lay off!"

"Good-bye, Toni," April called to the girl's retreating back. "If you need anything, call me."

Without looking back at them, the girl raised one hand in a lazy wave.

Jeremy backed out of the driveway and glanced at April, whose eyes seemed unnaturally bright.

She really cares about that bratty girl, Jeremy thought in wonder.

As if she sensed how Jeremy felt about Toni, April defended the girl. "Toni tries to hide it, but she really likes those kids."

"Maybe that's because they like her, too," Jeremy said. "From what you tell me, not many people ever have."

April looked almost grateful. "That's true. You must understand that Toni isn't nearly as tough as she tries to act. If she's sent to reform school. . ."

"Let's hope she won't be," Jeremy said when April seemed unable to finish the thought.

April looked doubtful. "Do you really think you can keep her from being sent away?"

"I'm going to try my hardest. But we need to talk about your being her guardian."

"Toni wants it and I'm willing. What's the problem?"

"The DHR, for one thing. Before they give up custody, they'll want to make sure you can handle the responsibility."

April raised her head in the way that Jeremy was coming to see as characteristic when she encountered something she did not like. "I won't have to do it by myself. Many people at my church have already promised to help."

Jeremy nodded. "I suppose you mean the Community Church?"

"You saw me there yesterday," April said, making it a statement.

"I wasn't sure you knew I was there," Jeremy said, a little disappointed that April had not made any effort to speak to him.

April hesitated, then decided to tell the truth. "I didn't until I saw someone who looked like you leave the parking lot in a big hurry. Later, Mr. Statum told me that your folks had built the original building."

"That was a long time ago." Neither spoke as Jeremy pulled away from a traffic light and stopped in front of Statum's Family Restaurant. He shut off the motor and turned toward April. "You didn't tell me you could sing," he said.

April already had her hand on the door handle, but she turned around and stared at Jeremy. "When was I supposed to do that?" she asked.

Then leaving Jeremy to stare after her open-mouthed, April got out of the car and hurried into the restaurant just as the clock atop the Rock County courthouse struck five times, and with a loud clap of thunder, a deluge of rain fell.

Jeremy realized he had upset April by speaking of her singing. It was too late to go after her now, but he could come back later.

It's time I had supper at Statum's again, anyway. I'm tired of my own cooking, Jeremy told himself.

When Jeremy returned to the office for a file he wanted to review, he was surprised to find Randall Bell still there. He came into Jeremy's office and sat down as if he intended to stay awhile.

"Guy Pettibone called," he said.

Jeremy had never mentioned his name, but from Randall Bell's expression, Jeremy was certain that he knew who Guy Pettibone was and exactly what he did for a living.

"Did he say I should call him?" Jeremy asked.

Mr. Bell nodded. "Among other things. Your uncle told me you had some political ambitions, but I had no idea that you were this serious about them."

Jeremy tried to ignore the implied criticism in Mr. Bell's tone and made his own reply more a statement than an apology. "I was taught to believe that anything worth doing at all is worth doing well."

"Guy Pettibone is the best at what he does, all right. You did well to consult him, but you should have told me about it from the first. He was surprised that I didn't know your plans."

Jeremy felt faintly uneasy. "I would have told you when the time came," he said, then added, "You two must have had a long conversation."

Randall Bell shrugged. "Long enough. The gist of it is I agreed to get in touch with my Montgomery contacts and see what might happen when Harrison resigns."

"I see. That's very kind of you." Jeremy tried not to sound as dismayed as he felt. He knew he needed Randall Bell's help, but he did not want the older man to take charge of his life—and he feared that that might be about to happen.

"Not at all. When I told Joan you might run for office, right away she said she wanted to help you. I'm glad that you two are getting along so well. Men have had a way of disappointing my daughter. It's about time Joan found someone worthy of her trust."

Jeremy swallowed hard and searched for the right words. "Your daughter is a wonderful person, and you've both been more than kind to me," he said as impersonally as he could. "You should know how much I appreciate it."

"Umm." Mr. Bell steepled his fingers and looked appraisingly at Jeremy. "I've always thought that actions speak louder than words. You're being watched, Jeremy, by more people than you know. Be careful what you do."

It was not the first time Jeremy had heard such advice, and he did not have to ask Mr. Bell what he meant because he knew all too well. "Yes, sir. I don't think you have anything to worry about."

Randall Bell stood and glanced at his watch. "Well, in any case, I'm not the one who wants to run for Congress. Mr. Pettibone said for you to call him."

"Yes, I'll do that. Thanks."

Jeremy waited until he heard Randall Bell leave the building, then he let out his breath in a long sigh before he punched in Guy Pettibone's beeper number.

∞

Not long before closing time that evening, April was in the kitchen when she heard Tom Statum greet someone warmly. She looked out and saw him shaking Jeremy Winter's hand. "Have a seat. April will be with you in a minute," she heard Tom say.

April emerged from the kitchen, picked up a menu, and arrived at Jeremy's booth just as he slid into it.

"See, I told you," Tom said. "How's that for fast service?"

"Great. It beats eating at home alone, anyway."

"That's what all our reg'lars say," Tom declared. "Only thing is, you ought to come in earlier. By this time, we're usually out of some of the daily specials."

"I'll keep that in mind," Jeremy said.

"I thought maybe you didn't like the food here," April said when Tom left and went over to the cash register to take a diner's check.

"Not at all. I eat at home most of the time, but I'm afraid I'm not much of a cook," Jeremy said.

April had to struggle to keep her usual friendly waitress smile from revealing her true feelings. "I'll get your water and be back in a minute to take your order," she said.

When April went behind the counter to the ice machine, Tom Statum joined her. "You oughter go out of your way to be nice to that young man. He could use a friend."

April looked at Tom in surprise. "What makes you say that?"

"Never mind. Just remember what I said."

When April returned to the table with the water, Jeremy handed her the menu even before she could ask what he wanted to order. "I'll take whatever you recommend."

"Everyone says the baked chicken and dressing is good. It comes with green beans and sweet potatoes. I think there's enough left for at least one more serving."

Jeremy nodded. "Then I'll have it."

April started to leave, then turned back to ask another question. "Roll or corn bread?" she asked.

"I thought corn bread came with all the plates," Jeremy said. "At least, that's what you gave me when I was here before."

He remembers that? April thought. "You have a choice," she said aloud.

"Then make it corn bread."

"All right." April nodded and started to turn away until Jeremy reached out a detaining hand.

"There's one more thing, April."

The tone of his voice and the touch of his hand were unsettling, but April made herself look at Jeremy and spoke in a firm voice. "Yes? What is it?"

"When you're through here tonight, can I take you home?"

April felt as if the breath had been knocked from her body, so unexpected was his request. *Oh, yes, Jeremy, I'll be glad to have you take me home,* she wanted to say. But her natural reserve would never allow her to speak so frankly. "If it's about Toni. . . ," she began, but he shook his head.

"No, this has nothing to do with her," he said.

April glanced back at Tom. "Mr. Statum usually takes me home when it's raining."

"Tell him you already have a ride."

April nodded. "All right." Then she withdrew her hand from Jeremy's. "Your order will be ready in a few minutes," she added in her best professional waitress tone.

But back in the kitchen, April felt far from professional, and even the cook noticed her expression.

"You look mighty happy, Miss April. Somebody musta give you a mighty big tip."

"Something like that," April said.

Something better than that, she thought. *Dear Lord, don't let me feel this way about Jeremy Winter unless something good can come of it.*

Chapter 8

Jeremy, accustomed to dining alone and in haste and often scarcely heeding what he ate, made himself slow the process as much as he could until finally he was Statum's Family Restaurant's last remaining diner.

At five minutes until nine, Tom Statum reversed the OPEN sign and locked the door. "I'll finish up. You can leave whenever you're ready."

April glanced at Jeremy. "Can I get you anything else?"

"No, thanks."

April nodded and went into the kitchen, Jeremy supposed to take off her apron, and he stood and reached for his wallet.

"How was everything?" Tom asked at the cash register.

"Very good," Jeremy said, although in truth he had paid far more attention to April than to what she had served him.

Tom handed Jeremy his change, then leaned forward slightly and spoke with a lowered voice. "That April's one fine girl. She could use a friend like you about now."

Not knowing quite what to say, Jeremy merely nodded. April came out of the kitchen and told Tom good night, then walked to the front door and opened it with her key before Jeremy could offer to do it for her.

"See you later," Tom called after them as Jeremy and April went outside.

It occurred to Jeremy that he and April were alone together after dark for the first time, and he wondered if that was why she seemed so uneasy. "My car is over there across the street." Jeremy opened the passenger door for April, then took his seat behind the wheel and inserted the key into the ignition without starting the engine. "Is there someplace else you'd like to go?"

April's laugh was barely audible. "In Rockdale at this hour, there's only Scooter's."

Jeremy recalled the roadhouse's unsavory reputation. "I'm sure that's not the kind of place either of us needs to be seen," he said.

"Just take me home." April sounded so tense that Jeremy feared he had somehow offended her.

"I don't know where you live," he said.

"Fifteen twenty Harrison," April said. "It's near Dale Boulevard."

With a jolt, Jeremy realized that April's apartment, which Toni had broken into, was located in Rockdale's only low-rent housing complex. Harrison Homes had been so named for the congressman who had helped get it built and whom Jeremy now wanted to replace in Washington.

74

Small world, he thought. Jeremy would have said so to Joan Bell, but April knew nothing about his political ambitions, and for now it seemed better to leave it that way.

"This whole area was an eyesore for years," Jeremy said. "The housing project is one of the best things that Harrison ever did."

"Harrison?" April's tone made it clear that she did not know who he was.

"The congressman from this district. The project wouldn't have been built without his help."

"Turn here. It's the last unit on the right," April said.

Jeremy shut off the ignition and surveyed the one-story brick apartment, distinguished from its neighbors by the small grapevine wreath studded with dried flowers on the front door.

"The place looks nice," Jeremy commented.

April sighed. "It's still public housing." Then she turned to Jeremy and spoke with anxiety in her voice. "Will living here hurt my chances to become Toni's guardian? Because if so, I've been saving up. I should have enough for a deposit on a better place."

Jeremy wanted to take April's hands, now clasped together under her chin in an attitude of supplication, and reassure her that it did not matter, but he could not give her any false hopes. "That's just part of it," he said. "You don't have a car, and that's a disadvantage," Jeremy said.

"Tom Statum's looking for a used car I can afford. In the meantime, he or Tim Brown take me wherever I can't ride my bike."

"I hope he finds something for you soon," Jeremy said.

April looked around uneasily. "We should go inside," she said. "Someone's likely to offer you a hit if you stay in the car."

"A hit?" Jeremy repeated. Although he knew quite well that April referred to a drug deal, Jeremy was surprised to think that such things could happen in a quiet place like Rockdale, and he said so.

"I'm afraid there aren't many safe places left anymore," April said with a note of sadness.

"It sounds like you speak from experience," Jeremy said.

When April quickly opened her door and got out of the car, Jeremy guessed it was in part because she did not want to talk about her past, whatever it might have been.

Jeremy followed April into the apartment and waited at the door while she switched on a table lamp and illuminated a clean and neat but very sparsely furnished room. From his vantage point just inside the front door, Jeremy could see all of the apartment's rooms. A small kitchen opened to the left of the living room, with a bedroom and bath visible to the rear. Two mountain bikes leaned against the apartment's front wall.

"You have two bikes?" he asked April.

"I keep one here for when Toni visits. She likes to ride, too."

I'd feel cramped in this place, even by myself, Jeremy thought. "Do you really have enough room for Toni?" he asked aloud.

April looked surprised at his question. "Of course," she said. "The couch makes into a bed, and Toni doesn't need much space. You should see where she has to stay at the Potters' house."

"Foster homes aren't usually luxurious," Jeremy said, "but from what Toni says, she'd rather stay in one than go to reform school."

April started to speak, then seemed to remember her role as hostess. "Please, sit down. Would you like a cup of coffee?"

"Thanks. That sounds good," Jeremy said.

A few minutes later, when April brought out a tray set with two cheap stoneware mugs and a couple of slices of homemade coffee cake on a chipped plate, Jeremy could not help comparing her and Joan Bell as hostesses. Both had tried to make Jeremy comfortable and had given him the best they had to offer. April's apartment lacked the expensive furnishings and fine china of the Bells' home, but somehow Jeremy felt more comfortable in it.

"This is delicious. When do you have time to bake?" Jeremy asked.

His praise seemed to embarrass April. "I enjoy it. Toni wants to learn how to 'cook fancy,' as she puts it. There's lots of things like that we could do together."

Jeremy nodded. "I'm sure that's so, but if you don't mind, I'd rather not talk about Toni tonight."

April seemed momentarily flustered. "Can I get you more coffee?" she asked.

"Yes, thanks. It's good." Jeremy noticed that April's hand, which no doubt effortlessly poured dozens of refills each day, shook slightly as she refilled his cup. *I'm making her uncomfortable,* he realized and decided to make his apology.

"I didn't mean to upset you when I said what I did about your singing. It was stupid of me. Of course, you don't go around telling strangers that you have a gorgeous voice. I was trying to pay you a sincere compliment, and if I seemed out of line, please forgive me."

In contrast to his usual well-thought-out speeches, Jeremy spoke in a rush, and when April lowered her head as if she could not stand to look at him, Jeremy thought he had made matters even worse and added, "Okay?"

April nodded her head, then raised it and looked at Jeremy in a way that made his heart seem to skip a beat. "I've never had many compliments, so I don't rightly know how to take them," April said. "I don't sing anywhere except church," she added, her tone suggesting that he might try to argue the point.

"God has given you a wonderful talent," Jeremy said sincerely. "I don't blame you for wanting to use it for Him."

April's eyes widened slightly. "I didn't expect. . .I mean, you don't have to apologize to me for anything," she said.

"Good. No matter what happens with Toni's hearing, I hope we can still be friends."

"So do I," April said.

Jeremy glanced at his watch and stood. "I'd better go now. I'll see you at the hearing?"

"Yes, but we're having a sunrise service on Warren Mountain Sunday morning. You're welcome to come."

I want you to be there, her eyes told him, and Jeremy smiled.

"All right. I'll try to make it," Jeremy said. "Thanks for the coffee."

April walked to the door ahead of Jeremy and opened it for him. "Good night," she said.

"You, too." Jeremy lingered at the door, aware that he did not really want to leave. He wanted to cradle April's face in his hands and kiss her.

Instead, he took her hand in his and held it. Their eyes met, and Jeremy hoped that the intensity of his gaze would speak for him before he released April's hand and turned away.

"Stay safe," April said so faintly that Jeremy was not sure whether he had really heard her or had merely thought the words that his grandmother had said to him so often over the years.

You stay safe, too, sweet April. By the time Jeremy could turn back to give voice to the words, April had closed her door.

Thinking April just might be watching him, Jeremy waved once more before he turned back and got into his car.

∞

The next day, Jeremy walked into the office to the sound of his ringing telephone and picked up the receiver to hear Guy Pettibone's secretary say that he had been trying to reach him. "I'll put him through now, Mr. Winter," she said.

"I called your beeper number yesterday," Jeremy said when Mr. Pettibone came on the line. "I'm sorry I missed you."

"Big things underfoot, boy. The word is that the governor's calling a meeting in Montgomery next week to discuss what to do about Harrison's seat. Nothing public yet, but all the movers and shakers will be there, and so should you."

"I haven't been invited," Jeremy said.

Guy Pettibone snorted. "Boy, don't you know that line about the timid heart never won the fair lady? Randall Bell will be there. Just make sure that you go with him."

Jeremy felt a bit dazed. He sank down into his chair and swallowed hard. *I seem to be losing control of my life to Guy Pettibone and Randall Bell,* he thought. "When did he tell you that?" he asked.

"Last night. When I couldn't get you at home, I called him. Bell's a good man, and he knows the right people. But you really need a beeper. A cellular phone's no good if you don't answer it."

Jeremy tried hard not to sound defensive. "I'm sorry I missed your call. I ate out and didn't get home until late. Mr. Bell can fill me in on the Montgomery meeting."

"Yes, but in the meantime, I've put out some other feelers that he doesn't know about. Bell's going strictly with his party, and you don't want a party label just yet. Someone without that baggage might just slip right in while the good ole boys are still fighting each other, doing business the old way."

"So I shouldn't commit to anything yet?"

"Nothing except getting your name and face known. Go on to Montgomery, but don't let on like you even recognize Harrison's name. You understand what I'm telling you, boy?"

Although Mr. Pettibone always managed to make Jeremy feel about ten years old, he cleared his throat and tried to sound sure of himself. "Yes, sir, I understand. Shall I call you when we get back?"

"Yes, or even sooner if anything changes. What's decided in the next few weeks will be critical. Stay on top of it, you hear?"

"Yes, I'll do that."

As usual, Guy Pettibone hung up the telephone almost before Jeremy could say good-bye. *Mr. Pettibone's not a man to waste words,* he thought.

Then Jeremy heard Randall Bell speaking to Edith, and he wondered what the two men had said about him. *I should hear Mr. Bell's version in about ten seconds,* he thought, but it actually took the older lawyer no more than seven seconds to rap lightly on Jeremy's office door.

"Hello there, Jeremy," he said. "Where did you get to last night? That Pettibone man was fit to be tied when he couldn't get hold of you."

"I went out to eat, but there weren't any messages on my machine when I got home."

"I suppose he doesn't like those contraptions any better than I do," Randall Bell said. "Anyhow, we had a nice talk about your chances for Harrison's seat. He thinks you ought to go to Montgomery with me next week."

Jeremy nodded. "I know. . .I just talked to him. What day is this meeting?"

"I'm not sure yet, but except for the Miller deposition on Monday and the Schmidt hearing, your calendar looks clear. We can probably postpone the Schmidt thing."

Jeremy thought of how disappointed both April and Toni would be if her hearing were further delayed. "I hope that won't be necessary," he said.

Randall Bell raised a questioning eyebrow. "That's small potatoes compared to what's happening in Montgomery. You won't ever get anywhere if you let small-town cases tie you up."

"You seem to like it here well enough," Jeremy dared to say.

Mr. Bell looked thoughtful. "I'll grant you that there's a lot to be said about being a big frog in a little pond, but if I had it to do all over again with the advantages you have. . .well, I just might be Senator Bell right now."

That Randall Bell might have had his own political ambitions had not occurred to Jeremy. "What happened that you didn't try for it?"

Mr. Bell shrugged. "Several things, including Joan's mother. She made it clear that she wanted no part of politics, and if I did, I'd have to do it on my own."

"Which means in those days you couldn't do it at all," Jeremy said, understanding Mr. Bell's dilemma.

"Those days or these, it's all the same. A man who wants to run for anything, from dogcatcher right on up the line, needs his wife's support. Without it, he hasn't much chance."

He sounds like Mr. Pettibone, Jeremy thought with some discomfort. *The next thing I know, Mr. Bell will be telling me how lucky I am to have a woman like his daughter to help me campaign.*

"It's not too late," Jeremy pointed out. "You're hardly dead with old age, and I'm sure your daughter would be a great help to you."

Randall Bell laughed ruefully. "I'm afraid too much water's already passed under that bridge for me. But you're right about Joan. She's not at all like her mother. When it comes to politics, Joan likes a good fight. You'll see."

Jeremy was saved from having to comment on that when Edith came to the office door to say that Evelyn Trent, Toni Schmidt's social worker, wanted to make an appointment to see him.

"The DHR office is closed for Good Friday, but she says she's willing to come in on her own time," Edith added.

Good Friday. April had invited him to come to the Easter sunrise service, so Jeremy should have realized what this day was.

"Tell her I can see her at ten o'clock," Jeremy said.

"We'll close the office at noon ourselves," Randall Bell said when Edith withdrew. "Hardly anybody stirs from noon on."

"Will there be special church services?" Jeremy asked.

"Not at First Church. Some of the others do something, I think, but most people stay home and rest up for Easter. That's the big day. First puts on quite a show. I think you'll enjoy it."

A church service shouldn't be a show. Jeremy would have said so, but he had learned that a political aspirant never talked about the specifics of his religion. It was good to be seen attending a solid, "mainstream" church but not to talk about it too much.

"Will there be a sunrise service?" Jeremy asked.

If he had asked if the aisles would be turned into bowling lanes, Mr. Bell could hardly have looked more shocked. "Of course not," he said, "but there'll be a big crowd at the regular service. You have to come early to get a place to park."

"I'll keep that in mind," Jeremy said.

"I've a few files to go over, then I'll be leaving. If I don't see you again before then, Joan said to tell you she hopes you'll join us at the country club for brunch after church."

"Thanks, but I'm not sure of my Sunday plans," Jeremy heard himself saying.

"Then you can call Joan and tell her that yourself. She'll think I didn't ask you nicely enough."

I don't want to call Joan Bell today or any other day, was Jeremy's first thought, but he knew that that was not entirely true. His political career needed a woman like Joan Bell, and he was extremely fortunate to have her on his side. Only a reckless fool would totally disregard her.

"I'll do that," Jeremy promised.

When Randall Bell left, Jeremy turned his attention to Toni Schmidt's case. What was Evelyn Trent's concern, coming to see him on her day off? *Whatever it is, I doubt if it means anything good for Toni,* Jeremy thought as he opened the file and referred once more to the social worker's notes.

∞

In her twenty-five years with the DHR, Evelyn Trent had seen it all, from child abuse to welfare fraud and everything in between. She took pride in her ability to keep her emotions out of her work and seldom did anything that was not strictly according to the book. But Toni Schmidt's case was different, and she did not like the way it had been going ever since Randall Bell turned it over to his young associate.

"Thank you for seeing me on such short notice," Evelyn Trent said when Jeremy invited her to have a seat. "I'm sure you want to quit work early today, so I'll make this brief."

"I'm in no hurry, Miss. Trent. What seems to be the problem?"

Evelyn Trent's fair face flushed slightly. "I don't have a problem, but you will if you go to court and petition for April Kincaid to be Toni's guardian."

Even though he was caught off guard, Jeremy tried not to show it. "How did you know about that?"

"Toni took great pleasure in telling me that soon she wouldn't have to do what we told her to because April was going to be her guardian. Is that what you intend?"

That wasn't very smart of Toni, Jeremy thought, but he masked his concern with a shrug. "I haven't decided yet," he said. "Would DHR object to that?"

The social worker nodded vigorously. "We certainly would. Toni needs a more mature and stable influence than a young woman like April Kincaid."

"Miss Kincaid seems to be both mature and stable," Jeremy said.

Evelyn Trent pursed her lips. "How much do you know about her past?"

"Evidently not as much as you seem to," Jeremy said, the need to defend April momentarily overriding his professional judgment. "Perhaps you'll enlighten me?"

"I don't repeat gossip and hearsay," Evelyn Trent said somewhat stiffly. "I'm merely suggesting that you ask the court to let Toni stay with the Potters."

"The DHR would have no objection to that?"

"We would go along with it on a continuing probationary basis. Should Toni get out of line again, we'd again petition for her to be remanded to the custody of the state."

In other words, Toni would be summarily shipped off to reform school. Jeremy did not have to say the words aloud; he knew Evelyn Trent was quite aware of the possible consequences.

"I'll consider what you've said, and I appreciate your concern," Jeremy said.

Miss Trent stood and nodded her head briefly. "I'm sure you do. After I've had my say the rest is up to you."

"Thank you for coming in," Jeremy said with studied politeness. "I suppose I'll see you in court next week?"

"I wouldn't miss it for the world," Miss Trent said with a hint of sarcasm.

Neither would I, Jeremy thought. There was no way he could ask for a postponement now. The longer Evelyn Trent had to spread doubts about April, the more difficult it would be to keep Toni in Rockdale with or without April's being her guardian.

"Have a happy Easter," Miss Trent said over her shoulder as she left his office.

"You, too," Jeremy responded automatically. But Evelyn Trent's mention reminded him that he had been invited to the Community Church's Easter sunrise service.

I won't have far to go. It's on Warren Mountain, Jeremy thought. April Kincaid would be there, and he could hear her sing.

"I'll be there for sure," Jeremy said aloud.

Chapter 9

Warren Mountain had never completely belonged to the Warrens, but since they had been the first to build on its flat ridges and gentle slopes, their name had been given to the entire range that stretched for several miles in a generally south-southwesterly direction. A natural amphitheater had been cut from the rock on the peak just beyond the Warren family cemetery, and it was there, where the sun's first rays touched the land, that sunrise services were traditionally held.

Jeremy could have walked up the mountain even in the predawn darkness, but he drove so he could offer to take April home afterward. From the number of cars that had already passed the house before he left, Jeremy correctly guessed that the informal parking area at the base of the amphitheater would be crowded. He backed into a space in the grass and followed a large, mostly silent crowd up the hill. At first it was hard to make out faces in the chill grayness, but as the time of sunrise grew closer, Jeremy recognized a few people, including Tom Statum. April was nowhere in sight, however, nor were the pastor and the song leader.

They're probably waiting to make a grand entrance, Jeremy thought.

As one, every face turned toward the top of the peak at their right, where a bright glow announced the arrival of the sun. At the very moment that its first beams penetrated the grayness, three women in long robes walked out of the woods and stopped before a low structure that had been built to represent Christ's tomb. Within it, another figure, dressed in white, was barely visible.

"Where is our Master?" asked one of the women.

"What have ye done with Him?" said another.

" 'Be not affrighted: Ye seek Jesus of Nazareth, which was crucified: he is risen; he is not here: behold the place where they laid him. But go your way, tell his disciples and Peter that he goeth before you into Galilee: there shall ye see him, as he said unto you.' "

The women turned and went back in the direction from which they had come, and Jeremy felt his scalp prickle as April stepped out from behind the representation of the tomb and the first triumphant notes of a familiar Easter hymn by Charles Wesley soared into the dawn.

Christ the Lord is risen today,
    Al—le—lu—ia!

Sons of men and angels say,
    Al—le–lu–ia!
Raise your joys and triumphs high,
    Al—le–lu–ia!
Sing, ye heavens, and earth reply.
    Al—le–lu–ia!

At the end of the first verse, the song leader joined April and motioned for everyone to sing. When the hymn ended, April took a seat in the front row, and the service proceeded with prayers, a short sermon, and more joint singing. The fully risen sun was bathing them all in its light when April stood once more.

Slowly, she walked to stand before the representation of the empty tomb, raised her radiant face to the sun, closed her eyes, and began to sing, unaccompanied.

"I know that my Redeemer liveth," she began.

A murmur of appreciation swept through the congregation, and even those who might not recognize Handel's soaring melody knew they were hearing something special on this, the most important day in the Christian calendar.

If it weren't for Easter, there wouldn't be any Christians. Jeremy could not recall the first time he had heard that, but he had long since accepted it as truth. If Christ had not risen from the dead, then He would be remembered, if at all, as another in the long line of prophets who brought their messages to a sinful world, then died and were buried and forgotten.

But as the words of April's song declared, Jesus, who took on all sins for the sake of the world His Father had created, did rise from the dead to live forevermore and to bring eternal life to all who believed in Him.

"Amen!" Jeremy heard himself saying with the others when the last long, true note faded away into the morning.

The service quickly concluded with another prayer and a praise chorus, then as silently as they had come, as if still under the spell of the joyful solemnity of the occasion, the worshipers began to leave.

Jeremy caught up with April and the red-haired music leader at the parking area and spoke softly to April. "Can I take you home?"

April looked at Jeremy almost blankly, as if struggling to recall who he was, then she nodded. "Yes. . .thanks," she said, almost in a whisper.

Silently, Jeremy took April's hand and led her to his car, and even after they started down the mountain, neither spoke. But when Jeremy left the procession of cars and turned into his own driveway, April looked at him in surprise.

"This isn't where I live," she said.

"I offered to take you home. I just didn't say whose."

"I've often wondered what this place looked like on the inside," April said when they got out of the car. "It's such a pretty old house."

"Old, anyway. After I get it painted, it'll look a lot better. Come inside and

I'll make us some breakfast," Jeremy added.

April looked uncertain if she should accept his invitation. "I could have fed you at my place," she said.

"Then I'll let you do the cooking," Jeremy said. "I usually just have those toaster pastry things."

April wrinkled her nose and shook her head. "If you can handle the coffee, I'll see what I can find."

A few minutes later, as they ate in companionable silence, Jeremy thought that April's cinnamon toast and omelet made the most wonderful breakfast he had had in years. And certainly having April sitting across from him at the old, green-painted kitchen table did not hurt, either.

"You make good coffee," April said after a while.

"And this is a mean omelet, lady," Jeremy replied. "Seems like you can cook about as good as you sing."

April's cheeks pinkened briefly, and she rose abruptly and carried her plate to the sink as if embarrassed by Jeremy's praise.

He followed her and got out the dishpan and put it in the sink. "I'll wash and you can dry," he said, but she shook her head.

"No. You know where things go and I don't. I'll wash and you can dry."

That's the way Joan did it, too. Jeremy wondered what had made him think of that.

"Evelyn Trent came to see me Friday," Jeremy said after a moment. April's shoulders stiffened, but when she said nothing, Jeremy continued. "Apparently Toni told her you wanted to be her guardian."

April groaned. "Oh, no! I thought Toni knew better than to talk to Miss Trent about anything. What else did she say?"

Jeremy wiped a dish thoroughly and put it into the cabinet before he turned back and looked into April's eyes. "She says the DHR's willing to let Toni stay with the Potters but not with you. She hinted that there would be trouble if we petitioned for you to be her guardian."

April lowered her eyes and, with studied diligence, resumed washing the dishes. "Did she say why?" she asked after a moment.

"She thinks you're too young and not stable enough."

Jeremy thought he detected a note of relief in April's voice. "Is that all?" Then she turned to face him. "Is that what you think?"

Almost automatically, Jeremy's arms went out to circle April's waist. "This is what I think," he said, then pulled her close and kissed her.

After a soft cry of surprise, April brought her hands out of the dishwater long enough to lay them lightly on Jeremy's shoulders. At first she answered his kiss with a light pressure, then she pulled away, picked up a dish towel, and dabbed at his shirt in the place where her hands had rested only a moment before.

"I'm afraid I got your shirt wet," she said.

"I don't mind." Jeremy caught April's hands in his and bent down to kiss her again. She did not resist, but when he would have deepened and prolonged the contact, she once more pulled away.

"Take me home now," April said levelly.

Jeremy matched her tone. "Of course." He did not attempt to apologize for kissing her. Although as a lawyer he knew he should not become involved with a client, Jeremy had enjoyed kissing April too much to pretend he had been wrong to do it.

April said nothing on the drive to her apartment, and when they reached her door, she turned and offered her hand to Jeremy. "I'm glad you came to the service this morning. . .and thanks for the breakfast."

"Thank you for inviting me. It was really special." *"And so are you,"* Jeremy wanted to say, hoping that his eyes spoke for him. "And thanks for making breakfast. I liked that cinnamon toast."

"Now you know how it's done, anyway." April hesitated a moment, then looked down at the key in her hand as if it might hold the answer to some important question. Without looking at Jeremy, she spoke in a low voice. "About the hearing. . . If DHR doesn't want me to be Toni's guardian, I'd rather withdraw my petition."

"You don't have to do that—" Jeremy began, but April's stricken look silenced him.

"I think I do," she said quietly. "But I'd rather tell Toni myself."

Jeremy nodded. "All right. But—"

April looked at her watch and gasped. "I didn't realize the time. We still have another service today. So long, Jeremy."

April let herself into her apartment, and Jeremy glanced at his own watch as he walked back to his car. He could still make the First Church service. The Bells were expecting him, and it would be a good time to put in another appearance at First Church. After all, many people would be there today who would not come to church again until next Easter. . .people whose votes he might soon need.

With that thought, Jeremy started the car and left without looking back at the window where April stood, watching him.

∞

The first thing that Jeremy noticed when he entered the First Church sanctuary was the almost overpowering scent of lilies, which seemed to be everywhere. His nose twitched and his eyes watered, and Jeremy wondered briefly if he might be allergic to lilies. The second thing he noticed—Joan Bell in her new finery— soon made him forget the first. Jeremy searched for a name for the shade she was wearing: pale lavender or was it mauve? The dress was of some soft, flowing stuff, topped by a hat of the same material and adorned with what looked at first glance to be real spring flowers.

"They're silk," Joan explained when she saw Jeremy's puzzled expression.

"I'm glad you're here," Randall Bell said when Jeremy sat down between him and Joan. "I have some news about Montgomery."

"Oh? What's happening?" Jeremy asked, but with the first notes of the organ, Mr. Bell shook his head and put his index finger to his mouth.

"I'll tell you later," he said.

Jeremy nodded as the service began with the rather spectacular entrance of the choir coming down the center aisle, singing the same hymn that April had sung earlier.

First Church does put on a good Easter show, Jeremy had to admit as the service progressed. *But it can't hold a candle to what took place earlier on Warren Mountain.*

As he had done before, the First Church minister delivered a short sermon, and even with all the extra singing and what Jeremy called "parading around," the service still ended almost on the stroke of twelve. Again Jeremy was greeted by and in turn greeted many people who seemed gratified that he had remembered their names. So many stopped to talk to Jeremy that he and the Bells were almost the last to reach the church parking lot.

"Daddy, you can go on. I'll ride with Jeremy," Joan announced at the last minute.

"Jeremy and I have things to discuss," her father said.

"You can do that any time," Joan said breezily. "It is all right if I ride with you, isn't it?" she asked Jeremy, somewhat tardily.

"Of course," he said and hastened to unlock and open the passenger door for her.

"You lock your car even at church?" Joan asked when Jeremy slid in behind the wheel.

"I lock it everywhere. . .force of habit," he replied. "You never know when someone might take a notion to steal it."

"Daddy says if thieves want a car, they'll take it, and it's too much trouble to lock it all the time," Joan said. "Besides, you're not in Birmingham now. Rockdale doesn't have a problem with car thieves."

Joan Bell continued to chatter about how safe Rockdale was, and once again Jeremy was keenly aware of the subtle scent of her perfume, which seemed to be everywhere and nowhere all at the same time. If April Kincaid wore perfume, he was not aware of it, yet she always smelled sweet and fresh.

I mustn't keep trying to compare Joan and April, Jeremy told himself, but at every turn, he found himself doing just that.

"Have you heard a word I've said?" Joan demanded when they reached the country club.

"Certainly," Jeremy replied. "The gist of it all is that Rockdale is a wonderful place to raise a family."

Jeremy did not realize the effect of what he had said until Joan's face turned red and she got out of the car without waiting for him to assist her. *If I say anything else, I'll only make matters worse*, he thought. Instead, Jeremy took Joan's arm and escorted her into the country club, aware that many eyes followed their progress with interest.

"Don't they make a lovely couple?" the dowager, Minnie Reed, whispered to her longtime friend, Estelle Johnson, as they passed their table.

"That's a wedding just waiting to happen," Estelle said in a stage whisper that reached not only Jeremy and Joan, but just about everyone else in the dining room.

Neither Jeremy nor Joan made any reference to what they had overheard, but Jeremy had to agree with the first part. No matter what else anyone might say about them, he and Joan did, indeed, look good together.

Despite his earlier mention of news from Montgomery, Randall Bell waited until Joan had left the table after lunch before he told Jeremy what was happening.

"Due to the holiday weekend, hardly anyone's left in Montgomery, but my contacts tell me that the meeting to discuss Harrison's replacement is expected to take place later on this week. Keep your calendar clear so we can go down there when something breaks."

Jeremy's first reaction was relief. "That's good. I won't have to postpone the Schmidt hearing, after all," he said.

Randall Bell shook his head slightly. "You really are involved in that case, aren't you?"

"It's different from anything I've ever done before," Jeremy said, but he suspected that Mr. Bell knew there was more to it than that.

"Well, for the firm's sake, I hope you win, but don't be too surprised if it should go the other way."

Jeremy looked at Mr. Bell in surprise. "What makes you say that? If you know something that I don't—"

"I know the way this town works," he interrupted. "It doesn't know what to do with incorrigible juveniles."

Before Jeremy could protest that Toni was hardly incorrigible, Joan returned to the table, effectively closing the subject.

"It's such a lovely day, I think we ought to go somewhere," Joan said.

"Seems more like a good afternoon to rest and get caught up on some reading," Randall Bell said. "You two go on and do what you like," he added.

Joan smiled at Jeremy. "How about it? Are you game?"

"That depends. What do you have in mind?"

"I haven't hiked in a while. I thought we might explore your mountain."

"If you mean Warren Mountain, it's not mine," Jeremy said.

"Part of it is, though, and with the redbuds and dogwoods in bloom, it ought to be spectacular."

"I suppose so," said Jeremy, who had only vaguely noted the pale green, interspersed with white and pink, that now formed a backdrop on the hills behind his house.

Joan laughed, a rich sound that Jeremy still found appealing. "Don't sound so enthusiastic. You lawyer types tend to stay inside too much. A little fresh air will do you good."

"Surely you can't refuse such a flattering invitation," Randall Bell said wryly.

"Oh, I'm not," Jeremy said. He had no real reason to turn down Joan's suggestion, and in any case, to do so would be quite rude.

"Good. I'll come to your place in an hour or so, then."

∽

April had made plans to spend Easter with Toni, beginning when the Potters brought the girl to the regular Community Church service on their way to their own place of worship.

"I feel like a dork in this dress," Toni muttered to April, who had given her the simple challis print the week before.

"You don't look like one, though," April assured her. "You should wear it to the hearing. It makes you look a lot older."

Toni brightened perceptibly. "Yeah? If I look old enough, maybe the judge will let me do what I want."

"Nobody ever gets that old," April said. "Come on and sit down. Our song is near the first."

"I don't know about this," Toni said. "Suppose I mess up?"

"You won't. We've practiced it enough to be perfect."

"Yeah, but that was just the two of us. In front of all of these people. . ."

"Close your eyes and they'll go away," April said. "That's what I always do. Hurry, put your bag down there by the umbrella stand and let's get inside."

When the time came, April took Toni's hand and led her to stand before the altar to sing "The Old Rugged Cross" the way she had taught her.

"On a hill far away. . ."

The girl's alto began a bit shakily, but her voice steadily gained assurance until, by the refrain, it was almost as strong as April's.

"Yes, I'll cling to the old rugged cross, And exchange it some day for a crown."

There was no doubt that the congregation enjoyed and appreciated their song, and many people told Toni so after the service ended.

"I'd sure like to have you in the choir as a regular, Toni," Ted Brown said as he took them back to April's apartment.

"So would I," April replied, but her heart ached with the knowledge that it might never come to pass.

At April's apartment, they changed clothes, packed a picnic lunch, filled their water bottles, then walked their bikes to the street.

"Where are we going today?" Toni asked.

"I thought we might ride up on Warren Mountain. I'll show you the place where we had the sunrise service."

"Cool," said Toni, who would have been at the service if the Potters had been willing to take her there.

That they would have to ride past Jeremy Winter's house had nothing to do with her choice, April tried to tell herself, but her heart knew better.

Chapter 10

Jeremy had not given any thought to what his house looked like when he had brought April there on the spur of the moment, but with Joan Bell, it was different. After he got home, Jeremy changed into jeans and a sweatshirt, and he had barely finished some intensive cleaning and straightening when Joan's red sedan pulled into the driveway.

Jeremy went out to greet her. "Right on time, I see," he said.

"It's a habit with us schoolmarms," Joan said.

Jeremy smiled. As with everything else he had seen Joan wear, her jeans fit perfectly, neither tight nor baggy. She wore a blue turtleneck tee shirt over which she had layered a cotton denim shirt. "You don't look much like a schoolmarm in those jeans."

"Good. I'll be glad when I can leave that occupation."

Jeremy decided it was better not to ask Joan what occupation she might prefer to teaching. "Would you like to come inside for a minute before we start hiking?" he asked instead.

"Oh, yes. I've been dying to see what you've done with the house," Joan said so quickly that Jeremy realized that that had probably been her main motive in coming over.

"I'm afraid you'll be disappointed. I intend to paint inside and out, but I haven't had the time."

They entered the house through the kitchen doorway, and Joan stopped and looked around thoughtfully. "This room cries out for wallpaper. It'd look really great with a chair rail and paper above it."

"I'm afraid wallpapering is out of my league," Jeremy said.

"Not mine. I'll be glad to help you if you like."

"Thanks. I'll keep that in mind."

As they walked through the other downstairs rooms, Joan had suggestions for improving each. The faded draperies in the dining room could be replaced by wooden shutters; the original wide-planked floors in the living room ought to be refinished and left uncovered; the dark hallway should be painted white.

"Are you taking notes?" Joan asked.

Jeremy knew he must look as overwhelmed as he felt and smiled ruefully. "I doubt if I have that much paper in the house," he said.

Joan laughed "Don't worry. I'll remember every detail. Shall we go now?"

"Yes, let's, before you find anything else to do to the house."

∞

The afternoon sun felt pleasantly warm on their faces as they walked up the road to a trail that Jeremy remembered from his childhood.

"It leads to the spring where Grandmother said her parents always got their water," he said.

"I'll be thirsty by the time we get there," Joan said after they had climbed almost vertically for a few minutes.

Eventually, they heard the splash of water hitting rocks, and near the top of the ridge, they saw the spring, issuing like a miniature waterfall from a cleft in the rocks.

"Beautiful!" Joan exclaimed. Cupping her hands, she leaned forward and drank deeply.

"Cold, too," Jeremy commented when she stepped aside to allow him to drink.

"Let's find a sunny place and sit down," Joan suggested.

"I thought you wanted to hike," Jeremy said. "We've just gotten started."

"This isn't an endurance contest," she reminded him. "Look, I see a nice, flat rock over there."

Something sunning on the rock scampered away into the underbrush at their approach, and Joan shrieked and grabbed Jeremy's arm. "I hope that wasn't a snake. I don't like snakes," she said anxiously.

"No, it was just a little lizard. I used to try to catch them, but I was never quite quick enough."

Joan nodded in agreement. "I know. A trap is the only way you can catch really fast things like that," she said.

Like men, Jeremy thought. *Women often attempt to trap a man if chasing him doesn't work.* But of course, that had nothing to do with him and Joan.

By now, Jeremy was fairly certain that he would not have to run very fast to catch Joan, and if he didn't make the move himself, she just might find some way to trap him.

"Trapping sounds rather cruel," Jeremy said.

"But sometimes it's necessary," Joan said, and the way she looked at him made Jeremy know that she was not really talking about wild animals.

Did she move or did I? Jeremy wondered. Suddenly, he felt surrounded by her presence, enveloped in her scent, so close to her that he could almost feel her breath on his cheek.

"Oh, Jeremy, you don't know what you need," Joan said. Her arms circled his neck, her head found his shoulder, and she sighed softly.

She expects me to kiss her now, Jeremy thought. *And if I don't, she'll probably kiss me.*

Joan Bell had already shown that she was not shy about taking the lead in such matters, but for the time being, she seemed content merely to be close to

Jeremy and let him make the first move.

She's going to have a long wait, Jeremy told himself.

∞

"I'm out of water and I'm thirsty," Toni said halfway down Warren Mountain. "Do you have any to spare?"

April held up her water bottle to show that it, too, was empty. "No. We're near a spring that has the best water you ever tasted, but the trail is almost straight up so we'll have to walk in."

"Suits me," Toni said.

They pedaled the short distance to the trail's start, then left their bikes in the underbrush, out of sight of anyone passing on the road.

"You weren't kidding when you said this was a steep trail," Toni said a few minutes later. Both she and April were hot and panting from their exertion by the time they reached the spring. April let Toni fill her bottle first, then filled her own and drank deeply.

"What's up there?" Toni asked, pointing to the crest of the hill.

"There's not much of a view, but it's a good place to rest."

"Let's check it out, then," said Toni.

April took the lead on the narrow path, but at the crest of the hill, she stopped so suddenly that Toni ran into her. Then Toni saw what had made April stop. "Oh!" she exclaimed.

Oh, indeed! thought April. Perhaps she had suggested going up Warren Mountain in the hope of seeing Jeremy Winter, but she certainly had not expected to find him holding Joan Bell in his arms.

The instant that Jeremy realized they were not alone, he stood, causing Joan to lose her balance and topple over on her side. Toni's first impulse was to laugh, but April's face told her she did not find anything funny about the situation.

"Excuse us," April said at the same time that a surprised Jeremy spoke her name.

"April. . .and Toni. I didn't expect to see you two today."

"No doubt," April said coolly.

"Uh. . .you know Joan Bell, I believe? Joan, this is Toni Schmidt."

Having recovered both her balance and her poise, Joan nodded at Toni. "How do you do? I've heard that Jeremy is defending you."

"Representing, not defending," Jeremy corrected. "Toni isn't a criminal."

The girl laughed shortly. "That's not what most people in Rockdale think," she said.

"How nice that you have a good friend like April," Joan said.

"She's gonna be my guardian, too, right, Mr. Winter?"

Jeremy looked at April, but she did not return his glance. "That remains to be seen," he said.

"The hearing's coming up soon, isn't it?" Joan asked. "I'm sure you'll all be glad to have this thing settled."

"Let's go, Toni," April said.

"We just came up here for some water," Toni volunteered. "Sorry if we bothered y'all."

"No bother at all," said Joan.

∞

April's face still felt warm when she and Toni reached her apartment. With shame, she admitted that she had begun to trust Jeremy enough to allow herself to care for him. Coming upon him with Joan Bell had been like a slap in her face.

Or maybe it's a wake-up call, April told herself. At any rate, she had no time to think about Jeremy Winter. For now, April had to find a way to tell Toni that she could not be her guardian, after all.

Dear Lord, give me the strength to do this, and give Toni the grace to accept it, she prayed.

Even so, April knew that the next few days would not be easy for either of them.

∞

The moment that Joan Bell looked up from Jeremy's shoulder and saw April Kincaid, she realized two things: April seemed to have some sort of romantic feelings for Jeremy, and even worse, he seemed to return them. At any rate, whatever mood Joan had managed to create between herself and Jeremy that afternoon had been totally destroyed when April and that wild Schmidt girl appeared on the scene.

"I suppose we should be getting back," Joan said when the intruders departed. Jeremy made no protest, and he said little else as they made their way back to his house. Once there, he did not suggest that Joan should come back inside.

"I'm sorry our hike was cut short," he said.

"So am I," Joan said sincerely. "We must finish it soon. Perhaps after this hearing and your business in Montgomery, we'll have more time."

"You know about Montgomery?" Jeremy asked.

Joan's laugh hinted that she knew many things of which he was unaware. "Daddy told me all about it." Her smile faded, and she adopted a serious tone as she spoke again. "He said something else, but I didn't believe it until this afternoon."

"Oh? What's that?" Jeremy asked.

"It was about April Kincaid. For your own sake, I hope you won't keep on seeing her after the hearing."

Jeremy made no effort to hide his surprise. "Your father told you I was going out with April?"

"You are, aren't you? No, don't answer. I won't make you lie. Good-bye, Jeremy. I'll see you around."

In a single fluid motion, Joan opened her car door and slid into the driver's seat. With a final wave, she turned the car around and drove away.

In near despair, Jeremy watched her go. He knew Joan had wanted him to reassure her that he cared nothing for April, but he had not been able to bring himself to do so. Even worse, the way April had looked at him when she saw him and Joan together made Jeremy know that whatever feelings she might have developed for him had probably been badly damaged if not completely destroyed.

Furthermore, April obviously had not yet told Toni that she would not ask to be her guardian. *Maybe that's because she still wants to try for it,* Jeremy thought.

"What a mess," he said aloud, then sighed, turned, and went back into his unpainted, unwallpapered, and suddenly quite empty house.

∽

Jeremy's desire for a meal he did not have to cook himself was not the only thing that sent him to Statum's Family Restaurant on Monday evening. He wanted to see April again, to try to smooth over the awkward scene that had resulted when she and Toni had found him and Joan Bell in each other's arms.

He went deliberately late, only a few minutes before Tom Statum would turn the OPEN sign to CLOSED, and he sat in the booth that he had already come to think of as his.

April was obviously uneasy, but when Jeremy asked to take her home, she did not refuse.

Only April's clasped hands betrayed her tension when, in her small living room, Jeremy began to try to speak something of what was on his heart.

"I've given some thought to what I said about your not asking to be Toni's guardian," he said. "Since you haven't already told her, it might be best to go on and try for it. Judge Oliver can certainly see your sincerity."

For a moment, April's cheeks grew pink as conflicting emotions played across her face. Then she lowered her eyes and shook her head. "I doubt that. Anyway, it's too late. I've already told Toni."

April's expression told Jeremy what he had already guessed—that Toni had not taken the news well. "I'm sorry. I shouldn't have tried to tell you what to do."

"No, I'm glad you did. There are some things that are better left alone."

Guessing that April must be referring to her past, Jeremy leaned forward and spoke earnestly. "Would you like to tell me about it? Maybe I can help."

April shook her head. "You're Toni's lawyer, not mine," she said.

Jeremy rose and knelt before April. "I'm not here as your lawyer," he said.

April looked at him levelly. "We both know that you shouldn't have anything to do with me. You're Toni's lawyer, and I'm her friend. Let's just leave it that way, okay?"

Jeremy took both of April's hands in his and pressed them as he spoke. "I know nothing of the sort, April. You—"

April jerked her hands from his and stood. "Don't say anything else," she pleaded. "Just do your best for Toni, and leave me alone."

"I mean you no harm," Jeremy began, but April was already holding the door open, and the set of her mouth told him that further pleading would be useless. "You know where to find me if you should change your mind," Jeremy said.

"I won't," she murmured and firmly closed the door after him.

Jeremy barely resisted the impulse to kick his front tire as he got back into the car. *I really blew it this time,* he told himself.

But he would not give up. After Toni's hearing, perhaps April would be willing to give him another chance.

∞

The insistent ringing of the telephone interrupted a dream in which Jeremy was attempting to make his first speech on the House floor, but no one seemed to be there except Guy Pettibone and Joan and Randall Bell.

With his eyes still shut, Jeremy groped for the telephone on his bedside table, spoke first into the wrong end, then reversed the receiver, tried again, and heard a voice he did not recognize.

"Mr. Winter? I'm sorry to bother you at this hour, but I thought you should know that Toni Schmidt is missing."

Jeremy opened his eyes wide and sat up in bed. "Who is this?" he asked.

"I'm sorry. I suppose I thought you'd know. This is Evelyn Trent. The Potters called me about midnight to say that Toni had apparently left the house after putting their younger children to bed. We both thought she might be at April Kincaid's apartment, so I went there first, but April says she hasn't seen Toni since Sunday night."

Jeremy squinted at his clock radio and saw it was just after two o'clock on what must be Tuesday morning—and Toni's hearing was scheduled for Wednesday. "Who else knows about this?" he asked.

"No one yet, but the Potters want to call the police. Toni rode her mountain bike home on Sunday and it's gone. They're afraid something might have happened to Toni on her way to April's."

"I'll call the police now. Thanks for calling, Miss Trent. I'm sure you'd like to get some sleep now."

"As a matter of fact, I would," she replied. She hesitated for a moment, then added, "Toni has her faults, but I don't want to see anything happen to her."

"Neither do I," Jeremy said. As he replaced the receiver and climbed out of bed, he realized that the crusty-appearing social worker probably felt far more emotion than she admitted, even to herself.

She might turn out to be Toni's friend, after all, he thought. But for now, his thoughts centered on someone who would need a friend of her own. After calling the police, Jeremy put on jeans and a well-worn college pullover that Mr. Pettibone's wardrobe specialist would never approve of and which might even cause Joan Bell to lift an eyebrow. But Jeremy figured that April would not even notice what he wore.

She must be frantic, Jeremy thought, driving faster than usual through

95

Rockdale's deserted streets. However, when Jeremy reached April's apartment and saw no light showing, he felt a prickle of apprehension.

Surely she didn't go out on her own to look for Toni, Jeremy told himself, but when his repeated knocking at the door brought no response, he felt real fear.

"Dear God, don't let anything happen to her," Jeremy said aloud, scarcely aware that, for the first time in a long while, he was praying.

∞

Even before April told Toni, she feared how Toni might react when she learned that April was not going to ask to be appointed her guardian. April knew Toni was in for a rough time, but after they prayed together about it, April thought that Toni had accepted the situation, although grudgingly.

However, the instant Roger Potter and Evelyn Trent appeared at her door at one o'clock on Tuesday morning, April knew she had misjudged the situation.

"We hoped to find Toni here," Mr. Potter said after telling April that the girl had been missing for several hours.

"I wish you had, but I don't know where she is, either."

"She's apparently on her bike. Where else would Toni go besides your place?"

April shook her head. "I don't know."

"Well, if she should turn up—"

"I know what to do," April finished for him. Once before, not long after Toni went to live with the Potters, she had made April an unplanned visit, and April had promptly returned the girl.

After Mr. Potter and Miss Trent left, April dressed and went to the corner phone booth. She had enough change to make only one call, and although April wanted to call Jeremy Winter, she did not. Mr. Potter had mentioned that Evelyn Trent was going to contact Toni's lawyer, and April did not want Jeremy to feel that he was beholden to her for anything. Besides, he was powerless to provide the kind of help she needed at a time like this.

April dropped her coins into the slot and dialed the number she had first called months before. *Don't let him have his answering machine on,* April prayed, and after four rings, she was rewarded when a familiar although sleepy voice answered.

"Yes?"

"Pastor Hurley, this is April Kincaid. Toni's gone off somewhere, and I don't know what to do."

"Will you be at your apartment?" he asked.

"Yes."

"Keep the door locked. I'll be there as soon as I can."

"Thank You, Lord," April murmured as she left the phone booth. In a crisis, there was no one she trusted more than Pastor Hurley. She would not have come to Rockdale if it had not been for him, and she certainly could not have stayed here without his continuing help.

His and the Lord's, April amended. She knew she owed them both more than she could ever repay.

Now April was not asking for help for herself but for Toni. *Lord, just as You let Pastor Hurley help me, so let us both help Toni now.*

Back at her apartment, April looked up some of her favorite scriptures, the ones that had seen her through much turmoil. It was not the first time April had faced a crisis nor, she knew, would it be the last. But now, at least, she knew, as the hymn she often sang said, in whom she believed. And she was persuaded that He was able to keep her and guide her and that all things would, indeed, work together for good in her life. But waiting for them to do so was not always easy, especially when she often felt so alone.

If only Jeremy Winter...

April did not let herself finish the thought. What could she have possibly hoped for from Jeremy, whose background was so different from hers and whose plans obviously could never include her?

I was wrong to let myself hope that we could ever have a future together, April thought. Nothing could change the record of what she had once been, and it seemed that her past sins would always find her out. What April had done to herself then was bad enough; she could not let what she had been hurt anyone else.

By the time Pastor Hurley rapped on her door, April knew that her time in Rockdale, as precious as it had been, had come to an end.

Chapter 11

Tuesday was one of the longest and most difficult days that Jeremy Winter had ever faced. From the time Evelyn Trent's phone call awakened him at two that morning, Jeremy dealt with one frustration after another.

Not only had Toni Schmidt disappeared, but no one seemed to know what had happened to April Kincaid, either. Early speculation that they were together faded when the police found that April's bike was still in her apartment, along with what seemed to be most of her clothes.

Tom Statum was equally mystified. On Tuesday morning, he had found a scrawled note on the restaurant's back door saying that April would not be at work for a while.

The police took the note and spent several hours dusting April's apartment for fingerprints, giving rise to all sorts of rumors that something might have happened to her.

"Have you contacted Judge Oliver yet?" Randall Bell asked Jeremy when they went out for lunch at a nearby cafe.

"About what?" Jeremy asked, at first not realizing what his partner was talking about. In his concern for Toni and April, he had temporarily forgotten everything else.

"The Schmidt hearing, of course," Randall Bell said. "It occurs to me that April Kincaid's mysterious disappearance and the girl's running away must have had something to do with their not wanting to appear before the judge."

"April wasn't going to petition to be Toni's guardian, and that could be why Toni ran away. Toni certainly didn't want to stay with the Potters. But April didn't know that Toni was gone until Mr. Potter and Evelyn Trent told her."

Randall Bell raised his eyebrows. "As late as Sunday afternoon, Joan heard Toni say that she was going to live with April. What makes you think that April didn't plan for the two of them to run off somewhere together?"

"For one thing, it's not like April to be underhanded. It's my guess that Toni decided to leave when she found out that April wasn't going to ask to be her guardian."

"Then where is April?"

"Looking for Toni, I suppose," Jeremy said, but even he was beginning to have his doubts, especially when the police said April's bike was still there and no one else had seen her all day.

But late that afternoon, Edith returned from the post office with the news that the police had received a call from April Kincaid.

"You have good connections with the police department," Jeremy said. "See what else you can find out about it."

The secretary hesitated for a moment. "The hearing's already been called off. What difference does it make where they are?"

"What makes you think they're together?" Jeremy asked, annoyed at Edith's lack of concern.

"Birds of a feather," she said laconically. "I'll call the chief," she added, seeing that Jeremy had not liked her remark.

A few minutes later, she returned to say that April had told the police that she was all right and urged them to concentrate on finding Toni Schmidt.

"I don't suppose they traced the call, did they?" Jeremy asked.

"Not likely, but they seem to think that April was nearby. At least they said it didn't sound like a long distance call."

"As if they'd know the difference," Jeremy muttered under his breath. "Thanks, Edith. I think I'll go now. When Mr. Bell gets back from the courthouse, tell him I'll see him tomorrow."

"May I ask where you're going?" Edith asked.

"It's none of your business," Jeremy wanted to say, but he made an effort to be polite. "It's been a long day. I'm tired and I'm going home."

"Yes, I'm sure that's a good idea," Edith said approvingly. "Shall I forward your calls?"

"Only if they concern Toni or April," he said.

∞

Jeremy had just changed into his jeans when the telephone rang. Hoping to hear that Toni had been found, he answered eagerly.

"Mr. Winter? This is Ed Hurley. Can you come to my house this evening?"

Ed Hurley? At first, Jeremy's mind drew a blank, but then Jeremy recognized the minister's distinct voice.

"What is this about?" Jeremy asked.

"Several things. I know you must be concerned about both Toni Schmidt and April."

A surge of hope quickened Jeremy's pulse. "Do you know where they are?"

"We'll discuss that when you get here. Do you know where I live?"

Jeremy took down the address. "I'll be right over," he said.

Pastor Hurley must know something, Jeremy told himself. *Let it lead me to April,* he added as he grabbed his keys and left.

∞

"Come in," Mrs. Hurley invited, opening the door of the modest frame house even before Jeremy could knock. "I just made some lemonade. Would you like some?"

"No, thanks." Jeremy looked over her shoulder and saw her husband enter the living room alone.

99

The men shook hands, then Mrs. Hurley excused herself and left them alone.

"Sit down, Jeremy. I hope you don't mind if I call you that. I'm so used to hearing April speak of you that way."

"April talks about me?" Jeremy asked, surprised.

Pastor Hurley smiled briefly. "Oh, yes. . .among other things."

"Do you know where April is?" Jeremy's tone made it a question.

"I can't tell you that, but she's all right."

"What do you mean, you can't tell me?" Jeremy's concern made his tone harsh, but the pastor did not seem to notice.

"April asked me not to tell anyone where she is, but she wants you to know that she's safe."

"What about Toni?"

Pastor Hurley shook his head. "I'm sorry to say that I don't know anything about her. I'm sure that this wasn't the best time for her to take off."

Jeremy laughed without humor. "That's for sure. Judge Oliver reset the hearing for next week. If Toni isn't there, he'll issue a bench warrant for her. When she's found, she could be sent to the state school for girls without any further delay."

Pastor Hurley looked shocked. "But Toni's hardly more than a child! April was doing her so much good. I can't believe that the law would be so hard on her."

"That's the way it is, though. And that's why it's so important for us to find Toni."

Ed Hurley nodded. "Yes, April is quite aware of that."

Jeremy looked closely at the minister. "Pastor Hurley, I know April must be looking for Toni and that you're probably helping her. I don't blame you for that. But as her friend, I really care what happens to Toni, and I want to help April find her."

The minister put his hand on Jeremy's shoulder for a moment. "You care about April, as well, perhaps more than you realize. You must have patience and know that God is at work even in this."

Jeremy shook his head. "That's hard to believe," he said.

"Yes, in the midst of a storm, it's hard to imagine that the sun can ever shine again, but it's there all the time."

"And this will pass away, also," Jeremy said, his tone more bitter than accepting, as he stood to leave.

"As a matter of fact, it will, perhaps even sooner than you expect."

Jeremy went to the door, then turned back. "I'd like to know any news from either April or Toni," he said.

"Of course. And don't look so worried, Jeremy. Things are rarely as bad as we convince ourselves they're going to be."

That's easy for him to say, Jeremy thought on his way to his car. *He's not in love with April—*

Overwhelmed by what he had just admitted to himself, Jeremy almost stopped in his tracks. As unlikely, inconvenient, and inappropriate as it might be, Jeremy's feelings for April had grown so strong that now nothing else seemed more important than finding her and telling her so. On his own, however, he was not getting anywhere at all.

All right, God, help me find April, and we've got a deal.

Just what sort of deal, Jeremy did not take time to spell out; in any contract, there had to be a basic agreement before the details could be worked out.

He was willing to start from where he was, as long as the path he traveled led him to April.

∞

Dusk had yielded to darkness when Jeremy returned home, and his headlights disclosed a car in his driveway. Not just a car, but Joan Bell's sporty sedan.

"That's all I need," Jeremy muttered. He had neither seen nor talked to Joan since their somewhat awkward parting on Sunday. He knew that at some point they would meet again, but he had not expected it to be this soon.

Jeremy got out of his car, expecting Joan to be waiting for him in her sedan. The car was empty, however, and when Jeremy looked toward the house, he saw lights illuminating the kitchen.

I'm sure I locked up when I left, Jeremy told himself when he opened the back door.

Joan stood before the stove, stirring something that filled the room with a spicy aroma.

"How did you get in?" he asked accusingly.

"I'm glad to see you, too," Joan replied mildly. "Did it occur to you that you might have left the door open?"

Jeremy shook his head. "No. I remember locking it before I left. You couldn't have found it open."

Joan's laughter was warm. "You're hard to fool, Jeremy Winter. Daddy still has a key labeled 'Warren rental.' So you see, I didn't have to break in."

"I'm sorry if I sounded short," Jeremy said. "It's just that I don't usually come home to find my supper being cooked. I presume that is what you're doing here?" he added.

"Of course. Don't look so serious, Jeremy. Daddy told me that you're taking this Toni Schmidt thing pretty hard, and I thought you could use some cheering up. It also occurred to me that you might be hungry."

"I suppose I am," Jeremy said, so obviously uncheered that Joan shook her head in mock despair.

"I was going to save my good news for dessert, but since you look so down—"

"What is it? Do you know something about April or Toni?"

Joan gave Jeremy a strange look. "How odd that you should mention April first when Toni is your client."

Jeremy felt his face warm. "In a way they're both clients, since April wanted to be Toni's guardian. Is there news about them?"

"No, but Daddy talked to some people in Montgomery today."

"Oh, that." Jeremy made no effort to disguise his disappointment.

"You don't sound very excited for someone who just might be handpicked to replace Harrison."

"What?" Jeremy asked.

"Go wash up. When you come back, we'll eat and I'll tell you all about it," Joan said.

Joan had made pasta, heated and added some more seasonings to some bottled spaghetti sauce from Jeremy's cabinet, and made a salad from fixings she found in the refrigerator. She had brought a loaf of homemade bread and a quart of chocolate mint ice cream, both of which she knew Jeremy liked.

"Everything is good, but I'm not very hungry," he told Joan a few minutes later when she scolded him for not eating much. "I've had a lot on my mind, having to cancel Toni's hearing and. . .and everything," he finished lamely, aware that he should not mention April's name again.

Joan leaned across the table and smiled at Jeremy, and the subtle fragrance she wore wafted toward him. "Maybe the latest news from Montgomery will help restore your appetite," she said.

Jeremy pushed his chair back from the table and folded his arms across his chest, his body language unconsciously proclaiming that he was not as excited about developments in the state capital as she was. "What's happening?"

"Daddy's been on the phone with several important people. They're having a big meeting soon, and Daddy says they want you to come and see them."

It was the kind of break that Guy Pettibone and Randall Bell had both worked on to give Jeremy a once-in-a-lifetime chance to make a good impression with some of the most powerful people in the state. The ambitious part of Jeremy's mind told him he should be turning cartwheels, yet his heart still felt strangely detached from the good news.

"Any idea what 'soon' means?"

Joan sighed as if his reaction had disappointed her. "This week, I presume."

The telephone rang, and Jeremy bolted from the table to answer it, hoping to hear April's voice. Instead, it was Guy Pettibone, who repeated what Joan had just told him and added another piece of information.

"Harrison's called a press conference for Friday morning. It's presumed that he'll announce his retirement then. Get on down to Montgomery and be ready to strut your stuff, boy."

"Suppose the governor has already decided to appoint someone as a political payback?" Jeremy asked.

"It won't matter. Whoever it is will still have to run again when the term's up, but the sooner you get some state backing, the better. You understand what

I'm saying, boy? You don't sound right."

"Yes, sir, I understand," Jeremy said. "It's been a long day, and I'm just a little tired."

"Perk up and get on down to Montgomery. Call me from there."

Jeremy hung up the receiver and came back into the kitchen. When he saw Joan at the sink, it was all he could do to not tell her to go home and leave him alone. *You're a nice woman, but you're standing where April stood.* Jeremy remembered quite well how he had kissed April there and how for one breathless moment, she had returned his kiss.

Joan turned to face Jeremy. "Any news?" she asked.

"No. Look, Joan, it was great of you to make supper, and I appreciate it. But if you don't mind—"

"I know. You can't wait to get rid of me," she interrupted, "and I'll go as soon as we've done the dishes. Get a towel and start wiping. I'll wash."

Feeling guilty that he had been so cool when Joan had gone out of her way to be nice to him, Jeremy pretended to be interested as she talked about some of the people he would meet in Montgomery.

When the dishes were done and Jeremy walked Joan to her car, he even leaned over to brush her cheek with a thank-you kiss.

"You can do better than that." Joan put her hands to Jeremy's face and placed her lips on his for a long moment, leaving no doubt that his apparent lack of interest had not discouraged her.

"Joan, you should know—" Jeremy began.

"We both know all we need to know," she said enigmatically. "One of these days, you'll realize what you really need."

I already have, Jeremy thought, but he let Joan get into her car and leave without telling her so.

When April came back—he would not allow himself to think she might not—he would have to tell her how he felt about her. He hoped—even prayed—that she would share his feelings.

But in any case, Jeremy knew that if his political ambitions were to be realized, he would still need Joan and her father's help. To say anything about April now would be premature and probably even disastrous.

You're a coward, Jeremy Winter, he told himself in disgust.

But for the moment, he did not think he had any other choice.

Chapter 12

Wednesday began little better than the day before and became even worse when police in nearby Fort Payne found a mountain bike fitting the description of Toni Schmidt's abandoned near the bus station.

"They think she rode it there intending to take a bus out of town," Randall Bell told Jeremy shortly after noon.

"Does anybody remember seeing her?"

"Not at the bus station, but the driver of a wrecker on an accident call saw someone about Toni's size walking along the side of the road and guessed she was hitchhiking."

That doesn't sound at all good, Jeremy thought. *However, if April were, indeed, looking for Toni, she should know about this latest development. I'll make sure that Ed Hurley hears about it,* he decided.

Aloud, he told Mr. Bell that he was about to leave the office. "I have to deliver the Morgan mortgage papers, then I think I'll go on home."

"Why don't you come for supper tonight? I'm sure Joan won't mind, and we need to talk about strategy for Montgomery."

"Thanks, but I'm not up to it tonight."

"Then we'll expect you tomorrow night. . .unless the call comes from Montgomery before then."

Jeremy did not really look forward to seeing Joan again, but in the meantime, other things—and one certain other person—totally occupied his mind.

∞

The Community Church parking lot contained quite a few cars when Jeremy pulled into it early that evening. He had not been to a Wednesday night church service in many years, but Pastor Hurley had urged Jeremy to come, saying that the whole congregation would like to hear the news he had about Toni Schmidt.

"That little girl kind of got next to a lot of us," Mrs. Hurley said when she saw Jeremy enter the church. "Come on down and sit with me," she added.

About half the people who attended on Sundays were present for this Wednesday service, but they made up in fervor what they lacked in number. The opening hymns, "What a Friend We Have in Jesus" and "Sweet Hour of Prayer," set the tone for the rest of the informal service in which requests for prayer produced a number of earnest petitions.

After several people's needs had been noted and prayed for, Pastor Hurley asked Jeremy to join him at the pulpit and share what he knew about Toni Schmidt and April Kincaid with them all. When he finished and sat down, Pastor Hurley spoke again.

"We may not know where Toni is, but we know whose she is, and we know that He shares our concern for her safety. As you are led, pray now for Toni Schmidt."

Several men and women did so before their pastor concluded with his own prayer in which Jeremy was surprised to find himself mentioned.

"Finally, Lord, we thank You for Jeremy Winter and for the help he has been so willing to give Toni. Lead this fine young man in the paths of righteousness and bring him to know Your perfect will for his life. Amen."

"Amen," everyone murmured, then someone, Jeremy supposed it was Tim Brown, began "Blest Be the Tie That Binds," and the members of the congregation joined in as they hugged one another in farewell.

"May the Lord bless you and keep you," Mrs. Hurley murmured when she embraced Jeremy.

"You, too." Instead of moving toward the door with the others, Jeremy stayed behind, feeling that he had some unfinished business there. He wanted to kneel at the altar and rest his head on the polished rail as he had done as a boy. In those days, his grandmother had told him that his prayers flew straight to God and what he asked, believing, he would receive. But she had added something else—as long as it is in God's will for you.

Jeremy had no memory of moving to the altar, but there he was, kneeling before it, its smooth wooden rail comforting his forehead as he poured out his heart to God. For the first time, Jeremy questioned whether his political ambitions, which had always seemed so right, were really in God's will.

I believe, Lord. Help Thou my unbelief.

With the admission came the first peace that Jeremy had known since April and Toni had disappeared. Some time later—Jeremy could not say how much longer—he heard a distinct and clear voice apparently addressing him directly.

"Do not concern yourself about April and Toni. They are resting in God's care, and so should you be."

Startled, Jeremy looked over his left shoulder to see who had spoken and saw no one. He stood, but his legs were so stiff from the unaccustomed kneeling that they almost gave way.

"Come over here and sit down," Pastor Hurley said from a pew on the right side of the church.

Jeremy wondered how long he had been watching him, but it did not really matter. "April and Toni are all right," he said when he joined the pastor.

Ed Hurley nodded. "That's not the only thing you found out here tonight, is it?"

"No," Jeremy said. He paused for a moment, struggling to put his feelings into words. "It's almost like coming home to kneel at this altar again and feel, actually know, the power of something outside myself again."

"That's the joy of your salvation at work," Ed Hurley said.

"I'm not sure I understand it," Jeremy admitted. For another half hour, he and the pastor talked, then prayed, and Jeremy found himself telling Ed Hurley that his political ambitions now seemed vain and inconsequential. "What matters most to me now is finding April and Toni," he concluded.

Ed Hurley looked closely at Jeremy. "We all share concern for Toni, but I must ask. . .how do you feel about April?"

Jeremy replied without hesitation, "I love her. I can't imagine my future without her."

The pastor nodded. "I think April knew that before you did. She asked me not to tell you where she was, but now I believe I should."

"You really know where she is?" Jeremy asked.

"Yes. She borrowed Mrs. Hurley's car and went to Chattanooga to look for Toni. Earlier today she called to say that Toni wasn't at her aunt's house, but she thought she might still show up there."

"April's in Chattanooga?" Jeremy glanced at his watch. "I can get there in a couple of hours—"

"Just a minute," Pastor Hurley cautioned. "Before I tell you where to find April, there's something you should know about her."

"April never said anything about her past, but apparently she thinks she has something to hide. Is that what you mean?"

"Yes and no. Jeremy, as a lawyer, you're used to seeing things in terms of right and wrong, black and white. What April might once have done has nothing to do with the beautiful person that she is today, but she doesn't want her past to hurt your career."

"I don't care about what April might have done. . .just tell me where to find her."

Ed Hurley regarded Jeremy gravely. "In God's eyes, every saint has a past and every sinner has a future. Can you really accept that fact?"

"I already have," Jeremy assured him.

"Then I think it's time for you to tell April so."

∽

Jeremy's first impulse was to go directly to Chattanooga without letting anyone know, but he stopped in the parking lot of a darkened business and punched the Bells' number into his cellular telephone.

"Are you all right? Daddy's been trying to reach you for hours," Joan said as soon as she heard Jeremy's voice.

"I'm fine," Jeremy said. "I have a lead that Toni Schmidt might be in Chattanooga, and I'm going to follow it up. Tell your father that I'll call him tomorrow."

Joan sounded almost frantic. "You can't leave town now. Daddy talked to the

Montgomery people this evening, and they want to see you tomorrow."

"What time?" Jeremy asked.

"About noon, I think Daddy said."

Jeremy reviewed what he had to do and mentally calculated the driving time from Chattanooga to Huntsville and then to Montgomery. "Tell him I don't think I can make it."

Joan sounded exasperated. "Have you suddenly taken leave of your senses? This could be your big break, Jeremy. You'll need these people—"

"Look, Joan, I have to go now," Jeremy interrupted. "Just tell your father what I said."

"All right. I hope you know what you're doing."

"Oh, yes. For the first time, I really do."

∞

It was nearly midnight when Jeremy pulled into the driveway of a modest frame house in the Brainerd section of Chattanooga. He was disappointed not to see Mrs. Hurley's car in the driveway, but so many lights burned in both the upper and lower floors that Jeremy thought that Ed Hurley must have called to tell his sister that Jeremy was on his way to see April.

However, it was obvious that the man who turned on the porch light and peered out the door at Jeremy did not know who he was, and only after Jeremy explained that Pastor Hurley had given him directions to the house did the man relax his guard and open the door to him.

"Who is it now?" a female voice called out, and Jeremy saw a middle-aged woman resembling Ed Hurley join her husband.

"I'm Jeremy Winter, Mrs. Watkins. Pastor Hurley told me that April Kincaid was here."

"What do you want with April? Are you some kind of policeman?" Mr. Watkins asked.

"Oh, hush," his wife said. "This must be the young fellow that April talked about so much. If my brother told you she was here, then I'm sure it's all right."

"The thing is, she's not here now," Mr. Watkins added.

"Don't look so worried," his wife told Jeremy. "She had a call from Toni's aunt that the police were holding the girl, and she went to try to get her released."

"When did that happen?" Jeremy asked.

"About ten o'clock, I think. I told her to wait until Mr. Watkins got home—he works second shift—but she said she could handle it herself and off she went."

"I see," said Jeremy, who could, indeed, imagine April's impatience to go to Toni. "Where is this police station?"

"I could tell you, but it'd be easier if I rode with you," Mr. Watkins said.

"Let's go, then."

Mrs. Watkins followed them to the car. "Tell April that I've made up a bed for Toni."

"God willing, we'll we back soon with both of them," Mr. Watkins said.

"How long have you known April?" Jeremy asked on the drive to police headquarters.

"Several years now, I reckon," he replied. "Mrs. Watkins met her when she was doing some mission work at a homeless shelter. She was so taken with April that she asked Ed Hurley to keep looking after her when she was ready to go out on her own."

"April lived in a homeless shelter?"

Mr. Watkins cast Jeremy a worried look. "She didn't tell you? Well, it's nothing she's proud of, I'm sure, but you have to give her credit for what she's made of her life since the bad times."

"I know," Jeremy said. "April is a wonderful person, and she's been a big help to Toni."

"You're Toni's lawyer?"

"Yes. But I also think of Toni as a friend."

"And April?"

Jeremy hesitated for a moment, then for the second time in only a few hours, he repeated a truth he had only lately come to admit. "I love her."

∞

The desk sergeant did not seem to know where Toni and April were, but another officer told them that Toni was being held for pickup by the juvenile authorities. April had tried to get Toni released to her custody, but the request had been denied.

"Where is Miss Kincaid now?" Jeremy asked.

"At the pay phone, I suppose. She said some lawyer in Alabama represented the girl, and she went to call him to come after her."

Jeremy adopted his most authoritative voice. "I'm Toni Schmidt's lawyer, and I'm here to take her back to Rockdale, where she has a court hearing pending."

Jeremy thought the officer looked almost relieved to have an excuse to be rid of her. "I'll get the paperwork started," he replied.

"Where are the pay phones?" Jeremy asked, looking around and seeing none.

"Down the hall and to the right, beside the lockers. You can use my desk phone if you like—"

But Jeremy was already gone.

∞

April stood by the graffiti-filled wall beside the pay phones, speaking in a voice that was strained but under control. "I'm sorry to call so late, Pastor Hurley, but I've found Toni. . . . Yes, praise the Lord, indeed. She's all right, just tired and scared. But the police won't let her go with me. I tried to called Jeremy Winter, but I got his answering machine. Will you keep trying to reach him and tell him— What? Are you sure?"

At the same moment that Pastor Hurley was telling April that Jeremy

Winter was on his way to Chattanooga, possibly was already there, Jeremy touched her lightly on the shoulder, and April almost dropped the receiver when she turned and saw him.

Jeremy took the receiver from her hand. "Pastor? I'm here, and the police are going to release Toni to me. We'll be coming back to Rockdale tomorrow. Yes, sir, I agree. Thank you. Good-bye." He hung up and turned to April, confident that the love and joy that filled his heart must surely show in his face.

"Jeremy—" April began before he swept her into his arms and held her in a fierce embrace.

All the way to Chattanooga, Jeremy had rehearsed what he would say when he saw April. He would speak logically and tell her he did not care what might have happened in her life before they met. But now that she was in his arms at last, all other words fled except the only ones that mattered.

"I love you, April."

April pulled slightly away and looked at Jeremy, revealing the tears in her hazel eyes. "You shouldn't," she almost whispered. "I'm too far out of your league. I'd just drag you down—"

"Let me worry about that." Jeremy silenced her further protests with a long, tender kiss and felt her gradually relax in his arms. Even before she whispered the words, April's response told him how she really felt.

"God help me, I love you, too, Jeremy Winter."

Jeremy's sudden laughter startled April, and she looked at him in alarm before he hugged her close again.

"God will help us both," he corrected. "I know that now."

"I'm glad," April said simply.

When she kissed him again, Jeremy quietly acknowledged that knowing and finding God's will for their lives would always be the most politically correct thing they could ever do.

Epilogue

On the last Tuesday in August, some four months after Jeremy returned to Rockdale with Toni and April, the voters of Rockdale went to the polls to elect a number of local and state officials. Jeremy and April cast their ballots early in the day, then joined a group of Jeremy's supporters at Statum's Family Restaurant to await the outcome.

"Don't call it a victory party," Jeremy warned when Tom Statum told him about his plans for the gathering.

"Everybody in town knows that you're the best man for the job, but I'll just call it an election celebration if that's what you want."

As they entered, the number of people who had come to Statum's Family Restaurant surprised Jeremy. He had expected to see the Bells (accompanied by a man rumored to be "really serious" about Joan) and Edith Westleigh from the law office. He knew Evelyn Trent and her ward, Toni Schmidt, who had worked tirelessly for his campaign, would be there, along with the pastor, choir, and a great many members of Community Church, where Jeremy and April would exchange marriage vows in September. But he had not expected to see so many others, from the country club set to the residents of Harrison Homes, that filled every table in the small restaurant and stood along the wall or sat on the floor.

Jeremy's entrance brought a cheer from the crowd to which he waved in reply.

"Get ready to make a speech when the results come in," Tom Statum said as if he had been managing political campaigns all his life.

Jeremy and April took their reserved places at the counter, from which Tom was dispensing more of the free lemonade that had been the main symbol in Jeremy's campaign.

"When life hands you a lemon, you'd better learn how to make lemonade" was a slogan that Jeremy had borrowed from April, who in turn had heard it from some anonymous worker at the homeless shelter in the darkest days of her life.

When the people in Montgomery decided to appoint Mrs. Harrison to fill out her husband's unexpired term, Jeremy had not wasted any time feeling sorry for himself. By then he had discovered several ways in which Rockdale could improve itself, and when Randall Bell urged him to run for mayor, Jeremy had been surprised at the support he had been given. Dallas Alston, Rockdale's long-time mayor, had been merely going through the motions for several years, and the town was ready for a change.

Jeremy ran on a platform of civic improvement, with emphasis on finding ways to keep the young people occupied and providing help for those who got into trouble, improving the police department, and attracting the right kind of new business to insure an adequate tax base to pay for it all. Among those who had become interested in his campaign was the millionaire Jackie Tyler, who had never before participated in Rockdale's civic life. He financed a barbecue at which a number of his well-known musician friends performed a catchy campaign song featuring the words, "Win with Winter."

"Wait until Mr. Pettibone hears this," Jeremy told April, who looked at him questioningly.

"I thought you fired him."

"I tried to, but he still wants me to run for Harrison's seat when his widow gives it up."

"Even though you'll have a wife with a juvenile record?"

"I explained that you ran away from a bad family situation and got in with the wrong crowd for a while, and Mr. Pettibone said that as long as we were up front about it, no harm would be done. In fact, he admires the way you've overcome your past." Jeremy paused, seeing the doubt in April's face. "But that's still a long time off, and in the meantime, if I win this election, I'll have all the politics I can handle right here in Rockdale."

"With them fancy electronic machines they use now, it seems to me that they should be done with the counting by now," Tom Statum said a few minutes after Jeremy and April's arrival.

Just then the telephone rang, and the noisy babble of dozens of conversations stopped as he picked up the receiver and listened for a moment. Then Tom's face broke into a wide grin, and everyone cheered the results they knew he must have heard.

Tom hung up the telephone and pounded Jeremy on the back. "Congratulations, Mr. Mayor. You won in a landslide!"

After a few minutes of applauding and cheering, the crowd silenced when Jeremy stood to speak to them.

"Thank you all for being here and for your support these past few months. Most of you know I decided to run for mayor when I realized how few opportunities Rockdale has for young people and after the folks at Community Church and First Church urged me to get involved. With your hard work and the help of the Lord, we all won today. You know I'll be new at this, and April and I will need your continued support as well as all your prayers to serve all the people of Rockdale. Thank you again, and praise God!"

When he sat down, Jeremy noticed that April's eyes were damp with tears of joy.

"I have so much to be thankful for, starting with you," she said softly as if they were the only people there.

Jeremy squeezed her hand. "We both do," he replied.

Their brief private moment was interrupted by a number of well-wishers.

"Nice job, Mr. Mayor," Joan Bell said sincerely. Once she had finally accepted the fact that Jeremy really intended to marry April Kincaid, Joan had become a staunch friend of them both.

Jeremy nodded. "Thanks. I know I wouldn't even have run for mayor if you and your father hadn't pushed so hard."

"Remember, we'll still be around for your next race."

After Joan, Jackie Tyler offered his hand. "Congratulations, Jeremy." Then he turned to April and spoke with sincere admiration. "My offer still stands, young lady. I'm about to produce a new album, and I sure could use a voice like yours to sing backup."

"I'll keep your offer in mind," April said, but her tone left no doubt that she would not be likely to take him up on it.

Mr. Tyler grinned and slapped Jeremy on the back. "I hope you know how lucky you are," he said.

"Blessed, not lucky," Jeremy corrected.

It's true, Jeremy thought as he spoke the words. No matter what lay ahead, Jeremy felt certain that the firm and sure hand of the Lord would continue to be in control of his life.

As if she knew and shared his thoughts, April squeezed his hand.

For now, Jeremy Winter would try to be the best mayor Rockdale ever had. If God had another political job for him to do later on down the road, then so be it.

Jeremy and April would be ready.

Toni's Vow

For Rebecca Blackwell Drake of Raymond, Mississippi,
meticulous historical researcher and writer,
excellent photographer, and tireless preservationist.
Thank you for your generosity and encouragement—
and most of all, for being my friend.
Special thanks to Mark Morrison, whose Waterfall Walks
and Drives in Georgia, Alabama, and Tennessee
(H.F. Publishing, Inc., Douglasville, GA)
is a marvelous guide to the natural beauty of DeSoto State Park
and Little River Canyon National Preserve.
Thanks also to Travis Overstreet of Leawood, Kansas,
for his expert assistance in musical matters.

Chapter 1

Ten years?

Toni Schmidt frowned slightly. No, it had been ten years since her graduation from Rockdale High School, just over nine years since she had last lived in Rockdale—and three years since her last, brief visit. Yet here she was, on her way back to live in a town she had once despised.

Toni maneuvered her compact SUV around a slow-moving logging truck. The road to Rockdale lay somewhere ahead, and assuming that the truck was bound for the Rockdale lumber mill, Toni had no desire to follow it through the winding, two-lane road that had been at least partially responsible for the town's relative isolation.

In her desire to put distance between her vehicle and the truck, Toni almost missed the Rockdale turnoff and had to brake at the last minute. Gravel sprayed as the SUV's rear wheels strayed onto the shoulder. Toni slowed and straightened the vehicle, glad that no one had witnessed her screeching turn.

"That wild Toni Schmidt—as reckless as ever." Toni could imagine the reaction of some of the town's gray heads. What would they think if they knew that "that awful juvenile delinquent," as Toni had once been called, was returning to the place that had once scorned her?

Toni sighed at the memory of the awkward ugly duckling she had been at fifteen. She lifted her chin to glance at her reflection in the rearview mirror. "Not that you're any great beauty now," Toni told herself aloud. Never one to dwell on her appearance, she knew that her straight mouth made her appear somewhat severe, but otherwise her looks were unremarkable. In recent years, her light brown hair had darkened, making a pleasing contrast to her ivory skin. Her hazel eyes no longer regarded the world with fear and suspicion, but the inner wariness Toni had learned in those days hadn't entirely disappeared.

She spread the neatly manicured fingers of one hand across the steering wheel and recalled how she had once bitten her fingernails to the quick. That was just one of her many bad habits that Evelyn Trent had helped Toni change.

Toni reached the posted speed of fifty-five miles per hour, leaned back in the seat, and reviewed the chain of circumstances that had led her to this day. Because of E-mail and the instant accessibility of her cell phone, Toni rarely wrote or received personal letters. She checked her Atlanta post office box only a few times a week and seldom found it full. Therefore, several months ago, Toni had been surprised to find two letters with a Rockdale, Alabama, postmark.

One she recognized at once; Evelyn Trent's distinctive handwriting hadn't changed since she'd served as Toni's guardian. They now kept in touch through exchanging Christmas letters—interspersed with infrequent telephone calls and E-mails—but in the first few years after Toni left Rockdale, Evelyn's letters had been an important lifeline. The other letter, with only a Rockdale post office box for its return address, Toni put aside. Fearing the worst, she opened Evelyn Trent's envelope immediately.

Toni still remembered every word of the brief note:

Dear Toni,
    You must be wondering why I'm writing this time of the year. I enjoyed your Christmas card. You certainly seem to be busy enough, but I sense you're not completely happy in Atlanta.
    I want to discuss an important matter with you. Please call me soon.
                                           Evelyn

Months later, Toni still remembered how puzzled she'd felt. The note sounded nothing like Evelyn's usual letters, and Toni feared that something was seriously wrong.

Toni resolved to call Evelyn that evening, then opened the second envelope, which contained a quite different message.

DEAR GRADUATE OF ROCKDALE HIGH,

it began, screaming in capital letters.

    Can you believe it has been ten years since we walked its halls? Well, now it's time to get together, so mark your calendars for the third weekend in July! A picnic and dance and many surprises are in store at Rockdale High School. Details will follow.
                                  Your Reunion Committee

Toni smiled, recalling how she had cringed over the idea of the reunion. *No one would notice my absence,* she had thought, then dropped the notice into the trash receptacle.

Toni had no wish to renew any connection with Rockdale High School. She hadn't kept in touch with the few friends she'd had there, and she certainly didn't want to see the snobs who had once disdained or barely tolerated her.

Toni called Evelyn that night and immediately voiced her concern. "Are you all right?"

"Of course I am—but thanks for asking."

"Then why did you ask me to call?"

"I plan to retire this summer. I'd like for you to consider taking my place."

At first, Toni hadn't thought Evelyn was serious. Whatever her former guardian's age, Evelyn Trent seemed far too young to retire from a job she so obviously enjoyed and did so well. Even when Evelyn had made it clear that the paperwork was already in place for her to leave her office on the first of August, Toni could not imagine replacing her mentor. In many subsequent conversations, she told her so repeatedly.

"For one thing, I'm not licensed to do social work in Alabama," Toni had pointed out.

"A license is just a piece of paper. You have the necessary education and experience."

Toni thought of how Evelyn had used her considerable powers to persuade Toni, almost grudgingly, to agree to pray about it. In the end, those prayers had been the deciding factor.

Recalling the hours she had spent on her knees asking the Lord to show her His will, Toni still felt a sense of awe. She hadn't experienced a heavenly vision or heard a clear voice from the clouds telling her to go to Rockdale, but over the next few weeks, several things worked together to point her in that direction. Her work duties were changing in ways that she didn't like; her apartment building was to become a co-op, and since she couldn't afford to buy her rental unit, she'd have to move. Then in the same week, two of her friends announced their engagements, further diminishing the number of singles she knew.

∞

A month after she received Evelyn's first letter, Toni agreed to apply to the Alabama Department of Human Resources for a social worker license. Another two months of red tape, including an interview at the state DHR headquarters in Montgomery, followed before Toni received her license—and shortly after, the offer of work in the Rockdale DHR office.

Almost before she realized she had traveled that far, Toni rounded a curve and crossed the bridge over Dale Creek, which marked Rockdale's city limits. The road looked pretty much the same, but Toni noticed that the bridge had been widened.

"Congressman Winter takes good care of us," Evelyn Trent had written Toni a couple of years after Jeremy Winter's election to serve his district in Washington, D.C. Jeremy's wife, April, was Toni's first—and for a long time, only—friend in Rockdale. Toni still thanked God for the kindness they had both shown her in this place then and had continued to show her since.

April Winter telephoned to express her delight that Toni was returning to Rockdale. "Wonderful news! Jeremy and I look forward to seeing you the next time we're home."

Home. Ironically, neither April nor Jeremy had been born in Rockdale, yet there was no question that they considered the old house that had been Jeremy's grandmother's to be their only real home. Toni hadn't come to the town until after her twelfth birthday, yet Rockdale was the closest thing to a hometown she'd ever known.

Toni entered the main downtown area and stopped for a traffic light near the courthouse where Jeremy Winter had persuaded a skeptical judge to allow Evelyn Trent to become Toni's guardian. A lump formed in her throat as she recalled how close she had come to being declared incorrigible and sent to reform school. What her life might have been if that had happened, Toni could only guess—but it could not have been good.

I owe Evelyn a great deal, Toni realized. That sense of debt had been at least partly responsible for her decision to return to Rockdale.

She knew it wouldn't be possible for anyone to replace Evelyn Trent.

But with God's help, I'll do my best.

It was a vow Toni intended to keep.

Chapter 2

Evelyn Trent still lived in the house where she had grown up. Her much younger brother hadn't objected when their parents deeded the house to Evelyn in return for her continuing to care for them for the rest of their lives.

Although Evelyn never married, like many single schoolteachers, she was often called "Ms. Trent." When they first met, Toni thought Evelyn Trent was a cranky old maid, set in her ways, and interested only in her work, which seemed to involve a lot of prying into other people's lives. With no children of her own, Evelyn had surprised many people—and perhaps herself—by taking in terrible Toni Schmidt when almost everyone else in town had given up on her.

Toni remembered the sinking feeling that had hit the pit of her stomach when she realized she would be totally at the mercy of a middle-aged, rather severe-looking social worker who had the power to send her to reform school at any time. Toni had feared the worst, yet Evelyn never mistreated her, as her biological parents, two stepmothers, and a series of foster parents had all done.

Not that her life with Evelyn had been a bed of roses. Toni had to behave herself and do her share of the housework without any talking back. Confused and unhappy, Toni had no choice but to obey her guardian, to whom she could give only a grudging respect.

Toni had enjoyed living in Evelyn's house from the start, however. The modest, three-bedroom frame bungalow with its single bathroom, small kitchen, and boxlike living and dining rooms seemed palatial compared to the succession of run-down house trailers, dingy public housing, and crowded foster homes that Toni had known all her life.

Second only to having her own room, Toni loved the deep front porch, which Evelyn had made comfortable with rocking chairs and a wicker swing. She decorated it in the summer with hanging baskets of ferns and all sorts of fragrant and colorful flowers.

On this summer day, years later, when Toni parked at the curb in front of 210 Maple Street, Evelyn was in the porch swing, apparently waiting for her.

"I figured you might get here about now," Evelyn said when Toni started up the porch steps. She waved toward a wicker table bearing a frosty pitcher covered by a hand-embroidered tea towel. "I thought you might like some lemonade after that long drive."

"Thanks—that sounds good. I see you recovered the swing," Toni added. "I like the green stripes."

Evelyn stirred the lemonade as she spoke. "Like a lot of things around here, it was time for a change."

But you haven't changed a bit, Toni would have said if she hadn't feared embarrassing Evelyn. The once faint lines in her former guardian's face had deepened since Toni's last visit, but Evelyn still didn't look nearly old enough to retire.

"Sit down," Evelyn invited after she poured their lemonade. "I remember you said you liked this front porch better than anywhere else on earth."

"As if I'd been all that many other places at that time," Toni said somewhat ruefully. "You certainly had to put up with a great deal from me."

Toni leaned forward and spoke quickly, aware that her words would embarrass Evelyn. "I hope you know how much I appreciate everything you have done—and are still doing—for me."

Evelyn's fair cheeks colored briefly, and she looked down at her glass. "I only did what I thought was needed," she said after a long moment. Then Evelyn looked at Toni in the intent way that meant she was about to say something important. "Anyway, it wasn't a one-way street. Seeing the world through your eyes made me less rigid, so we both benefited. You've made a wonderful start in your career, but now I'm concerned about your future."

"I supposed that was why you brought me back here and offered me your job. Of course, if you've second thoughts about this whole retirement thing—"

Evelyn shook her head impatiently. "Not at all. If I didn't want to retire, I wouldn't do it. And if I didn't believe you could handle the work here, you'd still be in Atlanta. But I don't want to see you put your whole life into it, as I did."

In her surprise, Toni blurted out the only thing that occurred to her. "I always thought you were happy."

Evelyn nodded. "I was—I am. I've been blessed in many ways, but I never married or had a family of my own. The older I get, the more I regret putting my work above everything else. I sense that you might make the same mistake."

Faced with this unsettling revelation, Toni scarcely knew what to say. "I don't know what you mean."

Evelyn sighed. "For too many years, work was my whole world. I was too wrapped up in it to let anyone else in. By the time I realized my mistake, it was too late. I'm afraid this old maid wasn't a very suitable role model."

Toni raised her chin in an old gesture of defiance. "I don't intend to get married," she said, more emphatically than she intended.

Evelyn laughed ruefully. "Oh, Toni, you sound like you did the first time I saw you, fifteen years old and both fists up, ready to take on the world. I kept hoping you would make a good marriage, but when year after year you wrote that you weren't seeing anyone special, I had an idea it might be on purpose."

Toni's voice was thick with emotion. "My mother's troubles began the day she met my father. I saw them end only when she finally overdosed on the drugs he brought home. I vowed then that no man would ever have the chance to mistreat me like he did her and the women he brought home afterward."

Evelyn laid her hand comfortingly on Toni's shoulder. "I know you went through some terrible things as a child, but surely you realize that marriage doesn't have to be like that. Look at April and Jeremy Winter. April had a rough start in life, too, yet you've seen how happy they are."

Not liking the turn the conversation had taken, Toni tried to change it. "Yes, they are, and I'm glad. But Jeremy Winter's already taken, and I haven't met anyone half as interesting. Since you think I should marry, maybe you've already picked out a likely candidate?"

Evelyn looked embarrassed. "Of course not. I just want you to keep an open mind. As much as you enjoy your work, your life ought to be measured by more than just your job."

"You haven't 'just had a job'—it's been more like a mission. I only hope to do half as well."

Evelyn rose, signaling her readiness to drop the subject. "Of course you will, and more. In the meantime, it's good to see you on this porch again. Bring in your things and rest awhile, if you like. At six, we're having supper with some people who want to see you."

Toni's heart sank at the thought that at least one of the "people" would probably be an eligible male. It was ironic that Evelyn Trent, who always declared that she was perfectly happy living alone, had now decided that no one else should.

I respect you, Evelyn, but I don't need a matchmaker. I will not be put on inspection like a hunk of meat.

Something in Evelyn's expression prevented Toni from voicing her objections. "I've had a hard week, getting ready for the move, so I hope it won't be a late evening," she said instead.

"No, this will be a relaxed supper, very informal. What you're wearing will be fine," Evelyn added before Toni could ask if she should replace her denim jumper for something more formal.

∞

Evelyn had reserved a large table at the rear of Statum's Family Restaurant, where April Kincaid had worked as a waitress when she and Toni first met. Of all the places in Rockdale, it was providential that Toni had picked April's apartment to rob. It wasn't something she thought of often, but now, as she was greeted by Tom Statum, she wished that Evelyn had chosen another restaurant.

Still, Toni knew she had to get used to seeing people who remembered her from those days. She was an unhappy runaway the night she'd broken into April's apartment. Toni was quite certain that her past sins had been forgiven in heaven, if not by everyone in Rockdale.

"There she is!" A man with fiery red hair rose from the table and held out his arms in welcome.

"Ted! Evelyn didn't tell me you were going to be here."

"Good thing—Toni might not have come at all," Janet Brown put in as her husband and Toni exchanged a brief hug.

"Do you still direct music at Community Church?" Toni asked.

Ted nodded. "Yes, and we're still on the lookout for new talent. When Evelyn told me you were going to be here tonight, I made her invite us."

Evelyn glanced toward the door. "Here come the others."

Toni turned, fully expecting to see at least one unattached man. Instead, two women entered the restaurant.

The older one was slender, dressed and coifed to perfection. Her face was familiar, but her name escaped Toni. The other, Toni's age and a bit more than pleasingly plump, wore a bright red linen dress and smiled brightly. Toni recognized her immediately as Mary Oliver, the daughter of the judge who had appointed Evelyn as Toni's guardian.

"Mary! How good to see you," Toni said, meaning it.

"Same here. It's been way too long since you've been in Rockdale," Mary replied.

Toni turned to the other woman, who held out her hand in greeting. "Margaret Hastings. You may not remember me, but I worked in Congressman Winter's campaign."

"Of course—and didn't you become mayor when he went to Washington?"

"She did, and she's still doing a good job in that office," Evelyn answered for Margaret.

Seated between Mary Oliver and Margaret Hastings, enjoying Tom Statum's special fried chicken dinner and sweet lemon-flavored tea, Toni felt like a spectator at a tennis match as each attempted to carry on a completely different conversation with her.

Mary wanted to tell Toni all about the upcoming tenth reunion at Rockdale High, which Toni gathered she had helped put together. Mayor Margaret kept relating various problems the town faced, as if Toni might have some power to make them go away. Across the table, Ted Brown tried to tell Toni about the growth of the church and embarrassed her by going on about how much everyone would enjoy hearing her sing there again.

By the time Tom served his famous Southern pecan pie and chicory-flavored coffee, Toni's head was swimming.

"I hope you enjoyed the evening," Evelyn said as they drove home.

"Yes, it was fun. But why do I have the feeling that I was on the menu, too?" Toni asked.

Evelyn laughed. "Because in a way you are. Anyone new in Rockdale or coming back after a long absence has to go through a few rites of initiation into small-town life. Tonight was just a sample of what's to come."

Toni groaned. "You told me how much everyone wanted to see me. You didn't warn me that they all wanted something from me, as well."

"Not all do. But small-town life is a two-way street, you know," Evelyn added.

"Right now, I feel as if I'm going the wrong way on a one-way street."

Evelyn maneuvered her old sedan into the detached garage and turned off the engine. "You'll feel better after a good night's sleep," she promised.

I hope so, Toni thought, too tired to say so. Yet as weary as she was, when she said her evening prayers, Toni felt enfolded in an almost palpable sense of peace.

God means for me to be here, and He will take care of everything. Comforted by that thought, she slept.

∞

"We'll go by the office this morning," Evelyn said when Toni joined her for breakfast.

"I thought I wasn't supposed to start work until next week."

"True, but I promised the others to bring you by today, and I have to go to the courthouse on a matter that just came up. I hope you don't mind."

"No, of course not. It'll be a good learning experience."

Evelyn laughed shortly. "That's one way to put it, but after nearly thirty-five years in this work, I'm still learning myself. Don't be discouraged if it doesn't all fall into place at first," she added.

∞

The Rockdale Department of Human Resources office occupied the lower floor of an ancient brick building on the courthouse square. Over the years, many wanted the DHR to acquire a new building, preferably on Dale Boulevard, where parking was more accessible. Funds were never available for that, and Evelyn had said she was glad because she liked the convenience of the courthouse square location. After a dilapidated furniture store behind them was razed and the site made into a parking lot, talk of moving the office had stopped.

First Toni met Anna Hastings, the mayor's blond sister-in-law, who occupied a desk in a sunny front window.

"She's officially the secretary and receptionist, but she also makes very good coffee and fills in wherever she's needed," Evelyn explained as she introduced Anna.

"I hope you're planning to work here many more years," Toni said so seriously that Anna laughed.

Edwinna Borden, the food stamps and other entitlements manager, overheard Toni's remark. She emerged from her small office next to Evelyn's and extended her hand. "More years than I'll be here," she said.

Toni had the impression Edwinna Borden was a brusque, businesslike woman in her late forties—the kind of person she'd far rather have as a friend than an enemy. "I'm happy to meet you," Toni said, returning her firm handshake.

Edwinna nodded toward Evelyn. "Same here, but I'd be a whole lot happier if having you here didn't mean losing Evelyn. I don't know how we'll manage without her."

Neither do I, thought Toni, then dismissed the negative thought. She could do the work—Evelyn had told her so, and in a way, so had the Lord.

"Don't start that again," Evelyn said, and Toni guessed the DHR office staff shared Toni's initial surprise that Evelyn actually intended to retire.

"Any calls?" Evelyn asked Anna.

"Just the judge's secretary, wanting to make sure you'd come over this morning."

"We're on our way," Evelyn said. "Hold down the fort, ladies."

"They seem to know their business," Toni said after they left the office and crossed the street, bound for the courthouse.

"They do. Anna started working for me right after you went off to college, and Edwinna has been here about two years."

"Why didn't either of them apply for your job?"

"Anna isn't qualified, and Edwinna lacks your experience. Besides that, her son requires specialized care, so she needs regular office hours and wants no more responsibility."

"I hope they can put up with me while I learn my way around," Toni said.

"Don't worry. You'll be fine."

"The courthouse hasn't changed," Toni said as they mounted its worn stone steps.

"The doors were painted last year. Otherwise, it's the same old building."

Toni hadn't been inside the Rockdale County courthouse in years, but even blindfolded, she would know the musty document smell that greeted her the moment she stepped over the threshold. She felt the flesh crawl on her arms as they mounted the worn wooden steps to the courtroom where Judge Oliver—Mary's father—had heard the testimony that led him to grant Evelyn Trent's petition to become Toni Schmidt's guardian.

Toni recalled how at first it seemed that she had escaped reform school only to wind up in a different kind of prison. Evelyn had cut her very little slack. As her ward, Toni attended school every day and always had a part-time job afterward. Although Toni resented the unaccustomed discipline, she soon came to like her structured life. She made good grades, and for the first time, Toni had spending money that she hadn't stolen.

"The judge is in his chambers," Evelyn said, leading Toni through the vacant courtroom to the judge's office.

It doesn't look nearly as large as it did when I was fifteen, Toni thought.

In those days, Toni had regarded Judge Wayne Oliver as an old man. Now, as he came from behind his desk to greet them, she saw that he was far from elderly. He still had the same salt-and-pepper hair and appeared to be as vigorous as ever, despite the extra pounds the years had added to his ample frame.

"Judge, you remember Toni Schmidt," Evelyn said, and from the way he looked at her, Toni knew that this was not the first time her former guardian had mentioned her to the judge.

"Of course. Nice to see you, young lady. You'll probably be involved in the case I asked Evelyn here to discuss, so it's a good thing you came along. Have a seat, ladies."

This could very well be the same chair where I sat when my own case was being discussed. Except for the age of the child, the file from which the judge read might also have been her own. Toni hadn't come into the Rockdale jurisdiction until she was fourteen, but she had already been to juvenile court in Tennessee several times before that. The little girl in this case was eight years old and was apparently being fought over by her parents. Her father had taken her out of state in violation of the divorce decree, and the mother, charging kidnapping, had sued for full custody.

"Is the child still missing?" asked Evelyn.

Judge Oliver nodded. "When she's returned to our jurisdiction, DHR will need to investigate and prepare a report for the preliminary hearing."

"What does the child want?" Toni heard herself ask and, from the way the others looked at her, immediately knew she should have remained silent.

"That is not the question, Miss Schmidt," the judge said as if a small child had just revealed her woeful ignorance.

"It's now a criminal matter," Evelyn added. "When the child is returned, I'm sure her feelings will be taken into account."

"I see," said Toni, who did, but she had never understood why "the system" had to function as it did. *No one ever asked me what I wanted when I was that age and being beaten black-and-blue and living hand-to-mouth. If they had, it would have saved a great deal of later grief.*

The judge continued discussing the particulars of the case for a few more minutes before he rose, shook Toni's hand again, and assured her that he looked forward to working with her.

"I hope to see you again before you really retire and leave Rockdale," he told Evelyn.

"If I go. I haven't quite decided about that," she said.

∞

"You told the judge you might not leave town," Toni said as they stepped from the gloom of the courthouse into the glare of the sun. "I thought you planned to become a world traveler."

"I do, and I will, but all in good time. I'm not much for burning my bridges."

"Neither am I—although I have burned quite a few by coming back to Rockdale."

Evelyn glanced at Toni as if to make sure she spoke seriously. "That will make it easier to build new bridges here."

Evelyn stopped at the DHR office and handed Toni a key to her front door.

"I had this made for you. Go on back to the house, and I'll be along as soon as I check on some things."

"Do you want me to make lunch?" Toni asked.

"No, that won't be necessary."

Evelyn entered the DHR office, and Toni stood on the sidewalk, staring after her for a moment. Evelyn almost seemed eager to get rid of her, but Toni had no idea why.

In any case, she welcomed the short walk back to Maple Street in the still-mild summer morning. Two blocks from the courthouse, she entered one of the oldest residential areas, where home owners took obvious pride in their property. Toni had forgotten, if she ever knew, the names of most of the colorful flowers that bloomed in beds, planters, and window boxes all along the way, but she enjoyed their fragrant beauty. Nothing like this ever grew around her Atlanta apartment.

She exchanged greetings with several residents who waved from their yards or porches as she passed. No one called her by name, but Toni recognized Jenny Suiter, an older woman she remembered as a notorious gossip.

Toni hadn't had any nosy neighbors in Atlanta. The few she actually knew by name were far too occupied with their own lives to worry about hers. It wouldn't be that way in Rockdale. With a small town, the bad came with the good.

Toni was still speculating about her possible reception among people like Mrs. Suiter when she turned onto Maple Street and continued to walk, head down, toward Evelyn's house. She was almost there before a glance at the front porch stopped her in her tracks.

A man occupied the wicker swing, and Toni knew he must have been watching her for some time. Transfixed, she saw him slowly unfold his long legs and stand.

Toni's mind automatically registered that, at well over six feet, this man made an imposing figure. Furthermore, he was handsome. In fact, Toni couldn't remember when she had seen any man whose appearance appealed to her so instantly.

Another thought followed immediately: *Evelyn is probably responsible for his presence*—and Toni wanted no part of her matchmaking.

With that in mind, Toni raised her chin and started up the porch steps, grimly resolved not to smile.

Chapter 3

I hope I didn't frighten you," the man said.

Toni glanced at his outstretched hand just as she stumbled on the top step. She reached for the handrail, missed it by inches, and would have fallen had he not caught her.

Toni shrugged free immediately and leaned against a porch pillar, embarrassed by her clumsiness and her tongue-tied reaction to the concern reflected in the man's intense blue eyes.

"Are you all right?" he asked.

Toni managed to nod. "I was just startled."

"You're trembling," he said almost accusingly. "Sit down and catch your breath."

When he put out his left hand to help her to the swing, Toni noted almost automatically that he wore no rings, adding to her suspicion that Evelyn had set up this meeting. *I don't care how good-looking he is, I won't let him rattle me,* she vowed as he sat down next to her.

"Put your head down if you feel faint," he said when Toni remained silent.

His strong features and firm chin match his forceful voice, she thought. He spoke as if accustomed to giving orders, but Toni had no intention of taking orders from him—or any other man, for that matter.

"I've never fainted in my life," she said firmly. "I am not the fainting kind."

His sudden smile revealed brilliant white teeth. "I believe you, Miss. . . ?"

Nettled that he hadn't offered his name first, Toni spoke rather shortly. "Should I know you? I'm afraid we haven't met."

The man's smile faded, and for the first time, Toni felt in control. After all, she was on Evelyn Trent's front porch as an invited guest, while for all she knew, this man could be an ax murderer.

"I'm sorry." He held out his hand again, and this time his smile, although not quite so dazzling, appeared genuine. "I'm David Trent. Evelyn is my sister."

Toni knew that Evelyn had a brother, but she was certain she had never seen his picture. She wouldn't have forgotten a face like that, even as a teenager.

"And you are?" he prompted.

Toni's initial suspicion that Evelyn might be playing matchmaker grew to an irritating certainty, and she knew how she'd like to reply: *I am Toni Schmidt, single by choice, and at this moment I am planning to boil your sister in oil for pulling this trick on me.*

The girl she had once been wouldn't have hesitated to say that and more, quite

127

loudly, but the young woman Toni had become had learned to curb her tongue. She lifted her chin and looked him straight in the eye. "I am Toni Schmidt," she said with rather more force than necessary.

"Glad to know you." David Trent extended his hand, and Toni had no choice but to take it. She sensed he had the strength to crush it had he wished, yet his touch seemed almost tender. When he seemed in no hurry to break the contact, Toni withdrew her hand.

Looking at him more closely, Toni realized that his eyes and mouth somewhat resembled Evelyn's. However, David Trent's rugged good looks were unmistakably masculine.

In return, David leaned back in the swing and studied Toni's face, frowning as if trying to place her.

Evelyn must have told him to come today, Toni thought at first, but now she believed that either this man didn't recognize her features or her name or else he was a great actor.

"Toni Schmidt," he repeated, then nodded as the light of understanding showed in his eyes. "Now I remember. Aren't you the girl who lived with Evelyn for a while?"

Great! Now that he knows my name, I'm dismissed as a girl. Although Toni knew her irritation was probably both irrational and unwarranted, she made no effort to hide it.

"I was fifteen, not exactly a child, when I came to live with Evelyn. I stayed here for just over three years."

David Trent pretended to count on his fingers. "Let's see. I was in Korea when Evelyn wrote she had taken you under her wing, so that must be—what? Close to thirteen years ago?"

Toni briefly inclined her head. With the distinct feeling that she had been bested, she tried to regain an advantage. "Now that you know my name and have computed my age, it's your turn to tell about yourself—and why you've shown up on Evelyn's front porch today."

David's eyebrows lifted slightly as if her bluntness surprised him. "You don't mince words, do you, Miss Schmidt? I wasn't trying to guess your age, but for the record, I'm single, I'm teetering on the downhill side of forty, and I'm on my sister's front porch in Rockdale because I wanted to visit her."

He spoke pleasantly, but Toni sensed that he believed her bluntness revealed a lack of manners. Rather than attempt to alter that impression, Toni pressed on, her tone almost accusing. "Evelyn didn't tell me you were coming."

He shrugged. "She's had a lot on her mind lately. She probably forgot it. Or maybe she wanted to surprise you."

He seems to be telling the truth, Toni thought. Evelyn might not have mentioned her to David, but Toni still suspected that she had somehow contrived their meeting.

"If Evelyn meant to surprise both of us, she seems to have succeeded," Toni said. "I take it you don't live around here?"

"No. I left Rockdale when I was eighteen and never came back or wanted to until now."

That sounds familiar—I could say the exact same thing myself. Unwilling to share anything so personal, Toni asked another question. "What kept you away all those years?"

Her question seemed to amuse David. "I presume you're not interested in a detailed résumé. Let's just say that I joined the army to see the world, and in a little over twenty-one years, I've pretty well done so."

The army—I was right about him, from his bearing to his close-cropped brown hair.

Toni nodded. "You look military."

David almost winced. "Is it that obvious?"

Yes, especially the way you order people around, Toni almost said.

"You mentioned being in Korea when I came to live with Evelyn. I vaguely recall her mentioning she had a brother stationed overseas."

He nodded. "Not just Korea. I went to Japan, Germany, Saudi Arabia, and Kosovo. The United States Army showed this country boy a whole new world, all right."

He doesn't sound like a country boy—he doesn't even sound southern, Toni thought. But if she said so, David Trent might think she was flirting. Toni took pride in the fact that she had never flirted with any man, and she certainly didn't intend to start with this one.

"Where are you stationed now?"

"I'm not. Like my sister, I decided it was time to retire. Since we seem to be playing twenty questions, it's your turn now. What is someone from Atlanta doing in Rockdale?"

"How do you know I'm from Atlanta?" Toni asked, suspecting Evelyn had told him so.

David jerked a thumb toward Toni's SUV, parked at the curb. "That's yours, isn't it?"

Toni nodded and for the first time noticed the silver pickup parked behind it.

"It doesn't take much detective work to figure that a Cobb County, Georgia, license plate on a vehicle strongly suggests that its driver lives in Atlanta."

"Lived," Toni corrected. It might not be David Trent's business, but he'd soon know the whole story, anyway. "I'm going to work in the Rockdale DHR office."

David's mouth fell open. "You're going to take my sister's place? I had no idea—that's quite amazing."

Toni looked down at her hands. "Evelyn is an amazing woman. No one who takes that job can ever replace her."

"Maybe not, but I'm sure you'll give it a good shot."

Rattled by the hint of admiration in David's voice, Toni rose abruptly. "Evelyn should be back any minute. I'll unlock the door so you can wait inside."

"Thanks. I want to get something from my truck first."

Toni watched David stride from the porch and idly noted that his full-sized pickup had four doors. Big man, big truck, she supposed. He took a package wrapped in brown paper from the passenger side of the front seat and returned to the porch.

Toni put Evelyn's house key into the lock and jiggled it several times before the door finally opened.

"That lock seems to be balky," David said. "I'll fix it while I'm here if Evelyn will let me."

A voice behind them startled both Toni and David.

"What is it I'm supposed to let you do?" Evelyn asked, apparently trying to sound cross.

David turned to Evelyn and smiled. "Lots of things I didn't know how to do when I lived here, big sister."

Evelyn turned to Toni. "I'd introduce you, but you seem to have met."

Yes, thanks to you.

"You've been holding out on me," David said accusingly.

"Not really. Don't stand there with the door open. I can't afford to air condition the whole town. Let's go inside. How are things in Virginia? Did you have a good trip down?"

As David assured his sister that all was well, Toni wondered if his home was now in Virginia or whether he'd been visiting someone there.

I know very little about David Trent, after all, was her first thought. The second—that he intrigued her more than any other man she'd met—Toni quickly suppressed.

He's Evelyn's brother. He's come for a visit; then he'll be gone.

Toni set her lips in a grim line. She didn't have a man in her life now, and she wanted it that way.

I don't care how handsome he is. I won't let David Trent manipulate my feelings—and that's a vow.

Chapter 4

David stopped in the middle of the living room and looked around. "I see you got rid of the flowered wallpaper. Otherwise, everything looks about the same."

"You haven't seen the sunroom. Ed Larkins enclosed the back porch last year. Toni, pour some lemonade for yourself and David. You two can chat in the sunroom while I get lunch together."

Evelyn pointed toward the sunroom on her way to the kitchen. David inspected the new addition and entered the kitchen, nodding his approval.

"Looks like Ed did a great building job, and you've got it decorated like something in one of those fancy magazines."

"I'm sure you read lots of those," Evelyn said, her dry tone not masking her obvious pleasure at his approval.

David took the lemonade from Toni, and Toni set her glass on the table. "You can drink it in the sunroom in peace—I'll help Evelyn," she said.

Your lemonade trap didn't work, Evelyn. Toni smiled at the thought, then quickly changed her expression when Evelyn looked annoyed.

"I've managed this kitchen just fine without you for going on ten years now. If I needed your help, I'd ask."

Toni washed her hands and dried them on a paper towel before replying. "Actually, I have fond memories of the time we spent in this kitchen."

Evelyn chuckled. "Even when you tried hard not to help?"

"Only at first, when I didn't want to admit that I didn't know how to do anything in a kitchen. You changed that in a hurry, though."

Evelyn set a bowl of potato salad on the table. " 'Slave labor,' I think you muttered under your breath a few times."

Toni laughed. "Probably many more times than you knew."

Evelyn removed a platter of cold cuts from the refrigerator and pointed to a plastic-wrapped relish tray. "There's lettuce in the crisper, ready to go on the tray. I'll put out the bread, then we can eat. David's probably hungry."

"From all this food, you must have known he was coming today."

Evelyn turned away and busied herself with the bread. "Not really. Anyway, I couldn't let you go hungry. Tell David lunch is ready."

Toni turned to find David standing in the kitchen doorway, holding out his glass. "How about a refill? I don't know when I've had such delicious, homemade lemonade."

131

"My, you're full of flattery today," Evelyn said dryly. "The pitcher's on the table—help yourself. Lunch is ready."

"Where do you want me to sit?" David asked.

Evelyn looked surprised. "Why, at your usual place," she said as if it had been days rather than years since they'd shared a meal in this kitchen.

David looked approvingly at the table. "You outdid yourself, Evelyn."

He made a move toward the potato salad bowl, then stopped when he saw his sister's folded hands.

"Sorry," he murmured.

"This isn't a mess hall," Evelyn reminded him. "Will you return our thanks?"

Toni read David's expression to mean that he didn't really want to, but he nodded, bowed his head, and mumbled a brief, formulaic grace.

"It must be hard to realize that you're a civilian again after all these years," Toni said in the ensuing silence.

"It hasn't quite sunk in yet," David admitted. "Right now, I feel a little guilty, almost as if I'm AWOL."

"Absent without leave?" asked Toni.

"Yes. I never had that on my record, although I came close on my first tour in Germany. I went on leave to the salt mines at Salzburg and missed my ride back to base. I almost lost a stripe before I got that straightened out."

Evelyn turned to Toni. "David was already a two-stripe sergeant by then, one of the youngest in the army." She looked back at him. "He retired with the highest enlisted rank."

David shrugged. "I was one of many sergeants major serving at brigade level."

"Tell Toni about some of the interesting places you've been," Evelyn prompted.

David's glance at Toni confirmed that he thought Evelyn was making far too much of his military career. "She already knows. We covered all of that before you got home."

Evelyn seemed pleased. "I'm glad you had the chance to get acquainted. I can't tell you how much it means to have you both under my roof again."

"I'm happy to see you, too, Sis, but I'm not staying under your roof," David said.

Evelyn frowned. "Why ever not? I can make up the day bed in your old bedroom. It'll be just like when you lived here as a boy."

David shook his head. "No, thanks. Everyone will be more comfortable with me at the Rockdale Inn."

Evelyn sighed. "I see that you're still stubborn as ever. At least tell me how long you plan to stay."

"I just got here, and you're already talking about getting rid of me," David complained.

"No chance of that," Evelyn said. "You never stay long enough to wear out your welcome."

Listening to them, Toni felt a pang of envy at the obvious love they shared. Her chaotic childhood had been a universe away from the normal family life which Evelyn and David took for granted and for which Toni had longed in vain. She never had a chance to bond with the assorted foster and stepchildren with whom she had briefly lived. She rarely saw happy families then, and even when she had finally found a measure of peace with Evelyn Trent, it wasn't like being in a real family.

David finished eating and stood. "I'll be right back." He returned shortly to hand Evelyn the package Toni had seen him take from his truck. "I thought this might come in handy in a few weeks."

Evelyn removed the brown paper, revealing bright wrapping paper. "For your retirement days," she read from the card. "It's too small to be a rocking chair and too big to be a gold watch," Evelyn observed. "What can it be?"

"Open it and you'll see," urged David.

Carefully, Evelyn withdrew a hand-tooled burgundy leather travel diary and matching passport cover, both with her name embossed in gold. "Oh! I've never had anything with my name on it."

"I know you like to keep records. The travel diary has all kinds of maps and information about time zones and currency and common words and phrases in fifteen languages. I think it'll come in handy."

Evelyn smiled ruefully. "It looks as if you're determined to get me out of the country."

"You always said you wanted to travel," David pointed out. "Now that you have the opportunity, I hope you'll do it."

In the silence that followed, Toni recalled something Evelyn had told her years before. *I always wanted to see what lay beyond these mountains, but my responsibilities kept me here. I suppose it's just as well.*

"Thank you," Evelyn finally managed to say. "It's a beautiful gift. You'll have to help me plan my first trip."

"Gladly. Just say the word."

As if remembering Toni, Evelyn turned to her with an expression that seemed to say, *Isn't my brother wonderful?*

"It seems I'll have to travel now," she said.

"And you can certainly do so in style," Toni remarked.

David stood and stretched. "Speaking of traveling, I'll go on to the inn now and grab a shower. When should I come back to take you ladies to dinner?"

Evelyn sighed. "There's not a reason in the world that you can't stay here. He won't put us out, will he, Toni?"

It would definitely be awkward sharing one tiny bathroom with a strange man—Evelyn's brother or not.

Toni addressed David with as much sincerity as she could muster. "No, of course not. After all, this is your home. Evelyn will be disappointed if you don't accept."

David looked at Toni, his expression suggesting that he both knew and shared her true feelings about the matter. "You're both kind, but my mind's made up, and as my sister will tell you, it's not easily changed."

"So I gathered," Toni murmured, relieved that David Trent wouldn't be intimately involved in her daily life.

"All right, if you must. Come back around five thirty," Evelyn said.

"Yes, ma'am. And good-bye, Miss Schmidt. Nice to meet you."

"Same here," Toni said to his back as he and Evelyn went outside.

From the living room, Toni saw them standing beside his truck, engaging in an apparently serious conversation.

She's probably telling him I'm a perfect match for him, Toni thought, although she hoped it wasn't so. A man was the last thing Toni needed, particularly now.

The telephone rang, and Toni went into the hall and picked up the old-fashioned receiver. "Trent residence," she said, as Evelyn had taught her so many years ago.

"Toni, is that you? This is Ted Brown. I know it's short notice, but I hope you'll sing for us this Sunday."

Picturing the redheaded minister of music who had first encouraged her to sing in public, Toni smiled. "I've scarcely unpacked my bags."

"I know, but Janet wants you to come about eleven thirty tomorrow for lunch. We can rehearse afterward."

Toni hesitated. She might not have been so quick to accept Ted's invitation, but it would keep her from being stuck with David Trent at least for a few hours.

"All right, Ted. Tell me where you live now."

Evelyn returned as she hung up the phone. "Who was that?"

"Ted Brown. I agreed to have lunch with him and Janet tomorrow, if that's all right."

"Of course, but I wanted to show you and David around so you can see what's changed in the last few years. We could pack a picnic lunch and make a day of it."

"I'll take a rain check. Maybe you should give David the tour tomorrow, since he probably won't be here very long."

Evelyn sighed. "David hasn't said when he's leaving, but I hope to persuade him to stay awhile."

Toni quickly changed the subject. "Ted wants me to sing on Sunday morning, so after lunch we'll go to the church to rehearse. I'll probably be gone all afternoon."

"I'll plan something special for tomorrow night," Evelyn said. "I'd better call Edith and see if she can do my hair this afternoon. Do you want me to make you an appointment?"

"No, thanks," she said, wondering whether Evelyn thought she should look more glamorous to suit David's tastes. "My last trim will do for a few more weeks."

Evelyn went to the telephone, and Toni returned to the kitchen to clear away the lunch dishes. As she worked, she thought how natural it seemed to be back in this house, how easily she had fallen back into their old routine.

If it weren't for David Trent, it would really be like old times. But his rather disturbing presence threatened to change everything.

Nothing is going to happen, Toni assured herself. She had no interest in David, and she suspected he wasn't overly impressed with her, either, despite what Evelyn might hope.

∞

Toni and Evelyn were sitting in the porch swing when David pulled up in his truck at five thirty on the dot. In neat tan slacks, an apparently new cotton shirt, and polished loafers, he looked even more handsome than he had that morning.

I'll give him that, Toni thought grudgingly. Never swayed by anyone's outward appearance, she was prepared to ignore his good looks.

"Right on time," Evelyn said approvingly.

David nodded. "It didn't take too long for the army to persuade me to be prompt. I see you're ready—where shall we go?"

"How about Statum's? The food's good, and it's close."

David shrugged. "It's all right, but I wanted to take you somewhere fancier. I had the restaurant at DeSoto State Park in mind."

"We'll do that some other time." Evelyn held out the keys to her aging sedan. "We can go in my car."

David ignored her outstretched hand. "According to the ads, four adults can ride in my truck in perfect comfort. I said I'd pick you up. That means I will also drive."

"Let him," Toni said quickly. "I can't go with you, anyway. I have to call some people in Atlanta I can't reach during the day."

"Surely that can wait," Evelyn said.

"No, I don't want to put it off," Toni said. "Besides, I'm sure you and David could use some time to yourselves."

"Sorry you can't join us," David said, but what Toni read in his eyes confirmed that he probably had no more interest in his sister's matchmaking than did Toni.

Evelyn pocketed her car keys and shrugged. "All right, if you insist." To Toni she said, "We'll bring you something."

"No, thanks. I'm not really hungry—I'll have the lunch leftovers later. You'd better hurry or Statum's will be filled up."

"That's true," Evelyn agreed. "Come on, David. I guess we know when we're not wanted."

"See you later," David called over his shoulder as he and Evelyn started down the porch steps.

Not if I see you first, buster.

Wondering why she was unaccountably rankled by the man, Toni suppressed the flip remark and waved good-bye instead.

Just ignore him, and he'll soon go away.

But as David opened the truck door for his sister, Toni knew that might be easier said than done.

Chapter 5

Toni expected David Trent to come to the house for breakfast the next morning, but Evelyn said he had taken his truck to Fort Payne for service. "He probably won't be back for hours. It's just as well, since I'll be busy nearly all day myself."

I should have saved the lunch date with Ted and Janet for another day, Toni thought. However, since she had promised to sing on Sunday, she needed to rehearse with them today.

"I don't know when I'll be home," Toni said, "but I'll have my cell phone on if you need to reach me."

Evelyn looked amused. "I recall you once fought leaving a phone number when you went out."

"I fought a lot of things, but eventually, I realized your rules had good reasons behind them."

"Maybe I had too many rules, but I always tried to do what I thought best for you."

Toni spoke lightly. "I suppose it worked. Here I am, all grown up and not in jail, and you're about to go out and see the world."

"Not quite. I'm not officially retired yet. In fact, I have to stop by the office this morning."

"Want me to go with you?" Toni asked.

"No, thanks. You'll be working there soon enough. Enjoy your freedom while you can."

∞

Later, as she drove to Ted and Janet's apartment, Toni thought it ironic that Evelyn would, on the one hand, encourage her to marry while on the other say she should enjoy her freedom. For Toni's mother, marriage had meant the end of both her freedom and her life. Toni wanted no part of that for herself.

If freedom means doing work I enjoy, then I am already free. And I intend to leave well enough alone.

Her route took Toni past Rockdale High School, the site of a great deal of activity. The campus message board proclaimed the reason:

WELCOME, TENTH REUNION ALUMNI

Of course—at Statum's Restaurant, Mary Oliver had urged Toni to attend the reunion, even though she hadn't registered or paid for the events. Toni hadn't given Mary a definite answer, but now attending the reunion seemed like an attractive alternative to being with David Trent.

I'll call Mary this afternoon.

Ted and Janet Brown lived on the second floor of a large brick apartment complex nestled into the base of Warren Mountain near the church where Ted led the music ministry.

Janet opened the door to Toni's knock and greeted her warmly. "I'm so glad you could come."

Toni surveyed the spacious living area dominated by Janet's grand piano. "What a lovely room!"

"It's also our studio," Ted said. "Janet gives piano lessons, and I have a few voice students."

"Do you still play for church services?" Toni asked Janet.

"Yes, but we've gone high-tech. You won't believe our new sound system."

Over lunch, Ted and Janet updated Toni on Community Church news, then made her the topic of conversation.

"We're surprised that you haven't married yet."

"Why 'yet'?" Toni asked, nettled by Janet's presumption that she would marry.

Janet looked surprised. "With so much to bring to a marriage, it seems some nice man would have claimed you by now."

Toni didn't try to hide her annoyance. "I don't need to be 'claimed,' thank you. My life is quite full enough as it is."

Ted and Janet regarded Toni with a mixture of sadness and pity, as if she'd just said she had a fatal disease. "You may think that now, but isn't it possible that God has already chosen the perfect partner for you?" asked Ted.

"If so, He hasn't shared that information with me," Toni said. The moment the words left her lips, she realized how flip they sounded and tried to make amends. "What I mean is that a long time ago, certain circumstances convinced me that marriage wasn't for me. I pray to know and stay in God's will. I believe He intended for me to return to Rockdale, but that's as far as I've been led."

"We don't mean to sound critical," Janet said. "Our marriage has been so fulfilling, we wanted the same for you."

"That's right. At least keep all your options open," Ted urged. "When your own will is so strong about something, it's hard for God to get through with any other message."

"Not that we'd presume to tell you what to do, of course." Janet spoke so earnestly that Toni smiled.

"Of course you wouldn't. Except that Ted has presumed to tell me I'm to sing on Sunday," she teased.

Ted seemed relieved Toni had shifted the conversation to safer ground. "You are, and we need to rehearse. If you didn't bring any of your own tapes with you,

I have some at the church I'd like you to hear."

"Can't Janet accompany me on the piano?" Toni asked.

"She can, but tapes with background vocals often work better with a voice like yours."

"If that's a polite way of saying I don't sing loud enough, I can raise the volume," Toni quipped.

"We'll try it both ways," Ted suggested. "Let's go."

∽

The moment Toni stepped inside the cool dimness of the Community Church sanctuary, she felt a strong sense of homecoming. She recalled how April Kincaid had almost literally dragged her to her first Sunday morning service so many years ago. In this place, she had accepted Christ as her Savior. And here, April, the best soprano in the choir, had encouraged Toni to join her in a shaky duet.

"Do you remember the first time you sang here?" Ted asked.

"I'll never forget it. I was trembling so much, April had to hold me up, or I know I would have fallen. We sang 'Whispering Hope,' and somehow the Lord got us both through it."

"He has a way of doing that," Ted said. He was silent for a moment, then pointed to the upper rear of the sanctuary. "The new sound booth is up there. Come on, I'll show you around."

∽

By the time they had chosen a background tape and rehearsed it a few times, it was almost five o'clock. When Toni returned to Evelyn's, David's truck was nowhere in sight, and Evelyn wasn't in the house. She had left Toni a note on the telephone message board, however.

Dinner out at six. Wear something nice.

Toni sighed. She didn't look forward to an evening she suspected had been engineered to bring her and David together. However, she had no plausible excuse to stay home.

The telephone rang, and when she answered, she heard Mary Oliver's lilting voice.

"Hi, Toni! I've been so busy, this is the first chance I've had to call. I hope you're coming to the reunion tomorrow."

"I meant to call you about that," Toni said. "I never sent any money—"

"I told you the other night that doesn't matter," Mary interrupted. "We're meeting in the auditorium at ten, followed by a picnic. The banquet's tomorrow night. Everyone on the committee is dying to see you."

I'm sure they are, Toni thought dryly.

"I can't make the banquet, but I suppose I could come to the morning meeting and stay for the picnic," Toni said.

"Great! Do you need a ride?"

Toni smiled, remembering the times Mary had taken her places in their teen years. "No, thanks. I'll see you at school at ten."

Toni showered and dressed in the beige linen two-piece dress she called her "uniform," suitable to wear almost anywhere. By then, it was nearly a quarter of six, and Evelyn still hadn't come home. She'd said she was going to the hairdresser's in the afternoon. She must have had some other errands to be this late.

Toni had just settled into a comfortable chair in the sunroom with the weekly *Rockdale Record* when the front door opened, and she heard Evelyn and David talking.

Toni joined them in the living room in time to hear Evelyn say, "I'm sorry, but you'll have to go to dinner without me."

"If your head is hurting that much, maybe you should go to the emergency room," David said.

"What's happening?" asked Toni.

Evelyn turned, her face contorted with pain. "I have a headache, that's all. If I don't lie down and stay in the dark, it could turn into a nasty migraine."

"You're still having those?" Toni asked, concerned about Evelyn and fearing she would have to dine with David alone.

Evelyn shrugged. "I don't have as many bad headaches as I once did. I have pills to take for it, but the best medicine includes rest in a quiet, dark place."

"I don't think we should go off and leave you here alone," David said.

"That's exactly what I need, however," Evelyn insisted. "Don't worry about me. The dinner reservation at the country club is for six o'clock. Run along now."

∞

"By my watch we're already late," David said when they left the house.

"The country club isn't likely to be overrun on a Friday night. I doubt they gave away the reservation," she said, half hoping they had.

"I haven't been in this place since my senior prom," David said a few minutes later when they entered the stone and cedar foyer of the Rockdale Country Club.

"I didn't go to my prom," Toni said, then wanted to bite her tongue. She had no intention of discussing her personal life with David Trent, and she was glad when the pert, young hostess distracted his attention.

The girl looked at David as if Toni didn't exist and smiled. "Dinner for two?" she all but purred.

"Actually, Evelyn Trent made a reservation for three, but it'll just be the two of us this evening."

The hostess made a mark on her list and called a waiter. "The special lakeside table, please." To David, she added, "Enjoy your dinner."

The waiter led them to a table overlooking a small lake, which shimmered in the moonlight. Tucked away in an alcove, their table was hidden from other diners.

"Very cozy," David remarked when the waiter left.

And very romantic. Toni wondered if Evelyn had arranged that, as well.

"It's also very dark in this corner," she remarked. "How are we supposed to read the menu?"

"We don't need to. Evelyn told me that prime rib is the Friday night special. Will that suit you?"

"I've never been picky about what I eat," Toni said, immediately wishing she hadn't. *I sound like an idiot,* she thought, then wondered why she cared.

"I'm not picky, either. I can thank the army for that. You wouldn't believe what I've had to eat over the years."

"Are K rations as bad as their reputation?"

"It's MREs now—meals ready to eat. Some aren't bad. All are light years better than my first army meal."

Toni relaxed a bit, glad to find a safe topic of conversation. "That sounds like a story that needs telling."

"Are you sure? I wouldn't want to spoil your appetite."

"You won't."

"All right. When I joined the army, several of us from Alabama rode from daylight into dark on an uncomfortable olive drab school bus. We finally got to Fort Jackson about ten o'clock, and the bus stopped at a mess hall. Everyone was tired, and we were all hungry, at least until we saw the food."

David stopped when the waiter appeared to take their order. After assuring them that the prime rib special was an excellent choice, he bowed and departed.

"So what was it?"

"Think of the worst food you can imagine," David invited.

"I don't care much for dried fish or anchovies."

"This was much worse. Everything was either cold, straight from the walk-in coolers, or room temperature. Green beans from a can; greasy, stiff French fries; and the entrée was," he said, pausing for effect, "cold fried liver."

Toni smiled, then found herself laughing as David continued to relate more stories about army life, and she finally dismissed her suspicion that Evelyn had contrived this private dinner. When David asked her about her life in Atlanta, he appeared to be entertained by her stories, as well.

Unlike the army food David described, their prime rib dinner was perfection. By the time they finished a final cup of coffee, Toni realized that the evening had turned out to be a rather pleasant diversion.

However, on the drive back to Evelyn's, David's mood sobered, and he expressed concern for his sister's health.

"Evelyn has worked hard all her life. She deserves a happy retirement. Now I wonder if her health will let her enjoy it."

"I think she's perfectly well. She's had occasional headaches ever since I've known her. They never last long."

"I still think she should see a doctor."

"She probably won't want to."

"I know, but I can outstubborn my sister if push comes to shove."

David pulled up to the curb and turned off the ignition. As he had done at the country club, he came around to open her door and help her from the truck. *David Trent has good manners—I'll give him that.*

"Would you check on Evelyn and let me know how she's doing?" David asked when they reached the front door.

"I suspect she's asleep, but I'll look in on her."

Moments later she returned; the soft snores issuing from Evelyn's bedroom had assured Toni her assumption was correct.

"Everything's fine."

"That's good. Tell Evelyn she missed a great dinner. I don't know when I've laughed like that. You're good company, Miss Toni Schmidt."

So are you. Toni almost voiced the words. "Good night, Sergeant Major Trent," she said instead.

"Just David," he corrected.

"And Toni," she added.

With a wave, he was gone, and Toni went back into the dark house, almost sorry she had enjoyed herself so much.

Toni cast a glance at Evelyn's door and sighed. *Why,* she wondered, *did David Trent have to come to Rockdale and complicate things?*

And what, if anything, did Evelyn have to do with it?

Chapter 6

As Toni expected he would, David rang Evelyn's doorbell just after breakfast.

"How's the patient?" he asked when Toni answered the door.

"Having coffee in the sunroom. Come on back."

Evelyn greeted David with a smile. "As you can see, I'm fine. All I needed was a little rest."

"What about those dark circles under your eyes?"

"With a touch of makeup, they'll be gone. Have you had breakfast?"

"Yes, but if you're offering, I'll take a cup of coffee."

"I'll get it," Toni said. "Black, no sugar."

Evelyn raised her eyebrows. "Now how did you know that?"

Toni groaned inwardly. *Why did she always say too much when David Trent was around?*

"We had coffee after a very good dinner last night," David answered for her. "I'm sorry you missed it."

"So am I, but Toni tells me you did just fine without me."

∞

When Toni returned with his coffee, David was telling Evelyn he had something to see to that morning.

"Come back and have lunch with me afterward," Evelyn invited. "Toni has other fish to fry today."

David glanced at Toni. "I see you're dressed up. What's the occasion?"

Toni had chosen her navy slacks and a red, white, and blue knit top with the reunion picnic in mind; the outfit was hardly "dressy," even by Rockdale standards. Obviously, David Trent had a limited knowledge of women's fashion.

"My Rockdale class is having a reunion this morning."

"I never went to any of mine," David said. "I suppose it might be worth it to see how old everyone else looks."

"This is my first reunion—and likely it will be the last." Toni glanced at her watch and stood. "I should be on my way. Don't overdo yourself," she warned Evelyn.

Evelyn sounded irritated. "I told you I'm fine. You all don't need to treat me like an invalid."

"I'll be right back," David told his sister. When they reached the front porch, he asked Toni what she really thought about Evelyn's health.

Toni hesitated. She wasn't about to share her renewed suspicion about the true cause of his sister's indisposition. "Evelyn says she feels well, and I believe her."

David sighed. "I hope you're right."

He looks troubled, Toni thought as he turned away. She had noticed the lingering sadness in his eyes, even when he smiled. David hadn't mentioned the dark side of his army service, but Toni presumed he must have had his share of trauma over the years.

That's another thing we have in common. But Toni would never tell him so.

∞

"Toni! Over here!" Mary called when Toni reached the front entrance of Rockdale High. "Come in and register. I saved a seat for you in the auditorium."

Toni followed Mary to a table in the front hall, where a slightly familiar bleached blond presided over the check-in. Betty Simpson Lewis, according to her name tag.

"You remember Toni Schmidt, don't you, Betty?"

She glanced at Toni without interest. "Sure. Do you have a married name?"

"No, she doesn't. Toni and I are the only girls from our class who have never been married," Mary said for her.

Betty handed Toni her name tag and a copy of the class roster. "You never been married yet," she said. "Y'all still have plenty of time to find yourselves a man."

"If we were looking," Mary said shortly. "Come on, Toni."

"Everybody around here seems to think a single woman must want a husband," Toni said.

"Tell me about it! I don't know why they think we won't be happy until we have that M–R–S in front of our names."

"Maybe misery loves company," Toni said.

The auditorium was noisy with the squeals of recognition and drone of dozens of simultaneous conversations. It was already ten o'clock, but almost no one was seated.

Mary stopped near the front and pointed to a chair with its seat turned up. "I saved this place for you. I have to be on the stage, but I'll see you after the program."

Toni glanced around. The auditorium was bright with fresh paint, but the wooden seats were as uncomfortable as she remembered. As had been the case in her student days, everyone else seemed to be having a good time talking with friends, while Toni sat alone and told herself she should never have agreed to come.

While Toni waited for the program to begin, she skimmed the class listings to see what had happened to the other graduates in her class. Two were deceased, several served in the armed forces, and six hadn't been located. Some lived as far away as California and Alaska, but a surprisingly large number had stayed in or near Rockdale.

"Hello, Toni. I hoped I'd see you here."

Toni turned toward the speaker, a tall brunette whose periwinkle blue linen pantsuit set off her slender figure, and recognized Joan Bell Timmons, a former social studies teacher who now lived in Atlanta.

"I almost didn't come," Toni confessed. "Sit down. Do the teachers come to this reunion thing every year, too?"

"No. This is the first class to invite me."

Earl Hurley, the master of ceremonies, came to the microphone and quieted the crowd. "The Rockdale ROTC color guard will now present the colors. Please rise and remain standing for the invocation."

Toni glanced at her program. Earl Hurley, son of the Community Church pastor and the first boy she ever dated, was now Rockdale's police chief. However, his prayer of invocation indicated that he could easily have followed his father's footsteps into the ministry.

Earl then introduced the reunion committee, which included his wife, Audra, the daughter of the former Rockdale High principal. Audra had led the "in" crowd, a clique whose members delighted in making outsiders like Toni miserable.

Loud applause greeted Mary Oliver's introduction; evidently she was a great deal more popular now than back in high school, when she had been teased about her weight.

After everyone on the stage had been acknowledged, Earl pointed to the rear of the auditorium. "They wouldn't join us on the stage, but there's somebody else here I'm sure you all want to see. Congressman Jeremy Winter, you and your wife come on down!"

To laughter, applause, and a standing ovation, Jeremy and April Winter made their way down the aisle, frequently slowed by well-wishers.

Toni felt rare tears gather behind her eyelids at the unexpected sight of her first and oldest friends.

"He just gets better-looking every year," Joan murmured as Jeremy and April stood on the stage.

Toni knew Joan Bell had wanted her father's young law partner for herself. Instead, Jeremy Winter fell in love with April Kincaid, whom he met while representing Toni before Judge Oliver. After helping elect Jeremy as mayor of Rockdale, Joan met and married a prominent Atlanta neurosurgeon. A few years ago, she had been instrumental in hiring Toni to work in the nonprofit agency on whose board she sat.

"Small world," Joan had said to Toni then.

Too small at times, it seemed to Toni. Especially in Rockdale, with its closed network of friends and relatives.

∞

The picnic turned out to be far more enjoyable than Toni had expected. She was pleasantly surprised that so many of the classmates who had shunned or ignored her in the past now made it a point to welcome her back to Rockdale. Once Jeremy and April sat down at the table with her and Mary, so many people came by to speak to the congressman that Toni had no chance to talk to her old friends.

"I wish Jeremy and I didn't have to be in Fort Payne this afternoon," April told Toni. "We have so much to catch up on."

"Maybe we could meet somewhere for dinner tonight," Toni suggested.

"We're eating at home for a change. Come over about six," April invited, and Toni agreed.

Jeremy glanced at his watch and stood. "Mary, that was a great barbecue. Thanks for inviting us."

Mary looked disappointed. "Do you have to go so soon? I thought maybe you'd want to address your constituents."

Jeremy laughed. "I want to make a speech even less than these folks want to hear one. I have a speech to deliver in Fort Payne, though, and if we don't leave now, we'll be late."

"There goes a really happy couple," Mary said in the silence following their departure. "Maybe some marriages really are made in heaven."

"The trouble is, they have to be lived on earth," Toni said.

∞

Toni stayed to help the reunion committee clean up and returned to Evelyn's around four o'clock. Toni had half expected David to be there, and she was strangely disappointed not to see his truck.

She found Evelyn peeling potatoes in the kitchen, which was fragrant with the aroma of roasting meat.

"You're cooking?"

"Don't sound so surprised—I haven't forgotten how. I thought David would like a home-cooked meal tonight."

"Where is he?" Toni asked, then immediately regretted the show of interest.

"I'm not sure, but he'll be here for supper."

"I won't be, though. I saw April and Jeremy Winter at the reunion, and April invited me to supper at their house. It's been ages since we've had a long visit."

"If I'd known the Winters were in town, I could have invited them to join us here tonight."

Toni smiled. "Their twin boys are almost six. It's better for me to go there."

"All right, but David and I will miss you," Evelyn said.

Sure. He'll miss me about as much as a toothache.

Or would he?

∞

Toni hadn't seen April for several years, but the moment she walked into the old Warren house, it was as if they'd never been apart.

"You look great," April told Toni. "Could it be you're in love at long last?"

"Hardly," Toni said tartly. "You know how I feel about that."

"I know how much you were hurting when we met, but your life is so different now, I hoped you had changed your mind about marriage."

"I haven't. Where are the boys?"

"In the kitchen with Gladys. You'll see them soon enough."

"I'm glad you still have her," Toni said, remembering the older woman Jeremy had hired to help April when Warren and Kincaid were born.

"So are we," affirmed Jeremy. "Now sit down and tell us what you've been up to."

∞

Toni thoroughly enjoyed seeing the twins, who were distinctly different individuals. Their dark hair and eyes reflected their father's Cherokee blood, while their facial features more resembled April's. They were lively but well mannered, making only a mild protest when April told them it was their bedtime.

The twins hugged their father, then held their arms up to Toni, as well.

"You must be very proud of those two," Toni said to Jeremy after April excused herself to put them to bed and hear their prayers.

"We are. They bless our lives every day."

When April returned, she and Jeremy took turns trying to convince Toni it was time for her to marry a good man and raise a family of her own.

"No, thanks. My life is happy just as it is."

"It could be a lot happier," April said. "It's time you knocked that chip off your shoulder."

"Yes," agreed Jeremy. "Like my grandmother used to say, 'Don't cut off your nose to spite your face.'"

"Or borrow trouble," Toni said. "End of discussion."

However, when April saw Toni to the door, she returned to the subject. "I know you don't want to hear this, but you're missing so much by not giving love a chance."

"You're right—I don't want to hear it. I don't feel I've missed a thing."

Toni spoke confidently, but on her way home, she considered her friends' counsel. April's relative youth hadn't allowed her to become Toni's guardian, but Toni had always looked to her as a role model and valued her advice—at least about most things.

April is wrong about this, though. I'm the best judge of what I should do.

Chapter 7

D avid just left," Evelyn said when Toni entered the living room shortly before ten o'clock. "He said to tell you he was sorry he didn't get to see you tonight."

"Too bad I can't be in two places at the same time," Toni said lightly.

"Tell me about the Winters. I'd love to see their twin boys again."

Toni and Evelyn chatted for a few minutes before Toni rose and stretched. "I'm going to call it a night. I need to be at church early tomorrow for a final rehearsal."

"David and I will come to the worship service."

Toni felt a tingle of apprehension. A pillar of First Church, Evelyn had allowed Toni to continue attending Community Church with April, but she had visited it only a few times when Toni sang. "Are you sure First Church won't collapse if you don't show up tomorrow?"

"I'm hardly that important," Evelyn said. "Besides, the church will have to do without me soon enough. They might as well get used to it."

∞

"We have a full house today," Ted Brown commented when he and Toni entered the sanctuary from the choir room just before eleven o'clock.

"The word must be out that I'm singing," Toni said with a touch of the sarcasm, which had been a shield in her teen years.

"Could be," Ted agreed. "Sit on the first pew. I'll hand you the mike when I cue the tape."

"I know the routine," Toni said.

"Just like old times, right?" Ted asked.

Not quite. In those days, there was no David Trent in the congregation.

Toni closed her eyes in silent prayer. *Lord, help me to be calm and sing only to You. Amen.*

When the service began, Toni immersed herself in it, shutting out everything else. She had asked Ted not to introduce her, but when she rose to sing, a murmur of recognition swept through the sanctuary. Toni felt a moment of near panic when she spotted Evelyn and David.

Help me, Lord.

Then, with the first note of "His Eye Is on the Sparrow," everything else dropped away, and Toni sang, as always, to honor her Creator.

Why should I feel discouraged?
     Why should the shadows come?
Why should my heart be lonely,
     And long for heav'n and home,
When Jesus is my portion,
     My constant Friend is He;
His eye is on the sparrow,
     And I know He watches me.

I sing because I'm happy,
     I sing because I'm free;
For His eye is on the sparrow,
     And I know He watches me. . .

After the last triumphant chorus, the final strains of the taped accompaniment died away, followed by a reverent silence. As Toni returned the microphone to Ted, she saw David regarding her intently and wondered what he was thinking.

Not that I care, she tried to tell herself, but the words did not quite ring true.

∞

After the benediction, Evelyn and David stood waiting in the vestibule for Toni while she made her way up the aisle through a crowd of well-wishers.

"That old hymn is one of my favorites," Evelyn said. "I can't believe how much richer your voice has become in the last few years."

"It's beautiful, and you use it well," David said.

He spoke sincerely, and Toni responded in kind. "The Lord gave it to me. I sing only for His glory."

The music leader joined them in time to hear Toni's testimony. "Mrs. Taylor said it was all she could do to keep from shouting 'Hallelujah!' when she heard you sing, Toni. I'm sure she had plenty of company." He turned to David and held out his hand. "I'm Ted Brown, and you must be David. Toni told me you were visiting your sister."

David shook Ted's hand, looking surprised that Toni had spoken about him. With a final wave, Ted departed, and Toni and David followed Evelyn outside.

"You and David can go in your car," Evelyn directed Toni. "I'll follow in mine."

"Where are we going?" Toni asked Evelyn's retreating back.

"To the DeSoto State Park restaurant," David said. "Do you want me to drive?"

"It's my car," Toni said, less graciously than she intended.

He seemed amused. "So it is."

"I'm used to driving myself, I mean," she added.

"I am, too."

Toni winced inwardly. *I'm doing it again. It seems I cannot carry on a simple conversation with this man without sounding like a fool.*

"Why isn't Evelyn riding with us?" Toni asked.

David shrugged. "She said something about wanting to get home early."

Toni said nothing, but she suspected she knew the reason.

Evelyn is trying to get David and me together.

∞

"It has been years since I've been to the state park," Toni commented to fill the silence between them as she drove.

"Me, too, but when I was a kid, I knew it like the back of my hand. The Scouts used to pitch tents at the campground and hike all the trails. We'd pretend it was the 1540s and we had come from Spain with Hernando DeSoto. We fancied we were the first Europeans to see all the falls and the Little River Canyon."

"I never had a chance to do anything like that," Toni said, aware too late how wistful she had sounded.

"Back then, roughing it was fun."

"These days, people think of that as having to watch a black-and-white television set," Toni said. *How stupid can you get? David must think I'm a dunce at making small talk.*

"Slow down! You're about to miss the turnoff."

David's cry startled Toni, and she applied the brakes so hard, the tires squealed. *Take it easy, buddy. I'm not in the army, and you're not my commander.*

As if he had read her thought, David apologized. "Sorry. I didn't mean to sound like a drill sergeant."

"Then don't talk like one," she said shortly.

To Toni's surprise, David smiled. "Duly noted."

A few moments later, they passed through the entrance gates, and Toni parked in the lot near the lodge. Evelyn pulled up beside them almost immediately.

"It must be at least ten degrees cooler up here," David commented as Evelyn joined them.

"That's one reason I like to come up here," she said. "The other is, the food is worth the wait," she added when they saw the large number of people lined up for the buffet.

"I hope so," David said. "I had my fill of standing around waiting to be fed in the army."

"I daresay not many mess halls are like this," Evelyn said.

Toni welcomed the ensuing conversation about recent renovations to the lodge and cabins, followed by the food in the buffet in particular and southern cooking in general. All safe topics.

"That food was definitely great," David said when he finished the last bite of his meringue-topped banana pudding.

"So is the scenery, and you don't have to wait in line for it," Evelyn said. "You and Toni should walk some of the trails."

"What about you?" Toni asked, anticipating the answer.

"I'm going home and take my usual Sunday afternoon nap. Stay here as long as you like. I have nothing planned for the evening."

"Now, that's a switch," David said after Evelyn left. "My sister seems to think I must be kept constantly occupied."

"Same with me. I suppose she wants to be a good hostess."

"Do you really want to go hiking?"

Toni pointed to the two-inch heels on her shoes. "These are hardly made for hiking."

"They'll do for DeSoto Falls. We can park not four hundred feet from it."

Toni hesitated, then handed David the keys to her SUV. "You drive, since you know the way."

David looked as if he might want to say something but took the keys without comment and opened the passenger door for Toni.

Neither spoke during the short drive, but even before David pulled into the parking lot, they heard the distant sound of falling water. "We must be getting close," Toni said.

"You'll soon see."

A constant roar came from the water spilling over the dam, which had been built in 1925 to provide electricity to the Lookout Mountain area.

They watched it for a moment, then started out on the path to the lower falls. It seemed natural when David took Toni's hand on the sometimes rough path and continued to hold it when they stopped at an overlook. They stood quietly, enjoying the view of the huge half circle of rugged cliffs—in shades ranging from brown to rust and white—surrounding the falling water. Below, a seemingly bottomless pool made a circle some 250 feet in diameter. In the fissures of the cliffs, stunted scrub pines and tufts of grass and wildflowers added their colorful accents.

They took in the scene in comfortable silence for some moments. "Awesome, isn't it?" David said over the roar of the water.

Toni nodded. "Every time I see something like this, I think of Psalm 42:7: 'Deep calleth unto deep at the noise of thy waterspouts.' It really shows us a tiny part of God's awesome power."

"You seem to be close to Him."

Toni searched for the right words. "Not as close as I want to be."

"I suppose everyone could say that. There was a time. . ." David broke off speaking and motioned toward a broad rock a few steps away. For a while they sat in silence and watched the magnificent scene. Rainbows played around the spray as the clear water fell in a breathtaking, headlong rush into the pool below them.

"Evelyn is missing a treat," Toni said.

David turned to face her. "I'm glad she didn't stay. I wanted to talk to you alone for a change."

For a change? You've had many chances, Toni almost said but checked herself. "What about?"

"I'm leaving tomorrow morning."

Toni looked at him in surprise. "Does Evelyn know?"

He shook his head. "Not yet."

"I'm sure she'll be very disappointed."

"I doubt you will. You don't seem to like me very much."

I didn't want to like you, but I think I do, anyway. "What makes you say that?" Toni asked.

David shrugged. "Your body language, for one. You always seem so skittish. I can tell I make you uneasy, but I don't mean to."

He spoke with such sincerity that Toni felt compelled to reply in kind. "It has nothing to do with you personally."

"Evelyn told me some bad things had happened to you when you were a child. I hope that's all it is."

Toni felt her cheeks warm. "I don't know what she said, but there's no need to feel sorry for me. That was all a long time ago. Besides, I got the impression that you were uncomfortable with me."

He looked surprised. "Not at all. In fact—"

Before she quite realized it was happening, David brought Toni into the circle of his arms and kissed her. Without stopping to think, she returned the brief kiss, then drew back.

Whatever possessed me to do that?

"Oh," she murmured.

David regarded her steadily. "I'll be back soon."

"For another visit?"

"Yes, but I've been talking to some people about buying into a business in Rockdale."

"So you could become more than a visitor." Toni tested the idea. She had thought he would soon be gone. How could she ignore David if he continued to be nearby?

"I hope so." He paused before he spoke again. "When I come back, I'll bring the children."

A thousand waterfalls roared in Toni's head, drowning out all intelligent thought.

"Children?" she repeated. "You have children?"

David looked stricken. "Evelyn didn't tell you?"

Toni shook her head. "No," she said, wondering why. Then the implication hit her. "I suppose these children have a mother?"

David's jaw tightened. "My wife died last year—that's why I left the army."

"I'm so sorry," Toni mumbled, chagrined.

"I suppose I should have mentioned them earlier."

You just forgot to mention them when you were telling me all about your life over a romantic dinner, right? Toni rose and stood, her legs trembling unexpectedly. "Why?

You thought I already knew. We'd better leave now."

"Wait," he called, but she had already started toward the path. "I'm sorry for the misunderstanding," he said when he caught up with her.

Misunderstanding?

David looked so contrite that Toni felt inclined to believe him.

"Tell me about your children," she said with as much interest as she could muster.

"Mandy—short for Amanda—is twelve, and Josh is six."

David removed two pictures from his billfold. One showed a smiling blond woman holding an infant; beside her stood an unsmiling little girl.

"That was taken when Josh was just a baby, before Jean got sick."

"Your daughter doesn't look very happy," Toni said.

"Mandy wouldn't smile because she'd lost her front teeth. This one was taken last year."

Toni saw what she took to be the same two children, several years older and photographed against a fake Christmas scene, the girl still unsmiling. "Nice-looking," she said.

David seemed disappointed as he replaced the pictures. "I take it you don't care much for children."

Toni groaned inwardly. *There I go again, saying the wrong thing.* "I wouldn't have lasted very long in social work if I didn't care about kids."

"That's not what I meant," David said.

Toni faced him, her chin high. "Then what did you mean?"

He opened his mouth, then closed it and shrugged. "Nothing. More of the misunderstanding thing, I suppose."

They continued to walk toward the parking lot, but this time David didn't take her hand, and once again Toni wished she knew what he was thinking.

"You can drive home," she said when he offered her the keys.

I know it's a peace offering, David's expression told her, *but I'm not fooled.*

On the drive back, Toni attempted to get David to talk about his family. "It must have been hard on the children when their mother died. Who takes care of them?"

David's mouth formed a straight line. "Jean's mother and stepfather."

"In Virginia?" she guessed.

"Yes. I really thought Evelyn had already told you all of that."

No, but she will.

They drove to Evelyn's house in an awkward silence. David shut off the ignition, handed Toni her keys, and came around to open the passenger door for her.

"Aren't you coming inside?" she asked when he started toward his truck.

"No. Tell Evelyn I'll call later."

It's just as well, Toni thought as she hurried into the house to confront David's sister.

Chapter 8

Toni entered the house primed for an immediate showdown. Disappointed to find Evelyn's bedroom door closed, Toni went to the sunroom. As her mind replayed the scene at the falls several times, Toni became increasingly convinced she had every right to be upset.

Evelyn came out of her room a half hour later, obviously surprised to find Toni alone. "Where's David?"

"At the inn, I suppose. He said he'll call you later."

Evelyn looked disappointed. "I expected you two would make an afternoon of it."

"We didn't."

"You look upset. Is something wrong?"

Toni took a deep breath. "Why didn't you tell me about David's children?"

Evelyn's expression reflected genuine surprise. "I've always mentioned David and his family in my Christmas letters. I took it for granted that you knew."

Toni assumed she'd remember if she'd read anything about him, but that didn't mean Evelyn hadn't written it. "I suppose I might have dismissed the family details since I didn't know them," she admitted, making a mental note to be more attentive in the future.

"Even so, it seems the subject would have come up naturally before now."

"David and I talked about our careers, but we never talked about our personal lives, and I gathered he wanted it that way as much as I did. But today when he said he would bring the children with him next time he came, I felt blindsided."

"I'm sorry. You and David seemed to hit it off so well."

"You invited him to Rockdale just to meet me, didn't you?"

Evelyn shook her head. "David has always had a standing invitation, but he was out of the country a lot; then after Jean became ill, he didn't have a chance to go anywhere."

"Didn't you think it odd that David didn't come here when he got out of the army?"

"Not really. His wife had just died, and he had a lot on his mind."

"You're certain you didn't just happen to invite him to come to Rockdale the very week I arrived?"

Evelyn threw up her hands. "You'd make a good prosecuting attorney," she said ruefully. "The only thing I told him was that I planned to retire soon and do some traveling."

"And some matchmaking," Toni added. "Surely you can't deny that."

Evelyn shrugged and shook her head. "Obviously, your mind is made up, but I wish you could accept my brother's presence at this time as a coincidence."

Toni's initial outrage had evaporated, leaving her drained and weary. She attempted a feeble smile. "So that's your story and you're sticking with it."

Evelyn stood. "I have to—it's the truth. I'm going to the inn. I don't suppose you want to come with me?"

Toni could think of nothing she wanted any less at that moment. "No, thanks."

"Is there anything you want me to tell David?"

Tell him it is probably just as well that our brief acquaintance came to an end before it could hurt us both.

Toni didn't know what brought such a thought to her mind, but she would never voice it. She shook her head. "Nothing except good-bye."

Evelyn started out, then stopped to glance back at Toni. "You look tired. Try to get some rest. Things will look different in the morning."

Yes. David will be gone then.

∞

Evelyn had already left when Toni got up Monday morning; a note on the telephone table said she was at the DHR office.

"I ought to go there, too," Toni said aloud. After breakfast, she showered and dressed in a comfortable lemon-lime shift. She had just closed the front door behind her when David's truck pulled up to the curb.

Toni's heart lurched, then began to hammer. She presumed David had already left Rockdale. In any case, she must be the last person he wanted to see.

"Evelyn's at the office," she called from the porch.

David turned off the motor, got out of the truck, and mounted the porch steps. "I know. We said good-bye last night."

Just go away and leave me alone, Toni wanted to say. "I'm on my way to the office myself."

"I won't keep you long. I couldn't leave Rockdale without apologizing for the way I acted yesterday."

Toni attempted to conceal her confusion with a veil of sarcasm. "Is that your idea or Evelyn's?"

"Mine. She said I should have talked to you about the kids from the start, but that's not easy for me. . . ."

David stood so close that Toni could see the pulse in his neck. *He's struggling to say the right thing. It wouldn't kill me to forgive and forget.*

"I can understand that. You don't need to apologize."

"About that kiss—"

"It never happened," Toni said quickly.

David's mouth twisted. "I was kind of hoping it had." For an instant, she thought he was going to kiss her again. Instead, he put out his hand. Almost automatically, Toni extended hers, and he pressed it gently. "Good-bye, Miss Toni Schmidt. It was nice meeting you."

He turned to go, and Toni barely resisted the impulse to follow him. "When will you be back?" she called from the safety of the porch.

"I'm not sure. Evelyn can fill you in on my plans. You two take care of yourselves."

"You take care, too," she murmured, too low for him to hear.

Toni felt a rush of conflicting emotions as he drove out of sight. Her hope to see David again struggled briefly against the knowledge that she was well rid of him. She had never allowed any man to get close to her, and David Trent should be no different.

That was a vow she still intended to keep.

∞

Evelyn Trent had always seemed to guard her emotions, and she seldom spoke to anyone of personal matters. But that evening when Evelyn brought out the scrapbook containing pictures and mementos of her family, Toni saw how deeply she cared for them. Toni was touched to see several photos of herself among Evelyn's pictures of the Trents.

"What a mess I was in those days," Toni said of a snapshot taken soon after Evelyn had become her guardian.

"You just needed a little cleaning up." Evelyn turned the page. "See how much better you look in your graduation picture."

Toni gazed at the image of herself at eighteen—an unsmiling young woman, her chin slightly raised, ready to take on a world that had been less than kind to her. "At least you made me comb my hair before going out in public."

Evelyn turned to another page. "This is Jean and David when they married in Virginia. She was a civilian employee at the base where he was stationed."

More pictures followed—of Mandy as a baby; as a toddler with an Easter basket; standing beside her mother, who held her baby brother.

"David showed me that picture," Toni said. "Jean must have been quite lovely."

"I never really knew her; she never came to Rockdale."

"Were they overseas when she became ill?" Toni asked.

"Oh, no—Jean went to Germany with David after they married, but she came home to have Mandy and never went back. David was on a four-year stateside tour when Josh was born, then he was sent to Kosovo. Jean became sick while he was there, but he didn't know how ill she was for a long time. Here are the children with their grandmother after the funeral."

"They all look so sad," Toni murmured.

"They were. Even Josh knew something was wrong, but his mother was ill for so long, he scarcely knew her."

Toni picked up a more recent picture of David's daughter. Skinny, straight hair, and unsmiling, she looked uncannily like Toni at that age. "What about Mandy?"

Evelyn sighed. "David is concerned about both children. The Websters—Jean's mother and stepfather—did their best, I suppose, but David left the army to be with his children. He wants to put down roots and make them feel like a real family again."

"When do you think that will happen?"

Evelyn closed the album and leaned back in her chair. "David has business to take care of in Virginia, but he asked me to find something he can rent here."

"What about this house? It would make more sense for me to rent an apartment and let them live here."

Evelyn smiled faintly. "I offered to let them live here with me after Jean's death and again the other day, but he turned me down again. He thinks this house—where we grew up—is too small." She sighed as if resigning herself to never understand her brother's reasoning.

"I'll gladly move if he changes his mind." Toni spoke sincerely. "I hope things will work out for them."

Evelyn sighed. "So do I. They all deserve better than what they've had."

∞

For the next two weeks, Toni stayed so busy learning the DHR routines and procedures she had little time to think of anything else. Soon Evelyn would be gone, and while Toni knew she could never replace her, she wanted the transition to be as smooth as possible. She felt pleasantly surprised when some of the people who had once called her JD, short for juvenile delinquent, now went out of their way to make her feel welcome. She also enjoyed her renewed friendship with Mary Oliver.

"It's so good to have someone I can talk to," Mary told Toni over a salad at Statum's one evening.

"From the reception you got at the reunion, I'd say you have a whole bunch of friends."

"I teach some of their children—that could have something to do with it. They like me in that role, but I know some of them also feel sorry for me. They think my life will be a big zero unless I get married."

"And you disagree, of course," said Toni.

Mary paused her fork in midair and leaned forward. "I wouldn't say this to just anyone, but I think you'll understand. I believe God called me to be a teacher and has let me remain single so I can give all my love to my first-graders—especially the ones who don't get much attention at home."

"I believe I was called to do social work, too," Toni said, "but that has nothing to do with my decision not to marry."

Mary was silent for a moment, as if recalling what she knew about Toni's background. "You haven't gotten over what happened to your mother, have you?"

"How could I? Believe me, her mistakes taught me lessons about men and marriage I can never forget."

"Maybe you should try to let go of your bitterness," Mary suggested.

"I'm not bitter," Toni insisted. "I just don't intend to get married."

"Not even if the right man comes along?"

"That hasn't happened."

Mary smiled. "At least not yet."

"Not ever. Case closed."

They went on to talk about other things, but that night Toni pondered Mary's words. Toni had never thought of her feelings about marriage in that way, but even if it were true, didn't she have every right to be bitter?

Maybe you should pray about it.

Although she had not voiced the words, Toni shook her head violently.

"There's nothing to pray about," she said aloud but without a great deal of confidence.

Her confusion was all David Trent's fault. He would soon be back in Rockdale, but after Evelyn left town, he would be easier to avoid—and her life would be much simpler.

Chapter 9

Toni expected David Trent would surely return to Rockdale to attend his sister's retirement dinner. However, he still hadn't arrived by the time Evelyn and Toni left for the country club that Friday night.

Evelyn thought only Toni and her fellow workers would be there; she did not know her "small dinner" would turn out to be held in a ballroom packed with well-wishers. Judge Oliver, who served as the master of ceremonies, ushered an astounded Evelyn to the dais, where Congressman Winter, Police Chief Hurley, and Mayor Hastings were already seated. After dinner, each delivered a short speech expressing their own and Rockdale's appreciation for Evelyn's years of service. Finally, President Newman Howell of Rockdale Bank brought in a set of luggage, which he presented to Evelyn along with tickets for a Caribbean cruise.

"We wanted to help you get started on all that retirement travel you've talked about for so long."

Obviously moved, Evelyn could not immediately speak. "Of course I thank you all, but I suspect you people really want me to get out of town."

Toni joined in the standing ovation that followed, touched by the obvious affection the town Evelyn Trent had served so long now bestowed upon her.

David should be here to see this. Toni had supplied Judge Oliver with David's telephone number, so he must have been invited. She felt a moment of uneasiness that something might have happened to him, then Evelyn spoke again.

"Thank you, thank you—please sit down. And now, there's someone here I want to make sure you all get to know."

Evelyn gestured to Toni, and again the crowd applauded. Toni felt the blood rush to her face as she made her way to the dais to stand beside Evelyn. She had refused Judge Oliver's earlier suggestion that she sit there, telling him the evening was Evelyn's and she alone deserved attention.

"This is Toni Schmidt, my most able replacement. I trust you will give her the same support that you always gave me."

More applause followed, along with a few scattered cries of "Speech!"

"Say something," Evelyn urged. She propelled Toni to the microphone and grasped her arm as if to make sure she stayed there.

When the applause died down, Toni looked at Evelyn, then at the audience. "I join you all in wishing Evelyn Trent a happy retirement, but let me correct one thing she said. I may sit in the same office behind the same desk, but I think we all know that no one could ever replace this great lady."

"Well said," Judge Oliver declared to more applause. "Thank you all for coming." He turned from the microphone and spoke to Evelyn. "Stand by the door and let everyone greet you on their way out."

Evelyn held Toni by the arm. "Stay with me. I want to make sure you meet everyone."

Toni had no choice but to do as Evelyn directed. By the time the last person had filed by, Toni's hand ached from being enthusiastically shaken.

"I don't know how you politicians do it," she told Jeremy Winter, who had lingered to talk to Judge Oliver. "I've smiled so much my face is about to crack open, and my hand's ready to drop off."

Jeremy chuckled. "I'll share our secrets with you sometime."

"How long will you and April be here?"

"We head back to Washington next week."

"Tell April to call me—maybe we can get together after church."

"Will do." He turned to Evelyn. "In case April and I don't see you again before we leave, know that we wish you the best."

"So do we all," echoed Margaret Hastings, bringing up the rear.

∽

"This evening has been a bit overwhelming," Evelyn admitted to Toni on the way home. "You knew they were going to do that to me, didn't you?" Without waiting for her confirmation, she went on. "I wish someone had told David this dinner would be such a grand affair. He should have been there."

Toni opened her mouth to say that David knew, then stopped, unwilling to get into something that was none of her business. *David Trent can make his own excuses.*

"The mayor's assistant videotaped the speeches, so he can see what happened," Toni said. "That's something else you didn't expect."

Evelyn sighed. "I never dreamed anyone would want to make such a fuss over me."

"You deserve every bit of it. You've always done much more than you were paid to do," Toni said.

Evelyn drove her sedan into the garage, shut off the motor, and turned to Toni. "You'll do a good job, too, and someday, God willing, you'll have your own retirement dinner. I just pray that long before then, you'll also have a good husband to share it with. That's about the only thing that could have made this night better for me."

Toni was surprised that Evelyn still felt so much sorrow that she had remained single. She considered saying so, but Evelyn left the car before Toni had the chance.

It's just as well. Evelyn doesn't understand how I feel about marriage and probably never will. That's one subject better left alone.

∞

David Trent returned to Rockdale on the Friday of Toni's first full week in his sister's former position. She discovered he was back over lunch at Statum's when she heard Nelson Neal, the manager of Rockdale's only condominium complex, tell Tom Statum that he'd finally rented his last vacant unit.

"Evelyn Trent paid the deposit last week and the tenants showed up this morning—a man and two kids. I believe the fellow's Ms. Trent's brother."

Tom nodded. "Yes, David Trent's been here several times lately. I didn't know he had kids."

Toni smiled inwardly. *That makes two of us, Tom.*

"Yep, a girl about twelve and a boy who looks about five. Didn't either of them seem real happy about moving here."

"Carryout up," a waitress called from the kitchen, and the condo manager took his food and left without further conversation.

Toni's mind whirled. Evelyn hadn't said anything more about when David would return—in fact, they hadn't spoken of him at all since the night of the retirement dinner, and Toni suspected it was deliberate. That morning, Evelyn had said she might not be back by the time Toni got home from work; she had several things to see to before leaving on her cruise next week. Toni wondered whether David might be the cause of at least one of those errands.

Evelyn had walked to work in all but the worst weather, and Toni planned to do the same. On her way home that evening, she thought of the first time she'd seen David Trent, waiting on the front porch—for her or for Evelyn, she never knew which. Was it possible that David would be there now?

It's not likely. He and the children will have had a long day, and he probably already knows Evelyn isn't there. He has no reason to go to her house.

Toni had so convinced herself that he wouldn't be there that she felt a jolt of surprise when she turned down Maple Street and spotted David's truck parked in front of the house. Then she saw David sitting in the front porch swing just as he had the day they met. The man was every bit as handsome as she remembered, but when he stood to greet her, he seemed unusually grave.

"Where are the children?" Toni asked.

"In the yard out back. How did you know they were with me? Not even Evelyn knew exactly when we were coming."

"The famous Rockdale grapevine," Toni said.

David pointed to Toni's briefcase. "I see you're already hard at work."

"Yes, last Friday was Evelyn's last day. I'm on my own now."

Had David's eyes always been so blue? Toni swallowed hard and tried to concentrate. "Rockdale gave your sister a wonderful retirement dinner. She was disappointed that you missed it."

"The judge called me with a heads-up, but I couldn't have gotten everything packed for the move that soon. Besides, it was Evelyn's night to shine. I would have been in the way."

"So you're here to stay now?"

"If you could see all the stuff I unloaded today, you wouldn't have to ask. Even without furniture, I managed to fill a pretty good-sized moving trailer with our stuff."

"I suppose you know Evelyn's not home."

"Yes, but I hoped you could join us for pizza tonight."

I want you to meet my children, and I don't quite know how to go about doing it, Toni read in David's expression.

She hesitated. Her mind urged her to say no now and keep on declining David's invitations until he finally got the message—she wanted nothing to do with him or his children. However, her heart, which had betrayed her by beating faster the moment she saw him, spoke for her, instead.

"All right." Toni glanced at her dry-clean-only business suit. "I'd better change first."

David relaxed visibly. "Sure, take your time. I'll round up the kids."

From inside the house, Toni heard David calling and the children's voices answering, but she couldn't make out any words. She exchanged her office outfit for blue jeans and a white shirt and started back to the front porch. Hearing the children's voices through the screen door, Toni stopped to listen. David stood with his back to her, blocking her view of the swing where the children sat.

"I'm huuungry," the little boy whined.

"I'm starved," the older girl complained. "How much longer do we have to wait before we can eat?"

Taking the cue, Toni opened the screen door and stepped onto the porch. "Not much longer," she said.

David looked relieved. "That didn't take long." He stepped aside and pointed out the children with the flourish of a painter unveiling a portrait. "You've seen their pictures, now here they are in the flesh—Joshua David and Amanda Jean Trent. Kids, this is Miss Toni Schmidt."

The boy scowled. "Daddy, you know my name's Josh."

"And I'm really Mandy," the girl corrected.

Toni nodded and shook their hands in turn. "You may call me Toni."

David gave them a weak smile. "Seems I didn't get anyone's name right, but now that the introductions are over, who wants pizza?"

"Me!" Josh jumped out of the swing and ran down the steps, followed closely by his shrieking sister, each determined to get to the truck first.

"They're not always this loud," David said apologetically. "It's been a long day, and they're used to having supper an hour earlier in Virginia."

"They obviously have good lungs." *That was a stupid thing to say. Why do I always say idiotic things around David Trent?*

David walked beside Toni to the truck and opened the passenger door. "While you were changing, I used my cell phone to order a couple of pizzas with the works. I hope that's acceptable."

I'm not fond of pizza, I don't usually eat supper this early, and if those kids keep up their carrying on, I'm sure to have a fine case of indigestion. Toni's better nature told her to be civil.

"Yes, that's fine. I'm not a big pizza eater, though. Maybe you'll have enough left for another meal."

"Not with Josh around," Mandy said.

"You eat lots more 'n I do," her brother protested.

"Don't either!"

"Do so!"

"That's enough," David said sternly.

Except for some furtive pinching and poking between them, Josh and Mandy behaved during the rest of the drive to the pizza restaurant.

"Did you used to come here when you were a kid, Daddy?" Josh asked when they had been seated.

"Pizza probably wasn't even invented that long ago," said Mandy.

"Actually, I think pizza goes back quite a few centuries," Toni said, then wanted to bite her tongue. *I sound like a prissy schoolmarm.* It appeared that the trouble she had talking to David also applied to his children.

Fortunately, the pizzas arrived soon after they were seated, and the children devoted their full attention to eating. Toni noticed their table manners could use a little work, but she didn't call it to David's attention. They were his children; teaching them the rudiments of etiquette wasn't her job.

"You'll have to come by and see the condo," David invited. "It's no palace, but it's within walking distance of both their schools, and that's a plus."

"That's right, school will be starting soon, won't it?" Toni recalled Mary Oliver's recent complaint that summers seemed to get shorter every year.

Mandy made a face. "I don't want to go to school in this dinky town."

"Dinky, stinky!" Josh sang out until silenced by David's glare.

Toni tried again. "Rockdale may be a small town, but the schools are excellent."

Mandy rolled her eyes at Toni's pronouncement. "Not as good as my school back home in Virginia. All my friends are there."

"Virginia isn't our home anymore," David said gently.

"That's what you say. I don't care where you make me and Josh live, we'll always want to go back to Virginia."

Seeing that Mandy was on the verge of tears, Josh apparently decided to cry, too. "Home! I wanna go home!"

"People are looking at us," David said. "You know how to act better than that."

In spite of herself, Toni felt sorry for David. *He seems to want to be a good father, but he doesn't know how.*

"Go wash your face," David told Mandy when the last of the pizza had been eaten. "It's wall-to-wall pizza."

"Josh has more on his mouth than I have on my whole face," Mandy said.

"Do not!"

"I'll tend to your brother," David said pointedly, and Mandy flounced off in a huff. "Come on, Son, let's repair the damage."

"I don't wanna have my face washed!"

David lifted Josh from his chair, set him on his feet, and hugged him against his hip, minimizing any arm-flailing as they headed toward the rest room. The boy squealed loudly and attracted a lot of attention.

Some of the diners looked at Toni as if to say that she was a rotten mother, David was a rotten father, and their children were just plain rotten.

Spoiled rotten. It didn't take a child psychologist to figure out how David's children had gotten that way. Their father had been absent much of the time, and Toni guessed their mother hadn't been a disciplinarian even before she became ill. After they went to live with their grandparents, they were probably allowed to do pretty much what they wanted. To get back on the right path, they needed a loving but firm father—and someone to be a mother figure.

Their aunt was the ideal candidate, but Evelyn probably wouldn't be around them enough to have much influence.

I guess that conveniently leaves just you, doesn't it? Toni's pesky inner voice inquired.

"Be quiet," she told it, and for the moment, it obeyed.

Mandy returned with a clean face and a more subdued manner, and Toni stood. "My face probably needs attention, too. I'll be right back."

"I think we're ready to call it a night," David said when Toni rejoined them.

The children had talked earlier of going for ice cream after the pizza, but fatigue had erased it from their minds. Mandy managed to walk to the truck under her own power, but David had to carry Josh, who was already half asleep.

Toni felt strangely moved by the quiet child in David's arms. *Josh looks like a little angel. It's too bad he won't stay that way.*

Both children were sleeping when David reached Evelyn's house. Lights inside confirmed she was there, but Toni correctly surmised that David wouldn't go inside.

"Tell Evelyn we'll see her tomorrow."

Toni grasped the door handle. "Thanks for the pizza."

"Wait."

David came around to the passenger side and helped Toni out. Aware of every detail—the scent of his aftershave, the warmth of his hand on hers, the fact that he stood so very close—Toni felt oddly breathless.

It couldn't have been more than a few seconds, but it seemed ages to her before David spoke. "Thanks for putting up with the kids. I'm afraid they weren't at their best tonight."

Toni ignored the strange fluttering in her chest and adopted her best social worker tone. "I understood that they were tired and stressed. Moving to a new place is never easy."

David's intense gaze suggested that he saw through her attempt at detachment. "Do you think there's any hope for us?"

Toni felt a thrill of alarm. *Which us is he talking about?* But it made no difference, since she would not be a part of David Trent's "us."

Toni raised her chin and spoke firmly. "You and the children will do just fine. Good night, David."

And we will be quite fine without each other, as well, Mr. Trent.

Trying to believe it, Toni turned and went into the house.

Chapter 10

As Toni suspected she would do, Evelyn headed for her brother's condominium early Saturday morning.

"He'll need some help getting things straight."

Relieved that Evelyn hadn't urged Toni to go with her, she volunteered to bring their lunch.

"Thanks. Come around noon. David's is the first ground floor unit on the left."

Toni hurried through her usual Saturday chores, then called Tom Statum and ordered sandwiches and fixings for three adults and two children.

After she showered, Toni put on a cotton shift and filled a cooler with cold sodas. She put paper plates and napkins and disposable utensils in a plastic bag in case they were needed.

"You must be headed to David Trent's condo," Tom said when he handed Toni her order. "I put in a little something extra for the kids," he added.

Toni didn't want Tom to think she and David Trent were spending time together. "Thanks. Evelyn has been over there all morning—I'm delivering their lunch."

"Tell David I'm glad he decided to come back home," Tom said.

Even without Evelyn's directions, Toni would have had no trouble finding David's condo. His truck stood alone in the first parking spot on the left, and a rental trailer partially blocked the sidewalk in front of the corresponding unit.

"Daddy, she's here!"

Josh had apparently been kneeling on the couch, watching for her from the front window. When Toni came in, he threw both arms around her legs, almost tripping her. "What you got? I'm hungry."

"Lunch, but the drinks and plates are still in the back of my SUV."

David came from the adjacent kitchen and took the sack from Toni. Even in his ragged cutoff jeans and a sweat-stained, olive drab T-shirt, David still looked attractive.

"Thanks. Did you say there's more to bring in?"

"Yes. Mandy, would you like to help me?"

"I guess so," she said without enthusiasm.

"I'll do it!" Josh exclaimed. "Let me, let me!"

"She didn't ask you, dummy—all you do is drop things," Mandy said.

"Josh can help, too," Toni said quickly.

Mandy muttered under her breath. "Sure, whiny baby always gets his way."

166

Pretending she hadn't heard, Toni led the way to her SUV and handed Mandy the cooler.

Josh danced up and down. "My turn, my turn," he sang.

Toni tied the handles of the plastic bag together so he could carry it more easily. "These are the paper plates and napkins. We can't eat without them."

Mandy left with the cooler, but Josh stayed and watched Toni close the rear hatch. For the first time, she noticed how blue the boy's eyes were. Just like his father's. *Josh is going to be a handsome young man.*

The boy obviously wanted to say something but seemed to be having a hard time getting it out. "What is it?" Toni prompted.

"Are you our new mommy?"

Toni felt her jaw slacken in shock. *Did Josh really say what I thought I heard?* "What makes you ask that?"

"Daddy said we'd get a new mommy when we came here."

"When did he tell you that?"

Josh shrugged and shifted the bag to his other hand. "I dunno—a long time ago."

Not knowing how to answer, Toni asked him a question. "Do you want a new mommy?"

Josh's blue eyes filled with tears. "I want my old mommy to come back from heaven. I want to go back home to Nana Alice."

Lord, show me what to say to this child.

Toni put her hand on his shoulder and spoke earnestly. "I know how much you must miss your mommy, but heaven is a wonderful place, and I'm sure your mommy is happy there. I know you miss your grandma, too, but we don't always get everything we want, Josh. Things work out if we wait and have patience first."

Josh wiped his eyes with the back of his hand and wrinkled his nose. "I don't like to wait."

"I know you don't, and neither do I. You know what? I'm ready to eat. How about you?"

His face brightened. "Me, too!"

Josh ran ahead of Toni and handed the bag to Evelyn, who stood in the doorway. "I was on my way to see what was keeping you. We're all about worked out." Like David, Evelyn looked hot and tired.

"So I see." Toni moved a couple of boxes from the kitchen table and dealt out paper plates and cold soda. "I'm not sure what Tom sent, David, but he said to tell you he's glad to have you back in town."

"I suspect he'll get a lot of our business," David said. "Cooking isn't my favorite thing."

Evelyn piled the wrapped sandwiches and packaged chips in the middle of the table. "There's enough here to feed a small army."

The children needed no invitation to come to the table. Mandy was in the act of unwrapping a sandwich when Evelyn stopped her. "Maybe you haven't been doing it where you lived before, but here we thank God for our food before we eat. Don't we, David?"

David looked surprised, but he nodded and bowed his head. The children followed suit, although Josh watched his father intently.

"Thank You for bringing us here safely, Lord. Thank You for this food and all our other blessings. In Jesus' name, amen."

Not bad, Evelyn's glance suggested.

Toni sighed and wished that Evelyn wasn't going away. She'd have her brother and his family under control in no time, just as she had once straightened out Toni.

"Did you and Josh go to church in Virginia?" Evelyn asked Mandy.

The question produced a moderate amount of eye rolling. "Sometimes Nana Alice took us, but mostly she didn't," Mandy said. "Larry never went."

"Larry?" asked Evelyn.

"That's what Jean's stepfather wanted to be called," said David.

"Larry says there's too many hippos in church," Josh explained.

Toni tried not to smile. She'd heard it said that churches were filled with hypocrites, but she'd never heard them called "hippos" before.

Mandy was quick with an ungracious correction. "Hippos are big, ugly animals. Hypocrites are people who pretend to be good but aren't. You don't know what you're talking about."

Evelyn spoke before the argument could escalate. "You should take the children to Sunday school tomorrow, David."

Josh made a growling sound. "Ugh, school! I hate school!"

"You don't know anything about school, dummy. I've told you before, kindergarten isn't real school."

"It is so, too!" Josh said.

"Be quiet, both of you," Evelyn said. "Mandy, don't ever call anyone 'dummy' again. Your brother is every bit as smart as you are, and calling other people names only makes you look bad."

Mandy sighed loudly. "He's always saying dumb stuff, though."

David finally found his voice. "You're the big sister and should know better. You should help Josh, not put him down."

Evelyn's sudden laughter startled them all. "Oh, David, you sounded so much like Dad just then. He was always reminding me what an obligation a big sister had to her little brother."

Josh's eyes grew large. "You're my daddy's big sister?"

Evelyn nodded. "Yes, just like you and Mandy."

Josh looked puzzled. "I thought you were my daddy's mommy."

For a moment, Evelyn looked as if she didn't know whether to laugh or cry, then she rose from the table and laid her hand on Josh's shoulder. "I saw something in the bottom of the lunch sack I think you might like."

Tom's brownies were a big hit, and the children seemed almost calm after eating. They helped clear away the trash without complaint and even followed Evelyn's suggestion to go to their rooms to rest.

"I wish you could stick around longer," David told Evelyn, echoing Toni's sentiments. "You're so good with the kids."

Evelyn spoke with some severity. "I'm an old maid who never had any children of my own. Everyone knows we don't know beans about raising children."

"They can't say that about you." David gestured toward Toni. "There's living proof that you know how it's done."

As she always did when a conversation turned personal, Toni felt uncomfortable. *Leave me out of this, please.*

Evelyn seemed to answer Toni's mute entreaty. "We're talking about your children, not Toni. They've been through a hard time, and they'll need all the help they can get. Start by taking them to Sunday school. They can meet some children before school starts, and making friends in a new place is important."

"I'll think about it," David said. "We should get back to work now."

"Leave me out of that 'we,' " Evelyn said. "I have some things to do at home. Maybe Toni will stay awhile."

Here we go again. Will her matchmaking never cease?

Yet, in all fairness, Toni knew Evelyn hadn't started packing for her cruise, and time was growing short. Still, intentional or not, it created another chance for Toni and David to be together.

"Don't feel you have to stay," David said quickly.

I think I want to. The admission surprised Toni, and she adopted a tone of indifference. "I suppose I could help for a little while."

Evelyn looked smug. "Good-bye, you two. Want to meet somewhere to eat tonight?"

"I don't think the kids and I are up to another dinner out just yet," David said. "Maybe tomorrow?"

"Toni arranged for us to meet the Winters at DeSoto State Park after church. You and the children can join us."

"Anywhere but there," Toni half expected David to say, but he nodded. "Sure—the kids will enjoy seeing the waterfalls."

"We can ride together—but try to take the children to Sunday school first." David smiled. "Yes, Granny."

"You're lucky I don't have anything to throw at you, Sonny," Evelyn grumbled.

"You don't really look old enough to be David's mother," Toni assured her.

"Tell Josh that. I'll see you at supper, Toni."

"I won't be here that long," Toni called after her.

"I realize you have much better things to do on a Saturday afternoon, but it would really help to get the kitchen things put away," David said.

David told her that Evelyn had unpacked and washed the dishes and glasses and left them on the counter near the cabinets where she thought they should logically be stored.

"I can reach the top shelf, so if you can hand me the things, I'll put them away," David suggested.

It appeared to be safe enough, but Toni soon found the task perilous. Their hands inevitably brushed, and Toni couldn't deny the pleasant sensation of David's touch.

Does he feel it, too?

Toni glanced at David, but he seemed totally absorbed in the orderly, almost military, placement of each item. They moved from cabinet to cabinet, working together in a smooth rhythm, until the counters were empty.

"That takes care of that job," Toni said. "Anything else you need me to do?"

"Nothing, thanks."

This would be a good time to tell David what Josh said to me about getting a new mommy, Toni's inner voice suggested, but she quickly dismissed it. That was a subject best left alone, particularly given Josh's tendency to get things wrong.

Toni gathered her keys and purse. At the door, she turned and spoke again. "Will you be taking the children to First?"

David's jaw tightened almost imperceptibly. "Their things haven't been unpacked, and I don't know where their good clothes are. Tell Evelyn we probably won't make it."

"But you will meet us at the park?"

David gazed at her intently. "Yes, I'll be at the park—again."

Maybe things will work out better this time, his expression said.

Don't count on it, thought Toni.

"Good-bye, then."

Toni was aware that David stood at the door and watched her leave; once again, she wished she knew what he was thinking.

∞

Toni ran a few errands and came home to find Evelyn in the sunroom, reading the newspaper.

"I've packed everything I can for now, and it's too hot to sit on the porch," she said before Toni could ask.

"Air-conditioning is a blessing on a day like this," Toni said. "This must be the warmest day we've had since I got back."

"Another good reason to go to DeSoto tomorrow." Evelyn paused, and Toni sensed the subject was about to change, probably for the worse. "Now that you've met them, what do you think of David's children?"

For starters, they are spoiled brats, Toni could have said, except it would not be a fair assessment. In any case, she was reluctant to criticize them to their aunt.

Toni chose her words with care. "I haven't been around them much. They're livelier than they looked in their pictures. Both are attractive and intelligent—and obviously something of a challenge. I'm sorry you won't be around to help David with them."

"My brother knew I'd be going away for long periods of time. Besides, I made it clear I had no intention of raising his children."

"They're going to need someone's help."

Evelyn sighed. "I had hoped. . . ," she began, then stopped. "That's one reason the children should become involved in church activities. Having good teachers during the school week and moral instruction in Sunday school will go a long way to get those two on the right track."

"David said not to expect them at church tomorrow. He said they hadn't unpacked their clothes yet, but I also got the feeling that he doesn't really want to go himself."

"I think you're right. David grew up going to church, but after he went into the army, he drifted away. He won't talk about it, but I suspect Jean's illness and death tested his faith severely."

"I had already guessed as much," said Toni. "I'm surprised that you got him to come to Community Church."

Evelyn smiled. "That wasn't my doing—he wanted to hear you sing."

"He went to be polite."

"There are none so blind as those who will not see," Evelyn quoted the adage. "I've noticed the way David looks at you, Toni. He needs you—and his children need you."

His children need a mother, you mean. And I seem to have been nominated and elected without ever knowing I was on the ballot.

Toni determined to end a conversation that had become increasingly uncomfortable. "What I need is the freedom to do the best possible job I can at the Rockdale DHR office. That's the only work I came here to do."

"Maybe so, but if the Lord intends something more for you, don't stubbornly close the door to His will."

Evelyn's words were a heartfelt expression of her unspoken affection, and Toni accepted them in the same way.

"If I see God's purpose at work, I'll do it," she promised, and Evelyn seemed satisfied.

Long after they had gone on to other topics, Evelyn's advice stayed in Toni's mind. She had felt God's leadership in her choice of social work and again when she made the decision to come to Rockdale.

Could God have something else in store for me now?

And if so, would she be willing to accept it?

Chapter 11

I t was one thing to agree that Toni and Evelyn, the Winters, and David and his children would all meet at DeSoto Park for lunch on Sunday; working out the logistics was another matter.

Since the Winters would be at Community Church, Toni left her SUV parked there and rode to the park with them and the twins. David was to pick up Evelyn when she got home from the service at First.

The morning had been hot and muggy, and by the time the Trents arrived at the park, thunderheads had begun to build in the western sky.

"I don't like the looks of those clouds," Toni heard Evelyn say to David as they approached the verandah where she sat with Jeremy and April. Josh spotted the twins playing under a huge oak tree nearby, and Mandy nearly stumbled over him when he stopped to stare.

"A summer storm could blow in later. Maybe it'll clear the air down in the valley," David answered Evelyn.

"Jeremy, I don't think you've met my brother, David," Evelyn said.

The congressman extended his hand. "No, but Toni's been telling us about you."

David shook Jeremy's hand, then glanced at Toni as if speculating about what she had said.

"This is my wife, April," Jeremy added.

"Hi, David. Toni and I have been friends for ages."

Evelyn called to Josh and Mandy, who were looking at the acorns the twins had gathered. "Come here, kids."

All four scrambled onto the verandah, and Toni made the introductions.

"Warren and Kincaid, meet Josh and Mandy."

The twins, sons of a politician, were accustomed to meeting people and solemnly shook hands all around. Josh had never met any twins; he was fascinated that the boys looked so much alike and also had the same birthday.

Evelyn herded the children toward the dining room. "You'll have more time to play after lunch. Let's go inside before the buffet line gets any longer."

Jeremy and April's entrance into the dining room initiated a ripple of conversation as first one person, then another, recognized them. Some diners waved in greeting, while others came up to speak to their congressman. Several older women fussed over the boys, embarrassing them and slowing the family's progress through the line.

"Is it always like this when you go out?" David asked when the Winters finally joined the others at a large table in the rear of the dining room.

"No, sometimes it's worse," April replied. "It's altogether different in Washington. No one pays us any attention."

"There's lots of kids to play with there," added Warren, the more outgoing twin.

"There aren't many children in our Rockdale neighborhood," Jeremy said.

"The next time you're here, our boys should get together," said David. "Josh is just about their age."

"I'm the oldest," Kincaid declared.

"I'm the smartest," Warren boasted.

"I'm gonna be in first grade," said Josh, not to be outdone.

Toni smiled at the children's banter, then noticed David regarding her with the intense expression she'd seen before. Embarrassed, she turned her attention to her plate, listening to but not entering the eddy of conversation swirling around her.

Jeremy leaned across the table and said, "David, Toni says you're back in Rockdale to stay. What are you going to do?"

"It's still up in the air, but when the children are settled in school, I expect to close a deal on a business."

Toni tried to pretend she hadn't heard and wasn't interested. *What David Trent does is his business and none of mine.*

"I've always believed the small businessman is the backbone of the American economy. If my office can help you in any way, just let me know," Jeremy said.

"I knew David needed to meet you," Evelyn said. "He hasn't told me exactly what he's up to, but I'm glad he's come home."

"So glad that she's leaving town," David countered.

"I heard about the cruise you were given," April told Evelyn. "Congratulations—you deserve a happy retirement."

Evelyn smiled ruefully. "You didn't feel that kindly toward me when I wouldn't let you become Toni's guardian."

"You're not going to hold my inexperience against me, are you?" April teased.

David looked puzzled, so Jeremy explained. "Maybe you didn't know that your sister thought April wasn't mature enough to take charge of someone only a few years younger."

"Toni was already my friend, and I wanted to help her," April added. "But Evelyn was right, as always."

Toni spoke with an edge of irritation. "I wish you all wouldn't discuss me as if I'm not even here."

The children had been talking among themselves, but Mandy raised her head at Toni's remark and looked at her with a spark of recognition.

That's exactly the way people treat me, her expression seemed to say.

"Sorry," April said. "All of that was a long time ago, anyway." She looked around the table. "It seems we've all finished eating. I wonder if anyone here would like to see a waterfall."

Immediately, all three boys jumped from their chairs, waving their hands in the air and calling out, "Me!" "Me!" and "I do!"

"I wish I had half their energy," Evelyn said. "If you don't mind, I'll do my communing with nature from the verandah."

The sun was still shining, but the western sky had darkened ominously by the time they left the lodge. Evelyn chose a rocker near the lodge entrance. "If you hear thunder, grab the kids and run. You don't want to get caught in a lightning storm up here," she told David.

"That's for sure. We'll go to the Lodge Falls—it's not far."

Jeremy and April started down the path, with the children running back and forth ahead and around them like a pack of playful puppies.

"It must be hard to have a happy marriage and raise a family under the pressures of Jeremy's job, but they seem to be succeeding," Evelyn remarked.

"April turned out to be a stronger person than anyone gave her credit for," Toni might have said if David hadn't been there.

"I'm thankful for good men who are willing to take up politics, but that isn't for me," said David.

"What is? When are you going to tell us about the business you mentioned to Jeremy?" asked Evelyn.

David shrugged. "Nothing has been settled, so it would be premature to say anything yet. But don't worry, you and Toni will be the first to know."

Don't include me—your plans are not my concern.

"I hope so," said Evelyn. "I don't want to have to hear it from Tom Statum."

"You won't." David turned to Toni. "We should go on now. The others will wonder what happened to us."

"Won't you come along?" Toni asked Evelyn. "It's an easy path."

"No, thanks. I'm right where I want to be. I'm practicing for my cruise."

And three's a crowd? Toni wondered.

"I suppose I should catch up and help keep my kids in line," David said soon after they started on the path.

"April and Jeremy can handle them. Have you noticed how well they've behaved around the twins?"

"You mean compared to the bratty way they usually act?"

Toni felt her face redden and regretted speaking at all. "All children need to be with others their own age. They'll be happier when school starts."

David dug his hands into his jeans pockets and sighed. "I hope you're right. In the meantime, maybe you could show us some of the bike trails where you and April used to ride."

Toni felt a prick of alarm. David seemed to know so much about her, compared to what she knew about him.

"I suppose Evelyn told you about that."

"She mentioned you liked bicycling. I thought it was something I could do with Mandy and Josh that would also be good exercise."

"I'm afraid I'm pretty rusty. I didn't have the time to ride much when I lived in Atlanta."

"Then it's time you got started again," he said.

In the gloom of the level forest through which they walked, they saw Mandy in the far distance but could barely hear her faint call. "Hey, you slowpokes! Hurry up! Come on!"

When David raised his hand, signaling she had been heard, Mandy turned back and went on. "I suppose Mandy thinks the falls will stop running if we don't get there in the next five minutes."

"Could be she's right."

Unaccountably, a vestige of the old, "wild" Toni surfaced. "Want to race?" she asked, already running before David had a chance to answer her challenge.

The path led through a forest floor carpeted with last year's leaves and strewn with acorns, pinecones, and small limbs. The flat-heeled shoes that had served her well on pavement skidded on the path's surface and offered Toni no traction. She rapidly lost ground to David, whose hiking boots were far more suited for the terrain. Aware he was close behind, Toni redoubled her efforts. She saw Mandy just ahead, standing to one side of the trail. As Toni ran past, Mandy stared at her as if she had suddenly gone stark, raving mad.

Mandy might not be far off the mark, she thought.

Toni scarcely had time to consider that possibility before another concern took its place. She was aware of a distant flash of light, followed by a low, rumbling sound that seemed to begin in the bowels of nearby Little River Canyon and rise, amplified by the beating of her heart, to fill her head.

Toni tried to stop, but the path suddenly tilted downhill, and she had built up so much momentum she had to keep running. Panting from the unaccustomed exertion, Toni had almost managed to brake her headlong rush when she stumbled. As if in slow motion, she saw the ground rushing up to meet her and closed her eyes, bracing for the inevitable impact.

Instead, she felt David's arms encircle her, drawing her close to him. They hit the ground, with David's body absorbing most of the shock.

He spoke roughly. "Are you trying to break every bone in your body?" He breathed hard, and when she raised her head, Toni saw on his face a mixture of anger and some other emotion she could not read.

She struggled in his grip, trying to sit up. "It seems you're doing that for me quite nicely."

His grasp loosened and he sat back. "I'm sorry if I hurt you, but if I hadn't stopped you—"

April ran up to them, concern evident on her face and in her voice. "Are you all right?"

"Of course I am." Toni looked at David, who was still recovering his breath. "I was just winning a race."

"It looked more like you were playing football," April said.

Jeremy reached them, trailed by the children. All were out of breath from running.

"I hope you have enough wind left to get back to the lodge," Jeremy said. "That thunder sounds like it means business."

"I don't wanna go. I didn't see all the falls yet," Josh whined.

"You'll get to do that another day," April assured him.

"What a baby!" Mandy muttered.

Another peal of thunder shook the ground, persuading even Josh it was time to leave.

They hurried toward the lodge to stabbing flashes of lightning and almost constant thunder.

Toni soon found she had turned her left ankle and fell behind. David dropped back and put his arm around her waist, enabling Toni to move somewhat faster.

A few hundred feet from their goal, a pelting rain sent the group sprinting for the safety of the verandah, where they collapsed, gasping for breath. The children laughed, relishing the sport.

"I was afraid you might get caught in the rain," Evelyn said. After satisfying herself that the children were all right, she shook her head over Toni's disheveled state. Bits of pine straw and twigs clung to her dress and legs, and Toni felt a streak of mud on her forehead. "I suppose I shouldn't ask what happened to you," Evelyn said with a wry grin.

David's unexpected smile twisted Toni's heart. "Nothing," he said. "Miss Schmidt just won a race."

She began to shiver, and April took her arm. "Come on, let's find some paper towels and dry off."

"She looks drownded," Josh offered.

"There isn't any 'ded' in drowned," Mandy corrected.

∞

"Those are some kids David has," April said when she and Toni reached the privacy of the ladies' room. "They'll likely lead you a merry chase."

Toni glared at April. "Not me! They're not my responsibility."

"That's too bad. A little love would go a long way with those two."

April blotted rain from Toni's hair for a moment in silence. "David Trent seems to be a fine man. You should get to know him better and see where it leads."

"It wouldn't lead to the altar, if that's what you're thinking. You of all people should know how I feel about that."

176

"Yes, but I hoped by now you might realize how foolish the vow you made years ago really is," April said.

"It's not foolish to me."

"So you say. 'The lady doth protest too much, methinks.'"

Toni realized nothing she could say would change her friend's mind. "The lady hath a headache, and methinks she needs go home."

April smiled. "You whine almost as well as Josh. All right, brat—let's go."

Brat, indeed! Toni adopted an injured tone. "And you are supposed to be my friend."

"I am," April said sincerely. "And as your oldest and dearest friend, I hope you'll take my advice. Don't allow yourself to be afraid of David Trent."

"I'm not afraid of him." Toni's denial was quick, though not entirely accurate.

"Then prove it—let him into your life."

That night, reflecting on April's words, Toni thought it was just as well that the Winters were going back to Washington—and that Evelyn was leaving, too.

With those matchmakers out of the way, dealing with David Trent would be a great deal easier.

Chapter 12

In the last few days before leaving on her retirement cruise, Evelyn spent as much time as she could with David and the children, as well as making herself available for Toni. Although Evelyn had officially retired, she graciously made sure that Toni could handle everything that might come her way at the DHR.

The first few nights of that week, Toni came home to find David and the children there for supper. Along with food, Evelyn skillfully gave the children a few needed lessons in table manners—reminding Toni of her own similar experience as Evelyn's ward. Toni learned that Evelyn also took them to the offices of her medical doctor and dentist, introduced them to the staff, and picked up new patient forms for David to fill out. "It'll save time to complete these now," she advised David. On every form, Toni was listed as the backup person to be notified in an emergency, since Evelyn wouldn't always be in town.

On Wednesday, Evelyn went with David to register the children in their new schools. Josh seemed impressed when David mentioned they would be in the same schools he had attended as a child.

That night at supper, Mandy aired a major complaint. "They start school too soon here. We didn't go back until after Labor Day in Virginia. It's not fair."

"That means you'll get out earlier next summer," Toni pointed out.

"The schools are all air-conditioned now, so going back in August doesn't make any difference. Now, when I was in school. . . ," Evelyn began.

"Spare us the ancient history," David teased.

The night before Evelyn was to leave, David invited them to come to the condo for his "killer chili," apparently the only main dish he knew how to make. Toni had a good excuse not to go, since Thursday night was the time for Community Church's fellowship supper, prayer meeting, and choir practice.

"Can't you play hooky one time?" Evelyn asked.

"We're getting some new music, and I really should be there. Besides, it's the last time you'll be with David and the children for a while, and that should be a family time."

"It would be with you there. You may not realize it, but you're as much a part of the Trent family as if you'd been born into it."

Perhaps to you, Evelyn. I doubt the other Trents would agree.

∞

After extensive planning, which involved the aid of David and several travel agents, Evelyn was finally about to fulfill her dream to travel to faraway places, and Toni would truly be on her own at work. On the third Friday in August, Toni joined Evelyn on her front porch swing—now surrounded by her new luggage—and waited for David to arrive to take her to the Chattanooga airport.

Toni looked at the itinerary Evelyn had organized with her usual efficiency. Today she would fly to Miami, the port where her Caribbean cruise would begin. After the cruise, Evelyn would travel cross-country by train to spend some time in California with her recently widowed college roommate. Both planned to fly to Hawaii for two weeks before touring New Zealand and Australia, finally returning to California six weeks later.

"From there I'll decide where to go next," Evelyn said.

"Surely you'll be ready to come home by then."

"That remains to be seen. I have a lot of years of staying home to make up for. I still want to see the Canadian Rockies and Yosemite and Yellowstone, for starters."

"I knew you planned to travel, but I wish you could have waited until I felt more secure in your job."

"It's your job now, and having me around would be a crutch you don't need. For that reason, it's providential that the cruise leaves so soon."

"I'm sure David wishes you'd stay longer, too. When you get tired of living out of suitcases, we'll be glad to have you back."

Evelyn smiled faintly. "That's at least one thing you'll be doing together." She glanced at her watch. "Speaking of David, he should be here by now."

As if on cue, David's silver truck pulled up to the curb. Three of its doors opened, and the children jumped out onto the walkway. Evelyn's brother was punctual, if nothing else.

David took the porch steps in a couple of strides and picked up Evelyn's largest bag. "It looks like you might be aiming to go somewhere."

The children scrambled onto the porch. Josh struggled to pick up the second suitcase, which Mandy tried to wrest from him. "You're not big enough to carry that," she scolded.

Josh stubbornly held on to one of the bag's handles. "I am, too!"

"I'll take it." Toni settled the argument by carrying the bag to the truck. She felt a pleasant tingle when David took it from her, and once more she wondered if he felt it, too.

"Thanks." David looked as if he wanted to say more, but he turned away to receive Evelyn's carry-on bag.

"I hope you can handle all this luggage by yourself," he said.

"Oh, yes—I practiced to make sure. The big suitcase has wheels and a pull-out handle the others ride on. Quite efficient."

David secured the luggage in the truck bed, herded the children into the backseat, and opened the passenger door for Evelyn.

Her voice held a note of wonder. "I can't believe I'm really leaving."

Toni smiled. "It certainly looks that way."

"You have the list of people to call if anything goes wrong with the house?"

"Yes, and I'll make sure to pay the bills on time."

"Drive the sedan at least once a week—I left the key on my dresser."

"Don't worry about a thing. The house and car and the DHR office and I will all get along just fine."

Evelyn smiled ruefully. "Thanks for the reminder I'm not indispensable. Good-bye, Toni."

"Have a good flight and a wonderful cruise—and a fantastic adventure. Drop us a postcard now and then, okay?"

In a rare display of affection, Evelyn hugged Toni and David in turn before he helped her into the truck and closed the door.

"I'm sorry you can't go with us," David told Toni.

I'm not. "The DHR calls," she said.

He glanced into the backseat. "All buckled up? Good. Let's hit the road."

Toni stepped back from the curb and waved. After David's truck rounded the corner and disappeared from sight, she went back inside.

Suddenly, the house seemed very empty. *Everything looks the same, yet so much has changed.* With Evelyn gone, Toni would have no one to turn to for help with the DHR office.

"You can handle it," Evelyn had assured Toni, and she wanted to believe it was so.

On the plus side, Evelyn won't be here to push David at me.

Toni wondered how much difference that would make. She hadn't forgotten Josh's question. Had David really promised they'd have another mother when they moved to Rockdale, or was it a case of a little boy's imagination?

Toni sighed. Josh and Mandy needed a mother, all right—but anyone who expected her to step into that role was sadly mistaken.

Toni picked up her briefcase and squared her shoulders. She faced a full day at the DHR office, and she didn't intend to start it by coming in late.

∽

Her generally warm reception in Rockdale had surprised and heartened Toni, but she knew not everyone approved of her or would like her actions. Some thought she was too young for so much responsibility, while others would resent anyone who took Evelyn's place. That fact had become evident even before Evelyn left, when Toni denied renewal of a day care center's license. The irate owner demanded that Evelyn Trent make the inspection herself, since her replacement obviously didn't know what she was doing.

Evelyn had set the woman straight in no uncertain terms; but now she was gone, leaving Toni to fight her own battles.

"You can't waver," Evelyn told Toni. "Stick to your guns and never allow anyone to intimidate you. I know you can do it."

Yes, but only with the help of the Lord, Toni realized, in this as in everything else. Otherwise, she would surely fail.

"Mrs. Norris wants you to call her," Anna said when Toni walked in the door.

"Did she say why?"

"She wants a reinspection—she says she's 'taken care of the so-called deficiencies' in your report."

"I have a custody meeting this morning and a foster home visit after lunch. Tell her I'll get there when I can."

Despite its occasional headaches, Toni liked her work and the sense of accomplishment that came with helping someone. Pleased that the day had gone well, she locked the office door shortly after five o'clock and started walking home. The nearer she got, the more her thoughts turned to Evelyn—and David.

No doubt David is back by now. I'm sure Evelyn made it to the airport on time. She'll call tonight, so there's no need for me to contact David.

As she reached the porch, Toni heard the telephone ringing. She dug out her door key and hurriedly unlocked the door, which David had repaired as promised. She was a bit breathless when she answered and even more so when she heard David's voice.

"I thought I'd given you time to get home, but it sounds like you had to run to the phone."

"I just got here—it's been a busy day. Did Evelyn get away all right?"

"Yes, the plane left almost on time. We haven't been back long ourselves. Evelyn asked me to bring over a gift she got for you; then I thought we might grab some food."

Toni listened in silence, suspecting more of Evelyn's matchmaking behind the "gift" and supper invitation. "That's very kind, but you've already had a long day. You don't have to bring the gift over tonight." *And you most certainly don't have to feed me.*

"Oh, but I do," David insisted. "I promised Evelyn I'd deliver it right away. The kids like barbecue, so we can swing by your place on the way to Pitt's Place. You might as well go with us."

Evelyn no doubt told him how much I like that barbecue. "I haven't eaten at Pitt's Place in years," she admitted.

"Neither have I. I'll be there in fifteen minutes."

David hung up before Toni had a chance to reply. She started to call him back to tell him not to come, but that seemed rather foolish. Since David was determined to come by anyway, she would wait until he arrived to tell him she wasn't going with them.

Toni changed into chino slacks and a comfortable knit top. She ran a comb through her hair and went to the front porch to wait for the now familiar silver truck to pull up to the curb.

Minutes later, Josh scrambled out of the pickup and ran up onto the porch, holding out a clumsily wrapped package. "This is for you."

"We didn't get it wrapped very well," Mandy said as she and her father climbed the steps.

David handed her an envelope. "This goes with it."

Toni scanned Evelyn's brief note:

Toni—This is for your desk.

"Open it, Toni," urged Josh.

Toni removed the wrapping to reveal a polished mahogany desk nameplate, with TONI SCHMIDT, DIRECTOR lettered in gold script.

"It's beautiful, but why didn't Evelyn give it to me before she left?"

"She ordered it from a store in Chattanooga a few weeks ago, and it just came in. We picked it up on the way home."

"I didn't expect anything like this," Toni said.

"I suppose Evelyn thought it might make you feel more in charge," David said. "Now that it's been delivered, we can go to Pitt's Place."

"I don't think I ever said I was going," Toni said.

David seemed surprised. "Of course you are. Put your gift away, and we'll be on our way."

Toni was aware that the children were watching as if waiting to see if she would give in. *David needs to know he can't just order me around. I should stay here and prove that point.*

But she had to eat sometime, anyway, and she sure liked Pitt's barbecue. After all, hadn't Jeremy Winter warned her not to cut off her nose to spite her face?

"I'll be back in a minute," she said.

Chapter 13

Pitt's Place seems to be popular as ever," Toni commented when David pulled into the graveled parking lot. Many of the cars and pickups parked haphazardly around the ancient frame building bore license plates from nearby Alabama counties, with a smattering from nearby Tennessee and Georgia.

Mandy read the sign over the front entrance aloud. " 'THE BEST RIBS AND PULLED PORK IN THE WORLD.' Is it really that good?"

"You can judge that for yourself," David said.

"Wow, look at all these people!" exclaimed Josh.

"From the size of the crowd, we'll have a long wait to get a table," said Toni.

David eased the truck into a narrow space between a new luxury car and a battered pickup. "If you don't mind eating it at home, I can order at the takeout counter."

Toni was about to tell him they could wait for a table when she noticed several of the people standing near the entrance were drinking beer. When she was a teenager, Pitt's Place had not sold beer. From her own bitter experience, she knew that kind of atmosphere was not fit for children. "Yes, that would be better."

"I know what the kids want. What about you, Toni?"

"I always liked the pulled pork barbecue plate special with sides of beans and slaw—no fries."

"If they have it, you'll get it. Sit tight, kids. This could take awhile."

Josh called after his father. "Hurry up fast! I'm hungry."

"You're always hungry," Mandy said with disdain.

"Josh is a growing boy," Toni commented.

"I don't know where," Mandy said. "He eats and eats and stays skinny. I'd be too fat to get in the door if I ate half of what he does."

Josh giggled. "Mandy, Mandy, two by four, can't get through the kitchen door," he singsonged.

His sister jabbed him in the ribs with her elbow. "That's not funny."

"Ow, that hurt!" Josh flailed at her with open hands, and Toni decided it was time to intervene.

"Stop that, you two!"

Both stopped hitting to stare at Toni in surprise, then Josh burst into tears.

"I wanna go hoooome," he howled.

So do I. I wonder what would happen if I howled, too?

"We'll be going home in a few minutes," Toni said instead.

Josh quit sobbing and raised his head. "Not that home—I mean home to Virginia."

"I know you miss your friends, but you'll make new ones here."

Mandy sounded as if she might be on the verge of tears, too. "Nana Alice and Larry aren't here."

She might not ask David anything personal, but she welcomed the opportunity to learn about their grandparents from the children. "How long did you live with them?"

"Forever and forever," Josh said dramatically.

Mandy spoke impatiently. "You don't know anything. We went to live with Nana Alice when Daddy had to go out of the country to someplace we couldn't go with him. I was halfway through the second grade then."

"Nana Alice needed a daddy, so she got Larry."

"Larry is her husband, dum—" Mandy caught herself just in time.

Toni knew she shouldn't pump the children for information, but she wondered how much David really knew about their situation.

"Did you like Larry?"

"Larry marry, scary Larry," Josh sang.

"Larry isn't scary," Mandy corrected.

"Do you like him?"

The moment Toni spoke, she realized she had probed too much. The rays of the late summer afternoon streamed through the truck's open windows and highlighted the stubborn set of Mandy's chin. Her body language spoke her thoughts with silent clarity: *It's none of your business, Nosy Miss Toni.*

"Mommy didn't like Larry," Josh offered. "That's why she told Daddy—"

Mandy quickly covered her brother's mouth. "You know what Daddy says about talking ugly about people."

Josh slapped at Mandy's hand, and she took it away. "Ouch! That hurt! 'Sides, I wasn't talking ugly."

"No, but you were about to."

"Let's not start a fight," Toni said quickly.

"She hits me all the time," Josh complained.

"I do not! You're always hollering, then I get the blame."

They squabbled on for a few more minutes until Josh remembered that he was hungry and started whining again.

Mandy sighed. "Maybe you should go see what's taking Daddy so long," she suggested to Toni.

"I wouldn't dare leave you and Josh alone—you might hurt each other," Toni imagined herself telling Mandy. *If they were my children—*

Toni stopped the thought in its tracks. *They are not mine, and they are not my responsibility.* However, she would still treat them with patience and respect. "You can see how crowded the place is. It takes the kitchen help awhile to get so many orders put together, but it shouldn't be much longer now."

Toni hoped she sounded confident, but she was hungry, too. It had been hours since the scant lunch she'd eaten at her desk, and the tantalizing aroma of smoke rising from the open hickory wood pit made her stomach rumble.

"Maybe Daddy will let us eat in the truck," Josh said.

"Not hardly." Mandy looked at Toni almost defiantly. "The condo is a mess. I don't think you'd want to eat there."

"We can go to Toni's house," Josh said. "House, mouse!"

Toni smiled at the boy's mercurial mood change. "I don't have a mouse in my house," she said.

"Where Nana Alice lives, they say, 'There's a moose in the hoose, get it oot,'" Mandy said.

"That sounds like the Tidewater regional accent. I've heard some Canadians talk that way, too."

Mandy and Josh stared at Toni as if she were speaking Urdu. *There I go, saying stupid things again.* She was glad to see David striding across the parking lot with their food.

"Hey, crew, did you think I wasn't coming back?"

"I thought Toni should go inside and see what was happening," Mandy said.

David glanced at Toni, who quickly focused her attention on stowing the carryout sacks around her feet. "The food smells wonderful," she said.

"We're gonna go to Toni's house to eat," Josh announced when David started the truck's engine.

David cast a sidelong glance at Toni and smiled. "Thanks for the invitation—I'm afraid our place isn't fit for company just now."

I didn't invite you. Although it was the truth, Toni knew it would sound ungracious to say so. "No problem," she said.

"This reminds me of old times," David said a few minutes later when they entered Evelyn's kitchen. "I wish I had a dime for every meal I've eaten at this table."

After the children washed their hands, Toni asked them to set the table with the everyday stoneware, aware that flimsy paper plates would be no match for the ribs and barbecue. Their hunger made them finish the task quickly. David poured milk for the children and opened cans of soda for himself and Toni. When everyone was seated, Toni glanced at David questioningly.

He looked back and answered her unspoken question. "Our hostess will bless the food," he said.

Another presumption that bordered on a command. But this was one order Toni did not intend to dispute.

"All right. Let's pray." Mindful that the children watched her closely, Toni folded her hands and bowed her head. "Dear Lord, thank You for this day and all its blessings and for this food. May it strengthen our bodies and fit us to do

Your service. In Jesus' name, amen."

"Now can we eat?" Josh asked plaintively.

Laughing, David put a slab of ribs on the boy's plate. "Have at it, little buddy."

Toni transferred Mandy's food to a plate and served herself last. The children were too busy eating to tease or fight with one another, and she and David savored their own food in quiet appreciation. As they ate, the thought occurred to Toni that anyone who didn't know better might think these four belonged together in this place.

We look like a family.

Almost as soon as Toni acknowledged that thought, she canceled it with another: *This is David Trent's family, not mine. I do not belong to him, and this is not our house.*

"What's for d'ert?" asked Josh, who had put away an amazing amount of ribs and fries but spurned the accompanying coleslaw.

"Dirt?" Toni repeated.

"He means 'dessert,' " Mandy supplied.

"I don't know where you'll put it, but I have store-bought cookies and chocolate ice cream. Will that do?"

David pretended surprise. "What, no homemade goodies?"

"Like we ever have any at our house," Mandy said.

The girl's tone was a bit too saucy to suit Toni, but since David said nothing, she would not make an issue of it herself. "Trust me, they're better than nothing, which is what you'd have if you waited for me to bake cookies in this hot weather."

"Help Toni clear the table first," David told the children. "What about the dishes?" he asked Toni.

"They go in the dishwasher—you don't have to rinse them first. I'll get the ice cream while you're doing that."

"We didn't have a dishwasher when I was growing up," David said. "That was the first thing Evelyn added when she remodeled the kitchen."

"You mean you had to wash dishes by hand?" Mandy asked in mock horror.

"Yes. And even worse, when I was your age, we didn't have a color television set."

Toni entered into the spirit of his banter. "I'm sure your father also walked five miles to school each way through snowdrifts tall as this roof."

Josh's eyes grew round. "I don't wanna walk to school. I don't wanna go to school. I wanna go back home."

Mandy regarded her brother with disgust. "Toni was just teasing. You never really had to do anything like that in Alabama, did you, Daddy?"

David shook his head. "No, and neither will you, Josh. Remember that walk we took to your school the other day? It's five minutes away, not five miles."

"Ugh. Don't talk about school," said Mandy.

Toni handed each of the children a bowl of ice cream, wishing she'd thought through her comment before opening her mouth. "Here's your d'ert," she told Josh. "When you finish it, I have something to show you."

David looked interested. "What is it?"

"You'll see," Toni said. "Anybody want a cookie?"

"I'll take two, store-bought or not," David said.

When they finished eating, Toni invited David to sit on the living room couch between Josh and Mandy.

"What happens next?" he asked.

Toni took Evelyn's photograph album from the shelf and handed it to David. "I thought the children might like to see the pictures Evelyn has of some of their relatives," she said.

David opened the album to the first page. "I haven't seen these pictures in years. That one's of Grandpa and Grandma Trent on their golden wedding anniversary—you're named for him, Josh. Those are my parents—your grandparents, kids—when they got married."

"Their clothes look funny," Mandy remarked.

"Yours will look peculiar to your grandchildren one of these days, too," David said.

Mandy wrinkled her nose. "I won't ever be that old," she said.

"That's me!" Josh exclaimed when David turned the page.

Without comment, Mandy looked at the picture of their mother holding Josh.

"Remember why you aren't smiling in this one?" David asked.

"I guess I didn't want to be a big sister."

"I heard you'd just lost your front teeth," Toni said.

"Or your last friend," David said. He turned the page. "You look a lot happier in these."

"Is that Mommy? She looks sad," Josh said.

"You were too little to notice, but she was already sick then," Mandy said matter-of-factly.

"I miss Mommy," Josh said. Tears came into his eyes, and Toni felt her heart constrict when David hugged his son close, then put his other arm around Mandy.

They all need the Comforter. If only David understood how to fill the void in their lives—

David closed the photo album and stood. "We'd better be getting home. Thanks for the use of your kitchen." David's countenance suggested he could have done without that walk down memory lane.

"And thanks to you for furnishing the food." *I didn't intend to make you feel sad,* she hoped her expression conveyed.

Toni followed them out onto the front porch. In the deep summer twilight,

Venus hung on the horizon, surrounded by a few bright stars. "God has given us another beautiful night," she said.

Josh looked puzzled. "I thought the weatherman did that."

David seemed to suppress a smile. "The men you see on television report what their charts show. They don't make the weather."

"Nobody does that," Mandy said. "Weather just happens."

"Get in the truck, kids," David ordered, and each tried to be the first.

"Your children have some interesting notions," Toni said. "I agree with Evelyn—it's time you started taking them to Sunday school."

David regarded her levelly. "And I think you're beginning to sound like my sister." He started toward the truck, then turned back briefly. "Good night, Toni—I'll call tomorrow."

Chapter 14

Toni arose early Saturday and went to the sunroom for her daily quiet time. The morning was still cool, and she raised the windows to get a better look at the birds congregating around the backyard feeder. A pair of robins splashed in the ancient stone birdbath until a scolding blue jay swooped down, temporarily scattering them and causing several finches to rise in unison from their perches on the feeder. At the tip of the tallest pine tree in the yard, a mockingbird burst into song.

At times such as this, Toni wondered how anyone could view these marvels of God's creation and still deny His existence. It never ceased to amaze her that God had always loved her, even when she scarcely knew He existed. She recalled the words she had sung so recently: *His eye is on the sparrow, and I know He watches me. . . .*

Toni opened her prayer journal to a blank page. She usually listed her concerns rather quickly. This morning, however, she sat still for a long time before she began to write.

> *David's children need spiritual help, and I can't turn my back on them.*
> *I suspect their father does, too, but I don't want him to misunderstand how*
> *I feel about him.*

Toni put down her pen and gazed into the distance without really seeing anything. If she had to characterize the way she felt about David Trent, it might be summed up in a single word: confused.

Toni sighed. Through the years, she had gone out with a number of men on casual dates that never developed into anything more. She had worked with still others she considered her friends. Yet, no man had ever so instantly appealed to her or had been more difficult to ignore than David Trent. Toni had resolved to shut him out of her life completely—until she saw him again and met his children.

This isn't getting me anywhere. She put the prayer journal aside and opened her daily devotional guide. The day's scripture—Proverbs 3:5—all but leaped at her from the page: "Trust in the Lord with all thine heart; and lean not unto thine own understanding."

Maybe that's what I have been doing—depending on my own weak understanding. Toni bowed her head in earnest prayer. *I don't understand what I should do, and I know I can't handle this alone. Give me Your understanding, Lord, so I can help David's children.*

∞

The telephone remained silent throughout Saturday morning as Toni went about her usual chores. David had said he would call, but when he had not done so by one o'clock, Toni decided her comment about taking the children to church had probably made him shy away.

In any case, Toni was not sorry she'd said it. Evelyn wasn't there to set her brother straight, and somebody needed to do it. On that point, at least, she felt no confusion. She was debating whether to call and tell him so when the phone finally rang.

David spoke without preamble. "Hi, Toni. Ready to go for a bike ride?"

He sounded friendly, and Toni decided that if he harbored any ill feelings, he certainly hid them well.

"I've been working at home all morning, and I still have to buy groceries," she said.

"You can do that later. This is the last weekend before school starts, and the kids haven't had a chance to ride their bikes any distance at all since we got here. We hope you'll join us and show us an easy ride."

Toni hesitated briefly. "I'll make a deal with you. I'll ride with you and the children today if you'll promise to take them to church tomorrow."

David sounded amused. "You drive a hard bargain."

"Take it or leave it."

"I suspect my sister's hand in this, but I agree to your terms. Can you be ready in half an hour?"

"Yes—and thanks for asking."

This time Toni hung up first, savoring her small victory. Instead of telling her when he would be there, David had given Toni some say in the arrangements.

David Trent is learning—even if I don't want to be his teacher.

∞

"Where to?" David asked when he had added Toni's bike to the other three in the truck bed.

"Josh and I should start with an easy trail. How about the top of Warren Mountain?"

"I hiked around it some as a kid, but I never took my bike there," David said.

"April and I often rode all the way to the top. It was one of our favorite places."

"Isn't Warren Road where she and the congressman live when they're in town?"

"Yes. Their house is about a quarter of the way up the hill, before the road gets so steep. The top of the mountain is almost flat."

"All right—next stop, Warren Mountain."

David turned onto Warren Road and passed Ted and Janet Brown's apartment complex, then the entrance to an expensive, gated subdivision. "I can't believe all this new development," David said.

"The area has changed a lot, but I hope Warren Mountain itself will stay undeveloped." She pointed out the ridge ahead. "That's where we're going," she told the children.

On the other side of the Winters' house, the road steepened and began to twist and turn on its way to the summit.

"I wouldn't want to ride my bike up here," Mandy said.

"I would," said Josh.

Mandy spoke with scorn. "You have trouble pedaling five feet on the sidewalk. You can't climb a hill."

"Yes, I can!"

"Can't!"

David turned and gave both children a warning glance, then he spoke to Josh. "It's not entirely a matter of strength. Your bike doesn't have gears, and it would be hard for anyone to ride uphill without them."

The boy still looked downcast, and Toni tried to reassure him. "Don't worry, Josh—you can ride your bike just fine where we're going."

"I'd forgotten how great the view is from up here," David said when the road leveled out. From the western summit of Warren Mountain, Rockdale looked like a miniature village nestled against the larger backdrop of Lookout Mountain.

"Turn at the amphitheater sign. You can leave the truck in the parking lot," Toni said.

Moments later, the children raced to the edge of the shallow amphitheater and peered down at the rows of seats that had been cut from the rock of the largely undeveloped eastern side of Warren Mountain.

"This place wasn't here when I was growing up. What's it used for?" asked David.

"Mostly bluegrass concerts and fiddling contests in the fall and spring. Community Church holds a sunrise service here every Easter. Seeing the resurrection story unfold just as the sun comes up over that bluff is breathtaking. The children should see it next Easter."

Toni took David's nod to mean that he would at least consider it. "Come on, kids. Put on your helmets. We're about to do some serious bike riding."

The logging road Toni remembered bicycling on with April more than a decade ago was now so overgrown, they were forced to ride single file. Toni led the way, followed by Mandy, then Josh, with David bringing up the rear. With every turn of the wheels, Toni remembered why she enjoyed riding so much, and even Josh, although his steering was a bit erratic, kept up and rode well.

Toni tried to lead them around the roughest areas, but the going was far from smooth.

"I take it loggers don't use this road anymore," David said.

"No one does. The original timber stands were exhausted years ago. The Warrens replanted the slopes, and if Jeremy Winter has anything to say about it, they'll never be clear-cut."

It was cool at the top of the mountain, especially in the places where trees on either side of the trail met to form a shadowy canopy. The riders dodged an occasional fallen limb, as well as thorns from the blackberry and winterberry bushes that grew at the road's edge.

At one point they encountered a swarm of persistent gnats. "It's a good thing we put the bug stuff on before we started out," David said.

Josh made a face. "Bugs taste yucky."

"You're not supposed to eat them," Mandy said with disdain. "Anyway, they can't get in if you keep your mouth closed for a change."

"Then close yours," Josh said.

Although Toni expected David to reprove the children, he remained silent, and she decided he must have chosen to ignore all but their worst arguments.

A bit farther on, they encountered a stretch so wet they had to walk their bikes around several mud puddles.

"I'm tired," Josh whined after a few steps.

I wondered how long it would take him to start that. Aloud, Toni assured him a beautiful clearing lay ahead. "It's on the right, not very far away. We'll stop there for a break."

"I don't see anyplace like that," Mandy said after a while.

They had reached a dry stretch of the logging track, and Toni got back on her bicycle. "Let's ride on a little farther. I'm sure we're almost there."

"I'm tired," Josh whined.

Mandy didn't sound much better. "Look how these briars are scratching my legs."

David looked at Toni. *You obviously don't know where you're going,* she read in his expression. "Maybe I should mount a scouting patrol," he said.

Why did I ever agree to do this? Toni wondered.

Josh shrieked as if he'd already been abandoned. "Don't go, Daddy! Don't leave!"

Something rustled in the underbrush, and Mandy screamed. "Is that a rattlesnake? I don't like snakes."

A lone chipmunk scampered across the path, and David laughed. "There's your snake, Mandy."

While looking to see where the chipmunk went, Toni caught a glimpse of green and walked her bike toward it. "There's the clearing—it was just a little farther than I remembered."

They entered the small, grassy meadow—now bright with purple asters and yellow black-eyed Susans—where Toni and April had often rested when they rode up Warren Mountain.

Mandy leaned her bike against an oak tree and stood still, listening. "I hear something."

"So do I," said Josh.

"Sounds like water." David glanced at Toni. "It's the Warren spring, isn't it?" Toni nodded. "Let's go see it."

On the other side of a gap in the trees, water fell a few feet from a cleft in a small ridge and splashed into a rock-lined pool before joining a narrow stream.

Josh clapped his hands in delight. "It's a little waterfall!"

"Where does the water come from?" Mandy asked.

"There's an everlasting spring just behind those rocks," Toni said. "You remember meeting Kincaid and Warren Winter. A long time ago, their ancestors got all their water here."

David put his hand into the flowing stream issuing from the rock. "It's ice cold."

"I'm thirsty. I want a drink," Josh whined.

"The spring water is probably safe to drink, but I think we should use the bottles we brought with us," Toni said.

"I'm hot," Mandy complained.

"April and I used to take off our shoes and put our feet in the pool to cool off," Toni said.

Josh jumped up and down, his fatigue temporarily forgotten. "I wanna do that. Can I, Daddy?"

"I suppose so." David looked at Toni, his expression clear: *This is your idea, so you can carry it out.*

"Sit down and I'll help you take off your shoes and socks," Toni directed.

Josh tugged vainly at one of his sneakers. "I can do it by myself!"

"Not likely," said Mandy. "I made sure to tie the strings tight, then I double knotted them."

David knelt in front of his son. "Here, buddy, I'll help you."

When Josh allowed him to do so without protest, Toni detected a gleam of victory in Mandy's eyes. *I won,* her look seemed to say. *You're not the boss of us.*

"How about you?" David asked Toni. "Want to take off your shoes and join the kids?"

Toni shook her head. "No, thanks. I'll get the water bottles."

"I'll help you carry them." David gave the children a stern look. "Don't budge an inch. I'll be right back."

"Hurry up! I'm thirsty!" Josh called after them.

"I don't suppose they'll drown while we're gone," David said.

"I'm afraid not."

David looked at Toni and spoke with the same ironic tone. "So the truth comes out. You really don't like kids, after all."

Embarrassed, Toni busied herself with retrieving Mandy's water bottle. "You know that's not true."

"I'd like to think so." David put his hand, still cold from the spring water, on hers. Toni shivered at his touch, not wholly from the cold. Once more, he regarded her with the intent yet guarded expression she did not understand.

"I care enough to want them to be in church tomorrow."

David removed his hand and stepped back. "That again," he said flatly.

Toni lifted her chin. "Yes. I know you went to First Church when you were growing up. Your children deserve the same foundation."

"I know who told you that, but the truth is, I haven't set foot inside First in years."

"That doesn't matter. My friend Mary Oliver teaches Sunday school. She'll be glad to see that Josh and Mandy get put into the proper groups."

"I don't know," David said. "The children aren't used to going to Sunday school."

"All the more reason to take them."

"That's what Evelyn said."

"You promised," Toni reminded him.

"I agreed to take them to church. I didn't say where. I suppose Community has Sunday school classes, too?"

Toni felt mixed emotions. Getting Josh and Mandy into Bible study was a step in the right direction, but she had expected they would go to First. The prospect of seeing them at her church every Sunday was a bit daunting. "Yes, the church has a full program for all age groups."

David gave her a peculiar look. "You won't mind having them there?"

"Of course not. I just wish—"

Josh's plaintive cry interrupted Toni. "I'm still thirrrsty!"

"Water's on the way," David called back.

Mandy regarded them suspiciously when they returned. "What took you so long?"

David handed the children their water bottles. "We were making plans for tomorrow."

Josh groaned. "I don't wanna ride bikes again!"

"Me, neither," said Mandy.

"We won't. You're going to Toni's church for Sunday school tomorrow."

Mandy rolled her eyes but said nothing.

"Are you gonna be there?" Josh asked Toni.

Mandy muttered something under her breath that Toni thought sounded like "I hope not," which David apparently did not hear.

"My feet are cold," Josh said.

"Mine, too," added Mandy.

"I'll get something to dry them with," David said.

Toni was surprised. "You brought a towel?"

"Sure. I also have a first aid kit in my bike saddlebag. I told you I was a Boy Scout."

∞

While the children were putting on their shoes, Toni glanced at her watch. "If everyone's had enough riding, I need to get back to town and do some shopping."

"I think we're all ready to leave," David said, tucking the damp hand towel into his saddlebag.

"If you go on a few hundred yards west, you'll see the main road," Toni told David. "It's—"

"I know where we are now," he interrupted. "The road's steep, but quicker than going back the way we came. I'll get the truck and meet you at the road."

"Hurry up, Daddy," Josh said. "I'm hungry."

"You're impossible," Mandy said.

And so are you, Toni might have added.

Yet, in spite of it all, Toni admitted she really cared about David's children.

It must be because I see myself as a child in them, Toni told herself. *David Trent certainly has nothing to do with it.*

Chapter 15

After Toni finished her shopping and had a late supper, she got a telephone call from Mary Oliver. They chatted for a while, then Mary asked Toni to come to lunch after church on Sunday.

"Once school starts, there's no telling when we can get together again."

Toni thought of previous Sundays she and David had shared. He had not asked her to go anywhere after church with him this Sunday, but if he should, she now had a good excuse to refuse. It wouldn't hurt David Trent to understand she had a life of her own. "All right—I'll be there around twelve thirty."

∞

Although Toni feared he might change his mind, David brought the children to Community Church for Bible study on Sunday. Toni met David outside the welcome center, where he turned the children over to Mark Elliott, Community Church's educational director.

"What now?" David asked.

"You can go with me to the Seekers class."

"If there's an entrance exam, I'm sunk. I haven't been in Sunday school for more than twenty years."

"This isn't an old-fashioned Sunday school—it's a very informal Bible study, and no one will hassle you. I've been only a few times myself, but everyone has made me feel welcome."

The Seekers met in a part of the fellowship hall close to the kitchen, where coffee, juice, and pastries were readily available. A dozen men and women were already there when Toni and David arrived. When Toni introduced David, she found he already knew several of them, including the group's leader, Greg Harmon, one of David's childhood friends.

Toni soon realized that God was answering her prayers for David in ways she never imagined, from the fact that he knew the leader to the current Bible study topic. Toni noticed that David seemed intensely interested in Greg Harmon's opening words.

"The world is so full of suffering and grief that even Christians sometimes feel overwhelmed and discouraged and don't know where to turn. In the next few weeks, we're going to look at what the Bible says about why God allows suffering. We'll talk about handling grief brought on when we see others suffer, as well as from our own losses. Let's ask God to be with us now as we seek His answers."

Toni bowed her head and added her own prayer. *Lord, I thank You that David brought his children today. Help him take what he needs from this study.*

She did not pray for herself or her needs; at the moment, she wanted nothing more than God's peace for David and his children.

∞

Toni had to leave for the choir room before the children got out of Bible study, but when the choir came in, she saw them sitting where David and Evelyn had been the month before. David sat between the children and nodded almost imperceptibly when he saw Toni watching them. She translated his expression as *We're here, as promised* and smiled in reply.

Mandy sat with her arms folded in an attitude of bored resignation, while Josh seemed to be interested in everything around him. He swiveled in his seat and craned his neck.

As the service continued, Toni found it difficult not to keep looking at them. Her gaze seemed attracted to David Trent like steel filings to a magnet, and nearly every time she stole a glance at him, Toni found him looking at her.

After the service, David and the children were waiting to one side when Toni reached the vestibule.

"You didn't sing," Mandy said almost accusingly.

"Daddy said you would sing," Josh added.

Toni looked at David, who shrugged an apology.

"I did sing—in the choir. I don't sing all by myself very many Sundays."

"That's too bad," said David.

Toni ignored David's compliment and turned to the children. "What about you? Who wants to tell me what you did in Bible study?"

"I do!" Josh exclaimed. "We had cookies and punch and learned a song about a little man named Zeekus and I drawed his picture." He held up a messy finger painting of a stick figure in a skeletal tree, which Toni took to represent his idea of Zacchaeus.

"You drew his picture," Mandy corrected.

Josh sighed, clearly exasperated. "That's what I just said."

"If you don't want people to think you're dumb, you have to learn to talk right," Mandy said. "It's drew, not drawed."

Toni suppressed a smile. *Mandy sounded just like me there for a second.*

"What about your class?" she asked Mandy.

"It was all right, I guess."

David and Toni exchanged a glance, confirming the obvious: For Mandy, that was high praise.

"Can we come back next week, Daddy?" asked Josh.

"Do you want to?"

Josh hopped up and down on first one foot, then the other.

"Yes. I had fun."

Toni smiled. "I wish I had time to hear more about what you did, but I have to go now."

"Why?" asked Mandy.

"I'm having lunch with a friend."

David looked surprised and disappointed in turn. "I suppose we'll have to ask you sooner next time."

Next time, maybe you won't take me for granted.

Josh tugged at David's hand. "I'm hungry." His pitiful tone suggested he had not eaten in days.

Toni glanced at her watch, then at David. "I must be going. I'm really glad you all came today. I'll see you later."

She hurried to her SUV and inserted the key into the ignition, then her hand suddenly began to tremble.

David and the children had participated in Bible study and worship, which was what she had wanted for them.

Toni wasn't automatically having lunch with them, which was what she had wanted for herself. Both could be considered victories.

Why, then, did she feel so miserable?

∞

The first time Toni saw Mary Oliver's house, it seemed like a palace. She was sixteen then and still afraid of Mary's father. As the man who had allowed Evelyn Trent to become her guardian, Judge Oliver could have, with the stroke of a pen, sent Toni to reform school. Despite her past, he had allowed his daughter to befriend Toni and invite her to their home.

The Olivers' hundred-year-old white frame house contained eleven spacious, high-ceilinged rooms, including a separate servant's quarters. In Toni's teenaged eyes, the house was so elegant, she could not imagine an ordinary mortal like herself living there.

Mary had soon set Toni straight about that. "This place is cold in the winter and hot in the summer, there isn't much closet space, and something's always falling apart or breaking down."

Even after Toni realized Evelyn Trent's cottage was much more comfortable, the Oliver house continued to represent both a luxury and a family tradition she could never claim for herself.

Now, years later, the house and its grounds seemed far smaller than Toni remembered them. She still admired the home's stately Victorian architecture and carefully tended landscaping, but Toni no longer envied Mary for living in it.

Toni had just parked her SUV when she heard a distant rumble of thunder and looked up to see a lone thunderhead building in the summer sky. Toni wondered where David might be taking the children to eat. Statum's, his favorite restaurant, did not open on Sunday. The country club served brunch, but David was not yet a member. She thought it unlikely he would return to DeSoto so soon—especially without her. *I should have told him about the buffet at—*

That thought was immediately replaced by another: *I am not responsible for where David Trent eats. He can certainly make his own dining decisions.*

Toni hurried down the brick walkway flanked by giant boxwoods. She breathed in their fragrance and resolved to have shrubs like that of her own someday.

Mary waited at the door. "Sounds like a storm's brewing—I'm glad you made it here before the rain."

"It's probably only a passing shower. Where's the judge?" Toni added, seeing only two places set at the dining room table.

"He and the Harrisons went to brunch at the country club, so we have the house to ourselves."

"I hope you didn't go to a lot of trouble on my account," Toni said.

"Not at all. I made chicken salad yesterday, and we're having it on a croissant with fresh fruit on the side."

"With your special iced tea." Toni pointed to the frosty pitcher on the sideboard. "I remember how much I liked it."

"It's brewed tea, mixed with sugar and orange juice and crushed mint. The mint gives it that special taste."

Mary brought out their plates, filled their glasses, offered a brief grace, and turned to Toni. "I'm surprised you've haven't already told me about David Trent."

Toni took a sip of her iced tea before replying. "There's nothing to tell."

"I hear that he's quite handsome."

"Who told you that?"

"Several people. You know how it is—any unattached man sends all the matchmakers into a tizzy. Rockdale doesn't have many widowers."

Toni laughed. "I know. Evelyn has her own opinion of women who bombard widowers with so many cakes and casseroles they have to marry again in self-defense."

"Have you been making cakes and casseroles for David Trent?"

"Of course not. Evelyn asked me to help him with the children, and that's it."

"According to Jenny Suiter, it's all over town that Evelyn Trent's brother is spending a lot of time with her former ward."

"She probably started that story in the first place. Gossips like to make much ado about nothing."

Mary did not sound convinced. "Yes, but where there's smoke there might be fire, right?"

"Wrong—especially when there isn't even any smoke."

Mary was still skeptical. "Time will tell about that."

Toni seized the opportunity to change the subject. "Speaking of time, you don't have much free time left before you go back to work, do you?"

"None, actually. I've spent the last few days getting my classroom ready, and tomorrow all the Rockdale teachers gather for a joint meeting. We'll work in our schools on Tuesday, then our little darlings arrive on Wednesday."

The thought of teaching a roomful of Joshes made Toni shake her head. "I don't see how you do it."

"Sometimes, neither do I. Teaching is my calling, but that doesn't mean it's always easy."

"Josh Trent will be starting the first grade," Toni said. "I hope his teacher will be patient with him."

"So do I." Mary paused, then smiled. "I saw the class lists Friday. Josh Trent is in my room."

Toni smiled and clasped her hands together. "That's an answer to prayer! His father will be happy to know that Josh will be in such good hands."

Mary's tone was faintly sarcastic. "I'm sure you can't wait to share the good news with him."

"No. He'll find it out for himself. Now, not to change the subject, but I'd like to have the recipe for this excellent chicken salad."

"The way to a man's heart—"

"I told you I'm not interested in going there," Toni insisted.

She had no sooner spoken than a bright flash of light illuminated the sky, followed by thunder that rattled the house.

Both women jumped, and Mary laughed, "Somebody must think you're not telling the truth."

"You of all people should know I'm not interested in getting a man," Toni said.

Mary nodded. "I know what your mouth says, but I'm not sure your heart still believes it. You can fool other people, Toni, but don't try to fool yourself."

"I'm not."

Or are you? a nagging inner voice asked Toni.

Chapter 16

For the next few days, her work at the DHR office kept Toni too busy to think about much else. However, throughout the day on Wednesday, she wondered how the children were getting along on their first day in their Rockdale schools. She was reluctant to call David, but she reasoned it would be all right if she asked to speak to the children.

Soon after she came in from work, Toni had her hand on the telephone to call them when it rang. She let it ring twice again before she picked up the receiver.

David spoke with his usual directness. "Ready for a school report?"

"Is it a good one?"

"Let's say the reviews are mixed. I promised the kids takeout pizza tonight in honor of the occasion. If you like, I'll come by for you after I pick it up."

Toni hesitated. As much as she would like to talk to the children, she did not want to appear to assume the status of a member of the family. "Thanks for the invitation, but perhaps that's something you and the children should share."

"We will, but having a friend there will make it even better."

A friend? David must not have seen the way Mandy looks at me—and Josh is usually too busy whining and hanging on to his father to pay much attention to anyone else. Toni suppressed an ironical laugh.

"I didn't know the children thought of me as their friend."

"If they don't, they should—anyway, please say you'll join us."

"All right, but you don't have to come by for me."

"It's not out of the way—I can be at your place around six o'clock."

Toni felt an edge of irritation. *There David goes again, telling me what he's going to do rather than listening to me.*

Toni's tone made her meaning clear. "If I come at all, I will drive myself." *Take it or leave it.*

David sounded genuinely puzzled. "Hey, if that's what you want, I don't have a problem with it. I was just trying to make it easier for you to say yes."

"I appreciate your concern, but your condo isn't exactly at the ends of the known earth, and I know how to get there. What time should I arrive?"

David was silent for a moment. "If you won't let me pick you up, come about a quarter of six. You can visit with the kids while I go for the pizza."

Considering the way they had behaved in the pizza restaurant, Toni would not be surprised if David did not want them anywhere near it again, especially when she was available to baby-sit.

"I'll do my best to keep them from hurting each other," Toni promised.

She sensed David's smile. "I hope that won't be necessary. You may be surprised how this day at school has affected them."

Pleasantly surprised, Toni hoped.

∞

With punctuality that matched David's, Toni reached David's condo a few minutes early. He came to the door with his truck keys in hand and seemed genuinely happy to see her.

"I asked the kids to set the table while I'm gone so we can get right down to eating when I get back."

"Honk your horn when you get here, and we'll open the door for you," Toni said.

"That's my job!" said Josh.

"Sounds like you've had takeout pizza before."

"Among other stuff," Mandy said, with the tone of one growing weary of fast food.

At the door, David paused. "Thanks for coming tonight," he said privately to Toni. "Behave yourselves," he called to the children.

Toni closed the door behind David and turned to survey the condo's interior. "The last time I was here, boxes were stacked everywhere. I'm sure it took a lot of hard work to get it all unpacked and put away. It looks as if you've always lived here."

"It doesn't feel that way," Mandy said.

"I know," Toni said. "It always takes awhile to get used to a new place."

Mandy regarded her with curiosity. "Daddy said you used to live in Atlanta. Rockdale must seem like a hick town compared to it."

Toni smiled. "If I had grown up in a big city, I might feel that way, but I like a smaller town."

"My new teacher said she went to school with you," Josh said, his tone suggesting doubt.

"Yes, Mary Oliver and I graduated from Rockdale High School the same year." Toni decided not to add that his teacher was her good friend.

"Miss Mary's a lot bigger 'n you," Josh said.

"People come in all sizes. What they look like on the outside has nothing to do with who they really are inside."

You're preaching again, Mandy's pained expression told Toni, and she realized Mandy had a point.

"We'd better get started on the table," Toni said. "Who wants to get out the plates?"

Mandy's tone questioned Toni's intelligence. "I do, of course, since I'm taller. Josh puts out the little stuff."

"It's good you're learning to help out." Toni had meant to pay the children a compliment, but the moment she spoke, she realized she merely sounded patronizing.

If I'm all they have as a friend, these two would probably say they don't need any enemies.

The table eventually got set, and Toni was pouring milk into their glasses when they heard a horn blast.

"There's Daddy!" Josh exclaimed.

"Open the door," Toni said, but Josh had done so almost before she could finish speaking.

David entered carrying two boxes, quickly filling the room with the unmistakable aroma of freshly baked pizza. "Looks like everything's ready. Good job, gang."

"Wash your hands, Daddy," Josh said when David had set the boxes on the counter.

David noticed Toni's amusement. "We help remind each other of these important things."

A few minutes later, when they were seated around the table, Toni was heartened to see the children apparently waiting for grace to be said without being told.

David pointed to Josh. "It's your turn tonight, big boy."

Josh looked from him to Toni and back again. "Do I have to?"

"It's your turn," David repeated.

Josh sighed and put his hands together. "All right, but everybody has to close their eyes. No peeking."

"We're not playing hide-and-seek," Mandy murmured.

When Josh was satisfied with their attention, he prayed. "God is great. God is good. Let us thank–Him–for–our–food–amen." After speeding through the last portion, he glanced at Toni as if seeking her approval.

"Very good," she said.

"You might make a good auctioneer one of these days," David told Josh.

"What's a actioneer?" he asked.

David's mouth was full, so Mandy answered for him. "Auctioneer. That's a man who talks real fast when he sells things."

"Close enough," said David.

"Not all fast-talking salesmen are auctioneers, and some auctioneers are women," Toni observed.

Mandy rolled her eyes, obviously finding the conversation too boring for words.

"Have you told Toni about school yet?" David asked Mandy.

"There's nothing to tell," said Mandy. "Rockdale Middle School is just one big zero."

"Zero means nothing," Josh put in. "I learned that in kiddygardent."

"Kindergarten," David corrected automatically. He looked at Mandy. "Show Toni your class schedule. It doesn't look like a zero to me."

Mandy sighed in martyred resignation and pulled a wrinkled computer printout from her jeans pocket. Toni read aloud: "Amanda Jean Trent has home room with Mr. Bates; first hour, English with Mrs. Marshall; second hour, math with Mr. Barnes; third hour, physical education with Staff; fourth hour, lunch and social studies with Mrs. Franklin; fifth hour, study hall with Staff and sixth hour, activity period with Staff."

"That Staff must be one busy teacher," said David, but his attempt at humor failed to amuse his daughter.

" 'Staff' means I'll have a lot of substitutes until they hire more teachers."

"What about your other teachers?" asked Toni.

"They all look mean."

"Good," said David. "Mean teachers keep order, and you can't learn without an orderly classroom."

"How about the other students? Did you meet any potential friends?" Toni asked.

Mandy shook her head. "I'm the only new one in my home room and probably in the whole school. Everybody else has known each other forever. One of the girls from the Bible study spoke to me in the hall, but we don't have any classes together."

"Give it a few days, and I'm sure you'll begin to make some friends."

Josh had been waiting impatiently for an opening in the conversation and now spoke. "I saw a new friend today."

"Who's that?" Toni asked.

"His name is Jeff. He was in my class at church."

"That must be Jeff Elliott," Toni said. "Tell me about your teacher."

"She said we could call her Miss Mary. She asked if we could tie our shoelaces. I told her I already know how to read, but she said she'd rather hear if we could tie our own shoes."

Mandy laughed. "Wow, are you going to be in trouble!"

"His sister has always tied Josh's shoes," David explained. "It didn't occur to me that it might not be best for him."

He spoke seriously, and Toni tried to hide her dismay. *Oh, David—how can a man so smart in so many ways be so clueless?*

Toni pulled a guess from thin air. "By this time next week, I predict you'll be tying your own shoes."

Josh looked hopeful. "Really?"

"Yes, but you'll have to practice a lot. Your sister will show you how, won't you, Mandy?"

"I've tried to, but little baby brother here always whined so much, it was easier to do it for him."

"I don't whine," Josh whined, then looked surprised when everyone laughed.

"When you make a sound like that, you're whining," Toni said. "Now that you're a big first-grader, you can learn not to do it."

"Who's gonna teach me?"

"Nobody. You can do it for yourself."

"I'm too little," Josh wailed.

"You are not!" Mandy retorted. "You act like a baby just to get attention."

"I know you can quit whining if you want to." Toni caught David's eye. *Be patient with him, and he'll come around.*

David's expression reminded Toni of his son's plea: *I can't do this by myself. Help me, Toni.*

Toni returned her attention to Josh. "Tell me something else about your day," she invited.

Josh looked sad. "Everybody else's mommy brought them to school."

Toni's heart constricted. *I know how you must have felt, Josh. I wish you could have been spared that pain.*

"You know, it's very special to be the only one who had a daddy there," Toni told him.

Josh regarded her solemnly. "That's what Miss Mary said."

"I think Josh is fortunate to have such a wise teacher," David said.

Josh nodded and stretched out his arms. "Yeah, she's this wide."

"Daddy said wise, not wide!" Mandy corrected, and David and Toni fought to keep straight faces.

"She has a lot of rules, too," Josh said.

"That's the way school is, Josh. Get over it," Mandy said.

Is there anything you like, Miss Negative? "Look for the good things—they're there," Toni said, but she doubted either child understood.

David stood and began collecting their plates, empty except for a few pieces of crust. "It's time to police the kitchen."

Mandy put the pizza boxes in the trash, and Josh collected the napkins while David loaded the dishwasher. When Toni started wiping the table and counters, she noticed David watching her with that strange expression she had never quite understood.

If David is thinking of me as a permanent part of his life because I can put up with his children and know my way around a kitchen, he's seriously mistaken. But how could she make him understand that without sounding presumptuous?

"Can I go to my room now?" Mandy asked when the kitchen was clean. "I want to write to Nana Alice."

"Yes, that would be a good thing for you to do. Tell her I said hello."

"You said I could watch my new tape," said Josh, not quite whining.

"And so you can. I'll set it up for you," David said.

"I can do it myself," Josh insisted.

"I'm sure you can, but I'll have to find it first." He turned to Toni. "Make yourself comfortable—I'll be right back."

Toni glanced at her watch. She had done what David requested; she had all but guaranteed a case of indigestion by eating two large slabs of David's favorite "kitchen-sink" pizza; she had heard his children's complaints about their first day of school. The evening was still early—she would stay a few more minutes to be polite, then leave.

While she waited for David to return, Toni examined the condo's living area more closely. The unit had come with average quality furnishings in reasonably good shape, to which David had added a few personal touches. A large calendar hung on the wall above the telephone; most of the squares for the current month were still empty. A business card was clipped to one edge. Something to do with that business David talked about buying into, maybe.

Above a table in the foyer hung a picture Toni had not seen before, and she walked over to look at it. The slightly enlarged photograph showed a pretty young woman in a full-skirted party dress. Toni guessed at the faded signature at the lower right-hand corner even before she leaned closer to read it: YOURS ALWAYS, JEAN.

Mandy will resemble her mother more when she gets older. She will be a beautiful young woman someday.

From Josh's room, the sound of lively music became louder when David opened the door, then faded again when he closed it behind him and returned to the living room. Mandy's door was also closed; for all practical purposes, Toni and David were alone.

Toni shivered when the sleeve of David's shirt brushed her bare arm, but he was apparently too absorbed in looking at the picture to notice.

"Your wife was a beautiful woman. Mandy is going to look a lot like her in a few years."

David seemed almost surprised. "I think she looks more like Jean's mother, Alice. Jean wanted the children to have this picture to remind them of what she looked like before she got sick—especially Josh. He was too small to remember her when she was well."

Toni felt tears forming from the knowledge that Jean Trent had not lived to see her daughter enter the seventh grade and her baby boy become a first-grader.

"I know losing their mother has been very hard for them. They shouldn't ever lose her memory."

"Thank you for being here tonight." Once again, Toni felt David must have read her heart, and she felt ashamed that she had almost refused to come.

Toni turned from the picture to look at David. "Your children are very special to me. If there is ever anything I can do for them, I want you to let me know."

David's voice was husky. "You don't know how much that means, Toni. I realize I'm not much good as a father. I'm trying to learn, but there are some things

I can't handle by myself. Mandy's at an age where she needs a woman to talk to."

Toni smiled wryly. "I know all about that. When I was her age, my life was a mess, and it continued that way until April and Evelyn took me in tow. I didn't trust anyone, and I sure didn't want to be told what to do. Looking back, it's a wonder I lived through it."

David regarded her tenderly, and Toni felt a moment of panic when she suspected he might kiss her. "I'm glad you survived, and so are the kids," he said. "You help us all just by caring."

Toni sought the right words to tell David not to expect more from her than she intended to give. She attempted to speak lightly. "I suppose that's the social worker coming out in me. Evelyn always believed that an ounce of prevention was worth a pound of cure when it came to dealing with children, and in my line of work, I've seen the truth of that statement many times."

"Nothing personal," he said, almost making it a question.

Toni lifted her chin and looked him in the eye. "I can't afford to make it personal."

A muscle worked in his jaw, but otherwise David's expression was impassive. "I understand."

Realizing she had been holding her breath, Toni exhaled deeply. "Thanks for dinner. I have some reports to review, so I'll be going now."

David walked with Toni to her SUV and waved as she drove away into the deepening August twilight.

On her way home, Toni reviewed their conversation. Did David really understand she would not allow their association to become personal? And more importantly, would she be able to keep it that way?

Chapter 17

After Toni got home from David's condo, she tried to work on a critical report due in Montgomery the following day, but she found it hard to concentrate and soon gave up. Her mind kept reviewing the strange way David had looked when she tried to tell him there would be nothing personal between them. She wondered if what she took as his disappointment could actually have been an attempt to disguise his relief.

This is ridiculous—I can't let David Trent interfere with my work.

She would have to see him again fairly often, since she had promised Evelyn—and David—to help with Josh and Mandy. She was a family friend and nothing more. The sooner all concerned accepted that truth, the easier it would be for Toni to be with them.

∞

When she reached the office Thursday morning, Toni asked Anna Hastings to hold her calls while she finished the report. She filed it before the deadline, leaving a backlog of other work to catch up on.

Evelyn warned me it would be like this, Toni recalled early Friday when an emergency foster care situation promised to take up much of the day. It turned out to be the kind of day when everything that could go wrong did. As a result, she was physically and emotionally exhausted when she left the DHR office late Friday afternoon.

As soon as she got home, Toni soaked away the day's tensions in a leisurely bubble bath. She had no commitments for the weekend and no plans to go anywhere except church on Sunday. She had made no plans to see David or the children, which was just as well. As much as she enjoyed his company, she and David had no future together, and the more she saw him, the harder it could become to remember that.

∞

Although Toni kept thinking David might call, her telephone remained silent Friday night. Rain started early Saturday morning, making bicycle riding impossible. By Sunday morning, Toni fully expected David to bring the children to Community Church again and invite her to eat with them afterward. Like Evelyn, she wanted to see the children in Bible study, and she believed David would also benefit from it. But that did not mean she had to go anywhere with them afterward.

When she arrived at church on Sunday morning, Toni looked in vain for

David's truck in the parking lot. Seeing Mark Elliott, the educational director, she asked if he had seen the Trents.

"Not today. Jeff told me he and Josh are in the same first-grade classroom. I hope Josh will join Jeff's Bible study class, as well."

"So do I."

Toni was disappointed that the children had not come to Bible study, but she still hoped David would bring them to the worship service. From the choir loft, Toni could view the entire sanctuary. If David and the children were there, she would see them.

The service began, the choir sang, and the announcements were made before Toni acknowledged that last Sunday's visitors were not going to make an appearance at Community Church on this day.

The realization grew into a sense of guilt. *I was so concerned David might ask me out, it never occurred to me to make sure his children came to church. If I had offered to pick up Josh and Mandy, they probably would have come. It's wrong of me to allow my vow not to become romantically involved with David to keep me from helping his children.*

When the pastor opened a session of silent prayer, Toni raised her own earnest petition.

Lord, You know I haven't been the faithful witness I could have been. Lead me in the right direction and show me how to deal with Josh and Mandy and their father. Let them find the joy and comfort of Your love and may they know Your healing peace.

When Pastor Hurley said, "Amen," Toni added her own "so be it." She had no doubt her prayer had been heard, but she also knew she had to do her part in its answer.

Even if it meant seeing more of David Trent than she would prefer.

∞

After the worship service, Toni was hanging up her choir robe when Janet Brown engaged her in conversation.

"We were hoping to see Evelyn Trent's brother today," Janet said.

So was I. "Apparently he and the children couldn't make it."

"Ted thinks David Trent looks like a baritone. Does he sing?"

"I have no idea."

Janet smiled. "From what I hear, you must be getting to know that family pretty well. I'm glad."

"As you know, Evelyn asked me to help the children as a sort of substitute aunt."

Janet seemed amused. "What does that make their father?"

"A friend," Toni said. "That's all."

"For now, maybe," Janet said. "Come home with us. Ted plans to grill a few hamburgers."

And you will no doubt grill me about the Trents. "Thanks, but not today."

"Tell David we hope to see him next Sunday."

209

"If I see him," Toni said pointedly.

"Oh, I imagine you'll see each other before then."

"Don't count on it. Despite what some people in this town seem to think, we're not a couple."

Janet grinned. "I'll see you at choir practice."

∞

Toni went home to a lunch of leftovers, still irritated at Janet's presumption about her relationship with David. Toni did not want to appear to be pursuing him, but she felt an obligation to find out the reason for the family's absence from church.

Maybe one of the children is ill and that's why they didn't come. After what I said the other night, David might not even let me know.

Toni dialed David's number and got a busy signal. *Maybe he's trying to get in touch with a doctor. I'll wait a few more minutes and try again, and if the line is still busy, I'll go over there and see what's happening.*

A few restless minutes later, Toni had her hand on the telephone to try the call again when it rang, startling her.

She picked up the receiver, and although Toni expected David to be the caller, she answered in her most professional manner. "Schmidt residence," she said crisply.

The familiar female voice at the other end sounded a long way off. "Hello, Toni. I wasn't sure you'd be at home this afternoon."

"Evelyn! I can hardly hear you. Where are you?"

"At the cruise line dock in Miami—we just came in and the place is a madhouse."

"How was your cruise?"

"Most enjoyable, but we can talk about that later. Tell me how you and the DHR office are getting along. Any problems?"

Toni briefed Evelyn about her work, concluding with the information that her first state reports had been filed on time.

"And thank you for the gift. The desk nameplate is beautiful. It almost makes me feel like I really belong there."

"That was my intention. I ordered it over the telephone and didn't get to see the finished product, but David said they did a good job and you liked it."

"When did you talk to him?" asked Toni.

"Just now. I was glad to hear you went biking with him and the children. They spend far too much time indoors. I hope you can go riding with them regularly."

"I will when the weather cooperates. It rained yesterday, and, of course, the children have started school now, so they won't have as much free time."

"From what they told me, Josh and Mandy don't like school very much."

"They've been going only three days, and Rockdale is still a bit like a foreign country. With a little more time, I'm sure they'll adjust to living here."

"I hope so. It'll help if you keep urging them to go to church."

Toni wondered exactly what David had told his sister. "I intend to."

"Good. They'll listen to you, and so will David. What about the house? Are you having any problems with it?"

"Everything is fine. Don't worry about us."

Static crackled on the line, followed by the distorted sound of a loudspeaker in the background. "I must go now—I'll call again when I get to California. It means a great deal to me to know you're there for Josh and Mandy—and for my brother. I'm proud of you, Toni. Keep up the good work."

Toni replaced the receiver and sighed. Evelyn obviously took it for granted that her involvement not only with David's children, but also with their father would continue. Evelyn might no longer be there in person, but in a way, she was still playing the role of matchmaker.

All right, Evelyn. I intend to help the children as much as they'll let me, and I'll do what I can to keep them coming to Bible study. But don't expect me to fall into their father's arms in the process.

Toni had just picked up the newspaper when the telephone rang again. *That must be David, wanting to talk about Evelyn's call,* Toni guessed.

"Hi, Toni, it's Mary. Have you got a minute?"

"Sure. How are you holding up after the wear and tear of the first days of school?"

"I took a nap after church. The first few weeks are always hard—and this year's class could be quite a challenge."

Toni was beginning to suspect the reason for Mary's call. "Is Josh Trent part of that challenge?"

"Unfortunately, yes. As you know, he's a darling little boy and quite intelligent."

"I also know he's a whiner who can't tie his own shoes," Toni said.

Mary laughed. "I see a lot of those in my line of work. That's not his main problem, though."

Toni felt uneasy. She didn't like the drift of the conversation and wondered if they were betraying Josh and David by having it. "Have you spoken to his father?"

"Not yet. I won't tell David Trent I talked to you, but I thought you should know that Josh is telling everyone he's getting a new mommy soon. Friday, Eddie Moore accused him of lying, and Josh became so angry, I had to separate them."

Toni feared the worst. "Did Josh name this supposed new mommy?"

"No, but who else could it be but you?"

"His imagination, I suspect. Josh told me he wants to go back to Virginia and live with his grandmother again."

"Yes, he likes to talk about all the fun things he did in Virginia. It could be that seeing everyone else with their mothers on the first day of school triggered a bit of wishful thinking. I wanted your input before I talked to his father."

"What will you tell David?"

"The same thing I told you, but mostly that Josh needs to learn how to control his anger before it gets him into serious trouble."

Even though she knew Mary's assessment was fair, Toni rose to Josh's defense. "His family has been through a lot in the past couple of years. I really don't know how much more David can do for the boy."

"Other than helping him with anger management. . . ," Mary paused, then spoke lightly, "he can get Josh a new mommy. I could mention a certain social worker as an ideal candidate."

"No, thanks. Short of that, I do want to help Josh. He's been to a Bible study class at Community once, and now that he's in first grade with Jeff Elliott, I hope he'll want to go every Sunday."

"Good. If Evelyn had stayed here, she would probably have brought the children to First Church. It's better for both of us for Josh not to be in my Sunday school department. No child should have to face the same teacher six days a week."

"I hadn't thought of that, but it makes sense. When will you talk to David?"

"Today, I hope. I'm calling all my students' parents to set up a home visit, but I never discuss behavior problems in front of the children."

"I know you make those visits on your own time—anyone who thinks teachers are overpaid doesn't know many like you."

"I could say the same about social workers. People don't go into our types of work for the money."

"They shouldn't, anyway. Do me a favor—if Josh gets into any more trouble, will you let me know?"

"You're listed as the emergency contact if David can't be reached, but if anything serious happens—which I don't anticipate—I'll let you know."

"Thanks. When you have time for us to get together again, give me a call."

"I will. And one more thing. . ." Mary paused.

"What?" Toni prompted.

"Don't be too hard on Josh's dad. He needs you, too."

Mary hung up before Toni had a chance to reply, which was just as well. *What makes Mary think I'm being hard on David? I want to help his children, but despite what everyone in Rockdale seems to believe, I'm not pursuing David Trent.*

Toni returned to her newspaper, but when she found herself rereading the same paragraph several times, she put the paper down and went to sit on the front porch. She would have to talk to David eventually, but she would give Mary time to call him first.

Even as Toni rehearsed what she should say to David, she heard him call her name. Surprised, she saw David and the children riding their bicycles on the sidewalk in front of the house.

"Get your bike and come with us," David invited.

Toni remained in the swing with her arms crossed. "That sounds a lot like an order." *And you know by now I don't take orders well.*

212

He looked contrite. "I meant it as an invitation."

Toni looked at Mandy, who was obviously less than thrilled to be there. "Where are you going?"

"To some park with a playground. Daddy says there's one around here somewhere."

"The only one I know about is on Jackson Street, on the other side of your condo. You've already come several blocks out of your way."

"Daddy said you'd go with us if we came and got you," said Josh.

Toni spoke directly to Josh. "I didn't see you at church this morning. Jeff's daddy said your friend hoped you'd be at Bible study."

"We didn't go 'cause Mandy couldn't go," Josh said.

Toni shifted her attention to Mandy. "Why not?"

"I didn't feel good."

"Mandy calls me a baby, but she's the one always cryin'," Josh said.

Toni looked at David for verification. *I'm sorry,* his expression said.

"I wanna go to the playground. Please come with us, Toni." Josh spoke emphatically but without whining.

"All right, since you asked nicely. I'll get my helmet and bike."

When they reached the playground some ten minutes later, David and Toni sat at a shady picnic table and watched Josh run toward the swings. "Push me," he demanded of Mandy, and to Toni's surprise, she did so without complaint.

"Something must be wrong with Mandy," Toni said. She spoke ironically, but David took her seriously.

"I'm afraid so. I've caught her crying several times since school started, and this morning she literally cried herself sick."

"I take it she still doesn't like Rockdale Middle School."

"That's putting it mildly. She keeps comparing it to her last school, and I have a feeling if anyone tried to be friendly, she'd shoot them down."

"It'll get better with time. At her age, girls tend to cry at the drop of a hat."

"I hope that's all it is."

Toni saw an opening and took it. "What about Josh? How is he doing?"

David's expression told Toni he had heard from Mary Oliver. "Josh doesn't cry—he just gets into fights. So far, I'm batting zero on my theory we'd feel like a family again once we came to Rockdale."

"Don't be so hard on yourself—or them. They're good kids, and they'll come around, probably sooner than later."

David reached for Toni's hand and held it loosely. "You know, I really misjudged you."

"How?"

His blue eyes held her gaze. "At first I believed you didn't like my children. Now I see you handle them better than I do. You couldn't do that if you didn't feel something for them."

"I am fond of Josh and Mandy, but don't put yourself down. You're learning together, and you love each other. That goes a long way."

"I still need a lot of help. I'd like to know that you'll set me straight when I need it and be there for the kids when I can't be." David searched Toni's face as if to gauge her reaction. "I know that's a big imposition," he added.

"I don't consider helping Josh and Mandy an imposition. In a way, I suppose you could say I'm taking Evelyn's place with them, just as I took her place at DHR."

David released her hand and rubbed his chin. "I suppose Evelyn called you—she said she was going to."

Toni nodded. "I assured her everything was all right here."

"She asked me to take care of you. I told her it seems you're doing all the caretaking so far."

Toni raised her chin. "Evelyn knows I'm used to being on my own. If I need help, I'll ask for it."

David smiled. "I won't hold my breath waiting for that."

"Good. You might turn very blue. While we're on the subject, Evelyn asked me to do something else."

"If you're talking about getting them into Bible study at Community, I told her I would."

"Even if Mandy cries and doesn't want to go?"

David sighed. "Yes, Toni, even then. I know I should have put my foot down this morning, but I felt so sorry for her, I just couldn't."

"Don't worry about it, but I think you'll find the rest of the week goes better after you've been in God's house. It always works that way for me."

"That's a good thing—otherwise, I doubt you could put up with the likes of us."

Josh came running back then, as eager to leave the playground as he had been to get there. "It's hot. I want to go home."

"Try that again without the whiny voice," David said. When he did, David and Toni applauded, and for once Mandy had nothing sarcastic to add.

This might be a good time for me to try to talk to her. The thought grew, and when the children reached the condo ahead of them and went inside to cool off, she decided to act upon it.

"If you don't mind, I'd like to borrow Mandy for a few hours."

David looked surprised. "What for?"

"I want to show her something. We can ride to my house, and I'll bring her and her bike home."

"I'll tell her," David said. *I don't know what you're up to, but I think it will be good*, his expression said.

I'm not sure myself, but I have to try, Toni answered silently.

Chapter 18

It was just past four o'clock when Toni and Mandy reached Evelyn's house. Mandy had readily agreed to come along, even though Toni had not specified where they were going. Josh had also wanted to go, and David had to promise to take him somewhere special, too.

"Leave your bike in the garage beside mine. We'll take the SUV," Toni directed.

"I'm glad you didn't let Josh come with us," Mandy said when they pulled away from the curb. "He's such a baby."

"Josh has a lot of growing up to do," Toni said.

"I suppose you think I do, too," Mandy said. "I'll be glad when I am grown up and people quit telling me how to act and what to do all the time."

Toni laughed. "I remember saying something like that to my friend April once. She told me no one has ever lived that long." Then seeing the hurt in Mandy's eyes, Toni added, "I know what you mean, though, because I felt that way myself when I was your age."

I doubt it, Mandy's expression said. "Where are we going?"

"Down memory lane, you might say. Like you, I was twelve when I came to Rockdale. I haven't been back to the first place where I lived in many years."

"I never saw this part of town before," Mandy said when Toni turned down a pothole-pocked street lined with ramshackle, unpainted houses. Rusting appliances and automobile bodies dotted many of the untended, weed-choked yards. "I suppose it looked a lot better then," she added diplomatically.

"Not much." Toni slowed before a shotgun house at the end of the street. Its boarded windows and sagging roof testified the house had been abandoned. "I lived here for several months."

Mandy wrinkled her nose in distaste. "Where did you go to school back then?"

Back then—to Mandy, any time before she was born is ancient history. "Nowhere, for a long time. It was spring when we moved here, and we stayed through the summer and moved again when. . ." Toni stopped herself. Mandy didn't need to hear all the sordid details. "When we found another place."

"Who's 'we'? Who was in your family?"

I didn't have a family, Toni could have said. "At that time, it was my stepmother and my father. He drove a truck and didn't come home very often."

"So you had a stepmother?"

Toni nodded. "Several, as a matter of fact."

Mandy was silent for a moment. "When Daddy marries again, Josh and I will have a stepmother."

Not "if" but "when." It's obvious Mandy has been thinking about a "new mommy," too. Not wanting to comment on that subject, Toni pointed out the roads leading to Community Church and Warren Mountain as they passed them.

"I'd like to ride my bike all the way up that mountain without Josh this fall."

"Some of the girls in your class would probably go with you if you asked them," Toni said.

"Or not," Mandy said.

"You'll never know until you try."

Mandy remained silent until they passed a battered metal sign obviously used for target practice. "NOW LEAVING ROCKDALE," she read out loud.

"That's a very old city limits sign. I don't know why it's still there. As you can see, we aren't really out of town at all."

Toni pulled into an aging mobile home park. "This is the next place I lived."

"It doesn't look much better." Mandy blurted out the words, then looked embarrassed.

"It wasn't," Toni said. "There's the lot—the one with the big tree stump in front. Of course, that's not the same house trailer. I'm sure the one I lived in was junked years ago. It wasn't in very good shape to begin with."

"Did you have a bike then?"

Toni blinked at Mandy's non sequitur. "No. April Kincaid gave me my first bicycle."

"Were you living here then?"

"No. I'll show you the last place I stayed before I went to your aunt Evelyn's house."

Mandy remained silent as Toni left the mobile home park and drove back to the center of town. Circling the courthouse, she drove south to Potter Road, on the outskirts of town.

"The Potters were my foster parents," Toni said. "They had several children of their own and also took in strays like me." Toni slowed, then stopped in front of a large, white farmhouse that had seen better days.

"The mailbox says R. Johnson. The Potters must not live here anymore," Mandy said.

"That's right. They left town before I did," Toni said.

"It doesn't look like such a bad house," Mandy said cautiously.

"It was all right, but it never felt like a real home to me. The Potters had several young children, and I looked after them. I didn't mind, though, since I never had any real brothers or sisters."

Mandy was silent for a moment. "Aunt Evelyn never said anything about where all you'd lived."

"There was no reason for her to." Now that Toni had Mandy's attention, she spoke earnestly. "God has led me on an amazing journey. From the time I was your age until April Kincaid came into my life, I got into a lot of trouble. I ran away several times. I broke into April's apartment to steal a blanket because I had been sleeping outside and I was cold. I believe God sent me there because He knew I needed a friend. With His help and the help of April and your aunt, I turned my life around." Toni stopped, overcome by unexpected emotion.

Mandy spoke quietly. "Does Daddy know about all of that?"

"He hasn't seen the places where I lived—but he knows how I lived before his sister took me in."

"Daddy likes you a lot," Mandy said matter-of-factly.

What can I say to that? Help me, Lord.

"I like all of you a lot, too, and I want you to be happy living here."

Mandy began to cry, her tears running unchecked down her cheeks. "It's been so hard. . . ."

Toni lifted the center console and handed Mandy a tissue from the box she kept there for such situations. "I know, Mandy. But God knew what He was doing when He brought you here, and He'll help you through anything if you ask Him."

Mandy dabbed at her eyes. "I asked God to make my mother well, but she kept getting sicker, then she died. I don't think God listens to me."

"I've felt that way myself many times. We don't understand God's ways, but Proverbs 3:6 tells us, 'In all thy ways acknowledge him, and he shall direct thy paths.'"

"I never heard that before," Mandy said.

"I hadn't heard it when I was twelve, either. I remember I was surprised to find the Bible had so much practical advice in it."

Toni's cell phone rang, and she looked at the caller ID feature and sighed. "It's the police chief," she told Mandy.

After a brief conversation with Earl Hurley, Toni turned to Mandy. "I'm sorry, but I must make an emergency placement. I'll have to take you home now." Toni put away the cell phone and headed the SUV back toward town.

"What's an emergency placement?"

"When a child needs to be removed from a dangerous or harmful situation right away, DHR is notified. In this case, both parents have been arrested on drug charges, and there's no one to take care of their two-year-old daughter."

"I want to go with you," said Mandy.

"First I'm going home to call around until I find a foster parent who can take the child. Then I'll pick her up and make the transfer."

"What if nobody can take her?" Mandy asked.

"Do you remember seeing the crib in your aunt Evelyn's spare room? That's why it's there."

"I didn't know you had to do that," Mandy said.

"Fortunately, it seldom happens, but that's part of my job."

Toni stopped in front of her house, and Mandy got out.

"You don't have to take me home. I can ride my bike."

"Thanks. I do need to start calling right away. I'm sorry we didn't have more time to visit."

"So am I."

Toni opened her arms, and Mandy came into them and hugged her warmly.

"Thank you, Toni."

Thank You, Lord, for showing me what to say to Mandy. Now help me find a home for this other little girl.

∞

Toni was halfway down her calling list before she found a foster parent willing to take on a two-year-old child, even temporarily. By the time she had picked up the little girl at the police station and settled her in the foster home, it was well past suppertime. She did not feel particularly hungry, but Toni picked up a fast-food sandwich on her way home.

The day had been exhausting, but Toni's sense of accomplishment more than compensated for her fatigue. Seeing the answering machine's message light flashing in the dark, she hoped it wouldn't be another emergency call.

"Call me when you get in," David's voice ordered.

What does he want now? Something in the tone of his voice made her uneasy, and she called him back immediately.

"Toni—I was worried about you. Is everything all right?"

"Of course—why wouldn't it be?"

"Mandy told me you had an emergency. I think she was a little spooked."

"I don't know why. Tell Mandy everything went well. It was a routine emergency placement."

David sounded less tense. "If an emergency can be routine. Anyway, thanks for spending time with Mandy."

"What did she say about it?"

"Not much—she mentioned you took her to some places where you used to live."

"I intended to take her to supper, too—maybe next time we won't be interrupted."

"She knows it wasn't your fault."

Toni suppressed a yawn. "That's good."

"I won't keep you any longer—you sound tired."

"Thanks for your concern. Tell Mandy I enjoyed her company."

"I think it was mutual. Good-bye, Toni. I'll see you soon."

∞

Toni spent most of Monday working on the necessary legal procedures to turn the previous day's emergency placement into a more permanent arrangement. She went to the jail to interview the parents to make sure there were no family members who could take custody of their daughter and asked Judge Oliver to expedite the hearing giving DHR the power to act in the child's best interests. Finally, Toni checked the regular list of foster parents and found a couple who had just lost a foster child to adoption—a happy result not seen often enough in the foster care system.

Toni came home Monday night pleased with the way her first emergency had turned out. Since Mandy had seemed so interested, Toni called to give her a report.

"How long will the little girl be away from her parents?" Mandy asked.

"That's hard to say. Their case has to go through the courts. There will be a trial, and if they're acquitted and want her back, we'll decide what to do then. If they go to jail, DHR will look after the child until the parents are released and can prove they can provide a good, safe home for her."

"Poor little girl," Mandy said. "I hope the people she's with will be good to her."

"We check our foster homes regularly—she'll be fine."

"Thanks for letting me know. Oh, Daddy says he wants to talk to you," Mandy said when Toni was about to hang up.

David sounded about as excited as she had ever heard him. "You won't believe this, but I just found a perfect baby-sitter living right next door." Toni's image of a gum-chewing teenager faded quickly when David told her Mrs. Tarpley was a widow and had recently retired. "She was away visiting one of her children when we moved in, but she came over with a plate of cookies this afternoon. She's agreed to stay with the kids after school tomorrow."

"What's happening then?"

"I'll be tied up with some business. I wanted to let you know Mrs. Tarpley would be here."

"I'll come by and check on them after work, just in case," Toni said.

"They'd like that—and you can meet Mrs. Tarpley. I think you'll like her."

"Your neighbor sounds like an answer to prayer."

"You really mean that, don't you?"

"I pray for you and the children every day. I believe Mrs. Tarpley is there because you need her."

"I hadn't thought of that, but I suppose it's possible. Keep praying. We need all the help we can get."

"You can pray, too, you know," Toni reminded him.

"What makes you think I don't?"

Toni heard Mandy's voice in the background, and David turned away from the telephone. "I'll be right there," she heard him say, then he came back on the line. "Sorry, but Mandy needs help with math."

"Give Mrs. Tarpley my work, home, and cell phone numbers and tell her to call me if she needs anything."

"She will. You're first on the list of emergency numbers. Good-bye, Toni—and thanks."

Toni continued holding the receiver even after David broke the connection. *Thanks for praying for them?*

Every time Toni thought she was beginning to understand David Trent, he managed to do something else to show how much she still had to learn about him. If he wanted to accept her as a family friend and emergency contact, that was fine.

She wanted nothing more.

∞

The children seemed genuinely glad to see Toni after work on Tuesday. Mrs. Tarpley was a calm, country-bred woman whose sharp eyes missed nothing; the children would not be likely to get away with anything when she was there. *Just what they need,* Toni thought and once again thanked God the woman had come their way.

After Toni asked Mandy what kind of schoolwork she had done that day, she showed her a project she and another girl were doing for their social studies class. "We're going to work on it at her house after school tomorrow," Mandy said.

"That's one way to make friends," Toni said.

"I know everyone in my class," Josh said. He proudly displayed a primary pad on which his first name was printed in crooked letters.

"Won't you stay for supper?" Mrs. Tarpley invited when Toni started to leave. "I cooked us a pot roast, and there's aplenty."

Toni was tempted to accept, but she did not want to be there when David came home. "Thank you, but I must be going." At the door, she paused and looked from Josh to Mandy. "Whose turn is it to say grace tonight?"

"Mine!" exclaimed Josh.

"No, it's not—you said it last time."

"You can both say a blessing, then," Toni suggested.

Mrs. Tarpley laughed. "I can think of worse things for them to be arguin' about."

"So can I," Toni agreed.

Toni felt reassured by her visit. The children seemed to be getting along better with each other and at school, and they were doing their homework. She had told David things would be better; perhaps they were already turning in that direction.

∞

On Wednesday, Toni had been reviewing case files all morning without a break when Anna Hastings knocked on her office door.

"Lunchtime."

Toni looked up in surprise. "Already? It can't be."

"It's nearly noon."

Toni glanced at her watch. "So it is, but I want to do a few more files. If you're going out, would you bring me back a sandwich?"

"There's a caller here with a different idea," Anna said.

"A caller?"

"A gentleman caller," Anna emphasized.

Toni reluctantly left her office. That David Trent waited in the reception area was no surprise; he was the only man in Rockdale likely to expect Toni to drop everything to have lunch with him.

David smiled engagingly. "I know you're busy, but you still need to eat. Let's go to lunch."

"I really don't have time," Toni said.

"We can grab a quick sandwich. I have something to show you."

"What is it?"

"I can't tell you—you have to see it for yourself."

Toni wavered, then capitulated when her curiosity won out. "All right, but it had better not take long."

After telling Anna she would be back in thirty minutes, Toni followed David into the oppressive midday heat of late August. The leather seats in his truck were hot to the touch, and the blast from the air conditioner felt more like a blast furnace.

"I don't know why I let you talk me into this," Toni said.

He smiled. "It must be because of my great charm."

Or my idiocy.

When he stopped in the Loading Zone Only space in front of Statum's Family Restaurant, Toni's heart sank. If she and David were seen together again, Toni could imagine what the Rockdale rumor mill would grind out. *Have you heard? Evelyn Trent's good-looking brother is courting Toni Schmidt. Why, every time you see one, there's the other.*

Again, David seemed to anticipate Toni's reaction. "Stay here. I'll leave the motor running so you'll have the air-conditioning. I won't be gone long."

Toni tried to sink out of sight in the seat, but Jenny Suiter spotted her and did a double take. She waved at Toni and went inside the restaurant. *Where she will see David and speculate why I'm sitting here in his truck when I ought to be in the office, tending to DHR business.*

"I must be getting paranoid," Toni said aloud. As long as she knew she was in the right, what others might say had never concerned her. However, gossip about her and David was both different and unwelcome.

David returned in a few minutes, a Statum's takeout bag in one hand and two containers of lemonade in the other.

"Where are we going?" she asked when he pulled away from the curb.

"You'll see."

David made a right turn, then another, bringing them to a parking lot almost directly behind Statum's Restaurant. He pulled into a shady space and turned off the engine. "Here we are."

"We're having lunch in a parking lot?"

"No." David came around the truck and opened her door. "Your balance is better than mine—you can carry the drinks. We're going over there."

Toni followed him across the parking lot to the side entrance of a one-story brick office building. David unlocked the door and motioned for her to enter.

Toni looked around the room, which was about the size of her DHR office. The furnishings, a haphazard collection of styles and materials, consisted of a large desk with a swivel chair, two side chairs, a filing cabinet, and a long table on which several stacks of papers awaited stapling. A plastic tablecloth set with paper plates and disposable cutlery covered the desk.

"Where am I?" she asked.

David laughed. "Certainly not in Kansas."

Toni pointed to another door to the right of the filing cabinet. "Is the Emerald City of Oz on the other side?"

"Look and see."

Aware that David watched in amusement, Toni opened the door onto a much larger, mostly unfurnished room. Its only occupant, a man in coveralls, stood with his back to them, carefully adding another name to the one already on the large front window.

Toni read the backward letters of the top name: N–O–S–N–E–B. "This is the Benson Insurance Agency?"

"It was. Fred Benson Senior died last year. I heard his son needed a partner, and we were able to work out a deal."

Why didn't you tell me about this? The question was on her lips before Toni realized it was not her concern. "I had no idea," she said, instead.

David looked pleased. "I knew as soon as my name went on the window, everyone in town would see it, but I wanted you to be the first to know."

Toni looked around the office, mentally calculating the amount of work ahead to bring the agency back to life. "Congratulations, I think."

"Thanks, I think. I'll tell you about it while we eat—I know you have work to do."

"Does Evelyn know about this?" Toni asked when David had filled in the details.

"She knew I was negotiating with someone, but I asked her to keep it quiet until we closed the deal, which we did yesterday."

"What do you know about the insurance business?"

"Enough. Jean's stepfather has an agency in Virginia, and I lived there long enough to learn the ropes. I'll have to take a few courses and pass a test, but Freddy Benson will do the paperwork until I have my license."

"I suppose this means you're in Rockdale to stay."

David smiled wryly. "After paying what all this will cost, the only other place I can afford is the poorhouse."

"Which is where I could end up if I don't get back to work."

∞

"Thanks for your time," David said when he pulled into the DHR parking lot.

"Thanks for the lunch—it seems you're always feeding me." She felt as if "I don't know how to deal with all this attention" was written all over her face.

"It's no big deal." His gaze seemed to respond, *When will you realize that I like being with you?*

Toni hurried back to her desk, aware not only that her promised thirty-minute absence had lasted far longer, but that Anna and Edwinna had no doubt been discussing her involvement with David Trent. Telling them the truth might not stop their speculations, but Toni decided it was her best defense.

"David Trent has bought into the Benson Insurance Agency, and we had sandwiches in his new office. If Judge Oliver calls, tell him I have some papers he needs to sign."

Back in her office, Toni stared blindly at the file before her, wishing her mind and her heart could agree about David Trent. She didn't know whether to feel dismayed or flattered that David wanted her to be the first to see his new office. It implied a closeness she had not sought and did not want.

Toni had vowed they could have no future together, but the more she saw him, the harder it would be to remain his friend.

Chapter 19

The moment Toni arrived at choir practice on Thursday evening, Janet Brown greeted her with the latest rumor.

"Word is you and David Trent were seen in the parking lot behind Statum's Restaurant yesterday. What was that all about?"

"Nothing worth mentioning. David has bought an interest in the Benson Insurance Agency, and he was showing me the office."

Janet nodded knowingly. "That sounds as if you two are getting to be something more than friends."

"Don't believe everything you hear. You know I have no romantic interest in David Trent—or anyone else."

Janet sounded doubtful. "Are you sure about that?"

"He's a good man, and I promised Evelyn to help with his children. I consider us to be friends—and that's all."

Ted Brown had been listening to their conversation and now joined it. "From what Mark Elliott says, David Trent is looking for more than a friend."

"What makes him say that?" asked Janet.

"Josh Trent is in Jeff Elliott's first-grade class. He told Jeff he was getting a new mommy real soon—any day now."

Toni groaned inwardly. *Not that "new mommy" business again!*

"Josh said something like that the first day of school, but I doubt anyone took him seriously."

"Jeff apparently did, but he said some of the other children laughed at Josh and said he should stop telling such stories."

Unaware Josh was still repeating the new mommy story, Toni tried to downplay it while concealing her own concern. "You know how children tend to exaggerate. This story seems to have taken off on its own."

"This is one story I'd like to turn out to be true," Janet said. "You would make a great new mommy for Josh."

Toni made no effort to hide her irritation. "I'm not about to be, and I would appreciate it very much if you both would make that clear to anyone who brings it up."

Janet sighed. "All right, but you shouldn't close your mind to the possibility."

"Places, everyone," Ted called out. "We have a great anthem to rehearse tonight, so let's get started."

"Good," Toni muttered. She had heard more than enough talk about Josh's new mommy for one day.

∞

On her way home, Toni decided David should know the extent to which Josh's original "new mommy" story was being spread. His father should also know that Josh was still being teased about it.

When she went to the telephone to call him, Toni saw the answering machine light blinking. *David. What does he want?*

His message was terse. "Call back when you get home."

There was an edge in David's voice Toni had seldom heard, and her first thought was that something had happened to one of the children. Toni called him back immediately, and he picked up the telephone on the first ring.

"I'm coming over," he said with his usual directness.

"Is something wrong?"

David hung up without replying, so Toni went outside to wait in the porch swing. When David's truck pulled up to the curb, she saw he was alone. Even in the dim glow of the corner streetlight, David looked troubled.

He ran up the walkway and took the porch steps in several strides. "Let's go inside."

Toni closed the front door behind them and turned to face David. "Where are the children? Are they all right?"

"What? Oh, yes. They're both in bed, and Mrs. Tarpley's there."

Toni pointed to the couch. "Sit down. Can I get you something? I have lemonade in the refrigerator."

"No, thanks." David sat on the edge of the couch. "I don't know what I'm going to do about Josh. He got into a fight on the school playground at recess this morning and had to sit in the principal's office the rest of the day. Mary Oliver said if it happens again, Josh could be expelled."

Toni put her hand to her throat. "I can't believe the school would do that to Josh. What was the fight about?"

"It goes back to something Josh said on the first day of school. I suspect the other kids in his class have been egging him on to keep the story going."

Although Toni thought she already knew the answer, she had to ask the question anyway. "What did Josh say that was bad enough to start a fight?"

"Do you remember how upset Josh was that first day when all the others in his class came with their mothers?"

Toni nodded. "Yes, but we talked about that. I thought Josh understood having his daddy with him made him special."

"Not special enough, apparently." David looked away from Toni. "Josh told everyone he was getting a new mommy of his own. Some of the children believed him, but others kept taunting him. Today he had enough of it and pushed one of the boys hard enough to knock him down. The child wasn't hurt, but Mary

Oliver said he came close to hitting his head on a metal slide. He could have been seriously hurt."

"What does Josh have to say about what happened?"

"Not much. He doesn't seem to understand what all the fuss is about, since no one was hurt."

"Josh apparently told the same story at his Bible study class, except there he said he was getting this supposed new mommy right away."

David looked up, surprised. "Why didn't you tell me this before?"

"I just heard about it at choir practice tonight. I told the person who said it I didn't know where Josh got such an idea and said it isn't worth repeating."

David shook his head. "The damage had already been done, I'm afraid, and it's all my fault. There's something about this you don't know. I should have told you, but. . ."

Toni shivered under the intensity of David's gaze, and her heart beat faster as she waited for him to speak. "I'm listening," she prompted.

David's jaw muscle tightened. "This is hard to talk about. Bear with me, and I'll try to get through it."

He took a deep breath and glanced at Toni. "Jean wanted me to leave the army when Josh was born, but I was up for a big promotion, so I stayed in. I was overseas when Jean got sick, and I blame myself for not being there when she needed me. She worried more about the children than herself. The sicker she got, the more she worried about them. Her mother and stepfather loved the children, but they let them do more or less as they pleased. Everything just got worse. . . ." David paused for a moment, his eyes bright with unshed tears, and Toni's heart went out to him. When she put her hand in his, he grasped it and continued to speak.

"When I finally got leave to come back to the States, Jean was in the hospital. She'd been almost too weak to talk at first, but that day she seemed so much stronger, I thought God had finally granted the miracle I had prayed for so long and so hard. She wanted to see the children, so I got permission to bring them in. I lifted Josh to sit in the bed on the side away from the IV tubes. Mandy and I stood on the other side. Mandy stroked her mother's cheek, and I held Jean's hand. She asked the children what they had been doing, and they talked to her for a while. Then Jean told them she had something important to say, and she wanted them to hear and remember it."

David stopped again, and Toni felt tears coming into her own eyes as she pictured the scene. She squeezed his hand in encouragement, and he took a deep breath and began to speak more rapidly. "Jean said—her exact words— 'David, I know you'll do your best to take care of our children, but you can't do it alone. I want you to vow to me and to them to marry again and give them a new mother.' The children cried and told her they didn't want another mother, and I had to take them out of the room. I tried to tell them their mother would be all right, but that night, she went into a coma. Jean lived for several more weeks, but she never spoke again."

"Of course, you made that vow."

David released Toni's hand to wipe his eyes. "Of course I did—what else could I do? I knew the children needed me, so I left the army as soon as I could."

Toni took a deep breath. David's story had changed her perception of several things. Evelyn had more in mind than romance for David. Toni could almost hear what Evelyn must have told him. *"Toni lost her own mother at an early age. She knows what it's like, and she loves children. She would make Josh and Mandy a wonderful stepmother. . . ."*

"So you came to Rockdale to find a mother for your children," Toni said flatly.

David shook his head. "I couldn't leave them with the Websters, and I couldn't think of a better place than Rockdale for us to put down new roots. I've never spoken of that day with the children, and I'm not sure Josh remembers it. I thought he told his classmates he was getting a new mommy because of what happened the first day of school."

David spoke so sincerely, so obviously from his heart, that Toni felt moved to respond the same way. "I wasn't going to tell you this, but I think Josh does remember. The first day I met the children, he asked me if I was his new mommy."

David stared at Toni. "I had no idea—what did you tell him?"

"I asked Josh if he wanted a new mommy, and he said no, he wanted his old mommy to come back from heaven. I acknowledged how much he must miss her, then I told him that heaven is a wonderful place and that she is happy there. That seemed to satisfy him."

"You always seem to know the right thing, while I. . ."

David broke off, despair mirrored on his face. "I want to be a good father, but I don't seem to know how. I don't know how to deal with my son."

Moved by his anguish, Toni put her hand on his arm. "Things aren't that bad. Mary Oliver can help us with Josh."

David looked surprised. "Did you say 'us'?"

"Us," she repeated. "I love Josh, too, you know."

"Oh, Toni. . ."

David pulled Toni into his arms and hugged her almost breathless, then drew back slightly and touched her cheek with the back of his hand.

"I don't know how I would manage without you."

"Very well, I imagine." Toni's voice sounded strange in her ears, and she realized she was trembling.

"We both know better."

David drew her close again, and with her head against his chest, Toni heard the steady beating of his heart. He stroked her hair and traced the line of her chin, then he kissed her tenderly. In response, Toni put her arms around his neck and hugged him briefly before drawing back.

"Thanks," David said huskily.

Toni smiled. "For what?"

David stood. "For everything—for being you—for being here for me."

"And the children," she added.

David regarded Toni with the intent look she had never quite understood. "How willing are you to help Josh?"

"What?"

"If you want to help my son, make his story come true. Marry me."

Toni felt her world spinning out of control. "I can't."

David's face clouded. "Why?"

"There's something you should know about me, too. Years before you vowed to marry again, I vowed never to marry at all."

"Evelyn told me about your vow and the reason behind it. But you must know I could never hurt you the way your father hurt your mother."

Toni stood and went to the front door. "I think you should go now."

David looked baffled. "I don't understand you, Toni."

"Sometimes, neither do I. Good night, David."

He lingered at the door. "If you change your mind. . ."

I won't. Toni almost voiced the words but stopped. *Don't say anything you'll regret later,* something warned her.

"Good night, David," she repeated.

∞

The next two days, Toni vacillated between hoping David would call her and fearing he might. She reviewed all the times they had been together and everything that had happened between them from the beginning.

Toni admitted she had been falling in love with David all along, even though she'd denied it. Had he asked her to marry him in any other way or at another time, she might have given him a different answer. She loved his children and wanted the best for them, but she also knew it would not be fair to them or to her if their father married her only to give them a mother.

What should I have done that I didn't?

It was not a question Toni could answer on her own, and during her quiet time on Saturday, Toni reflected on the degree to which she had let God guide her decisions. When she prayed, Toni knew she had a tendency to ask for her own will to be done rather than allowing the Holy Spirit to guide her. Tears filled her eyes as Toni recalled the many things she had stubbornly held on to rather than turning them over to God.

On a day like this, rote prayers had no meaning. Toni sank to her knees and shared her heart with the only One whose help was always there.

"Lord, You know why I made that vow not to marry. You know how much I was hurt from all the bad things that happened to me."

"Yes, Child. Give it all to Me, and I will heal your heart."

"Lord, if You mean for me to be David's wife, even though he doesn't love me, I will. And if the answer is no, grant me Your peace."

"My peace you always have. My grace is sufficient. Trust Me."

"I want to, Lord. Help me."

"I will, My child."

Chapter 20

Even though Toni had dismissed David's proposal of marriage, she realized he could never be out of her life as long as they both lived in Rockdale. In such a small town, avoiding David altogether was impossible, especially since she intended to maintain a relationship with his children. Not only would David and Josh and Mandy never be completely out of her sight, they would remain in her mind and heart. And at the moment, Toni was concerned about Josh.

Is he really in danger of being expelled, or is David overreacting? Toni glanced at her watch and decided it was not too late to call Mary Oliver.

Her friend answered on the first ring and did not seem surprised to receive Toni's call. "Hi, Toni. I suppose you heard what happened to Josh."

"Yes, but I thought we had an agreement that you'd let me know if Josh got into serious trouble."

"I would have, but the way things developed, I didn't have time. I knew you had choir practice that night, and I figured David Trent would tell you, anyway."

"He did, but from what David said, the child Josh hit wasn't hurt. I can't believe he's in danger of expulsion."

"Unfortunately, he is. The Rockdale school board adopted a zero tolerance policy a couple of years ago. Teachers are expected to enforce each part of every rule, no matter the circumstances. It doesn't help that the boy Josh knocked down is Cody Marshall, a nephew of the school board president. Sam Marshall called me at home that night to say if Josh so much as touches another child, out he goes."

"David is really upset about this. He had talked to Josh about controlling his temper and thought everything would be all right, but apparently when someone pushes Josh, he pushes back."

"Shoves back is more like it. I don't have any magic solution, but Josh might listen to you. In case you didn't know it, the little guy is quite attached to you."

"I suppose I can try," Toni said.

"One more thing—I hear that you're seeing a lot of Josh's father. That can't be anything but good for all of you."

If you only knew what happened that night, you'd never say that. "Don't believe everything you hear. Good night, Mary—and thanks."

Her conversation with Mary had only confirmed Toni's belief she should maintain her relationship with David's children, at least until their aunt returned home—or their father came up with a more willing candidate to be their new mommy.

∞

Despite everything that had happened, Toni wanted David to follow through on his promise to bring the children back to Community for Bible study. To let him know he should still do so, Toni decided to call the children and remind them she wanted to see them at church the next day. The telephone at the condo rang four times before David's recorded voice invited her to leave a message.

"This is Toni. I hope you've had a great day today. I'll look for you all at Bible study tomorrow morning."

Her message was short and to the point—and she prayed it would be heeded.

∞

Toni was a few minutes late arriving at Community Church Sunday morning. When she spotted David's truck in the parking lot, she offered a prayer of thanks that he had not let what happened between them keep him and the children from Bible study.

When Toni entered the Seekers class, a discussion about grief was well under way. Without looking at David, she slipped into a chair beside Linda Travers. When one Seeker said he had always heard grief was sinful, Linda pointed out that Jesus was without sin, yet He wept with Mary and Martha over the death of Lazarus.

"Jesus expressed grief at other times, too," Greg said. "Let's look at those scriptures." After a thirty-minute discussion, Greg summarized the main points. "Grief is a normal reaction to tragedy and death, but it doesn't last forever—and God is always there, ready to wipe away every tear."

"If we let Him," said Susan Harmon, Greg's wife. "Some people hold on to their grief until it beats them down and wears them out."

"I like what Psalm 30 verse 5 says about how joy comes in the morning," Linda said.

"That's right, 'weeping may endure for a night, but joy cometh in the morning,'" Greg quoted the King James Version.

"That's it." Linda turned to Toni. "Isn't there an anthem about that?"

"Yes—it's called 'Joy in the Morning.' In fact, the choir is singing it this morning—and I'll be late if I don't go now."

And if I leave now, David won't have to speak to me.

When Toni entered the choir loft and saw David sitting in the congregation with his children, she felt a strange tug at her heart. *They could so easily be my family.* But they weren't. In keeping an old vow, she had refused both David and his children.

Toni stood with the rest of the choir to sing about the heavenly joy that comes in the morning after a night of weeping.

Let David take this message to heart, Lord. He's had more than his share of weeping. It's time for him to reclaim the joy of his salvation.

When Ted Brown had asked Toni to present an offertory solo for that

Sunday, she had chosen music that spoke to her own heart. But when she rose to sing that morning, she realized it not only echoed that day's Bible study, but also had a message David needed to hear.

Lord, I thank You for what You have done for me. Help me sing to Your glory.

With Janet Brown accompanying her on the piano, Toni began to sing "A Day of New Beginnings." The words of the song spoke of a new life in Jesus—of God making all things new.

"Amen!" someone said when the last piano note faded.

Amen, Toni's heart echoed.

∞

Toni did not expect to see David and the children after the service, but they were waiting for her when she emerged from the choir room.

"You sang pretty," Josh said.

"I'm glad you liked it," Toni said.

"That was a cool anthem. I might join the junior choir," Mandy said. "They go on tours and do stuff."

"I never had a chance to do that myself, but it sounds like fun." *And a great way for you to make new friends.*

"We're gonna take a picnic to Soda Park. Come with us, Toni," Josh said.

Toni looked at David. *Is this his idea or yours?*

"Everyone wants you to come," David said pointedly. "We're going home to change clothes. We'll pick you up in twenty minutes."

There you go, giving me orders again. I should say no for that reason alone. But Toni had a reason to go—she needed to have a talk with Josh.

"All right. Can I bring anything?"

"No, thanks. Mrs. Tarpley insisted on doing it all."

∞

"Slow down, Daddy. We're s'posed to turn off right up there," Josh said when David neared DeSoto State Park's main entrance.

"I know, but the park has over five thousand acres. Today we're going to a place you've never been."

Leaving the truck in a turnout, they hiked down a fairly steep trail. As they went, David pointed out hickory, black and chestnut oaks, pine, poplar, dogwood, and sassafras trees he had learned to identify as a Boy Scout.

At the bottom of the hill, they came to a quiet pool fed by a small waterfall several hundred yards away. With no rain in the last few days, the waterfall was more of a trickle than a torrent, but the pool, outlined by oak leaf hydrangeas and lichen- and moss-covered rocks of all sizes, was beautiful.

"Stay away from that poison oak," David warned. "Those red winterberries are good to eat, but watch out for the thorns."

David set the picnic hamper on a large rock in the clearing. "I hope you like fried chicken and potato salad," he told Toni. "Mrs. Tarpley chose and cooked the menu, and Mandy packed our sodas."

"I put in the cookies," Josh said.

"The ones you didn't eat, that is," Mandy returned.

Toni smiled. *Mandy will always tease her little brother, but she seems much gentler with him, at least.*

After they finished eating, David handed the children small buckets and told them to fill them with small, flat rocks. "I'll teach you how to make them skip across the water later."

"Come on, Josh. I'll help you look. Let's walk down the path and see what we can find," Toni said.

Mandy started to follow them, but David called her back. "You can help me look around here." Toni understood his unspoken message: *I trust you to talk to Josh alone.*

"We can find more, can't we, Toni?" Josh tugged her hand impatiently. "Hurry up!"

Toni let Josh lead her down the path to a place where many small rocks had washed up beside the pool. Josh picked up a few small pebbles, then he found a larger rock and threw it at a nearby tree. A startled blue jay flew from one of the limbs, scolding loudly.

"Pow! Take that, you rat!" Josh picked up an even larger rock, but Toni stayed his hand. "Never throw rocks like that. You almost hit that bird. You could hurt an animal or a person very badly doing that."

Josh dropped the stone and dug the toe of his sneaker into the loamy soil. "I was just playin'. I didn' mean to hurt nothin'."

"I know that, Josh. You weren't thinking just then. But sometimes when you get really mad, you might forget and do things you shouldn't."

Josh looked up at Toni with tears in his eyes. "Cody's uncle says I'm a bad boy."

Toni knelt and put her arms around Josh's thin body. "No, you're not. Getting mad doesn't make you bad, but you should never let the way you feel inside make you do bad things."

"I can't help it," Josh said.

"Yes, you can. When you feel yourself getting mad, just walk away, and nothing bad will happen."

"You mean I should put myself in time-out?"

"Time-out?"

"That's where Miss Mary makes us go when we do something wrong."

"She sends you out of the room?"

"No, there's this special chair in the corner behind a screen. We hafta sit there until we get over bein' bad."

"That's a wonderful idea, Josh—giving yourself a time-out if you get mad. I'm proud of you for figuring that out."

Josh grinned, apparently proud of himself as well. "Hurry up, or Mandy and

Daddy'll find more skippin' rocks."

Josh wants to be good, Lord. Help us show him how.

∞

"Come on," David called a few moments later. "You should have enough rocks by now."

"I don't know how to do it," Josh said. "Teach me, Daddy."

"Neither do I," Toni admitted.

David demonstrated his skill first by sending a pebble skipping in graceful arcs across the pool. Then he showed each of the children how to hold and throw their stones for maximum distance. Mandy caught on quickly and began to help Josh.

When Toni's first few efforts sank rather than skipped, David put his hand over hers and guided her through the correct motions. Feeling the familiar, almost electrical jolt that accompanied any close contact with David, she moved away.

"Now try it on your own," he said.

The stone hopped once, twice, then sank out of sight. "I guess I don't do very well on my own."

Toni read the question in David's eyes. "Nothing personal, of course," she added.

David glanced toward the children, who had moved some distance away and had their backs to them. Satisfied they were absorbed in skipping stones, he turned to Toni.

"It seems every time we come up here, I manage to upset you."

"I'm not upset."

"Maybe you aren't now, but ever since the other night—"

"I want you to know that Josh and I had a good talk just now," Toni put in before David could say anything else. "I think he really can tell when he's about to lose his temper. He told me he's going to put himself in a time-out when that happens. I think that's real progress. You might want to talk to him about it yourself."

"Thanks. I will. You're so good at handling things like that. I'm not. I'm no good at saying how I feel. What I should have said the other night—what I'm trying to say now—is that the minute I saw you, I knew you were special. Sure, I was glad you and the kids got along, but even if I didn't have them, I'd still want you."

David took her hands in his and spoke slowly. "I love you, Toni, and I want to marry you. For my sake, not theirs."

She felt breathless, as if she had been underwater a long time and needed air. David was looking at her in the familiar, intent way. She now understood its meaning, but it was hard to comprehend that David loved her. When Toni finally managed to speak, her voice was a breathy whisper. "You do?"

David nodded and squeezed her hands. "I know you don't love me yet, but—"

She raised her chin and looked David in the eye. "Who says I don't?"

234

He looked stunned. "I thought you did."

"I never said that—you assumed it."

David reached out to draw Toni close. "Say it, then."

"You're giving me an order again," she murmured. She pulled back to smile at him. "But in spite of that and everything else, I love you, David."

He kissed her deeply once, then again and again. He finally released Toni with a shout that reverberated through the trees and brought the children running toward them.

Josh's eyes were wide. "What is it, Daddy?"

"Did you see a snake?" Mandy asked anxiously.

"No, kids. That was a happy shout. I want you to meet someone."

He pointed to Toni, and Josh and Mandy exchanged puzzled glances. "We already know Toni," Josh said.

"Yes, but she's going to be Mrs. David Trent. Josh and Mandy—meet your new mommy."

When the meaning of their father's words sank in, Josh grabbed Toni's knees and hung on for dear life, while Mandy gave her a more subdued hug. "I'm so glad," she said.

Josh let go of Toni to jump up and down. "I told everybody I was gonna get a new mommy!" He stood still and looked at Toni. "I'm glad it's not Mrs. Tarpley."

"So am I," David said.

"Amen," added Toni.

And thank You, Lord, for directing all our paths to this day.

Epilogue

On a sunny Saturday in early March, after her leisurely exploration of Mexico, Evelyn Trent returned to Rockdale for the first time since Christmas. Evelyn had declared that nothing could keep her from Rockdale when her brother and her former ward exchanged their marriage vows.

David and the children met Evelyn at the Chattanooga airport and took her to her house. Since David had to take Josh and Mandy to their activities that afternoon, David excused himself soon after he brought Evelyn's luggage inside.

"Thirty minutes?" David asked Toni.

"Better make it forty-five."

"What's that all about?" Evelyn asked.

"Our schedules. Sometimes it seems we're going in different directions."

"From what they said on the way home, Josh and Mandy are involved in a lot of different things. I hope they also have time to just be kids."

Toni nodded. "They do. Many of the planned activities revolve around their church groups, and both play seasonal sports. They've made friends and seem happy."

"I see so much difference in the children—and their father—since you came into their lives."

"It's God's work, not mine. Once David realized he could give his guilt and grief to the Lord, he found real peace. The children's involvement in the church has done wonders for them, too."

"That's exactly what I'd hoped. I couldn't be prouder of them—and of you, Toni."

"I had a good role model." Evelyn's praise embarrassed Toni, and she quickly changed the subject. "If you feel up to a short ride, I want to show you something."

"I've already traveled several thousand miles today. I suppose I can handle a few more."

A few minutes later, Toni drove out Rockdale Boulevard, bypassed the gated community near Warren Mountain, and turned onto a street where several new houses were in various stages of construction.

Evelyn expressed her surprise. "When did all this happen? I didn't know anything like this was out here in the woods."

"How could you? You've hardly been here since you retired."

"That's going to change. I've enjoyed all my travels, but I plan to stay home for a long while."

Toni turned into a cul-de-sac and stopped in front of a two-story red brick house at the end of the street. A SOLD banner stretched across the builder's sign in the front yard.

"Here we are."

Evelyn gaped, as close to being speechless as Toni had seen her since her retirement dinner. "This is yours?"

Toni nodded. "Ours and Rockdale Federal's."

"David told me when I was here for Christmas you were thinking of building, but he never said a word about this all the way home from the airport."

"That's because the children don't know about it yet. We just closed the deal the day before yesterday, and we want to surprise them."

"I don't know about Josh and Mandy, but you've certainly surprised me."

Toni stopped on the brick walkway and used her hands to sketch their landscaping plans. "I want boxwoods for both sides of the walk. In the beds in front of the house, David will put in azaleas and rhododendrons, butterfly bushes, hydrangeas, and chrysanthemums. This fall, we'll plant lots of daffodil and tulip bulbs."

Evelyn looked amused. "Those are mighty ambitious plans from someone who didn't know a tulip from a toadstool a year ago."

"You can thank David for that. He's been poring over catalogs and trying to teach me a few gardening basics."

"He's always liked digging in the dirt, and I know he missed doing that in the army."

They reached the covered entryway, and Toni unlocked the leaded-paned front door and ushered Evelyn into the stone-tiled foyer.

Evelyn looked into the living and dining rooms flanking the foyer, then her gaze followed the sweep of the spiral stairway. "I had no idea you and David could afford anything so grand."

"Neither did we. We've been looking at houses for several months, but most were either too small or too expensive. David sold construction insurance to the builder. He told David he would reduce the price for a quick sale and accepted our offer."

Toni led Evelyn through the downstairs rooms. "The kitchen is large enough to eat in, and there's a covered porch behind it that we'll screen in. There's the master bedroom—the other three are upstairs."

After walking through the second-floor bedrooms and a large room over the garage destined to become the children's playroom, Toni and Evelyn returned to the foyer.

"That was quite a tour. I must say I'm quite impressed by the David Trent mansion," Evelyn said.

Toni smiled. "The Evelyn Trent house once seemed like a mansion to me. Neither David nor I have owned a house before, and we both felt led to this one.

We want to make it a true home for Josh and Mandy and, God willing, any children David and I have together."

"I'm sure it will be. God certainly had a hand in bringing you and David to Rockdale at the right time."

"With a little help from a certain social worker," Toni said.

Evelyn sighed. "You'll always think what you like about that, I suppose. The main thing is you were finally able to rescind your vow to never marry."

"For a long time, I used it as a shield against the pain of what happened to my mother. When I asked God to show me the way I should go, He led me to make a far better vow to David."

"I believe Jean would agree that David couldn't have found a better mother for her children. I'm glad the Websters are coming to the wedding. Josh and Mandy should keep in touch with their mother's family."

"We agree. The children will go to Virginia for a visit this summer."

The doorbell rang, startling them both. Toni opened the door to David, who put his arm around her waist.

"Has Toni shown you around?" he asked Evelyn.

"Yes. It's a beautiful house, and you are both—" Evelyn broke off, choked by sudden emotion.

"We are all truly blessed," David said.

"Amen and amen," added Toni.

Anita's Fortune

*To Carol Benjamin, Peggy Farmer, Lee Marsh, Edna Waits, and Ellen Woodle,
fellow writers and faithful friends, with affection and appreciation
for everything we have shared through the years.*
Muchas gracias *to Marjorie Masterson,
Spanish teacher and former exchange teacher to Barranquilla, Colombia,
for her considerable expertise.*

Chapter 1

"Tell me about Christmas when you were a little girl, Mama."

Anita Muños de Sanchez smiled at her daughter, Juanita, whose dark eyes shone in anticipation of the story she never tired of hearing.

In the tones of "Once upon a time," Anita began to recite how their house in Colombia filled with fun and laughter, and aunts and uncles and grandparents brought gifts of candy and books and clothes. Her mother cooked for days, making the special treats they had at no other time of the year. They went to church for special programs and made a manger scene in the house to celebrate the Christ Child's birth. Then, the day after Christmas, Anita and her brother took some of their gifts to an orphanage as a way of giving thanks for everything they had received.

"I wish we could have Christmas like that now," Juanita always said at the end of the story.

"We have our own special Christmas, and one day you will be telling your little girl stories about making cookies for the people in the homeless shelter and wearing pretty wings as an angel in the pageant."

"I wish I had aunts and uncles and grandmothers to talk about," Juanita said.

"You can tell your little girl about all our friends at church," Anita said. "For now, it's time for prayers and bed."

Later, sitting alone in the living room, illumined only by the lights on their small tree, Anita recalled the last Christmas she had spent at her childhood home. For the first eighteen years of her life, Christmas had been a happy time. Surrounded by a loving family who understood the true meaning of the celebration of the birth of the Christ Child, she had nothing but happy memories of the holidays, which her evangelical parents kept as true "holy days." She was willing to share the stories of those days with her daughter, but Juanita knew nothing of the tragedy that had followed the happy times.

Looking back, Anita realized the signs that all was not well had been beneath the surface for some time. Sometimes her parents quit talking when she entered the room. Strange telephone calls came at all hours, including the middle of the night. "Wrong number," her mother would say the next morning, but even after her father chose to have their home telephone number unlisted, the calls continued. Maria Borda de Muños's usually cheerful countenance often looked sad and drawn, and Ricardo Muños spent more time away from home "on business" than ever before. Yet when Anita asked them what was wrong, they assured her everything was fine. Her older brother must have noticed something strange was happening, but when she shared her concerns with him, Enrique told Anita she was imagining things.

"Study hard and do not worry about anything else," her mother told Anita when she entered her senior year at American High School. "God will care for us."

Anita liked school, and she always made good grades. Her human physiology teacher, Señora Marjorie Ledford, an exchange teacher from Virginia, took Anita aside one day and asked if she had any career plans. Everyone assumed Anita would go on to a university, as most of American High School graduates did. Some even traveled long distances to attend colleges and universities in the States, but Anita had no desire to leave Colombia.

"My brother is taking a general diploma at the Atlantico. I suppose I will do the same."

"Enrique will work in your father's warehouse business, so that is fine for him. But with your great aptitude for the biological sciences, you should consider a medical career."

Dr. Anita Muños. Anita imagined herself in a white lab coat, a stethoscope around her neck, saving lives. *Maybe I could become a medical missionary and bring the good news to many who have never heard of the Great Physician.*

However, when Anita mentioned she might like to study medicine, her parents exchanged a strange look and said they would have to look into it. A few weeks later, they told her they had enrolled her in a nursing school in Bogotá.

"If you still want to be a physician after that, we will see what can be done," her mother said.

Anita had welcomed her parents' decision; medical school would take years and years, but as a nurse, she could start helping people much sooner.

Before Anita left for her first term in a large teaching hospital in Bogatá, Ricardo Muños gave her a notebook-sized metal lockbox attached to a length of chain with a separate lock.

"Put your valuables inside this box and chain it to a heavy piece of furniture like your bed frame in such a way it cannot be easily removed. Keep the keys on a chain around your neck at all times."

"Are you sure such a thing as this is necessary?"

"I am sure. The sealed envelope inside is to be opened only in case of a dire emergency. Do you understand?"

Anita had a few pieces of heirloom jewelry she had planned to leave in her room at home, but her father told her to put them in the lockbox. She guessed the fat envelope inside contained a fairly large sum of money. The whole business made her feel uncomfortable, but Anita did as she was told. She chained the box to the metal frame of her bed in the nurses' dormitory and wore the key around her neck under her uniform.

First-year students were allowed a brief vacation the week before Christmas.

When Anita called to tell her parents when her flight would arrive, her brother answered the telephone. In a strained voice, he told her not to come home.

"Stay in Bogotá, 'Nita. I will let you know when it is safe to come here."

Anita had tried to find out what was wrong, but Enrique hung up after repeating, so urgently that she had to believe him, that she must not come home.

After the initial shock wore off, Anita called her mother's older sister, her favorite aunt. When she repeated Enrique's message, Aunt Rita told Anita it did not surprise her.

"Your parents are having problems. Enrique is right. You must stay where you are."

Anita found it impossible to consider that her parents' marriage could be in trouble, yet Aunt Rita refused to give any more information. "Can I stay at your house, then?"

"No, that cannot be." Anita heard the fear in her aunt's voice and shivered. "Stay in Bogotá," Aunt Rita said again, then hung up abruptly.

Something is going on, and I must know what.

Anita made several more vain attempts to contact her parents, both at home and her father's office, before she decided to go to Barranquilla despite being warned to stay away.

The next twenty-four hours were forever branded into Anita's memory. She had prayed for her family all the way from Bogotá to Barranquilla, yet when she saw the burned-out hulk of what had been her home and was taken to the morgue to identify the bodies, Anita felt so abandoned by God, she could not even attempt to pray.

Her family was dead, and nobody seemed to care. Certainly not the authorities, who quickly ruled her parents and brother and a servant had perished in a fire of unknown origin. She could not reach any of her relatives; her aunts and uncles and grandparents seemed to have disappeared into thin air.

Everyone was suddenly afraid of Anita, including her oldest friends. After quick expressions of sympathy, they closed their doors to her. Anita went to Señora Ledford's apartment near the American school, but the doorman told her the teachers had left for the holidays. Pastor Robales refused to take her in even temporarily, advising her to leave the city immediately. "Go with God," he added as he closed his door. Anita realized the bitter truth. The life she had always known was gone forever, and she had nowhere to turn.

When Anita tried to find out who was investigating the fire, she was told the case was closed. On her way out of the police headquarters building, a detective took her aside and offered chilling advice.

"Leave Colombia as soon as you can, señorita. The people who did this to your parents and brother will not rest until they kill you, too."

"What people? My parents did nothing wrong. I have done nothing—"

"Ricardo Muños did not cooperate with some very influential people—that is all I can say. Trust me in this. You are in great danger. You must get away immediately."

Anita flew back to Bogotá as soon as she could get a flight. That night, she retrieved the lockbox from beneath her bed and left the nurses' dormitory without saying good-bye to anyone. Instinctively, Anita realized others could also be in danger because of her.

Let them think what they will. I will not pass this way again.

An hour later, in the privacy of a stall in the ladies' rest room at the Bogotá airport, Anita opened the lock box. Her eyes blurred with tears when she saw her father's familiar handwriting on the envelope. *Soledad por Emergencia.*

With trembling fingers, she had opened it. . . .

∞

"Mama!"

Jolted back to the present, Anita turned to see her daughter holding the infant Jesus that belonged to the manger scene.

"Is it time for the baby Jesus to be born yet?"

Anita glanced at her watch's luminous dial. "It is not quite midnight, but if you promise to go right back to bed, you may put Him in His crib now."

Juanita nodded. Carefully, she placed the Christ Child into the manger atop the dried grass she and Anita had gathered for the purpose. "Sleep well, Baby Jesus," she whispered.

Anita carried her daughter back to her bed and kissed her good night. "Sweet dreams, Muchacha."

"Sweet dreams to you, Mamacita," Juanita murmured drowsily.

Anita returned to the living room and glanced at the manger scene. She treasured her daughter's love for Jesus and prayed that Juanita's faith would grow as she matured, as her own had. In the dark days after her eighteenth Christmas, her belief in God had been tested as never before.

Thinking back to that time, Anita marveled at her father's foresight. His envelope contained American money, as she suspected, but beyond that, Ricardo Muños had given Anita detailed instructions on what she should do and concluded by saying she should always ask God to help her. "Remember Hebrews 13:5–6. 'He hath said, I will never leave thee, nor forsake thee. So that we may boldly say, The Lord is my helper, and I will not fear what man shall do unto me.' "

At the bottom he had added these words: *Todo se pasa. Dios no se muda.*

Anita repeated the words from St. Teresa of Avila she had memorized as a child: "Everything passes. God does not change."

Even though her life had been turned upside down, Anita still had the assurance of her faith. "Go to the American embassy in Bogotá," her father's note instructed. The officials there knew about his death and did not seem surprised to see her. They cut through the customary red tape to get her out of Colombia quickly. She would fly to the United States and be enrolled in a nursing program at an Arizona hospital.

"When can I go back to Barranquilla?" she asked.

The embassy official shook his head. "I'm afraid it may never be safe here for you, señorita. You are young, and you speak English well. You have a rare opportunity to make a new life in the United States. I advise you to take advantage of it."

I tried to do that, Anita told herself.

But the embassy hadn't warned her about men like Juan Sanchez.

Chapter 2

Anita knew she should turn off the Christmas tree lights and go to bed, but she couldn't get Juan Sanchez off her mind. She had been in Arizona for almost a year when he appeared at her apartment house and tried to engage her in conversation. She had every intention of ignoring him, just as she had other men who showed interest in her, but about that time, Anita started getting disturbing notes. Written in Spanish, they were filled with vague threats. When the authorities dismissed them as a prank and refused to take any action, she had told Juan about it.

"I am a private investigator with connections in the highest places, and I can help you," he said, and Anita believed him. Juan was handsome and charming, ten years older than Anita and a refugee from Guatemala. When she told him her family had been killed by men she suspected were big-time drug dealers, he convinced her they were probably after her, as well. However, he was willing to help her escape their clutches.

"Come with me away from this place. Here, your every move is known. I will take care of you. Trust me."

Unfortunately, she had. Juan seemed so sincere, so interested in her welfare, Anita never suspected he might have set her up. She didn't love Juan, but she was grateful for his help, and when he asked her to marry him, it seemed the best way to escape from her family's killers.

In Anita's childhood dream, she would be married in her church, surrounded by her family friends. She expected to wear a traditional white wedding gown and veil and carry her mother's bridal Bible. In reality, Juan stopped in New Mexico just long enough to get a justice of the peace to perform the hurried ceremony.

"You are safe now," Juan told her, but Anita soon realized that was not the case. Eventually, she learned the truth: Knowing Anita was the only surviving child of wealthy parents, Juan had thought she must surely have a fortune stashed away somewhere, and he wanted to get his hands on it. They never stayed in one place very long. Sometimes Juan had money, but more often he did not. When he drank, he had a tendency to become violent, and occasionally he struck her.

Long before their first anniversary, Anita realized marrying Juan had been a terrible mistake.

Except for Juanita.

The child sleeping in the next room had been a gift from God. Loving and caring for Juanita had kept Anita going during the long months after Juan had been sent to prison.

Juanita had just begun to walk then, and she had no memory of her father. When she was old enough to ask about her daddy, Anita told her he had to go away for a while and would come back one day.

She both counted and dreaded the days until he would be released on parole. Then, a week before Juan would have come home, a violent riot broke out in his prison block, and Juan was killed. Anita tried to console herself that he might have been trying to stop the riot, since a man about to be released would have no reason to cause trouble. In any case, Anita Muños de Sanchez had become a widow with a four-year-old daughter to support. She told Juanita the father she didn't remember was in heaven, and they were going to live in San Antonio, Texas. In San Antonio, Anita had found a nursing school that would let her work for her tuition while she finished the requirements to become a registered nurse.

She had found something else there—a church much like the one she had known in Colombia, whose members accepted and supported Anita and her daughter. Now Juanita was a happy and healthy first-grader.

I have much to be thankful for this Christmas. May I never forget my many blessings.

∞

Anita had not meant to, but she fell asleep in her chair. When she awoke, the lights still burned on the little Christmas tree, and Juanita was tearing into the small store of presents beneath it.

"Look at my huggy doll, Mama! It's just what I wanted."

Anita grabbed her daughter and held her close. "And you're my huggy doll!"

The soft-bodied doll had long black hair just like Juanita's. She wore a blue print dress, detachable blue shoes, and a permanent smile. "I can't wait to show Dora to Beth," Juanita said. "Can I go over there now?"

"Wait until after breakfast. So you named your huggy doll Dora?"

"Yes, 'cause I just adore her. I picked out her name a long time ago."

"Dora is also a short form of 'Theodora,' which means 'gift of God,'" Anita said. "Remember the Bible verse you learned last week?"

Juanita wrinkled her brow. "Something about every good and perfect gift."

"Close. 'Every good gift and every perfect gift is from above.' That's from the book of James. And what is the greatest Christmas gift ever?"

Juanita pointed to the manger scene. "Jesus. Everybody brought Him gifts, but He's the bestest present."

Anita hugged her daughter again and wished, as she so often did, that her parents had lived to see their precious grandchild. But of course, if they had lived, Anita wouldn't have come to be in this place.

"You haven't opened your presents, Mama. The one in the red paper's from me."

Anita knew Beth's mother had helped Juanita shop; she was not surprised to see the white sweater.

"This will be perfect to wear on a chilly winter night. Thank you."

"Dora and I are hungry," Juanita said a few minutes later.

"So am I. Which do you want, pancakes or waffles?"

Juanita held up her doll. "Dora says she likes pancakes best."

"Then pancakes it will be. You can help mix the batter."

∽

Beth lived a few hundred yards away in the next building of their apartment complex, but Anita never let Juanita walk there or back alone. She visited for a while with Beth's parents, Tim and Amy Sherrod, who were also fellow church members, then excused herself.

"Call me when you're ready for Juanita to come home."

"We'll drop her off on our way to my folks' house," Amy said.

Back at her apartment, Anita cleared away the Christmas wrappings, leaving the opened gifts displayed around the tree. She had just picked up a book of devotions, a gift from her nursing supervisor, when the telephone rang.

"Sanchez residence," Anita said.

"Mrs. Juan Sanchez?" a male voice asked.

Anita drew her breath in sharply. She had been careful not to use Juan's first name in San Antonio; very few people knew it. "Who is this?"

"A friend of Juan's. We need to talk."

His voice grated like fingernails on a chalkboard, and Anita felt a chill of fear. "I do not talk to people I do not know."

"You should know me. Juan Sanchez was my partner."

"Partner in what?"

"Like I said, we need to talk."

"About what?"

"You sure do ask a lot of questions. I'll be there in fifteen minutes."

"I do not want to see you," Anita said, but the caller had already hung up.

She replaced the receiver and brought her hands together in an attitude of prayer. Anita did not recognize the man's voice, but whoever he was, she wanted nothing to do with anyone who claimed to be Juan's partner.

As far as she knew, Juan worked alone—if deception and stealing could be called "work." He never told Anita where he was going or what he was going to do. When the police came to arrest Juan on a theft charge, he denied any wrongdoing. It was all a misunderstanding, he insisted. But the evidence had been enough to bring him to trial and persuade the jury hearing the case and the presiding judge to the contrary.

Through it all, Anita never heard Juan or anyone else say he had not acted alone.

What could this man want?

Anita glanced at the clock. Whoever he was, she did not want Juanita to see him. She probably had an hour before the Sherrods brought her daughter back home. If he really got there in fifteen minutes, he should be gone before Juanita returned.

Even though she expected it, the sound of the doorbell startled Anita. Through the peephole in the front door, she saw a fair-skinned, sandy-haired Americano of average height and weight. Even after years in the United States, Anita still automatically registered everyone she met as Latino or Americano. In all the places she and Juan had lived, there had been many Latinos. This man was a stranger, and as Anita opened the door as far as the chain lock allowed, she wondered if Juan ever had anything to do with him.

"Feliz Navidad, Señora Sanchez. I trust you are having a pleasant holiday."

Anita spoke through the narrow opening in the door. "I do not know who you are or what you want. I doubt my husband knew you, either."

"Oh, he knew me all right. Like I said on the phone, we worked together. My name is Bill Rankin; I need to talk to you."

Bill Rankin. The name stirred a faint near-memory, but she could not attach it to anything substantial. "You have five minutes. After that, I expect you to leave."

"I understand."

Anita unchained the door to admit Bill Rankin. Observing people had become second nature to her from work as an emergency room nurse, and Anita noted he had watery blue eyes and a faint, crescent-shaped scar over his left eye, possibly made by a broken beer bottle.

She remained standing, determined to make this man's visit short and uncomfortable.

"What really brings you here, Mr. Rankin?"

"Cut right to the chase, don't you? Juan warned me you were that way."

"You have less than five minutes now. I am listening."

"Maybe we ought to sit down."

"No. Get to the point."

Rankin's eyes searched the living room, and too late Anita realized her daughter's gifts were still on display. "Juan said you had a kid. Must be four or five years old by now, right?"

Anita swallowed hard and hoped Rankin didn't notice the fear she felt for Juanita. "Whatever you have to tell me, do so and leave."

Rankin shrugged. "The fact of the matter is, I never got my cut from our last partnership. Juan said you would give it to me."

Anita tried to disguise her alarm. "I have no idea what you are talking about. My husband is dead. He left me nothing."

"Yeah, I heard about that prison riot—tough way to go. But Juan Sanchez didn't die broke."

"I told you I know nothing. I want you to leave now."

Rankin picked up a Bible puzzle book from beneath the Christmas tree. "Juan said you went to church a lot. Last I heard, lying is still a sin. I believe you need to think real hard about that, Anita."

His use of her first name reddened her cheeks, but Anita forced herself to speak calmly. "I am not lying. You have not told me what it is you think Juan owes you."

Rankin's lips compressed. "No, think about it. Juan Sanchez cheated me out of a fortune. We both had a key to the storage unit where we stashed it. We was going to split it after things calmed down, but then I got collared on a parole violation and Juan got sent up on some other robbery thing. I got out last week and went to the unit, but my key didn't work. The manager said a dark-haired woman cleaned it out months ago. The way I figure, it had to be you. Half that stash is mine, and I intend to get it."

Anita shook her head. "I never rented a storage unit, and I do not have what you want. You are mistaken."

"And you're mistaken if you think you can get away with this, lady. Juan said his wife was smart. If that's so, you'll cooperate with me."

Despite her inner turmoil, Anita spoke with calm assurance. "I cannot give you what I do not have. Please leave now."

"All right, but don't think this is over. I'll be back. One way or another, I intend to get what's mine."

Anita closed and chained the door behind Bill Rankin and leaned against it. Her heart pounded and her head swam from the enormity of what she had just heard.

Bill Rankin obviously believed she had collected some sort of fortune her husband had denied him. Yet, Anita had told the truth. She had never known Juan to rent a storage unit, nor had she taken anything from one.

"One way or another, I intend to get what's mine," the man had said.

The doorbell rang and Anita shuddered, fearing Rankin had returned.

"Mama, let me in," Juanita called out. Relieved, Anita unchained the door and swept her daughter into her arms. Then she had a chilling thought: *Bill Rankin hasn't been gone very long. He could have seen Juanita coming to the apartment door.*

Dear Lord, show me what I must do to keep my daughter safe.

≪≫

After Juanita went to bed, Anita assessed her situation. Bill Rankin was convinced Juan Sanchez's widow had something of value that belonged to him. In an attempt to get it, he could be more than willing to harm Juanita. Calling the police would be a waste of time. Even if the authorities took his implied threats seriously, Bill Rankin had not actually harmed them, nor had he broken any law. By the time he did so, it might be too late.

As she always did when faced with a problem, Anita turned to the scriptures.

Her Bible still lay open to the second chapter of Matthew's Gospel, where she had read Juanita the story of the coming of the wise men, ending with the twelfth verse. She continued reading the passage, which suddenly took on new significance:

> *And when they were departed, behold, the angel of the Lord appeareth to Joseph in a dream, saying, Arise, and take the young child and his mother, and flee into Egypt, and be thou there until I bring thee word: for Herod will seek the young child to destroy him. When he arose, he took the young child and his mother by night, and departed into Egypt.*

Anita buried her head in her hands and prayed earnestly. *Be with me, Lord, and help me protect my child. Grant me the wisdom to know what to do and the strength to carry it through.*

Chapter 3

The next few days were the longest in Anita's life. With God's help, she had made a good, secure home for her daughter in San Antonio. Now, a stranger from her husband's past threatened to destroy everything. He would be back; that was certain. She had no choice—she and Juanita would have to leave. . .and soon.

But where could they go?

Anita still kept her valuables in the lockbox her father had given her. Of its original contents, only a few pieces of jewelry remained and those only because Anita had refused to let Juan pawn them. She had a small amount of cash on hand and not much more in a savings account in the credit union of the hospital where she worked. The rent on her furnished apartment was not due until mid-January. Her ten-year-old automobile had long since been paid for, although she had used part of her reserve cash to keep it running. The car could hold their absolute necessities; the rest of their belongings would go to the homeless shelter supported by her church.

Anita had enough monetary resources to leave, but she lacked a destination. She had no desire to return to any of the places she and Juan had lived before he went to prison. It was better to make a fresh start. She and Juanita would head east, but no one in San Antonio must know the real reason.

"We are going to take a trip in the car to a new place," she told Juanita when nearly all the arrangements had been made.

"Can Beth come with us?"

"No, sweetie. We might not be back for a while. You can take as many of your toys as you can fit in this duffel bag. We will give what is left to the boys and girls at the rescue mission."

Juanita was accustomed to giving away her old toys, but she found it hard to part with some of the newer ones. In the end, Anita let her pack another small suitcase with things she could play with while they traveled.

Anita gave the apartment manager notice she would not be renewing her lease and resigned from her hospital job by telephone. She left the phone connected, however. If Bill Rankin called again, she did not want him to know she had left town. She told her pastor and Beth's parents that she and Juanita were going to visit relatives and might not return to San Antonio. They were surprised, but no one seemed to doubt her. The last thing Anita needed was for someone to report her and Juanita missing—and then to be found by Bill Rankin.

Finally, all the arrangements were in place. In the predawn darkness of the Saturday after Christmas, Anita dressed her sleeping daughter and carried her to the car. For the second time in her life, Anita Muños de Sanchez headed into the unknown, guided only by her faith.

∞

"Where are we going, Mama?" Juanita asked when she awoke.

"Toward the sunrise," Anita replied.

"Where's that?"

"I can show you on the map when we stop for breakfast."

A hundred miles later, Anita pulled into a fast-food restaurant and opened the map she had marked the night before. "We are here," she said, "and this is where we are going."

Anita's finger traced the route, east on Interstate 10 through Houston and Baton Rouge, then northeast on Interstate 59 and Interstate 81 into Virginia.

"Will we get there today?" Juanita asked.

"No, it will take several days."

Juanita held out her huggy doll. "Dora's hungry."

"So am I. We will have a nice breakfast."

∞

As mile after weary mile unfolded, Anita began to doubt the wisdom of attempting to travel all the way to Virginia. She had picked that destination in part because she remembered it was the home state of Señora Ledford, her American schoolteacher, but mostly because it was so far from any connection with Juan Sanchez.

What Juanita had initially welcomed as an adventure turned into an endurance contest after the novelty of travel lost its appeal. Anita drove as many hours each day as she dared, stopping only to eat, sleep, and buy gas. In that manner, she reached the mountainous terrain between Birmingham and Chattanooga shortly after noon on the third day. Anita turned off the interstate in a steady, cold rain and pulled into a truck stop for gas. When she went inside to pay the cashier, she overheard truckers talking about the ice storm that was rapidly working its way south.

"How is the road to Chattanooga?" she asked one of them.

"Probably not very good, ma'am. A semi's already jackknifed outside Chattanooga, and it wouldn't surprise me if they closed the interstate."

"Is there any other way to get there?"

"U.S. 11 runs parallel to the interstate. It's still open, but it'll probably get icy, too."

Anita dug the map from her tote bag. "Show me where we are now."

The trucker jabbed his finger at an unnamed interstate exit. "Go back over the interstate and take the first left. It'll get you to Chattanooga, but it has a sight more curves than the interstate."

Anita thanked him and returned to the car. She had planned to get at least as far as Chattanooga that night, and since the rain had let up, she decided to use the alternative road.

"Where are we now, Mama?" Juanita asked when she saw they weren't returning to the interstate.

"I am not sure, sweetie, but we are headed in the right direction to get to Chattanooga."

A few minutes later, Anita thought the rain had stopped and turned off her windshield wipers. Soon she realized the precipitation had merely changed to sleet, which was forming a thin sheet of ice over everything. Anita had driven on many mountain roads before but never when they were coated with ice. She ran the blower on the defroster at full speed and turned the wipers back on, but they were fighting a losing battle against the gathering ice.

Anita weighed her options. She had seen little traffic on this road, and if she stopped, she might be stranded on it. She did not know how far Chattanooga was, but it seemed obvious she could not get there any time soon.

Ahead on the right, a state road sign pointed to Rockdale. She pulled over and finally found the town on her map. Rockdale was not as large as Fort Payne, which lay to the south, but it was the only place of any size in the vicinity.

Cautiously, Anita turned onto the Rockdale road. Even narrower than the one she had just left, it descended in a series of curves. Although the turns were well banked, the accumulating ice made them treacherous. Anita felt her car fishtailing in the first few turns and managed to steady it. Then another deeper curve caught her off guard, and she felt the car skidding. On one side, a thin guardrail separated the shoulder of the road from a sharp drop-off. On the other, a solid bank of rock rose vertically. Anita kept her foot off the brake in hopes the car might slow on its own. But the turn tightened, and when she touched the brake lightly, she felt her tires losing traction. She did not trust the fragile guardrail to keep her vehicle from plunging over the embankment, but she did not want to collide with the massive rock bluff, either.

Knowing she was about to lose control of the vehicle, Anita clenched her jaw and gripped the steering wheel.

Help us, Lord, she prayed, just as the car spun around sickeningly and skidded off the road.

∞

Weekday shifts were usually quiet for Rock County deputy sheriff Hawk Henson. On a normal day, he might serve a few subpoenas, investigate a few citizens' complaints, and enforce traffic laws in the jurisdiction. But from the moment the National Weather Service in Birmingham issued a Winter Storm Watch about ten that Monday morning, Hawk knew the day would be far from routine.

A steady rain had fallen all morning and saturated everything. Now the drops encountered an Arctic cold front that had broken through the high-pressure barrier that would normally have kept it away. When such a storm occurred in the mountains of northeastern Alabama, the rain often turned to sleet, causing ice to build up on every exposed surface from bridges and overpasses to trees. Ice-coated tree limbs were beautiful, but all too often they broke beneath the unaccustomed weight and fell onto power lines, leaving thousands of people without electricity. Sometimes it was days before households in remote areas had their power restored. As a member of the county's emergency response team, part of Hawk's job was to see that people who needed it had help.

"Looks like we're in for a bad one," Sheriff Lester Trimble said when he came back to the courthouse after lunch.

"I'm afraid so," Hawk agreed. He had sensed this storm brewing for several days, but he knew better than to tell his new boss. *That's just more of that Injun superstition of yours*, Sheriff Trimble would have said. Trimble, formerly the chief deputy, had been elected to the post in November, when Asa McGinty, the long-time sheriff who had hired Hawk, retired.

Fresh out of the army after serving in the military police for eight years, Hawk could have joined any number of big-city law enforcement agencies. However, he had come back home to Rock County, where his Cherokee ancestors had lived since finding sanctuary from the Trail of Tears. In the years since, the mountains that had protected the Cherokee survivors had also furnished many of them with a living.

"Word just came that I-59's closed south of Chattanooga. An eighteen-wheeler jackknifed in the rain. State troopers are trying to keep everyone from driving on the roads around Lookout Mountain," Hawk reported.

"Yeah, so I heard. Tom Statum had the radio on at the restaurant. There's enough warning out now. People know not to drive in this kind of weather."

"Locals do, but we should check the road coming into town."

Sheriff Trimble shrugged. "Anybody fool enough to be trying to drive on it in this weather deserves what they get. Unless it's an emergency call, you should stay put."

That wasn't an order, Hawk told himself when Lester Trimble left for the day an hour later. The sheriff lived on the side of Warren Mountain; his wife was there alone, and he wanted to make sure she could start the emergency generator if their power failed.

"Call me if you need me," the sheriff said in parting, but Hawk knew he really meant: *It's all yours now. Don't bother me.*

"You can leave, too, if you want," Hawk told Sally Rogers, the sheriff office's receptionist and dispatcher for more than twenty years.

"Thanks, but I'll stay until the end of my shift," she said.

Hawk looked out of the office window at the darkening sky. Sleet rattled against the windows, and the top of the hills surrounding Rockdale were already turning white.

Check for traffic on the road into town.

Hawk jerked his head around, for a moment convinced that someone had spoken the words aloud. But Sally sat quietly at her desk, and no one else was in the office.

Similar cautions had been given to Hawk several times over the years. The voice he heard so clearly usually warned him of danger to himself or someone else. The first time it happened, Hawk had told his mother about it. "It is a gift from God," she said. "Do not be afraid to listen and heed what it tells you."

Hawk Henson took his leather jacket from a hook near the door. "Hold down the fort, Sally. I'm going to make a final traffic check on the road into town."

She looked surprised. "Shouldn't be anything out there by now."

"Maybe not, but it won't hurt to look. You can forward my calls to the cruiser."

Hawk left Sally shaking her head and walked, head down, against the peppering sleet to his Rock County Sheriff's Department vehicle. The weather was worsening. Sally was probably right. No one in their right mind would still be on that road.

Hawk glanced at the mountain rising above the town.

But if anyone up there needs help, I'm on my way.

∞

Anita heard her daughter's scream and added her own at the same instant her car made contact with, then scraped along the guardrail until it jolted to a halt. Even though Anita's car did not have an air bag, her safety belt held her in place. Securely strapped into the backseat, Juanita wailed in shock and fright.

Shakily, Anita got out of the car. "Do not cry, sweetie. Everything's all right." She quickly satisfied herself that her daughter was largely unhurt. Anita's left elbow sported a bruise, while Juanita had escaped with only a tiny scratch on her arm.

Juanita clutched her huggy doll. "Dora didn't like that."

"Neither did I. But God is looking after us. He kept us safe, and He will send someone to us soon."

Anita cautiously walked around to the passenger side of the car to survey the damage. Her heart sank when she saw the crumpled fender and broken headlight. The right front tire was flat, but even worse, the rear of the car partially blocked the roadway. Anyone coming around the curve might not see her wrecked vehicle in time to avoid it. She feared being hit, but sleet still fell, and the car was their only shelter.

"You and Dora can sit up front with me, and we will keep each other warm," Anita said. She had turned off the ignition immediately after the crash and did not want to risk starting the motor to run the heater unless it became absolutely necessary.

"It's getting dark, Mama," Juanita said after a few minutes.

"The skies are just cloudy. It is still a long time until night."

Juanita's lower lip trembled. "Suppose nobody comes?"

"Someone will. Let us close our eyes and thank God for keeping us safe so far and ask Him to send help. You go first."

Minutes after Anita added her petition to her daughter's, she heard an approaching automobile.

"It's a policeman, Mama," Juanita said when the black-and-white vehicle rounded the curve, slowed to a stop, and turned on its blue light bar.

SHERIFF, ROCK COUNTY, ALABAMA, Anita read on the side of the cruiser. *We will not make it to Tennessee tonight.*

A man in a dark brown uniform came toward Anita as she got out of the car. "Are you all right?" he asked.

Even in the waning daylight, she saw he had dark skin and hair. Not Latino exactly, but not the usual Americano, either. Native American, she guessed.

"Yes, but the car is not."

"So I see." He returned to the cruiser and spoke into the two-way radio at some length before returning. "A wrecker's on the way from Rockdale. I reckon that's where you were headed."

Anita nodded. She was accustomed to hearing south Texans, but this man's speech had an unexpected softness. "Actually, I wanted to go to Chattanooga, but a trucker told me the interstate might be closed."

"It is, but you couldn't get to Chattanooga on this road, either."

"I know. I was on U.S. 11. When the weather turned bad, I decided to stop in Rockdale, instead. I did not know I would have to go down a ski slope to get there."

He smiled and extended his hand. "I'm Hawk Henson, Rock County deputy sheriff. Something told me to check on this road before I clocked out."

"That was God," said Juanita, who had scrambled out of the car in time to hear his last remark.

"I am Anita Sanchez, and this is my daughter, Juanita."

Hawk Henson's eyebrows rose perceptibly, and Anita could imagine what he must be thinking. It would not be the first time that her Hispanic name had caused people to regard her with a mixture of curiosity and repulsion.

The deputy sheriff released Anita's hand and shook her daughter's. "In any case, you're getting chilled out here. Hop in the backseat of my car, Miss Juanita. It's nice and warm, and I'll take you and your mother to town after the wrecker gets here."

"That is very kind of you, Deputy," Anita said.

"Just call me Hawk. Get what you need for the night from the car. Everything else will be safe for now."

Anita took their overnight bags from the backseat and handed them to the deputy. "How large is Rockdale?" she asked when he had stowed their things in his patrol car.

"It's no Chattanooga, but we have several nice places to stay. I recommend the Rockdale Inn. It's not fancy, but it's near everything, including Hovis Batts's repair shop. And speaking of that, here he comes."

In short order, the affable garage man had hooked Anita's car to his wrecker and started back down the mountain to Rockdale.

"I hope you don't wreck your car, too," said Juanita as the deputy eased down the road, keeping a safe distance from the wrecker.

He glanced at her in the rearview mirror and smiled. "That would put us in a pretty pickle, wouldn't it?"

Juanita giggled. "I never saw a pretty pickle. I don't like pickles."

"Neither do I," Hawk agreed. He continued to drive slowly, and several times during the drive to Rockdale, the radio crackled, followed by a spate of unintelligible words.

"I suppose you must be used to driving on ice," Anita said.

"Nobody ever gets used to ice, ma'am. Best thing is not to drive on it at all, but this cruiser has special tires, and I know the danger spots. That curve that did you in is the worst one on the road."

"I was not expecting ice in Alabama," Anita said.

Hawk seemed amused. "Obviously, south Texas is a lot different from northeastern Alabama."

"How do you know where we live?" asked Juanita.

"I don't, but your car is licensed in San Antonio, Texas, and it isn't stolen."

Anita considered his words. "You must have called the tag number in on your radio."

"Yes, ma'am. Don't take it personal, though. That's routine when a traffic call involves an unknown subject."

An unknown subject. As far as Rockdale, Alabama, knew, Anita was completely unknown.

She found that thought comforting.

Chapter 4

The moment Hawk Henson stepped from his patrol car, he knew the petite brunette standing beside her wrecked car wasn't a local. Her first words combined with her appearance to place her into a broad frame: Hispanic. Hawk Henson had been stationed at Fort Hood long enough to recognize the ethnic source of the young woman's dark hair and eyes and clear olive skin.

He was not surprised when he heard her last name. Sanchez was a common Mexican name, both in Texas and, for several years now, on nearby Sand Mountain in Alabama. The majority of those Mexicans were males who worked hard in niche jobs, kept to themselves, and sent most of their pay back to their families in Mexico. However, he was almost certain that this Anita Sanchez had no connection with them. She had an air of refinement, and the formal way she spoke English without using contractions suggested she had studied the language rather than learning it by ear after coming to the United States.

The little girl looked just like her mother and had the same lilt to her voice. They were different, all right, and Hawk had no trouble determining he would do all he could to help this intriguing young woman and her soft-eyed daughter.

∞

"When are we going to get there?" Juanita asked when they had been in the patrol car for a short while.

"Look, sweetie. The sign says WELCOME TO ROCKDALE," Anita said. Soon, they crossed a bridge, and Anita realized the mountain's trees and rocks had been replaced by houses and businesses, and rain had replaced the sleet. The roads in the valley were wet but apparently had not yet iced over.

"Here we are in Rockdale, Alabama," Hawk Henson announced. "That big building yonder is the Rock County courthouse." He turned left and slowed down in front of Hovis Batts's Garage. "There's the wrecker. Hovis will take your car around to the back lot for the night. The Rockdale Inn is right down the street. I can take you to the inn and bring the rest of your luggage over later."

"I suppose we should not leave anything in the car." Anita had not thought that far ahead, but she was glad to have someone else helping her to make decisions for a change. Even before Juan went to prison, Anita had borne most of the responsibility for their household.

"Yes, ma'am. Most of the folks around here aren't likely to steal, but it's not good to put temptation in their path."

Hawk Henson slowed to a careful stop in front of the Rockdale Inn and removed their overnight bags from his patrol car. "Watch out. Those stone steps are probably getting slick."

"They just look wet," Anita said, but her first step convinced her he was right.

"You can't see glare ice. We get that kind of black ice around here a lot, and it's dangerous to drive or walk on either one. Here, I'll help you."

The deputy steadied Anita's arm with his until she reached the top step, then he went back and carried Juanita and her huggy doll up the steps and into the inn. The lobby was deserted, but when Hawk rang the bell on the counter, a plump woman wrapped in a purple sweater emerged from a door marked OFFICE. She glanced from Anita and Juanita to Hawk Henson, obviously trying to make some connection.

"Hello, Deputy. What can I do for you?"

"Evening, Mrs. Tanner. These folks had some car trouble on their way down the mountain, and they need a place to stay."

"For how long?"

"Until my car is fixed," Anita said.

Mrs. Tanner glanced at the deputy. "When do you reckon that'll be?"

"We don't know yet. Hovis Batts just towed it in, but from the looks of it, it could take awhile."

Mrs. Tanner pointed to the rates posted on a sheet under the glass counter-top. "You can pay by the day or week. If you give me a charge card, we can work out the details when you know more."

Anita felt a stir of uneasiness. "I do not have a charge card."

The deputy frowned. "I hope you don't carry a wad of money around."

"No. I have traveler's checks."

Mrs. Tanner's grin showed a gold tooth Anita hadn't previously noticed. "That's good as cash any day of the week in my book. Let's get you registered and into a room."

Instead of the kind of single registration card Anita had been filling out at motels along the way, the Rockdale Inn used a bulky guest register ledger. While she filled in the necessary information, Hawk Henson took the luggage to room 115, at the rear of the ground floor. He returned and gave Anita the key but did not leave.

"You can get breakfast here, but you'll have to go somewhere else for your other meals. Statum's Restaurant has good food and it's close, but the sidewalks will be getting slick. I'll clock out and come back and take you to the restaurant."

Anita hardly knew how to respond to the deputy's offer, which sounded almost like an order. Perhaps Hawk Henson was merely doing his duty as a deputy sheriff, but she detected at least a glimmer of personal interest.

"Dora and I are hungry, Mama," Juanita said.

Anita noticed the fatigue in her daughter's voice and sighed. "Thank you, but we don't want to put you out. We can take a taxi to the restaurant."

Both Hawk Henson and Mrs. Tanner, who had been listening to their conversation, laughed. "Honey, there's one taxi cab in this whole town, and I guarantee it won't be running in this kind of weather," Mrs. Tanner said. "You'd better take the deputy up on his offer before he changes his mind."

"All right," Anita said.

The deputy turned to Mrs. Tanner. "I'll bring some rock salt for those steps. Somebody could break a leg out there tonight."

"I didn't know it was getting that cold," Mrs. Tanner said.

Anita and Juanita started down the hall, and Hawk called after them, "I'll be back in fifteen minutes."

Anita turned and waved. "We will be ready."

∞

Statum's Family Restaurant, usually crowded by five thirty on a weekday evening, held only a handful of diners when Hawk Henson led Anita and Juanita to a booth near the back, beyond the cold, plate glass windows.

The worsening weather was the universal topic of conversation among the few patrons. The waitress who came to take their order asked Hawk what he knew about road conditions.

"Hi, Rita. The roads are bad and getting worse on Lookout Mountain. It's warmer in the valley, but I suspect we'll get some ice here tonight, too."

Anita saw that the attractive, young, red-haired waitress seemed to be trying hard not to stare at her and wondered if the deputy noticed. She was glad he did not feel he had to introduce them, but from the curiosity in his own glance, Hawk Henson inevitably would raise questions. Although long accustomed to evading men who wanted to know her better, Anita braced herself for the encounter.

"What can I get you this evening?" Rita asked.

"I'll have the blue plate special," Hawk said. "It's usually good," he added to Anita.

"All right, I will take that, too, with water to drink. Do you have a child's plate?"

The waitress pointed to the bottom of the menu. "Chicken fingers or a small hamburger with fries and applesauce."

"She will have the chicken, but leave off the fries and bring her a glass of milk."

Juanita looked distressed. "I don't want to eat fingers."

"You will not be, sweetie. It is the same as chicken planks. You like those."

The waitress looked at Hawk. "Will this be on separate checks?"

"Yes," Anita said quickly. "I will pay for ours."

Rita nodded and tucked the order pad into her apron pocket. "I'll be right back with your drinks."

"So you were on your way to Chattanooga," Hawk said as if resuming a previous conversation. "Business or pleasure?"

That is none of your concern. Anita hesitated to say so, however; after all, the deputy had rescued them from the storm and been nothing but kind since. She could be polite, at least.

"Neither. Chattanooga seemed to be a good place to stop for the night."

"We're going to Ginny," Juanita said.

Hawk raised his dark eyebrows in the gesture of inquiry she'd noticed before. "Ginny? Is that in Tennessee?"

"She means Virginia," Anita said reluctantly.

"You still have a long way to travel, then."

Anita nodded but said nothing. From experience, she had learned not to volunteer information.

The waitress brought their drinks, and Hawk immediately took a sip of his steaming hot coffee. Rita hadn't furnished any creamer; apparently she knew Hawk took his coffee black.

"You ought to have coffee. It'll warm you up in a hurry," he said. "Ice water only makes you feel colder."

"I am quite comfortable," Anita said. She could not tell him why she always ordered water. In addition to coffee's extra cost, no brew in the States had ever tasted as good as the coffee she remembered in her native Colombia.

Hawk glanced at the thin gold band on Anita's left hand. "I suppose your husband couldn't make the trip with you?"

"No," Anita replied, truthfully enough. She felt no sentimental attachment to Juan Sanchez's wedding ring, but she continued to wear it. She didn't want anyone to think Juanita's mother hadn't been married. The band also protected Anita from men who might think any single woman was fair game.

Juanita set her glass of milk on the table. "Mama doesn't have a—" She stopped when she saw Anita's warning glance.

"Never tell strangers anything personal." Anita had repeated the warning for many years, and Juanita seldom forgot. Obviously, her daughter already considered the deputy to be their friend—and that could be dangerous.

Tom Statum, the restaurant's owner, emerged from his office and came over to greet Hawk. "Don't tell me Sheriff Trimble's got you working the second shift now."

"No, sir. I've clocked out for the night."

Tom Statum looked at Anita and Juanita, then back to Hawk. "Who do you have here? I don't remember seeing these young ladies in here before."

"This is Anita and her daughter, Juanita, and Juanita's daughter, Dora. Their car had a little problem with ice on the road into town this afternoon."

"I hear it's bad from here to Lookout Mountain," Tom said. "I'm thinking of closing early, before it gets any worse here."

"That might not be a bad idea. I checked with emergency response about thirty minutes ago. They don't expect much trouble here in town, but the power company trucks are ready to go if they're needed."

"If it gets much colder, they will be." Tom moved away from the booth as the waitress approached with a laden tray. "Here comes your food. I'll let you folks eat in peace." He nodded to Anita and Juanita. "Nice to meet you ladies," he added.

Had Tom Statum noticed the deputy had not mentioned their last name? Anita was almost certain Hawk had not forgotten it, but whatever his reasons, she was glad for the omission. It made her feel safe to be anonymous, at least for the present.

The waitress dealt out their plates and put extra napkins on the table. "Holler if you need anything else."

Juanita put her huggy doll's soft arms together and nudged Anita. "Look, Mama. Dora wants to say the blessing."

Hawk's eyebrows rose, but he made no comment.

"Fine," Anita said. Without looking at Hawk, she laid her right hand over Juanita's and bowed her head.

"Thank You, God, for everything. Bless our food. Amen."

"Dora, that was a very nice table grace," Hawk said.

"It was a blessing," Juanita corrected.

"That is the same thing, sweetie," Anita said.

Hawk smiled. He was obviously comfortable around Juanita, and he seemed to enjoy her insistence on praying in the restaurant. Anita busied herself, helping Juanita with her food and giving her a portion of the vegetables from her own blue plate special.

As they ate, Hawk talked about the usual winter weather in this part of Alabama. "How do you like the food?" he asked when he exhausted that topic.

"It is very good."

"I see Miss Juanita isn't eating much," Hawk said.

"She is tired. This has been a long day."

"Travel isn't easy for little kids," Hawk said, although Anita doubted he had any firsthand knowledge.

When the waitress returned to refill Hawk's coffee mug, both refused her invitation to try a dessert.

"No, thanks, Rita. I'll take the check now," Hawk said.

Anita noticed the waitress went out of her way to hand her bill to her directly, as if afraid the deputy might try to take it if she left it on the table. It was obvious to Anita that Rita regarded Hawk as more than a regular patron of Statum's Restaurant, but the deputy seemed blissfully ignorant of the waitress's interest.

"Y'all take care tonight," Rita said. The words were plural, but addressed directly to Hawk.

"You, too. Tom said he'd close early. You should go home and stay there."

Rita smiled. "I won't be having any late dates tonight; that's for sure."

Anita reached the cash register first. When she opened her billfold, she had the distinct impression that Hawk Henson might be looking over her shoulder at her driver's license.

The deputy seems to be trying to figure me out, Anita thought, almost too tired to care.

"The sleet seems to have stopped," Hawk observed when they left the restaurant.

Anita wrapped her cloth coat around her and shivered. "The air seems much colder."

"So it does. Let's get your luggage before the weather turns worse."

"Is he still here?" Anita asked when Hawk stopped at Hovis Batts's garage. A single overhead light burned in the office, but both garage bay doors were closed.

"Hovis is always here. He lives in an apartment upstairs."

Hawk called the garage man on his cell phone, and a few seconds later, the outside floodlights came on, and Hovis Batts opened the gate to the back lot.

"Stay in the warm car, sweetie. We will be back in a minute," Anita directed. Juanita was already curled up like a kitten, so nearly asleep she barely nodded.

"Here it is," Hovis said unnecessarily. Anita's car had been removed from the wrecker, and in the glare of the floodlights, it looked even worse than she remembered.

Anita dreaded hearing his answer, but she had to ask the question. "How much will it cost to fix?"

Hovis stroked his chin and cocked his head to one side. "Hard to say before I can get it inside the garage for a better look. Offhand, I'd say you're looking at anywhere from a couple hundred to a couple thousand dollars."

Anita's heart sank. His words were not unexpected, but she did not understand the dollar spread.

"What's the bottom line?" Hawk asked.

Hovis shrugged. "If all the lady wants is to get back on the road, it could cost as little as the price of a new headlight assembly and tire. I doubt anything major's messed up under the hood, but I won't know until I get a better look. Repairing the body damage would cost a lot more." Hovis looked to Anita. "Do you have insurance?"

"Just liability."

"I don't reckon the guardrail will sue you for running into it," Hovis said.

Hawk ignored the garage man's attempt at humor. "Open the trunk. I'll get the rest of their luggage out of your way."

Anita had filled every usable inch of the automobile's spacious trunk. Hawk's eyebrows lifted in surprise when he saw all the suitcases, cardboard boxes, and plastic bags to be removed.

"My patrol car won't hold all of this. I'll take what I can now and come back for the rest of it."

"I am sorry to be so much trouble," Anita said.

"You're not. It's all in a day's work."

"I never seen a trunk packed with so much stuff," Hovis commented. "Looks like you're moving."

Anita made no comment and avoided looking at Hawk, who must have reached a similar conclusion. When the deputy found the metal lockbox, Anita could almost see the suspicion in his eyes.

There are no drugs inside, she wanted to say, but denying an unspoken charge might only make her appear guilty.

He gave Anita the box. "You'd better take this."

"My traveler's checks are in it," she said.

Hawk's eyebrows rose again, and Anita wondered if he believed her. "Looks like you'll be needing them."

And then some.

Forty-five minutes later, Hawk had finished transferring everything from the car to room 115 at the Rockdale Inn. Mrs. Tanner was nowhere in sight, for which Anita was thankful.

"Thank you," she said when the deputy piled the last of the luggage into the room. "I do not know what we would have done without your help."

Hawk spoke as if reading from a cue card. "I'm glad I could be of service, ma'am."

Are you really?

Even as Anita locked the door behind the deputy, she had the distinct impression she would see him again.

Anita wrestled her sleeping daughter into her nightclothes and tucked her into one of the room's two double beds, then she knelt to pray.

As bone-tired and half-asleep as she was, Anita would not rest until she had thanked God for keeping them safe and delivering them into what appeared to be good hands, then she concluded with her perennial plea for guidance.

Continue to be with us, Lord, and help me to know what I should do.

∽

A few blocks away, Hawk Henson let himself into his rented duplex, chosen for its proximity to the courthouse. Removing only his shoes, he stretched out on the bed. The threat of bad weather had lessened, but if an emergency arose, he wouldn't have to waste time getting dressed to respond.

Hawk pillowed his hands under his head and peered into the darkness. His bedroom wall became a screen for the film produced by his mind, a replay of the hours he'd spent in the company of Anita Sanchez and her daughter.

Hawk had never been attracted to anyone he met in the line of duty, but then he'd never run across anyone like Anita Sanchez. Despite her beauty, she'd made no attempt to flirt with him. She seemed independent yet vulnerable, and Hawk found himself wanting to put his arms around her and assure her he would take care of her. Although his law enforcement experience strongly suggested she probably had something to hide, Hawk's instincts made him doubt she could be guilty of any sort of criminal behavior.

Given the damage to her car, she would likely be around for a while. One way or another, Hawk Henson determined he would find out more about Anita Sanchez.

Chapter 5

"Look, Mama, the sun's shining."

Anita struggled awake and opened the covers to let her daughter crawl into bed beside her. "So it is. Did you and Dora sleep well?"

Juanita nodded and kissed her huggy doll. "Dora had a bad dream, but then she went right back to sleep. Now she's hungry."

Anita glanced at her wristwatch and was surprised to see it was almost eight o'clock. "Get dressed, sweetie. After breakfast, we will come back and have our baths."

Mrs. Tanner sat in the lobby, drinking coffee and watching a television news channel. She pointed toward the adjacent breakfast room. "Help yourselves."

"What is the weather forecast?" Anita asked.

"Clearing and warmer. Even Lookout Mountain should be thawed out soon."

"That is good news," Anita said, thinking it would be even better if she could get into her car and drive away.

Surveying the Rockdale Inn's array of dry cereal, milk, juice, coffee, and cinnamon rolls, Anita realized Dora was not the only hungry one.

After she filled their plates, Anita sat at one of the small tables and held hands with Juanita while she thanked God for the food. When she raised her head and saw Mrs. Tanner watching, Anita did not look away. Recalling the way the people in the restaurant had regarded them, Anita decided staring at strangers must be a major source of entertainment in Rockdale.

"I hope you have a nice day," Mrs. Tanner said when Anita and Juanita started back to their room.

"It is good to see the sun again, at least." Anita hesitated, then decided she should tell Mrs. Tanner about the extra luggage in the room. "Deputy Henson thought I should not leave anything in my car, and last night he helped me bring the rest of our things to my room. I thought you should know in case the maid might say something."

Mrs. Tanner looked interested. "The maid doesn't work nights. If anyone saw you and the deputy going into your room, it wasn't Millie."

"I did not mean that," Anita said quickly. "It is hard to move around the room for all the luggage. We have no need for daily room service, anyway."

Mrs. Tanner shrugged. "Whatever you say. Just let me know when you find out how long you'll be here." *And the sooner you leave, the better I will like it,* Anita thought her tone suggested. More than once, in ways both subtle and open, landlords had let her know "her kind" were unwelcome. While she had long since steeled herself to ignore such slights, they still hurt.

Anita returned to the room and tried to view their things as the innkeeper might. By volunteering unnecessary information, she had practically insured that Mrs. Tanner would snoop around the room as soon as they left. She didn't think the woman would take anything, but that would not stop her from drawing unwelcome or inaccurate conclusions.

Anita left the bathroom door open while Juanita played in the tub. She made up both beds, then got down on her hands and knees to chain the lockbox to her bed frame. Satisfied it was hidden by the dust ruffle, she replaced the box's key on the gold necklace around her neck.

Having done all she could to protect their possessions, Anita said a silent prayer, asking God to be with her and Juanita through whatever the day might bring.

∞

"Where are we going, Mama?" Juanita asked when they left the Rockdale Inn about an hour later.

"To the garage to see about the car."

The midmorning air was brisk but not uncomfortably cold. Anita turned her face up to the sun, enjoying the welcome warmth. With Juanita's hand in hers, they walked past a variety of buildings in the direction of Hovis Batts's garage.

Adjacent to the Rockdale Inn parking lot, an old frame house had been converted to a law office. On the other side was a vacant brick store with a FOR SALE sign in one the large front windows. Then came a dry cleaning business, a parking lot, and another vintage frame house now used as a boutique. After crossing a side street, they came to a combination gas station and convenience store, another parking lot, and a hardware store. Anita walked slowly, partly so as not to tire Juanita, but also so she could take everything in. Anita had never lived in a small town, and she was curious about this place in which they had found shelter from the ice storm.

"Are we there yet?" Juanita asked after they crossed yet another side street.

"Almost, sweetie."

The garage had not seemed so far when they had ridden to the inn from it the night before, and Juanita was not the only one glad to see the BATTS GARAGE sign halfway down the next block.

Hovis Batts sat at a cluttered rolltop desk in his office, entering figures into a calculator. When Anita entered, he stood to greet her and Juanita. "'Morning, ma'am. Hello there, little lady."

"Have you looked at my car yet?" Anita asked.

"Did that first thing, knowing you was anxious to get back on the road. Would your daughter like to go to the customer lounge? Little ones usually like watching the tropical fish swim around the aquarium."

Juanita looked to her mother for permission, and Anita nodded.

"How bad is it?" Anita asked after Juanita left.

"The good news is everything under the hood looks okay, and you can drive it just fine without fixing the body damage." He paused.

"What is the bad news?"

"Not as bad as it could be, but probably not as good as you'd like. You already know you need a new tire and headlight. The A-frame suspension, front shocks, and part of the headlight housing all need to be replaced. I checked around, and nobody local has all the parts on hand."

"Can you order them?"

"Sure, but it'll take awhile to get here, and you'll need to pay up-front before I order anything."

"How much?"

"I was just figuring all that up. A new headlight assembly runs about two fifty, but you might be able to get one from a junkyard. Add the shocks and new tire and the labor—this is just a rough estimate, but I'd say you're looking at around twenty-five hundred dollars."

Anita had braced herself for bad news, but this figure was worse than her expectations. She knew to the penny how much money she had. When she left Texas, Anita figured she would already have found a job in Virginia before her savings ran out. Wrecking her car had not been part of her plans.

"I cannot pay that much all at once," she said.

"You can use plastic. I take all the major credit cards."

Anita shook her head. "I do not have a charge card."

The garage man looked surprised. "These days, I thought everybody had at least two or three. Maybe you could ask somebody to wire you money? I used to send my boy cash that way all the time."

I have no one to ask. That was a truth Anita did not care to reveal.

"How much money will you need to order the parts?"

"Five hundred down would do it."

"How much is the towing charge?"

Hovis Batts seemed embarrassed. "You don't have to worry about that. Deputy Henson's already been in this morning and taken care of it."

It was Anita's turn to be embarrassed. "He has?"

"Yes. He said to tell you he's on duty today if you need anything."

Anita spoke as much to herself as to Hovis Batts. "I suppose I should thank him. Do you know where I can find the deputy?"

"The sheriff's department works out of the courthouse. He'll be there unless he's out on a call."

"I remember seeing the courthouse yesterday. It is back that way, is it not?"

Hovis Batts jerked his thumb in the general direction of the square. "Two blocks down and two to the left—you can't miss it. About that up-front money—

the sooner I get it, the quicker I can order the parts."

"Will you take traveler's checks?"

"No, but you pass the Rock County Bank on the way to the courthouse. They can cash them for you there, for sure."

Anita called to Juanita. "Come on, sweetie. Time to go."

"Is the car fixed?"

"Not yet, but Mr. Batts is working on it."

"Can I come back and see your fishes again?" Juanita asked him.

"Any time." Hovis Batts looked at Anita. "Whenever I get uptight about things, I go in there and look at those fish. Calms me down every time."

"Maybe I should try it myself," Anita said.

Yet, as they walked to the courthouse, Anita realized she did not feel as tense as she probably could given the circumstances. She had asked God to help them and guide her, and she believed He would. The sun was shining, and she and Juanita had found at least one friend in Rockdale.

For these blessings, Lord, accept my thanks.

∽

The sheriff's department occupied cramped quarters on the ground floor of Rock County's aging courthouse. Signs in front of a half-dozen parking spaces around the building proclaimed they were reserved for the official vehicles of the sheriff and his deputies. VIOLATORS WILL BE FINED. Rock County Sheriff's Department cruisers occupied three of the places, leaving the others vacant.

"Look, Mama, there's Deppy Hawk's car," Juanita exclaimed when she saw the cruisers.

"Deputy," Anita corrected automatically. "All the patrol cars look alike. His might not be there."

"The dep'ty is nice. I hope we get to see him again."

So do I. "We can go inside and see if he is here," Anita said.

Only a few steps into the courthouse, Anita saw heavy black lettering on a frosted door:

ROCK COUNTY SHERIFF'S OFFICE
LESTER TRIMBLE, SHERIFF

Anita opened the door and went inside. At one of the four desks in the room, a balding deputy sat with his back to her, talking on the telephone; the other desks were empty. A woman in a uniform similar to Hawk Henson's sat at a desk, surrounded by a switchboard and several computers. SALLY ROGERS, DISPATCHER, according to her nameplate.

She looked up when Anita approached the desk. "Can I help you?"

"I would like to see Deputy Henson."

"He's out on a call, but Sheriff Trimble's here."

"When do you expect the deputy to return?"

The dispatcher glanced at a notebook on her desk. "That's hard to say, ma'am. He could be back soon, if you care to wait."

Anita looked around. The only available seating, a hard wooden bench, did not look at all inviting, but they were already here, and she still wanted to thank Hawk Henson. "Come on, sweetie. We can sit over there and rest a minute."

The balding deputy was still talking on the telephone. From where they sat, Anita couldn't see the nameplates on the other desks, but she noticed all but one of the desks was strewn with papers and empty food containers. Anita felt almost certain Hawk Henson's work space would be the neat and orderly one.

"Look at the big fishie, Mama." Juanita pointed to a mounted fish on the wall behind the desks.

A trophy fish, body curved, had been captured by the taxidermist in the act of jumping out of the water.

Poor thing. "I have never seen a fish like that," Anita said aloud.

Other examples of a hunter's attempt to preserve his kill lined the walls. Anita recognized a many-antlered buck deer, then shuddered along with her daughter at the hideous head beside it. She had never seen one alive, but from its curved tusks and piglike face, Anita guessed the trophy to be a wild boar.

The dispatcher saw them looking at the heads and spoke with pride. "All those came from right around here in Rock County."

Anita wondered if Hawk Henson had killed them and tried to think of a tactful way to ask. "Someone who works here must be a good hunter," she said.

The dispatcher nodded. "Most every man in the county likes to hunt and fish. See that boar's head over there?"

How can we miss it? Anita wanted to say but simply nodded.

"A ten-year-old boy bagged that one bow-hunting."

Juanita's eyes widened. "Like an Indian's bow and arrow?"

"No, he used a crossbow."

The dispatcher might have told the stories of the other trophies, but the door to the sheriff's private office opened, and a large, mostly bald, middle-aged man came out. He stopped and stared at Anita.

"Who do we have here?"

"The dispatcher said we could wait for Deputy Henson."

The sheriff's eyes narrowed in appraisal. "What business do you have with him?"

"I want to thank him for his kindness to me and my daughter."

"And what might that be?"

"My car wrecked on the road into town yesterday. The deputy came to our rescue."

The sheriff's blue eyes gleamed. "So you're the one. What were you thinking about, driving in that kind of weather? My deputy could have lost his patrol car up there on that mountain."

The sheriff's tirade shook Anita, but she was determined not to show her discomfort. "I assure you I did not have the accident on purpose, sir. I was trying to find a place to spend the night, and Rockdale was the closest town."

"Where are you from? You don't sound American."

Had the sheriff smiled or said the words lightly, Anita could have dealt with them in the same way. Yet however much his rudeness and implied prejudice stung, Anita knew she could not afford to lose her temper.

"I have lived in Texas for many years." *The last time I looked at the map, it was still in America.*

He spoke under his breath, but Anita still heard his words. "Wetback, huh. Might have known it."

Anita was still biting her tongue when Sally Rogers called to the sheriff, and he turned away.

"Sheriff Trimble? Your wife's on line one."

"I'll take it in my office."

The sheriff glared at Anita once more, then closed his office door with a great deal more force than necessary.

"Mama, why is that man so mad?"

"Some people are just naturally angry. We must pray for them and not become angry ourselves."

Juanita thought about her mother's words for a moment. "That's hard to do."

"I know, sweetie. That is where the praying part comes in."

"Dora doesn't want to stay here," Juanita said.

Neither do I. Anita still intended to thank Hawk Henson, but she had worn out her welcome with Sheriff Trimble, and she wanted to hear no more from his sharp tongue.

"We can see the deputy later," Anita said.

"You decided not to wait?" Sally Rogers asked when they stood to leave. Anita thought she detected a gleam of sympathy in the woman's eye and knew she must have heard the sheriff's comments.

"We need to be going," Anita said.

"I'll tell Hawk you came by, Mrs.—?"

"He will know," Anita said.

And he knows where to find me.

Chapter 6

Anita returned to the Rockdale Inn to retrieve her cache of traveler's checks. She was about to leave the lobby to go to the bank when a Rock County Sheriff's Department cruiser stopped in front of the inn.

"Look, Mama, it's the dep'ty," Juanita said.

"So it is." Anita glanced at the empty reception desk, glad Mrs. Tanner was elsewhere at the moment.

Hawk Henson hurried up the steps, head down, and Anita noted his surprise when he opened the door and saw her and Juanita standing in the lobby, wearing their coats.

"Looks like I caught you just in time," he said. "Sorry I missed you earlier. Sally said you came by the office. Is something wrong?"

"No. Mr. Batts told me you took care of the towing bill. It was kind of you to do so, but I intend to pay you back."

Hawk's lips compressed, and Anita saw her words displeased him. "I wanted to do it. I expected nothing in return, so please say no more about it."

Anita had been brought up to accept gifts graciously, but it had been such a long time since anyone had given her anything, she was out of practice. "In that case, Juanita and I thank you."

Juanita held out her huggy doll. "Dora thanks you, too."

Hawk took one of the huggy doll's limp hands in his and shook it. "I am glad to see Dora has good manners." He looked back at Anita. "Can I give you ladies a lift?"

"I want to cash some traveler's checks. The bank is close enough for us to walk there."

"It's also less than a block from the sheriff's office, which is where I'm heading. You might as well ride while you have the chance."

"Dora and I like your car, Dep'ty Hawk," Juanita said.

"I hope you are not breaking any rules," Anita said when she saw several passersby gaping at the sight of Deputy Henson assisting his unusual passengers into the patrol car.

"Not one," Hawk said, but Anita doubted Sheriff Trimble would agree. "Hovis Batts tells me it might take awhile to get your car fixed," Hawk said when they passed the garage.

And a lot of money. Although Hawk did not say so, Anita realized the garage owner had no doubt shared that news, as well.

"He has to order some parts," she said.

"I know. It would save you a chunk of money if we could find a headlight assembly on a junked car, though."

We? Anita swallowed hard. "I would not know how to find a junked automobile."

"I know enough for both of us. I'm off tomorrow, and I have nothing better to do. I'll make a few calls first, then check out likely salvage yards. There are several around Fort Payne and more up on Sand Mountain."

I should not let this man put me any further in debt to him. Even so, Anita pushed the thought aside. "If you are willing to do that, I would be grateful."

Hawk smiled, and once more Anita noticed how white his teeth were. "I'll tell Hovis to hold up on ordering that part."

"I can tell him myself, since I have to take the money to him when I get the checks cashed," Anita said.

"Fine." Hawk pulled into the bank parking lot and turned off the ignition. "I'll come in with you and then take you to the garage."

Anita raised her eyebrows. "Are the streets here that unsafe?"

"No, but it doesn't pay to take unnecessary chances." Hawk looked as if he might say more had Juanita not been present.

The few people in the bank lobby looked up when they entered, and Anita guessed they wondered what business one of their deputy sheriffs had with the unfamiliar woman and child with him. Hawk walked over to the far teller window, where a dark-haired, dark-eyed teller greeted him warmly. DEBORAH HAWK, her nameplate said.

"Hi there, Chief. What can I do for you this morning?"

"Nothing for me, princess. But this lady wants to cash some traveler's checks."

The teller looked at Anita, then back at Hawk. "I don't reckon I need to ask if she has an account with us."

"Doesn't matter," Hawk said. "Traveler's checks are just as good as cash, aren't they?"

The teller ignored Hawk to look at Anita. "I'll have to see some ID."

Anita opened her purse and handed over her driver's license. "Will this do?"

"Texas, huh? By way of the Rio Grande?"

"That's none of your business." Hawk made his words a mild reprimand, and the teller surprised Anita by sticking out her tongue at him.

Behind her, Anita heard Juanita's quick intake of breath and was grateful her daughter did not blurt out what she probably thought. *How come that lady stuck out her tongue at Dep'ty Hawk? Doesn't she know that's not nice?*

"Just give her the money," Hawk said.

"I will, but she has to sign the checks in my presence first. How many checks do you want to cash, Ms. Sanchez?"

"Five, each for one hundred dollars."

"How do you want the money?"

"Give her a cashier's check made out to Hovis Batts," Hawk said before Anita could reply.

"What kind of scam you got going with Hovis?" the teller asked, her tone making it clear she was teasing.

"The lady's car needs parts, and he's got to have up-front money before he'll order them. Oldest scam in the world."

"Car trouble takes a bundle of money, all right," the teller said. "That fender-bender I had two months ago cost me over three thousand dollars and ruined my insurance rating."

"It would help if you didn't drive like a maniac," Hawk said.

"That last accident wasn't my fault, and you know it. Those crazy Mexicans—"

"Never mind," Hawk interrupted. "Shouldn't you be making out the check?"

"Thanks for telling me how to do my job," Deborah Hawk said dryly. "The drill is I have to wait until all the traveler's checks are in my possession before I can legally negotiate them."

"Here is the last one." Anita pushed the signed checks toward the teller, who made a display of inspecting each before she put them inside her cash drawer and turned away to the check-writing machine.

"Debbie's my cousin," Hawk said as if answering a question Anita had not asked.

"Hawk is a family name?"

"Yes. My mother and Debbie's father were brother and sister, and we grew up together. She has a sharp tongue at times, but she's all right. Next time you come in here, she'll take good care of you."

"I hope I will not have to ask her to cash many more checks," Anita said.

"I suppose that depends on how long you intend to stay," Hawk said, almost making it a question.

"Or on how long my money lasts."

"Here you are, Ms. Sanchez. Hovis can cash this any time he likes without a waiting period."

Anita inclined her head. "Thank you."

"Thanks, princess. Watch that lead foot, now."

"You watch out, too, Chief."

Something about the way the teller looked at Anita suggested that she might be warning Hawk about her.

Do not take offense where none is intended, Anita reminded herself. She had first heard those words from her mother, and many times since leaving Colombia, she had taken them to her heart as a talisman against the hurt of being considered "different."

When Anita handed Hovis Batts the cashier's check, she thought she detected a new respect in his eyes. "I'll get on ordering the parts right away."

"Hold off on the headlight assembly," Hawk said. "I'll try to find one locally."

"All right. When will you be able to look?"

"I'm off tomorrow. If nothing turns up, I'll let you know."

"How long will it take the parts to get here?" Anita asked.

"That's hard to say with New Year's coming up. I'd say it'll be at least four or five days."

Anita did some mental arithmetic and arrived at an inevitable conclusion—given that and the time it would take Hovis Batts to install the parts, it could be a long while before she could resume her journey.

The pager on Hawk's belt beeped, and he sighed. "It's back to the office for me."

"Can we go with you, Dep'ty Hawk?" asked Juanita.

"I'm afraid not. But I'll give you and your mama a ride back to the inn if she'll let me."

Anita shook her head. "No, thanks. We can walk from here. Thank you again for all your help."

"That's a nice young man," Hovis Batts said when Hawk left. "If he can find a headlight from a junker, it'll save you quite a bit of money."

"I hope he can," Anita said.

"Dora's hungry, Mama," Juanita said when they left the garage.

Anita glanced at her watch, surprised to see that the morning was nearly spent. Aware that each passing day would cost more of her savings, she decided to pick up sandwich makings at the convenience store near the garage.

"We can have a picnic in our room. Let us see what we can find to eat."

Anita was glad to discover this particular convenience store had a fairly extensive food section. "What kind of jelly do you want with your peanut butter?" she asked Juanita.

"Dora wants grapen."

"Grape, not grapen." Anita made the correction almost automatically. She picked up a loaf of bread and a flat of bottled water, then added a couple of apples to her basket. Seeing Juanita eyeing them with longing, she also took a box of animal crackers. Not exactly a feast, but enough to tide them over until supper—when, she supposed, they would eat in the only restaurant within walking distance of the Rockdale Inn.

The clerk looked up from her tabloid magazine when Anita placed her choices on the counter. "Will that be all?" she asked.

"Yes." Anita opened her purse, her hand on her billfold.

"We don't take checks—just cash or major credit cards," the clerk said, pointing to a large sign to that effect.

Why does she think I am going to give her a check? Anita quickly dismissed the sudden edge of irritation. "How much do I owe?" she asked instead.

The clerk said the sum slowly, took Anita's money without comment, failed to add the standard "Thank you and come back," and immediately returned to her reading.

"That lady wasn't very nice," Juanita observed when they left the store.

"She was reading something interesting, and we took her away from it," Anita said. Privately, however, she suspected the clerk had simply not liked their looks.

Neither had Hawk's cousin. Anita realized that if Hawk had not gone into the bank with her, she might have had trouble getting her traveler's checks cashed. She was a stranger in town, true enough, but Anita felt there was more to it than that.

Why did so many people in Rockdale seem to mistrust her?

She would ask Hawk Henson the next time she saw him.

∞

When Hawk returned to the office, Sally Rogers told him the sheriff wanted to see him.

"He had another round with Mrs. Trimble while you were gone, and he's not in a very good mood," she warned.

"Thanks for the heads-up."

Hawk paused at the sheriff's office door, mentally bracing himself. Sheriff Trimble was unpleasant most of the time, but when he was in a really bad mood, sparks flew and his deputies tried to find some excuse to leave the office. Hawk knocked and announced himself, then was greeted with a roar from within.

"Come in, Henson."

The sheriff remained behind his desk as if to remind Hawk he was in charge. "I hear you've been messing around with that fool woman who wrecked her car during the ice storm. I don't want her and that kid of hers hanging around my office."

As he so often had to do in the sheriff's presence, Hawk recalled a familiar verse from Proverbs: "A soft answer turneth away wrath: but grievous words stir up anger."

"Mrs. Sanchez and her daughter had an unfortunate accident. She came to thank us for helping them. I doubt if you'll see her around here again."

"Sanchez. If there's one thing this town don't need, it's a bunch of Sanchezes moving in. I don't want what happened on Sand Mountain and Fort Payne repeated in Rock County. Those Mexicans come in illegally to begin with, and then the next thing you know, you've got three, four families living in one house, taking jobs away from decent people, carousing around, and causing all kinds of trouble."

Hawk ignored most of the sheriff's tirade, only part of which he knew to be true, but he could not let Anita go undefended. "Mrs. Sanchez is not an illegal Mexican immigrant. She and her daughter are American citizens, and they have just as much right to be here as anyone else."

"How do you know she's legal? Just because she batted her pretty brown eyes at you don't mean anything she told you is true."

Hawk hesitated, wondering how much he dared say to the sheriff. "Mrs. Sanchez didn't tell me she's a citizen. I found that out when I ran a routine check on her car tag. According to Texas records, she is a native of Colombia, South America."

"I wouldn't be surprised if she didn't come up here to run drugs. When's she leaving town?"

"I don't know, but her car is in pretty bad shape." Hawk paused, then decided to give the sheriff something to consider. "Rock County can't afford a discrimination lawsuit. If Mrs. Sanchez should decide to stay here, we don't have the authority to make her leave."

Sheriff Trimble scowled. "We don't have to ask her to stay, either. Get it, Henson?"

"I think we understand each other," Hawk replied levelly. It was not the first time he and his boss had locked horns, and given each man's temperament, Hawk knew it would not be the last.

"Fine. Tell that woman to stay out of my department."

"Don't worry. After the way I suspect she was treated this morning, I doubt that will be a problem."

∞

After lunch, Juanita yawned and announced that Dora wanted to take a nap. Anita tucked them both in and put the food away in the cooler she had retrieved from the car the night before.

Juanita fell asleep almost immediately, and Anita sat at the small table and opened her Bible. She needed time to think about everything that had happened that day and to consider what she should do next.

Virginia was still a long way off, and the chance she could find her former teacher was slim. In addition, she did not know how long it would be before her car was ready to drive—and by then, even more of her savings would be gone.

Anita had made a clean break from San Antonio, and she felt sure Bill Rankin could not track her. For her purposes, Alabama would serve as well as Virginia, and from what she had seen of Rockdale, it could also be a good place to bring up her child.

That is, if the people could get over the prejudice some of them seemed to harbor against her.

Anita bowed her head and prayed for guidance. She had felt the strong presence of the Lord on every step of her journey, even when she wrecked her car.

Send me a sign, Lord. Let me know what I should do.

Chapter 7

Although Anita half-expected Hawk Henson to call or come by, he had not done so by the time Juanita announced that Dora was getting hungry.

"Put on your coat, sweetie. We will walk over to the place where we had supper last night."

"Will the dep'ty be there?"

"I doubt it," Anita replied.

However, they had no more than been seated when Hawk Henson entered Statum's Restaurant and immediately spotted them.

"Is this seat taken?" he asked Juanita, who giggled and obligingly scooted over to make room for him in the booth.

"You look different," Anita commented. Hawk had exchanged his uniform for a brown cardigan worn over a sports shirt with a buttoned-down collar, blue jeans, and hand-tooled cowboy boots.

"Better or worse?" he asked.

"Neither—just different."

The same red-haired waitress from the previous night came to take their order, but this time Hawk made it clear he would be paying.

"It seems I am always having to thank you for something new," Anita said when the waitress left.

"I can afford it," he said easily. "You'd be surprised how much a Rock County deputy sheriff pulls down these days."

"How hard is it to get work around here?" Anita found herself asking.

"It depends. What kind of work do you have in mind?"

Anita lowered her head. She had already said more than she had intended, but she trusted Hawk to tell her the truth. "I am a nurse, but I could take a fast-food job if necessary—anything to make a little money."

Hawk's eyebrows lifted in surprise. "What about your husband? Can't he send you something?"

Anita glanced at Juanita, who seemed more interested in a little girl who had just come in with her parents than in her mother's conversation. "No," she said simply. "That is not an option."

"I see," said Hawk. "You're running away from him, right?"

"No," Anita said, then stopped before she made matters even worse.

"Look, Mama. That little girl has a huggy doll almost like Dora," Juanita said.

"So she does, sweetie."

The children looked at each other, and when Juanita raised one of Dora's hands in a wave, the other huggy doll waved back.

"That's Jack and Cynthia Tait," Hawk said. "Jackie's about Juanita's age."

"I wish I could play with her," Juanita said wistfully.

"That could probably be arranged." Hawk slid out of the booth and went to the Taits' table.

Anita could not hear what he said, but in a moment, the family came to the booth, and Hawk made the introductions.

"So you're at the Rockdale Inn?" Cynthia Tait asked Anita.

"For now, at least," Anita said.

"Jackie's getting restless, and with another week of Christmas vacation left, I'd be happy to have your little girl come over to play."

"I am sure Juanita would like that, but I have no way to get her there at the moment," Anita said.

Cynthia Tait waved her hand, displaying a number of rings on each finger. "I can come after her. How about ten o'clock tomorrow morning? I'll bring her back about two, if that's all right."

Juanita turned pleading eyes to her mother. "Puhlease, can I go, Mama?"

Anita smiled at her daughter's eagerness. "It is kind of you to ask, Mrs. Tait. Juanita and I thank you."

"Just call me Cynthia," the woman said.

"And I'm Jack," her husband added.

"That worked out well," Hawk said when the Taits returned to their table. "Juanita has a new friend, and her mama can help me look for a headlight assembly tomorrow."

Anita started to protest, then thought better of it. Why not go with Hawk? It would give her a chance to tell him as much of her background as he needed to know.

Besides, Anita had come to enjoy his company.

∞

December 31.

Anita looked at the date on her calendar and thought about how much had happened in the last few weeks. Until Bill Rankin had come along, it had been a good year. Since then, just about everything that could go wrong had. But tomorrow, another year would begin. Each day was a gift from God, another new chance to change her life.

Even now, on this last day of the old year, Anita had something to look forward to. A trip to a junkyard did not sound very thrilling, but if it saved any of her precious store of money, it would be well worth it.

Juanita was excited about playing with her new friend, and her eyes shone as she kissed her mother good-bye and went off with Cynthia Tait.

When her daughter left, Anita returned to their room to dress for her junkyard expedition. Hawk had told her to wear old clothes, but when she came into the lobby in the coveralls she kept in the car in case she had to change a tire, he seemed surprised. With her hair in a ponytail beneath a baseball cap, she knew she must look quite different from the young woman Hawk was accustomed to seeing.

"Will this do?" she asked.

"Sure, but I hardly knew you in that getup. You look like a teenaged boy ready to work on his hot rod."

Although Hawk smiled when he said it, Anita felt oddly embarrassed, as if she had broken some unwritten rule. "I can change—"

"No need for that—you look fine. Let's go."

"I must be back before Cynthia Tait brings Juanita home."

"Don't worry about that. If we're delayed, I can call Cynthia and ask her to keep Juanita there. Besides, a lot of places close early on New Year's Eve. We should be finished by noon. I brought a thermos of hot chocolate and a couple of sandwiches for lunch."

"I hope your vehicle has a heater," Anita said when she saw how much colder the air had become since the day before.

"It's a Jeep 4x4—and yes, it has a heater. I also keep a few blankets and extra jackets in back. The weather around Lookout Mountain can go from good to terrible with little warning."

Hawk opened the door for Anita, then walked around and started the engine.

"Where are we going?" Anita asked.

"To a junkyard in Georgia first."

"All the way to another state?"

"Tennessee, Alabama, and Georgia all come together not far from here," Hawk said. "If the first place doesn't work out, we'll try a salvage yard on Sand Mountain."

They had been climbing out of Rockdale for several minutes when Hawk slowed and pulled to the side of the road. He pointed to the dented guardrail that had stopped Anita's car. "Look familiar?"

Seeing the scene on a clear, sunny day, Anita shivered, realizing how easily her accident could have been much worse. "Without that guardrail, I would probably not be here now. God was with us."

Hawk nodded. "I agree."

He drove on, from time to time pointing out sites of interest along the way—strange rock formations, then an everlasting spring that gushed from the side of the mountain only to disappear into a supposedly bottomless pit a few feet farther on.

"The spring never runs dry, even in the worst drought," Hawk explained. "The Cherokee say it is a gift of God."

Hawk slowed, then turned into a narrow dirt lane guarded by a NO TRES-PASSING sign on the trunk of an oak tree. He pulled in beside a long-abandoned log structure.

"This is called a 'dogtrot' cabin because dogs slept on the wide-open hall between the rooms. When I was a kid, I spent a lot of time here."

"It looks very—" Anita paused, searching for a word that would convey her meaning without insulting Hawk.

"Primitive?" Hawk supplied. "It was. No electricity, and the water comes from a spring. My great-grandfather built a better house down the road a ways, but I still like this place best."

"You do not still live up here?"

"No. We came down from the mountain when I was twelve, but the house is still back there. I check on it from time to time."

Anita imagined Hawk as a young boy growing up in what seemed to be a wilderness. "I think you would still like to live here."

Hawk nodded. "In a way, I would, but it's too far from town."

He pulled back onto the highway, and before they had gone much farther, Anita saw a flash of tan in the underbrush beside the road. She felt her body lunge forward as Hawk braked heavily, just seconds before a magnificent buck deer loped across the road, followed by a couple of does.

"Sorry for the sudden stop, but if we'd hit those deer, my Jeep would be in even worse shape than your car."

Seeing the deer, Anita was reminded of the trophies in the sheriff's office. "Do you hunt them?"

Hawk nodded. "Occasionally, but not for sport."

"So the buck's head in the sheriff's office is not yours?"

"No. My father taught me to respect all animals. It's part of my Cherokee heritage. God gave them to us, and He expects us to use them wisely. When I kill deer, I dress the meat and cure the hide."

"I suppose you did not catch the fish on the wall, either."

Hawk laughed. "No. I eat my catch."

After they climbed out of the valley, Hawk turned onto the road that Anita knew led to Chattanooga, then turned onto another road. A few minutes later, he stopped at a dilapidated salvage yard in the middle of nowhere. PETE SCOTT—BEST JUNKERS IN GEORGIA, the crude, hand-lettered sign announced. A chained Doberman barked to announce their arrival, bringing the owner out of the shack that passed for his office.

"Howdy, Hawk. It's been awhile. Good to see you."

Hawk shook the man's hand and nodded toward Anita. "Pete, this lady needs a right headlight assembly for her Olds. You told me over the phone you have one."

"Yep, but that car come in some time ago, and it's pretty well buried out back."

"We'll find it."

Hawk took a sack of tools from the Jeep, and Anita followed him through the weed-choked lot. Hundreds of wrecked automobiles lay where they had been dumped, some little more than rusty hulks, others fairly new models. "How will you ever be able find anything in here?" she asked.

"By looking. You can help. Pete said the car was blue. Be careful of sharp edges," Hawk added when a jutting fender threatened to rip a hole in Anita's coveralls.

After fifteen minutes, she was ready to give up, but Hawk persisted. "I think I see the car. Stay where you are, and I'll check it out."

Hawk disappeared behind the yellow hulk of an ancient school bus, then emerged moments later, shaking his head. "I found the car, all right, but the right headlight's cracked."

"It cannot be used?"

Hawk shook his head. "No, but all is not lost. I have another prospect on Sand Mountain."

"Where is that?"

"On another ridge not far from here."

"You are very kind to go to all this trouble for me," Anita said after they pulled away from the junkyard.

"It's no trouble. I should thank you for giving me a good excuse to prowl junkyards again. It's been awhile since I allowed myself that pleasure."

"You call it pleasure? I would call it hard work."

"As a kid, I used to help my father rebuild wrecked cars."

"Was that his business?" Anita asked, immediately regretting she had asked such a personal question.

"One of them. Mostly, he ran a bush hog."

Anita had no idea what a bush hog was, but she refrained from asking. Something in his voice gave Anita the feeling Hawk's father was dead and that he still grieved the loss. *As I do for my father and mother and family and always will.*

Anita shivered, and Hawk reached over to turn up the heater fan. "Warm enough now?" he asked after a few minutes, and she nodded.

After making several more turns onto narrow, winding back roads, Hawk reached U.S. Highway 431, a busy four-lane route. "We're on top of Sand Mountain now," he announced. "We should find your headlight here."

A tall fence surrounded the salvage yard where Hawk stopped next. Once more, the owner greeted him like a long-lost friend, and again Anita followed Hawk through a tangle of auto bodies and parts. Eventually, they reached an Oldsmobile Anita thought could be the twin of hers, even to the paint color. The back of the car had been badly mangled ("Train hit it," the salvage owner told them), but the front was intact.

"This will do," Hawk announced, and for the next few minutes, Anita served as mechanic's assistant, handing him the requested tools and helping him remove the headlight assembly.

While Hawk took the part to his Jeep and stowed his tools, Anita paid the salvage man, grateful to find the cost was only a fraction of what Hovis Batts had quoted for the same new part.

"Now, for lunch," Hawk said when they were back in the Jeep. "If you want more than a sandwich, we could stop at one of the many restaurants along this road."

Anita glanced at her coveralls and shook her head. "I am not properly dressed to go to a restaurant. Your sandwiches will be enough."

"You look better than half the people you'd see inside," Hawk said, then let it go at that.

This part of Sand Mountain was built up, with one town seamlessly melding into another. Anita noticed the area had many small Mexican restaurants and grocerias, and most of the other businesses had prominent SE HABLA ESPAÑOL signs.

"Why do so many places say they speak Spanish?"

"Because so many Mexican immigrants live here now. It started as a trickle with migrant labor in the summers; then a new chicken processing plant opened. When word got around they were hiring Mexican workers, more and more poured in."

"Do the local people accept them?"

"Some do, others don't. The Mexicans tend to keep to themselves."

Hawk had not said, nor had Anita asked, but she suspected enough of these newcomers were illegal aliens to make them all be viewed with suspicion. *Perhaps that is why so many people in Rockdale look at me in such a peculiar way—they think I am one of these immigrants.*

"I am not from Mexico," Anita said aloud.

Hawk parked in a deserted roadside park and turned to face her. "I already know that. But I don't believe you have a husband."

Anita felt her face warm. Hawk Henson had been extremely good to her—far better than any other man she had met in America. She did not want to lie to him, but she could not share the real reason she had left Texas with anyone.

Anita took a deep breath. "I will tell you about Juan Sanchez."

Chapter 8

Seeing the pain reflected in Anita's eyes, Hawk almost wished he hadn't said anything about her husband. Juan. Of course, Juanita Sanchez must have been named for her father. Hawk wondered why he hadn't already guessed that himself.

Anita paused as if searching for the words to tell him about this phantom husband. Hawk opened the thermos and poured her a cup of hot chocolate. She looked at him with gratitude, then took a sip. She gripped the cup tightly, then spoke slowly, in a voice devoid of emotion.

"I married Juan Sanchez soon after I came to America. He had trouble finding work, and we moved around a lot. After he died, I moved to San Antonio. After Christmas, I decided to visit a teacher I knew when I lived in Colombia." Anita paused and took another sip of chocolate.

"You were on your way to Virginia to see this teacher when you had the accident?"

"Yes."

Hawk's heart twisted in sympathy at the sorrow in her eyes when she lifted her head. It was obvious Anita Sanchez didn't want to talk about her late husband, and Hawk resolved not to question her further about him. But the supposed friend in Virginia was another matter.

"Have you tried to contact this person since the accident?"

Anita shook her head. "No. I—I really do not know where she lives."

Hawk leaned back against the window and shook his head. "Let me get this straight. You took off from San Antonio with everything you own packed into your car without knowing where you were going?"

Anita looked him in the eye. "I know it must sound strange, but that was the way of it. I had to leave San Antonio."

"Too many memories?"

Anita nodded. "Yes. It was not a good place for us anymore. I planned to start over in Virginia, but nothing worked out as I expected."

Hawk barely resisted the impulse to reach out and comfort Anita in her obvious distress. He would never take advantage of a grieving widow, but this woman obviously needed someone's help. Even if Anita Sanchez was still hiding something from him, as he suspected, Hawk couldn't turn away from her.

"You can start over anywhere. Let's talk about it while we have our lunch."

∞

By the time Hawk dropped Anita off at the Rockdale Inn, her head was spinning with the ideas he had proposed. He had spoken quietly, answering every objection she had raised with logic and gentle persuasion.

Not only did Hawk Henson believe Rockdale was an ideal place for Anita to make a new start, he knew people who could help her every step of the way.

Glad to have some time alone before Juanita returned from playing with Jackie Tait, Anita took off her junkyard garb and stepped into the shower. Her body felt tired, but Hawk's words had lifted her spirits. He had not insisted on knowing more about Juan Sanchez, for which Anita was grateful. Then when Hawk started talking about the possibility she might stay in Rockdale permanently, he had made it all sound so possible, so—Anita searched for the word—so right.

She had asked God for a sign, and she believed He might have given her one. *"You can find peace in this valley, My child."*

The words had not been spoken audibly, but Anita's heart heard them clearly.

Show me what You want me to do, dear Lord. I am Your servant.

∞

When Hawk returned in the evening, he took them to a pizza restaurant, much to Juanita's delight. She loved pizza, but their budget seldom allowed it. The music was too loud for much conversation, but Juanita obviously was having a glorious time.

"I'm sorry we can't celebrate New Year's Eve properly, but I have to try to keep the drunks off the road tonight," Hawk said when they left the restaurant.

"Juanita and I could never stay awake until midnight, anyway," Anita said.

When they reached the inn, Hawk accompanied Anita and Juanita into the lobby. "I can stay a little while longer," he told Anita. "Can you get Juanita settled and come back? We need to talk."

When Hawk had left her at the inn earlier that day, Anita had promised to think about the possibility of establishing a new life in Rockdale, and she suspected he wanted an immediate answer.

Anita listened to her daughter's prayers and silently added one of her own. *Let me say what I should. Let my decision also be Your will.*

When Anita returned to the lobby, Mrs. Tanner was talking on the telephone behind the registration desk. Anita suspected as soon as that conversation ended, the innkeeper would probably try to overhear theirs.

"We can sit in the breakfast area," Anita suggested.

Hawk took a chair opposite her at one of the small tables and leaned forward. "What about it? Are you ready to stay in Rockdale?"

"I cannot make that decision now—it is too soon. I have always prayed to know God's will for my life. I have to trust Him to show me if I should stay."

"Show you how?"

"It is hard to say. Ever since I left Texas, I had the feeling God was guiding us. If He means me to stay here, I believe I will know if I can find a job and a place to live."

"I can help you with both."

"I appreciate all you have done for us, but I must stand on my own two feet."

Hawk frowned. "If you think I expect anything in return for helping you—"

"No, no, it is not that. I do not wish to become dependent on anyone. I—I think it would be better if you did not do so much for me."

Hawk's lips compressed. "Speak for yourself, Anita."

It was the first time Hawk had addressed her by her first name when they were alone, and somehow he managed to make it a verbal caress. Anita made herself look directly at him and hoped he would not notice how much his simple use of her first name had affected her.

"I do speak for myself—and for my daughter."

Hawk sighed and reached into his shirt pocket for a small notebook. He wrote a couple of names, then removed the page and offered it to her. When their hands brushed, Anita knew she was right to insist on keeping her distance from Hawk Henson. The attraction she had felt for this man from the first had steadily grown. His touch kindled sparks that traveled all the way from Anita's hand to her heart. As much as she enjoyed the sensation, Anita knew she could not afford to have it repeated. She had trusted one man and had been badly hurt. She did not intend to allow herself to make that mistake a second time.

"These are the people you told me about today?"

"Yes. Toni Trent heads the local Department of Human Resources office. She can tell you what services are available and how to get them. Phyllis Dickson does the hiring at the hospital. You can walk to the DHR office from here, but the hospital is a couple of miles on the other side of the courthouse."

"To me, that is also walking distance." Anita looked at the names and noted Hawk's handwriting was exceptionally neat. She tried to imagine what would happen if she asked these women for help. *They might take one look at me and tell me to go back to Mexico.*

"The DHR office and just about everything else will be closed tomorrow, but you can see Toni first thing on Friday. I'll call tomorrow and tell her you're coming."

"Are you sure—"

"They'll treat you right," Hawk interrupted. Seeing her hesitation, he wrote several telephone numbers on another sheet of paper and pushed it across the table. "Let me know how it goes. Here are the numbers where I can be reached. The top one is my cell phone, then the sheriff's office, and the last one is my home number."

"Will you have to work tomorrow also?" Anita asked.

Hawk smiled without humor. "Yes. Sheriff Trimble made out the holiday work schedule according to the football bowl games he wanted to see. It's no holiday for law enforcement, though. A few people always get hurt shooting fireworks, but drinking causes most of our New Year's calls, ranging from drunk driving to domestic violence."

Yes. I had my share of bad holidays when Juan Sanchez drank. It was not a subject Anita cared to remember.

"You cannot see the football games yourself, then?"

Hawk shrugged. "Football is almost a religion to some people around here, but it's just a game to me. I can watch the portable TV in the office between calls. What will you and Juanita do tomorrow?"

"We like to watch the parades before the football games. After that, we will rest and count our blessings."

"That's not a bad way to spend any day." Hawk glanced at his watch and stood. "I have to go now. Call me on Friday?"

"I will."

As soon as the door closed behind Hawk, Mrs. Tanner called to Anita. "Any idea how much longer you'll be here, Mrs. Sanchez?"

Anita thought Mrs. Tanner's emphasis on "Mrs." spoke volumes. *She must believe I am a bad woman, up to no good with Deputy Henson.* However, she spoke politely.

"I do not know, but I can pay you now for this week if you like."

Mrs. Tanner waved her hand. "That's all right. You can wait until Friday to take care of the bill."

"I will give you the money then. Good night." When Anita turned to leave, Mrs. Tanner spoke again.

"Happy New Year, Mrs. Sanchez."

"The same to you, Mrs. Tanner."

Back in her room, Anita considered the timeworn phrase. Happy New Year. With God's help, it would be a happy year.

And soon she would take the first steps to make it so for her and her daughter.

∽

"Do you have any plans for the day?" Mrs. Tanner asked when Anita and Juanita finished their breakfast.

"We will probably stay in our room and watch the parades on television," Anita replied.

"You might as well watch them on the big-screen TV out here," Mrs. Tanner said. "I don't care about the football games unless Alabama or Auburn are playing, but I enjoy the pretty floats and all the music."

"Can we, Mama?" asked Juanita, as if she feared Anita might refuse.

"Of course, sweetie. Thank you, Mrs. Tanner."

Mrs. Tanner popped corn for them around lunchtime, then surprised Anita by inviting her and Juanita to have supper with her in the cramped apartment behind the inn's registration desk.

"I don't suppose you know about eating black-eyed peas and hog jowl for luck on New Year's," the innkeeper said when they were seated around the small table.

"Hog jowl?" Anita repeated, unsure what that meant.

"The meat around a pig's jaw—but I cook my peas with a ham hock. They taste even better that way."

Juanita eyed the main dish warily. She had been trained not to make comments about food she was served, but Anita guessed the source of her concern. *Do I have to eat those dirty-looking peas?* Juanita's eyes asked.

"See the black dots in the middle of each pea? They look like little eyes, do they not? That is why they are called black-eyed peas," Anita explained.

"So you have had them before?" Mrs. Tanner sounded almost sorry she would not be the first to introduce the peas to Anita.

"I have seen them in the frozen food section at the market, but I do not know their taste."

"Now's your chance." Mrs. Tanner put the rest of the food on the table—a tossed salad and a pan of corn bread hot from the oven—and sat down. "You want to say a blessing?" she asked Juanita, who had already folded her hands.

Suddenly shy, Juanita shook her head. "This is your house. You do it."

Mrs. Tanner imitated Juanita by folding her hands and bowing her head. "We thank You for this food, Lord," she said after a pause.

"Amen," added Juanita.

As they ate, Mrs. Tanner confided that she didn't like her first name (Lois) and recounted in some detail the story of how she had met and married Mr. Tanner, who had left her the inn at his death some years ago.

"We never had any children. Your little girl must brighten your life, Mrs. Sanchez," she concluded.

"Please, call me Anita. Yes, Juanita is a gift from God."

"She's getting sleepy," Mrs. Tanner observed. "Maybe you should take her on to bed now."

Anita felt a twinge of guilt for not helping her hostess with the dishes, but she could see Juanita was tired, worn out by the unusual events of the past week. "Thank you for the meal," Anita said. "We enjoyed it very much."

Mrs. Tanner looked embarrassed. "I knew everything was closed for the holiday, and I couldn't let anyone under my roof go hungry. Besides, eating alone isn't much fun."

That I know, Anita could have said. On the way back to their room, Anita realized she had been wrong about Mrs. Tanner. She had thought the innkeeper to be a nosy busybody, but now she realized she was probably lonely. If Anita had misunderstood this woman, it was no wonder that so many others also misunderstood her.

"Judge not, that ye be not judged." The verse, a favorite of her mother's, came to her mind unbidden. Never become so concerned with others' faults that you do not see your own.

"I will try to do better," Anita said aloud.

"What, Mama?" Nearly asleep, Juanita spoke in a whisper.

"Nothing, sweetie. I was thinking out loud."

"It sounded like you were praying," Juanita said.

"In a way, I suppose I was." Anita unlocked the room and closed the door behind them. "Brush your teeth and wash your face. When you're ready for bed, I will hear your prayers."

The preparations took the edge off Juanita's sleepiness, and when Anita leaned over to kiss her good night, she smiled up at her. "You know what, Mama?"

"No, what?"

"I think we are in a good place."

"So do I, sweetie."

Thank You, Lord, for bringing us here.

Chapter 9

Hawk called Toni Trent around four o'clock in the afternoon on New Year's Day. From the background noise, he guessed she and David had probably invited several friends over. She put him on hold until she could pick up a telephone in a quieter room.

"I hope this isn't a child endangerment call," Toni said.

"No, things have been pretty quiet so far. Men don't usually start beating up their families this early in the day. I have a friend who needs a favor, though. She'll be coming to the DHR office tomorrow, and I wanted to give you a heads-up."

Toni reached for the notepad and pencil she kept beside every telephone. "Would this friend happen to be the beautiful brunette you've been seen with several times lately?"

Hawk groaned. "Where did you hear that?"

"Where didn't I hear it? Tom Statum was the first to mention it, I think—anyway, who is this friend, and what can I do for her?"

"Her name is Anita Sanchez. She's a widow with a young daughter. She wrecked her car in the ice storm the other day, and it'll be awhile before Hovis Batts gets it put together again. She doesn't have much money, and she can't afford to stay at the Rockdale Inn much longer."

"Her name is Sanchez?" Toni repeated.

Hawk sighed. "Yes. What about it?"

"I just wondered if she would be eligible for food stamps. The rules are rather strict."

"I don't know about that, but I doubt she'd take anything she thought was charity."

"Food stamps aren't charity—they are a federal government entitlement for people in need."

"Whatever you say. If you can help her find a place she can afford, it would be a great start."

"I'll see what I can do." Toni paused. "It's about time you had a lady friend. I hope this one works out. Happy New Year, Hawk."

"Hey, wait a minute," he protested, but Toni hung up before he could deny Anita was his "lady friend." Silently, he rehearsed the arguments in his imaginary defense. *Anita Sanchez and her daughter need help, that's all. What kind of person would I be if I failed to do what I could to make their lives a little better?*

Hawk sighed. He could assure everyone else his motives were entirely pure, but deep down, he realized Toni Trent was closer to the truth than he cared to admit.

"It's about time you had a lady friend." Toni could have been teasing, but he knew she wasn't. Ever since his return to Rockdale, Hawk had earned the reputation of being a loner. He had dated several women, but he seldom went out with the same one more than two or three times, and those not consecutively.

It was a fact: In the few days he'd known her, Hawk had already spent more quality time with Anita Sanchez than with any of the forgettable women he'd dated in the past few years.

Maybe it's just as well Anita believes I'm doing too much for her. Hawk tried to tell himself he should keep his distance to quiet the gossip, but he didn't care about that.

Hawk Henson had never made a New Year's resolution in his life, but at four fifteen on the afternoon of the first day of the new year, he decided to continue to help Anita Sanchez—and to see her as often as she would allow.

∞

Bill Rankin was not having a happy New Year's Day at all. As he sat drinking beer in a smoky bar in San Antonio, he decided it was probably among the most miserable days of his life. Worst of all, he had no one to blame but himself. He now realized he had handled Anita Sanchez badly. If he had it to do over, he would have tried to befriend her first and make her believe he wanted to help her get all the money she was due from her no-good husband.

Bill shifted his weight on the barstool and sighed. He had been too impatient to claim the fortune that was rightly his to take the time to charm her into giving it to him. *I could have done it that way*, Bill told himself. He had talked more than one lonely woman out of her money, but something in Anita Sanchez's eyes warned him she would never allow herself to be such an easy mark. *Why, then, didn't I figure she would try to run?*

"I thought she'd stay here because of the little girl," Bill mumbled. He had badly misjudged Anita Sanchez, and as a result, she had managed to slip away—and no one would tell him where she had gone.

She and her fortune, the money that was rightfully his.

Bill raised his beer and made his own private New Year's resolution. *I will find Anita Sanchez and her brat, and I will get every penny she owes me.*

The daughter would be the key to Anita's fortune. Her mother had shown she would do anything to protect her—even if it meant giving up everything else.

I will find her. The trail was cold now, but sooner or later, Anita Sanchez would make a mistake that would lead him straight to her.

Comforted, Bill raised his mug again and toasted his inevitable victory.

∞

Anita had expected to take Juanita with her to the DHR office, but when Mrs. Tanner found out where she was going, she offered to let Juanita stay at the inn with her until Anita returned.

"Juanita has some new coloring books. She could use them at one of the tables in the breakfast area, if that is all right."

"Even better, she can stay with me right here behind the counter," Mrs. Tanner offered. "I'll clear a space for her."

Juanita seemed so pleased with the idea, she scarcely waved good-bye when Anita left.

The morning air was brisk but not unbearably cold. The night's light frost had melted in the morning sun, and the cloudless sky promised a lovely day.

May it be a good day for Juanita and me, as well. Anita fingered the plain gold cross hanging from a delicate gold filigree neck chain. According to family legend, the first Muños man to seek his fortune in Colombia many generations ago had brought the chain with him from Spain. When she was sixteen, her father put it around Anita's neck and reminded her of its history. "The cross is not a worldly bauble to be worn with pride, my daughter, but a reminder to be humble in remembrance of the price the Savior paid for your salvation."

Anita had removed the cross from the lockbox that morning to wear as a symbol of the source of her courage and strength. Along with it, she took the document certifying Anita Muños Sanchez to be a naturalized citizen of the United States of America.

At the DHR office entrance, Anita stopped and took a deep breath. *Be with me now, Lord,* she prayed, then went inside.

The receptionist looked up when she entered, but before she could ask Anita's business, a woman emerged from a door marked DIRECTOR and greeted her.

"Good morning, Mrs. Sanchez. Hawk Henson told me to expect you."

Anita had imagined the DHR director would be old and gray or perhaps fat and frumpy. However, the young woman who extended her hand to Anita was trim and attractive. From her short brown hair to her tailored brown business suit and sensible pumps, she looked every inch a professional. Yet her smile was warm, welcome proof she truly cared for others.

"I am pleased to meet you, Mrs. Trent."

"We can talk in my office. Alice, hold my calls, please."

Anita sat on the edge of the chair Mrs. Trent offered. Instead of going behind her desk, the DHR director pulled up another chair to sit beside Anita.

"I understand you could use help," Mrs. Trent said.

"I do not know what Deputy Henson told you, but my daughter and I need a place to live. I cannot afford to stay at the Rockdale Inn much longer."

"Yes, Hawk said housing was your main problem. Can you tell me a little about yourself, Mrs. Sanchez? If you're a qualified alien, you might be eligible for several benefits."

Anita felt her face warm. *Why do so many Americanos automatically presume anyone with a Latino name must be an illegal alien?* She opened her handbag and removed the precious paper. "I am a naturalized citizen of the United States.

Here is the proof."

Mrs. Trent looked uncomfortable. "I'm sorry—it's my job to ask. You're eligible for several programs, including food stamps."

Anita shook her head vigorously. "I still have some savings. I need a job and a place to live. I have not come here to beg for food stamps."

"I understand. We usually refer clients who need work to the State Employment Office. However, I believe Deputy Henson said you're a nurse?"

"Yes. I have emergency room experience."

"In that case, you should see Phyllis Dickson—she's the hospital's head of personnel. For a place to live, I can refer you to Harrison Homes, Rockdale's only low-rent apartment units. What do you have in mind?"

"Something small for my daughter and myself. We have no furniture."

Toni Trent made a note on the legal pad. "I'll talk to the rental agent and get back to you. Tell me about your daughter."

"Juanita is six years old."

"You'll want to register her for school. I can help you do that, too," Toni added, seeing Anita's stricken look.

"There are so many things to consider in a new place," Anita said.

"I know. I came to Rockdale as a stranger once myself." Toni asked a few more questions and made notes on a yellow legal pad. "I believe I have everything we need," she said, then paused. "Unofficially, I'm curious about why you decided to come to Rockdale."

"The deputy did not tell you?"

"No. He said you were a friend who needed help, that's all."

Anita touched her gold cross. "I was caught in an ice storm a few days ago. My car wrecked on the road into town, and Deputy Henson found me. He has been helping my daughter and me since."

"So you have decided to stay here because of the deputy?"

Anita hesitated, then shook her head. "Not really. I know it might sound strange, but I believe God might have led me to this place."

Toni Trent did not seem surprised or taken aback. "I noticed your beautiful cross. You and your daughter would be welcome at our church Sunday."

"Thank you, but my car has not yet been repaired."

"I suspect Deputy Henson would give you a ride."

Anita tried to suppress her alarm. She did not want to be seen in Hawk's company anywhere else. "Maybe later, after we are settled," she said.

Toni stood. "It has been a pleasure to meet you, Mrs. Sanchez. I'll talk to the rental agent and let you know about an apartment."

"Thank you very much. I would like to see the lady at the hospital now, if you will please tell me how to get there."

"I can do better than that." Toni Trent led Anita from her office and stopped at the reception desk. "Where are the abuse report forms for the hospital?"

The receptionist pointed to her "Out" box. "I was going to mail them when I went to the post office."

"I'll hand-carry them. If anyone calls, I should be back in forty-five minutes." Toni turned to Anita. "You can ride to the hospital with me."

"That is not necessary. I do not mind walking," Anita said.

"When you see how far it is to the hospital, you'll be glad you rode."

"Hawk told me it was about two miles," Anita said, then wished she had not used his first name.

Toni smiled. "Men aren't always accurate about distances."

They got into Toni Trent's SUV, and after they had traveled a few blocks, Toni pointed out a series of one-story red brick buildings. "That's the Harrison Homes apartment complex. It's a low-rent housing development where most tenants behave and take care of their apartments. Dwight Anders is a good manager."

Anita looked at the monotonous sameness of the apartments, typical of all government-sponsored housing projects. She and Juan had lived in such places, and Anita had been very happy to get out of them. Still, the smallest apartment here would be better than their cramped room at the Rockdale Inn. "They look very nice."

A few blocks later, Toni pulled into the parking lot of the Rockdale Hospital, a three-story yellow brick building that occupied the entire block. *A one-hundred-bed hospital,* Anita guessed. An ambulance stood on the emergency-room apron, its doors open as its occupant was removed. *The patient will be taken to a cubicle for evaluation and treatment. Those first few minutes will be important.* ER procedures were universal, and Anita could already picture herself working there. *Let there be a place for me here if it is Your will,* she prayed.

Anita realized Toni Trent was addressing her. "The personnel office is on the right as we go in. I'll take the abuse report forms to the administrator and meet you in the lobby after you see Mrs. Dickson."

Seeing Anita enter with Toni Trent, the receptionist quickly ushered her into Phyllis Dickson's office. Had the social worker not been with her, Anita doubted she would have been granted such speedy access.

The personnel director at the San Antonio hospital had been a stern and large-boned, middle-aged woman with iron-gray hair. Anita was pleasantly surprised when Phyllis Dickson turned out to be an attractive blond, and she hoped she would be as kind as Toni Trent. However, from the moment the personnel director laid eyes on her, Anita had the feeling she was being weighed in the woman's private scales and found wanting.

"You say you are a nurse?"

Anita nodded. "Yes. I trained in Arizona and Texas. I worked as an emergency room triage nurse in San Antonio."

"Do you have proof of past employment and an Alabama nursing license?"

"I can give you the address of the hospital where I worked until after

Christmas, and I have a copy of my Texas license."

"At the present, money is short. We aren't hiring nurses."

Anita tried not to show her disappointment. Everything else had gone so well that day, she had hoped this would, also. "Is there any kind of work I can do?"

The personnel director looked through a slender stack of papers on her desk. "A temporary position will be available in the day surgery area when one of the staff goes on leave in a couple of weeks."

"I will take it."

"It's janitorial work," Mrs. Dickson said. "Do you still want it?"

Janitorial work. The most menial job, with the worst pay, in any hospital. Anita swallowed hard and tried not to show her distress. *It is only temporary, and perhaps a nursing job will open soon.*

Anyway, in her position, Anita did not have many choices.

"I need to work. Whatever the job is, I will do it."

Chapter 10

Toni Trent was waiting in the lobby when Anita emerged from Mrs. Dickson's office. "Does she have anything for you?"

"A woman in day surgery goes on maternity leave in a couple of weeks. I will take her place for a couple of months."

"Day surgery," Toni repeated. "Nursing?"

"No—cleaning."

"At minimum wage?"

"A little over. It is not what I hoped for, but it is a start."

"Good. Mrs. Dickson's certifying you will be employed will help with your housing application."

"How long does it usually take to get an apartment?" Anita asked when they reached Toni's SUV.

"That depends on whether there's a waiting list. Since we're so close already, let's find out."

Toni turned into Harrison Homes and parked in front of the housing office. "Wait here. If Dwight Anders isn't in his office, I can still get a housing application."

A short time later, Toni returned to the car, accompanied by a rather stout man Anita judged to be around forty. "Mrs. Sanchez, this is Dwight Anders. He's going to show us a one-bedroom apartment."

Anita got out of the car and joined them. "Is the apartment available now?" she asked.

"It will be after we finish cleaning and painting it. The last tenants left before Christmas, and what with the holidays and all, we haven't had a chance to get the work done."

Dwight Anders led them to the unit, one in a row of seemingly identical apartments. When he unlocked the door and motioned them to step inside, Anita was surprised to see Toni Trent put her hands to her face, apparently overcome with some emotion.

"I know this apartment well. Being in it again brings back a lot of memories."

"Why? Did the DHR have to come here for some reason?" Dwight Anders asked.

"No. I stayed here with April Kincaid part of the time when I was fifteen. We kept our bikes against that wall over there."

The manager looked blank. "April Kincaid?"

"You probably know her as April Winter, Congressman Jeremy Winter's wife."

Dwight Anders looked impressed. "She once lived here? No wonder the congressman is so willing to help us get the funds to repair and update the units."

"This one looks as if it could use some help," Toni said.

From the small living room, Anita could see almost the entire apartment. The kitchen was to the left, open to the living room. The bedroom was straight ahead, with the bathroom behind the kitchen. Small as it was, Anita would be glad to live in it, except for one thing.

"There is no furniture?" Anita asked Mr. Anders.

"No, this unit rents unfurnished."

"Do you have anything you could put in it?" Toni asked.

"Only bits and pieces tenants left when they moved—mostly junk. The unfurnished units rent for less," he pointed out.

"Then don't try to furnish it," Toni said. "Assuming Mrs. Sanchez qualifies, when could she move in?"

"That depends on the paperwork. The apartment should be ready in a couple of weeks." Dwight Anders turned to Anita. "Get your application in as soon as you can, Mrs. Sanchez. The larger units have a waiting list. You're lucky you can use a small apartment."

The Lord's plan has nothing to do with luck, Anita wanted to say. "Thank you, Mr. Anders. I will start on the papers right away."

The housing director returned to his office, and Toni and Anita got back into the SUV. "What do you think about the apartment?" Toni asked as they drove away from the Harrison Homes. "Is it large enough for you and your daughter?"

"Oh, yes, thank you. But I cannot afford to buy much furniture."

"You won't have to. I stored a set of twin beds and matching dresser last fall when my stepdaughter got new furniture for her room. My sister-in-law is about to replace a sofa. We'll be glad to see them put to good use."

"I do not think finding furniture for me is part of your job," Anita said.

"My job is to help others any way I can, just as I have been helped. I was a messed-up teenager when I met April Kincaid. I'm in social work now because of people like her and my sister-in-law, who for many years had the job I have now."

Looking at the poised DHR director, Anita found it hard to picture Toni Trent as a troubled teenager. "I became a nurse to help others, myself," she said. "I hope I will yet be able to do that in Rockdale."

"So do I." Toni stopped in front of the Rockdale Inn and handed Anita her business card. "You can call my cell phone if you have any questions about the housing application. Bring it to my office Monday so I can review it before we turn it in."

Anita regarded Toni Trent with gratitude. "I wish I had the words to tell you how much I thank you, Mrs. Trent."

"You don't need words—your eyes speak for you. I'll see you Monday?"

"Yes, Mrs. Trent."

When Anita entered the lobby, Mrs. Tanner and Juanita were nowhere in sight, and for a moment she feared something might have happened to Juanita.

She was about to knock on Mrs. Tanner's apartment door when she saw it was slightly ajar. She heard Mrs. Tanner say something indistinguishable, followed by the welcome sound of her daughter's laughter.

"Mrs. Tanner? I am back," Anita called.

The innkeeper came to the door, wiping her hands on a kitchen towel. Behind her stood Juanita, enveloped in an apron which covered almost her entire body.

"That took less time than I expected," Mrs. Tanner said. "Juanita and I are making soup."

"It's veg'able soup, Mama, and I put in the words," Juanita said.

"The words?" Anita repeated.

"Small pasta letters, actually—to make it alphabet soup," Mrs. Tanner explained.

Anita hugged her daughter. "I know it will be good, then."

"Come back around noon, and we'll have it for lunch."

"Thank you, we will. And I also thank you for watching Juanita."

"It is my pleasure," Mrs. Tanner said, obviously meaning it.

Later, when Anita said grace, her heart felt lighter than it had for days. She welcomed the opportunity to thank God, not only for the soup, but for all the other blessings the day had brought.

∞

After lunch, Juanita needed little persuasion to lie down for a rest. After her daughter fell asleep, Anita returned to the lobby and gave Mrs. Tanner a capsule version of the day's events.

"I hope to get into an apartment at Harrison Homes soon, but that will probably take another two weeks," Anita concluded. "How much will I owe you in all?"

"Pay me for the first two weeks, and we'll call it even," Mrs. Tanner said. "I know you and Juanita need more room, but I'll be sorry to see you leave."

"I want to pay the entire bill. I do not like to be in debt to anyone."

"You won't be if you'll agree to sit behind the desk and answer the telephone while I'm out. It would be a big help to me."

"I suppose I could," Anita said. "Until I start working at the hospital, I will not have anything else to do."

"It's settled, then."

"One more thing," Anita said. "I promised to let Deputy Henson know what I found out today, but Juanita is sleeping, and I do not want to awaken her."

"You can use the phone in my apartment. It's a private line. Do you know his number?"

"Yes, thank you."

Mrs. Tanner led Anita into her neat combination sitting room and bedroom and pointed out the telephone beside her recliner. "Take your time," she said, then closed the door behind her.

Presuming Hawk would be at work, she tried his office number. "May I speak to Deputy Henson?" she asked when Sally Rogers answered.

"He's out on a call. Is this Mrs. Sanchez? He said to tell you he'll call you when he has the chance."

Anita thanked her and hung up. She was not surprised the receptionist recognized her voice, but she wondered what Sally Rogers thought when Hawk told her Mrs. Sanchez would call him, and she felt frustrated she had not been able to tell Hawk her news. After all, if it had not been for him, her life could well have taken a totally different turn.

"That was a short conversation," Mrs. Tanner commented when Anita returned to the reception desk.

"The deputy is out of the office," Anita said.

"I always liked Hawk Henson. Some folks around here act like they're ashamed they have Indian blood, but Hawk's family has never been like that."

"From what he said, he has kept up some of the old ways. That cannot be easy in these days."

"I suppose not." The inn telephone rang, and when Mrs. Tanner went to answer it, Anita waved and returned to the room.

Juanita stirred when she opened the door, then sat up and announced she had slept long enough. "Can we go outside, please, Mama?"

"We can walk to the garage. I want to see how the work is coming along on our car."

"And I want to see the fishes."

∞

Hovis Batts greeted them warmly and assured Juanita the fish had been waiting for her return.

With her daughter engaged in fish watching, Anita asked about her car. "Was the salvage headlight all right?"

"Perfect—even down to the color. In fact, I put it on this morning. The parts I ordered ought to come any day now. You'll be back on the road again before you know it, Mrs. Sanchez."

"I have decided to stay here, at least for a while, but I will need the car when I start working at the hospital."

Hovis Batts's face registered surprise, then curiosity. "I thought you was anxious to get out of here. What made you change your mind?"

Hawk Henson. But Anita knew he was not the only reason.

"The people where I was headed might not be as kind as those I have met here. Besides, I would have run out of money by the time I could have gotten there."

"I suspect people are about the same everywhere, when you get down to it.

Some folks around here won't give you the time of day, but don't let them bother you none."

Sheriff Trimble for one, Anita thought. But Hovis Batts was right: Anyone looking for a slight would be sure to find it, no matter where they lived.

"Let me know when the car is ready."

"I will, but I hope you'll bring the little lady here anytime you like. My fish like to have visitors."

"In that case, I will watch them with my daughter for a while and let you get back to work."

Juanita sat in front of the aquarium, transfixed. "Look, Mama," she said when Anita entered the room. "That one mean fish is chasing all the others. See how scared they look?"

"Yes. But look, here comes another fish to chase that one."

"I want the good fish to win," Juanita said.

"So do I, sweetie."

They watched the chase for several minutes until both fish tired of their sport and retired to the elaborate underwater castle, leaving the other aquarium inhabitants to go about their business.

For some reason, the aggressive fish reminded Anita of Bill Rankin. A few weeks ago, she had run away like one of those poor fish to escape a man she felt to be evil.

Now, praise God, Bill Rankin was half a continent away and no longer able to hurt her and Juanita. And in Hawk Henson, they had a champion who would protect them.

Now, we are safe. May it always be so.

Chapter 11

"H enson? Come in here," Sheriff Trimble bellowed from his office.

Hawk hung his coat on the rack beside the door and sighed. He had spent much of the day driving all over Rock County on a wild goose chase. An informant claimed knowledge of a crystal methamphetamine lab operating in the wilderness, but Hawk had found nothing. He knew meth labs were out there, all right—they had replaced the growing of marijuana as the major source of local illegal activity throughout northeast Alabama. Rock County law enforcement officers were increasingly faced with problems the rural county had never had before and for which they were largely unprepared.

Now what? Hawk hoped the sheriff wasn't about to send him out on another patrol. "Yes, sir. What is it?"

"Sit down. Find anything?"

"Not in any of the places I looked—and I covered a lot of territory."

"I'm not surprised. We don't know enough about all this new stuff. Asa McGinty applied for several drug training grants before he retired. I reckon that's why we got this letter."

Hawk skimmed the paper the sheriff handed him. A narcotics training academy in North Carolina had accepted the Rock County Sheriff's Department application to send an officer for extensive training. He returned the letter to the sheriff and nodded. "That sounds like a good course. When will you go?"

Sheriff Trimble snorted. "Never. I'm too old for that kind of stuff. I'm giving them your name. They'll let you know when the next class starts."

Only recently Hawk would have embraced the opportunity to attend such a school, not only for the training, but also to get away from Rockdale for a while. A change of scene never hurt, and every time he left it, he always returned refreshed and with a new appreciation of his beloved county.

But things had changed. Hawk realized he didn't want to go anywhere now. Since Anita Sanchez had come into his life, nothing had seemed exactly the same.

"Shouldn't you send one of the other deputies? They have more seniority."

"Maybe so, but they all say you are the best one to go, and I agree."

Hawk understood perfectly. *Nobody else wants to do this, so I'm stuck with it.* Having to make do with everyone else's leftovers was nothing new to Hawk, but he resented the sheriff's easy assumption he would automatically agree to do anything he was asked. "Suppose I don't want to go, either?"

Sheriff Trimble scowled. "If we don't use this grant, it won't look good when the time comes to ask for more training money, and the druggies will keep on outsmarting us. Turning down training like this won't look good on your record, either."

"I never said I wouldn't go. How long is the course?"

"I'm not sure, since they have more than one. Most are five days; others are longer. It'll take you a day to get there and another day to get back. You'll get your regular salary and all expenses, including travel."

"You can turn in my name. Is that it?"

"Not quite." Sheriff Trimble leaned back in his chair and folded his arms across his chest in the manner of a man about to deliver a reprimand. "Your foreign girlfriend called you here while you were out. This is a business office. Tell her not to do that again."

Hawk forced back an angry reply. It had been a long day, and he was tired, but that was no excuse to lose his temper. "If you mean Mrs. Sanchez, she isn't my girlfriend, and she isn't 'foreign.' I asked her to call me, not the other way around."

"I don't imagine she's 'Mrs. Sanchez' when you're alone, is she, Henson? Like I said before, we don't need her kind around here. For all you know, she could be a drug runner herself."

"Anita Sanchez is a widow who's had a hard time lately. She is no more a drug runner than you are, Sheriff."

"I reckon that remains to be seen, Henson. Close the door when you leave."

∞

As the afternoon passed and Hawk did not call, Anita began to wonder if something could have happened to him. In San Antonio, she had worked with a woman whose husband was in law enforcement. Although her friend accepted the fact he had a dangerous job, Anita noticed her anguish when he went undercover and disappeared for days at a time.

Anita had experienced similar pain with Juan, except when her husband left for a long period of time, it usually meant he was either in trouble or looking for it.

What would life with Hawk be like?

Anita cut the thought short, upset she had allowed herself to think of Hawk as anything more than a friend. He had been good to her, but he had his own life. She and Juanita were not a part of it now, nor would they ever be—

The telephone rang, startling her. It was almost as if thinking of Hawk had caused him to call, and Anita took a steadying breath before she picked up the receiver.

"Hi, Anita. Sorry I couldn't get back to you sooner, but this is the first chance I've had to call all day. What did you find out?"

"Quite a bit." Briefly, Anita told him about her day.

"You already have a job offer and a place to stay? That's great. We should celebrate tonight."

"It is too early for that. The job isn't very good, and it does not start for a couple of weeks. I might not be approved for the apartment, either."

"Don't borrow trouble. We'll talk about it tonight if you and Juanita will have dinner with me."

Anita hesitated. She meant it when she told Hawk they should not be seen together so much, but she had much to tell—and ask—the deputy. "I would rather go out of town."

"So would I. There's a restaurant in an old house near Mentone. It's not a fancy place, but the food is good."

"Where is Mentone?"

Anita sensed Hawk's smile. "Out of town a ways. I'll be by for you ladies at six o'clock."

∞

Although she kept trying to convince herself Hawk was just a family friend, Anita felt fluttery as a teenager on her first date when she dressed for the evening. She had a limited wardrobe, in part because she had always worn uniforms to work but also because she spent most of her clothing budget on her growing daughter. She had one dress for special occasions and a couple of other everyday outfits, plus several separates, all suited for the San Antonio climate. Taking Hawk's word that the place they were going was not fancy, Anita decided to pair her black slacks with a long-sleeved white blouse and her only woolen jacket.

Juanita had several like-new hand-me-down outfits her friend Beth had outgrown, including a few long dresses she loved. Bypassing the ones with ruffles and bows, Anita chose the red-and-green plaid dress Juanita had worn to church the Sunday before Christmas.

"You look pretty, Mamacita," Juanita said when both were ready.

"So do you, sweetie."

"Looks like somebody's going to a party," Mrs. Tanner observed when Juanita twirled in front of her, showing off her dress.

"Dep'ty Hawk's coming to get us," Juanita said.

Mrs. Tanner glanced at Anita. "Where's he taking you this time?"

"To a restaurant in an old house in Mentone, I think he said."

Mrs. Tanner raised her eyebrows. "Mentone, eh? There's some high-class inns and eating places around there."

"He said it was not a fancy place."

"If it's the one I think, it's got a real pretty view, but, of course, you won't be able to tell that at night."

"Mama, here he is!"

Hawk greeted Mrs. Tanner, then helped Juanita put on her coat. "Isn't Dora going with us?" he asked.

"No. She's tired. She has to stay here and sleep."

Hawk directed his attention to Anita. "Will that jacket be enough?" he asked, seeing she did not have her coat.

304

"It will if the car is warm and we will not have to walk very far."

"My heater works, and it's only a few steps from the parking lot to the restaurant—but it's another cold night."

"Good-bye," Mrs. Tanner called after them. "Have a good time."

"You have a good time, too!" Juanita responded, leaving the innkeeper smiling.

∞

Once more they climbed out of the valley onto Lookout Mountain and traveled on a series of winding, two-lane roads. With the dark asphalt pavement beneath and an almost starless sky above, they rode through a tunnel of light made by the Jeep's headlights.

"It sure is dark out here," said Juanita.

"We'll come back in the daytime so you can see everything." Hawk waved his hand toward invisible sites. "DeSoto State Park and Little River Canyon are just over there, and Sequoyah Caverns is nearby."

"Are those caves?" Anita recalled the thousands of bats she had seen in a New Mexico cave and shuddered.

"Yes. The caverns are named for the Cherokee who made an alphabet for the Cherokee language. We know Sam Houston visited the caverns—he left his name on one of the pillars in 1830."

"Sam Houston from the Alamo?" Juanita asked.

"The same. The caverns belong to the Echota Cherokee tribe, so in a way, I'm one of the owners."

"Can we go there tonight, Dep'ty Hawk?"

Hawk chuckled, a rich sound that started low in his throat and grew into a full laugh. "It's closed at night, but I'll take you there some weekend soon, all right? For now, look at all these lights."

Many Christmas decorations were still up throughout the area, and in the resort town of Mentone, clear lights festooned nearly every building and twinkled in the still night air.

"Pretty!" Juanita exclaimed. Although it was far too dark to see it at night, Anita took Hawk's word that Mentone offered a magnificent view from the bluff on which it sat.

"I'll show you our ski resort next time."

"Skiing in Alabama?" asked Anita. "Surely it is not cold enough here for that."

"The mountain elevations get more snow than Rockdale, but it wouldn't be enough without a little help. It's interesting to watch the machine make snow."

"Do you ski, Dep'ty Hawk?" Juanita asked.

"No," Hawk said emphatically. "I'd rather keep both my feet on solid ground."

Hawk slowed and turned into a narrow graveled driveway beside a Victorian frame house. In addition to lights around the circling verandah, a single candle shone in every window.

"Look at all those pretty lights, Mama!"

"I see them, sweetie."

The display reminded Anita of the San Antonio Riverwalk, and for a moment she felt a pang of loss for the culture she had left behind. Being Hispanic in San Antonio, she was one among many, and no one noticed she spoke English with an accent. In Rockdale, however, everyone knew she was not one of them, often before she said a word.

Live in the present, she reminded herself. This day, which had been good so far, was not yet over. Perhaps the best was yet to be.

The full parking lot made it appear they might have a long wait for a table. However, when they entered the wide entrance hall, a dark-haired hostess in a long red wool dress hugged Hawk and led them to a table in what had been the house's library. Shelves filled with a mixture of books and unglazed pottery rose to the tall ceiling, and a cheerful fire blazed on the hearth.

Even as Anita speculated the hostess might be Hawk's girlfriend, he introduced her as his cousin, Amitola.

"That's a pretty name," Juanita said.

"It means 'rainbow' in Cherokee," Hawk said. "Amitola, these are my friends, Anita and Juanita Sanchez."

The girl nodded to acknowledge the introductions. "Do you live in Rockdale?"

"We are there at the present," Anita said.

"Sorry I don't have time to visit—we're really busy tonight. Your server will be along in a minute."

"You made it sound like you're in Rockdale temporarily," Hawk said when Amitola left.

"We may be. I do not even know if we will have a place to stay in Rockdale."

"I wouldn't worry about that. Toni Trent has been known to work wonders when it comes to finding housing."

"She is a wonderful lady. Thank you for speaking to her on my behalf."

"Toni would have welcomed you even if I hadn't called her first. You're right—she is a great lady. We came back to Rockdale about the same time after being away for a while. Our paths crossed when DHR needed a deputy to help remove a child from an unsafe situation. It turned out to be the first rescue case for us both, and we've been friends ever since."

"Who's DHR?" Juanita asked.

Anita's look flashed a warning for Hawk to watch what he said. She did not want Juanita to be concerned about children being taken away from their homes.

"The DHR is a place where people go for all kinds of help," Hawk said.

"You went there this morning, didn't you, Mama?"

"Yes, sweetie. Mrs. Trent is in charge there. She took me to the hospital, then to see an apartment."

Juanita's eyes grew large and her lower lip trembled. "Is she going to take me away, too?"

"Of course not!" Anita reached over to hug her daughter.

"No one is going to take you away from your mother," Hawk said. "I won't let them."

The server appeared with the menus, diverting Juanita's attention. Even though she said nothing more about her fears, Anita realized she had not protected her daughter as well as she thought; Juanita had probably known more about their sometimes precarious situation than she had let her mother know.

Someday, when Juanita was old enough to understand, Anita would tell her daughter the truth about her life in Colombia and her marriage to Juan Sanchez. For now, she wanted her to be happy and feel safe in their new life in Alabama.

∽

Prompted by Anita's questions about Cherokee history, Hawk did most of the talking during dinner, but he volunteered no information about himself.

"You seem to have many cousins. You must have a large family," Anita said.

Hawk smiled. "All the Cherokee around here consider ourselves to be kin, whether we're close blood relatives or not. The girl at the bank is my true first cousin. Amitola and I are third cousins, I think. The Old Ones somehow kept up with it all. I never have tried."

Do Cherokee have to marry within their tribal family? Anita would not ask the question, but her daughter came close.

"Dep'ty Hawk, do you have a Cher'kee wife?"

The question seemed to amuse him. "No, Miss Juanita. I have never had a wife of any kind."

"Amitola's pretty. Why don't you marry her?"

"Juanita! You should not say such things," Anita protested.

Hawk smiled. "I don't mind. I can't marry Amitola because she already has a husband. In fact, she and Joel have a three-year-old boy and a girl about your age."

Anita had repeatedly told herself Hawk Henson could never be more than a friend, yet she felt foolish relief at his reply.

"I'd like to play with Amitola's little girl," Juanita said.

"That would be hard to arrange, since she lives on the other side of Mentone. You'll have lots of kids to play with when you start school, though."

Juanita looked excited. "I like school. When can I start?"

Anita wished he had not brought up the subject, since she had done nothing about enrolling Juanita. "We will talk about that later, sweetie."

Mercifully, their server arrived with the bill at that moment, and they left the restaurant and started back to Rockdale without further conversation.

"I think we just lost a passenger," Hawk said a few minutes later when a glance in the rearview mirror revealed Juanita had fallen asleep.

"It is past her bedtime, but riding in a car always makes her sleepy. When she was a baby, it was sometimes the only way to get her to fall asleep."

"What about your husband? Was he still living then?"

307

Anita hesitated. She could not lie to Hawk, but neither was she ready to tell Hawk where Juan Sanchez had been during that time. "Yes, but he was not with us very much."

"It's hard to raise a child alone," Hawk said. "My mother did her best, but she was never the same after my father died."

"How old were you then?"

"Twelve. Mother would have liked to stay on the mountain, but we had to move back to town when he got sick."

Anita tried to picture Hawk at twelve. "You did not want to leave?"

"Not at first, but I knew we had no choice. I thought we'd return when I got old enough to do all the heavy work. But by then, my mother wasn't well enough to go back."

"She is not still living?"

"No. She died on my eighteenth birthday." Hawk cleared his throat and glanced at Anita. "What about your folks?"

From long practice, she had learned to be brief and matter-of-fact. "I lost them both when I was eighteen."

Hawk took his right hand from the steering wheel and briefly touched Anita's arm in a gesture of sympathy. "What happened?"

They were murdered because they would not cooperate with a drug ring. Anita could not bring herself to speak the whole truth, so she said as little as possible. "Our house burned while I was away in school."

"That must have been terrible for you. You came to America afterwards?"

"Yes."

Hawk considered her words for a moment before he spoke again. "You lost your family and then your husband, yet you didn't give up. You're a brave lady, Anita."

Hawk's praise disturbed her. She had not told him the whole story, and she felt completely unworthy of Hawk's admiration. "When I was a little older than Juanita is now, I asked Jesus Christ into my heart. I have faith He will help me, and He always has."

Hawk nodded. "Some Power was definitely with you during that ice storm. Most women would have fallen to pieces after wrecking their car, but you didn't."

If I were really as strong as you seem to think, I would never have agreed to see you tonight. Anita smiled ruefully. "I know I have been blessed, but I am still feeling my way in this place. Some things have worked out, but much still has to be done."

When Hawk glanced at her again, Anita lowered her head, embarrassed. "You know I will do whatever it takes to help you any way I can," he said.

"Yes, and I appreciate the offer. But as I told you, I must do as much as I can on my own."

Hawk seemed ready to pursue their conversation further, but as they crossed the bridge back into Rockdale, the glare of the street lights woke Juanita.

"Where are we?" she asked drowsily.

"Almost home," Hawk said.

When they stopped in front of the inn, Hawk carried a groggy Juanita through the lobby. After Anita unlocked the door, he laid the girl on a bed inside the room.

"Good night, Hawk. Thank you for a wonderful evening."

Anita's hand was on the door, ready to close it after him, until Hawk covered her hand with his and took a step toward her.

"Come back out after you put Juanita to bed. I have something to say to you."

Anita started to ask what it was, but his intent look silenced her. "I won't be long."

Shortening her daughter's usual bedtime ritual, Anita helped Juanita into her nightgown and tucked her into bed.

What does Hawk want to say to me? Her heart beating unaccountably fast, Anita squared her shoulders and left the room.

Chapter 12

When Anita entered the hall, Hawk took her hand and led her to a nearby alcove containing the ice and vending machines. It offered relative privacy.

"What is it?" Anita looked into his dark eyes and felt her throat tighten. Her heart was beating so rapidly, she felt sure he could hear it.

Hawk stroked her cheek with the back of his free hand. "I admire you for wanting to be independent, but please don't shut me out of your life just to prove you don't need anyone."

Anita shivered at his touch. Hawk's voice, his words, the intense way he was looking at her—they all suddenly overwhelmed her. *I could never shut you out of my life, Hawk. I am afraid I am falling in love with you, and I do not know how to deal with it.*

Unwilling to say what was really in her heart, Anita stammered a reply. "I. . . you are wrong. I do not mean to shut you out. I cannot thank you enough for being a friend to Juanita and me. You will always be an important part of our lives."

Hawk frowned. "You think of me only as your friend? I hoped—" He sounded troubled, and Anita feared what he might say next.

"Please understand. Juanita and I have had no one to help us for so long— it is not easy to break old habits."

"In time, do think you might change your mind about me?"

Hawk sounded so wistful, it was all Anita could do not to throw her arms around his neck. She had never had such strong feelings for a man, but Anita could never forget the hard lessons she had learned when she misplaced her trust in Juan Sanchez. Her heart told her Hawk was different, but her mind was reluctant to believe it.

"Perhaps it does not need to be changed." Anita rested the palms of her hands on his shoulders and stood on tiptoe to brush his cheek with a light kiss. "I promise to pray about it."

Hawk looked startled, then he smiled faintly. "I will be doing some praying myself. For now, promise to call me if you need anything or when you can stand to have me around again—whichever happens first."

Reassured by his teasing tone, Anita returned his smile. "I will."

Hawk hugged her in the same brief, almost impersonal way he had earlier embraced Amitola. "Take care, Anita," he said, then walked away.

Anita stayed in the alcove for a moment, considering what had passed between them. While her heart urged her to confess her true feelings for Hawk, her mind warned her it would be too soon for both of them.

She believed God had led her to this place and perhaps to this man. *Dear Lord, if You mean for us to be together, let me know it in Your own time.*

As Anita returned to the room where her daughter slept, she felt as if a burden had lifted from her shoulders. Many important things would require her full attention in the next few days, and while she was resolved not to allow Hawk Henson to distract her, she thanked God for this man's willingness and ability to help her.

∾

Toni Trent had offered to help Anita complete the Harrison Homes application. Anita did not know how to answer some of the questions, so she took Juanita with her to the DHR office. After Toni showed Anita how to finish the form, she turned her attention to Juanita.

"If you're like the little boy at my house, you're probably ready to start back to school."

Juanita looked to her mother, uncertain how she should answer.

"I have not enrolled her," Anita said.

"This would be a good time to get that done." Toni glanced at her watch. "I don't have to be in court for almost an hour. I can take you to Rockdale Elementary. You can walk back to the inn from there," she added, seeing Anita was about to protest.

At the school while Anita filled out the registration papers, Toni Trent conferred with the principal. She came out of the office looking pleased.

"Juanita will be in Mary Oliver's class. She's an excellent teacher. My stepson had her for the first grade, and he loved her."

"Miss Oliver is in her classroom, working on materials for the next term. I've called her on the intercom," the principal said.

After Toni greeted the teacher and introduced Anita, Miss Oliver stooped to shake Juanita's hand.

"I am happy to meet you, Miss Juanita Sanchez. Would you like to see our classroom?"

Anita was reassured by the woman's warm, motherly manner, but a suddenly shy Juanita nodded and said nothing. However, when she saw the names of the other students above their material cubbyholes, Juanita broke into a big smile.

"I know her!" She pointed to Jackie Tait's name. "I played at her house."

"You'll soon know all the other boys and girls, too," Mary Oliver said. "Let me show you some of the things we'll be doing."

While her daughter was thus occupied, Anita turned to Toni with a new concern. "Juanita stayed at her Texas school until I could pick her up after work. Is that kind of day care available here?"

"Not yet, although several parents have asked the school board to look into starting it. However, I know someone who might keep her for you."

When they left the school a few minutes later, Toni drove to a nearby condominium and introduced Anita and Juanita to Mrs. Tarpley, an older woman who reminded Anita of her grandmother.

"What a pretty little girl!" Mrs. Tarpley exclaimed. "How old are you, darling?"

Juanita's shyness seemed to have evaporated. "I am six years old. I'm in the first grade."

"She'll be in Mary Oliver's class," Toni said. "When her mother starts working at the hospital in a few weeks, she'll need a place to stay for a few hours after school."

"I reckon Josh would be glad to have some company. We can try it for a while and see how it goes."

"Thanks," Toni said. "We'll get back to you about it in a few days."

"I like her," Juanita commented when they left.

"So do I," Anita agreed. "Once again, I do not know how to thank you," she told Toni.

"Think nothing of it. As I may have mentioned, I know what it's like to be a stranger in Rockdale."

Not really, Anita wanted to say. *At least no one ever thought you were an illegal alien.* "Most people here have been kind," she said, instead.

"I'm glad to hear it. As for those who haven't welcomed you, give them time. Old notions sometimes die hard."

Anita knew about those "old notions." Not only in Rockdale, but almost everywhere she had lived in America, a few ignorant people always seemed ready to judge her and Juanita according to their preconceived notions of Hispanics.

"Such people do not bother us," Anita said, hoping it would continue to be true.

∽

The next week passed in a blur. Juanita started school and appeared to be making a good adjustment, and Anita appeared before the Harrison Homes housing council for a formal interview. Despite her concern she might not have made a good impression, her application was approved a few days later. That news added to Anita's feeling that their staying in Rockdale was in God's will.

She stayed at the inn most of the time, filling in for Mrs. Tanner. Anita had seen Hawk only briefly since the night they went to Mentone, but he called almost daily. When Hovis Batts finished the repairs on her car, Hawk checked it out to make sure it was safe for her to drive.

"Hovis did a good job," he said when he delivered the vehicle to the inn. "You'll need to get an Alabama car tag and driver's license soon," he added.

Anita groaned. "Add that to the utilities and telephone deposit, and my first paycheck will be gone before I even start working."

"Your Texas tag doesn't expire for a few months, so you can get by with keeping it awhile longer. You have thirty days to get an Alabama driver's license, but for ID purposes, you might not want to wait that long."

"Where do I go to get a driver's license?"

"The office is in the courthouse. You'll have to take a vision test and show a valid ID."

Anita went to the courthouse the next day, but the form required a permanent address, and she did not know the street name or number of her Harrison Homes apartment. "I will have to come back when I have all the information," she said.

The clerk raised her eyebrows. "She probably can't reada the Engleesh," she heard the woman tell another applicant.

With their laughter still ringing in her ears, Anita walked past the sheriff's office. She thought about stopping to see Hawk, but not wanting to risk a repeat of her encounter with the sheriff, she went on.

On the Thursday before Anita was to report for work at the hospital, Dwight Anders called to tell her the work on her apartment had been completed. "The keys are in my office. Since you've already paid the deposit, you can move in anytime you like."

Anita called Hawk's cell phone to deliver the good news.

"Great. I have Saturday off. I'll be there at eight o'clock to help you move."

"It should not take long. You know we have very little."

"That doesn't matter. I can't think of a better way to spend my day off than with you and Juanita."

It will be good to see you again, too. "Thank you," she said, instead.

To Anita's surprise, the Trents arrived in David's truck about the same time as Hawk. "We do not need this much help," she protested.

"Many hands make light work," Toni said. "David got a key yesterday and moved the furniture I told you about. I can't wait for you to see it."

When Anita finally stood in the living room of her new home, the sight almost overwhelmed her. "You told me about the beds and sofa. What about all this other furniture?"

A small dinette set, a couple of chairs, a pair of end tables, lamps, even a small television set filled the apartment. In addition, a dozen cartons were stacked on the kitchen counter and against the walls, waiting to be unpacked.

"The Seekers class at Community Church rounded up some things we thought you might need, and Hawk donated the end tables and a couple of chairs," Toni explained.

Tears came to Anita's eyes as she examined the contents of the boxes. They were filled with sheets, towels, kitchen utensils, and dishes—many of the things she had planned to buy when she had the money.

"All this—it is too much," she finally managed to say. "You know how I feel about taking charity."

Toni shook her head. "This is not charity. Most of it is used, and everything here was offered in the spirit of Christian love. Please accept it in the same way, and help someone else one of these days."

"I will," Anita said. "Please tell your friends I thank them from my heart."

"When you get settled, I hope you will come to Community and tell them yourself," Toni said. She glanced at Hawk. "That goes for you, too."

"You know I have to work a lot of Sundays. I've used my lunch break to come to the worship service, but there's no way I can get to Bible study as long as Sheriff Trimble makes out the work schedules."

"You two go to the same church?" Anita asked.

Hawk nodded. "Yes. In fact, one of my mother's cousins donated the land Community Church sits on."

"That must mean you're related to Jeremy Winter," Toni said. "I didn't know that."

"Hawk has many cousins." Anita and Hawk's exchanged smiles did not go unnoticed.

"It seems you're getting to know our deputy pretty well," Toni said.

"He has been very good to Juanita and me," Anita said.

"All in the line of duty, of course," David Trent teased.

"Mama, which bed is mine? Dora wants to take a nap."

"You decide, and I will find sheets for it."

With the help of Hawk and the Trents, the unpacking went rapidly. At noon, David went out for pizza. Anita was touched when his thanks for the food included the request that God would bless this home she and Juanita were establishing.

When they had done all they could, Toni and David Trent left, and soon afterward Juanita fell asleep on her chosen bed with her huggy doll clutched in her arms.

"She was too excited to sleep much last night," Anita said.

"You look exhausted yourself. Try to get some rest."

Anita walked to the door with Hawk. "I know you must be tired of hearing me say it, but again, thank you for your help."

"I could never get tired of hearing you say anything, Anita."

Hawk's eyes looked into hers, and Anita's breath caught in her throat as he bent his head to hers. When their lips met, Anita's arms circled his neck almost as if they had a will of their own.

"Thank you," Hawk whispered against her cheek. He held her close for a moment, then released her. "Call me if you need anything."

"I will."

Anita watched him walk away, more certain of the bond they shared. Juan Sanchez had only pretended to be concerned about Anita's welfare so he could take advantage of her. From the first, however, Anita had instinctively known

Hawk Henson was different. She had come to believe she could trust him with her life—and perhaps even her heart.

The Lord has truly been my Shepherd. The words of the Twenty-third Psalm came to her mind. Only recently, she had walked in the valley of the shadow of death. Now, in so many ways, Anita could say with the psalmist, "My cup runneth over."

Yet, even as she praised God for her blessings, Anita knew she should never take them for granted.

Chapter 13

The Rockdale Hospital day surgery was the most recent addition to a building that had been added onto several times since it opened in the 1930s. Anita reported to work on the first day with mixed feelings. She was grateful to be employed at all, but working in a hospital setting without being able to use her training was frustrating. Her orientation had dealt with standard hospital procedures for safe handling of bodily wastes, the meaning of various codes, and the like, things she already knew.

However, when head custodian Jean Vinson presented Anita with a detailed list of her duties, Anita felt far less at home. The woman's attitude indicated she doubted if anyone with a Spanish accent had the intelligence to follow her directions.

"Your job is to keep the entire day surgery area as clean as possible at all times, but you must never go in an operating area when it is in use."

After a few more instructions, Jean Vinson took Anita to the janitorial supply closet and showed her the cleaning supplies. "Don't even think about taking any of this home. Everything is checked out from central supply, and you'll have to pay for any shortage. Understand?"

Anita inclined her head. "Yes, Mrs. Vinson, I understand."

"I hope so. If you can't handle this job, lots of local people would like to have it."

"I will do my best. I want you to tell me if I do anything wrong."

Mrs. Vinson blinked, taken aback. "No doubt you will," she muttered. "Here's a cart. Take it to your area and get started."

The first week was the worst. Strong physically, Anita was no stranger to hard work, but it was a challenge to clean such a large area both thoroughly and quickly. She did her job without calling attention to herself and spoke only when spoken to.

Hawk stopped by to see Anita several times during the first week. She did not think his work usually brought him to the hospital so much, and she suspected he had come to offer moral support.

On Tuesday of her second week at the hospital, Hawk invited Anita to have lunch with him in the cafeteria.

"What is the occasion?" she asked.

"The prisoner I brought to the ER for treatment was admitted for surgery. I don't have to go back to the office for a while. How are things going? You look tired."

"Everything is fine. Juanita enjoys school, and she likes staying with Mrs. Tarpley until I get off."

"You shouldn't be doing janitorial work when the ER really needs you."

"Why do you say that?"

"My prisoner had to wait in the ER far too long before anyone saw him. The desk clerk said someone had called in sick and a couple of others have quit lately, so they're understaffed."

"Mrs. Dickson told me the hospital was not hiring nurses."

"They ought to be. My prisoner's appendix almost burst this morning. I'm going to register an official complaint."

Anita appreciated Hawk's righteous indignation, but she doubted the personnel director would. "Please do not mention me in any way. Mrs. Dickson could think I asked you to complain because I think I am too good to scrub floors."

"I don't intend to. As part of the county's emergency preparedness team, it's my duty to make sure the hospital is prepared for any kind of disaster. At the moment, the ER can't handle even routine cases."

Anita considered Hawk's words. "Mrs. Dickson knows I have ER experience. I wonder if she has checked my references yet?"

"If she hasn't, I predict she will soon."

∞

Anita was cleaning the rest room in the day-surgery waiting room a couple of days later when word came that Phyllis Dickson wanted to see her immediately. She prayed all the way to the personnel office. *Whatever happens, let me accept it.*

This time, Mrs. Dickson seemed almost cordial. "I have checked your credentials, Mrs. Sanchez. The Alabama Nursing Board has agreed to accept your Texas license on a temporary basis, pending approval of your application. If you're still interested, we have an immediate opening for a triage nurse in the ER day shift."

Anita checked the impulse to hug Phyllis Dickson, but she could not keep from smiling at her. "Oh, yes, I want the job."

"You can start Monday. In the meantime, I'll have to find someone to cover your day-surgery duties." Phyllis Dickson's expression softened. "Mrs. Vinson says you're a hard worker. She'll be sorry to lose you."

"I did not think she liked me," Anita said.

"She liked the way you did your job, and that's what matters around here. Go back to day surgery now, and I'll send payroll the change right away."

∞

When she got home that evening, Anita called to thank Hawk. "If you had not complained to Mrs. Dickson, I would probably still be a cleaning lady."

"I can't take all the credit. I wasn't the first to bring the situation to her attention. It was only a matter of time before she would have had to hire more nurses."

"I am happy it was sooner rather than later."

"And I am happy for you."

Anita thought Hawk's voice sounded strained. "Is something wrong?"

"Not exactly. I have paperwork to finish tonight, but I'd like to come by around nine o'clock, if that's all right."

"Of course. I will leave the outside light on for you." *Something is bothering Hawk,* Anita thought as she hung up the phone, and she wondered what it could be.

"Is Dep'ty Hawk coming to see us?"

"Yes, sweetie, but not for a while. Wash up and you can help me set the table."

Juanita wanted to stay up until Hawk arrived, but after doing her homework and taking a bath, she let Anita hear her prayers and tuck her into bed. "Tell the dep'ty to come back in the daytime," she said sleepily.

"I will. Good night, sweetie."

Hawk arrived shortly after nine o'clock, still in his uniform.

"You must have had a busy day," Anita said.

He nodded. "You might say that."

"Would you like something? I have hot chocolate and soda."

"No, thanks." Hawk sat on the couch and patted the cushion beside him. "Sit down."

Anita had never seen Hawk look so serious. "You seem troubled tonight. What is wrong?"

"Nothing—but I have to be away for a while."

"Why?"

"The sheriff's department got a grant to send an officer to North Carolina for drug enforcement training, and Sheriff Trimble decided I would be the one to use it."

"That sounds like a good thing," Anita said.

"Oh, the training will be great, and we need all the help we can get in learning to deal with illegal drugs. I just wish someone else had wanted to take it."

He does not want to leave because of me—and I do not want him to go, either. "How long is this training?"

"Five days plus travel time. I leave tomorrow."

Anita felt relieved. "You will be away only a week?"

"I don't like to be out of touch that long. I'll have my cell phone, but from the course description, we'll be in the field most of the time."

"Juanita will miss having you around. She wants us all to go to Mentone again."

The intense way Hawk regarded Anita made her realize he was about to say something highly personal. He smiled slightly and squeezed her hand. "I'd like to think her mama might miss me just a little bit, too."

I will miss you a great deal, Hawk. I cannot imagine a day without seeing your face or hearing your voice. Anita could not bring herself to say the words aloud, but she returned his smile. "Of course I will."

"When I come back, we'll make a day of it—we'll see Sequoyah Caverns and the ski slopes and then have dinner at another mountain restaurant."

"I will tell her. And we will pray for your safe return."

Hawk put his arms around Anita. "I will pray for you, too, Anita," he whispered against her hair. Releasing her, he stood. "Take care of yourself."

Anita smiled faintly. "It is what I have always done."

At the door, Hawk turned and lightly kissed Anita's forehead. "That's for Juanita." He cupped her face in his hands and looked into her eyes. "And this is for you."

Hawk's kiss was long and sweet, and Anita gladly returned it.

"See you soon," he said and was gone.

Anita closed the door behind her and leaned against it, her knees suddenly weak. *He loves me—and I love him.*

The words had not yet been spoken, but in her heart, Anita knew as surely as she had ever known anything that they would be.

∽

Anita's first day of work in the ER was not physically exhausting, but her coworkers were not enthusiastic about adding the cleaning woman from day surgery to their staff. Tom Duffey, the male charge nurse, let Anita know she would be reassigned if she didn't work well with the ER team.

It was a fairly light day, and Susan Endicott, the female emergency medicine doctor who supervised the ER, had time to check Anita out on the use of various life-saving equipment and pose hypothetical questions about ER cases.

By the end of the day, secure in the knowledge she had earned Dr. Endicott's approval, Anita breathed a prayer of thanks.

Except for missing Hawk, her life could hardly be better.

∽

"You say you are investigating Mrs. Anita Sanchez?"

Janet Foster, a junior personnel assistant at the San Antonio hospital where Anita Sanchez had last worked, leaned back in her chair and considered Detective Martin's request. It was her first day of filling in for the absent chief of personnel, and she didn't like the way this burly detective was trying to intimidate her.

"Yes. Mrs. Sanchez was under suspicion for drug trafficking when she left town with a large sum of stolen money. We need your help to find her."

Janet Foster picked up a file jacket tabbed Sanchez, A. M., and scanned the contents. "Mrs. Sanchez had good evaluations, but it appears she resigned without the usual notice."

"Like I said, she was in a hurry to get away from the law."

"I'm afraid we can't help you, Detective. Mrs. Sanchez left no forwarding address."

"What about her last salary check? Where was it sent?"

"The staff was paid for their work to date at the end of the week before Christmas. No other money was coming to her."

Detective Martin leaned over the desk. "Are you sure there's nothing else in that file?"

Janet Foster turned the jacket upside down, and a telephone memo fell out. "Apparently someone from another hospital called to verify her past employment."

"When was that?"

"About a week ago."

The detective was obviously excited. He took a pen and notebook from his coat jacket. "Exactly where was the call from?"

"I don't know. It just says 'Rockdale Hospital.' "

"Thank you, Miss Foster. You have done the public a great service. I'll see that you are commended for this."

The detective left the office hurriedly, and Janet Foster replaced the Sanchez file in the jacket.

∽

In the privacy of his cheap hotel room, Bill Rankin put his fake ID card and detective's badge in an envelope, then sealed it and stuck it in his breast pocket. The fake credentials had cost an arm and a leg, but they had been worth every penny. Now, thanks to them and the help of a not-too-bright hospital paper-pusher, he knew where to begin to look for Anita Sanchez. There couldn't be many Rockdale Hospitals in the United States. Soon, he would find her—and the fortune she had stolen from him.

Chapter 14

H awk's drug enforcement course covered a great deal of territory and was much more demanding, both mentally and physically, than he had expected. Anita Sanchez was on his mind all week, but he had no opportunity to call her from the field. The hour was late when he got back to the base of operations Thursday night, and he didn't want to risk waking her.

Friday morning, Hawk discovered his cell-phone battery had died. He borrowed a cell phone from his roommate but hung up when he got Anita's answering machine. It wasn't quite eight o'clock in Rockdale, but he realized Anita would already have left to take Juanita to school.

After the brief graduation ceremony on Friday morning, Hawk started the long drive back to Rockdale. He felt an odd sense of urgency, prompted not only by his desire to see Anita, but also by a feeling something might be wrong. He knew it was unreasonable—Anita took pride in being able to take care of herself and her daughter, and everything seemed to have worked out for her. *Anita has a good job and a place to live, her car has been repaired—and I think she knows how I feel about her.*

"If she doesn't, she soon will," Hawk said aloud.

∞

"Mrs. Sanchez? Mrs. Dickson wants to see you right away," the ER receptionist said when Anita came back from lunch Friday afternoon.

Anita's heart sank. Had someone complained about her? Although Tom Duffey still regarded her with suspicion, she felt her first week in the ER had gone well.

"You asked to see me, Mrs. Dickson?"

"Yes, Mrs. Sanchez. Come in and close the door behind you."

Phyllis Dickson pointed to Anita's personnel folder. "Your application for employment states you are a widow. Is that correct?"

Anita nodded, mystified. "Yes. My husband died several years ago."

"His name was Juan Sanchez?"

Again Anita nodded. "Why do you ask?"

"I just had a telephone call from a man who claimed to be your husband. He asked if you worked here."

For a moment, Anita could not speak. "It could not be my husband."

"I didn't think so. This man didn't have a Mexican accent."

"Did he call himself Juan Sanchez?"

"No. He said his name was John Martin, and he needs to get in touch with you concerning your child."

Bill Rankin. Somehow, that man has found me. Anita was almost afraid to ask, but she had to know. "What did you tell him?"

"Nothing. Hospital personnel records are private."

Anita released her breath in a long sigh. "Thank you."

"Do you know who this man is?" Mrs. Dickson asked.

"I think it is someone Juan Sanchez once worked with. Do you know where he was calling from?"

"No. The reception faded a few times. I suppose he was using a cell phone."

Anita shivered. Bill Rankin could be on his way to Rockdale this very minute. "Thank you for letting me know."

Phyllis Dickson stood, signaling the end of the interview. "I don't want any trouble at the hospital."

"Neither do I."

Mrs. Dickson's warning numbed Anita. She did not want to lose her job because of Bill Rankin, but knowing her daughter could be in danger from him was far worse. If only Hawk were here—he would know what to do.

Anita prayed for a calm spirit and the wisdom to make correct decisions, and when she could do so in privacy, she called Toni Trent.

"I believe a man I knew in Texas is coming here. I am afraid he might try to harm Juanita."

Thankfully, Toni did not seem surprised or press her for personal details. "Give me his name and a general description."

After Anita did so, Toni promised to call the school and Mrs. Tarpley. "They'll make sure that no one has access to Juanita that they don't know personally. Local law enforcement should know about him, as well."

"Hawk is still out of town. I do not think Sheriff Trimble would listen to me."

"I'll call him, and I won't mention your name. I'll also talk to Earl Hurley, the Rockdale chief of police."

"Thank you. It might turn out to be nothing, but—"

"Better safe than sorry," Toni finished for her. "Call me right away if anything else comes up."

Somehow, Anita made it through the rest of her shift and picked up Juanita at the usual time. The girl's happy chatter made Anita even more determined to protect her daughter from Bill Rankin. As soon as she was sure Juanita was asleep that night, she tried again without success to call Hawk. His cell phone was out of calling range or he was unavailable, the robotic voice at the other end repeated each time.

When her own telephone rang a few minutes later, Anita hesitated to answer it, although she had asked for an unlisted number. Her answering machine was programmed with an anonymous male voice, and she let it take the call.

"Anita, this is Toni. If you're there, pick up."

"Hello, Toni. I was afraid it might be—someone else."

"Has the man contacted you yet?"

"No, and as I told you, I do not know for certain he will."

"Earl Hurley found no outstanding arrest warrants for anyone named Bill Rankin. Unless he actually commits a crime, their hands are tied."

"Perhaps this will come to nothing. He is not here yet—he might not even be planning to come. As the Bible says, 'Sufficient unto the day is the evil thereof,'" Anita quoted.

"That's a fine scripture, but you must be careful, Anita. I've dealt with domestic violence, and I know how ugly it can get. Women should never be too afraid or ashamed to ask for help."

I should have done that when I was married to Juan, but domestic violence is not my problem now. Anita realized the social worker must think her current problem was related to domestic violence, but she could not deny it without telling Toni the whole sordid story of Bill Rankin's connection to Juan Sanchez—and she did not want to do that.

"God is with us. I will be all right. Good night, Toni."

∞

Hawk made better time coming back than he had going to North Carolina, but it was still almost midnight when he crossed the bridge into Rockdale, too late to call Anita.

I'll see her first thing tomorrow, Hawk promised himself.

Road-weary, he fell into bed and slept deeply until the insistent ringing of the telephone jarred him awake. He managed to pick it up just before his answering machine clicked. He was surprised to see it was almost eight o'clock.

"Henson," he said.

"Hawk—I thank God you are back. I thought I would have to leave a message on your answering machine."

Anita's voice sounded strained, and he sat up in bed, now fully awake. "What is wrong?"

"I need to talk to you."

"Has something happened to Juanita?"

"No. She is with Toni Trent. I will tell you why when I see you."

"I'll be over right away."

Hawk showered and dressed quickly, speculating all the while what could make the normally calm Anita Sanchez sound so afraid.

Whatever it was, Hawk prayed he would be able to help her.

∞

"Thank you for coming," Anita said when she opened the door to admit him.

Hawk looked at her closely. Anita didn't appear to have been crying, but she was clearly troubled. "I intended to come by this morning, but I got in late last night, and I overslept."

"You have not had breakfast?"

Hawk made a gesture of dismissal. "I'm not hungry. What's wrong?"

"It is too long a story to hear on an empty stomach. I will make you breakfast."

Seeing Anita was determined to feed him, Hawk sat at the table and watched her move efficiently around the kitchen, pouring juice and coffee and whisking eggs to make an omelet.

Hawk wanted to tell Anita how much he had missed her, but the misery in her eyes silenced him.

"I didn't think you drank coffee," he said when Anita poured a cup for herself and joined him at the table.

"It is not as good as the coffee I had in Colombia—but this brand is acceptable."

"Thanks for that great breakfast. Now tell me what's going on."

When Anita lowered her head momentarily, Hawk thought she might be praying. Then she looked at him and squared her shoulders. "There are some things about me you do not know," she began.

∞

Anita started at the beginning, briefly recounting the tragic events that had led her to leave Colombia. She traced how Juan Sanchez had persuaded her to marry him because he could protect her from the people who had killed her parents.

"I now believe Juan made up the threats himself. He thought I could claim my parents' fortune as my own until he realized it no longer existed. He turned to petty crime and was arrested and sent to prison. He died there in a riot not long before he would have been released."

As heartbreaking to hear as her story was, Hawk knew Anita was telling the truth. He reached across the table to take her hands in his. "I had no idea you have had that many terrible things happen to you."

Anita shrugged. "God has helped me through it all. Juanita and I had a good life until a man Juan had done robberies with showed up on Christmas Day. He claimed I stole a fortune belonging to him."

"You didn't, though?"

Anita shook her head. "I knew nothing about it. He said a woman who looked like me took his share of the money from a storage unit before he got out of prison. He wanted me to give it back."

"That's why you left San Antonio—you were running away from this guy?"

Anita nodded. "I did not think he could find us, but Mrs. Dickson said a man claiming to be my husband called the hospital Thursday to ask if I worked there. It has to be Bill Rankin. He knows where we are. I am afraid he will try to harm Juanita when I tell him I cannot give him the money."

No wonder she looks so troubled. "I had a feeling you were hiding something, but I never suspected anything like this. You should have told me."

"I would have when I knew you better, but I feared you might think less of me if you knew the whole story."

"Why? You shouldn't be ashamed of what Juan Sanchez did. You've risen above a lot of bad things in your life. If anything, I admire you even more, Anita."

Her face reddened. "I am so glad you are back," she whispered.

"Come here." Hawk stood and opened his arms, and Anita entered into his embrace. "Everything will be all right." He stroked her hair and comforted her as he would a child. He was willing to let her cry into his shoulder as long as she liked, but soon Anita pulled away and faced him, dry-eyed.

"What happens when Bill Rankin comes here looking for me?"

As a man in love, Hawk wanted to tell Anita he would protect her, no matter what. But as a law enforcement officer, he knew Rankin could be a dangerous foe. "The first thing is to keep Juanita away from him. You say she's at the Trents' now?"

"Yes. I called Toni yesterday, and she offered to take Juanita today. She also contacted the sheriff and the Rockdale police chief. He told her Bill Rankin is not currently wanted for any crime, and they cannot do anything unless he commits one here."

"You did well to call Toni, and she took the right steps. How much does she know about the situation?"

"I told her Juanita might be in danger from a man from my past. She does not know why I fear him."

"That doesn't matter—the main thing is, Juanita should stay away for the time being. Pack a suitcase with enough clothes to last her a few days, just in case, and I'll see that Toni gets it this afternoon."

"What about me? What should I do?"

Hawk glanced around the apartment. "Rankin mustn't know Juanita lives here. If he asks about her, say she's still in Texas. Take her artwork off the refrigerator and hide her toys.

"Then what?"

"We wait for him to show up. And we pray—a lot."

Chapter 15

Anita reached Toni by her calling her cell-phone number. "We've been shopping, and we're about to come home for lunch. Juanita can stay with us as long as necessary," Toni assured her.

"Thank you, Toni. Hawk has Juanita's suitcase. You can get it from him later today."

"I'm glad Hawk's back. He's a good man to have on your side in a crisis."

"I know," Anita said. She hung up and turned to Hawk. "Toni said Juanita can stay there indefinitely."

"I thought she would. Toni's a good woman to have on your side in a crisis."

Anita managed a feeble smile, her first in many hours. "That is exactly what Toni said about you. Juanita and I are blessed to have such good friends."

"Toni and I have worked together on several crisis situations involving children."

"I wish you could stay here," Anita said when Hawk stood to leave.

"So do I, but I have work to do at the sheriff's office, and I must get a new battery for my cell phone. It quit on me in North Carolina."

"I do not want to be out of touch with you, especially now."

"Don't worry, I'll borrow a phone if I can't get mine fixed. If you can't reach me, call Toni."

"I will."

Hawk kissed her briefly, and when he left, Anita locked and bolted the door behind him.

She felt the need to pray, yet she could not concentrate enough to frame an effective prayer. *God knows what I need. I must trust Him to provide it.*

∞

Anita had never known time to go by so slowly. When the telephone rang, her heart hammered, and she waited in dread for the answering machine to take the call.

"Pick up, Anita."

"Where are you?" she asked, relieved to hear Hawk's voice.

"At my desk in the sheriff's department. I have a new battery for my cell phone, but it'll be awhile before it's charged up enough to use. In the meantime, you can call me here at the office."

"Yes. I will let you know if anything happens."

"Are you all right? I can barely hear you."

Anita cleared her throat and tried to speak louder. "I am fine."

"Stay that way. I'm working on a plan to deal with this guy. I'll talk to you again in a little while."

Anita hung up the telephone, but in minutes it rang again. She waited warily until she heard Toni Trent's voice.

"Hi, Anita. Somebody here wants to talk to you."

"Guess what, Mama!" Juanita exclaimed as she got on the phone. Without waiting for Anita to speak, she continued in a rush. "We had hot dogs, and then Miss Toni took me and Josh to her church, and she played a tape in a big machine and tried out this real pretty song. She's gonna sing it tomorrow. She says I can stay over here tonight and go to church with them and hear her sing if you'll let me. Can I, Mama?"

Hearing her daughter's excitement, Anita thanked God for a friend like Toni Trent, who had the ability to keep Juanita safe without letting the child know she was in danger. Now it was up to Anita to play her part. "Are you sure it is all right with Miss Toni?"

"She wants me to stay."

"Let me speak to Miss Toni."

When Toni came on the line, Anita thanked her for the invitation as normally as she could. "Hawk has her suitcase. He was at the sheriff's department when he called a few minutes ago."

"David can pick it up—he's going out again, anyway. Let me know when you want us to bring Juanita home."

You mean, when it is safe to bring her home. "I will." *And dear Lord, let it be soon.*

∞

The third time the telephone rang an hour later, Anita took a deep breath and braced herself, certain this time the call would be from Bill Rankin.

"It's Hawk. Any word yet?"

"No. You must wonder if Bill Rankin even exists."

"He's real, all right—I looked up his record. Rankin was released from prison on parole in December and supposedly returned to the Houston area."

"We lived in Houston when Juan went to prison."

"That makes sense. That's probably where the money he thinks you have was stashed away."

Anita shivered. "What will happen when he finds me?"

"Nothing, if I have anything to say about it. My guess is he'll drive here. He probably won't get here before Sunday evening. I have to work until eleven tonight, but I'm off Sunday. I'll be over tomorrow morning. If you need me before then, call my cell phone. Try to get some sleep tonight."

"Thank you, Hawk."

∞

Before she went to bed, Anita read through many of her favorite psalms. Gradually, the peace which passeth all understanding allowed her to have a restful night. She felt much calmer when she opened the door to Hawk around ten o'clock on Sunday morning.

"You look much better today," Hawk commented after embracing her briefly.

"I prayed a lot, and I slept well last night. Now I wonder if Bill Rankin is really coming here."

"I'm almost certain he'll show up. I dug around in the Texas records a bit more. Juan Sanchez and an unknown accomplice committed a robbery in Dallas. Juan went to prison, the other man got away, and the money they took was never recovered."

"Juan was already in prison before I knew about the robbery. I never heard how much money was involved."

"The company they robbed didn't make the amount public, but I found it in the police records. If they agreed to split the money, Rankin's share would be twenty-five grand."

Anita's eyes widened. "I had no idea it was so much. I wish Juan had never told that man he had a wife."

Hawk squeezed her hand. "I know you hoped you'd never see this Rankin again, but if he comes here, we'll make sure he's put away where he can't bother anyone again."

"I just want him to go away and leave me alone."

"That won't work. Rankin tracked you to San Antonio, and he knows you're in Rockdale. When he gets here, you have to let him into the apartment and talk to him. It won't take him long to incriminate himself."

"It will be my word against his," Anita said.

"Not this time. I'm getting you a remote recording device called a wire. Every word you and anyone near you says will be sent to a receiver and recorded."

"Where?"

"In my Jeep."

Anita thought of what lay ahead and shook her head. "He believes I have his money. When I keep telling him I do not, I think he might hurt me."

"I won't let that happen. I'll hear every word Rankin says and watch every move he makes. If he even looks like he wants to lay a hand on you, I can have him in handcuffs in a matter of seconds. But I doubt that will be necessary, because you won't tell him you don't have the money."

"Then what—"

"Here's the plan." Hawk spoke earnestly, answered Anita's questions, then asked her to repeat what she was to do when Bill Rankin arrived. "If he calls first, get him to come to the apartment. I'll stay here until I know he's on the way."

"What if he should come here directly?"

"He won't see me—I'll have time to go out the back door."

"You seem to have thought of everything," Anita said.

"I hope so. Juanita will have to stay at Toni's again tonight. I'll get the equipment together and come back later."

Anita followed Hawk to the door. "You know I can never tell you how much what you are doing for Juanita and me means to me."

Hawk smiled faintly. "As you recently pointed out, you've done a good job of taking care of yourself. But until Bill Rankin is back behind bars where he belongs, I'm glad you're letting me help."

∞

Knowing the Trents usually went out to eat after church, Anita waited until Sunday afternoon to call Toni.

"How is Juanita?" she asked.

"She's having a really good time. She enjoyed going to Bible study and church with us. The question is, how are you?"

"I am afraid I might be coming down with something. I do not want to expose Juanita to it."

"I understand," Toni said. "We'll be glad for her to stay over tonight, and I'll take her to school tomorrow."

"Let me tell her—I do not want her to worry about me," Anita said.

After a brief conversation that reassured Anita her daughter welcomed staying with the Trents another night, she hung up the phone with the hope it would be the last time she had to make such a request.

As much as she dreaded seeing Bill Rankin again, Anita was more than ready to face him if it meant he would be out of her life forever.

∞

Hawk returned to the apartment around three o'clock with a small plastic case containing a tangle of wires, a small battery, and a miniature microphone. He showed her how to put it on, then directed her to test it by talking.

"I'll be in the Jeep, checking to make sure it's working."

Anita entered the bedroom to untangle the wires. She wrapped them around her waist, then put on a bulky turtleneck sweater to make sure the wires were hidden, the battery was accessible, and nothing would muffle the microphone.

Back in the living room, Anita looked out the window at Hawk's Jeep and waved. "I have this thing on, but I do not know if it works."

In a moment, Hawk returned to the apartment. "I heard you loud and clear. You can turn off the battery for now—you're ready for Mr. Rankin."

∞

Tom Duffey worked as charge nurse for the Rockdale Hospital ER day shift four days a week and every other weekend. Compared to the more dramatic Saturday night cases, Sunday nights were usually calm. Shortly after seven o'clock on this Sunday, Tom was doing paperwork at his desk in the charge nurse's office when the receptionist called him.

"A man with a badge wants to see you," she said.

"What kind of badge?"

"Detective."

"Where's Dr. Drew?" Tom asked, referring to the Birmingham medical school resident who worked in the ER on weekends.

"The doctor said you should talk to him."

Tom sighed. "Send him back."

The man who approached Tom's desk didn't fit his idea of a detective. His clothes looked as if he'd slept in them, he needed a shave, and his horn-rimmed glasses gave him a peculiar, owlish look. However, he opened his billfold to reveal a detective's shield with "Martin" printed across it.

"I'm Detective John Martin. I want to see the charge nurse. Where is she?"

Tom was accustomed to people who didn't know male nurses existed and had stopped taking it personally. "You're looking at him. What can I do for you?"

"I need to question one of your nurses about an investigation—a young woman named Anita Sanchez."

Tom heard the name with mixed feelings. Professionally, he knew he wasn't supposed to reveal information about hospital employees, but personally, he hadn't trusted the Sanchez woman from the start, and he was curious to know why the detective wanted her. "Is she in some kind of trouble?"

"No, but she may have important knowledge about a current police investigation. Where can I find her?"

"I can't give out that information."

Detective Martin snapped his billfold shut and leaned over the desk. "Look, Mr. Duffey, don't make this hard. If I have to come back here with a warrant, interfering with a police investigation won't look good on your record."

Tom raised his hands in mock surrender. "No need for a federal case." Tom opened his desk drawer and withdrew the card marked SANCHEZ, ANITA M., from the file box. "She lives in Harrison Homes—the apartment number isn't listed." Tom copied the information on a memo sheet and handed it to the detective.

"This is just what I need. Have a nice night, Mr. Duffey."

The man almost swaggered as he walked away. *He didn't say where he was from,* Tom realized the moment the detective left. Everyone in law enforcement anywhere around Rockdale had been in the ER on business at one time or another, and Tom knew them all. Belatedly, he thought he should have checked the man out with the local police. However, to say anything now would be like locking the barn door after the horses were long gone.

He called Anita Sanchez a young woman—he must know her. Tom briefly thought he should alert Anita Sanchez about the man, but he didn't want to get on the wrong side of the detective.

"What did he want?" the ER receptionist asked when Tom returned from his office.

"Nothing important."

Chapter 16

The pale winter sun set early, and Anita turned on a single lamp beside the couch. Hawk brought in pizza, and after they ate, they remained at the kitchen table, near the back door. Although the blinds were closed, they could see the headlights of every car entering Harrison Homes. They watched at the window to see if any of the automobiles would stop in front of Anita's apartment.

"This place has a lot of traffic for a Sunday night," Hawk commented after the tenth car went on without stopping.

"For public housing, it is still a quiet place."

"Dwight Anders makes sure of that, but you and Juanita should have a better home."

"Getting this apartment was an answer to prayer. It is more than enough."

Hawk regarded Anita intently. "I know, but you and Juanita deserve to have the best of everything."

At the moment he moved to take her into his arms, another automobile turned into the apartment complex, then slowed to a crawl. The car passed the apartment, then the driver braked and backed up.

Anita whispered, even though no one outside could hear her, "It must be Rankin."

The automobile eased into a parking place between Hawk's Jeep and Anita's car. When the headlights went out, Hawk gave Anita a quick hug.

"Turn on the battery before you go to the door. He has no idea you know he's coming, so act surprised. You know what to do?"

"Yes."

"Remember, I won't let you get hurt."

Hawk closed the back door behind him just as a knock sounded at the front door. Anita switched on the battery and earnestly prayed she would be able to do what Hawk had told her.

Anita turned on the outside light and peered through the blinds. At first, she did not recognize the man standing there. His hair was a strange color, and he wore odd, horn-rimmed glasses. Once she looked at his features, however, Anita knew Bill Rankin had, indeed, found her. Taking a deep breath, she opened the door.

"Hello, Mrs. Sanchez." He jerked a thumb toward her car. "Looks like you ran into a little trouble on the way from Texas."

Anita had no difficulty looking shocked. "What are you doing here?"

Bill Rankin smiled smugly. "You know very well. I want no more than I did

331

before—and I won't take less. Aren't you going to let me in?"

Anita shrugged and opened the door wider to admit him. "It will not do you any good. I have nothing to say to you."

"Is that why you left town in such a big hurry?"

"What I do is not your business. Please go away and leave me alone."

"Not until you show some cooperation. Tell me, how does that pretty little girl of yours like Alabama?"

She glared at him. "My daughter is not here. I left her with friends in Texas."

"Even if you did, I can find her. You don't want to make me have to do that, do you?"

Rankin's smirk told Anita he enjoyed her discomfort.

She folded her arms and regarded him steadily. "If you do not leave, I will have you arrested."

Rankin's laughter was chilling. "Sure, you will. Look, Anita, you know we have to settle this sooner or later. If you try to run away again, I'll just follow you. I'm a reasonable man. Give me what is mine, and you won't see me again."

"You have never told me what, exactly, you want."

"Don't try to play dumb with me, girlie. We both know what Juan Sanchez did with my money. You beat me to Dallas and took it all from the storage unit. Now, I want my share."

"In San Antonio, you told me you did a robbery with my husband. He did prison time for it, and you did not. I do not think you deserve anything."

"I don't see it that way. You should know by now I mean business. You have my money, and I want it."

"If I had taken your ten thousand, would I be living in public housing?"

Bill Rankin's face reddened. "You have a lot more than that, and we both know it."

"I know no such thing. But. . ." Anita paused for a moment. "How much money would it take for you to go away and leave me alone?"

Rankin relaxed visibly.

He thinks he has me now. Anita's heart beat faster. *I must keep my nerve.*

"All I ask is my share of the take—for thirty thousand, you'll never see me again."

Anita shook her head. "I will not be cheated. Your share was less than twenty-five."

Rankin's smile made him look almost pleasant. "So you do have the money! I knew it." He glanced around the apartment as if looking for a possible hiding place.

"You will find nothing here," Anita said hastily.

"So where is it?"

Anita pulled her necklace from beneath the turtleneck and showed him the key attached to it. "This opens a safety deposit box at a local bank."

Rankin looked skeptical. "You would have to rent more than one box to hold a suitcase full of cash."

"No. Inside the safety deposit box is the key to a storage unit."

Bill Rankin folded his arms and shook his head. "You expect me to believe you went to all that much trouble to hide the money in this jerkwater town?"

"Believe what you like. The bank opens at nine. I will get the key and meet you at the Store-More on Rockdale Boulevard."

"Try any tricks, and my contacts in Texas will take care of your daughter. I don't think you want that to happen."

"What I want is to be rid of you, Mr. Rankin. That matters more to me than the money."

"Smart girl. See you tomorrow. Sleep well, Mrs. Sanchez."

Anita followed Rankin to the door and leaned against it, drained.

As soon as Rankin's car was out of sight, Hawk reentered the apartment through the back door. "You can turn off the microphone now."

"Did it work?" she asked.

"Perfectly. You were great."

"Is it enough to arrest him?"

"We have Rankin's verbal threats on tape, but when he shows up at the storage unit, it'll prove beyond all doubt he intended to extort money from you."

"What happens then?"

"The Rockdale Police will be on hand to arrest him." Hawk glanced at his watch. "I need to set things up with Chief Hurley tonight. Will you be all right here alone?"

Anita allowed herself a small smile. "I am accustomed to being by myself, but I am never alone—God is with me."

"I think you'll be safe tonight. I doubt Rankin will come back, but if he should, call me immediately—and don't let him inside."

Anita nodded agreement, and Hawk gathered her into his arms for a brief kiss. "Everything will be all right. Soon all of this will be over."

When Hawk left, Anita closed and locked the door behind him. His words had reminded her of her father's favorite quotation from St. Teresa. "Todo se pasa—Dios no se muda." Everything passes—but even more important—God does not change.

God will supply all the courage I need to play my part well tomorrow.

∞

Bill Rankin left Harrison Homes and headed toward the Courthouse Square. He was pleased with the way the evening had gone, but fatigue from his long drive from Texas was beginning to take its toll. He had originally planned to spend the night in his car, watching Anita Sanchez's apartment to make sure she didn't try to run out on him. However, his negotiations with her had gone so well, Rankin no longer thought that precaution was necessary.

Mentioning her kid had done the trick, he decided. Anita Sanchez might like to keep all the money, but even more than that, she wanted her daughter to be safe—and she knew Bill Rankin was smart enough to find her. Tomorrow, all his hard work would pay off.

In the meantime, he needed a place to sleep. Rockdale wasn't exactly overrun with motels, but Bill remembered a billboard on the edge of town advertising a place on Main Street, "in the heart of Rockdale." He reached Main Street and turned right. A few blocks later, he saw the Rockdale Inn, a square, two-story red brick building. From the few cars scattered around the parking lot, Bill Rankin figured he could get a room without any trouble. "This is your lucky day, my man," he said aloud.

The lobby was empty when Bill entered, but when he rang a bell on the counter, a woman emerged from a room marked OFFICE and greeted him. LOIS TANNER, MANAGER, he read on her name tag.

"I need a single room for tonight."

Mrs. Tanner quoted a lower price than he expected.

"In that case, I'll pay cash."

"Sign the register, and I'll get your room key."

Welcome to the dark ages, Bill thought when the innkeeper pushed the large ledger toward him. He hadn't seen one of those in a hotel for years. He had just written "John Martin" after the current date when a name at the top of the opposite page leaped out at him. Anita Sanchez. She had signed this very register only a few days after Christmas.

"I see a familiar name," Bill said.

"Oh? Who would that be?"

"Someone I knew in San Antonio—Anita Sanchez. Nice-looking brunette lady with a pretty little girl."

Mrs. Tanner beamed. "That would be Juanita. I hated to see them leave."

"They're still in town, though?"

"Oh, yes. Anita Sanchez works at the hospital. You can look her up there tomorrow, Mr.—" The innkeeper turned the ledger around to read his name. "Mr. Martin."

"I might do that. I suppose Juanita is going to school here?"

"Yes—Rockdale Elementary. She's a bright little girl." Mrs. Tanner rummaged around under the counter for a moment and brought out a photograph of a little girl with long, black hair, wearing an oversize apron. "I took this one day when she was helping me make soup."

"She still resembles her mother," Bill said.

"Isn't that the truth! Here's your key, Mr. Martin. Room 116's on the right. It's just across the hall from where the Sanchezes stayed."

"Thanks." Bill Rankin walked away from the registration desk, his fatigue suddenly replaced by anger. Anita Sanchez had lied to him. *Her daughter is here in Rockdale, after all.* There had been no sign of her in the apartment—Bill was certain of that. Someone must have tipped off Anita Sanchez.

She knew I was on her trail, and she played me for a sucker.

Bill entered his room, his mind racing. He didn't know what game Anita Sanchez might think she was playing, but she was about to lose—and her daughter would be Bill Rankin's winning card.

Chapter 17

Anita slept fitfully Sunday night and awoke long before dawn. She watched the sun rise in a cloudless sky on Monday morning and rehearsed the day ahead.

In a few hours, she and Bill Rankin were to meet one last time, and she prayed everything would go according to Hawk's plan. Anita did not know what the future might hold for her and Juanita after this morning, but she had no doubt Hawk Henson would play a large part in it.

When her telephone rang around seven o'clock, Anita answered right away, thinking it must be Hawk.

"Hello, Mamacita. Are you feeling better?"

Hearing her daughter's voice, Anita smiled. "Hi, sweetie. Yes, I am much better. I will not go to work this morning, but I will see you after school."

"All right. Here's Miss Toni. She wants to talk to you. 'Bye, Mama." Juanita made a kissing sound, and Anita could hear her daughter hand the receiver to Toni Trent.

"Good morning," Toni said. "Juanita and I wanted to know how you're getting along."

"As I told her, I will not go to the hospital this morning. I plan to pick her up after school, though."

Anita heard Toni cover the telephone while she talked briefly to someone, then she returned to the line. "The kids are making so much racket packing their lunches I could hardly hear you. They've closed the kitchen door, so we can talk in peace. Is everything really all right?"

"Yes. Hawk has the situation under control."

"I'm glad. If there's anything I can do, I hope you'll let me know."

"I will. Thank you for keeping Juanita. I know she has had a good time."

"The pleasure was ours. I should warn you—Mandy French-braided Juanita's hair last night."

"French braid?"

"You might have another name for it—her hair is plaited close to her head. French braids can stay in place for days. Mandy's aunt Evelyn taught her how to do it, and she loves to practice on anyone with long hair. I hope you don't mind."

"Not at all. Tell Mandy I might let her braid my hair sometime, too."

"I will." The call-waiting tone sounded on Toni's line. "Oops—I need to take this call. I'll check with you later."

Anita hung up, feeling much better. Her daughter was happy and safe, and soon she would see Hawk again.

When Bill Rankin was out of the way for good, life would be close to perfect.

∞

"I hope you slept well, Mr. Martin."

Bill Rankin looked up from his breakfast and belatedly realized he was the Mr. Martin the innkeeper was addressing. "Yes. I like a quiet place like this."

"Business is slow this time of year. If you want to stay longer, I can give you a very good rate."

"I'll keep that in mind. By the way, do you have a Rockdale map?"

Mrs. Tanner laughed. "It's hard to get lost around here, Mr. Martin. I can tell you how to get to just about anyplace hereabouts."

"I want to make note of some area addresses. A map would help."

Mrs. Tanner returned from the reception desk and handed him a dog-eared Chamber of Commerce map with the town of Rockdale grid on one side and Rockdale County roads on the other. "It's not new, but then not much else around here is."

"Thanks. I'll return it in a few minutes."

"Take your time. Checkout's not until noon."

Back in the room, Bill Rankin opened the map and began to make notes. He glanced at his watch, satisfied he had time to find Juanita Sanchez and still meet Anita at the Store-More.

Anticipating the look on the woman's face, Bill smiled in satisfaction. His situation was looking better by the minute. Not only would he get his cut of the money, but probably Juan's as well.

Bill patted the fat envelope in his briefcase. In a matter of hours, John Martin's passport and airline tickets would take Bill Rankin out of the country to a place where he could live like a king on almost nothing.

But first, he had to find Juanita Sanchez.

∞

Bill Rankin noted the location of the elementary school on Mrs. Tanner's map. Although it was within easy walking distance of the Rockdale Inn, he drove his car to within a block of the school's main entrance and parked. From his vantage point, he could watch every child enter. Even if he didn't see Juanita Sanchez go into the building, Bill Rankin believed the girl would be there that morning.

Just after eight o'clock, he would go inside, flash Detective John Martin's badge, make up a story about Juanita Sanchez being in danger, and walk out with his prize. On the way into town, he'd noticed a long-abandoned log cabin near the road. He would have enough time to take the girl there and still meet her mother at nine o'clock.

While he waited, Rankin idly watched the seemingly endless procession of vehicles depositing waves of children in front of the school. A pickup truck pulled to the curb in front of him and stopped. A boy and girl got out, and the male driver pulled away from the curb immediately and turned left into a cross street.

He must be in a big hurry, was Rankin's first thought. Then he looked at the children and felt a rush of adrenaline. He quickly dismissed the boy, who looked about eight or nine years old, and focused his attention on the petite dark-haired girl clutching a cloth doll. Her hair was in braids, but her features definitely matched the picture the innkeeper had showed him.

If that little girl isn't Juanita Sanchez, I'll eat my hat.

The boy walked rapidly toward the school, leaving his companion behind. Quickly, Rankin got out of the car and started after the girl. He saw a doll-sized blue shoe on the sidewalk and picked it up.

About the same time, the little girl stopped and turned around, apparently realizing her doll had lost one of its shoes.

Rankin smiled and held out the small blue object. "Hello, Juanita. I believe I have something that belongs to you."

Chapter 18

G ood morning, Anita. Any problems last night?"
Hawk's welcome voice made Anita smile. "No. Everything has been
very quiet. Dr. Endicott knows I will not come to work today. I plan to
be at the bank at nine o'clock."

"Good. Bill Rankin might not be trailing you, but you know what to do."

"Yes. I will stay in the bank a few minutes. Then I go to the Store-More on
Rockdale Boulevard."

"Correct. Rankin will show up there for sure, and when he does, we'll be
ready."

"If he has reason to believe I have called the police, I do not know what he
might do."

"He won't see us—besides, his mind will be on the money."

"I want this man to be out of our lives."

"We're almost there, honey. Hang on, and I'll see you shortly."

Anita stood holding the receiver for a moment, reviewing their conversation.
Hawk had called her "honey," not in the way southern clerks and waitresses did
as a matter of course, but with genuine affection. Having to deal with Bill Rankin
had preoccupied them both and postponed the time when their feelings for one
another could be openly discussed. Now, Anita had yet another reason to play out
the rest of her charade with Bill Rankin.

At twenty minutes before nine on Monday morning, Anita Sanchez entered
the Rockdale bank where she had recently opened a checking account.

Almost immediately, Hawk's cousin called to her. "Hi, Ms. Sanchez. You're
getting an early start. What can we do for you?"

"Good morning, Debbie. I would like to have my paycheck from the hospital sent here directly. Can I do that?"

"Sure, if you have an account with us."

"I opened a checking account last week, but I have not used it."

"I can give you the form to request direct deposit. It's very simple."

As Debbie Hawk got the form, Anita half-turned so she would see anyone
entering the bank. She did not expect Rankin would come inside, but if he did,
she would pretend to have been coming from the bank's safety deposit boxes.

"Here you go," Debbie said a few moments later. "I put your account number on the top line. Fill out the rest and take it to the hospital payroll office."

"Thank you." Anita took the form and had started to leave when Debbie spoke again. "I haven't seen my cousin around lately. Is he all right?"

The teller's casual presumption that she would know about Hawk both embarrassed and pleased Anita. "Hawk was out of town for a week. He is back now."

Debbie smiled. "The next time you see him, tell him I said hello."

"I will."

Her conversation with the teller temporarily distracted Anita, but when she emerged from the bank into the glare of the sun, she thought about what lay ahead and sighed deeply. With God's help, the nightmare Bill Rankin had brought into her life would soon be over.

∞

Wearing uniform coveralls provided by Rockdale Moving and Storage Company, Hawk and Rockdale chief of police Earl Hurley waited in the Store-More office for the subject of their stakeout to arrive. The third member of their team, Sheriff Trimble, was stationed inside a storage unit containing, among other things, the decoy suitcase.

Getting them together early on a Monday morning, especially with such short notice, had taken all of Hawk's powers of persuasion. Aware of past arguments over jurisdiction between the city and county law enforcement units, Hawk presented the situation as an exercise in interagency tactical training. Chief Hurley welcomed the opportunity to defend his town's turf, and Sheriff Trimble agreed to participate so he could claim some of the credit for capturing a dangerous criminal. Since neither routinely worked stakeouts, Hurley and Trimble were quite willing for Hawk, who had the most tactical experience, to take charge of the operation.

Early Monday morning, they met in the warehouse of a moving company owned by one of Hawk's cousins. After a brief run-through, the men put coveralls on over their uniforms and drove a small moving van to the storage facility.

"What happens if Anita Sanchez loses her nerve?" Earl Hurley asked Hawk.

"I don't think she will. In any case, she's an innocent victim and must be protected."

"She doesn't look all that innocent to me," Sheriff Trimble muttered. "If it wasn't for her and her kind, our jobs would be a lot easier."

Hawk wanted to defend Anita, but he knew he'd be wasting his breath on a man unwilling to part with his deep-rooted prejudices.

"Our job is to catch bad guys," Chief Hurley reminded the sheriff, "and I hope we can close the book on this one."

When the time neared for Anita and Rankin to meet, Hawk felt a rush of adrenaline. As he always did when facing a potentially dangerous situation, Hawk closed his eyes and offered a silent prayer for protection.

"Someone's coming," Earl Hurley said in a stage whisper, and Hawk opened his eyes to see Anita's car pull into the Store-More.

340

∞

Bill Rankin's errand had taken a little longer than he expected, but it would be well worth it. He had Anita Sanchez exactly where he wanted her, and very soon he would have her money, as well.

Rankin got back to Rockdale as the clock on the courthouse struck nine times. He spotted Anita's car in the parking lot of the bank and congratulated himself. *Perfect timing, Rankin. You ought to do this for a living.*

Chuckling at his wit, Bill Rankin drove toward the place he and Anita were to meet. Seeing a grocery store, he pulled into the parking lot and put Dora's shoe into a Rockdale Inn envelope, sealed it, and stuck it in his pocket. He waited a moment after Anita's car passed before he eased back onto Rockdale Boulevard. He didn't think she had alerted the police to follow her, but he'd done time more than once for taking too much for granted. He could smell a setup a mile away, and if anything looked out of the ordinary, he wouldn't even stop at the storage unit.

Seeing the Store-More sign ahead, Bill Rankin slowed even more. Although Rockdale Boulevard was a busy, four-lane road, the Store-More units were tucked away at right angles to the street, somewhat shielded from curious passersby. Except for an unattended moving van and Anita's automobile, the place was deserted.

Since everything looked legitimate, Bill Rankin smiled in anticipation as he turned into the parking area. If all went as well as he expected, Anita Sanchez was about to lose her fortune—and he was about to claim it.

∞

When Hawk had explained his plan to Anita the night before, it had sounded simple. Anita would meet Rankin near the Store-More office and lead him to a nearby unit where she would show him a suitcase supposedly containing the money. When Rankin took the suitcase, the law enforcement officers would come out of their hiding places and make the arrest. At no time would Anita be in danger. The case against Bill Rankin would stand up in court, and he would go to prison on a number of different charges ranging from a Texas parole violation to attempted extortion.

Now that the time had come to carry out the plan, Anita prayed for the ability to play her part well. Knowing Hawk was nearby reassured her. Although she could not see him and was not sure where he was, Anita knew he would protect her. When Rankin pulled in beside her, she did not hesitate to get out of the car and wait for him to join her.

"Good morning, Señora Sanchez," he drawled. "I presume you're here on this lovely day to do a little business."

"What kind of business is that?"

"The same as we agreed to last night. Something of mine is in one of these units, and when I have it, you'll get something you want."

"You will go away and leave me alone, yes?"

"That is not the only thing you want." Rankin reached into his pocket and pulled out an envelope with a pronounced bulge in the middle. "Take this."

"What is it?"

"Look and see."

Anita's fingers trembled slightly as she opened the envelope. When she saw the small blue object it contained, her heart lurched, and she felt dizzy. Dora's shoe. Juanita had taken her doll to the Trents' house. Wherever Dora was, Juanita would likely be.

"How did you get this?"

"That doesn't matter. You lied when you said your pretty little girl was in Texas. You'd better not be lying about the money. Give me what I want, and you'll get what you want—that's the deal."

"Where is my daughter?"

"In a safe place—for now. The quicker I get the money, the sooner you'll have her back."

Anita hesitated, her mind whirling. She knew Hawk was probably watching from the office, too far away to have seen Dora's shoe or heard Rankin's words. And even if he did, what could Hawk do differently? Bill Rankin had changed the script, but Anita had no choice but to play the part she had been assigned and pray everything would work out as originally planned. When that happened, Rankin would no longer be a threat to anyone.

"How do I know you have Juanita?"

"How do I know you have the money?"

"You will see. The suitcase is in that unit."

Rankin followed Anita down the line of identical storage units until she stopped at number seven. He looked around as if to assure himself they were alone. "Unlock the door and get on with it."

"That has already been done. It is open."

Bill Rankin frowned. "How did you have time to do that before I got here? This had better not be a trick."

Anita stood silent as Rankin seized the handle and raised the unit door. Hawk told her he would put an old brown leather suitcase underneath several boxes and other household items. In the time it would take Rankin to get to it, the officers would be in position to make the arrest.

When daylight flooded into the cubicle, Anita noticed a mattress leaning against the wall moved slightly and guessed one of the law enforcement officers was hiding behind it.

Fortunately, Rankin had not seemed to notice the movement. He glanced at the unit's contents and shook his head. "Where did all this stuff come from?"

"Different places," Anita replied truthfully enough. The unit was Hawk's and contained assorted odds and ends of furniture and household goods belonging to him and his late parents. She spotted the decoy suitcase Hawk had described, one of several pieces of luggage half-hidden beneath several cardboard boxes.

Silently, Anita pointed to it, then stood back and held her breath, expecting Rankin to reach for the suitcase.

Instead, he pointed to a nearby dresser. "Put the suitcase up there and open it."

Anita hoped the officers would come forward and arrest Rankin at any moment, but no one approached as she wrestled the suitcase free and laid it on top of the mirrorless dresser.

"Open it," he demanded.

Anita pressed her thumbs against the latches. They snapped open with a loud click, and she stepped away. "You do the rest," she said.

Rankin put both hands on the lid, ready to lift it.

Where was Hawk? Although the winter morning was unusually warm, Anita felt cold. She folded her arms across her body and grasped her elbows. She had no idea what, if anything, the planted suitcase contained, but she knew it was not the fortune Rankin expected, and she feared what might happen if he looked inside before he could be arrested. Only when he could not lift the lid did Anita notice the small keyhole in the center of the suitcase.

Rankin scowled. "It's locked. Where's the key?"

"I—I don't have it," Anita stammered.

Enraged, Rankin pushed Anita's jacket aside and reached for her neck. His hand encountered the necklace, and roughly he jerked it free and held it up, revealing the dangling lockbox key.

"What do you call this then?"

Chapter 19

I don't know what's going on, but I don't like it," Hawk said moments after Bill Rankin arrived.

Earl Hurley peered through the binoculars he used at Alabama football games and had thought to bring at the last minute. "The guy just handed her some kind of envelope. She's in the way—I can't see what's in it."

"They're spending too much time talking. I should have wired Anita."

"I can't read lips, but Rankin looks like he thinks he's got the situation under control."

"He'll soon find out otherwise."

When Anita turned away and started toward the storage unit, Hawk alerted Sheriff Trimble by walkie-talkie. "They're on the way. Don't make your move until Rankin has the suitcase in his hand."

The sheriff's voice sounded muffled and far away. "It's about time. I just turned off my flashlight, and I can't see a thing."

"There will be plenty of light when they open the door." Hawk switched off the walkie-talkie and stood. "Let's go. It shouldn't take Rankin long to find the suitcase."

Although they had agreed not to use weapons unless absolutely necessary, Earl Hurley and Hawk had concealed their revolvers in the side pocket of their coveralls, and Hawk assumed Sheriff Trimble had done the same. Neither man spoke as they approached unit seven.

"Put the suitcase up there and open it," they heard Bill Rankin tell Anita.

Rankin and Anita had their backs to them as she lifted the suitcase onto an antique dresser and opened the side clasps.

Hawk and Earl Hurley exchanged a concerned glance.

This isn't the way we planned it. Where is Sheriff Trimble, and what will he do?

They were still a couple of yards away when Bill Rankin tried to lift the suitcase lid, then snatched Anita's necklace. Hawk started running toward them, and at the same time, Sheriff Trimble stepped from his hiding place behind the mattress, which fell over and hit Rankin and Anita.

"Hands up!" the sheriff cried, waving his pistol wildly.

Rankin pushed the mattress back toward the sheriff, knocking him off balance. Grabbing the suitcase, he turned and ran into Hawk and Earl Hurley.

"Not so fast," the police chief said.

Bill Rankin's face reddened in fury. "What's going on here? Movers are robbing me in broad daylight? Where are the police?"

"We're right here." Hawk grabbed one of Rankin's arms, and the police chief held the other. Rankin continued holding onto the suitcase, and Anita's necklace dangled from his hand.

Sheriff Trimble joined them, holding his revolver with both hands. "It looks like you're the robber here," he said.

"You might as well drop the suitcase," Hawk said. "You won't find any money in it."

Anita remained inside the rental unit until Rankin was finally in custody, then she came out and stood beside Hawk.

"If you're the law around here, arrest this woman," Rankin loudly protested. "She's the thief, not me."

"That's not the way we heard it," Hawk said.

Chief Hurley cleared his throat to make a formal arrest statement, but Anita interrupted him. "This man has my daughter. Make him tell us where she is."

All three law enforcement officers stared at Anita. "What makes you think he's telling the truth?" Chief Hurley asked.

"This." Anita opened her shoulder bag and removed the envelope Rankin had given her.

Hawk recognized its contents immediately. "That shoe belongs to Juanita's doll. How did you get it, Rankin?"

"I found it," he said. "I don't know where the girl is."

When the men increased the pressure on their grip, Rankin winced and moved his shoulders to indicate his captors were hurting his arms. "Can we talk about this somewhere else?"

"Cuff him, and I'll call for a patrol car," Chief Hurley said. "If he's a kidnapper, the feds need to be informed right away."

Anita was closer to tears than she had been at any time since Bill Rankin found her. She looked from the chief to the sheriff in turn, her eyes pleading even more than her voice. "Please help me find my child—I have to know she is all right."

Hawk looked at Anita as if he wanted to take her into his arms and comfort her. "Don't worry. We'll find her."

Sheriff Trimble was obviously skeptical. "This man told you flat out he has your daughter?"

"More or less. He said he had something I wanted and he would give it to me in return for the money."

"Before we jump to any more conclusions, let's make sure the girl's really missing," Chief Hurley said. "Where is she supposed to be?"

Anita forced herself to speak calmly. "Juanita spent the weekend with the Trents. She should be at school now."

Earl Hurley jerked a thumb toward the moving van. "My cell phone's on the front seat. Call the school and see if she's there, then bring me the phone."

"Check with the Trents if she's not," Hawk added. "They might just be running late. Do you have the numbers?"

"Yes." Anita climbed into the moving van cab and called Rockdale Elementary School from the list she always carried in her handbag. Waiting for someone to answer, she prayed to hear good news. *Maybe Bill Rankin really did find the shoe, or more likely, he managed to steal it to frighten me into giving him the money. If so, Juanita will be at school. . . .*

"Rockdale Elementary, Mrs. Hurst speaking."

Anita had met the school secretary when she enrolled Juanita, and she remembered how patiently the woman had helped her fill out the paperwork. "Mrs. Hurst, this is Anita Sanchez. I need to know if my daughter, Juanita, is at school today."

"Just a moment and I'll check."

Anita heard the sound of papers being shuffled, followed by a long silence and a muffled conversation before the secretary returned to the phone.

"Mrs. Sanchez? Miss Oliver reported her absent. No one tried to check her out from the office—apparently she never got here today."

Anita's eyes filled with tears, but she managed to steady her voice. "She spent last night with the Trents. Is Josh also absent?"

"I'll find out."

In the silence, Anita tried to tell herself everything was probably fine. *Toni Trent sometimes has emergency calls. Perhaps such a call this morning delayed her.*

After another long pause, the secretary returned to the telephone. "Josh is here, Mrs. Sanchez. He says his mother had an emergency call, and his father took him and Juanita to within a block of school and let them out to walk the rest of the way. Josh went on ahead and thought Juanita was behind him. Perhaps you should tell the police."

"Thank you. I will do that."

Numb with worry, Anita left the van. Hawk, Sheriff Trimble, and Chief Hurley had removed the moving company coveralls and were in the process of putting Bill Rankin into the backseat of a Rockdale police cruiser.

Hawk turned as Anita approached. "What did you find out?"

"Juanita is not in school. Josh Trent is, but Juanita never got there." Anita brushed past Hawk and went to the patrol car where Bill Rankin sat in the backseat and addressed him in a voice choked with emotion. "What have you done with her? Where is Juanita?"

Even in custody and wearing handcuffs, Bill Rankin remained defiant. "Where is my money?"

Hawk reached inside and grabbed the lapels of Rankin's coat. "Aren't you in enough hot water already? Tell us where to find the girl, or you're going to be in a whole lot more trouble."

"Let me go. I can't tell you where she is."

Hawk stepped back, but there was no mistaking the fury in his eyes. "Can't or won't?"

Bill Rankin leaned back against the seat as if considering his options. "I might be able to show you a place where a child could hide."

Anita's eyes pleaded with Chief Hurley. "Let him take us there."

"Not until we book him."

Hawk spoke earnestly. "Look, Chief, this man kidnapped a six-year-old child this morning. Getting her back is more important at the moment than taking his fingerprints."

"I don't know what you're talking about," Rankin said sullenly. "Anita Sanchez robbed me. I haven't hurt anybody."

"That part had better be the truth," Hawk said.

"Where is my daughter?" Anita repeated.

Rankin jerked his cuffed hands in the direction of the mountain. "Up there."

"That's Rock County's jurisdiction," Sheriff Trimble said. "We'll go in one of our patrol cars."

"Mine is at the warehouse," Hawk said. "I'll drive the moving van there and be right back."

"Please hurry," Anita said.

Chief Hurley obviously didn't want to turn over any part of the investigation to Sheriff Trimble, but his jurisdiction technically ended at the city limits. "My patrol car will follow as backup, but I'll ride in the county car with the prisoner," the chief told Sheriff Trimble.

While Hawk was gone, the chief used his cell phone to report the incident to the FBI. "We have the situation under control," Anita heard him say, and she prayed it was so.

Some ten minutes later, they were on their way up the mountain. Hawk drove his Rock County patrol car, with Anita in the front seat. Still in handcuffs, Bill Rankin sat in the rear, wedged between Police Chief Hurley and Sheriff Trimble. Two city policemen followed in a Rockdale police cruiser.

Rankin had agreed to point out where they might find Juanita without admitting he had taken her there against her will, but he refused to answer any questions. "I know my rights. I'm supposed to have a lawyer. I don't have to talk to you."

"That's right, Rankin," Hawk said. "You don't have to say a word to show us where Juanita Sanchez is—just point in the right direction."

Bill Rankin chuckled as they drove past the guardrail crumpled by her car, and Anita's heart sank. Juanita would have noticed that. Maybe she even said something to him about it.

Hawk's quick glance told Anita he had noticed the guardrail as well and also remembered it as the place they had met. How long ago that now seemed. . . .

"There's nothing much along here except woods and logging trails," Sheriff Trimble said a moment later. "Did you take the girl to DeSoto State Park?" he asked Rankin.

When he remained silent, Hawk spoke. "I doubt he would go there. It's too public and too far."

"We must be getting close," Anita said. "He could not have gone very far this morning. He was at the storage unit just after nine o'clock."

"Good point," Hawk said. "Maybe you should consider a career in law enforcement, Mrs. Sanchez."

Hawk had spoken lightly, but Sheriff Trimble did not. "That's all we need, another fox to guard the henhouse."

Anita was not certain what the sheriff's statement meant, but she knew it was not complimentary. The sheriff had made his dislike for her plain enough.

"In a case like this, we need all the help we can get," Chief Hurley said.

Rankin remained silent, but a moment later, he leaned forward and peered ahead, then raised his cuffed hands in the direction of a NO TRESPASSING sign on the right.

Anita and Hawk exchanged a quick glance of recognition but remained silent.

"How do you suppose Rankin found this place?" Sheriff Trimble asked as Hawk turned into the narrow lane.

"He probably noticed it on the way into town and thought it would make a good hideout," Chief Hurley said.

"Chances are he was planning to kidnap the girl all along," the sheriff said.

"No," Bill Rankin said, apparently forgetting he had said he wouldn't talk.

As the patrol car slowed in front of the log cabin that had been Hawk's ancestral home, Anita leaned forward and clasped her hands. *Let Juanita be all right*, she prayed as she had from the moment she had seen Dora's shoe.

Anita wanted to run into the cabin, but even before the patrol car came to a complete stop, Hawk stayed her arm. "Wait outside. The sheriff and I will go in first."

Chief Hurley remained in the backseat with Bill Rankin, and Anita stood by the cabin door until, moments later, she heard a welcome voice from inside.

"Hello, Dep'ty Hawk. Have you seen Mama?"

Anita brushed past the men and knelt to sweep Juanita into her arms. The tears she had not shed in her anguish now flowed freely in her joy. "I am right here, sweetie."

"Don't cry, Mamacita," Juanita said when her mother finally released her. "God took good care of me, just like you said He would."

Anita threw back the blanket and cried out when she saw rope binding her daughter's thin ankles. "Hawk, look at this."

Hawk's eyes darkened when he saw the circle of rope burns around Juanita's ankles. "We'll have these off in a jiffy," he assured her.

To distract Juanita while Hawk loosened the ropes, Anita produced Dora's missing shoe and helped her slip it onto the huggy doll's foot. "There now. Dora has two shoes again." Then Anita took a closer look at the doll's hair. Once long like Juanita's, it was matted together. "What happened to Dora's hair?"

"I tried to do it in French braids, but it got all tangled."

Anita knew Mandy Trent had braided Juanita's hair, but she had not realized how much difference the French braids made. Having her hair pulled back made Juanita's face appear thin, and she looked older. "Don't worry, sweetie. We can fix it when we get home."

"All set," Hawk said. Having freed Juanita, he unhooked the other end of the rope and coiled it. "This will be added to the evidence against Mr. Rankin."

Anita examined Juanita's ankles, relieved the damage seemed superficial. As painful as they must be, the burns would have been much worse if Juanita had struggled against the rope. Although it must have seemed like an eternity to the child, Anita thanked God Juanita had been in the cabin a relatively short time.

"Let's get you home." Hawk scooped Juanita into his arms and carried her outside.

The Rockdale policemen were transferring Bill Rankin to the backseat of their cruiser when Anita came out of the cabin. Seeing her, he stopped and yelled, "You may think you can keep your fortune, but when I tell the police where it came from, you won't have a dime."

"I thought you weren't going to talk," Chief Hurley said.

Bill Rankin shrugged. "Anita Sanchez may have everybody in this hick town fooled, but believe me, she's no saint. That's all I'm saying until I get a lawyer."

Hawk was buckling Juanita in the backseat of his patrol car when Rankin made his outburst, and Anita hoped her little girl had not heard it. However, when Anita got in beside Juanita, she saw the girl looked troubled.

"That man said he was your friend, Mama, but he doesn't act nice at all. Dora's shoe fell off, and he took it and wouldn't give it back. He said he was taking me to see you, but you weren't here. Then he tied me up so I couldn't go outside and get chased by a bear. I wish he would go back to Texas and leave us alone."

"So do I, sweetie. We must ask God to keep him from bothering us again."

"That's one prayer request I believe God will grant," Hawk said.

Chapter 20

After they let Sheriff Trimble out at his office, Hawk offered to take Anita and Juanita directly to their apartment and return their car later in the day. "I imagine you ladies could use a little rest."

Anita shook her head. With the Lord's help, she and Juanita had walked through the valley of the shadow of death and come out unscathed. She had stayed strong then, and she intended to remain that way until she had seen the incident with Rankin through to its conclusion.

"Thank you for the offer, but I can drive myself home."

"I'm not tired," Juanita said. "You can take me back to school now, Dep'ty Hawk. Dora's s'posed to be my Show and Tell."

Anita smiled, grateful Juanita had apparently not been traumatized by the morning's events. "You can take Dora to school another time, sweetie. We need to get home and put medicine on your ankle."

Juanita nodded. "All right. Dora's a little tired, anyway. She's had a very bad morning."

So have we all, sweetie.

When they reached the Store-More, Hawk helped Juanita into the backseat and fastened her safety belt. "There you go, princess."

He closed Juanita's door and joined Anita, who stood beside her car with her keys in her hand, looking down the line of storage units.

"This is not over yet, is it?" Anita's eyes asked Hawk to assure her their ordeal was completely finished, but he could not.

"When the FBI gets here, you and Juanita will be questioned. You'll probably have to testify before a grand jury and at Rankin's trial, but I don't think he'll ever be in a position to bother you again."

"What about the money?"

Hawk looked puzzled. "What do you mean?"

"None of this would have happened if my husband had not helped Rankin commit a robbery. I would like to help the police find the money and restore it to the rightful owner."

"I have an idea who might have taken it, but the money has probably long since been spent."

"You can tell me about it later," Anita said.

Hawk glanced around, and seeing no one in the vicinity, he put his arms around Anita and pulled her to him. "Yes. I have several things to talk about.

Go home and get some rest, and I'll come by after work."

❦

Anita went home, but resting was another matter. Soon after Anita entered the apartment, Toni Trent came by with Juanita's suitcase.

Toni hugged Anita and Juanita in turn. "I couldn't believe you got her back so fast," Toni said after Juanita took the suitcase to her room and started to unpack.

"The Lord was with us," Anita said.

"Just about everyone in town was praying for both of you. David was in Statum's having coffee when he heard about it. He thought it was just a rumor at first."

Juanita came out of the bedroom, looking puzzled. "Mama, all my toys are gone. Did that man take them, too?"

It will be a long time before she can forget Bill Rankin. "No, sweetie. I put them away in the closet. You can get them out now."

"I can't tell you how sorry we are about what happened," Toni said when Juanita left. "David is devastated. The children were in sight of the school, and he had an important eight o'clock appointment. It never occurred to him anyone would snatch a child off the sidewalk in broad daylight in our little town."

"Please do not let your husband blame himself," Anita said. "I still do not understand how Rankin found out Juanita was in Rockdale."

"Perhaps he was already here, watching you even before he called the hospital."

"There are other things that do not make sense," Anita said but then was interrupted by the ringing telephone.

"I'll get it," Toni offered. "You don't need to be answering a lot of questions just now." Anita nodded consent, and Toni picked up the receiver. "Sanchez residence, Toni Trent speaking."

"Hello, Toni. This is Lois Tanner. Is it true that Juanita's been found and she's all right?"

"Yes on both counts, praise God."

"I felt just awful when I heard that sweet little girl was missing. It's funny—I was going to call Anita today, anyway—a man who registered at the inn last night said he'd known her in Texas."

"What was his name?" Toni asked, instantly alert.

"John Martin. He seemed to know Anita well. I showed him a picture I took of Juanita when they were living at the inn."

"Did he ask you questions about them?"

"Not that I recall—oh, he did ask if Juanita was with Anita and wanted to know if she was going to school."

"Lois, the police are going to want to talk to you. Call Earl Hurley and tell him what you just told me."

"Why?"

"That man could be the one who took Juanita."

"Oh, no! He seemed so nice—you know I would never willingly do anything to harm Juanita."

"Of course you wouldn't. We all know that. But you can help build the case against him."

"I'll call Earl Hurley right away. Tell Anita I'm sorry. I don't know what else to say."

"That's enough."

"If there's anything else I can do, I hope you or Anita will let me know."

"We will. Good-bye, Lois."

Anita had heard enough of the conversation to guess its content even before Toni repeated it. "One more mystery solved," she said. "The man who called Phyllis Dickson said he was John Martin, too."

"He is very clever," Toni said. "I suppose that's what attracted you to him in the first place."

"What?" Anita asked, then she realized she had never told Toni Trent the reason she feared Bill Rankin. "I want you to know what really happened. Maybe it will help me to understand it better myself."

"What about Juanita?" Toni asked.

Anita looked into the bedroom and saw her daughter had fallen asleep on her bed, Dora in one arm and her next-favorite doll in the other. She closed the door and rejoined Toni in the living room.

"This could take awhile. I will make coffee."

∽

After all the personnel in the sheriff's office who were involved in the day's operations had given their statements to the FBI agent dispatched from Huntsville, Sheriff Trimble called Hawk into his office. He was pleased with the way things had turned out, especially since the FBI agent had been quite complimentary of him and his department.

However, Sheriff Trimble seemed convinced that the morning's events, precipitated by Anita Sanchez, signaled the start of a massive crime wave.

"I still think that woman has some connection with drugs. She might be clean now, but she and her husband must have been involved with all kinds of drug dealings in Texas."

"No. Juan Sanchez never had anything to do with drugs. He had a criminal record, but she didn't know that when she married him."

"What about her relationship with Rankin? You know the old saying—a person who lies down with dogs gets up with fleas."

Hawk sighed, exasperated by the sheriff's attitude. "She had no relationship with Rankin. As I told you, she was trying to get away from him. Despite all the bad things Anita Sanchez has been through, she is a fine woman."

Sheriff Trimble shook his head. "It's obvious her pretty face has you completely taken in. Once the hullabaloo is over, I hope the woman will return to her own kind and let Rockdale get back to normal."

"If I have anything to say about it, Anita Sanchez won't be going anywhere."

Sally Rogers stuck her head into the sheriff's office. "Your wife's on line one, Sheriff."

Leaving the sheriff's office, Hawk clocked out and picked up his jacket.

"I was praying for the little girl," Sally said. "I'm happy she turned out to be all right."

"So am I. But keep the prayers coming, please. She and her mother still need all the help they can get."

∞

Knowing Hawk was coming over, Anita decided to cook dinner for him. She knew everyone in Rockdale would be talking about the day's events, and she did not want to burden Juanita with the added attention they would receive if they appeared in public so soon.

Even more than that, Anita wanted to be alone with Hawk so she could thank him for all he had done for her and Juanita. At the same time, she felt she had to make it clear she expected nothing more from him.

By late afternoon, Juanita was restless and looking for something to do, so Anita wrapped an apron around her and set her to work in the kitchen. By the time Hawk arrived, Juanita had tired of playing cook. She greeted him warmly, then pulled off her apron and handed it to him.

"Here, Dep'ty. You can help Mama now. Dora and I are going to practice our letters 'til it's time to eat." Juanita picked Dora up from the couch and went into the bedroom, closing the door behind her.

Hawk smiled. "I was going to ask how she is doing, but I think I just got my answer."

"Juanita does not really understand what happened today. We talked about what she will do if anyone ever again tries to make her go with them. I also told her Bill Rankin was only pretending to be our friend."

"For now, that is enough. She is a remarkable little girl—and blessed with a wonderful mother."

"Oh, Hawk—Juanita and I owe you so much. Please know you do not have to do anything else—"

Hawk stepped forward and took Anita into his arms. His lips stopped her carefully rehearsed speech with a knee-weakening kiss. Then he looked into Anita's eyes and said words already written on Anita's heart.

"I love you, and I want to marry you. I know I don't have much to offer—"

Anita put her hand across Hawk's mouth. "Do not say such things. You have much more to offer than I could ever deserve."

Hawk covered her hand with his and moved it to his cheek. "Does that mean you'll consider marrying me?"

"There is nothing to consider. I married Juan Sanchez for the wrong reasons. I hoped I would grow to love him, but it never happened. From the first time I saw you, I believed with all my heart that God sent you to help us. I appreciated what you did for Juanita and me in friendship, but when I got to know you better, I began to understand what real love should be like, and I realized I had never known it. Now I do."

Hawk reached into his pocket and brought out a small black jeweler's box. "In that case, this is for you."

Anita was close to tears when Hawk opened the box and revealed a ring set with a small solitaire diamond. Although she had never had an engagement ring before, she knew one when she saw it.

Anita held out her left hand and removed the wedding band from her marriage to Juan Sanchez. "I have continued to wear this ring for Juanita's sake. It stands for a vow I made in good faith, but I am no longer bound by it."

Hawk's hands shook slightly when he took his ring from the box and slipped it on Anita's finger. "I'm glad you feel that way."

"I do."

Hawk smiled. "I do, too, and I can't wait for the world to know it."

"Neither can I."

Hawk grinned widely, then embraced Anita again. They stood together, content in each other's arms, until the stove timer chimed. Startled, Anita pulled away and smoothed her apron.

"The food is ready. Tell Juanita to wash her hands and come to the table."

"Is there anything else I can tell her?"

"Not yet. Wait until after dinner—otherwise she will be too excited to eat."

Hawk kissed Anita's forehead and smiled. "I'm afraid that goes for me, too."

Saying her huggy doll wasn't hungry, Juanita came to the table without Dora. When all were seated, she reached her hands out to Hawk and Anita.

"Will you offer our thanks tonight?" he asked.

"All right. Bow your head, Dep'ty. Dear God, thank You for this food and for this day and for Mama and Dep'ty Hawk and Dora and everyone and make us all better. A-men."

"Very nice," Hawk said, reluctant to let go of Anita's hand.

"Not everything that happened today was good, but God looked after us as He always does. We should always remember to thank Him for all His gifts," Anita said.

Juanita noticed her mother's new diamond ring. "That's pretty, Mama. That man who found Dora's shoe said you had a fortune. Does that mean you're rich?"

"No, sweetie. He was wrong. We do not have riches, but we have good friends. They are worth much more than gold."

"So is being loved," Hawk told Juanita. "A lot of people around here love you and your mother. That ring shows I love her in a special way."

"We love you, too, Dep'ty. Can we eat now?"

∞

After the dishes were done, Anita invited Juanita to sit on the couch between her and Hawk. "We have something to tell you," Anita said.

"Wait! I want to get Dora."

Hawk smiled. "By all means. Everyone in the family should hear this."

Juanita returned with her huggy doll and climbed back onto the couch. "We're ready now."

Anita thought she was prepared to share their news with the whole world, but now that the time had come, she did not know how to tell her own daughter. When her eyes sent Hawk a mute appeal, he took one of Juanita's hands and spoke quietly.

"Your mother loves you very much, and so do I. We also love each other, and we want to be a family."

Juanita's eyes widened. "You mean get married?"

Anita nodded, uncertain what her daughter's reaction meant. "Yes, sweetie."

Juanita threw both arms around Hawk's neck. Then, not to slight anyone, she hugged her mother and Dora, as well. "Miss Toni is Josh and Mandy's stepmother, but they call her 'Mommy.' When you're my stepfather, can I call you 'Daddy'?"

Obviously touched, Hawk smiled. "If that's what you want, of course."

Juanita was so excited, she wanted to stay up past her bedtime, but soon she admitted she was tired. After Anita tucked her into bed, Hawk joined them to hear Juanita say her prayers. She asked God to bless just about everyone she knew in Rockdale by name, then added, "Thank You for sending us the dep'ty and making this the bestest day of my whole life."

When they returned to the living room, Anita tried to brush away her tears, but Hawk noticed. "Hey, what's this? Is the thought of marrying me so awful?"

"Oh, no—I agree with Juanita. This is the bestest day of my life, too."

"And mine three." Hawk held Anita close for a moment, then sighed and drew back.

"What is the matter?"

"I was thinking how sad life must be for people like Bill Rankin. His concern about money has made him overlook life's true fortune."

"You are right. As much grief as he has caused, we should pray for that man."

Safely folded in Hawk's strong arms, Anita quietly offered thanks to God. He had given them salvation through His Son Jesus Christ, and now Anita and Hawk had also received a great fortune—a love which would continue to increase through all the years ahead.

Epilogue

Small towns have long memories, and the story of a stranger who kidnapped a little girl in broad daylight passed almost immediately into Rockdale's folklore. Oddly enough, no one who told it mentioned the kidnapped girl and her mother were exotic Hispanic strangers themselves. They had become part of Rockdale now, and as such, anyone who tried to harm them had the whole community against them.

Anita and Juanita did not keep their Hispanic last names for long. Anita Sanchez became Mrs. Hawk Henson in an early summer wedding at Community Church, with Toni Trent serving as Anita's matron of honor.

By that time, their lives had undergone several changes. Hawk was promoted to chief deputy and moved into the condo next door to Mrs. Tarpley, where Anita and Juanita joined him after the wedding.

Even before he and Anita were married, Hawk filed a petition to adopt Juanita Sanchez.

"In my heart, you're my daughter already, but this will make it legal," Hawk told Juanita.

The little girl was delighted. "Now Dora and I will be Hensons, too."

When Congressman Jeremy Winter heard Anita's story, he arranged an investigation into the deaths of her brother and her parents. He found out that the drug lords who were responsible had been in prison several years, and they had shown no interest in her after she fled to America. As Anita suspected, Juan Sanchez was the sole source of the threats she thought had come from Colombia.

Best of all, Anita's aunt Rita had contacted the American embassy in Barranquilla several years ago in an effort to find her niece, and both women now looked forward to the prospect of a family reunion in the near future.

In July, Bill Rankin went on trial in Texas on assorted counts of parole violations, impersonating a law officer, and attempted extortion. Following those proceedings, he would be returned to Alabama to face many of the same charges, plus the most serious of all, kidnapping.

Anita chose not to go to Texas for the trial, but the prosecuting attorney who took her deposition promised to keep her informed about the proceedings. Exactly six months from the day Juanita Sanchez had been kidnapped, a call from Texas cleared up the last remaining mystery concerning the fortune Bill Rankin thought Anita had taken.

"Deputy Henson asked me if the Texas police had investigated the manager of the storage unit where Juan Sanchez put the take from the robbery. It turns out they knew each other, and when he heard Juan Sanchez was dead, the manager opened the unit and took all the money. When Rankin showed up to get his share, the manager made up the story that a Hispanic woman had taken it. Rankin had seen your picture and assumed it must have been you."

"What happened to the money?"

"We're still working on that. My guess is the company will recover at least part of it."

"Does this change your case against Bill Rankin?"

"It confirms the reason he came after you. Don't worry, Mrs. Henson. Texas has enough on Rankin to put him away for a long time, not counting a sentence for the kidnapping charge."

Anita let out a sigh of relief. "Thank you for letting me know about this."

"Sure. I'll call again when the trial is over, but there's no doubt of the outcome."

Hawk came in just as Anita hung up the telephone. "From that smile, that call must have been good news."

"Very good. The Texas prosecutor says the police took your suggestion about checking on the storage unit manager, and thanks to you, they know he took the stolen money. The company could get some of it back."

Hawk smiled. "Great. Now we know what happened to your fortune."

"That money was never mine." Anita put her arms around Hawk. "My fortune is right here."

AUTHOR'S NOTE

Although Anita Muños Sanchez is a fictional victim of domestic violence, she represents women everywhere who may need help to escape an abusive relationship. In real life, although most communities provide some kind of crisis counseling, many women may be unaware of these services or be unwilling to use them out of fear. Working with and praying for abused women can be a valuable ministry for Christian women. Even small acts of kindness can make a difference.

In the words of Dr. Amparo Vargas de Medina of Colombia, who has been a tireless campaigner against domestic violence in her own country and throughout Latin America: "Las pequeñas cosa en las manos de Dios, Èl las vuelve grandes"—God alone is able to take the smallest things and mold them into marvelous works.*

*Reprinted from the July 2003 issue of *Missions Mosaic*, published by Woman's Missionary Union, Birmingham, Alabama. Used by permission.

Mary's Choice

In loving memory of my grandmother, Mary Griggs Whitehead
("Mother Mary" to all who knew her),
and my mother, "Pinkie" Whitehead Oldham,
women whose lives reflected what they told me:
"Pretty is as pretty does."

Chapter 1

"Happy birthday, Miss Mary!" eighteen first-graders shouted more or less in unison when Mary Oliver entered her classroom at two o'clock on the third Friday in May.

Summoned to the principal's office fifteen minutes earlier, Mary had told Ann Ward, her student teacher, she couldn't imagine what Mrs. Martin wanted that couldn't wait until school was out. "Hold down the fort—I should be back soon."

Now Mary stood in shocked surprise and looked around. Dark pink crepe paper streamers and pink and white balloons decorated the room, and HAPPY BIRTHDAY TO OUR TEACHER was written in large letters on the chalkboard. The top of Mary's desk had been cleared to make room for a sheet cake on which thirty candles blazed. Smiling broadly, blond student teacher Ann Ward and brunette room mother Katie Pierce flanked the cake.

"Blow out the candles, Miss Mary!" Tommy Pierce shouted.

"Then she can see the presents and we can have cake," added his twin sister, Tammy.

Mary looked from the children crowding around her to the women beside the desk and shook her head. "I didn't think anyone knew it was my birthday."

"We thought you deserved to be included in the birthday calendar, too," Katie Pierce said. "Mrs. Martin agreed, and Miss Ward helped us."

"Hurry, Miss Mary! Blow out the candles before the cake burns up," Lance Hastings said.

"She has to make a wish first," Tammy Pierce said.

"I can't think of a thing to wish for," Mary said.

"You could wish for a husman, Miss Mary," Juanita Sanchez suggested.

"Husband," Mary corrected as a chorus of little voices joined to ask her to wish for a man. "I'd rather think of something nice for all of you, instead," Mary said.

"That's right, if Miss Mary wanted a husman, she'd already have one," Jackie Tait declared.

Mary's last shred of composure crumbled, and she laughed so hard she could scarcely take a deep breath.

"It's your birthday, so you can have three tries," Juanita Sanchez said when Mary's first effort extinguished only a few candles.

"I think you just made a new birthday rule," Katie Pierce said.

With a second breath, Mary blew out most of the remaining candles, and when her third attempt extinguished the rest, the children cheered and applauded.

"That means Miss Mary can have three husbands," Jackie Tait declared.

Katie Pierce smiled at the child. "One at a time, of course."

After having cake, the children gathered around Mary in the story area and watched her examine the two-page books each had made. All bore the hand-printed heading "My Teacher" and the student's picture of Mary. The second page, written using the classroom computer, contained an individual "story" about their teacher.

"What a fine job you all did!" Mary exclaimed as she held up each one for inspection. In fact, many of the boys and girls had gone out of their way to create a realistic portrait, complete with impossibly large green eyes. Some had given her two-toned red and yellow hair in an effort to capture Mary's unique strawberry blond shade. Some showed her with tiny feet and hands and a big head, while one budding Rembrandt depicted Mary as a snowman in a blue dress. Mary suspected they'd had more than a little help from their student teacher, who had spent several afternoons with the class during the past week while Mary held year-end parent conferences.

The students' stories contained sentiments such as "I like my teacher," "Miss Mary helps me," and "I love her."

Mary's eyes brimmed with sudden tears. She loved "her" children, too, more than they could ever know. "Thank you all for making this birthday very special."

"Your students really love you," Ann Ward said a few minutes later when the school day ended. "I hope I can be half the teacher you are."

You're already half my size. The flippant words almost slipped out. Mary judged Ann Ward to be a perfect size eight, in contrast to her own sixteen petite dress size.

"Thanks, Ann. My best advice to you is to follow the lead of the Master Teacher. If you can do that, you can't go wrong."

Ann nodded. "That's exactly what Jason said when I told him I wanted to be a teacher."

"Jason? I don't believe you've mentioned him."

"Jason Abbott—he's an older cousin. I haven't seen him since I was a college freshman, but I just found out he's coming to Rockdale soon."

Katie Pierce had been listening to their conversation and addressed Ann. "I had no idea you were related to Jason Abbott. He's been called to be my church's associate pastor."

"Toni Trent mentioned Community Church was adding to the staff," Mary said. "She'll be glad to know he's from a good family."

Ann smiled. "On my mother's side, anyway. When you get to know him, I'm sure you'll like him."

"Pastor Hurley can't wait for him to get here and start some new programs."

"My mother said Jason feels the same way," Ann said. "I'm sorry to be leaving town just as he's about to arrive."

When the classroom had been restored to order, Ann helped Mary take her students' gifts and the remaining birthday cake to her car.

"You'll probably have another birthday cake waiting when you get home," Ann said.

"I doubt it. My father and I are having dinner at the country club tonight, and that will be it."

"You don't have any other family around here?"

Mary opened the trunk of her aging Toyota, the first car she'd bought with her own money, and moved several book-filled plastic crates to make room for her students' birthday books. "Not really. The Olivers have scattered all over the map. About the only time we see them is on Decoration Day, when we tend the family cemetery on Memorial Day weekend. That reminds me—I still have a few more calls to make."

"You're in charge, I suppose?"

Mary shrugged. "Not officially, but I try to remind everyone."

"Dad's aunt Frances did such things in our family. She never married." Ann stopped suddenly, and Mary silently supplied *either*. Obviously, Ann assumed being single automatically made Mary the family record keeper.

"Thank you for helping with my party," Mary said. "The children and I will miss you."

Ann stepped back as Mary slammed the trunk shut. "I know I'm out of line to say this, but I think it's a shame you haven't married and had your own children. You'd make such a good mother."

Mary had heard similar statements before, and she gave Ann her stock answer. "I love being first-graders' school-hours mother. That's enough for me."

∞

She thought she sounded convincing, but Ann's comment echoed in her mind on her drive home. *You'd make such a good mother.*

Mary usually dismissed such statements without a second thought. Since feeling God's call in her teens to teach, Mary had presumed she would remain single.

Not that I ever had much choice. Overweight from childhood, Mary had avoided being hurt by rejecting the few men who didn't mind being seen with her. She had settled into a comfortable routine, working with children and making a home for her father.

"Home" was a turreted Victorian built by her great-grandfather Hugh Oliver. "A real southern showplace," the pages of a prestigious magazine featuring Alabama homes had described it. Mary had no illusions about it, however. The house tended to be cold in the winter and, despite strategically placed window air conditioners and fans in the high ceilings, it could also be hot in the summer.

Mary turned into the driveway and went around to the back where the original carriage house now served as a two-car garage and storage for the Olivers' lawnmower and gardening tools. She noted the absence of her father's stately black sedan. Judge Wayne Oliver had been hearing cases all week, and he would probably stay at the Rock County courthouse until well after five in an effort to clear the current docket.

Mary put her birthday gift books on the dining room table. In the kitchen, she scraped the lettering from the icing, double-wrapped the leftover cake in foil, and put it in the freezer. Later she could bring it out and share it with her father as an end-of-school cake. On the thirtieth anniversary of his daughter's birth, Wayne Oliver needed no more reminders of the day that also marked his wife's death.

Mary recalled how, when she was four, she had realized everyone else in her world had a real mother, while all she had was a picture of a pretty young woman in a white dress.

"Aunt Janie, where is my mother?" Mary had asked the black woman who had helped raise her mother and was now doing the same for her.

"Miss Grace be in heaven, Miss Mary. She loved the Lord, and His angels done took her right up there."

At the time, Mary made no connection between her birth and her mother's death, but when she was six, her aunt Lucy Austin had taken Mary to her first Decoration Day. Sylvia, Aunt Lucy's ten-year-old daughter, took Mary aside and showed her the family's burial plot.

"That's your mama's grave." Sylvia then read the inscription aloud.

"May 21—that's my birthday," Mary said.

"I heard my mama say your mama died 'cause something busted inside of her when you were born. If it hadn't been for you, Aunt Grace would still be alive 'stead of lyin' here under all this dirt."

That evening, Mary had climbed into Aunt Janie's ample lap and sobbed inconsolably.

"What's de matter, chile?"

"Sylvie Austin told me I killed my mother," she said between sobs.

"You never killed nobody, chile. Don't pay no attention to that gal, 'cause she don't have a brain in her head. You was born 'cause God wanted you here on earth, and He took Miss Grace to heaven 'cause He needed her there. It don't do to try to say why God does what He does. Come on, darlin'—quit cryin' and Aunt Janie'll give you a hunk of the chocolate cake I made for you this mornin'."

The cake tasted good and Mary felt better, at least for the moment. Whenever Mary got hurt or had a problem, Aunt Janie was always there with something good to eat. As a result, Mary had gone from toddler "baby fat" to a childhood of wearing hard-to-find chubby-size clothing. She began her painful teen years in ill-fitting women's plus-sizes.

Fatty, fatty, two by four. . .

Can't get through the kitchen door. . .

The taunting had started early and continued long after Mary had learned to close her ears to it. At a church camp in her fifteenth summer, the leader had taken Mary aside and used scriptures to show her how much the Creator God loved her, just as she was, just as she had been made.

"There is no such thing as an ugly body to God. He loves you in your body. His grace covers everything you see as a fault, just as His blood covered your sins when you accepted Jesus as your Lord and Savior."

From that day, Mary's attitude changed, not only about the way she looked but also about everything in her life. When she was no longer the center of all her thoughts, Mary found others who needed to know the peace she had found in accepting God's grace. One such person, Toni Schmidt Trent, had recently returned to Rockdale and was now Mary's best friend.

Once Mary understood what she had allowed food to become, she had begun to lose weight by learning to eat only when she was physically hungry. By popular standards, she was still overweight when she graduated from college, but Dr. Mason, who had tended two generations of Austins and Olivers, wasn't concerned.

"You're a healthy young woman. Get married and have lots of babies. Don't even think about trying to diet yourself to death."

Mary spread out the portraits the students had made of her and thought of the advice Dr. Mason had delivered almost a decade ago.

"Marriage isn't in the picture for me," Mary had told the doctor. Then, she had automatically dismissed all thought of marriage; now, she wasn't so sure.

"Mary—I'm home. Where are you?"

Judge Oliver came in through the kitchen, and Mary heard him put his briefcase on a table in the front hall.

"In the dining room. Come see what my students did."

Wayne Oliver shrugged out of his suit jacket and hung it on the antique walnut hall tree. Much taller than his daughter, he had a large frame, which carried only a few more pounds than it had in his football playing years at the University of Alabama. Like his daughter, the judge had the kind of round, high-cheekboned face which looked youthful even past middle age. His eyes were the same unusual shade of green as Mary's, while his close-cropped salt-and-pepper hair contrasted with his daughter's strawberry blond bob.

"I take it your class did something good?"

"With my student teacher's help. Every child in the class made a book for me."

Wayne Oliver's stern countenance, befitting his position as a judge, softened when he viewed the pictures. "Quite a collection of portraits," he said after a moment. "Looks like you have a pretty good crop of kids this year."

"As usual," Mary said.

Her father glanced at his wristwatch. "We have reservations at the country club for six thirty. We'll leave about six. Put on something nice."

Mary watched her father walk away, humming as he all but skipped up the stairs. He had been acting a bit strange lately. Usually she had to nag him to buy clothes, but a few weeks ago, he had gone to Birmingham on his own and returned with a new suit and several casual shirts and slacks. Last weekend he had disappeared for hours with no explanation. And oddest and most telling of all, he smiled a lot more these days.

He's up to something, all right—I wonder what.

Chapter 2

"Y ou look very handsome in your new suit," Mary said when her father came down the stairs promptly at six.

He glanced at it as if he hadn't noticed what he was wearing. "Do I? Thanks."

"Why are we going so early?" Mary asked as they left the house.

"You'll see."

Instead of turning right toward Rockdale Country Club, Wayne Oliver turned left toward town. He circled the courthouse and turned right, then right again.

Her father stopped the car in front of 210 Maple Street, a house she knew well. Toni Schmidt had lived there as a teenager after Evelyn Trent became her legal guardian and again when she'd returned to town a couple of years ago to take over Evelyn's job. Toni had moved out after marrying Evelyn's brother last year, and Evelyn had recently returned to town after a second round of extensive traveling.

"I'll be right back," her father said.

While he mounted the porch steps and rang the doorbell, Mary got into the backseat to allow Evelyn to sit up front. Apparently Wayne Oliver, who had avoided going out with women as long as Mary could remember, had invited Evelyn, the retired director of the Rockdale office of the Department of Human Resources, to accompany them to the country club. Not an official date, perhaps, but close.

Evelyn appeared at the door, trim and stylish in a long navy blue sheath. Her pearl necklace and earrings accented her blue eyes, silver-white hair, and smooth ivory skin. *This isn't the first time they've gone out,* Mary guessed. They must have kept it under wraps, because she hadn't heard even a whisper about it—and with all the busybodies and gossips in Rockdale, she most certainly would have.

Wayne Oliver offered Evelyn his arm, and they came down the steps looking like an elegant couple in an advertisement for something extravagantly expensive. A lump rose in Mary's throat as she saw how much they already looked as if they belonged together.

"Hello, Mary," Evelyn said when she had been installed in the front seat. "How's school? I suppose you're counting the days to the end of the term."

"In a way, but it's a bittersweet time. I've had really fine children this year, and I hate to lose them."

"I hear that every year," her father said. "One of these days, Mary's bound to have a class full of little stinkers."

"If so, I'm sure she'll turn them around. She certainly did a great job with my nephew."

"Josh was never a bad child—he just missed his mother. Once Toni came into his life, he blossomed."

"Speaking of Toni, she and David will be there tonight," Wayne Oliver said.

Evelyn half turned to address Mary. "Toni has certainly made a wonderful stepmother for my brother's children."

"When I remanded Toni Schmidt to your custody all those years ago, I never imagined where it would lead," the judge observed.

"Neither did I," Evelyn agreed. "The Lord, indeed, moves in mysterious ways."

∞

Mary expected they would sit in the main dining room, but the hostess told him some of his guests were already waiting in the Rock Room.

Lloyd Hastings, husband of long-time Rockdale mayor Margaret Hastings; Randall Bell, retired lawyer and lifelong friend of Wayne Oliver; and Realtor Walter Chance stood as Judge Oliver's party approached the large, round table in the private dining room.

Mary was surprised to see Walter Chance, a high school classmate with whom she'd worked on their tenth reunion. His perennial smile and brick-red hair made him look somewhat clownlike at first glance, but no one could deny he was serious about reviving his family's real estate business.

Walter smiled widely and pulled out the chair next to his for Mary. "That's a pretty dress."

"Thanks, Walter."

"Hello, Mary, Evelyn," said Margaret Hastings when they were seated. "You both look stunning."

Mary accepted the compliment, although she suspected it was intended more for Evelyn. Mary knew her green crepe dress—bought on sale for more than she cared to admit—set off her green eyes and ivory skin, and the long lines of the jacket added an illusion of height and made her seem pounds lighter. But stunning was not the word Mary thought anyone else would likely use.

"Red is definitely your color, Margaret," Evelyn observed.

"Thanks," said the mayor. "Look, here comes Toni Trent. I'm glad she didn't wear her hot pink dress tonight. When we wind up being seated together, those colors clash badly."

Mary turned to see Toni, wearing a light blue dress under a darker blue jacket, enter with David Trent, Evelyn's brother.

Once again the men stood, and Toni took the chair to Mary's left. "It's been too long since we got together."

Mary still considered Toni to be her best friend, but since Toni's marriage, they hadn't been as close. Being the last remaining single, never-married women in their

Rockdale High School graduating class had given them a shared bond when Toni had come back to Rockdale to live, determined not to marry. However, after Mary saw David and Toni together, she wasn't surprised when they became engaged, and she rejoiced in her friend's happiness.

"Our colors blend well tonight," Margaret Hastings told Toni. "I'm glad you didn't wear your hot pink dress."

"I probably would have, but I can't get into it now."

Mary glanced at Toni and saw her waistline had thickened considerably since she'd last seen her. Toni didn't seem to be upset by the change—in fact, her face glowed with happiness.

"Is there something we should know?" Mary asked.

David took his wife's hand and smiled broadly. "Toni wanted to keep it quiet as long as possible, but we're expecting a baby in October."

"How wonderful!" Mary hugged her friend. "Do Josh and Mandy know?"

"Yes, but we asked them not to tell anyone for a while. They can't wait to have a little brother or sister."

"You don't know which?" asked Margaret.

"No. We'll take whatever the Lord sends us and rejoice," David said.

"That's a good attitude," Randall Bell said. "Just paint the nursery all-purpose white. That's what my daughter, Joan, did with both of hers."

Just then Dr. Vance Whitson, pastor of First Church, and his wife arrived.

"This is quite an occasion," Lloyd Hastings observed when the couple took the remaining seats. "As long as I've known Wayne Oliver, I believe this is his first dinner party. I suppose you're responsible, Mary."

She shook her head. "No—I didn't know anything about it until we got here."

"I think I know who assisted Judge Oliver." Margaret smiled at Evelyn, whose cheeks flushed becomingly.

"The judge wanted to surprise Mary, and I offered to help," Evelyn said.

Randall Bell, a long-time widower, smiled at Evelyn. "Excellent choice. Maybe you should start catering, now that you've retired."

"No thanks, Randall. I stay so busy now, I really don't know when I ever had time to work."

Wayne Oliver tapped his glass with a spoon. "I'm glad you could all join us. Dr. Whitson, will you offer our thanks?"

A bit dazed, Mary bowed her head as her church's senior pastor provided a lengthy blessing for the food.

∞

Later, if anyone had asked about the menu that evening, Mary would have been hard-pressed to name even one dish. Walter Chance did his best to make entertaining small talk, while everyone at the table noticed the attention Wayne Oliver was paying Evelyn Trent, who sat beside him, blushing like a schoolgirl and laughing at his somewhat lame jokes.

This evening is about them, not me. Mary wanted her father to be happy, but seeing him and Evelyn together made her feel oddly alone. *He must have realized it would and invited Walter to keep me company.*

During dinner, conversation turned to rumors about changes coming to the town of Rockdale as outside interests sought to buy land or start new ventures.

"It's time we got together to decide how to deal with these things," Randall Bell said. "As much as some of us might want to, we can't stop changes from happening, but we ought to prepare to direct it for the good of everyone in Rockdale and Rock County."

Judge Oliver nodded in agreement. "Some of us have been considering what to do about this for some time—our mayor here, Newman Howell, Sam Roberts, and Dr. Endicott, to name a few. We agree it's time for everyone who's interested in managing Rockdale's growth to get together. Mayor Hastings has agreed to open the city council chambers next Tuesday night and serve as an ex officio chairman of a new organization to be known as the Rockdale Civic Improvement Association. Anyone who cares about what happens to Rockdale is invited to be a part of it."

"That sounds like a good idea," said Walter Chance.

"Be thinking about it. For the moment, there's a much more important item on the agenda," the judge said.

At the host's signal, the kitchen doors opened, and the headwaiter wheeled in a cart bearing a birthday cake. A buzz of conversation confirmed it was as much a surprise to the guests as to Mary.

Judge Oliver, who cheerfully admitted he couldn't carry a tune in a bucket, waved both hands in an attempt to direct a ragged rendition of the traditional happy birthday song.

Mary had no trouble looking surprised. Her face turned red, and although she wanted to slide out of sight beneath the table, she tried to smile. She was grateful someone had the good sense to put a single large candle on this cake, unlike the thirty small ones on her school cake.

The headwaiter stopped the cart beside Mary and stepped aside, and Toni tugged on her sleeve. "Stand up. You have to make a wish and blow out the candle."

With a strange feeling of déjà vu, Mary rose and blew out the oversized candle, bringing a round of applause.

Her father stood beside Mary and put his arm around her shoulders. "I don't know what my daughter wished for, but I hope she gets it. I'm proud of Mary, and it's time I told her so."

Mary hugged her father, too full of tears to speak, and when she sat down again and saw tears gleaming in Evelyn's eyes, she suspected the retired social worker had played a part in more than merely arranging the dinner.

The headwaiter cut a huge chunk of the cake for Mary, then his assistants moved in to serve everyone else.

"It's chocolate!" Mary exclaimed.

"I know that's your favorite. Your mother loved chocolate, too."

"Thank you. This is just what I wanted," Mary said, and they both understood she meant the sentiment, not the cake.

"You should have reminded us it was Mary's birthday," Margaret Hastings told Judge Oliver.

"That's right, Wayne. We would gladly have brought a gift if we'd known," Randall Bell said.

"I'm glad you didn't," Mary said.

Evelyn nodded. "I told your father you'd feel that way."

A few minutes later, when they went to freshen their makeup, Mary took the opportunity to speak to Toni. "That's great news about you and David. I'd like to give you a baby shower this summer."

"Thanks. We have a room in our house we've always called the nursery, but we don't have a thing in it."

"Look at your calendar and come up with a date—a Friday night in July or August will probably work for everyone."

"Will you be in town all summer?" Toni asked.

"Yes. I hope to have time to vegetate for a change."

"That's what I'll do if David has his way, but I want to work as long as I can. I'd rather stay home longer after the baby comes than to quit weeks before."

"As long as you feel well, I see no reason why you shouldn't keep working."

"That's what I told David. Besides, Evelyn has agreed to fill in while I'm on maternity leave, so my job will be in good hands."

Mary was silent for a moment. "Speaking of Evelyn, how long has my father been seeing her?"

"I don't know, but I think it's about time for them both."

"Lately my father has seemed rather preoccupied. Now I believe it's because of Evelyn."

"Do you approve?" Toni asked.

Mary shrugged. "I like Evelyn, but after all the years he's dodged well-meaning widows, it's strange to see him dating."

"David and I felt the same way about Evelyn at first, too. It should be interesting to see what happens."

∞

When the dinner ended and Walter Chance offered to take Mary home, she suspected her father had planned it that way.

"There are still a few hours left in your birthday," Walter said on the way to his car. "Maybe we should continue the celebration somewhere else."

Mary smiled. "In Rockdale? I don't know where that would be. Thanks, anyway."

Walter helped Mary into his sedan but made no move to start the engine.

He had parked beneath a bright security light, and Mary saw his expression was uncharacteristically serious when he turned to her.

"It really meant a lot for the judge to include me tonight. Since Mother's been gone, I've had to eat alone most nights."

Walter's mention of his mother made Mary feel uncomfortable. For years, Roberta Chance had done her best to make her only son into the kind of mama's boy no girl in her right mind would want to marry—and finding fault with anyone Walter showed even a slight interest in. Then a few months ago, Walter's mother had shocked Rockdale by eloping with a Georgia timber cruiser she'd known only a short time, leaving Walter in full control of the business his late father had started. Mrs. Chance's sudden departure had dumbfounded her son and set gossips' tongues wagging.

Although Mary privately thought it was probably the best thing that ever happened to Walter, she knew the sudden change in his life must have affected him deeply, and her sympathy was genuine. "I know this has been a difficult time. Where is your mother living?"

"Atlanta at the moment, but her husband travels all over the Southeast. There's no telling where they'll be next week."

"You're bound to miss her very much, but I'm glad to see you're getting on with your own life."

"I've been trying to. I'm glad you understand—most people around here don't."

Walter Chance was an old friend, and Mary couldn't help feeling sorry for him. "Everyone says you're doing wonders for Chance Realty."

Walter brightened. "I'm still working out some changes, but the business is doing well."

"Your father would be proud of you."

Walter grinned. "Your father sure must be proud of you, to throw you a dinner party like that."

"My birthday wasn't the only reason for it," Mary said. She meant the talk about forming a civic improvement association, but Walter apparently had another idea.

"I think the judge wanted to be seen with Miss Trent. Do you think they'll get married?"

The question startled Mary. "Can't they enjoy each other's company without assuming they're headed for the altar?"

"Not in Rockdale—you know that's the way it is around here. Anyway, I think they make a nice couple."

So did Mary, but she didn't care to discuss her father's personal life. "I'd like to go home. This has been a long day."

Walter was instantly contrite. "Of course you're tired after teaching all day. Forgive me for talking your ear off."

"You didn't—no harm done."

When they reached her home, Walter escorted Mary to her door. "I didn't know today was your birthday, but I intend to give you something, anyway."

"Please don't. Your friendship is gift enough."

Walter's eyes widened. "Really?"

Why did I say that? "We've been friends since kindergarten, I mean."

"We're not in kindergarten now." As if to prove it, Walter gave Mary an awkward hug.

She stammered in surprise. "I—I don't want you to give me anything. I mean it."

"And I mean what I say, too," Walter said cheerfully. "Good night, Mary."

She closed the door behind him and stood for a moment in the dark hallway. Moonlight streamed into the front windows, making everything seem somehow strange and unfamiliar.

Like this evening.

Mary believed her father was correct—Rockdale had resisted many outside forces for years, but change was inevitable. In fact, many such changes had probably already been set into motion.

And so it is with my father and me. It seems he's finally found someone to love.

Could Mary do the same? Perhaps Rockdale wasn't the only thing about to change.

Chapter 3

The last few days of the school year passed in a blur of reports and good-byes. Ann Ward, who was to graduate and move to Seattle that summer, repeated how much she'd learned from Mary.

"I hope you'll get to meet Jason soon," she added. "You two would get along great."

"I'm sure we would if he's anything like you," Mary said, but she thought it unlikely their paths would cross. Jason Abbott would be at Community Church, and Mary attended First Church. "And never the twain shall meet."

With school out of the way, Mary completed plans for the annual Decoration Day. Mary and her father never knew exactly how many relatives would show up to tend the family graves on the last Sunday in May, but everyone would come to the Oliver house for a light supper on Sunday evening.

"It seems fewer people turn out every year," Wayne Oliver remarked when they saw the half-dozen cars parked around the cemetery on Sunday afternoon. "This new generation doesn't seem to care about family traditions."

What new generation? Mary almost asked. She could count the relatives near her age on the fingers of one hand, and she was the only one who still lived in Rockdale.

The cemetery was situated on flat land at the top of Oliver Mountain, one of several ridges surrounding Rockdale. A stone fence surrounded the plot, and a hundred-year-old wrought iron gate marked the entrance. Many of the jumbled, weathered tombstones were shaded by oak, maple, and hickory trees, whose roots had caused cracks in several of the older stones. A spring-fed stream splashed on nearby rocks as it made its way down the mountain, and the soft wind sighed through the trees, the only sounds other than the songs of birds.

"This place is more beautiful every year," Mary remarked.

"And needs more attention. When I was here last week, I noticed the Austin headstones needed cleaning. You can start there."

Mary glanced at her mother's great-great-grandparents' graves, among the oldest in the cemetery. "The headstones look newly cleaned."

"So they do. The question is, who did it?"

"I plead guilty, Judge Oliver," a male voice said.

Mary turned to the speaker, a well-built, dark-haired man with startling, deep blue eyes. He wore jeans and a battered red shirt with "Alabama Football" stenciled on the front. Mary hadn't seen him in at least ten years, but she recognized him instantly.

Todd Walker. A distant cousin on her mother's side of the family, five years older, and football star at the University of Alabama. Throughout her teen years, Mary had had a secret crush on Todd, who had scarcely known she existed. Even now, years later, he still made her heart beat a bit faster.

"Todd!" Wayne Oliver exclaimed. "I had no idea you were back in Alabama."

"I've been working in Birmingham for a couple of months. I looked at the calendar Friday and realized it was time for Decoration Day, so I threw a few tools in the truck and drove over this morning. I took the liberty of cleaning a few stones before anyone else arrived. I hope you don't mind."

"Not at all. They look almost like new."

Todd turned his attention to Mary. "I was hoping to see you today, Mary Oliver—or do you have a different last name now?"

Mary shook her head, feeling as tongue-tied in his presence as when she was a love-struck teenager. "No."

"You kids can catch up with each other while you work," Wayne Oliver said. "As you can see, there's much to be done."

When her father called her and Todd "kids," Mary winced. She was thirty, and Todd had to be thirty-five. Granted, they weren't exactly dead with old age, but both were past being kids.

If Todd noticed her father's use of the term, he didn't show it. "Where would you like for us to start, sir?"

Us. Mary smiled inwardly at Todd's casual reference. In assuming he and Mary would work together, Todd made it sound as if they were a couple.

"Since you've already done the headstones, you might as well work in the Austin plot. There aren't many Austin kin left, and I doubt if any others will show up today."

"I see you came prepared," Todd said when her father left to greet a few late arrivals.

At first Mary thought he referred to the straw hat, blue jeans, and long-sleeved shirt salvaged from her father's wardrobe, then she realized he meant her heavy gloves and grass clippers. "I wear the gloves to weed and use the shears to trim places the lawnmower can't reach."

"Good idea." Todd spread out his hands, which were at least twice the size of Mary's and, like hers, ringless. "The gloves obviously won't fit me, but I can use the clippers while you pull weeds."

They began to clear the area around the newly cleaned stones. " 'Warren Austin,' " Todd read from the headstone. "According to my mother's family tree, he's a 'way back grandfather.' "

"Mine, too. He was my great-great-great-grandfather."

"So what kin does that make us?" Todd asked.

"Fifth cousins, I believe. Or maybe we're first cousins, five times removed. I don't know much about genealogy."

"Neither do I. But I'm much more interested in learning about my roots now than when I was a kid."

So Todd noticed her father's comment, after all. Mary returned Todd's slight smile and resumed her work without saying anything.

After a moment, Todd spoke again. "I take it you stayed here in Rockdale?"

"Yes. I teach first grade at Rockdale Elementary."

"I'm not surprised. You're just right for a place like Rockdale."

As Todd spoke, a stubborn sheaf of Johnson grass Mary had been tugging at a long while suddenly yielded, and Mary sat down hard. Embarrassed, she spoke quickly. "I always thought you'd go off and do great things in some big city."

Todd laughed. "So did I, but right now I'm doing rather small things in Birmingham. It isn't exactly a metropolis, but I wanted to get back to Alabama."

"I heard you were living in California. You didn't like it?"

"The weather was great—other things weren't."

Todd's tone warned her to avoid personal questions, and Mary was glad when he asked about present-day Rockdale. "I hear it's on the verge of a lot of growth. How do you feel about that?"

"Everyone says change is inevitable, but I hope Rockdale won't try to grow just for the sake of growth. I like it just as it is now."

"Nothing stays the same forever. Organisms must grow and change or they'll die. The same thing applies to towns."

"That sounds like something from Sociology 101."

Todd smiled. "You caught me there. People in Alabama who remember me at all probably still think I'm a dumb jock. I didn't want the Olivers to think that, too."

Mary had never thought of Todd as lacking intelligence, but his concern seemed real. "I don't," Mary said, "and I'm sure my father doesn't, either. He played football, too, you know."

"I'd almost forgotten. I'm sure no one would ever call Judge Oliver 'dumb.'"

"Not to his face, at least." Mary stood and stretched. "I think we've done all we can here. I'm thirsty—it's time for a break."

Several workers were already gathered around the cooler, pouring lemonade from gallon jugs.

"This is great stuff," Todd said.

"Mary makes this every year," said Nancy Oliver. "The lemonade and supper afterward are just bribes to get us here."

"Whatever works," Wayne Oliver said.

After a brief rest, Todd went to help Mary's father on the Oliver side. Although she had worn gloves, Mary found blisters forming on the thumb and index finger of her right hand, so she spent the rest of the afternoon cleaning headstones with Nancy.

By the time the sun went down behind Oliver Mountain, more than a dozen workers had trimmed around every grave and filled a number of trash bags with weeds, grass, and debris from the small cemetery. Satisfied with the result of their labors, Wayne Oliver thanked the participants for another successful Decoration Day and invited them to his home for supper.

"I hope you'll join us," Wayne told Todd as they left the cemetery.

"Sure. I can't miss the chance to see your wonderful house again," Todd said.

On their way back to town, Mary told her father she didn't recall ever seeing Todd Walker at their home. *As much as I admired him, I believe I would have remembered it.*

"Todd and his mother came to Decoration Day almost every year until she passed away. You must have been away at college the last few times they came together. Since Gladys died, Todd hasn't been back to Rockdale. Why do you ask?"

"No reason."

Mary had never told anyone how she felt about Todd Walker when she was growing up, and she saw no need to confess it to her father now.

The Decoration Day workers arrived at the Oliver house hot and tired. Mary brought minted iced tea to the long tables on one of the two screened-in porches, then returned to the kitchen for the platters of sandwiches and brownies she had made the day before.

Todd followed Mary into the kitchen and offered to help serve.

"You seem to know your way around a kitchen," she remarked a few minutes later.

"I've done my own cooking for years. It's become sort of a hobby."

Mary hesitated to say anything personal, but he had provided a good opening. "It sounds as if you live alone."

Todd directed his attention to removing the plastic wrap over a plate of deviled eggs. "Yes. I've had a few roommates, but they never worked out."

Were his roommates male or female? Mary was curious, but it was none of her business, so she kept silent.

"Leave the eggs on the counter so I can sprinkle them with paprika," she said after a few moments.

Todd watched Mary add the finishing touch to the deviled egg platter. "I remember seeing your housekeeper do that the last time I was here—I think she was called Aunt Janie. Does she still work for you?"

"Unfortunately, she died of a heart attack just before I graduated from college." The words were hard to say, even years later.

"Sorry. I know you were very close."

She was like a mother to me. I still miss her. Mary nodded. "You can take the eggs in now. I'll serve the brownies later."

"So you did all this by yourself?" Todd sounded impressed.

"Such as it is. We'd better get the eggs on the table so my father can bless the food."

While they ate, the relatives retold old stories and passed around information and pictures of absent family members. A motherless only child, Mary always enjoyed this annual opportunity to feel a connection with others who shared her heritage.

Todd sat beside Mary and seemed genuinely interested in each of the family stories. *Either he's having a good time or he's a good actor.*

Eventually, everyone moved to the front hall for long good-byes. Mary returned to the porch to find Todd Walker had already wrapped and refrigerated the few leftovers and was clearing the tables, putting paper plates and plasticware into a garbage bag.

"You don't have to do that," Mary said.

"It's the least I can do after enjoying such great hospitality."

Wayne Oliver joined them, apparently not surprised to find Todd there. "I didn't think you'd leave without saying good-bye."

"Todd's been cleaning up," Mary said.

Wayne Oliver unknowingly repeated her words. "You don't have to do that."

"It's my pleasure. I don't know when I've had a better time, Judge Oliver, or a better supper, Mary."

"I'm glad you remembered the day," Wayne Oliver said. "Now that you're back in Alabama, don't be a stranger."

Todd glanced at Mary. "I won't." He turned to shake her father's hand. "You may get tired of seeing me this summer. Good-bye, and thanks again."

The Olivers walked Todd to the front door and watched his sporty pickup truck pull away from the curb.

Wayne Oliver rubbed his chin. "I wonder what Todd Walker plans to do in Rockdale this summer. Come to think of it, he didn't say where he works."

"I don't know, either," Mary said.

Seeing Todd again reminded Mary of the way girls had always flocked around him. He'd had his pick of the prettiest and the most popular ones, and he would never be interested in anyone who looked like her.

However, Todd Walker was a mature man now, and Mary believed he had really changed. She had a strange feeling he actually wanted to see her again.

Is that possible?

Mary sighed. *More like wishful thinking,* she told herself. She wouldn't get her hopes up, only to have them dashed.

Chapter 4

The Rockdale Civic Improvement Association held its organizational meeting on the first Tuesday in June, and Judge Wayne Oliver was chosen as its leader. On the steering committee were Mayor Margaret Hastings; bank president Newman Howell; hardware store owner Sam Roberts; and Dr. Miles Endicott.

News of its formation received mixed reviews from Rockdale's citizens, who promptly dubbed it "the CIA." Some, like restaurant owner Tom Statum and Police Chief Earl Hurley, thought it was a good thing, while Sally Proffitt saw it as the beginning of the end of their town.

"I never saw anything with 'improvement' in it that didn't wind up costing us money," she told Oaks condo manager Nelson Neal in the checkout aisle at the Sack-and-Save grocery.

"I agreed and all I said to her was, 'We don't need any more taxes,'" Nelson explained.

But Sally Proffitt undoubtedly called Jenny Suiter as soon as she got home to report, "Nelson Neal says they're going to try to raise our taxes," because the rumor had spread through Rockdale like wildfire.

Seeing something must be done to clarify their position, Margaret Hastings suggested putting an article in the newspaper.

"We should also hold a public meeting to make sure everyone understands what we're trying to do," Sam Roberts said.

"Let's do both," Wayne Oliver urged. "With an article in this week's newspaper, we should have a good turnout for a meeting next week."

"Our work is cut out for us," Margaret Hastings said. "Judge, why don't you ask Mary to write the article?"

∞

In the nine years Mary had been teaching, she'd never had an entire, uninterrupted summer vacation. The old saying that June, July, and August were the three best reasons for being a teacher had never applied to her. Between going to school several summers to earn her master's degree, traveling to conferences, and working on projects like the tenth reunion of her Rockdale High School graduating class, Mary had filled each summer.

"This year I'm going to work in the garden and catch up on my reading and that's it," Mary told anyone who asked about her summer plans. However, even before her father asked her to help the Civic Improvement Association, Mary realized she'd probably get little reading or gardening done this summer, either.

Her calendar was already full. Anita Sanchez's bridal tea was coming up on Sunday, and Mary was to serve at the reception following Anita's wedding to Hawk Henson the next Saturday. Vacation Bible School would be followed by school workshops and Toni's baby shower.

"No rest for the weary," Mary muttered as she began writing the Rockdale Civic Improvement Association article. When the telephone rang, she let the answering machine take the call. Hearing Walter's voice, Mary was glad she had.

"Hi, Mary. I know you must think I forgot all about you, but I'm back in town now. Call me, all right?"

Mary sighed and returned to work. Until she turned in the article, Walter would have to wait.

∞

Later that morning, Mary called Margaret Hastings and read her the completed article. "Will it do?"

"Yes, thank you. It's great. If you can take it in right away, Grant can put it in this week's *Record*."

Mary did as Margaret suggested, and Grant Westleigh, the publisher of the weekly newspaper, promised to feature the article on the front page of the next edition.

"I hope the Civic Improvement Association will be successful. The more folks who get involved, the better it'll be for Rockdale," he said. "I'm glad to do my part."

Relieved that chore was done, Mary left the newspaper office and headed for Statum's Family Restaurant, where she and her father planned to meet for lunch. She'd walked only a short distance when Walter Chance came out of his realty office and fell into step beside her.

"Hi, Mary. I saw you leaving the *Record*. I called earlier and got your answering machine."

"I just left an article about the Civic Improvement Association with Grant."

"They picked the right person to do it. You sure did a good job organizing our class reunion."

"That's ancient history."

"Two years isn't all that long. Anyway, I called to tell you your birthday gift will be here in a few days."

"I told you I didn't want anything."

"Too bad," Walter said cheerfully. "You're getting it anyway."

When Mary walked past her car without stopping, Walter spoke again. "Where are you going?"

"To Statum's for lunch."

Walter brightened. "Good—we can eat together."

"I'm meeting my father." Seeing Walter's face fall, she added, "I'm sure he won't mind if you join us."

When they reached the restaurant, Wayne Oliver immediately invited Walter to sit beside him. "I'm glad to see you. I need to talk to you about the Rockdale Civic Improvement Association."

He did so at some length, then listened as Walter offered a few suggestions. However, from the way he kept glancing at her, Mary got the impression Walter would rather have her to himself. When Judge Oliver left to return to the courthouse, Walter seemed genuinely sorry he had an appointment to list a property.

"I'll call you when your gift comes in. I can't wait for you to see it."

"Comes in? What is it?" Even though Mary didn't want anything from Walter, she was curious.

He grinned. "You'll find out."

∞

"Walter Chance has a good head on his shoulders," Mary's father said that evening. "Now that his mother's out of the picture, he seems to be using it. He knows the local real estate market, and I can tell he'll be a big help to the Rockdale Civic Improvement Association."

That's probably what my father had in mind when he invited Walter to the dinner. "He seemed interested about it at lunch."

Her father looked amused. "When he wasn't making eyes at you, that is. I'd say Walter Chance seems to be smitten with you."

Mary shook her head. "You have it wrong. He's been lonely since his mother left town. He thinks of me as a good friend—that's all."

Wayne Oliver shook his head. "We'll see about that."

Mary glanced at her wristwatch and stood. "I have to make some Vacation Bible School calls, then I'm going to read awhile. I'll see you at breakfast."

In her room, Mary opened her Vacation Bible School notebook to the list of workers, but she found it hard to concentrate for thinking about her father's remarks.

I don't care what anyone says, Walter Chance is a friend, and that's all, she told herself.

Mary shook her head and sighed. God's call to teach His children was never far from her mind, and now she resolved to focus on the task at hand.

Lord, I put myself and all the Vacation Bible School workers in Your hands. Bless us and use us according to Thy will.

Then she made her first call.

Chapter 5

Mary had lost count of the number of bridal showers she had been involved with in the last ten years or so, but Anita Sanchez's was the fourth since the first of May. Mary had met Anita in January, when her daughter, Juanita, enrolled in Rockdale Elementary and was put in Mary's class. From the first, Mary had found Juanita to be a delightful little girl. When she made her usual visit to their home, Anita Sanchez had impressed Mary, as well. A widow living in public housing without much income, Anita had a quiet dignity that she managed to sustain even when a man who had followed her to Alabama from Texas kidnapped Juanita. The whole incident had lasted only a few hours, and the little girl had taken it in stride because, as she told her classmates, "God took real good care of me." Shortly afterward, when Juanita told Mary her mother and Rock County deputy Hawk Henson were getting married, they had rejoiced together.

Mary knew Hawk had encountered a certain amount of prejudice because of his Cherokee heritage, and she suspected he'd felt a bond with Anita Sanchez, the first Hispanic to settle in Rockdale, who also knew what it was like to be "different."

All that was behind them now, and entering Community Church's fellowship hall on the second Sunday afternoon in June, Mary was glad to see the petite bride-elect. Anita was the lovely center of attention in a yellow dress, which set off her dark hair and eyes.

Toni Trent, one of the hostesses, pointed out the serving table. "Juanita and Mandy are helping—I heard Juanita ask if Miss Mary would be here."

Mary glanced at the long, lace-covered serving table where Juanita handed out napkins and Mandy poured punch. Both girls were smiling and obviously enjoying themselves.

"Can I bring you some refreshment?" Toni asked Anita.

"No, thank you. I am too excited about seeing so many people today. I cannot eat or drink a thing."

Mary nodded in greeting to Margaret Hastings and Janet Brown, the wife of Community Church's music leader, then she and Toni walked toward the serving table. "Anita looks very happy," Mary commented.

"Believe me, after the hard time she's had the last few years, she deserves to be. She and Hawk both believe God meant for them to be together, and that's a wonderful foundation for their married life."

"Being in God's will is the best foundation for anyone's life," Mary said.

Toni glanced at her friend. "I know from experience God sometimes changes our perception of His will. I hope you're ready to accept it, should that happen to you. I think Walter Chance would like to be more than just a friend."

Mary ignored the comment and moved on ahead to greet Juanita and Mandy.

"This is a fun party, Miss Toni," Juanita said. "Miss Janet says they do this every time someone gets married."

"Just about," Toni agreed.

"Miss Janet told another lady Aunt Evelyn might need a tea soon," Mandy said.

Juanita looked puzzled. "But she's old."

Toni and Mary struggled not to smile. "Mandy's aunt isn't too old to be a bride," Toni said. "There isn't any age limit for that."

"Then when can I be a bride and have a party like this?" asked Juanita.

"When you're grown up and out of school," said Mandy, who enjoyed playing the role of big sister to Juanita.

"Let's get a glass of punch and sit down," Mary suggested to Toni. "You don't need to be on your feet all afternoon."

"You're as bad as David," Toni said. "He nags me all the time to take it easy."

They took their cups to a round table at the far end of the fellowship hall.

"Apparently the town has already decided Evelyn and your father will marry," Toni said.

"As I recall, the same thing happened with you and David. In your case, they were right."

Toni smiled. "So they were. Evelyn and Wayne obviously enjoy each other's company. I hope they'll be allowed to do so in peace."

"Changing the subject," Mary said, "my student teacher mentioned her cousin was Community's new associate pastor. I don't suppose he's here this afternoon."

Toni looked amused. "Jason Abbott? He hasn't officially started working, but even if he had, he'd hardly be at a bridal shower. And changing it back, you might as well get used to your father being part of a couple."

∽

Mary returned home after the tea to find an empty house and a brief note from her father: "I won't be home for supper. Don't wait up."

On an impulse, she called Evelyn Trent's telephone number. She was not surprised when Evelyn's answering machine took the call.

Mary smiled wryly. It seemed their roles had suddenly been reversed. Now it was the father who went out on a date, while his daughter was advised not to wait up.

She had just hung up when the telephone rang. *Walter,* Mary guessed correctly.

"I'm glad I caught you at home. I have your gift, and I'd like to bring it over tonight, if that's all right."

Mary glanced at the clock. "I'm afraid not. I just got in, and I have a lot work to do."

"How about tomorrow night?"

"All right—seven o'clock."

"Great! See you then."

Mary replaced the receiver and wished she felt as enthusiastic about seeing Walter as he sounded about seeing her. She'd always liked Walter, perhaps in part because he'd had such a hard time—first dealing with the death of his father and then with a mother who'd tried to smother him. Mary considered him a good friend, and she knew friendship was the basis for many successful marriages. She also believed Walter Chance would make an excellent father. For the time being, however, Mary didn't see him as her potential husband.

Mary spread the Vacation Bible School material on the dining room table and began to work, determined to be ready for the first meeting with her committee.

∞

Mary's father hadn't come home by the time Mary retired for the night, but following his admonition, she didn't wait up for him. Just before she fell asleep, Mary thought she heard his footsteps on the stairs, but she didn't get up.

By the time she came downstairs the next morning, her father had already left. "Early pretrial conference this morning and Bar Association dinner tonight," his note told her. "Home about nine."

By then, Mary hoped, *Walter will already be gone.*

∞

Mary reached First Church early, parked at the side of the building, and walked around to the front entrance. During the week when the sanctuary wasn't being used, it was closed off from the rest of the building to conserve energy, but it remained open for prayer.

Before the meeting, Mary went directly into the sanctuary. Having recently been at Community Church, Mary was struck by the contrast. She enjoyed attending special parties and programs at Community Church, and sometimes she went to a worship service when Toni Trent would be singing a solo. She rather admired Community's easy, informal style of worship, but for as long as Mary could remember, the more traditional First Church in downtown Rockdale had been an important part of her life.

From its Gothic-style native sandstone exterior to the massive oak double doors leading into the vaulted sanctuary, the building spoke to her of God's glory. As a child, she had spent hours studying the stained-glass windows on either side of the velvet-cushioned dark wood pews. Even if they hadn't been placed there by long-ago Austin and Oliver ancestors, the two windows bearing their names would still have been Mary's favorites.

The Austin window showed Jesus as an infant, flanked by Mary and Joseph, with several angels looking down from the top of the window. In the Oliver window, Jesus blessed several children crowded around Him. When Mary was about four years old, someone remarked she could have been the model for the chubby-cheeked little girl in the Savior's arms. Since the window had been placed there nearly a century earlier, the likeness was dismissed as an interesting coincidence. However, as a child, Mary had liked to imagine herself resting in Christ's arms. Even when she was a grown woman and no one noticed any resemblance between her and the child in the stained-glass window, Mary still felt a sense of peace and protection each time she saw it.

Passing by the Austin and Oliver stained-glass windows, Mary spent some time at the altar in prayer, asking God to help her concentrate on making this year's unusual VBS program a success.

"The traditional Bible story and crafts, juice, and cookies worked for generations of children, but we need to do something to get attendance back up to where it ought to be. See what you can find," First's educational director had urged during the March planning meeting.

Thus challenged by Reuben Martz, Mary and the committee had decided to adopt an entirely new concept for Vacation Bible School. Most of Mary's key workers had enthusiastically agreed, but a few grumbled they saw no reason to change anything.

Just like the town itself. Part of Rockdale seemed perfectly content with the status quo, while others clamored for progress at any price.

In the end, they had worked out a compromise: The basic VBS framework would remain the same, but the program itself would be more varied and give the children different things to do.

Mary rose from prayer and went into the educational wing, following the chattering female voices to the meeting room.

"Hello, Mary," Melanie Neal greeted. "We were beginning to wonder what happened to you."

"I was in the sanctuary." Mary looked around the room at the women. With the exception of herself and Melanie, a fourth-grade teacher at Rockdale Elementary, all were busy stay-at-home moms, and she knew they appreciated brief, to-the-point meetings. "Everyone's here except Alice Taylor, and she and her family are out of town this week. Let's have prayer, then we'll get started."

∞

"I like the setup for this year's Bible school. You've come up with some really good ideas," Melanie Neal told Mary after the meeting. "We've never tried a field trip before."

"It took some talking to persuade Reuben Martz it could be done within our budget, but it'll be something for the kids to look forward to on the last day."

"Ronnie can't wait for VBS. He started whining about being bored two days after school ended," Melanie said.

Veronica Smith joined them and voiced her agreement. "Cassie would say that, too, except she knows I can always find work for her when she complains of having nothing to do."

"Whatever happened to the days when kids could enjoy doing nothing?" Melanie asked rhetorically.

"Television and video games, for starters," said Mary.

"I've got to go now," Veronica said. "Mandy Trent's staying with the kids, and she has to be somewhere else by lunchtime."

"Me, too—I have several errands to run," Doris Atwood said.

"Ronnie's at day camp, so I'm free until three o'clock," Melanie said when the others were gone. "Want to go somewhere for lunch?"

"Sure. What do you have in mind?"

"If you have the time, we can go to DeSoto State Park," Melanie suggested.

"Fine. My father won't be home for supper. With a good lunch, I can do with a sandwich this evening."

"Since going out for lunch was my idea, I'll drive," Melanie volunteered.

Mary put her VBS materials in her Toyota's trunk and climbed into Melanie's SUV. "If this vehicle was any bigger, I'd need a ladder to get in."

"I know, but its size comes in handy when Ron and I haul Ronnie's soccer team all over Rock County."

As Melanie talked about the Neals' plans to take their son's team to a regional soccer tournament in Georgia, Mary felt the same near-envy she had begun to experience when women her age talked about their families. Last year, when Toni Schmidt had married David Trent and become an instant mother to Josh and Mandy, Mary's happiness for her friend had been mixed with a sense of regret that Toni had something Mary never expected to experience. Lately, Mary had found herself yearning to be part of that kind of family so often, she had begun to believe it might be God's way to let her know she should have her own family.

With a smile, Mary recalled her student's simple logic. *First, I'll need a husman.*

Chapter 6

I haven't been here since the weather turned warm," Mary said when they entered the DeSoto State Park lodge.

"Ron likes the Sunday buffet, but so does everyone else. I'd rather come during the week when it's not so crowded."

"It certainly isn't crowded now," Mary observed. Just before the noon hour, only a few tables were occupied.

"Let's sit by the window," Melanie said. "I love to feel I'm in the middle of all these wonderful old trees."

After going through the buffet line, Mary and Melanie took their plates to a table overlooking the path to Lodge Falls and watched the dining room slowly fill with the usual mixture of casually dressed tourists and local men and women who worked in Fort Payne, Rockdale, and other nearby towns. Mary had known quite a few of the diners all her life, but she didn't recognize the man who entered with the Community Church pastor.

"Who's that with Ed Hurley?" she asked Melanie.

"I don't know, but I suspect he might be Community Church's new assistant pastor. Ron's dad showed him an Oaks condo last week."

"My student teacher mentioned her cousin had been called to Community."

Almost as if Pastor Hurley had overheard their conversation, he brought his companion to their table. Although both men were casually dressed in short-sleeved sport shirts and summer slacks, the senior pastor bowed formally.

"Hello, ladies. Melanie Neal and Mary Oliver, may I present Community's new assistant pastor, Jason Abbott."

Of average height and size, with hazel eyes and wavy, light brown hair in need of cutting, Jason Abbott looked nothing like Mary expected. He wouldn't stand out in a crowd, yet something about him immediately appealed to Mary. His smile was infectious, and his grip was sure and firm when he shook her hand.

"Mary Oliver? My cousin Ann Ward told me to look you up. She said you were the best supervisor any student teacher could have," Jason said.

"Ann made my job easy—she's a natural teacher."

"I'm really glad to meet you, Mary," he said as if he meant it.

"It's a small world, isn't it?" Pastor Hurley asked rhetorically.

When Jason turned to shake Melanie's hand, Mary noted his shirt looked slept in and his slacks needed a good pressing. Unlike his always-neat cousin, Jason Abbott didn't seem to care how he looked.

Mary had scarcely made the judgment when a Bible verse came immediately to mind: *"The Lord does not look at the things man looks at. Man looks at the outward appearance, but the Lord looks at the heart."*

She had just met Jason Abbott, but Mary believed he must surely have a heart for the Lord—and that was what really mattered.

"Are you related to Nelson Neal?" Jason asked Melanie.

"He's my father-in-law. Will you be renting a condo at the Oaks?"

"Possibly."

"Mary also works with children at First Church," Ed Hurley said.

Jason Abbott regarded Mary with interest. "Really? Ann didn't tell me that. I'd like to talk with you about your Vacation Bible School. I understand First is trying something different this year."

"I'm not on the staff," Mary said quickly. "Reuben Martz is our educational director. He's in charge of VBS."

"Mary isn't a paid worker, but this is the third year Reuben has turned VBS over to her, and she also directs the children's Sunday school classes. She probably knows more about those programs than Mr. Martz," Melanie said.

Jason Abbott smiled. "You sound like Mary's agent."

"I just want to give credit where it's due," Melanie said.

"If you have time, I hope we can get together soon," Jason told Mary.

"Of course, for what it's worth."

Jason took a pen and small green notebook from his shirt pocket and wrote Mary's telephone number as she gave it. When he left their table, Jason nodded and smiled fleetingly. "Nice to meet you, ladies." To Mary, he added, "I'll call you."

When the men were safely out of earshot, Melanie turned to Mary. "What did you think of Jason Abbott?"

"He seems nice enough," Mary said cautiously. "My father would say he needs a haircut."

Melanie smiled. "I noticed that, too. He's not bad-looking, though, in a friendly puppy-dog sort of way."

"In any case, Community will probably like him."

∽

Mary returned home after lunch with Melanie to find three messages on the answering machine.

In the first, Walter Chance repeated he would be there at seven that night and added he couldn't wait for her to see his gift.

The second, from her father, reminded Mary he wouldn't be home for supper.

The third was a pleasant surprise.

"Hello, Mary and Judge Oliver. This is Todd Walker. I apologize for the short notice, but I'll be in Rockdale tomorrow and I'd like to take you both to lunch. I'll drop by the house about eleven. See you then."

Hearing Todd's mellow voice, Mary thought he could have been a radio announcer. Although he'd said he would be back to Rockdale often, Mary had doubted it. She listened to the message again, then left it on the machine for her father.

Todd would be here tomorrow. But tonight Mary was seeing Walter Chance.

&

As Mary expected, Walter arrived promptly at seven. He had been the only Rockdale High reunion committee member who was always punctual. "One of my worst faults," he had said cheerfully when Mary tried to compliment him.

On this night, Walter had apparently taken even greater care with his appearance than usual. His hair was carefully combed, and his cotton sport shirt appeared to be new. The crease in his trousers was razor-sharp, and his shoes were freshly shined.

Unaccountably, Walter's neatness made her think of Jason Abbott's untidiness. "You look very nice tonight," Mary said.

"You always do," Walter returned.

Mary's loose-fitting denim jumper had looked fine for the VBS meeting and lunch at DeSoto, but it was undeniably wrinkled, and she was embarrassed not to look her best when Walter had taken such obvious pains with his appearance.

"Come in," she said belatedly.

Walter entered the hall and looked around. "Is the judge here?"

"No—he had a dinner obligation."

The news seemed to please Walter. "Here—happy birthday. I'm sorry it took me so long to get this to you."

Mary set the lavishly gift-wrapped package on the hall table. "This looks too pretty to open right away. Can I offer you a brownie and some lemonade?"

"Statum's supper special tonight included pecan pie, so I'll skip the brownie. I'll take a glass of your fine Oliver lemonade, though."

"I'll get it."

Walter followed Mary to the kitchen. "How many hours do you reckon we spent working on the reunion at this table?"

"A lot. Looking up addresses, making flyers—it all took time."

"I enjoyed every minute, though."

When they finished their lemonade, Mary rose from the table. "We're not working tonight—we can sit in the living room."

"This is a wonderful house," Walter said. "It'd be perfect for a family with a bunch of children."

"It's not for sale," Mary said quickly.

"That's not what I meant." In the hall, Walter pointed to the package on the table. "Aren't you going to open it?"

"Of course. Let's sit down first." Mary took the gift into the living room, and Walter joined her on the sofa.

"I hope you like it. When I described you to the lady in the store, she said this should be just right."

It's probably just as well I didn't hear that conversation. Seeing the embossed gold seal of a prestigious Birmingham jewelry store on the package, Mary suspected Walter had spent more than he should have on her gift. When she removed the silver wrappings and looked at the contents of the rectangular, blue velvet-covered box inside, she was certain of it.

From a fine gold chain, a gemstone glowed with deep green fire. Mary had never seen anything like it, and she hardly knew what to say.

"Oh, Walter—this is far too fine."

"Not at all. I picked out the stone, and they set it just for you—that's what took so long. Here, I'll help you put it on."

Walter's fingers touched the nape of her neck when he fastened the clasp, and Mary shivered at the unexpected sensation.

Embarrassed, she went into the hall and stood before the mirror. The square-cut emerald brought out the green in her eyes and even added a touch of elegance to her denim jumper.

"It is a lovely necklace," she said, meaning it.

Walter smiled with pleasure. "It looks great on you, too. The stone is genuine—it came with papers."

"I've never had any jewelry with my birthstone," Mary said.

"Then it's time you did. I thought of your eyes the minute I saw this—I knew it would match them."

"I can't accept a gift like this," Mary began. She almost finished the sentence with "from someone I'm not engaged to marry," but stopped short.

Walter stood behind Mary with his hands on top of her shoulders, then bent to kiss the nape of her neck. Surprised, Mary shivered. Flustered, she turned from the mirror and into Walter's arms, where he held her close for what seemed a very long time.

"I'm not very good at this, but you must know I think a lot of you," he murmured. "The store is holding the matching earrings for you."

Mary felt almost comfortable in Walter's embrace, but his last words brought her back to reality, and she backed away from him. "You shouldn't have done that."

Walter touched the silver hoop in one of Mary's earlobes. "I want you to have the earrings, too, but I didn't know if you had pierced ears."

"Yes, since seventh grade, but—"

"The earrings dangle." Walter pointed to an antique lamp in the living room. "Sort of like the things hanging on that shade."

"They're called prisms. The earrings sound lovely, but I can't accept them, either."

Walter shook his head and sighed. "You sound just like you did when we worked on the reunion, expecting everyone to do things your way."

His accusation took Mary aback. "You're saying I'm bossy?"

"No offense intended—that comes from being a teacher, since kids need a firm hand."

"Yes, they do."

Walter stepped closer and spoke with quiet urgency. "Maybe you haven't given it much thought, since you stay so busy, but don't you ever think about wanting to have kids of your own?"

His unexpected question startled Mary into a quick response. "You're right—I haven't given it much thought." *And I don't intend to discuss it with you tonight, either.*

Walter lifted his arms in mock surrender. "I'm sorry if that was out of line. Maybe I should leave before you throw me out."

Although he smiled, Mary sensed she'd hurt his feelings. "I would never do that. I do appreciate your gift."

"You really like it?"

"Of course—but you should return it to the store. I don't deserve it."

"Let me be the judge of that."

At the front door, Walter turned to give Mary a brief peck on her cheek. "The necklace will stay right here. You can wear it when we go out to celebrate your birthday."

"No. Anyway, one birthday party a year is more than enough, and I've already had two."

"I won't call it a birthday dinner, then. Being with you makes any day a special occasion."

Mary heard his flowery words in disbelief. If Walter Chance ever had any romantic interest in her, he'd kept it well hidden, and she hardly knew what to make of the sudden change in him. "We had some good times working together, but—"

"We'll have even better ones in the years to come, I hope." Walter pulled Mary close and kissed her as if he really thought of her as more than his good friend. "I really do enjoy being with you," he said when he finally let her go.

Mary realized Walter probably expected her to offer a similar sentiment, but she could not. His kiss—and her reaction to it—had temporarily rendered her incapable of saying what she should. "Good night, Walter."

He smiled. "Take care, now."

Mary leaned against the door, relieved he was gone, at least for the time being.

His gift was by far the most valuable she'd received from any man other than her father. Even in the relatively dim hall, the emerald captured and reflected bursts of light.

Wondering if she looked as strange as she felt, Mary returned to look into the hall mirror. Color infused her cheeks, and her eyes glowed with the same hue as the emerald. The necklace became her, all right, but she should have refused it immediately.

Should she accept and wear Walter's gift, Mary felt it would send him—and everyone who saw it—a mistaken message.

Mary removed the necklace and replaced it in its velvet nest. She would show it to her father when he came home; but as lovely as it was, she couldn't keep it.

She would return Walter's gift with gratitude—and the heartfelt hope Walter Chance would understand.

Chapter 7

"I take it you got my messages about the Bar Association meeting," Wayne Oliver said when he came home that evening.

"Yes. However, I didn't know you were going out last night."

"I'd like to talk to you about that."

"I have something to discuss with you, too."

He smiled faintly. "Let's adjourn to the study, then."

Mary had always liked the mahogany-paneled room with its floor-to-ceiling array of books. When she was very small, she had longed for the day when she would be able to take a book from any shelf and read every word of it. By the time she was old enough to do so, Mary was disappointed to find most of the tomes had to do with the law—Wayne Oliver's father before him had also been a lawyer—and, in her opinion, the books made very dull reading. However, the room was furnished with a couch and several comfortable chairs. As a child, Mary had often done her schoolwork at a table beside the window while her father worked on the mysterious papers in his briefcase—"my homework," as he called it.

Her father moved one of the overstuffed chairs to face the other, as he had done through the years when he wanted to have a heart-to-heart talk with Mary. She always supposed it was so he could see her face and gauge her reaction to his words.

Wayne Oliver leaned back in his chair and steepled his fingers, much as he did when he was about to hear a case in his court. "I'm sorry if I caused you concern last night, but at the last minute, Evelyn decided she wanted to go to an arts festival in Huntsville. After we took it in, we stopped for dinner on the way home. We were gone a few hours longer than I expected. I suppose I should have called, but time got away from me."

"I wasn't worried—and I'm glad you and Evelyn are going out. You probably know it's causing some talk around town, though."

He nodded. "Unfortunately, some people have nothing better to do than talk about their neighbors. We knew gossip could be a problem, but Evelyn and I don't let it bother us."

"It doesn't bother me, either—and I wish you both well."

Her father leaned forward and touched Mary's cheek tenderly. "I'm glad you feel that way. I didn't think you'd mind, but this is a new situation for me."

Mary smiled. "Rockdale may be in for a lot of new things."

Her father settled back into his chair. "So it seems. Now it's your turn—what's on your mind?"

"I want to show you something."

"That's a mighty fancy box," her father commented when Mary returned with it.

"Walter brought it over this evening as a birthday gift."

"That was thoughtful."

"I'm not sure 'thoughtful' is the right word. Open it."

Wayne Oliver's startled expression confirmed Mary's belief the emerald pendant was no ordinary bauble. "The stone looks like the real thing. I'm surprised Walter Chance can afford a piece like this."

"Even worse, he wants to give me the matching earrings."

Her father shook his head. "I knew Walter cared for you, but this is more than an ordinary gift."

"I know—I tried to tell him he shouldn't have given it to me, but he wouldn't listen."

"You like Walter, don't you? You seem to get along well."

"Of course, but suddenly he seems to think we're much more than friends. Grandmother Oliver would say a girl shouldn't accept any expensive gift unless she and the man are engaged, and I've decided not to keep it."

Her father returned the box to Mary. "I hardly know what to say. Rules about accepting gifts have changed since my mother's day. Walter will probably feel hurt if you return it, but if it makes you uncomfortable, you shouldn't keep it."

"That's what I thought. I'll give it back tomorrow."

Wayne Oliver stood and winced as he rubbed the shoulder he'd injured playing football years before. "Is that all we have to discuss?"

"Yes," Mary said, then belatedly remembered. "One more thing—Todd Walker left us a message on the machine."

Her father looked puzzled after hearing it. "I wonder what brings Todd to Rockdale in the middle of the week?"

"I suppose we'll find out tomorrow."

"You'll have to do that on your own. With a full court docket, I won't have time to go out for lunch."

"Todd didn't leave a number where he could be reached," Mary said. "It would serve him right if he found nobody at home."

Her father smiled. "I doubt you'll allow that to happen. Maybe Todd will take you somewhere nice."

"Melanie Neal and I had lunch at DeSoto today, but Todd may already have something in mind."

"I suspect he does," her father said dryly.

∞

Tuesday morning found Mary with mixed feelings about the day ahead. While she looked forward to seeing Todd Walker, she dreaded the necessary encounter with Walter Chance.

During her morning quiet time, Mary prayed more earnestly than usual for God's guidance. She had always trusted His leadership, but lately Mary had felt confused about the source of her changing feelings about marriage.

"Never accept your own wishful thinking as the Lord's will. 'Thy will be done' must be part of every petition." Mary didn't remember where or when she'd heard the admonition, but it often came to her mind when she prayed for guidance.

Show me Your will for my life, Lord.

Mary didn't expect God to speak to her directly in a voice from above, but she trusted He knew what was best for her and would make it clear to her in due time.

For now, she still felt she had to return the emerald pendant. Even if Walter Chance should turn out to be the man God meant for her, Mary couldn't accept his gift now.

At nine o'clock, Mary called Walter's office and felt relieved to hear he had gone to a property closing. Since he wasn't there, she could return the necklace without seeing him—at least immediately.

Mary composed a quick note telling Walter she appreciated his thoughtfulness and valued his friendship, but she couldn't accept such a valuable gift. Signing it "Your friend always," Mary then printed Walter's name on a manila envelope, put the note and the jeweler's box inside, and sealed it with mailing tape.

Ten minutes later, she handed the package to Ellie Fergus, Chance Realty's forty-something receptionist, and asked her to give it to Walter.

"He'll probably be tied up until lunchtime. Do you want him to call you when he returns?"

"No—that's not necessary."

Mary knew Walter would probably try to contact her as soon as he opened the package, but by then she'd be with Todd Walker. For the moment, Todd was all that mattered.

∞

Mary surveyed the contents of her closet and debated what she should wear. Todd had already seen her in her worst baggy jeans and oversized shirt, so almost anything else would be an improvement. She wanted to look presentable without going overboard to impress him.

After several false starts, Mary finally chose a two-piece red linen dress she'd had for several years. With the proper accessories, it was the kind of outfit that could be worn anywhere, at any time. She almost hadn't bought it, thinking the color called attention to her size. Instead, the salesclerk had assured her it suited her coloring perfectly. "Red is a powerful color for women who can wear it, and you definitely can."

Today Mary chose simple silver hoop earrings and a slender silver necklace to complete the image of an independent young woman who wasn't afraid to dress boldly.

I don't know why I'm going to all this trouble. Todd Walker was out of my league when I was a teenager, and I'm past the point of playing dating games now.

When the telephone rang shortly after ten thirty, Mary's first thought was Walter had come back to the office early or that Todd wouldn't be there after all, leaving her all dressed up with no place to go. However, Mary relaxed when she heard a familiar feminine voice at the other end of the line.

"Mary, this is Janet Brown."

In addition to playing for Community Church's worship services, Janet gave private piano lessons to many of Mary's former first-graders and helped with Rockdale Elementary's annual musical program. Mary steeled herself, fearful Janet was about to ask her help with something.

"Hi, Janet. What's up?"

"I'm calling to invite you and Judge Oliver to a reception in the Community Church fellowship hall Sunday afternoon to welcome Jason Abbott, our new associate pastor."

Mary decided not to tell Janet she'd already met him, since it had no bearing on whether she and her father attended the reception. "What time?"

"From two until four. I especially want Pastor Abbott to meet you and the judge. We think he's a great addition to Rockdale."

"Thanks, Janet. We'll try to be there."

Pastor Abbott. It was the first time Mary had heard Jason called by his formal title. *He probably looks more dignified when he's in church.*

Mary wrote "Community, 2–4:00" in next Sunday's square on the calendar beside the kitchen telephone, then she surveyed the current week.

For Tuesday, Mary's father had written "RCIA Mtg 7:00." The Rockdale Civic Improvement Association would hold an open forum in the high school auditorium the next week, and Mary figured she'd be expected to attend the Tuesday night meeting and make notes for another article.

On Wednesday the Olivers usually attended the fellowship supper and midweek services at First Church. Mary had marked Friday night for the rehearsal dinner for Anita and Hawk's wedding and Saturday for the wedding and reception, at which she was serving.

Now, with the addition of Sunday's reception for Jason Abbott, Mary had managed to fill nearly every day with some sort of activity.

So much for a leisurely vacation.

Just as Mary capped her pen, the doorbell rang. On her way to answer it, her glance at the grandfather clock confirmed that Todd Walker was ten minutes early. No time to double-check her hair and makeup—but Mary supposed she probably looked as good as she ever would.

Todd had his hand extended, ready to ring the doorbell again, when she opened the door.

"There you are," he said. "I was beginning to think no one was home."

"Come in," Mary invited.

"Wow," Todd said when she turned to face him. His admiration seemed genuine, and Mary didn't know how to react.

"You look better, too." As soon as she said it, Mary wished she could take back the comment. However, it was true: From his dress shirt, worn without a tie and open at the neck, to his dark slacks and shined tassel loafers, Todd Walker looked every inch like a very handsome junior executive.

"Thanks. I've been told I clean up pretty well. Is the judge here?"

"No. He sends his regrets, but he doesn't have time to go out for lunch today."

Perhaps it was Mary's imagination, but she thought Todd looked pleased her father wasn't joining them.

"I was afraid of that, but I'm glad to see you."

"You almost didn't. This is a busy week, and I might not have been here. You should have left your number."

Todd shrugged. "It wouldn't matter. I had to be in the vicinity today, and I hoped lunch would work for us—and apparently it has."

Mary acknowledged the failure of her mild reprimand and returned his smile. "I'll get my purse, then we can go."

Chapter 8

"I don't usually have lunch this early," Mary told Todd as they made their way down the boxwood-bordered brick walk to the street.

"Neither do I, but it won't be so early by the time we get where we're going."

At the end of the walk, Mary stopped and stared at the vehicle at the curb, a fire-engine red convertible with the top down. "What happened to your truck?" she asked.

"Nothing, but this is a lot more fun to drive. Besides, it matches your dress." Todd opened the convertible's door for Mary. "I can put the top up if you like."

She shook her head. Although she didn't want to admit it to Todd, Mary had never ridden in a convertible, and she was curious to know what it was like. "Don't put it up on my account. My hair is so short, wind won't hurt it."

"You won't feel much wind in your hair in this car, but it's bright today—your eyes will need protection."

Her father had given Mary a stylish new pair of sunglasses for her birthday, and when she removed them from her purse and put them on, Todd whistled in appreciation.

"You look like a movie star, Miss Oliver. I can see myself reflected in your lenses, but I can't see your eyes."

Todd turned the key in the ignition and the car roared to life. To Mary, the motor had the rich sound of the stock cars she'd seen at a NASCAR race at Talladega. Directly across the street, Sally Proffitt must have had a similar thought, because she came out of her house and shaded her eyes as if looking to see what was making so much noise.

Mary groaned inwardly, aware that Sally Proffitt would probably waste no time calling Jenny Suiter. She had a good idea what Sally might say: "You won't believe this, but Mary Oliver just rode off in a fancy red convertible with a man."

By suppertime, the news would be all over town.

Mary didn't think Todd had noticed Sally Proffitt's neck craning, but after making a U-turn in the street and heading back toward town, he laughed. "Maybe we ought to go back and give your neighbor an encore performance. It's obvious she enjoyed the first show."

"That's Sally Proffitt. She's a widow without much to do since her children grew up and moved away. She thinks it's her job to know everything going on around here."

"I know the type," Todd said. "She's probably also tried to persuade the judge he needs a wife."

Mary smiled at his accurate depiction. "I think she did at one point, but Rockdale's widows gave up on my father a long time ago. He calls Sally Proffitt and her best friend Rockdale's two-woman gossip tag team. What one doesn't know, the other finds out. Then they share the results of their investigations with everyone who'll listen."

"I hope riding in my car won't ruin your reputation," Todd said lightly.

"Even Sally Proffitt couldn't do that," Mary replied. For better or worse, no one in Rockdale was likely to believe Judge Oliver's schoolmarm daughter capable of doing anything wrong.

When Todd turned onto the main road leading out of town, she reminded him he hadn't said where they were going.

"Since we don't have to worry about getting Judge Oliver back to court on time, there's something I want to show you."

"A new restaurant?"

"Not exactly. You'll see. Lean back and enjoy the ride."

It was a perfect early June day, and Todd maneuvered the red car expertly around the twists and turns of the road out of Rockdale. Mary liked the new sensation of openness and freedom of riding in the convertible. She relished the feeling she was one with everything around her—the welcome breeze, the cloudless sky, even the flickering shadows of passing trees.

On the other hand, Mary knew her unshaded face would soon be as red as her dress. *So much for glamour—it never was my style, anyway.*

"We must be going to Mentone," Mary said when they reached the main highway and Todd turned in that direction.

"Close."

He passed Mentone and turned the car into a rutted lane a few miles on the other side. The going was so rough, Mary grasped her armrest with both hands, convinced her safety belt was the only thing keeping her from being thrown out of the car altogether.

"Sorry," Todd muttered when they hit a particularly rough spot. "That was the worst part."

He continued driving until the road ended abruptly at a fencerow after a few hundred more yards. Several nearby trees had faded but still prominent signs that read: POSTED: NO HUNTING NO FISHING NO TRESPASSING. Behind them, dust stirred by the car's tires still hung in the air. Mary felt a thin film of grit when she ran her tongue over her dry lips—and imagined it had permeated every fiber of her suit, as well. *I got dressed up for this?*

"It's not as bad as it looks," Todd assured her. "This is as close as we can get to the gate—it's just up the way."

"The gate to what?"

"Something special. Watch your step, now—this is uneven ground."

You can say that again. Mary's open-toed sandals were no match for the loose dirt and sticks littering the ground. "I have to stop. I think there's a small boulder in my shoe," she said after walking a short distance.

There was no place to sit down, but Todd took Mary's left arm and held her steady while she balanced on one foot, cranelike, and removed debris from first one sandal, then the other. "You should have told me to change my shoes before we left the house," she said.

"I didn't think about it," Todd admitted. "Anyway, we're almost there."

Todd continued to hold Mary's arm, guiding her around a nest of fire ants and through a rusty gate. On the other side, a narrow, crooked path wandered toward a rock outcropping.

"That's a deer trail," Mary noted.

"I see you know your way around the woods."

Mary detected a note of respect in Todd's voice. "Yes, but I don't usually track deer while wearing open-toed sandals."

Todd chuckled. "I like your sense of humor. Most women take themselves far too seriously."

Maybe so, but full-figured women like me pretend to be jolly at all times—it's expected of us.

"So do some men," she said, and let it go at that.

If Todd heard her, he made no comment. They reached the rock outcropping, and Todd stepped up onto it and turned to help Mary. "Here we are."

If I fall now, I'll probably break something major and disgrace myself forever. Mary kept her eyes down and concentrated on keeping her footing. With a final effort, she found a secure foothold and pulled herself up to stand on the rock beside him.

"Well, what do you think?" Todd asked.

Mary looked up and gasped in admiration at the view before them. The rock on which they stood bordered a bluff overlooking a heavily wooded valley. To the right, a waterfall bisected an adjacent ridge. Its sparkling waters spilled over the top of the mountain, then cascaded into a meandering stream in the valley below. "It's beautiful," she said. "Where are we?"

"In one of those well-kept secret places locals keep to themselves."

"How do you know about it?" asked Mary.

Todd smiled. "I'll tell you about it over lunch, but I wanted you to experience it first."

"Thank you. A view like this is definitely worth a few rocks in my shoes."

"I'm glad you agree."

Todd smiled, apparently pleased with her reaction. He took Mary's hand to help her down, then continued to hold it on the walk back to the car. "Now we'll have lunch," he said.

Todd drove back to Mentone and stopped at a restaurant located in an old Victorian house near the bluff. Mary had been there several times, and she knew the rear windows offered a pleasant view of the valley below. However, the panorama they had just seen was much more spectacular.

The dining room was nearly filled, but the hostess led them to a just-vacated table in the rear.

Mary excused herself as soon as the waitress had taken their orders. "I'll be eating dirt and drinking mud if I don't wash the dust from my face first," she told Todd.

"I don't remember the lane being that dusty—I suppose it's because it hasn't rained here lately."

In the dim light of the mirror in the ladies' room, Mary dabbed a wet paper towel to her mouth and forehead and noted the sun had already affected her skin. *I'll probably be burned to a crisp by the time I get back home.*

Mary sighed. In her childhood, her fair complexion had freckled when she stayed out in the sun too long, but in recent years, her unprotected skin merely went from pink to red. She always used a high-numbered sunblock and wore a hat when she gardened or was outdoors for a long time. However, today she hadn't thought to do either. She'd enjoyed riding in Todd's convertible, but the resulting sunburn would be a different matter.

Todd stood when Mary returned to the table. "Feel better?" he asked.

"Much."

He looked at her closely. "The color in your cheeks is quite becoming, but I'm afraid you've gotten too much sun."

Mary felt she would be blushing if her face weren't already red. "I'm told I inherited my mother's fair skin. I should have worn my floppy-brimmed red hat."

Todd smiled. "You had on a country-gal straw hat at the cemetery. I can imagine you in a floppy-brimmed hat—Mary Oliver, southern belle, holding an armful of—of petunias or whatever pretty flowers you grow in that garden of yours."

Mary smiled at his fanciful description. She had never thought of herself as a southern belle, and she was sure no one else had, either. "I don't think you'd see me with an armful of petunias. Most of the flowers in our garden are perennials—since they come back every year, they require very little work. We usually plant several flats of annuals for color, but I rarely have armfuls of anything."

"Maybe you'll give me an educational tour of your garden. I admit to being an ignoramus when it comes to flowers."

"Most men are," Mary said. She was about to tell him her father had proved to be an exception when the waitress brought their food.

After a while, Todd looked out of the window and pointed to the patchwork of fields and woods in the valley below. "You know, this entire area is really one of the best-kept secrets in the country. I had almost forgotten how green Alabama is."

"I suppose it is, compared to much of the West."

"Some of California is naturally green, but I spent most of my time in the desert. There wasn't enough available water for nonessential irrigation, so most landscaping consisted of rocks and sand and cactus plants."

"That sounds grim."

"I thought so, too. I never really got used to it. Even the weeds around here look beautiful to me, so long as they're green."

"You were going to tell me about the place we just saw," Mary prompted.

Todd watched Mary dip her fork into the container of raspberry vinaigrette dressing beside her plate and then into her garden salad. "That's a good idea," he said. "Too much dressing spoils a salad's taste."

And cuts down the calories. Although true, it was not something Mary wanted to share with Todd Walker. "True. Now what about that bluff property?"

Todd poured ketchup on his plate and dipped a few french fries in it before he spoke.

"It's ten acres in all, too rocky to farm and too poor to support any livestock except goats. It's been in the Millican family for years, although none of them lives here now. Herman Millican tried to sell it about ten years ago, but nobody wanted to buy it then. His son inherited it, and when I finally tracked him down in Key West, he said he might consider selling for the right price."

"I don't suppose he's put it on the market?"

"No. It would have been snapped up by the first person who saw it."

"Assuming you're that person, are you going to buy it?"

Todd speared a french fry and pushed it around his plate, then looked back at Mary. "I'd like to buy it for myself, but actually I scouted it for my company."

His company? "I don't think you ever said where you work."

"Haskell Holdings—you probably never heard of it."

"You're right, but I don't know much about the business world."

Todd warmed to his subject. "Haskell Holdings is a large conglomerate composed of many separate companies, ranging from small to large. Among other things, it provides venture capital."

"Exactly what do you do for this conglomerate?"

"Lots of things. For one, I find opportunities for investment for the Holdings' companies."

"Like the Millican land?"

Todd smiled his approval. "You got it. I'm also going to be doing some scouting around Rockdale."

"For land?"

"Not necessarily."

Todd leaned toward Mary and seemed about to say more, but just then an attractive young woman with honey-blond hair appeared at their table. When she spoke Todd's name, he rose to greet her.

Mary inspected the newcomer. Almost Todd's height and reed-slender in white slacks and a designer top, she had the kind of tan probably acquired from lazing on white sand beaches. Her perfectly manicured nails made Mary want to hide her imperfect gardener's hands. From head to toe, the young woman oozed charm and self-assurance.

"I didn't expect to see you here today," she said.

Todd seemed slightly flustered. "Same here."

The blond looked at Mary. "I don't believe we've met."

"Sorry—I seem to have left my manners at home today," Todd said quickly. "Mary, meet Veronica Lindsay. Veronica works for Haskell Holdings, too."

Veronica took Mary's hand, but her expression suggested she thought Mary must have crawled out from under one of the local rocks. "Hello, Mary. And just what do you do?"

"Mary is a teacher," Todd put in quickly.

"How nice." Veronica's tone denied the words.

Mary's pasted-on smile flickered, then faded. She glanced at Todd, then looked back to Veronica. "He didn't mention my main claim to fame."

Todd and Veronica both seemed surprised. "Really? What is that?" Veronica asked.

"Todd Walker is my cousin."

Chapter 9

All her life, Mary had experienced bouts of what she called "foot-in-mouth disease." Especially under stress, Mary found herself saying things she instantly regretted and later agonized over. Her words occasionally hurt others, but for the most part, Mary bore the brunt of her own speech. She recognized herself in the third chapter of the book of James and often prayed for the strength to tame her tongue when it threatened to become "a flame of fire."

However, the looks on Todd's and Veronica's faces when she declared her kinship to Todd had been priceless. His mouth had dropped open, and Veronica seemed to be pleased.

"It was nice to meet you," she told Mary. "Sorry, but I have to run."

After Veronica drifted away, Todd sat back down and stared at Mary. "Why did you tell her that?"

"I don't know," Mary confessed. "At least it's the truth."

"It's more like a half truth. Anyway, I think you shocked Veronica."

Good. She looks like she needs some shaking up. But this time, Mary kept the thought to herself.

∞

When they left the restaurant, Todd put up the convertible top. "You've had enough sun for one day," he told Mary.

"I don't tan well," she said. *Unlike Miss Veronica.*

Todd smiled. "You turn pink very nicely, though."

"Did you say you work with Veronica?" Mary asked as they started back to Rockdale.

"She's at Haskell Holdings, but we don't report to the same boss."

"It's odd you both wound up in Mentone the same day."

He shrugged. "Coincidences happen all the time." His tone suggested Todd didn't want to talk about Veronica, and she took the hint.

"How long after you left California did you start working in Birmingham?"

"It was quite awhile. When I quit my job out there and came back to Alabama, I didn't have anything else lined up."

"That took a lot of faith," Mary said.

"More like a lot of stupidity. I studied the 'Help Wanted' ads and sent out dozens of résumés without ever getting a nibble. I was nearly broke and ready to take almost any kind of work when I ran into a guy I'd played football with at Alabama."

"I suppose he worked for Haskell Holdings," Mary said.

"Yes—how did you know that?"

"It was just a guess." Too late, Mary realized she should have let Todd finish his own story.

"Anyway, Kurt Talbott hired on there several years ago. He got me an appointment with his boss, and a week later I became part of the HH family."

Since Veronica also works there, does that mean she can also claim to be your kin? Wisely, Mary suppressed the sharp words.

After Todd spent several more minutes enumerating the benefits of his Haskell Holdings employment, Mary told him it sounded like a good place to work.

"It is. And best of all, it let me have a chance to take my favorite cousin out to lunch."

Mary saw no need to reply, especially since they had reached Rockdale and were only blocks away from her house. However, when Todd stopped the car at the curb and came around to open her door, courtesy demanded her to invite him to stay longer.

"I'll give you that educational garden tour now if you have time," she said.

"Sorry, but I don't. I still have to check in at the office this afternoon. Maybe I can take you up on it some other time."

"I hope you will. Thanks for lunch—and for letting me see that bluff property. I hope your deal works out."

"So do I."

Todd walked Mary to her front door and waited while she unlocked it. "I can remember a time when no one in Rockdale locked their doors," Todd said.

"Unfortunately, that's no longer safe, even here."

"Still, the town seems pretty much the same as it's always been."

"For better or worse." Mary started to tell Todd about the Rockdale Civic Improvement Association, then decided against it. He should get back to Birmingham, and she needed to go inside and treat her sunburn.

"Better, I think." Todd gave Mary a cousinly peck on the cheek. "I hope to see you soon," he said, then turned and walked back to his car.

I hope to see you soon. Was it merely a polite good-bye to a relative, or did Todd mean it more personally?

Todd turned and waved when he reached his car. Mary waved back, then glanced across the street. Sally Proffitt was sitting in her porch swing, no doubt having watched every move she and Todd had made.

That woman needs a pair of binoculars. She's headed for a bad case of eyestrain.

❦

"What's that white goop on your face?" Mary's father asked at supper that evening.

"Ointment. We went to lunch in Todd's convertible, and I got sunburned."

"Todd Walker has a convertible? You should have worn a hat. Where did you go?"

"To the restaurant in Mentone you like."

"I'm sorry I couldn't join you, but it's just as well I didn't try. I had to declare a mistrial in the Gessman case, and two other cases I'd expected to plead decided to go forward to trial."

Mary knew her father enjoyed discussing his work, since she kept what he said confidential.

"Did Todd say why he was in town today?" he asked when he finished recounting his day in court.

"Not exactly, but I think Haskell Holdings might be looking to buy property around Mentone." Mary decided against identifying the Millican land. It had nothing to do with Rockdale, and although Todd hadn't asked her to keep quiet, she gathered he didn't want others to know about the bluff land.

"So that's where Todd works."

"What do you know about it?"

"Not much. Haskell Holdings is a rather new megacompany with too many irons in the fire, in my opinion. Which division is he in?"

"I don't know, but apparently one of his Alabama football teammates who already worked there was responsible for his being hired."

Wayne Oliver chuckled. "Ah, the good old buddy system in action. There are some positive things to be said about collegiate sports, after all. I hope Todd comes our way again. I'd like to get to know him better."

So would I. Seeing Todd again had reminded Mary of the feelings she had once had for him. Those days of puppy love were gone, but her interest in Todd Walker was not.

"I hope you'll be here the next time he comes."

"What about Walter? I don't suppose you had time to see him today."

"No—I tried, but he wasn't in his office this morning."

"So you still have the necklace?"

Mary shook her head. "I asked Ellie Fergus to give it to him. So far, he hasn't called."

"I'm surprised," Wayne Oliver said.

So am I.

Her father looked at his watch. "I don't want to be late for the Civic Improvement Association meeting."

"I'd forgotten all about that."

"We need another article, and you did a good job on the first one. You should come with me tonight."

Mary didn't really feel up to going out. Her arms weren't quite as sunburned as her face, but when she'd put on a sleeveless shift after showering, the line where her red linen suit sleeve had ended and her sunburn began was quite clear. Ordinarily, she would have begged off, but this evening was different.

"Where is it, and who will be there?"

"The Endicotts'. It'll be me, Margaret Hastings, Newman Howell, Sam Roberts, and Miles Endicott."

Walter Chance wouldn't be there. "All right, but I hope the air conditioning works—my face feels like it's on fire."

∞

Walter didn't call that night, nor did Mary hear from him the next morning. She alternated between being glad he hadn't called to wishing he would so she could know the matter of the necklace had been resolved once and for all.

Mary tried to concentrate on writing the second Rockdale Civic Improvement Association article, an open invitation to all Rockdale residents to come to the high school auditorium for an informational meeting the following Tuesday night. However, since the committee wanted to make sure the article would arouse enough interest to produce a good turnout, Mary took special pains with it.

When she handed the article to Grant Westleigh, he looked it over and nodded his approval. "Just a minute," he said when Mary turned to leave. "Don't you also have an item for the 'Around Rockdale' personals column?"

Mary knew Grant was teasing her. She had a pretty good idea why, but she decided to pretend otherwise. "Not unless my meeting of First Church Vacation Bible School's steering committee qualifies for the Personals."

"I had in mind something more like this: 'Miss Mary Oliver recently entertained Mr. First Name Unknown, Last Name Unknown, of Birmingham, who took her for a ride lasting several hours in his red convertible. Miss Oliver is recovering from her resulting sunburn at the Oliver ancestral home in Rockdale.'"

Mary laughed. "I believe I know the source of that piece of information, but I wonder how she knew the unnamed mister lives in Birmingham."

"Maybe it's because she can read a license tag from a distance of, say, across a street. How about filling in the blanks?"

Mary knew she could trust Grant Westleigh to keep a confidence. "There's nothing secret about it, but it's hardly front-page news. The car in question is Todd Walker's. You probably remember him—he was a Rockdale High football star who went on to play at Alabama."

"Sure, I do. Isn't he kin to you?"

Only a relative would be taking someone like Mary Oliver for a ride in a convertible. Grant Westleigh might not think so, but she knew many others probably would.

"Todd and I are distant cousins."

Grant Westleigh grinned. "Kissin' cousins, as we say in the South. Is he moving back here?"

"No. Todd works for Haskell Holdings."

"Which, of course, happens to be in Birmingham."

"At least Sally Proffitt got that part right," Mary said ruefully.

The newspaperman put his index finger to his lips. "Hush, now. You know

I can't divulge my sources."

"I hope you won't repeat what I said to your 'sources,' either. Come to think of it, I suppose we should have told Sally Proffitt and Jenny Suiter there'd be a secret meeting of the Rockdale Civic Improvement Association. The word would be all over town a lot sooner than this article can be printed."

"At least in a garbled version. I've noticed that those ladies' stories always manage to get at least one detail wrong."

"Otherwise, they'd make a great addition to your staff. Good-bye, Grant. Thanks for your help."

"Glad to be of service. Take care of that sunburn."

Mary was still smiling as she left the *Record* office. Since Sally Proffitt had spread the news of what she'd seen all over town, she supposed it was better to laugh about it than to be bothered.

Mary was about to get into her car when Walter Chance came out of his office and almost literally blocked her way.

"Hello, Mary. Do you have a minute?"

Chapter 10

Here it comes—*Walter has found the envelope.* Mary glanced at her watch as if she had something pressing to do, but Walter ignored the gesture.

"I want to show you something. It'll take thirty minutes, tops."

Mary didn't know whether to be relieved or alarmed. *Surely he must have opened the envelope by now—or has he?* She decided not to bring it up first.

"I suppose I can spare that much time."

Walter finally noted her sunburn and did a double take. "Wow—how did you get that?"

"By not wearing a hat when I should have."

"You don't need any more sun."

Walter took Mary's arm and steered her toward his building. "My car's in the parking lot out back. I'll just stop and tell Ellie I'm leaving."

Ellie Fergus sat at her desk, talking on the telephone. She waved at Mary, then covered the phone's mouthpiece to speak to Walter. "This is a man who's staying at the Rockdale Inn and wants to see the Johnson house. When can you show it?"

Walter signaled for the telephone, and Ellie handed it to him. "Hello, this is Walter Chance. How can I help you?"

Mary leaned close to Ellie and spoke in a whisper. "Did you give Walter the envelope I left here yesterday?"

"I put it on his desk. Do you want me to see if it's still there?"

"No—it's not important."

Certain Walter hadn't opened the envelope, she didn't want him to do so yet.

Walter continued to speak with enthusiasm as he described a property Mary knew well. The vacant farmhouse on the edge of town had looked extremely run-down last July when she and Toni drove by it on their way to take the Trent children to pick wild blackberries. Mary and Toni had reminisced about the time Toni lived there in foster care in her teens, before Judge Oliver gave Evelyn Trent custody of the girl so many others had called "terrible Toni Schmidt."

"It's sad the house wasn't kept up after the Johnsons left town," Toni remarked that day, and Mary had agreed.

Hearing Walter's glowing account of the place, Mary recalled her father's words: "Walter Chance has a good head on his shoulders." He was certainly making a success of the family business, and Mary could see why he was regarded as a good catch.

"I can pick you up at one, if that's convenient. Good. See you then, Mr. Andrews."

Walter returned the telephone to Ellie, who noted the appointment on the office calendar. "I'll be out of the office for about thirty minutes. Don't call my cell phone unless it's a true emergency."

"Yes, Mr. Chance."

"Sorry for the interruption." Walter led Mary down the hallway, past a conference room, his office and those of the other two Chance Realty agents who worked there, and into the small parking lot.

Of the cars parked there, Walter's beige Towncar was the largest and most luxurious. Walter kept the exterior washed and waxed and the interior spotless as a matter of course. "My clients deserve to be pampered when I take them to see properties," he had told her when they worked together on Rockdale High's tenth reunion. As a gag, the reunion committee presented Walter with a special award for owning the largest automobile in their graduating class. He had accepted it with his perennial smile, but when someone asked him what he would do with the award, his expression turned serious. "I'm going to frame it, since it's the only kind of award I ever got from Rockdale High School."

Now, as Walter unlocked the car doors and helped Mary in, she asked him about it. "Did you keep the certificate the committee gave you for having the largest car at the tenth reunion?"

Walter's smile deepened. "Sure do. In fact, it's hanging in my office, between my brokers' license and Better Business Bureau membership plaque. Like I said, I'm ready for another reunion."

"And I'm still not rested up from the first one."

Walter turned his car onto Main Street. "I'm glad you came with me."

"I still don't know where I'm going."

"To see a piece of land that might be on the market soon."

"Why?" Mary asked. "I'm not interested in buying property."

"Maybe you should be. Land can be a great investment, you know."

Mary laughed. "My teacher's salary doesn't give me much extra money to invest."

"You and the judge could go in on it together."

"Go in on what?" Mary made no effort to mask the irritation she was beginning to feel.

"You'll see," he said.

Mary felt a touch of déjà vu at his words, so much like what Todd Walker had said the day before. For a moment, she wondered if Walter would also take her to the Millican bluff land. However, he'd told Ellie he'd be back at his office in thirty minutes, so they weren't going far.

Walter stopped at a traffic light at the precise moment Sally Proffitt emerged from the Clip and Curl Beauty Shop, where she had a standing Wednesday morning appointment. Jenny Suiter also had her hair done there by a different operator on Friday morning. Mary suspected the women compared notes on what each heard, but she doubted if they received more news than they imparted. In Mary's opinion, it was more blessed neither to give nor receive gossip, but apparently Sally Proffitt and Jenny Suiter thought it their Christian duty to share "news."

Sally saw Mary immediately. She must have recognized the car—Walter Chance had the only one exactly like it in Rockdale. She looked surprised, then smiled and waved at Mary, who nodded in greeting.

"Too bad you don't have tinted side windows," Mary told Walter when the light turned green.

"Why?" Since Walter obviously hadn't seen Sally Proffitt, she decided not to tell him. "Do not worry about tomorrow. . . . Each day has enough trouble of its own." Of course, Sally had nothing to tell the town; the fact that Mary Oliver and Walter Chance happened to be in the same vehicle on a sunny midmorning in June could hardly be headline news, even in sensation-deprived Rockdale.

"It would make the interior cooler," she said.

"I can crank up the air-conditioning." Walter reached out to change the temperature setting, but Mary stayed his hand.

"It's fine like it is."

"If you get uncomfortable, let me know."

The only thing I'm uncomfortable about is riding off to parts unknown with you. "I will."

"You probably know where we're headed by now," Walter said when he turned onto the narrow road leading to Oliver Mountain.

"Yes, but I don't know why. The only thing up here is our family's cemetery, and it isn't for sale."

Walter smiled faintly. "I didn't think it was."

He drove past the entrance to the cemetery and onto an even narrower unpaved lane, which ended abruptly at a grassy meadow. "Here we are," he announced.

Mary got out of the car, aware she wasn't dressed for hiking. She wasn't wearing a hat, so she risked further sunburn. Once again, her open-toed sandals weren't meant for uncertain terrain. Mary's slacks and knit top were more practical than yesterday's linen suit, but they offered no protection against the chigoes lurking in the weeds at the edge of the meadow. Unless Mary took precautions against the tiny pests, they delighted in burrowing into her skin, leaving red, itching welts all over her body.

Walter handed Mary a can of insecticide. "Spray this around your feet and ankles and on your arms. There are chiggers up here."

"I know. Thanks—I don't enjoy being eaten alive."

"I always carry bug spray," Walter said. "It comes in handy when I show rural property."

"I don't understand why you brought me here."

"You will."

Mystified, Mary followed Walter through a patch of weeds at the edge of the meadow and onto a rock outcropping overlooking Rockdale. The view, while not nearly so spectacular as the one Mary had seen at Millican's Bluff the day before, was impressive.

"A lot of people would think this is an ideal place to build a house."

A lot of people? Or Walter Chance?

Mary turned her head and glanced in the direction of the cemetery. "At least their neighbors won't be having any late-night parties."

Walter seemed slightly shocked Mary would speak so lightly of the last resting places of so many of her ancestors. "You wouldn't mind living up here? Many people wouldn't want a house close to a cemetery."

Mary spoke more seriously. "Maybe they don't want to be reminded of their own mortality. My eternal home is elsewhere, so cemeteries don't make me feel uncomfortable—especially not my own family's burial place."

"I know a contractor who could really build a fine house up here."

"Are you trying to tell me you want to build a house on our mountain?"

"No. This bluff land is far too valuable for a single home."

Mary felt the familiar irritation with Walter she'd encountered when they worked on their class reunion. Sometimes he could be downright—she searched for the right word—frustrating. "Do you mean someone wants to develop a whole subdivision up here?"

"No. Something much more profitable." Walter bent to scoop up a handful of loose stones from the rocks around them. "See this? Oliver Mountain is almost solid rock. That's unusual, because most of the ranges around here are riddled with limestone caves."

"Like Sequoyah Caverns," said Mary, who had recently gone there to arrange the Vacation Bible School field trip.

"Right. What we have here is a perfect location for a rock quarry."

Chapter 11

A rock quarry?

Mary had seen enough rock quarries to know they were unsightly. A quarry on the brow of Oliver Mountain would be fully visible to at least half of Rockdale, an ugly scar on the otherwise green landscape. "You believe someone plans to put a rock quarry in here?"

"I don't know for sure, but it's a pretty good guess."

Mary thought of the noise and dust a working rock quarry would generate only yards from her family's cemetery. "That would be awful. Does the Civic Improvement Association know about this?"

Walter tossed the pebbles out and over the edge of the hill and dusted his hands on the sides of his slacks. "No. I heard someone from out of town ordered a geological survey, but I don't know who, and I don't know who did the work. It's all based on rumor, but I thought the judge might want to look into it."

"I'm sure he will. I'll tell him." Mary took one last look around the peaceful Oliver Mountain meadow and shuddered at the thought it might eventually be whittled away to nothing. "A quarry here would be terrible."

Walter nodded. "To prevent that, this land should be zoned for single-family dwellings only. That would be a good thing for the Civic Improvement Association to look into. It could be their first accomplishment."

"I'm sure my father will want to look into it right away."

Mary turned to go back to the car, but Walter caught her hand and stopped her. "I wanted to see you today for another reason. I want to take you out to dinner tonight—your necklace will look really great with the dress you wore to your birthday dinner. How about it?"

Caught off guard, Mary glanced at her watch as if the present time had any bearing on his invitation. "Uh—this is Wednesday. Father and I have a standing dinner engagement at the First Church fellowship supper."

Walter released Mary's hand. "How about tomorrow night, then?"

Mary looked into his eyes and knew she had to tell Walter the truth. "There's something you need to know—I won't ever be wearing the necklace."

He looked bewildered. "Why not?"

Mary took a deep breath and looked heavenward as if for guidance. "I can't. I don't have it anymore. I put it in a manila envelope and left it at your office yesterday. It's probably still on your desk."

"Why did you do that? I thought you liked it."

413

"My father and I agree it's too expensive for me to accept."

"The judge told you to give it back?"

"No, but—"

"Don't worry about the money—I can afford it. I just wanted you to have something as special as you are."

Walter looked unhappy, and Mary spoke quickly. "I'm not that special. And I want you to know I appreciate it—and your friendship—more than I can say."

His face brightened. "Then you'll wear it when we go out tomorrow night?"

"No—anyway, I never said I'd go with you."

"Forget the necklace. I don't care if you wear it or not. I'm still taking you somewhere nice tomorrow night."

Confronted with a combination of Walter's determination and her own wish to spare his feelings, Mary nodded. "If you insist."

Walter smiled. "I'll look at tomorrow's appointments and let you know what time I can pick you up."

Back in town, Walter stopped his car in the street behind her Toyota. No one was around to see her get out of Walter's car, but Mary figured the harm was already done. Sally Proffitt had probably already told the world that Judge Oliver's daughter, who had been seen riding in a red convertible with one man, was now riding around with Walter Chance.

∞

When Mary got home, she left a message for her father to call her when he had the chance. She was preparing a salad for her lunch when he returned her call.

"What's up?"

"I ran into Walter today. He's heard something about Oliver Mountain you should know."

Mary repeated Walter's news without adding he had taken her to the site. "He said he didn't mention it to anyone on the Civic Improvement Association because it was hearsay, but he thought you'd want to follow up on it."

"This is disturbing—I'm glad you didn't wait to tell me. I'll see if I can find out who requested that geological survey. There won't be a quarry on that mountain, I can assure you."

"I hope not."

"Since you've seen Walter, I presume he knows you returned the necklace. How did he take it?"

"Not very well. I agreed to have dinner with him tomorrow night, and that seemed to make him feel better."

Mary sensed her father's smile. "I'm sure it did. I'll try to track down that survey after court adjourns, but it might take awhile. If I'm not home by five thirty, go to the church supper without me. I'll try to get there before the serving line closes."

"I hope you can find the information," Mary said.

"So do I. See you later, puddin'."

Puddin'—her father hadn't called Mary by her childhood nickname in years. *He's getting mellower with every passing day.*

Mary believed the change in her father could be summed up in two words: Evelyn Trent—and she would be at the church supper that night, too.

∞

Mary and her father seldom missed First's Wednesday night fellowship dinner. For Mary, it was a midweek break from cooking, and her father enjoyed being with his friends. Even when they arrived together, Mary and Judge Oliver usually sat at separate tables. On this night, when her father still hadn't come home by nearly six o'clock, Mary followed his instruction and went by herself.

After Mary came through the serving line, Jennifer Stokes invited her to sit with her and her husband at one end of the long table. Their children sat at the other end, as far away as they could get. Mary had scarcely put down her tray before Alice Taylor and her children joined them.

"Here come the Smiths," Jennifer said. "We could have a Vacation Bible School committee meeting on the spot."

"Count us men out of that, please," Dan Taylor said.

"Ron is helping Melanie with the recreation this year. You could give us some of your time, too," Jennifer said.

"Alice spends enough hours at church for both of us," said Dan Taylor.

Mary listened to the couples' good-natured banter as an outsider, glimpsing things she'd never experienced and therefore could never fully understand. Still, she thanked God for Christian friends who laughed with her, not at her.

When Mary returned to the table with her ice water, the adults at the table suddenly fell silent. Mary immediately assumed she was the topic of their conversation. Sally Proffitt must have struck again.

"What were you talking about?"

Alice and Jennifer exchanged a quick glance. "We were checking out the judge," Jennifer said.

Mary hadn't seen her father enter, and when she automatically glanced at the table he usually shared with a few old friends, she saw he wasn't among them. Jennifer pointed toward a rear table, where Wayne Oliver sat with his back to the rest of the diners.

He wasn't alone: Evelyn Trent, whose distinctive silver hair stood out in any crowd, sat beside him. They seemed to be deep in conversation, apparently oblivious to the rest of the world.

Mary smiled faintly. "My father told me to come on by myself because he might be late."

"Now we know why," Jennifer said.

Her tone made Mary feel she should defend him. "He had to work late. Besides, he and Evelyn Trent have been friends for years."

"True, but they never seemed to be quite this friendly," Alice said.

"You sound like Sally Proffitt," said Melanie.

Alice made a face. "Well, Miss Sally isn't here tonight, so somebody has to do her job."

They were all smiling, and Mary was glad no one seemed to expect her to say anything else about her father and the retired social worker. Mary thought of telling them she and Walter Chance were going out the next evening. That would change the subject in a hurry, but Mary remained silent.

"If women's gossip could be taxed, this town would have all the money it could use," Dan Taylor said.

"Women aren't the only ones who like to talk," Alice retorted. "What about all those stories you guys like to tell about the fish that got away and how many holes below par you shot playing golf?"

"Men talk about things of interest. We don't talk about other people behind their backs," Dan said.

"I'll remind you of that the next time you start discussing the mill manager," Alice said.

"Hey, that's not gossip—that's reporting facts."

Everyone laughed, but in a way, Dan's words hit the mark. Sally Proffitt and Jenny Suiter too often reached completely wrong conclusions about the "facts" they reported.

Mary hoped Sally Proffitt wouldn't be on her front porch when Walter came to pick her up.

∞

The families at Mary's table gradually drifted away, the adults to the sanctuary for the midweek service and the children to their special activities. Among the last to leave the fellowship hall, Wayne Oliver and Evelyn Trent joined Mary in the hallway outside the sanctuary.

"Did you find the information you were looking for?" Mary asked her father.

"Not yet. The firms doing that work are scattered all over, and many are one-man operations with answering machines. I meant to get home earlier, but as I told Evelyn, the time got away from me."

"I ran late tonight myself," Evelyn said.

"We were talking about the Rockdale Civic Improvement Association meeting," her father said, as if Mary had asked.

Mary didn't try to suppress her smile. "That must have been fascinating dinner conversation."

Evelyn nodded. "Actually, it was. He's trying to persuade me to join the steering committee."

"You should. You know everybody in Rock County."

"I did in the past, but I've been out of town so much since I retired, I'm behind the times."

"Rockdale still moves in the slow lane," Mary said. "You haven't missed much."

"So Wayne tells me."

When the first piano chords signaled the start of the service, Wayne Oliver led the way to the family pew. Seated between Mary and Evelyn, Mary's father handed her a hymnal and shared another with Evelyn. As they sang, Mary noticed he stood closer to Evelyn than hymnal sharing required.

Watching them, Mary felt a lump rise in her throat. Her father and Evelyn looked completely at ease with each other. *This is the way it's going to be from now on. It's only a matter of time until they marry. After that, our lives will never be the same again.*

Even without that prospect, Mary hardly knew how to handle the changes in her own life.

As Dr. Whitson led in prayer, Mary silently raised her own petition. *I thank You for bringing my father and Evelyn together, Lord. Help me to accept the changes going on around me. Help me to live constantly in Your will, not mine.*

When Mary opened her eyes, Evelyn looked at her as if she knew something of Mary's inner struggle and felt sympathy for her.

Evelyn Trent could become my stepmother. Mary tested the thought and found it was not at all unpleasant. She smiled at Evelyn, who smiled back.

Her father looked puzzled. "Why are you two smiling? Did I miss something?" he whispered.

"It's just a girl thing," Mary whispered back. At that, Evelyn bent her head and covered her mouth, her shoulders shaking in silent laughter.

Looking baffled, he muttered "Women!" under his breath, and Mary almost laughed aloud. Fortunately, the choir director announced another hymn, and somewhere during the second verse, she and Evelyn managed to regain their composure.

∞

After the benediction, Evelyn and her father left together, headed for the side lot where both had parked their cars, and Mary drove home from church alone. She was reading the newspaper in the living room when her father came in almost an hour later.

"You and Evelyn seemed to be having a good time tonight," he said. "What was that all about?"

"I believe Evelyn and I reached an understanding tonight. I wonder if you have."

Wayne Oliver looked mystified. "What do you mean?"

"How do you feel about Evelyn?"

He smiled ruefully. "It seems we've had this conversation before. We're very good friends, and I can assure you my intentions are honorable."

"If you're going to marry her, I'd rather hear it from you than get a garbled version from Sally Proffitt or Jenny Suiter."

"Those gossips! You can't believe anything they say."

"I don't—that's why I'm asking you."

"Evelyn and I enjoy each other's company. At first, the thought of a more permanent arrangement never entered my mind, and I'm sure she felt the same way. Evelyn's never been married, and she's used to being independent. So am I. But lately, we've grown closer. . . ."

When her father didn't finish his thought, Mary went over to his chair and gave him a brief hug. "I believe you should ask Evelyn to be your wife."

He looked uncertain. "You wouldn't mind?"

"How could I? It's obvious you're happy when you're together."

He looked relieved. "You don't know how much I've prayed about this. I'm not sure Evelyn will have me, but knowing you approve makes it easier to ask her."

"Be assured you have my blessing."

Her father's voice was husky with emotion. "Thank you, my dear. I only hope you'll know such happiness one day."

"I haven't been looking for it."

"Neither were Evelyn and I. Things change—we go along in the same rut for years, then the Lord moves us in an entirely different direction. When that happens to you, I trust you'll recognize it."

I think I am beginning to. "When, not if?" Mary questioned.

"When," he repeated. "I believe you're close to realizing I need some grandchildren."

Mary smiled, but she recognized the truth in her father's words. She had always assumed she would cook and keep house for her father as long as he lived. It had never occurred to her that he wished for grandchildren. He had never spoken of it, probably because it seemed so unlikely Mary would ever marry.

"I'll see what I can do about that one of these days," Mary said. "For now, I'm going to bed."

Late into the night, Mary considered the uncertain future ahead when her father and Evelyn married.

They'll have to live here—Evelyn's house is far too small. She'll want to bring some of her furniture and personal items, and that means rearranging everything.

Mary sighed. She believed God had a solution for every one of her problems. Now she prayed to find them.

Chapter 12

Her father came down for breakfast Thursday morning, humming and smelling of aftershave lotion.

"Beautiful morning, isn't it?"

Mary smiled at his good humor. "You probably don't care, but the weather forecast mentions scattered thunderstorms and heavy rain this afternoon. You'd better take your umbrella."

"Maybe the storms will be scattered somewhere else. Anyway, I'll be inside all day. This afternoon I hope to find out who tested land on our mountain. I'm glad Walter told you about it when he did."

"Remember I'm having dinner with him tonight, so I won't be here when you get home."

"Where's he taking you?"

"I don't know—out of town, though. He said he'll let me know later today when he can get away to pick me up."

Her father smiled. "Should I wait up for you tonight?"

"Hardly. Even if we go to Mentone, we should be back by nine."

"Ask Walter in when you get home. I'd like to discuss this quarry business with him."

"Maybe you should go with us." Mary could imagine the look on Walter Chance's face if her father did so.

"No, thanks. Three's a crowd."

∞

Walter called Mary shortly after noon. "Was the judge able to find out who owns the land on Oliver Mountain?" he asked.

"Not yet, but he's working on it."

"Good. I'll pick you up at five thirty."

The weather was fine when Walter called, but by five o'clock, the earlier sunny skies had been replaced by billowing thunderclouds, and the scent of rain hung heavy in the air.

Mary put on her red linen suit, then rummaged in the coat closet for her ancient black nylon taffeta raincoat. It wasn't glamorous, but Mary was more interested in keeping dry.

Walter rang the doorbell promptly at the appointed hour. "I'm sorry I didn't bring better weather, but I see you're prepared for the worst," he said when she opened the door.

"I call this raincoat 'Old Faithful'—I think I've had it since tenth grade."

"It still looks very nice—and so do you."

Walter had exchanged his usual casual attire for the kind of ensemble featured in department store ads. His beige sport coat, navy blue slacks, pale blue dress shirt, and beige and navy patterned tie looked new, and Mary caught the subtle scent of a spicy aftershave.

He must have shaved and changed clothes after work. The knowledge both unsettled and touched Mary, and she wished he wouldn't try so hard to impress her.

Thunder growled in the distance, and when they reached Walter's car, Mary glanced across the street. The empty front porch swing moved slightly in the rising wind, and the drapes at the front windows were closed. Mary was grateful Sally Proffitt wouldn't see Walter help her into his Towncar.

"I wanted to take you someplace better," Walter said as they headed out of town, "but with all the bad weather, I thought we should settle for DeSoto Park. Is that all right?"

"Of course. I haven't eaten there at night in a long time."

"The buffet is usually good, but we can order from the menu if you don't like what they have tonight."

Walter's obvious eagerness to please made Mary feel even worse. "Let's decide when we get there."

He nodded as if she had said something profound. "Good idea—but then, you always have good ideas. That's one of the many things I like about you."

"Here comes the rain," Mary said a moment later. A few dime-sized drops pelted the windshield, soon joined by hundreds of others in a sky-wide curtain.

Walter wasn't driving fast before the rain began, but now he slowed even more and turned on the car's headlights. Even at high speed, the windshield wipers were unable to keep up with the increasing volume of rain.

I hope Walter can see the road better than I can. Mary almost told him so, but she didn't want to break his concentration.

Mary peered out at the sky, a uniform dark gray as far as she could see. A bolt of lightning cut through the air nearby, followed almost at once by a tremendous thunderclap. Startled, she shivered. "That sounded like a sonic boom."

"Don't worry—a car like this is about the safest place you can be in a storm."

"I'm not worried." Afraid she had spoken too sharply, Mary tried to make amends. "You're a good driver."

Walter smiled at her compliment. "I try to drive safely all the time, of course, but especially when I carry such precious cargo."

Mary manufactured a sudden cough to cover her reaction. *Precious cargo, indeed!* At least he didn't put one of those 'Baby on Board' signs in the rear window. Walter's attempt at being gallant made her feel almost sorry for him.

Mary's fake coughing fit did not go unnoticed. "I keep a package of lozenges in the glove box. Help yourself."

She tried to look grateful and went through the motions of unwrapping one of the red disks without putting it in her mouth.

"All better?" Walter asked in a moment, and she nodded.

"Yes, thank you."

Mary sighed and glanced at her wristwatch. She had been with Walter fifteen minutes, yet it had already been a long evening.

∞

Mary hoped the storm would be spent by the time they reached the park, but the rain seemed to have followed them there, then increased in intensity.

Walter reached behind the driver's seat for the largest umbrella Mary had ever seen. "I came prepared. This will keep us dry."

As he spoke, lightning flashed again, followed closely by rolling thunder. Mary had never feared storms, but she flinched at the sudden noise. "Let's wait awhile. We didn't come all the way up here to be struck by lightning."

Walter laughed as if Mary had said something hilarious. "I've always enjoyed your sly sense of humor."

"You're only saying that because it's true," she said lightly.

This time, Walter didn't return her smile. "I mean it, Mary. I'm just not very good at this."

He spoke with great sincerity and reached for Mary's hand.

Afraid he would try to kiss her, Mary reclaimed her hand and pulled up her raincoat hood. "The lightning seems to be letting up. It's probably safe to go inside."

"If you say so. Stay right there."

Walter got out of the car and opened his black umbrella, on which CHANCE REALTY was printed in large red letters. He helped Mary out and put his arm around her on the pretext of sheltering her under his umbrella. He kept a firm hold on her all the way to the DeSoto Park lodge porch, and when he finally let her go to close the umbrella, he seemed to do so reluctantly.

He smiled. "That wasn't so bad, was it?"

It depends on what you mean. I could certainly have done without being hugged quite so much. "No. The umbrella kept me dry."

"Remind me to give you one. I keep a few in the car in case I have to show property in the rain."

Walter put his hand on the small of Mary's back and steered her into the dining area as if she couldn't find the way unassisted. Even though Walter was trying to be polite, the gesture embarrassed her.

Mary recognized the hostess, a senior the year she and Walter entered Rockdale High School. Sally something—Mary couldn't think of her last name.

"Good evening, Walter—hi, Mary—I guess y'all are dining together tonight?"

"Hello, Sally. We sure are, and I hope you have a nice, quiet table away from the traffic."

"There might not be much of that tonight, the way it's storming. I can seat you by a window if you like."

Walter looked at Mary. "How about it? Do you want to watch the rain?"

"No. I teach my first-graders to stay away from windows during a storm."

"Then I reckon we should, too," Walter said.

"Follow me." The hostess led them to a table tucked away in a corner, far from the windows. "Do you need a menu?"

"How about it, Mary?"

"The buffet will be fine."

"Two buffets, then? Your waitress will take your drink orders. Enjoy your meal."

"Sally Richmond," Mary said when the hostess walked away.

"What?"

"The hostess—her name is Sally Richmond."

"Was," Walter corrected. "She's married to Ted Morgan. I sold them a house near Warren Mountain a couple of years ago. In fact, it's in Toni and David Trent's neighborhood."

They fell silent again as the storm continued to rage. Lightning flashed almost constantly, accompanied by booming thunder. The dining room lights flickered a few times but never went out.

"I sure picked a terrible time to take you out," Walter said after an especially loud burst of thunder shook the building.

He sounded so forlorn, Mary tried to cheer him up. "This is a typical summer storm—it won't last long, and the rest of the evening will probably be fine."

The waitress arrived at their table before Walter had time to reply. "What can I get y'all to drink this evening?"

He answered without consulting Mary. "I'll take sweetened iced tea, and the lady will have ice water with a slice of lemon."

"How did you know that's what I wanted?" Mary asked when the waitress left.

"Easy. All those times the reunion committee met at Statum's, you always ordered water with lemon. You did it the other day, too."

"You have a good memory."

"It's good to remember the good times, but making happy new memories together is even better."

Mary began another effort to tell Walter not to read too much into her reasons for going out with him. "You really shouldn't—"

With uncanny timing, the waitress brought their drinks. "Here you are. Feel free to go to the buffet any time, and let me know if you need anything else."

Walter smiled. "How about it? I don't know about you, but I'm ready to tie on the old feed bag."

The old feed bag? Mary sighed. It seemed every time Mary began to feel closer to Walter, he managed to say or do something odd.

"Fine," she said aloud. "Lead the way."

∞

Mary's weather prediction proved correct. While they were eating, the black storm clouds moved on, and the sun came out again. Walter's mood lightened, and he began to talk about all the good things he hoped the Rockdale Civic Improvement Association would be able to bring about for the community.

"I might even run for city council if that's what it takes to get better zoning laws."

"Since you're in the real estate business, some people might see that as a conflict of interest. You could do more good working behind the scenes."

Walter nodded. "You're right—I hadn't thought of that. Somebody needs to step up to the plate and wake up the powers that be, or there's no telling what kind of mess Rockdale will wind up in. The quarry is just the tip of the iceberg."

"That reminds me—my father wants to talk to you about it tonight."

"I figured he would, but I hadn't planned to end this evening in Judge Oliver's company."

Mary wasn't sure she wanted to know what else Walter might have preferred, and she didn't ask.

Walter apparently took her silence to mean agreement. "Don't worry, we'll have lots of other evenings together."

Don't take that for granted, Mary almost blurted out, but Walter's expression made her soften her words.

"I've enjoyed dinner tonight, I really have. You're a very special friend, but that's all."

Walter seemed amused. "Don't be so serious. Being good friends was a good start for us, but it surely won't be the end."

Mary felt frustrated. Walter almost seemed to think she was playing hard to get. While she suspected nothing she could say would change his mind, Mary had to try. "In this case, I think it is."

To her chagrin, Walter smiled. "There's that dry sense of humor again. You're something else, Mary Oliver."

"So are you," Mary retorted, and he laughed aloud.

When the waitress removed their plates, Walter glanced at his watch. "We have time to walk down to the waterfall, if you'd like to do that now."

Mary shook her head, glad for a ready excuse. "The path will be slippery after all the rain, and I'm not wearing my hiking shoes."

"Of course—I wasn't thinking. I certainly don't want to do anything to cause you harm."

"Thanks," Mary said quickly. "Maybe we should get back to Rockdale now."

Walter flashed a big smile. "Your wish is my command, milady."

Stifling a sigh, Mary allowed Walter to steer her from the dining room.

Chapter 13

They reached Mary's house shortly after eight o'clock, and her father quickly invited Walter inside.

"I've made several inquiries, but no one seems to know anything about a geological survey on Oliver Mountain," he told Walter. "I want to know exactly what you heard."

"It's all secondhand, but I have a few ideas about it and some other things, too."

"Sit down and tell me about it."

Walter did, and for a while, Mary feared he and her father would talk all night.

A half hour into their discussion, she made some coffee and heated a plate of brownies she'd frozen after Decoration Day.

"These taste like you just baked them," Walter declared. "You sure know your way around a kitchen."

"That she does," Mary's father agreed. "Have another brownie."

Mary rolled her eyes and retreated to her room to read.

Walter finally left shortly before the ten o'clock news, which Mary and her father had watched together for years. She was putting their cups into the dishwasher when he came into the kitchen.

"Walter said something interesting while you were out of the room."

"What was that?"

Mary's father leaned against the kitchen counter and folded his arms across his chest. "Mr. Chance seems unwilling to take 'no' for an answer. He wants me to use my influence to persuade you to keep the necklace."

"I thought we agreed I shouldn't."

"Maybe it wouldn't be such a bad idea. Walter assured me he can afford it."

"I don't care. It's not the kind of gift one accepts from a friend."

"Surely you know he wants to be more than that."

Mary closed the dishwasher. "Is that what he told you?"

He laughed. "You two remind me of eighth-graders in the throes of a first crush. They can't talk to each other, so they have to let their friends talk for them."

"Believe me, I don't have a crush on Walter Chance."

"That's too bad. He all but asked me for your hand."

Mary studied her father's face and decided he was serious. "What did you tell him?"

"The truth. My daughter has a mind of her own, and I have nothing to do with her love life."

Mary didn't know whether to laugh or cry. "My love life! Please tell me you didn't use those words."

"Walter wants to be your personal Prince Charming. He's a nice fellow—if you can't love him, try not to break his heart."

∽

Mary wasn't surprised when Walter called the next morning to tell her how much he'd enjoyed going out with her. When he asked her to have lunch with him, she quickly refused.

"I can't."

"If you change your mind—"

"I won't."

Mary could picture Walter's baffled shrug. "Okay. See you later."

Being pursued was new to her, but Mary hoped Walter would soon realize she had no interest in being caught.

She had no sooner hung up than the telephone rang again. Thinking it might be Walter calling her back, Mary took her time answering.

"Mary Oliver? This is Jason Abbott."

Jason Abbott. Her heart lurched unaccountably, and she realized she'd been hoping he'd call. "Yes?"

"We met Monday at DeSoto State Park, and you were kind enough to offer to tell me about your children's programs."

"Yes, I remember."

"When would it be convenient for us to meet?"

"Do you have a specific time in mind?"

"I'm free the rest of today and tomorrow. After that, it would be sometime next week before we could get together."

"Around two this afternoon is fine for me."

"Good. I'd like to see First's facilities, if that's possible."

"I'll be happy to give you a tour. I can meet you in front of the sanctuary—it's on Spring Street."

"I know. Pastor Hurley pointed it out when we toured Rockdale."

Mary smiled at the thought of "touring" such a small town. *That must have taken all of a half hour.* "I'll see you there at two o'clock."

∽

The courthouse clock had just struck twice when Mary pulled into her usual parking place at the side of First Church. While she was unfastening her safety belt, a dark green Honda sedan pulled up beside her. A man wearing jeans, a knit shirt, and white athletic shoes got out and approached her. His hair looked freshly cut, and Mary suspected he had shaved that morning, but he still looked slightly shaggy.

"Thanks for agreeing to meet with me."

"I'm always glad to talk about our children's department. We've put a lot of work into it."

Jason followed Mary through the double front doors and pushed his sunglasses to the top of his head. Once inside the sanctuary, Jason stopped to look at the stained-glass windows. The afternoon sun streamed through them, casting multicolored beams of light across the pews.

"I wondered if the inside of this church could be as beautiful as the outside. Now I see it is. That's a great-looking pipe organ. Is it still used?"

"Every Sunday. The walls shake when Mrs. Harvey pulls out all the stops."

"I can imagine." Jason glanced at the walls on either side. "These stained-glass windows are extraordinary."

"Most of them date back to the late eighteen hundreds," Mary said.

"You can tell they were made with great care by a master craftsman." Jason walked around the pews to get a closer look at the western windows. "This one of Jesus with the children is superb."

"It's my favorite," Mary said.

Jason bent to read the placard beneath the window, then looked at Mary. "Are you related to the Olivers who commissioned this window?"

"Yes, and my mother's family gave the one beside it."

"It's beautiful, but I prefer the Oliver window. That one little girl looks as if she could step right out of the scene at any moment."

"She wouldn't want to, though. She would have stayed at the Master's side."

"Those who come to Jesus as children usually stay with Him their entire lives. That's why I want Community Church to introduce as many children to Christ as possible."

"We try to do that here, too."

They stood looking at the windows in companionable silence a few moments longer, then Jason spoke. "I could stay here all afternoon, but I suppose we should move on."

Mary led Jason from the sanctuary into the administrative area. "I would introduce you to Dr. Whitson, but our pastor leaves at noon on Fridays to work on his Sunday sermon."

"I expect we'll meet at the Rock County Ministerial Association dinner later this month."

Next, Mary led Jason into the children's area of the educational wing, stopping to explain each area. As they went, he took notes and asked a few questions.

"These are the preschool and kindergarten classes. The youth painted the wall murals over the last few summers. The work gave those who weren't helping with Vacation Bible School something positive to do."

"Good idea. You don't have a day care program?"

"No. We don't really have anywhere to put one."

"I'd like to start one at Community. What about after-school programs?"

"Some of our kids come for one-on-one tutoring a few times a week during the school year, and volunteers open the church library from time to time in the summer."

"Programs like that can be a great outreach." Jason Abbott replaced his notebook in his shirt pocket, and Mary assumed he had all the information he wanted.

"Is there anything else you want to know?"

"I don't want to be a pest, but I understand you're doing something different for Vacation Bible School. Can you tell me a little about it?"

"Sure, but all the material is at my house. If you like, you can follow me home."

Jason Abbott's sudden smile transformed his unremarkable features. "Like a stray dog? If it's not convenient, just say so. I don't want to impose on you."

"You're not. Besides, I'd like your opinion of what we're doing."

"Since you put it that way, lead on, Miss Oliver."

"The children call me Miss Mary, but for you, Mary will do."

"I've been known as Brother Jason, Pastor Jason, and Pastor Abbott, but to my friends, I'm just Jason—and I'd like you to call me that, too."

"All right, Jason. We can go out this side door by the office."

∞

Instead of turning into the Oliver driveway, Mary stopped in front of the house. Seeing Sally Proffitt sitting on her front porch, Mary waved to her.

"I want you to meet my neighbor," Mary told Jason, and they walked across the street together.

Sally Proffitt stood, obviously curious about the strange man with Mary Oliver.

"Mrs. Proffitt, I'd like you to meet Jason Abbott. He's the new associate pastor at Community Church, and he's coming to my house to see the materials we're using at our Vacation Bible School this year."

Jason smiled and extended his hand. "I'm pleased to meet you, Mrs. Proffitt. You look like someone with Vacation Bible School experience yourself."

Sally Proffitt looked pleased. "In my time I worked with little ones, but my arthritis got so bad, I had to give it up."

Jason looked sympathetic. "Being with children is such a blessing, I know you must miss it."

For once, Sally Proffitt had nothing to say, and Mary took advantage of her silence. "Maybe you and Mrs. Suiter will consider helping us with the VBS refreshments this year," Mary said.

Sally Proffitt looked embarrassed. "We'll think about it."

Mary and Jason went back across the street to the Oliver house, leaving an obviously deflated woman behind.

"What was that all about?" Jason asked when Mary stopped to unlock the front door.

"I wanted Mrs. Proffitt to meet you. Otherwise, she would have wondered why you were here."

Jason smiled. "I know women like her. Every place has a few."

Mary decided to say nothing more about her nosy neighbor as they entered the house, dim and blessedly cool in the midafternoon heat.

Jason Abbott looked around. "I love your house. They don't make them like this anymore."

"If you saw the utility bills, you might understand why. We'll sit at the dining room table, where there's room to spread out the materials."

Mary excused herself to get her folders, then she stopped by the kitchen and returned with a tray bearing a pitcher of lemonade and a plate with the remaining brownies.

"You shouldn't have gone to all this trouble," Jason said when she put the tray on the table.

"I didn't. I made the lemonade at lunch, and the brownies were on hand."

Jason bit into one. "Umm, a homemade brownie. This is a real treat."

The way to a man's heart is through his stomach. Mary didn't know why the old saying had popped into her mind. She took it for granted that a man like Jason Abbott was already taken, so they could have no more than a shared professional interest.

Mary sat down beside Jason and opened the first VBS folder. "Here's the schedule we plan to use."

Jason surveyed the stack of folders spread out before him. "This took a lot of work. I can tell you're an organized, can-do person."

"I didn't do it all by myself," Mary hastened to say. "My committee did much of the daily plans."

"Even so, someone has to take the lead. I hope to find some Mary Olivers at Community Church."

She smiled. "There's only one of me in Rockdale, but the Community congregation has many talented people who love the Lord."

Jason nodded. "So I'm told. Unfortunately, Mark Elliott went out of town about the time I got here and won't be back for a few weeks. It's hard to get the full picture of our children's programs without the education director."

"You must have many other things to do in the meantime," Mary said.

"Oh, yes—when I was interviewed, the personnel committee made it quite clear I'm expected to wear many hats. However, Pastor Hurley shares my heart for children, and meeting their needs will be a top priority."

"I believe God gave me a heart for children, too." Mary had never said those words to anyone, yet she felt perfectly comfortable saying them to Jason Abbott.

He nodded. "That's obvious." He paused. "I'm glad He gave you the heart to help me, too."

Chapter 14

The hall clock was striking five when Jason Abbott stood to leave. Time had seemed to pass so quickly, Mary was surprised to realize Jason had been there almost two hours.

"I didn't mean to spoil your entire afternoon," he said.

"You didn't. I enjoy talking shop."

At the door, Jason paused. "I hate to admit it, but I'm not sure how to get back to the Rockdale Inn."

"You're not living at the Oaks?"

"Not yet. I still have stuff to move from Georgia."

Mary gave Jason directions, and when he started down the walk, she noted Sally Proffitt watched him from her front porch. *No doubt she's timed every minute of Jason Abbott's visit.*

Jason pulled away from the curb seconds before Wayne Oliver's sedan turned into the driveway. Mary was collecting her VBS material when her father came into the dining room.

"Who was that?" he asked.

"Jason Abbott—the new associate pastor at Community. I was showing him our Vacation Bible School materials."

"Is he the one they're having a reception for Sunday afternoon?"

"Yes. From what I hear, they're looking forward to having him there."

Wayne Oliver glanced at his watch. "Shouldn't you be getting ready for that rehearsal dinner?"

Mary guessed the source of her father's concern. "Are you going out tonight, too?"

"Yes and no. Evelyn invited me to have supper at her house around six."

She smiled. "Tell her I said hello—and don't rush home on my account."

∞

Other than serving at the reception, Mary wasn't involved in Hawk Henson and Anita Sanchez's wedding, so at first she hadn't understood why Hawk Henson invited her to the rehearsal dinner. However, when he explained Anita Sanchez would have no family members there, she had agreed to fill in for them.

Told to dress casually, Mary chose a lime green pantsuit from her school wardrobe, paired with comfortable low-heeled shoes. Even though she knew no one would care what she wore, she added gold earrings. As they should, all eyes would be on the happy bride.

Mary had refused Hawk's offer to pick her up, preferring to drive herself. That way, she could come home whenever she liked. She had just arrived at Rockdale Country Club when a male voice called her name.

Jason Abbott had also changed his clothes. He now wore a light-colored sport jacket over a cotton dress shirt, and polished loafers had replaced his athletic shoes. He looked slightly rumpled, as if his clothes had been removed from a suitcase without being pressed.

"I didn't expect to see you tonight," Jason said. "I'm supposed to go to the Henson-Sanchez rehearsal dinner. How about you?"

"Me, too, although I'm not in the wedding."

"Neither am I, but something came up, and Pastor Hurley asked me to take his place tonight. I haven't met either the bride or groom."

"You'll like them both," Mary said. "Anita Sanchez is originally from Colombia, and she doesn't have any relatives here. Hawk Henson has a large family, and he invited me so she won't feel so outnumbered tonight."

"Thanks for the information. Shall we go inside?"

∞

When they reached the private dining room where the rehearsal dinner was being held, Mary found herself in the odd position of introducing Jason Abbott and Hawk Henson.

"Thanks for coming. Pastor Hurley told me you'd pinch-hit for him tonight." Hawk shook Jason's hand, then motioned for Anita to join them. "Anita, this is Pastor Jason Abbott."

She smiled and took his hand. "I am pleased to have the honor to meet you tonight, since Hawk and I will not be here Sunday afternoon for your reception."

"I won't ask why not," Jason said, and they smiled.

"Mary, you sit next to Toni," Hawk directed. "Pastor, you sit beside Mary and Anita. When my aunt and uncle arrive, I'll ask you to pray, then the food will be served."

Jason nodded. "Let me know when."

Mary greeted Toni, and they talked briefly about the *Record* article concerning the Rockdale Civic Improvement Association. After the last of his relatives arrived, Hawk introduced them to everyone, then announced Pastor Jason would offer an opening prayer.

Jason stood and thanked God for the food and the occasion and asked a special blessing on the couple who would be married the next day and on the home they would establish together.

"That was nice," Mary said when he sat down. "It wasn't long, yet it said exactly the right thing."

Jason looked amused. "Thanks. I'm glad you approved of my first official function on behalf of Community Church."

Mary realized she had seemed to critique his prayer. "I don't have a habit of judging public prayers. It's just that even though my pastor, Dr. Whitson, is a fine man and a wonderful preacher, he's given to rather long public prayers."

"I hate to interrupt you, but please pass the salad dressing," Toni Trent said.

Mary did so, and Jason turned away to talk to Anita Sanchez. "I went to Guatemala on a summer mission trip once," Mary heard him say, and later they exchanged a few sentences in Spanish.

"Our new associate pastor looks like a real winner," Toni told Mary. "We love Pastor Hurley, but it's good to have someone young enough to bring in new ideas."

Mary told Toni about Jason Abbott's visit to First Church to discuss children's programs.

"That's interesting," she said. "It's too bad Jason's engaged. He'd be perfect for you."

Engaged? Mary swallowed hard and hoped Jason hadn't overheard Toni's remark. "You sound like the other matchmakers—you of all people should know better."

"I know David and I are blessed to be together. If God means for a match to be, it'll happen."

Jason turned back to Mary in time to hear the last part of Toni's statement. "What's going to happen?"

"The rehearsal," Mary said quickly.

Jason looked puzzled but didn't pursue the subject.

∞

"We're having a very simple wedding. I don't see why we need to rehearse," Hawk said when they entered the sanctuary.

"You need to know what to expect," said Toni, who served as the unofficial director. "You and Anita should be familiar with the music cues."

Mary settled into a pew to watch. After conferring with Toni, Janet Brown took her place at the electronic organ and played the final chords of a piece by Pachelbel, the signal for Jason Abbott, as Pastor Hurley, to emerge from a side door with David Trent, Hawk's best man.

Janet continued to play as little Juanita Sanchez walked in slowly, scattering pretend rose petals from the beribboned basket she'd use the next day. When Juanita reached the front, David had to remind her to take a few steps to the left and make a half turn before she stopped. When Toni came down the aisle next, David smiled as if remembering their wedding.

When Toni reached the altar and made her half turn, the organ struck the opening chords of the traditional music that launched tens of thousands of brides down thousands of church aisles annually. Mary, who was substituting for the mother of the bride, was the first to stand as Hawk and Anita entered together.

Mary's breath caught in her throat from the emotional impact of the love that shone so clearly from the couple's faces. When they reached the altar, Jason opened Pastor Hurley's book.

"Dearly beloved, we are gathered here," he began. Although he looked as if he'd like to continue, Jason stopped reading and addressed Hawk and Anita. "And so on."

After going through the ring ceremony, Jason told Anita and Hawk that Pastor Hurley would pronounce them husband and wife. "Then you'll turn and face the congregation."

"They have to kiss each other first," Toni said in a stage whisper, and everyone laughed.

"If you insist." Hawk barely brushed Anita's lips.

After another run-through with music, Toni decided they were ready for the real thing and reminded everyone what time they should gather at the church the next day.

"Thank you for filling in for Pastor Hurley," Toni told Jason. "Will you be at the wedding?"

"No. I have to go to Georgia to see about something."

Toni smiled. "Or someone? Anyway, you must be back for your reception on Sunday."

"Don't worry, I will."

Mary and Jason left the church at the same time and walked out into the soft summer night together.

"I'm sorry you'll miss the wedding," Mary said. "It should be a beautiful service."

"I know."

Mary was on the verge of asking Jason when he'd be rehearsing for his own wedding, but she didn't want to seem to pry. "I'll see you Sunday afternoon, then. Journey safe."

"Thanks. Good night, Mary."

On her way home, Mary realized she had enjoyed this evening far more than she'd expected. Anita and Hawk practically glowed with their love, and so did Toni and David Trent. And Mary supposed when she met Jason Abbott's fiancée, she'd see yet another devoted couple. *I am happy for them all, I really am.*

Why, then, did Mary suddenly feel so lonely?

～

Compared to other weddings Mary had witnessed over the years, the Sanchez-Henson ceremony was small and simple, but it had a special charm. Anita looked beautiful in her ankle-length light yellow dress. Her short veil was attached to a headband covered with yellow roses, and Juanita performed her flower girl duties flawlessly. Hawk and Anita spoke their vows in strong voices, and even the sometimes tricky candle-lighting worked perfectly. Community Church was filled to capacity, and the guests burst into spontaneous applause when Ed Hurley introduced two previous individuals as Mr. and Mrs. Hawk Henson.

"What a lovely couple they make," said Phyllis Dickson, who had hired

Anita to work at the Rockdale Hospital when she first came to town.

"That marriage was absolutely made in heaven," agreed Pastor Hurley's wife.

From her post at the serving table, Mary heard those comments and others like them. Many of the women had wept openly during the vows, and their eyes were still red.

Walter Chance approached in his Sunday-best navy blue suit, smiling broadly. "Hello, Mary. You giving away that punch?"

Mary handed Walter a cup. "I didn't see you at the wedding."

"I was in the sniveling section on the groom's side. If weddings are supposed to be so wonderful, why do women cry?"

Mary smiled. "Not all do, but in many cases, I think it's an emotional reaction to the couple's happiness."

"Or maybe sadness because two more singles are no longer on the marriage market."

What marriage market? No such thing existed in Rockdale, but Mary would never say so to Walter.

He stepped aside to allow Mary to serve punch to others, then accepted a refill. "Since we're already dressed up, how about going to Mentone tonight? I still owe you a first-class dinner."

"You don't owe me anything, but I can't go in any case."

His face fell. "Previous plans?"

"You might say that." In a way, it was the truth—Mary had planned not to go out with Walter Chance again, at least not for a long time, and she steeled herself against his sad, lonely-Walter look.

"Oh, well, there'll always be another time," he said.

"Good-bye, Walter," Mary said pointedly, and he moved on.

Juanita Sanchez, still giddy from her performance as flower girl, held out her punch cup for a third refill. "Who was that man talking to you, Miss Mary?"

"Mr. Walter Chance. He has a real estate office."

Juanita looked disappointed. "I thought maybe he was the husman you wished for when you blew out your candles."

Mary tried not to laugh. "In the first place, I didn't wish for a husband. Besides, Mr. Chance and I are old friends."

Juanita didn't look convinced. "When you do get a husband, can I be your flower girl?"

Mary hugged the little girl. "You were wonderful today, and I can't think of anyone I'd rather have as my flower girl."

Juanita's dark eyes shone with pleasure. "Really?"

"Really. But let's keep that our secret, shall we?"

Juanita nodded solemnly. "All right, Miss Mary. I won't even tell Jackie Tait, and you know she's my bestest friend."

A commotion at the other end of the hall signaled Hawk and Anita's approaching departure, and Toni Trent came over to head Mary and Juanita in that direction.

"Hurry up, Juanita, so you can see your mother throw her bouquet."

Mary had never tried to catch a bride's bouquet, and she didn't intend to start now. She stopped at the edge of the half circle of young women whose arms were stretched out to Anita. Once, twice, and a third time, the bride made as if she would throw her bridal bouquet but did not. Then, as the women were laughing and out of position, she tossed it up and over them in a perfect arc.

Mary saw it coming toward her, and when she raised her arms in self-defense, the bouquet flew into them.

Everyone cheered and clapped when they saw who had caught the bouquet. "Good for you, Mary Oliver!" someone cried out.

"There's Rockdale's next bride!" another declared.

Juanita beamed with pleasure. "See, Miss Mary! I knew you were going to get a husband."

"That's just an old tradition. It doesn't mean anything."

Juanita would not be dissuaded. "Yes, it does. It means I can be your flower girl. I'll save my basket."

"Hold up the bouquet," the wedding photographer told Mary, and she had to oblige, aware the pictures would show her as pink-faced and unsmiling. The photographer's flash temporarily blinded her, and when the picture taking finally ended, Mary handed the bouquet to Janet Brown.

"Would you put this in the kitchen cooler? Anita might want to preserve it later."

"I will—that's a good idea."

When Janet left, Mary turned to see a grinning Walter Chance at her side. "Good catch!"

She shrugged, aware Walter probably wouldn't believe she hadn't wanted the bridal bouquet. Many women in Rockdale probably thought Walter Chance was a good catch for some lucky woman, since he had money and his shrewish mother was no longer meddling in his life.

Mary fantasized about putting a notice in the *Record*, addressed to all single-but-searching women in Rockdale and surrounding Rock County: Attention, ladies! Want a man willing to spend money on you? Contact Walter Chance at Chance Realty during normal business hours or leave him a voice-mail message.

Seeing Mary smile without knowing the cause, Walter apparently took new hope and squeezed her hand.

Chapter 15

Mary and her father had kept the same Sunday ritual for years. Both rose early and read favorite sections of the newspaper before going to First Church for Sunday school and morning worship. From there, they went to Rockdale Country Club's Sunday buffet. Lately, however—or, more specifically, since Evelyn Trent had become an important part of Judge Wayne Oliver's life, there had been fewer "normal" Sundays. Evelyn liked going other places to eat after church, often with her brother, David, and his family and sometimes with Mary's father.

On this Sunday morning, Wayne Oliver told Mary he and Evelyn were planning to have lunch in Chattanooga.

"You'll miss the reception for Community's new associate pastor," Mary pointed out.

"I've already met him, and so has Evelyn. You can have our share of the little sandwiches and cakes and doodads."

"There will be plenty of those, I'm sure—Community does such things well."

"You can give Abbott my best wishes—I don't remember his first name."

"Jason. Jason Abbott."

"A pastor with a name from Greek mythology?"

"Jason is the Greek name for Joshua. It's in the Bible—a man named Jason was the Jewish convert who took Paul in at Thessalonica."

"You know more about the Bible than I do—I'll have to take your word that this particular Jason isn't a heathen."

Mary knew her father wasn't serious, but his remark made her realize she knew nothing about Jason Abbott's background, except that he and Ann Ward were cousins. Not, of course, that she should. *He's at Community Church, and I'm at First. We share an interest in our churches' children's programs, period.*

∞

As the eleven o'clock worship service began, Mary wished Jason Abbott could hear the grand swell of the pipe organ and see the sun stream through the stained glass windows. It would never happen, though. He would always worship at Community Church and she at First. And that was that.

However, Mary went to Jason's reception. The number of cars in the parking lot suggested many of Rockdale's residents had turned out for the occasion.

On her way into the church, Mary saw Audra Hurley, a high school classmate married to Police Chief Earl Hurley, the son of Community's pastor.

"I can't wait for you to meet our new associate pastor," Audra gushed. "You'll just love him."

"We've met," Mary said.

"Oh, that's right. Earl mentioned Jason filled in for his dad at the rehearsal. Wasn't that the most touching wedding? I cried so much, I went through three tissues."

"It was a lovely ceremony," Mary agreed.

"I'll see you later—I'm a hostess."

A little of Audra goes a long way. In their high school days, Audra Benson had led the in crowd of girls who delighted in making Mary miserable. It hadn't been easy, but with the Lord's help, Mary had forgiven Audra and the others for the pain they'd caused her, often thoughtlessly. While Mary and Audra could never be close friends like she and Toni were, they'd worked together well on several community projects, including their high school class's tenth reunion.

When Mary entered the fellowship hall, Toni Trent greeted her. "I'm glad you came. I don't have to ask why your father isn't with you—I know he and Evelyn went somewhere after church."

"Chattanooga, I think. Anyway, he's already met Jason."

"So have you, but go through the reception line, anyway. I want Pastor Hurley to see all the non-Community people."

While she waited in line, Mary noticed Jason Abbott wore a dark gray suit that looked new but didn't quite fit. His conservatively patterned tie was a good choice, but he kept running his finger under the neck of his shirt, the way Mary's father did when his collars had too much starch. *Jason Abbott needs someone to oversee his wardrobe.*

Mary quickly dismissed the thought. He reputedly had found such a person, and in any case, the way he dressed was none of her business.

But where was his fiancée? Mary had presumed she would be at the reception, but apparently she hadn't come. Jason stood between Pastor and Mrs. Hurley to greet those who had come to meet him.

Mary noticed Jason looked into each person's eyes as if genuinely interested in knowing more about them, just as he had done with her. The people's smiles made it clear the new associate pastor was winning many friends.

When it was Mary's turn to be introduced, Jason told Mrs. Hurley they'd already met. "Mary shared some wonderful information about First's children's programs with me."

"Good," said Pastor Hurley. "I hope you'll continue to help us out. As I told Jason, seeing to the children will be his top priority."

Mary believed she'd already given Jason Abbott all the information he needed, but to be polite, she nodded. "Of course. If there's anything else I can do, please let me know."

Jason smiled. "As a matter of fact, I have several things to discuss with you."

He turned to meet the couple behind her, and Mary went to the refreshment table, which looked suspiciously like the one from which she'd served punch the day before.

"Recognize the tablecloth?" asked Toni. "Janet and I recycled it from the wedding reception. We put a sandwich tray over the stain where someone spilled punch."

"That was one of Hawk's twin teenaged cousins. Tom or Tim—I never could tell them apart," Mary said.

"You did a good job yesterday," Toni said. "In fact, things couldn't have gone better."

Audra Hurley came over to survey the refreshment table. "Hi, Toni and Mary. I'm supposed to tell the kitchen hostesses if we're low on anything."

"The cucumber sandwich tray needs refilling, but everything else looks all right," Toni said. "I'd say things are going well."

Audra snickered. "The refreshments are, anyway. See Mother Hurley's corsage? We ordered it for Jason's fiancée. We thought she'd be here today."

"Why isn't she?" asked Toni.

Audra shrugged. "I don't know. Pastor Hurley said no one was coming, period. No reason."

"She's missing a good chance to meet everyone," Toni said.

Mary wanted to hear more about Jason Abbott's phantom fiancée, but someone else spoke to Toni, and Audra returned to the kitchen.

"This is an excellent turnout," Janet said.

"Yes, it is." Mary glanced at the receiving line, where Jason Abbott continued talking to all comers. "He must be getting thirsty. Someone should give him something to drink."

"The punch is too sweet. I'll get him a glass of water. Thanks for the suggestion—I'm sure he'll appreciate it."

When Janet handed Jason the glass, she pointed to Mary. He mouthed "thanks" as he lifted the glass in a mock toast, and Mary returned his smile.

Toni noticed the exchange between them. "What was that all about?"

"Nothing. I thought Jason needed something to drink, and Janet apparently told him so."

"Jason Abbott's a really nice person—I can't imagine what would keep his fiancée from being here today."

Neither can I. "I should be going," Mary said.

"I'll see you at the meeting," Toni said.

For a moment, Mary's mind went blank, and she almost asked, "What meeting?" before she remembered. "Yes. I hope the Civic Improvement Association on Tuesday night will have as good a turnout as this reception."

"Maybe you should have announced Jason would be on the program," Toni said lightly. "He'd be quite a draw."

"Yes, since Rockdale folks are so curious about anyone new. Too bad we didn't think of it before."

Toni laughed. "I'll tell him you said so. Good-bye, Mary."

∞

Mary had just changed into more comfortable clothes and settled down to finish the Sunday paper when the telephone rang.

"Mary? I'm glad I caught you at home. Are you busy this afternoon?"

She recognized Todd Walker's distinctive radio-announcer voice immediately. "I have been—I just got home. Are you in Rockdale?"

"Next thing to it—I'm staying at DeSoto State Park. I'd like to come by if you'll be home this afternoon."

"I will, but my father isn't here."

"No matter—you're the one I want to see."

"I'll be here," Mary said.

"Good. I'm on my way."

Why would a handsome man like Todd Walker waste a beautiful summer afternoon on me?

"It can't be anything personal," Mary said aloud, but the sudden rapid beating of her heart betrayed her.

Mary had a matter of minutes to make herself presentable before Todd Walker arrived. She put on calf-length white cotton pants and topped them with a long red-and-white striped short-sleeved blouse. With the addition of red-and-white earrings shaped like anchors, her ensemble was complete.

"Not bad," Mary told the hall mirror, then shook her head at her vanity. She had learned to make the most of her positive attributes so her size wouldn't be the first thing anyone might notice about her. Yet Mary never expected to attract the kind of attention from men that other women could almost take for granted.

She turned from the mirror as the doorbell rang.

"You must have broken the speed limit to get here so quickly," she told Todd.

"I cheated. I was on my way when I called you on my cell phone."

Mary motioned Todd to come inside. He pointed to his white twill slacks and red-and-white plaid shirt, then to her outfit.

"Looks like we had the same idea about a color scheme today," he said.

"You already know how much I like red."

"You should—it's your color, no doubt about it."

The compliment embarrassed Mary, and she spoke quickly. "Thanks. Can I get you something to drink?"

"No, thanks. We'll have something later, if you like. Right now, we're going for a ride."

"Will hiking be required?"

"Not this time. I'm in the convertible again, though, so you'll want a hat."

Mary took a wide-brimmed white straw hat from the hall closet. "I'm ready," she announced.

"You look very fetching, Miss Oliver. Your carriage awaits."

When they started to his car, Mary glanced across the street and Todd smiled. "I don't see your neighbor. Too bad—I would have invited her to come with us."

Mary laughed and took her place in the front passenger seat. Todd started the engine and turned the car around in the street. "Have you made progress on the bluff property we looked at last week?"

"Yes. I hope to close the deal tomorrow, but I decided to come a day sooner."

"Any particular reason?"

Todd glanced at her. "I wanted to see you."

Mary opened her mouth, then closed it quickly when her mind didn't immediately provide her with anything intelligent to say.

Todd appeared to be leaving town, but on the other side of the bridge, he pulled into a pocket-sized roadside park and stopped.

"I subscribe to the Rockdale newspaper now. When my copy came on Saturday, I read a story about a meeting of the Rockdale Civic Improvement Association Tuesday night."

Thinking Todd hadn't meant anything personal by saying he wanted to see her, Mary felt herself relax. "I know—I wrote it."

Todd didn't seem surprised. "It's a good article, but I wonder how many of the people in the organization really want to improve the community."

"All of them, of course. That's the whole idea."

"Yes, but exactly what is their idea of improvement? We're going back into town and drive around. When we do, I want you to try to forget you live here."

"Why?"

"Because until you see a place as an outsider, it's hard to detect any need for improvement."

"Oh, I think many of us know Rockdale could be a better place to live. The only question is how to accomplish it."

"Go along with me on this, Mary. Close your eyes, and when you open them on my count of ten, you will be seeing Rockdale for the first time. Understand?"

"I suppose so." Mary sighed, then closed her eyes. As Todd began his countdown, she stifled an impulse to laugh. *Your eyes are getting heavy—you will hear only my voice and you will do what I say. . . .*

Mary had never been hypnotized, but she thought Todd's smooth voice was well suited for such a practice.

"Three—two—one. Open your eyes. You are now prepared to see Rockdale in an entirely new way."

Mary had no idea what to expect, but she was willing to try to do as he directed. As Todd drove slowly through town, he asked her what she saw.

"A beautiful old courthouse," Mary said when they reached the square.

"Now what?" asked Todd when they reached Rockdale Boulevard.

"I hadn't really noticed it before, but a few businesses along here do look a little shabby."

"How long has that building been for sale?" he asked when they passed a neglected storefront.

"I don't know—a few months. Daniel Smith's copy shop was there, and after he left town, no one wanted to take it over."

"Does Rockdale have any upscale restaurants?" he asked.

"No."

"How about grocery stores? Are they clean and well stocked and large enough?"

"I don't have any trouble finding what I need," Mary said somewhat defensively.

"Remember, you're supposed to see the stores as an outsider, maybe someone from a place with lots of different kinds of chain stores. Do you find them here?"

"No, but I like to shop with people I know personally. You don't have that advantage in a bigger place."

Todd shook his head. "You're not playing by the rules." He reached the end of Rockdale Boulevard and pointed to the mountain rising before them. "One of Rockdale's biggest problems is staring you in the face right now."

"Rockdale Ridge? What's wrong with it?"

"Do you know who owns it?"

Mary shrugged. "Some lumber company, I think. Maybe the state has part of it. Why?"

"There's a major highway not three miles on the other side of that ridge. If Rockdale Boulevard were to be extended to meet it, the town would boom."

"Not everyone wants Rockdale to grow," Mary said.

"Unfortunately, that's a problem. The city fathers should be thinking about the benefits of planned growth. It could transform this whole area."

Mary didn't understand Todd's enthusiasm. "What's your interest in all of this?"

"My roots are here. I want Rockdale to be the best place it can be."

"What do you propose to do about it?"

He put the car in reverse and turned it around. "We can talk about that over dinner."

"Not much is open around here on Sunday night."

Todd grinned. "My point exactly. We're going elsewhere."

Chapter 16

This time when Todd took the road out of town and kept going, Mary thought he might be going to Mentone again. Instead, he turned onto the road leading to DeSoto State Park.

"I'm surprised you're staying at DeSoto Lodge," she said.

"It's usually full this time of the year, but I got a cancellation. Since it's halfway between Rockdale and Mentone, it's an ideal location. The food's good, and I thought you might enjoy dining there tonight."

Again, Mary thought. "I will, thank you. You haven't said how long you plan to stay."

"As long as it takes to do what's needed." Todd pulled into the lodge's parking lot and shut off the engine. "You have a subtle way of asking questions."

Mary returned his smile. "That's what teachers do."

"Relax. This is summertime. You're not on duty now."

Todd opened the car door and took Mary's hand. "The dining room hasn't opened yet, so we have time to visit the falls."

Mary pointed to her shoes, the same open-toed sandals she'd worn when Todd took her to Mentone. "You said we wouldn't be hiking."

"We're not. You've been here often enough to know the path to the falls is more a walk than a hike. In fact, I checked it out earlier today, and I can certify it's sandal safe."

"In that case, I suppose I'll go. It's been a long time since I've seen the falls."

As he had done in Mentone, Todd held Mary's hand as they walked. The afternoon was warm without being oppressively hot. Neither spoke, and Mary sensed Todd was enjoying the beauty of God's creation as much as she was and, like her, hesitated to spoil it by speaking.

They reached the top of the path, where water cascaded over a series of small waterfalls. Todd continued to hold Mary's hand even after they were seated on a bench overlooking the foaming stream.

For a time, the only sounds were those made by the falling water and calling birds. Finally, Todd broke their long silence. "Do you know you're very good company?"

Mary shook her head. "I don't know why you'd say that."

"Because it's true. Many otherwise attractive females talk too much. I can't stand a chatterbox. You're not like that. When you talk, you have something to say. I like that."

441

As if to prove him right, Mary said nothing, unable to think of anything sensible. She thought of the blond she'd met in Mentone and wondered if Todd considered Veronica, his fellow Haskell Holdings employee, a chatterbox.

"I've told you something I like about you," Todd said after a moment. "You're free to return the favor."

Mary smiled faintly. She'd never tell Todd Walker he'd been the love of her young life, so she said the first thing that came into her mind. "I suppose you know you have a wonderful voice. I like to listen to it, even when I don't understand what you say."

Todd laughed. "You've obviously never heard me sing. As for what I say, I know I tend to get carried away at times. What I've been trying to tell you all afternoon is simple. I'd hate to see the town of Rockdale dry up and die because a handful of its people are afraid of progress."

Mary quickly defended Rockdale's leaders. "It's not that way at all—the Civic Improvement Association wants to manage change, not stop it."

"It remains to be seen how they'll go about doing that."

"What do you think they should do?"

Todd smiled wryly. "Lots of things. For one thing, Rockdale needs more than one road to the outside world. For another, Rockdale and all of Rock County need to capitalize on their natural resources. Except for a little logging here and there, the land's going to waste."

Mary didn't know enough about those subjects to agree or disagree with Todd. "Come to the meeting Tuesday night and say so. They really want people to speak their minds."

"I intend to be there as an observer. I haven't lived in Rockdale for years, and I wouldn't want it to seem like I'm sticking my nose where it doesn't belong."

"If you care enough to take time off from work to come to the meeting, you deserve to be heard."

Todd looked away. "I'm not exactly taking time off from work."

He almost looks guilty. "I don't understand. What does Haskell Holdings have to do with Rockdale?"

Todd looked back at Mary. "Nothing. I'm here to check out some things in the area, that's all."

The thought occurred to Mary that Haskell Holdings could be one of the nameless entities rumored to want to buy land around Rockdale. If so, had Todd come to Rockdale on his behalf—or theirs?

Before Mary could find a tactful way to ask him about it, Todd glanced at his watch and stood. "The dining room should be open now. I haven't eaten since breakfast, and I make it a policy never to say anything important on an empty stomach."

Mary realized he was teasing and smiled. "And I make it a policy never to say anything important to a man at any time."

Todd's finger sketched an imaginary line in the air. "Bravo! Chalk one up for Miss Mary Oliver. She may not say much, but when she does, watch out!"

Todd held her hand all the way back to the lodge. At the porch, he stopped. "I want to get something from my cabin. I'll be back in a minute. Wait in the lobby—the mosquitoes will be thick on the porch this time of day."

Mary went to the ladies' room and ran a comb through her hair and powdered her nose. The mirror reflected unnaturally bright eyes, and her cheeks glowed, partly with the remnants of the sunburn she'd gotten the last time she was with Todd. The other cause, she suspected, also had something to do with him.

When Mary came back into the lobby, the dining room hostess spoke to her. Sally Richmond, now Morgan, she remembered.

"Hello, Mary. Are you and Walter here again this evening?"

"Hi, Sally. I am, he isn't."

"You're alone, then?"

Todd arrived in time to hear their exchange. "No, Sally. The lady's with me."

Sally looked flustered, and Mary remembered she and Todd had attended Rockdale High at the same time. From the way Sally and Todd looked at each other, she guessed they had dated.

"Good. As you can see, we're not at all crowded tonight. You can sit where you like."

Todd pointed to a window overlooking the lawn, now deeply shadowed. "Over there will be fine."

Sally led them to the table where Mary had sat when she met Jason Abbott for the first time, not a week ago.

"Do you come here often?" Todd asked.

"Not really, but in the past week I've been here for both lunch and dinner."

"Then maybe you can tell me what to order."

"I don't know what you like."

Todd smiled faintly. "I hope you're beginning to."

When the waitress came to the table, Todd waved off the menu and ordered two catfish dinners.

"I presume you love fried catfish and hush puppies as much now as you did when you were a kid."

"When did you ever see me eat catfish?" she asked.

"At a family reunion at my grandmother's house. The men had gone fishing that morning, and the women fried their catch. I was about ten, so you must have been all of five years old. I remember my mother telling your father you were eating too fast, and you might swallow a bone."

Mary didn't remember ever having catfish at Todd Walker's grandmother's house. "I think you made that up."

Todd smiled. "I guess that day didn't make as much of an impression on you as it did on me. Anyway, I brought these to show you." He opened the briefcase he had brought from his room and handed Mary a sheaf of detailed architect's drawings.

She read the heading of the first aloud. "Millican's Bluff: Concept One."

"What do you think of it?"

"It looks like a new building trying to pretend to be an old farmhouse."

Todd looked delighted. "That's exactly what I think. Check out the others and tell me which you like best."

Mary examined the drawings, which she took to be increasingly elaborate treatments of someone's idea of what should be built on Millican's Bluff, ranging from a restaurant to a medium-sized hotel and a large resort. Then she handed them back to Todd without comment.

"Well?" he prompted. "If you were in charge, which would you choose to build?"

"None of them. I would leave that gorgeous view alone."

Todd looked disappointed. "You know that's not going to happen. The land's just going to waste now. Think of all the money this project will pump into the area—all the people it will put to work."

"I know—but I still don't like spoiling God's natural beauty with artificial things, and I wouldn't want anything like that for Rockdale, either."

Todd drew back as if she had slapped him. "There's no danger of that. But towns are like people. They move forward, or they wither and die."

Which am I, Todd, withering or moving ahead? "Since you feel so strongly about it, come to the meeting Tuesday night and say so." *And stop badgering me about it,* Mary's expression added.

Todd's sudden smile surprised Mary. "I like your style, Mary. You're not afraid to speak your mind."

"Thanks," she said dryly. Todd's compliment wasn't exactly the kind to flutter a female heart. But then, Mary acknowledged, for years Todd Walker had that effect on her without saying a word or doing anything—something he would never know.

"Two catfish dinners," the waitress said. "Careful, the plates are hot."

"I really missed this kind of food in California."

"They don't have catfish? No wonder you came back."

By the time they finished eating, the sun had gone down and the sky had deepened into a purple twilight. On the drive back to Rockdale, Mary raised her face to the cool evening air and let it blow through her hair. Todd put on a CD of big band era instrumentals, and Mary leaned back into the soft leather upholstery and closed her eyes, relaxing as the music and the wind swirled around her.

The next thing she knew, Todd was shaking her shoulder. "Wake up—you're home."

Mary opened her eyes and sat up. "I wasn't asleep," she protested, but she hadn't remembered crossing the bridge back into town.

Todd came around and opened the door. "Looks like I'm too late for the garden tour," he said when they started down the walk.

"I'm afraid it's too dark to see anything now, but you can probably smell the jasmine and honeysuckle."

"Oh, yes—no man-made perfume can beat the real thing."

In the near-darkness, Mary fumbled with her key, unable to see the front door lock.

"Let me do that." Todd's hand brushed hers, and when the door swung open, he put his arms around Mary.

"So soft," he murmured.

Surprised by his sudden move, Mary stood quietly and waited to see what would happen next.

When he tightened his embrace, Mary instinctively raised her face to accept a kiss which seemed to last a long time.

When Todd released her, Mary realized they were standing in the doorway, half in and half out of the house. "We should close the door."

Todd stepped into the dark hall, pushed the door shut with his foot, and kissed Mary again.

Leaving one arm around his neck, Mary reached for the light switch with the other. When the light came on, Todd jumped back, startled. "Who turned on that light?"

"I did."

Todd looked sheepish. "I thought maybe the judge was lying in wait with his shotgun. I'd better leave before he gets home."

Mary smiled. "I've never known my father to point a shotgun at anyone."

"I don't want to be the first." Todd started for the door, then stopped to kiss Mary again, this time quite briefly. "I'll call you," he said, and with a final wave he was gone.

Before Mary closed the door behind Todd, she saw Sally Proffitt on her porch swing, outlined in the faint glow of her living room windows. Mary sighed and went back into the house, aware of two things—a man she had once adored had just kissed her, and if, as she suspected, Sally Proffitt had seen it, everyone in Rockdale would soon know it.

Chapter 17

Mary had just gotten out of bed Monday morning when she heard the back door close, signaling her father's departure. When she went into the kitchen for breakfast, Mary found his note on the small corkboard by the calendar.

> *You were in bed when I got home and still asleep when I left. If you have time today, my tan suit needs to go to the cleaners.*

The note was typical of those they had exchanged over the years, brief and to the point. It said nothing about his and Evelyn's trip to Chattanooga or what time he'd gotten home. Of course, her father didn't know everything about Mary's time with Todd, either.

Mary glanced at the calendar for the week ahead. Except for an appointment for a haircut Tuesday morning and the Rockdale Civic Improvement Association meeting that night, the squares were blessedly blank.

"I can use some time off," she said aloud. Mary had books to read and letters to write, but her first priority for the day was the garden.

After breakfast she put on the jeans, oversized shirt, and straw hat she'd worn on Decoration Day and started weeding the front flower bed and cutting the woody stems of bloomed-out hostas. As she worked, Mary thought about Todd Walker. She suspected the interest he'd shown in the Olivers' garden was more feigned than genuine.

Like his sudden interest in me. Mary couldn't believe that a handsome man like Todd Walker, up and coming in the business world, had twice sought her out, taken her to lunch and dinner—and then kissed her. Mary reviewed every word he'd spoken the night before. "You're good company," he'd said.

Mary sighed. *So is a golden retriever.* Although Todd had seemed to want to kiss her, she knew she shouldn't entertain romantic notions about him. If, as she vaguely suspected, Todd Walker had some hidden reason for paying her attention, she would be neither surprised nor hurt.

Mary worked in the flower beds for two hours, went inside for water and a brief rest, then spent another thirty minutes on the small plot by the kitchen door where her father had put out a dozen tomato and red and green pepper plants. He called it "his" garden, but Mary usually wound up weeding and mulching it. Noting the tomato plants would soon need staking, she posted a reminder to that effect on the cork bulletin board.

Mary was in the shower when the telephone rang. Todd Walker was her first thought—he'd promised to call. Then she decided it probably wasn't Todd, since he had business to transact that day and wouldn't likely be free to call until evening, if at all.

Mary towel-dried her hair and dressed in slacks and a knit top before going to the answering machine. She hadn't noticed it when she came inside, but the display showed two messages.

The first was from Walter Chance. "Hi, Mary. I'm making reservations at Mentone for Thursday night, so go ahead and mark your calendar. I'll catch you at the meeting tomorrow night—I'll be pretty much tied up until then. Have a great day!"

Mary could picture Walter smiling eagerly as he recorded the message. She felt irritated he took it for granted she would go out with him, but almost everything Walter Chance did these days seemed to grate on her nerves.

Where is your Christian attitude? Mary's conscience asked. *You should be thinking kind thoughts toward this man who thinks so much of you.*

I can't be too nice. Given an inch, Walter will take a mile.

Mary's conscience eventually won every argument, and this was no exception. *All right, I'll be kind to Walter, but that doesn't mean I have to go to dinner with him Thursday—or any other time.*

Having settled her mind about that, Mary played the second message, which was from another familiar and more welcome voice. "This is Jason Abbott calling for Mary Oliver. Thanks for coming to the reception yesterday. When you have a minute, please call me."

He added the church phone number and his extension, which Mary wrote down and dialed immediately. She feared she'd get his voice mail, but after the phone rang a few times, Jason answered, sounding a bit out of breath.

"Did I catch you at a bad time?"

"I was on my way to see Pastor Hurley when I heard my office telephone ring. I didn't know I could still sprint so fast. Thanks for returning my call. I thought you might be taking a well-deserved vacation this week."

"I was gardening this morning."

"I don't want to impose on you, since you've already given me so much help, but our church leaders are planning to remodel the educational wing. They hope you'll give us some good ideas."

"I don't know anything about remodeling a church," Mary said.

"You don't have to. It'll be some time before we add to the present space, but in the meantime, could you look at what we have now and give us some suggestions for improvement?"

Mary visualized Jason bent over the telephone, speaking earnestly, perhaps running his free hand through his unruly brown hair, and knew she couldn't refuse. "I don't know what sort of help I'd be—I know Community has an excellent Bible study program."

"That's true, but the children's space needs immediate improvement. You can help us with that if you can spare the time."

Mary pictured her almost-blank calendar. "I'm free on Wednesday. I can come by Community that morning, if that's convenient."

"That'll be perfect—say about ten o'clock?"

"All right. And while I'm thinking about it, I hope you're coming to the Civic Improvement Association meeting at the high school tomorrow night."

"I don't know much about it, but Pastor Hurley mentioned I should go."

"Definitely. Rockdale is going to change, no matter what, and my father and some others think we need to decide what kind of changes we want and how we want them made."

"Sounds like a good idea. I hope to see you there Tuesday night—and at Community on Wednesday morning?"

"Yes. I'll be there at ten." Mary hung up the telephone and added "Community Church—10:00" to the previously blank calendar square for Wednesday. Mary didn't regard helping Jason Abbott as a chore. She was quite willing to share her knowledge with someone whose enthusiasm for helping children develop a relationship with their Creator seemed to match hers.

You wish he weren't already taken.

The idea came as clearly as if a voice had whispered it in her ear. As much as Mary would like to dismiss it, deep down, she admitted its truth.

∞

Mary's father called around noon on Monday to say the Rockdale CIA committee would meet that evening at their house. "I hope you don't mind, but I invited Walter to sit in with us if he's free."

"Thanks for the warning," Mary said. "What time?"

"Six thirty. Should I pick up something on the way home?"

"Did you promise to feed them?"

"I mentioned we might have a few sandwiches and your famous orange mint iced tea."

"I have all the makings for that, but I wasn't planning on having company tonight."

"You're not—the committee is hardly company and they won't expect a feast."

"I'll take care of it."

"Thanks, puddin'. I can always count on you."

Mary smiled at his use of her pet name as she hung up the telephone. Over the years, her father had often called at the last minute to say he'd invited someone to supper. She enjoyed cooking and liked to prepare special dishes for guests.

She wasn't eager to see Walter Chance, but if he asked again, she'd tell him she wasn't going to Mentone with him on Thursday—or any other time.

But kindly, her conscience reminded her.

∽

"Time to get started," Wayne Oliver announced shortly after six thirty.

"Where's Walter?" asked Mayor Hastings. "I wanted to hear what he had to say about the quarry."

"He had to go out of town, according to Ellie Fergus, but she says he'll be back for the meeting tomorrow night."

Mary felt momentary relief, even though Walter's absence only postponed the inevitable. "There are sandwiches on the dining room table and the tea's on the sideboard. Please help yourselves."

The committee members did so, then sat down to discuss about how the meeting should be conducted.

"We should have a good turnout," Sam Roberts said. "Everyone who has come into the store since the notice came out on Friday wanted to talk about it."

"I hear Rockdale folks might not be the only ones there," Margaret Hastings said.

"Who else is coming?" asked Dr. Endicott.

The mayor shrugged. "According to the grapevine, several big developers want to see what we're up to."

Mary immediately thought of Todd Walker, but she remained silent. She hadn't had a chance to talk to her father about Todd, and this was hardly the time to bring it up.

"I wish they would," Sam said. "I'd like to see them keep a straight face while they try to say big box stores won't ruin a dozen businesses like mine."

"Or that what they want to do to make money won't hurt the environment," said Newman Howell.

"We don't yet know that's the case," Wayne Oliver reminded them. "However, once we have tougher zoning laws, the big bullies will leave us alone."

"I'm all for that," said the doctor.

"We'll put zoning first on the agenda. What next?"

Mary dutifully took notes, but as talk about the next night's program swirled around her, she realized all three of the men who had recently shown some kind of interest in her would be at the meeting.

Walter, Todd, Jason—each man different, each with so much to offer.

"If Rockdale doesn't make good choices now, we might never have another chance," banker Newman Howell said as everyone stood to leave.

"I like that—we should use it as our slogan," the mayor said.

Maybe I should, too.

In her heart, Mary felt the community wasn't the only thing about to have to make hard choices.

∽

As the committee hoped, many people turned out for the open meeting of the

Rockdale Civic Improvement Association. Mary had lettered a banner inviting them to join the RCIA for a five-dollar donation, and she and Ellie Fergus sat at a table set up outside the auditorium doors. Mary took the money and Ellie added the names and addresses to the roster.

Among the first to arrive, Evelyn Trent had already made out her check. "I've heard so much about this meeting, I feel as if I'm on the committee myself. If your father talks about it as much at home as he does when we're together, you're probably tired of hearing about this association."

Mary smiled at Evelyn's resigned tone. "After tonight, I suspect he'll have time for other important things."

"Let's hope you're right."

"I always wondered what it would be like to belong to the CIA," a man said.

Mary recognized his voice even before she looked up and saw his warm smile. "Hello, Jason. I'm glad you could come."

"You've cut your hair—I like it," he said.

Surprised he noticed, Mary murmured her thanks. Jason signed the list and had scarcely gone inside before Todd Walker appeared. He bent close to speak to Mary as if he didn't want to be overheard. "The bluff deal is a 'go,' but it's run me ragged the past two days. I wanted to call you last night, but some of the bigwigs came up from Birmingham to celebrate, and I couldn't get away."

Mary hadn't forgotten Todd's promise to call, but she didn't want him to think she felt disappointed he hadn't. "I'm glad things worked out for you."

"We can have our own celebration before I go back to Birmingham," Todd said. "How about lunch tomorrow?"

Mary thought of her commitment to Jason Abbott and shook her head. "Sorry, I'm tied up all day."

Todd looked disappointed. "In that case, I won't stay around tomorrow." He looked at her more closely and smiled. "Hey, I like your hair. There's even less to blow in the wind now."

Mary said nothing, but after Todd signed the list and moved on, Ellie Fergus shook her head. "It looks like my boss has some serious competition. Men don't usually notice a woman's hair has been cut, much less compliment her on it."

Mary chose her words carefully. "Todd Walker is one of my Austin cousins."

"And also one of the best football players Rockdale High ever sent to the university. I see Todd has a Birmingham address—what's he doing in Rockdale?"

That's a good question. "His roots are here."

"Maybe his job is, too—I hear he works for Haskell Holdings."

"Yes. They just bought property around Mentone."

"Walter tried to get that land himself."

Maybe that's where he went yesterday. "I didn't know that. Where is Walter? I haven't seen him tonight."

"He came early to set up the sound system. I'm sure he'll find you before the night is over."

Unfortunately.

Mary was relieved when others arrived at the membership table, ending their conversation. She didn't like to discuss either Todd Walker or Walter Chance with Ellie or anyone else.

When they heard Judge Oliver calling the meeting to order, Ellie urged Mary to go inside. "Don't you need to write minutes or something? I'll stay out here for the latecomers."

"All the comments will be recorded, so I won't take notes. I doubt if any one person could possibly keep up with everything, anyway."

Ellie smiled. "Or with all your admirers?"

Instead of denying she had admirers, Mary answered lightly. "They're under control, at least for now. Chief Hurley and Deputy Henson are both here in case a fight breaks out."

Ellie's laughter followed Mary into the auditorium, where Mayor Hastings invited the crowd to stand for the Pledge of Allegiance.

Mary thought the committee had chosen an excellent way to begin the meeting. What it would accomplish and how it would end remained to be seen.

Chapter 18

The auditorium was crowded, and after each of the original Rockdale CIA members made their opening statements, half the audience seemed to want a turn at the microphone. Mary stood at the rear of the auditorium and listened. When Todd Walker came forward to speak, a ripple of conversation swept through the crowd as people recognized then applauded him.

"Thanks, friends," he said when the applause died down. "It's nice to know my hometown hasn't forgotten me. I haven't forgotten y'all, either, and that's why I'm here tonight."

Each speaker was limited to three minutes, but Todd talked much longer. Mary didn't know when or how he'd learned public speaking, but he obviously knew how to use his powerful voice.

"A town like Rockdale will grow or die. The right outside interests will bring jobs and offer advantages you'd never have otherwise. Don't make the mistake of trying to keep everyone out, just because you're afraid things will change. They're going to do that anyway. It's up to all of us to make sure the changes are good ones."

When Todd Walker finished speaking to restrained applause, Walter Chance took the microphone.

"What Mr. Walker says is true up to a point, folks. The thing is, he doesn't live here now, and we do. Rockdale is ours, and if we don't take steps to protect it from the wrong kind of change, it'll be too late to complain about what happens. In case you don't know it, our zoning laws are a mess. It won't do much good to talk about pie-in-the-sky progress when we're mired down in mud-pie zoning."

The crowd laughed and applauded Walter. He lacked Todd Walker's ease or grace, but he'd obviously impressed the audience.

Who would have suspected it? Now that he was on his own, Walter Chance seemed on his way to becoming a community leader.

Other speakers followed. Most were complimentary of the CIA, but a few called them "the same old crowd."

"They're trying to fleece the city while crying wolf, but we won't let them pull the wool over our eyes!" one man declared, miffed when his mixed metaphor drew unintended laughter.

When it was obvious every relevant point had been made, Wayne Oliver stood and asked those present to help those in authority make needed changes. "If you haven't already signed up with the Civic Improvement Association, stop by the table on your way out and put your money where your mouth is. If you're willing to help on any of the committees we've talked about tonight, we have sign-up sheets for that, too."

"We do?" Mary asked Ellie, who had joined her to hear the final speakers.

"I think your father made that up on the spot, but I brought several spare legal pads."

"We'd better get busy and put them out."

After calling another meeting in two weeks, Wayne Oliver adjourned the first Rockdale Civic Improvement Association general gathering. Enough people came to the membership table to keep Ellie and Mary busy for another half hour. Mary expected Todd Walker to stop by, but apparently he had already left.

Wayne Oliver came out of the auditorium as Mary and Ellie were tallying the evening's contributions. "We can count the money later. It's been a long day, and I'm tired."

"Go on, Judge. I'll take Mary home."

Mary didn't see Walter until he spoke. Remembering her promise to her conscience to be nice to him, Mary forced a smile. "You don't have to do that, Walter. I'm ready to leave. By the way, you did a good job tonight. I didn't know you were such an accomplished speaker."

Walter glowed. "You think so? Maybe I should have left out the mud-pie part."

"Not at all—it made your point well," Mary's father said. "Come on, Mary. Ellie and Walter can deposit the money in the RCIA account tomorrow, can't you?"

"Of course," Ellie said. "I'll make a copy of the deposit slip for you."

Undaunted, Walter grinned. "I'll even deliver it to Mary in person."

Good. I won't be at home.

"That won't be necessary," Wayne Oliver said. "Drop it off at the courthouse."

"I'll see you later," Walter added to Mary.

"Walter did well tonight," her father said on the way to his car. "It's too bad you don't return his feelings, but from what I hear, he's not the only fish on your string."

"What are you talking about?"

"Todd Walker. Apparently several people saw you with him Sunday."

Sally Proffitt strikes again. "It's not secret—as I told you, he dropped in unexpectedly. You could have gone to dinner with us if you'd been here."

"I don't think either of you would have liked that."

"Todd's my cousin," she reminded him.

"Kissing cousin, apparently. After his speech tonight, I'm convinced Todd's company has some kind of plans for Rockdale. I wish I knew what he was up to."

"Then ask him."

"The next time he comes to see you, I will." Wayne Oliver rubbed his shoulder. "This was quite an interesting night. I think change is definitely in the air."

"So it is," Mary agreed, but she doubted she and her father were thinking about the same things.

∞

Mary reached Community Church at precisely three minutes before ten on Wednesday morning and saw Jason Abbott waiting for her just inside the main entrance. Mary recognized the shirt and slacks he'd worn the day they met; neither seemed to have been pressed since.

Jason smiled and extended his hand. "Thanks for coming. I see you brought a clipboard."

"I like to take notes and make sketches when I tour a facility, and my clipboard serves the purpose well."

"Another good idea. Would you like coffee or a sweet roll before we start? Mrs. Hurley keeps us well supplied."

"No, thank you. I'm ready to begin the tour."

"Follow me, then."

Mary quickly understood why Community wanted to add more space. The church had grown tremendously in the last few years, and rooms which had once been adequate for infants, toddlers, and other preschool groups were now crowded. Children's classes had been moved into larger rooms recently vacated by older youth and adults, who now met in portables outside the church proper. However, nothing had been done to make the children's new spaces attractive.

As Jason had done at First, Mary asked a few questions and made notes as they went. "These halls would be perfect for Bible school murals."

"I don't know if our youth are as talented as the ones who did yours," Jason said.

"No talent required—I can show you how to take a sketch and enlarge it on a grid projected on the wall. From there, it's a matter of coloring in the lines."

When Pastor Hurley saw them in the hall, he invited Mary and Jason into his office, where they talked for some time.

"Tell your father I think the Civic Improvement Association is off to a good start," the pastor said when Jason and Mary stood to leave.

"He's worked very hard on it. He'll be glad to hear that."

"I thought it was a productive meeting," Jason told Mary when they left Pastor Hurley's office. "Rockdale seems fine the way it is, but I suppose there's always room for improvement."

Mary glanced at her wristwatch, ready to make a graceful exit, but Jason didn't seem to want her to go.

"I'll show you my office. After I check my messages, we'll go to lunch."

"Oh, no, you don't have to do that."

"I want to."

Mary followed Jason down a narrow hall to a small office filled with boxes marked "books."

"Excuse the mess. I seem to have a larger library than Community has shelves."

"Cozy," Mary commented. The word sounded better than her first impression: cramped.

"It's adequate. When the educational facilities are remodeled, I'm told I'll have a much larger office."

Mary stood near the door and looked around the windowless cubicle while Jason accessed the voice mailbox on his telephone. His desk was all but covered with assorted papers and folders. A small artificial African violet plant and a framed picture of a curly-haired child on one corner were the desk's only decorations.

"No messages," a hollow electronic voice reported, and Jason replied to it in the same robotic tones. "Thank you. Have a nice day."

Mary laughed. "You imitate your machine very well."

"Why not? Machines are always imitating us."

Mary pointed to the picture on his desk. "Who's the adorable child?"

"My nephew, Mack. That was taken last year just before his long curls were cut."

What about your fiancée? Where is her picture? Before Mary could summon the courage to speak, Jason asked if Statum's would be all right for lunch. "I'd rather go to DeSoto Park, but there isn't enough time for that today."

"You don't have to feed me at all," Mary repeated.

"I know, but I have a few more questions to ask about the primary department. Call it a business lunch."

Mary smiled faintly. "In that case, it's all right."

∞

Statum's Family Restaurant was filled with the usual assortment of workers from nearby businesses and offices. In addition to the seated diners, many others came in for takeout service.

When Mary and Jason entered, Tom Statum motioned them to a just-cleared booth at one of the large plate glass windows. "Hello, Pastor Jason, Mary. Have a seat. Rita will be with you in a second."

Several diners turned to greet Jason or Mary or both, their eyebrows raised in question. If Jason noticed, he made no comment, and Mary saw no reason to point it out to him. Every pastor lives in a fishbowl, Mary once heard. So does every teacher, she had thought at the time. In a small town, anyone in those fishbowls was bound to be a topic of conversation.

"You've no doubt eaten here many times. What's good?" Jason asked.

"The plate lunches are excellent, but I don't usually have that much for lunch."

"Neither do I—in fact, I sometimes forget to eat at all. Pastor Hurley said I should stock my office with fruit and crackers and instant soup so I won't waste away."

"I don't know where he thinks you'd put anything else in that office," Mary said.

When the waitress appeared to take their orders, Mary said she would have her usual. "I will, too, whatever that is," Jason added.

The waitress looked doubtful. "Most men want more than a fruit salad plate. Wouldn't you rather have fries and a cheeseburger?"

"No," he said firmly, "but make my fruit salad a club sandwich on whole wheat, light on the mayo."

"Can do." The waitress took the menus and departed.

"I suppose you and your father must know everyone in town," Jason commented when Mary introduced him to several people who stopped by the booth.

"In a place this size, that's not hard. You must have grown up in a big city."

"A few towns and several cities. My father was a minister, and we hardly ever stayed in any one place more than four or five years."

"So you're a PK? A preacher's kid who became a preacher, no less. Ann didn't tell me that."

Jason smiled. "She still can't believe I followed in my father's footsteps. So many people assume ministers' families are going to be rebellious, and a lot of them turn out to be."

"But surely you weren't ever that way yourself?"

Jason's smile faded. "Only with the Lord."

Before Jason could explain his meaning, Walter Chance entered the restaurant and made a beeline for Mary.

Mary's heart sank as Walter looked from her to Jason and held out his hand. "I don't believe we've met, but you're Justin Abbott, Community's new assistant pastor, right? I'm Walter Chance. Chance is the name, and real estate's my game."

"Jason," Mary corrected as the men shook hands. "It's Jason Abbott."

"Close," said Walter, then returned his attention to Mary. "Our Mentone reservation is for seven," he said clearly. "I'll pick you up around six."

Mary groaned inwardly, not only because of what Walter had said, but because Jason Abbott—and everyone else in the restaurant—had heard it.

"I can't go," she said, but Walter had already turned away to pick up his take-out order. It would only make matters worse if she followed him to repeat she wasn't going to Mentone.

"Nice fellow you have there," Jason said cautiously.

"He's not my fellow. I've been trying to tell him so for days, but he won't listen."

Did I actually tell Jason Abbott that? Mary closed her eyes and put her hands to her flaming cheeks in embarrassment.

She opened her eyes and saw Jason's amused look. "I don't know why anyone wouldn't want to listen to you. I certainly enjoy it."

You do? Mary sipped her water and felt her composure gradually returning.

Thanks to Jason Abbott. He had turned what could have been a humiliating experience into something positive.

"In fact," Jason continued, "I'd like it very much if you could show me some of the local sights tomorrow. I know you're a good tour guide."

"Tomorrow?"

"Yes. Consider it as a community service."

"In that case, I don't suppose I can refuse."

"Good. I have a couple of early appointments, but I should be free around ten. We can have lunch at DeSoto State Park after the city tour."

"Here's your order."

Until Rita set the platters on the table between them, Mary hadn't realized she'd been leaning forward, hanging on Jason's every word. Once more she felt everyone in the restaurant must have noticed.

"Is tomorrow settled, then?" Jason asked when Rita left.

"Yes. I look forward to it."

Mary meant every word.

Chapter 19

For her role as Jason Abbott's tour leader, Mary settled on a lime green pantsuit with a long, slimming top. She further prepared by wearing walking shoes, locating her straw hat, and putting bug spray in her purse.

Just before ten o'clock, Mary looked out and saw Sally Proffitt sweeping her front walk. A moment later, Jason's car stopped in front of Mary's house. She watched him get out of the car and wave to her neighbor and opened the front door in time to hear their shouted agreement it was a lovely morning.

"It seems you've made a new friend," Mary commented when they started down the walk.

"I hope so. Being new in town, I need all of those I can get."

Mary waved to Sally Proffitt while Jason opened the car door for her. Friend or not, Sally probably wondered what Jason and Mary were up to now.

"Where would you like to start your tour?" Mary asked.

"Pastor Hurley took me around the main streets and showed me the park, but I haven't seen the town from the ridges. Even though Community Church is right at Warren Mountain, I've never been to the top."

"We'll go there first."

"I talked to Ann last night," Jason said on the way. "She was happy to hear we'd met and said to tell you she's glad you're helping me."

"She'll be a wonderful teacher. I hope we can stay in touch."

"Ann feels the same way."

At the summit, Mary directed Jason to the grassy area used as a parking lot for the amphitheater built into the far side of the mountain. "Community has a beautiful Easter Sunrise service here every year. My father and I never miss it."

Jason was obviously impressed. "I can see why. This is a spectacular setting. The rock formation on the left looks like my idea of the garden tomb."

"Doesn't it? I get chills just thinking about it."

Jason took Mary's hand as they walked down the rough-hewn steps to the bottom of the hill. They looked out in silence over the valley below for a moment before returning to the car.

"I'm surprised this area isn't covered with houses," Jason said.

"We can thank Congressman Winter and his Warren kin for that. They still own a lot of the land and want to keep the top pretty much as it was when their Cherokee ancestors hid out here instead of being forced to walk the Trail of Tears."

"I understand Hawk Henson's ancestors came here for the same reason," Jason said.

"Some Cherokee living around the Tennessee River were rounded up, but others saw what was going on in time to get to the mountains. They had hunted here, and they knew no one would likely bother to look for them in this wilderness."

"That Native American removal was a terrible business," Jason said. "Now that I've seen Warren Mountain, I'd like to take a look at that ridge on the opposite side of town."

"It's called Oliver Mountain." From his smile, Mary decided Jason must already know that.

"Were your folks running from the soldiers' roundup, too?" Jason asked.

"No. Both sides of my family were living in Virginia in the late sixteen hundreds. They moved to North Carolina and Georgia before settling here around 1830. How about your family?"

"The Abbotts were English, but I don't know much more than that."

They reached the base of Warren Mountain, and Mary directed Jason to the street leading to the winding Oliver Mountain road.

"I don't see houses on this ridge, either," Jason observed as they neared the summit.

"Not now. The first Oliver and Austin families lived up here, but after a fire in the late eighteen hundreds, my great-grandfather moved off the mountain and built the house we live in now. Our family cemetery is here, so we'll never sell off any of our part."

"You don't own it all?"

"No. My mother's people, the Austins, had the parcel overlooking Rockdale."

When they reached the crest of the ridge, Jason parked the car, and he and Mary walked into the cemetery. "What a great last resting place—I know it takes hard work to keep a place like this up."

"Our relatives get together and clean it each Decoration Day, and my father and I work on it at times during the year."

"Tell me about the people buried here." Jason's tone indicated his interest, and Mary led him to the headstones Todd Walker had recently cleaned.

"Warren and Mary Austin were my great-great-great-grandparents on my mother's side. Theirs are the oldest graves here. Their daughter married the first Wayne Oliver. He and his wife are buried over there."

"What about all these smaller headstones?"

"Infants and small children. Many died young in the early days."

Jason stroked the weathered head of a cherub above a small child's grave. "After all these years, it's still sad to see these."

" 'The Lord giveth, and the Lord taketh away, blessed be the name of the Lord,' " Mary read aloud from an adjacent headstone.

"At least they had a strong faith. That's a great heritage for any family."

When they finished walking around the graves, Mary pointed to the road leading to the end of the ridge. "You can see a lot of Rockdale from here."

"Should I get the car?" Jason asked.

"No, it's an easy walk, but we need to take precautions against chigoes. The spray is in my purse."

"It seems I have a lot to learn about country life."

"Chigoes are good teachers." Mary used the spray and handed it to Jason.

Thus prepared, they started walking, and Jason again took Mary's hand. When they reached the meadow where she and Walter Chance had recently stood, Mary stopped short and put her free hand to her throat. Pink plastic ribbons fluttered from the top of a series of wooden surveyor's stakes.

"These stakes weren't here last week."

"It looks like somebody may be planning to build up here."

"I don't know why—the meadow is too far from the edge to get the benefit of the view."

"Who owns this land?"

Mary shook her head. "I don't really know—it's passed through many hands in the past century." *But this is Austin land, and Todd Walker's mother was an Austin.*

"Where's the view of the town you mentioned?"

"To the right—we're almost there." Disturbed by what she had just seen, Mary led Jason to the edge of the bluff. *I must find out who made that survey.*

"Wow," Jason said when they reached the edge.

Although Mary had seen the sight numerous times, she felt the same way. She pointed to the spire of First Church and the dome of the courthouse, both almost hidden by surrounding trees. "After the leaves fall, you can see much more."

"It's like looking down at the land when you first take off in an airplane." After a moment, Jason glanced at the ground and kicked at a loose rock beside his foot. "Anyone living here would have a spectacular view, but this rock outcropping would be expensive to build on."

Mary didn't repeat Walter's opinion that the land was suited for a quarry. The less said about him, the better.

"Not only that—I'd rather look up at the mountain and see trees than a house." *Or a quarry.*

"So would I. What else do you suggest I should see today?"

"Pastor Hurley probably took you out Rockdale Boulevard. Did he say anything about the ridge where it dead ends?"

"No. Is it special?"

"It could be." Mary repeated what Todd Walker said about adding a connecting road and developing the land around it.

"That would cost a ton of money. Who would pay for it?"

"Someone who thought the return would be worth it, I suppose. I can't imagine what Rockdale would be like if that happened."

Jason smiled faintly. "You sound like someone who wants things to stay the way they are."

"Some things."

"From what I heard last night, that might not be possible."

"I know, but I like Rockdale the way it is now."

"So do I. At least I like what I've seen so far."

Jason's smile made his comment personal. Flustered, Mary turned from the bluff. "We should go now. DeSoto fills up early for lunch this time of year."

∞

On the drive out of town, Jason asked Mary about the school system.

"Rockdale isn't perfect, but it's a good place for children to grow up," Mary concluded.

"With teachers like you, I can see why."

Jason spoke so matter-of-factly, Mary didn't think he meant to flatter her, as Walter Chance seemed so fond of doing. Mary admitted Jason's comment probably meant more to her than it should have, and she could think of no adequate reply. "You've never seen me teach," she finally said.

"I don't have to. Your eyes light up when you talk about children, and I've noticed the way you interact with them. All the programs in the world mean nothing if the teacher doesn't love children."

"Like 'a resounding gong or a clanging cymbal'?" Mary began quoting from 1 Corinthians 13.

Jason nodded. "Exactly."

They were still talking easily when they entered DeSoto Park Lodge, and Mary realized there had been no awkward silences between them. Even when neither spoke, the time between their conversations seemed comfortable.

Dining room hostess Sally Morgan raised her eyebrows when Mary and Jason entered. "Hello, Pastor Jason. Hi, Mary."

"Hello, Mrs. Morgan. Mary's been helping me plan the children's program at church. As I mentioned the other day, Pastor Hurley and I hope you and Ted will work with us on it."

Sally shrugged. "My husband doesn't think he can teach little children. He's afraid he'd be out of place."

"I disagree. Tell Ted we'll talk about it soon."

"That would help." Sally Morgan smiled slightly as she reverted to her hostess role. "Do y'all want the buffet today?"

"Yes, we do."

"Since it's not raining, you can have a window table."

"What did she mean by that?" Jason asked after they were seated.

"Sally knows I stay away from windows during storms."

"Another good idea. Maybe I should start writing them down."

Mary replied in the same light tone. "I don't think anyone would want them."

"That's their loss. I know a good thing when I see it."

Mary accepted his words as friendly banter. After all, a man like Jason who was engaged to one woman wouldn't seriously compliment another.

∽

Jason had never seen Lodge Falls, so after they ate, Mary took him on the now-familiar path. She felt a strong sense of déjà vu as they stood together and watched the water for a while, then sat in silence on the same bench she'd recently shared with Todd Walker.

Jason had held her hand on the path, but he released it when they were seated. He looked out over the water as if not really seeing it, and Mary wondered what he was thinking.

As easy as conversation between them had been, Jason had said little about his personal life and nothing at all about his fiancée. After sitting beside him in silence for some time, Mary decided their friendship allowed her to bring up the subject.

"I hope your fiancée will like Rockdale."

Jason looked startled. "My fiancée?"

"The woman you plan to marry. Everyone says you're engaged."

Jason's brow furrowed, and he shook his head. "I'm sorry about that. It was all a misunderstanding."

"You thought you were engaged, but you're not?"

"No. I mean I'm not engaged, and I never was. When Pastor Hurley interviewed me, he asked if I planned to marry, and I said I did. I meant it in general terms, but he took it to mean I was already committed to someone."

But he's not. Jason Abbott isn't taken, after all! Mary's heart soared. "That must have been embarrassing."

"It was. Especially last Sunday when they ordered a corsage for my nonexistent fiancée."

"What did you tell them?"

"I left it up to Pastor Hurley. He decided against making a public announcement, but if anyone asks, he confirms I'm not engaged."

"That should make a lot of Community Church women glad."

Mary's tone was light, but Jason's response wasn't.

"I told Pastor Hurley the truth. I believe God's plan for my life includes marriage and a family someday."

Mary's sincerity matched his. "Then He will let you know when that time comes."

"How about you? Do you believe God really wants you to remain single?"

His question caught Mary off guard. "I told you I was called to be a teacher. I haven't heard any further call."

"I wonder if you're listening."

Jason's query made Mary uncomfortable. "I—I hope so."

"I would have said the same thing once. When I was in college, I wanted a career in business so much, I didn't ask if God approved. When I landed a high-paying position with a big firm in Atlanta as soon as I graduated, I took it as a sign God blessed my choice."

"Obviously, you changed your mind," Mary said after a moment.

"No, God changed it for me. It didn't take me long to realize I'd always be miserable doing what I wanted. From the moment I gave Him all my life and sought His will in everything, God began to lead me into the ministry. The journey hasn't always been easy, but I felt His presence every step of the way."

"I always wanted to be a teacher," Mary said. "I felt that calling so strongly, I never even considered doing anything else."

"That doesn't mean God doesn't have something else in store for you. Three months ago, I'd never heard of Rockdale, yet here I am. I believe it's for a reason."

"So do I," Mary murmured.

Jason stood, signaling his readiness to leave. On the drive back to Rockdale, he described some of the part-time jobs he'd had while attending seminary, and Mary told him about the mission trips she'd taken while in college.

"At one time I thought of becoming a missionary, but God didn't open those doors, so I came back here."

"From all reports, your Rockdale first-graders are your mission field."

Mary smiled faintly. "That sounds like Toni Trent. She thinks of her work for Rock County in the same way."

"She's not the only one. Anita Sanchez—I mean Henson—can't say enough nice things about you. But even before they said anything, I knew from Ann you had a special gift for working with children."

"No, it's the other way around. The students I teach and the children at First are a precious gift. I try to do my best for them."

"I know—it shows."

The admiration in his voice embarrassed Mary, and as much as she had enjoyed being with Jason, she was glad they had reached her house. She thanked him for lunch and automatically invited him to come inside. He politely declined, then surprised Mary by shaking her hand.

"Thanks for the tour and for all the other help. You don't know how much I value your friendship."

Jason's words cut Mary as no knife could have. She wanted to tell him she was willing to be more than his friend, but he was gone before she could frame the words.

As she closed the door, Mary imagined what Sally Proffitt might tell Jenny Suiter this time. "From the way they shook hands when he brought her home, I'd say nothing's going on between Mary Oliver and that new Pastor Abbott, after all."

Chapter 20

Mary was still going over every detail of her day with Jason Abbott when Walter Chance called to say he'd pick her up at five o'clock.

Jarred back to the present, Mary spoke more harshly than her conscience liked. "No, you won't. I tried to tell you at Statum's I couldn't go."

"I guess I didn't hear you." Walter paused. "Are you all right? You sound funny."

I feel funny, too. "I'm fine, but I won't go out with you again, so please don't ask me."

"Is it the judge? I thought he liked me."

He probably likes you better than I do. However, Mary resolved to be kind. "My father believes you have a good head on your shoulders. Maybe you can help solve a mystery."

Walter sounded bewildered. "The way you're acting is a mystery to me."

"Who put those survey stakes on Oliver Mountain?"

Walter's slight hesitation spoke volumes. "What stakes?"

"I think you know."

"Don't worry about it."

"Walter Chance, don't try to hold out on me."

He laughed ruefully. "I'm not. I planned to tell you about it at dinner tonight."

It was Mary's turn to hesitate, but only momentarily. "Tell me what? If you know anything about Oliver Mountain, you should share it."

"That's what I was trying to do. Are you sure you can't go tonight?"

I won't go, not just can't. "I'm positive. Good-bye, Walter."

Mary hung up the receiver before Walter could say anything else.

When her father came home, Mary told him about the stakes she'd seen that morning.

"That's odd. Why would anyone survey that land?"

Mary debated how to tell her father the little she knew. "The stakes are on the meadow side, not the bluff. I'm beginning to believe Walter knows more about several things than he's told us."

"Such as?"

"Apparently he bid on the bluff land around Mentone that Todd Walker's company bought. I wouldn't be surprised if he's already taken options on the land at the foot of Rockdale Ridge."

Wayne Oliver looked thoughtful. "I suppose that might explain why he's pushing new zoning laws, but he agrees there can't be a quarry on Oliver Mountain."

"If you ask him about the stakes, he'll probably tell you what he knows."

"I want to see them for myself. Do you want to go with me?"

"No, thanks. I'll stay here and start supper. You'll need the bug spray—it's in my purse. Jason and I used it this morning."

Her father shook his head. "Jason Abbott, Todd Walker, Walter Chance—you're always going out with some man or the other these days."

"It only seems that way. Anyway, it doesn't mean anything."

He looked thoughtful. "Maybe it will. You know I'd like to see you marry."

So would I. Mary's realization she didn't want the Oliver line and heritage to end with her had been slow to come, but now Mary felt ready to welcome marriage—if it was in God's plan.

"I suppose stranger things have happened," she said.

∞

Shortly after her father left, the telephone rang.

"I hope I didn't catch you at a bad time," Todd Walker said.

What does he want? "I'm about to start supper."

"I'm sure it'll be something good."

"Join us if you're in Rockdale."

"Unfortunately, I'm not. I have business in Rockdale tomorrow, though. I'd like to see you."

"Why?"

"Do I need a reason to want to see you?"

No, but I'd like to know what you're really up to. "What time?"

"Around noon."

"All right."

Todd's tone lightened. "I like a woman of few words. I'll see you tomorrow."

Mary returned to her supper preparations, her mind in turmoil. She should be happy Todd Walker wanted to see her. Why, then, didn't she look forward to meeting him again?

∞

Over supper, Mary's father told her what he'd found.

"The stakes you saw today have nothing to do with the bluff property. I intend to find out why they're there."

"Walter didn't say who owns the meadow land. Do you know?"

"Yes."

"Care to share it with me?"

"Not just yet."

"I almost forgot—Todd Walker called while you were gone. He's coming to Rockdale on business tomorrow."

Her father raised his eyebrows. "Really? Have him call me. We have some matters to discuss."

∞

Mary didn't care to be seen with Todd Walker at Statum's, nor did she want to go out of town for lunch again. Instead, she put together chicken salad, fruit trifle, and orange mint tea and set the kitchen table with the everyday stoneware.

She doubted Todd Walker had come to Rockdale to see her, but when Mary opened the door to him, she realized anew how handsome he was. Any woman ought to be proud to be seen with such a man.

"Come in," Mary invited.

"No—come out and we'll go to lunch," he countered.

"We're eating here. I hope you like chicken salad."

"I do, but I planned to take you somewhere special."

"Too late! Your lunch awaits. We'll eat in the kitchen—you can wash your hands at the sink," she said cheerfully.

Mary feared she might have overdone being casual, but Todd didn't seem to mind. "I enjoy being treated like home folks."

"You are. After all, we're kin."

Todd smiled when she offered him a towel to dry his hands. "Kissing kin." He bent his head and brushed her lips lightly. "That's the best kind."

Without comment, Mary took her place at the table and offered grace.

"That was nice," he said, and Mary suspected it had been a long time since he had heard thanks returned.

"How did your business go?" she asked.

"Very well. It's not official yet, so you're the first to know. After I told my bosses Rockdale will support it, Haskell Holdings agreed to build a recreation complex at the foot of Rockdale Ridge."

"Something like that is certainly needed," Mary said.

While he ate, Todd spoke glowingly of the plans for a swimming pool, lighted tennis courts, and all-purpose recreation center.

A suspicion dawned in Mary's mind. "You must have been working on this for a long time." *That's the real reason you came here on Decoration Day.*

Todd tried to sound modest. "Other people had already drawn up preliminary plans. I helped site the final design."

And I suppose you also promised to get local approval, starting with the help of the influential Judge Oliver. "It seems you've earned another feather in your cap."

"That remains to be seen." He leaned back in his chair and smiled at her. "I don't know which was better, the food or sharing it with you."

That sounds a lot like something Walter Chance would say. "Are you ready for the garden tour now?" Mary asked.

"Later. I want you to see something. Get your hat and let's go."

Seems to me I've heard that before. Mary glanced at her sandals and sighed. "I'll change shoes and be right back."

∞

Todd was driving his truck, and Mary felt a sense of déjà vu when he turned onto the winding Oliver Mountain road.

"Are we going to the cemetery?" she asked.

"No."

Without comment, Todd drove to the edge of the meadow, where several sets of tire tracks gave evidence of recent activity in the area. As Todd helped Mary from the truck, the sun went behind a dark cloud, and the survey markers' plastic streamers danced in the freshening breeze.

Mary shivered, and Todd put his arm around her shoulders. "I used to play here in this meadow on Decoration Days while my folks worked in the cemetery."

"What do you know about these stakes?" she asked.

Instead of answering her question, Todd countered with another. "Look around, Mary. What do you see?"

"A flat meadow and a rocky bluff. Why?"

"From a height of twenty-five feet, the view of Rockdale would be terrific— the whole town would be at your feet."

Mary voiced her suspicion. "Does Haskell Holdings have something to do with these stakes?"

Todd sounded astonished. "Of course not. Why would you think that?"

"You work for them."

"Yes, but that's not why I had this plat surveyed. Don't you see? It's the perfect place for a house."

Mary felt confused. "I didn't know you owned this land."

"I don't."

"Who does?"

"You really don't know?"

Mary slowly shook her head. In the distance, thunder rolled. A hawk wheeled overhead, and somewhere a crow called. It seemed a very long time before Todd spoke.

"You do, Mary. Marry me, and I'll build you the finest house Rockdale's ever seen."

Chapter 21

Mary felt stunned. "If this is your idea of a joke—"

Todd pulled Mary to him and kissed her. "I've never been more serious about anything in my life. How about it?"

Mary detached herself from his embrace and stepped back a few paces. "I know it's a cliché, but this really is sudden. We barely know each other."

"I know all I need to about you, and if you want more time to get to know me, that's fine—it'll take some time to choose a plan and build the house, anyway."

Thunder sounded again, nearer and louder, and the wind bore the scent of rain. Todd took Mary's hand. "Let's go back to the truck before we get soaked."

The moment they got inside, heavy rain began to beat a tattoo upon the roof. "This reminds me of sleeping under Grandma Austin's tin roof as a kid," Todd said. "I hoped it would rain every time I stayed there."

Mary heard Todd speaking, but she scarcely took in what he was saying. She didn't know which was more preposterous, Todd Walker's sudden proposal of marriage or the revelation he wanted to build a house on land he apparently thought she owned.

There has to be something more than love behind this proposal.

"Aren't you going to say anything?" Todd asked after a while.

"You don't like chatterboxes," Mary reminded him.

Todd took her hand, the only contact the truck's center console allowed. "A simple 'yes' will do. How about it?"

"Not until you explain a few things."

Todd sighed. "I'll admit I haven't always been a saint, but I turned over a new leaf when I came back to Alabama. Now I want to settle down with you and raise a family in the place where I was born. What else do you need to know?"

It would help if you could say you loved me. "The rain's letting up—please take me home."

✀

Todd matched Mary's silence on the way back to her house. He drove his truck to the rear of the house and walked Mary to the door.

"When can I see you again?" he asked.

"I don't know. I need to talk to my father."

Todd grinned unexpectedly. "That's supposed to be my line. You're really something, Miss Mary Oliver. I'll call you tomorrow."

Mary closed the kitchen door and sighed. *He won't be coming back. Or if he does,*

I won't see him. I no longer have a crush on you, Todd Walker.

Feeling strangely detached, Mary went to her room and examined her reflection in her dresser mirror. She didn't look different, but she felt greatly changed by the last few weeks. She glanced at the yellowed index card she'd tucked in the mirror frame years before: "The Lord does not look at the things man looks at. Man looks at the outward appearance, but the Lord looks at the heart."

Once she had used the scripture to help her feel better about herself. Now, the familiar words had new meaning. Todd Walker's appearance was handsome, all right, but Mary believed the praise of men mattered too much to him.

On the other hand, no one could accuse the usually disheveled Jason Abbott of vanity. His priorities obviously centered more on the spiritual side of life than on the material.

Mary tried to picture herself as Jason might, a dedicated teacher who loves children. But he'd told Mary to listen for God to tell her if His will for her life included something more.

Turning from the mirror, Mary knelt beside her bed. Her standard, general prayer for guidance seemed somehow hollow. Recalling Jason's experience, Mary realized what had been missing from her own petitions.

Lord, I've been too busy thinking I'm doing Your will to listen to You. I thank You for using Jason Abbott to speak that truth to me. Forgive me for my presumption and for all the many other ways I have failed You. I promise to be a better listener, and I ask You to show me what I should do and trust You to help me do it.

∞

Some time later, the telephone rang. Mary was going to let the answering machine take the call, but when she heard her father's voice, she picked up the receiver.

"Is Todd still there?"

"No. He left some time ago. I'm sorry, I forgot to give him your message."

"I'm on my way home. We need to talk."

∞

Her father found Mary in the living room and wasted no time telling her what he'd discovered.

"Todd hired the survey crew that put those stakes on the mountain."

"I know. He told me."

"Did he say why?"

"He wants to build a house there."

Her father looked shocked. "What? He doesn't even own that land."

"Who does, then?"

Wayne Oliver sighed. "It was originally Austin land. Your grandfather Austin put the meadow lot in trust for your mother and her heirs when she was born. After her death, some of the other Austins wanted to add their shares to yours and develop it, but they couldn't touch it as long as it was in the trust."

"Why didn't you tell me?"

"I should have, of course. I didn't think you'd want to sell the land, although by the terms of the trust, you'd gain control of it on attaining the age of thirty."

Which I just did. "Todd obviously knows about the trust. Who else does?"

Her father shrugged. "Anyone with the patience to dig into the probate records, I suppose."

"Walter Chance," Mary murmured. "I think he must have found out, too. I don't believe anyone ever intended to put a rock quarry on Oliver Mountain. He wanted to make sure the land would be taken into the city and zoned residential so he could develop it himself."

"Aren't you jumping to conclusions? How would Walter get the land?"

"The same way as Todd—by marrying me."

Wayne Oliver looked stunned. "I knew Walter was leaning that way, but Todd? He actually asked you to marry him?"

"Hard to believe, isn't it? Walter hasn't gotten down on bended knee, but he's dropped some heavy hints. Todd proposed to me today on top of Oliver Mountain. What will you do about his survey?"

He shrugged. "Nothing, I suppose. The property isn't posted, and it's not illegal to survey someone else's land. Margaret Hastings complimented Todd— she said he's worked hard to persuade Haskell Holdings to build a recreation and entertainment complex in Rockdale."

Mary nodded. "I know, and the town needs it."

Her father looked at Mary closely. "Are you positive you don't want to marry Todd? I know you once liked him a great deal."

So he knew I had a crush on Todd, after all. "He said he wants to settle down in Rockdale and have a family. I felt comfortable with him before today, but I can't agree to a marriage based on deceit."

"All right. If Todd should ask about the land—"

"You can tell him it's not for sale," Mary said firmly.

∞

After the whirlwind of activity of the past few weeks, Mary should have welcomed the opportunity to do as little as she wanted, but she felt at loose ends all weekend. Vacation Bible School wouldn't start for ten days, the ground was too wet for gardening, and none of the books Mary tried to read held her interest.

When Walter called on Saturday, Mary told him the mystery of the stakes had been solved. "No one will be building anything on that land anytime soon."

"That's really a pity. You could have a beautiful view from the second story."

Mary hung up, shaking her head. She held nothing against Walter, and she hoped with all her heart he'd find someone to share his life—but it wouldn't be her.

Todd called later to apologize for the way he'd bungled his proposal. "Will you give me another chance? I'll be in Rockdale often, and I hope you'll agree to continue to see me."

"It wouldn't do either of us any good. I wish you well with the recreation project, but that's it."

Todd sounded genuinely sorry. "If you change your mind, you know how to reach me."

Yes, Todd, I have your number—in more ways than one.

The only man Mary really wanted to hear from did not call. At the very least, she hoped Jason Abbott would continue to ask her advice, but with every passing day, even that seemed more unlikely. Word of his availability had gotten out, and everywhere Mary went in the next week, she heard wild suppositions about why Jason and his fiancée had broken up, coupled with speculation about the women he might date now that he was "free."

Mary kept silent, not wishing to add fuel to a fire that was obviously already out of control. Again she thought of how the New Testament writer James had compared the tongue to a flame of fire. *When it's used to gossip, it can certainly destroy lives.*

Her father spent much of his free time that week attending various committee meetings of the Rockdale Civic Improvement Association and working with city council members on zoning laws and similar matters.

After what seemed a very long week, Mary held a final Vacation Bible School planning meeting on a cloudy Friday afternoon. After the others left, Mary entered the sanctuary. The moment she walked in, Mary realized she wasn't alone.

Jason Abbott rose from a pew nearest the Oliver stained-glass window. "Hello, Mary. I hope I didn't startle you."

"What are you doing here?" She blurted out the words, then tried to soften her reaction. "Obviously, you're looking at our windows."

"Actually, I came to see you, but I couldn't resist studying this stained glass again. It's surprising how much light filters through it even on a cloudy day."

"Yes. You wanted to see me?"

"Your father said you were here. I want to ask a favor."

Anything. Say it, and if it's in my power, I'll do it. "What is it?"

"I know your Vacation Bible School starts on Monday. I'd like to visit from time to time and see what you're doing."

"Of course. I assume you're still looking for ideas for Community's Bible school?"

Jason smiled faintly. "I've been nicely told plans have already been made for this year, but I'm looking ahead."

"I have no idea how all the new things we're trying will work out, but you're welcome to come by to observe any time."

"Thanks. I look forward to it."

They stood together beside the window, outlined in the colored light filtering in through the stained glass. Jason had said what he had come to say, and their business was over. Mary knew she should leave, yet she was reluctant to do so.

"How are things going at Community?" she asked.

Jason smiled ruefully. "I suppose you're aware each of us has been the talk of the town this week. I'll be glad when some other topic for gossip comes along."

Each of us? "What have you heard about me?"

Jason's smile faded. "I shouldn't have said anything. I don't like to repeat gossip."

"Now that you've brought it up, you have to tell me."

He sighed. "The word is you're about to get married."

"I am? To whom?"

"There's some disagreement. Some say Walter Chance, others Todd something—he spoke a long time at the meeting last week."

"Todd Walker," Mary supplied. "How do these wild stories get started?"

"You're not engaged?"

"No more than you were. I've heard several versions of why your fiancée broke off your engagement, by the way."

Jason smiled. "I won't believe what I hear about you if you'll do the same for me."

Mary smiled. "Agreed."

Jason lightly touched Mary's cheek. "I'm glad the gossips were wrong."

Her heart lurched, then began to beat more rapidly. "So am I."

"I have to get back to work, but I hope to see you soon."

He really seems to mean it. Thank You, Lord.

Chapter 22

Rain fell the first two days of Vacation Bible School, preventing the planned nature walks, but it still went smoothly. The weather didn't seem to affect the turnout for the second Rockdale Civic Improvement Association general meeting Tuesday evening, and Wayne Oliver seemed satisfied at the work that was being accomplished.

Jason wasn't at the meeting, and although Mary watched for him daily, she didn't see him again until near the end of Wednesday's Vacation Bible School session. After the children had been dismissed, he invited Mary to lunch.

"I'm sorry I couldn't get here sooner, but this has been a busy week. I brought a picnic lunch. I'll let you decide where we should take it."

Mary tried not to sound quite as joyful as she felt. "I know a great spot on Warren Mountain."

Mary directed Jason to an old logging road, from which they walked into a grassy meadow surrounded by wildflowers.

"Don't I hear water?" Jason asked.

"That's the everlasting spring. It appears to come out of the mountain and makes a neat little waterfall before it goes down the mountain and becomes the creek we cross to get into town. We can eat on the big rocks around it if you like."

"I brought a tarp, but this is much better."

When they were settled on the rocks, Jason opened a huge hamper filled with containers of food and bottles of water and soda. "Everything but the ants," he said when Mary commented on the seemingly endless supply of food. "My neighbor, Mrs. Tarpley, fried the chicken and made the brownies. The rest is straight from the grocery."

"Partaking of God's bounty surrounded by God's beauty. I can't think of a nicer way to have lunch," Mary said.

"Neither can I." Jason took her hand and offered a prayer of thanks for all God's gifts, particularly for their fellowship and the food that had been prepared for them.

"Amen," Mary echoed when he finished.

Jason seemed reluctant to release Mary's hand. "This is a perfect place for a picnic. How did you find it?"

"Toni Trent and I rode our bikes up here quite often when we were in Rockdale High."

"You two have been friends a long time," Jason observed.

"Yes. In fact, we were the only friends each other had in those days."

"It's hard to believe you and Toni weren't popular."

"About as popular as poison ivy. How about you? Were you voted the most anything when you were in school?"

"No. I felt awkward and ugly, so I made good grades instead of friends. I thought if I could earn a lot of money, everybody would like me."

Jason spoke matter-of-factly, but Mary understood the hurt he must have known. "Except for the money part, I felt the same way."

"My mother kept telling me I should look at myself through God's eyes and not my own or others'. Now I realize how self-centered I was then," Jason said.

"I know what you mean. I relied on the verse in First Samuel: 'Man looks at the outward appearance, but the Lord looks at the heart.'"

Jason spoke quietly. "When I look at you, I see a beautiful woman whose life reflects her love for God and His children."

Beautiful. No one had ever called Mary beautiful, and she tried to hide the depth of her pleasure.

"That's a fine compliment, but it doesn't sound like you're talking about me."

"Don't sell yourself short, Mary. I know God doesn't."

When they had finished eating, Jason took Mary's hands in his and looked into her eyes. "Have you given any more thought about what God wants for your life?"

Mary's gaze held his. "I've been praying about it."

"Good." Jason squeezed Mary's hands, then released them and picked up the picnic hamper. "I wish I didn't have to go back to work this afternoon. We'll have to do this again."

Soon, I hope. "Don't forget you're invited to the Vacation Bible School field trip on Friday."

"I haven't—and you can be sure if I'm not there, it won't be because I didn't want to be."

∞

Mary's prayers for a successful and safe trip to Sequoyah Caverns were answered. The hired buses got the children there and back on time without breaking down, and everything else went off as planned. Awed by the beauty of the cave's lake and gigantic rock formations, the kids behaved well.

Mary's only regret was that Jason Abbott wasn't there to enjoy it with them.

"Thank you for arranging this trip for us," Mary told Hawk Henson at the end of the day. "Seeing God's handiwork here capped off the whole week. This place is truly inspirational. I'm glad the Cherokee own at least this part of your ancestral land."

"So are we. I'm sorry Pastor Jason couldn't get away today. He's interested in planning a trip like this for our church's kids."

"I'll be glad to show it to him later."

Hawk remained silent for a moment. "It's too bad you're so committed to First Church. You and Pastor Jason would make a great team at Community."

I believe we could make a good team, period. "We're sharing information and programs as it is."

But after Mary got home that night, she considered Hawk's remark. "It's too bad you're so committed to First Church."

Mary wondered if Jason Abbot might have had the same thought. First Church had always been at the heart of her spiritual life, but she recognized it was only a building. *Its purpose is to help people worship God—and since He exists in Spirit and in Truth and not in bricks and stones and glass, I should never let it take the place of God.*

Mary now believed Jason Abbott had entered her life for a reason, but she wasn't so sure about what role, if any, she was meant to play in his. That night when she knelt to pray, Mary acknowledged her future still seemed in doubt.

Lord, I am wholly committed to You. You know how much I love First Church, but I love You more. If it is Your will for me to help Your servant Jason in his church, I will obey.

∾

Jason called Mary on Saturday to get her version of the field trip. "According to Hawk, it was a great success. He thinks Community should do the same for our Bible school."

"I'm sorry you couldn't come with us, but I'll be happy to take you to the caverns when you have time."

"Thanks—I'd like that. We've been busy preparing for the Fourth of July celebration. Toni will sing a solo, and after the service, we'll have an old-fashioned dinner on the grounds. I wish you could be here for it."

"Is that an invitation?"

"Yes, but I know you'll probably have obligations at First, particularly on the first Sunday after Bible school."

"Yes. I'm due to give the Vacation Bible School report to the church. Maybe some other time."

Jason sounded resigned. " 'Never the twain shall meet,' " he quoted.

Mary hesitated. "Never is a long time. Good-bye, Jason."

∾

On Sunday morning, Mary's father showed her the ring he intended to give Evelyn when they went to Mentone for lunch after church.

Mary admired the emerald-cut diamond set in white gold. "Does she know about this?"

"No. When she agreed to be my wife, Evelyn said she didn't need an engagement ring. However, I want her to have one."

"She'll love it." When Mary hugged her father, unexpected tears gathered in her eyes.

"Hey, you're not supposed to cry until the wedding," he said.

Mary smiled. "I'll probably cry then, too."

As soon as she reached the church, Mary sought out Melanie Neal. "I know it's short notice, but will you please read the Vacation Bible School report at the worship service?"

Melanie looked mystified. "You always give the report. It's your big moment."

"Not this time. I have something more important to do."

∽

Mary walked into Community Church on legs that seemed to have turned to jelly. Anita Henson saw her and took Mary's hand.

"Toni will be so happy you have come to hear her sing," she said.

Mary nodded, grateful for the excuse.

At their invitation, Mary sat between Anita and her daughter, who seemed delighted to see her. Hawk grinned and gave Mary the thumbs-up sign.

Hawk seems to understand why I'm here today. Will Jason?

The service began, and from his chair near the pulpit, Jason glanced idly over the congregation. When he saw Mary, he did a double take, then smiled.

Mary felt a surge of joy. He's glad I'm here—and so am I.

Community's informal worship service was different from First's in many ways, but Mary realized everything that really mattered was the same. Like First Church, Community consisted of a body of believers, united as brothers and sisters in Jesus Christ.

While Pastor Hurley prayed, Mary's mind and heart overflowed with praise, not only for all God had given her, but also for what He yet had in store.

After the benediction, Jason hurried to find Mary and took her arm.

"Where are you going, Pastor Jason?" little Juanita asked. "We're s'posed to eat now."

"Later. Miss Mary and I have to talk first."

Dimly aware of the curious glances they attracted, Mary allowed Jason to lead her through the hallway and into his office. He closed the door behind him and turned to her.

"What about your report?"

"I asked someone else to read it. I'm sure First Church is still standing."

"Even without one of its pillars?"

"God has let me know I can be a pillar anywhere He wants to use me."

"Even here?"

"Especially here."

"Hallelujah!" Jason's face broke into the widest smile Mary had ever seen just before he swept her into his arms and kissed her.

Still holding her tight, he whispered in her ear, "I pray God has also let you know you should marry me."

She pulled away to look at him. "Without first being asked?"

"Of course not, if you think it's necessary." Jason took her right hand in his and looked intently into her eyes. "Mary Oliver, I love you and I want to be your best friend, your life's partner, and your husband—as long as we both shall live."

"Amen," said Mary. "In that case, the answer has to be a yes."

"Thank You, Lord," he whispered, then kissed her again.

Folded in Jason Abbott's arms, Mary felt as if she'd come home after a long journey. She had no doubt God had led them both to this moment—and her to this man.

Thank You for helping me to make the right choice.

Epilogue

Everyone agreed Rockdale had never experienced such a summer. With the help of the Civic Improvement Association, new zoning laws were put into place to protect the town's natural beauty. Several projects that would offer more shopping, dining, and recreation choices and add tax revenue were in the works, and Haskell Holdings held a gala ground-breaking ceremony for the entertainment and recreation center. It was no wonder the entire town felt a sense of optimism.

The summer also brought changes in the personal lives of several Rockdale residents. Walter Chance had helped a pretty young widow with three children find a house, and soon it seemed evident they might be headed for the altar.

Todd Walker continued to work for Haskell Holdings. Still single, he had apparently dropped his plans to settle down in Rockdale.

Mary Oliver created quite a stir when she joined Community Church, and she and the associate pastor were seen together quite often. After Jason Abbott took Mary to Georgia to meet his parents, no one was surprised when their engagement was announced, with plans for a late December wedding.

After a short engagement, Judge Wayne Oliver and Miss Evelyn Trent were married at First Church in a simple but moving service. After the Olivers returned from their honeymoon cruise, Evelyn moved out of her house on Maple Street, and Mary moved into it.

On the day Evelyn's furniture arrived at its new home in the Oliver house, she and Mary noticed Sally Proffitt and Jenny Suiter watching from Sally's porch.

"Those poor ladies will have to find someone new to gossip about now, now that I'm married and you're engaged," Evelyn said.

"What they really need is to feel useful. Jason's asked Phyllis Dickson to involve them in some kind of volunteer work at the hospital."

"Good. Your Pastor Jason seems to have a gift for knowing exactly what people need."

"He does, doesn't he? I hadn't thought of that as one of his gifts, but it is."

"You know, it wasn't an accident you two found each other," Evelyn said. "Jason needed someone to support his ministry, and you needed to be a wife as well as a teacher."

"God knew I needed a stepmother like you, too—I really believe you and my father were meant to be together."

Evelyn smiled. "Isn't it amazing how—when we let Him—God leads us to make the right choices?"

A Letter to Our Readers

Dear Readers:

In order that we might better contribute to your reading enjoyment, we would appreciate your taking a few minutes to respond to the following questions. When completed, please return to the following: Fiction Editor, Barbour Publishing, Inc., P.O. Box 719, Uhrichsville, OH 44683.

1. Did you enjoy reading *Alabama*?
   ❑ Very much—I would like to see more books like this.
   ❑ Moderately—I would have enjoyed it more if _____
   _____
   _____

2. What influenced your decision to purchase this book?
   (Check those that apply.)
   ❑ Cover   ❑ Back cover copy   ❑ Title   ❑ Price
   ❑ Friends   ❑ Publicity   ❑ Other

3. Which story was your favorite?
   ❑ *Politically Correct*   ❑ *Anita's Fortune*
   ❑ *Toni's Vow*   ❑ *Mary's Choice*

4. Please check your age range:
   ❑ Under 18   ❑ 18–24   ❑ 25–34
   ❑ 35–45   ❑ 46–55   ❑ Over 55

5. How many hours per week do you read? _____

Name _____

Occupation _____

Address _____

City _____ State _____ Zip _____

E-mail _____

*H*EARTSONG ♥ PRESENTS

Love Stories
Are Rated G!

That's for godly, gratifying, and of course, great! If you love a thrilling love story but don't appreciate the sordidness of some popular paperback romances, **Heartsong Presents** is for you. In fact, **Heartsong Presents** is the premiere inspirational romance book club featuring love stories where Christian faith is the primary ingredient in a marriage relationship.

Sign up today to receive your first set of four, never-before-published Christian romances. Send no money now; you will receive a bill with the first shipment. You may cancel at any time without obligation, and if you aren't completely satisfied with any selection, you may return the books for an immediate refund!

Imagine. . .four new romances every four weeks—two historical, two contemporary—with men and women like you who long to meet the one God has chosen as the love of their lives. . .all for the low price of $10.99 postpaid.

To join, simply complete the coupon below and mail to the address provided. **Heartsong Presents** romances are rated G for another reason: They'll arrive Godspeed!